# WHITE PAGAN

❧*❧

Book 6 of the

Kestrel Harper Saga

❧*❧

Tamara Brigham

*Published by:*
*Tamara Brigham*
*PO Box 151*
*Clearlake, CA 95422*

*Printed and bound in the United States of America*

*First Edition*

*ISBN # 978-1-7371869-2-2*

*For Bo*
*Thank you for 14 beautiful years*
*If love could grant immortality*
*You never would have left me.*

♥

❧*❧

❧Chapter 1❧

"You know I will always be with you. Never fear that."

The gold and crimson clouds clawed the firmament, stretching upwards behind their backs to fade into the gathering twilight in the eastern sky. The Llaethlágárá, as ancient as the heavens, bled purple in the warmth of the ninth-month twilight, disappearing as the night devoured them. It would not be long before darkness passed into dawn again, leaving only memories of the passage of events that heralded another milestone in the bard's life.

Wortham's voice sounded weary, tight yet deflated, as the stretched thin day drew to a close. In Bhryell, the stooped-shouldered soldier had stood by him as Kavan watched his adopted son Sóbhán wed his niece, Chethá MacLyr, taking the young man further out of Kavan's orbit. They had never been bound by blood, but they were bound by their years together and the familial name Sóbhán had taken out of honor and respect for the man who had saved him from the streets of Rhidam, and likely death, and given him a life, an education, and a calling he might otherwise not have found. A search for his biological family had revealed that he was a foundling, that those Sóbhán had believed to be family had discovered him in their barley field, no more kin to him than Kavan was. He loved the people who had given him a start in life when they could have just as easily passed him on to some other family or the Faith to rear. But he felt a deeper bond to Kavan as the memories of those long-ago days softened and frayed. Sóbhán considered himself blessed to have been twice rescued and given life, and now thrice blessed by the healer who had accepted the place at his side as wife and closest friend.

Kavan likewise felt blessed and honored to have witnessed the union, to have been able to give Sóbhán something of himself and a start in the world that the Second Great Elyri Persecution had tried to steal. Going to Bhryell, being in Hes Índári, had been a risk, excommunicated from the Faith as he was, but after a lifetime of exclusion, most of the residents of his hometown now welcomed him; they would not turn on him. Kavan wholeheartedly believed it. Even if they had, if those who still shunned him took word of his trespass to the Faith authorities in Clarys, Kavan would have stood in Bhryell's náós to participate in the solemn, joyful occasion of Sóbhán's marriage. He had given Sóbhán life; he had been both obligated and blessed to release him to make the most of it.

With the majority of those the Lord of Alberni had mentored in recent years now moved on into adult lives of their own, Wortham knew that loneliness weighed heavy on the bard's shoulders. No matter the size of the crowd, no matter the wide-spread adoration that surrounded him from both men and women, young and old, wealthy and poor, Elyri and Teren, there was loneliness within the bard that was rarely filled save by a handful of individuals who held the White Bard dearest to their hearts.

The children had been amongst them, but with most now married, they came back to Kavan only rarely. Owain Lachlan, enemy turned dearest friend, had left them five years past, a mournful blessing as the extended illness in his lungs had dragged the prince through suffering that no healer, no miracle, had been able to lessen. Only his wife's care and the frequent visits from his son and grandson, supplemented by the music Kavan gladly gave, had eased his suffering. When Saint Kóráhm and the záryph came to collect the man's steadfast soul, letting him go had been the kindest thing Kavan could do.

But that loss, and the happiness of young lives pairing and starting anew, left Kavan one step closer to the sort of solitude he would not easily endure. Wortham knew this, even if Kavan did not speak of it. Even with his close attachment to those children still, and the abiding friendship that had grown over the past twenty-one years with the Queen's Chamberlain, Níkóá McCábhá, Wortham knew his cherished friend was suffering the melancholy of loneliness. He hated to see Kavan suffering. He would do anything to ease it.

Even if it meant promising the impossible.

"She was there, you know. On Káliel. Before you came."

"Who?"

Wortham showed no inclination to answer, causing Kavan to believe the statement, whatever it meant, to be unintentionally uttered. Instead, Wortham coughed once, a soft sound clearing his throat, and murmured, "I love you. You know that, don't you, Kavan?"

With the sound of his name on his friend's lips, Kavan reached to the side and covered the man's gnarled hand with his. Wortham's hand turned, met Kavan's touch, palm to palm, and intertwined fingers in a tight grip of devotion. So rare was it that Kavan initiated physical contact, or accepted it, from anyone other than children, that the gesture spoke of the strength of his reciprocated love with no need for the passing of words.

At the edge of the Elyri's senses, a host of presences gathered. In their midst was one that came too rarely now for Kavan's comfort. A breath escaped, long and soft and final, followed by the shudder of a passing Kavan could not mistake.

The clutching hand in his slowly slackened, the captain's hand growing gradually cooler within Kavan's, and the bard squeezed his eyes shut to block out the world. Doing so did little more than accentuate the company of those his eyes could not perceive, those who mourned with him as he whispered, "I know, sínréc." Tears broke the bonds of his pale lashes and slipped down his cheeks.

No one else had earned that title from him.

It was doubtful, the brief thought passed, that anyone else would.

The emptiness within screamed, but on the outside, there was little evidence of his turmoil. He did not need to look at Wortham to know the man's soul was gone. Two years. Two years separated them in age and yet Kavan appeared as the man's son or grandson, the longevity of the Elyri creating a visible distance between them where no other had ever existed. For nearly fifty years their lives, their souls, their hearts had been inseparable.

Now Wortham was gone.

The sun sank lower, dipping beneath the line of the Alberni manor house and eventually beneath the horizon, pulling the light with it, drawing night into place. In Kavan's open, empty palm, silver-blue moonlight pooled and gathered into a sphere, expanding, shrinking, brightening, and fading as the force of his grief expended through the unconscious release of power. Elyri were welcome in Enesfel once again, thanks to the Crown's diligence and perseverance over the last two decades, but few dared display Elyri power in public. Only within the security of his estate, sometimes in the Rhidam castle, or within the walls of St. Kóráhm's, did Kavan use his gifts without fear or restraint. Only with this man who had protected him as surely as Kavan had protected in return.

His hand again tightened around Wortham's.

Who would protect him now?

Hands on his shoulders. A familiar touch that spilled more tears, followed by the press of lips on the top of his head. The answer to his question, the protection of the Heretic-Saint who was always with him. But it was not the same, could never be the same, as having a companion of flesh and blood to lift him up, walk beside him, share the small trials and joys of each day. Kóráhm was most often there only in spirit, usually undetectable despite Kavan's beseeching prayers. Not like Wortham, who had shared everything from their first meeting until this last, devoted to Kavan's every need. Their love for him might not be different, nor Kavan's love for them, yet their ability to be consistently beside him had been. As before meeting Wortham for the first time aboard a Hatu ship off the coast of Káliel, Kavan now faced his days alone.

He did not know how he would bear it.

Yet bear it he must, he sighed, feeling the Saint's grief and comfort envelope him, the brush of feathered wings wrapped around him in a holy embrace. There were those who depended on him, the people of Alberni, those within the chellé hábhai, family, friends, and the Queen of Enesfel. People who, selfishly at times, expected too much. But he needed to be needed, needed to give as much as they desired of him, and in truth, he had no wish to give up his life, even so his soul could spend eternity with the one he loved so dearly. Nor would Wortham want that of him.

It was that knowledge, and his stubborn perseverance, that kept him seated beside Wortham throughout the cold hours of darkness, until long after all warmth had left the big heart of his best friend, until the weightiest portion of his grief had spent itself into the power of night, and the ball of moonlight in his hand faded into the air from whence it had been drawn. In its place, the pale pink and yellow of dawn tried to gather, but instead, it spluttered and went out when the surge of panic erupted as the arrival of day reminded him it was time to let Wortham go.

The stiffness of Wortham's joints kept his fingers curled around Kavan's, discouraging the bard from pulling away, and yet it was something that needed to be done. Remaining here, as the cold gave way to the warmth of another autumn day, accomplished nothing, and though he did not want to say farewell to the man at his side, what remained on the stone bench in the manor garden was no longer Wortham Delamo. It was a shell, a physical thing that held nothing but the memories Kavan poured into it.

"Lord Cliáth, mother…"

The footsteps along the garden path faltered, stopping far enough away that Kavan would be unable to touch the speaker if he tried, but near enough to bear witness to the secret Kavan had carried alone throughout the night. Head turning, his emerald eyes opened to take in the blissful expression of contentment on his friend's face, his gray hair and beard fluttering in the morning breeze, one of the last butterflies of the year perched on his knee, his good eye closed as if in slumber. Despite the ache it caused, Kavan swallowed the grief lump and looked at seventeen-year-old Rhyrdan Delamo with affection.

"He did not suffer." Despite the conviction behind them, the words stuck and struggled to break free. "Kóráhm saw him to his rest."

Rhyrdan's head of dark curls bobbed once. Though still of youthfully slight build, the broadness of his hips and shoulders heralded his father's bear-like physique and the mass of dark hair and stubbled growth upon his cheeks and chin suggested that, within a few years, Wortham's youngest son would bear a more striking resemblance to his father. Seeing that promise, reading both grief and adoration in the young man's cinnamon brown eyes, reminded Kavan that he was not as alone as he felt. He saw Wortham in Rhyrdan's eyes, a sight that filled him with both joy and sorrow.

"As did you," Rhyrdan murmured, coming closer to brush his father's hair from his forehead. The touch, gentle and loving, was accompanied by a hand that reached for Kavan's as well. "He would have it no other way. When…?"

Kavan's hand lifted, intending to take the one offered to him, then hesitated. One touch, he knew, and he would likely give in to the weeping he had thus far avoided. Yet the desire for connection he read in Rhyrdan's eyes, as if he might somehow touch his father's soul through the bard's hand, pushed Kavan to accept the hand with a difficult swallow past the burning knot in his chest and a force of will that kept the rush of tears at bay.

"Twilight…not long after we returned."

Rhyrdan nodded. Kavan and Wortham had departed the festivities as soon as the new couple retreated to Kavan's Bhryell home for their first night together. Others, villagers and family, from both Elyriá and Enesfel, had remained to celebrate together, sharing food and drink and music until sometime long into the night. The bard could not afford to stay longer, could not risk word of his presence spreading to Clarys and bringing members of the k'phóredhet or ecclesiastical guardsmen to interrupt the celebration and find him there. He stayed long enough to witness the joining, to give a song, his voice and harp so rarely heard in Elyriá now, to the new couple, and then he returned to Alberni where he would endanger no one. Wortham, of course, had insisted on accompanying him, knowing the bard's need for comfort and respite from the melancholy the marriage would inevitably create.

Or perhaps, Rhyrdan thought, meeting Kavan's gaze, his father had known the end was nearing and chose to come home and spend his last moments in the garden he loved with the man he loved more than his children, more than his wife, more than his life. While there were times when the elder son Madoc resented Kavan's preferential place in their father's heart, Rhyrdan never had. How could anyone resent and condemn a love as deep as was shared between Wortham Delamo and Kavan Cliáth?

Rhyrdan hoped that someday he would share that same bond with the man who had mentored him.

"Shall I tell Mother?"

Kavan opened his mouth but there was no sound. Perhaps he should be the one to break this news to Zelenka, but he did not think he could bear her grief. Besides, there were others he should tell. Prince Merrek. Dhóri. Madoc and Yóáná and those in Rhidam who had loved the man. And Sóbhán…although he had no wish to take this news to the couple at the dawn of their life as husband and wife. Perhaps it could wait a few more days. Burial could wait too, at least long enough for those who wished to share in it to arrive in Alberni.

A bell tolled, announcing the first service of the day. St. Kóráhm's. Yes. Wortham would be buried on those sacred grounds. Kavan would have it no other way.

With an effort of aching stiffness, Kavan pried his hand free of Wortham's and got to his feet, nodding to Rhyrdan's question. "I will bring him in…ask Emeria to ready a bed downstairs where he may…"

He could not put the man in the bed shared with his wife. Zelenka's superstitions would not permit it. But Rhyrdan's sister, like the boys, did not share those notions, at least not as profoundly, and so Emeria would feel no fear of the man's body resting nearby as he awaited burial. Besides, the choice would allow Kavan to enter the manor through the door of the servants' quarters and remain out of Zelenka's sight. Perhaps it would permit him to set about the duties of notifying others without having to face her.

Rhyrdan, after kissing his father's forehead, nodded and let go of Kavan's hand, turning with squared shoulders towards his familial duties. With Madoc serving Rhidam as Lord High Justice, Wortham's passing made Rhyrdan the man of the House and he was determined to prove to the Duke that he was willing and capable of assuming his father's place, filling his duties…every one of them…even if his cheeks were damp with running tears.

After the footfalls on the stepping stones retreated beyond the range of his hearing, and the door to the servants' quarters opened and closed without latching, Kavan forced the tension out of his shoulders. He had never learned to cope effectively with the sorrow of others, particularly in those instances when he carried so much of his own. Sympathy would be no easier to bear and yet would have to be faced. Enduring it from others would be preferable, he admitted stoically, to feeling that no one cared about his grief.

Elyri strength enabled him to lift his friend in loving arms, and as the sun peeped over the Llaethlágárá, Kavan carried Wortham one last time into the house. If only Wortham had been allowed another sunset.

One more would not have been enough. One more would always give birth to the longing for another and another.

Instead, Kavan would enjoy those sunrises, and sunsets, for him. But not this one. This rising would pass unappreciated, for the light of it could not touch the shadows of sorrow wringing Kavan's heart.

⁊Chapter 2⁊

There was an unsettled feeling in his center as Ártur stared through the open window towards the eastern horizon, searching the gradually brightening sky for something he could not identify. It was long after midnight when he and Syl returned to Rhidam, after saying farewell to their son, his wife, and various other family members who had attended the wedding and taking Prince Merrek to his home in Fiara. It had felt good to have so many of those he loved together, as scattered as their lives had become, and he was proud of the life his daughter Chetha was building for herself. She had chosen to serve as a healer in Bhryell, one of three in the small village now, to remain at her new husband's side. Sóbhán was a good man, intelligent, kind, and driven. His focus on the ancient skill of Cliáthan harp making had already won him accolades throughout Elyriá, to both Tám's pride and frustration. Not a Cliáth by blood, though one who had chosen to take the name as Kavan's adopted son, Sóbhán was proving to be a more structured, disciplined, and talented harp maker than Tám. Kavan might not have followed in his family's footsteps, but he had given the Cliáthan trade a craftsman like no other.

Now that young harp maker had married Ártur's daughter and they had set up home in Kavan's house until they could acquire a home of their own. As long as Kavan's excommunication held, he would not live in his hometown, in the house he sometimes called home, nor could he legally visit it. In the interim, it was fitting that someone the bard loved should fill the rooms with life, and more fitting that the house be maintained and controlled by the one Kavan called son.

Syl was called upon to attend the queen shortly after they emerged from the Gate into the upper oratory and had come to bed nearly an hour later. This was not the first time Diona had suffered difficulty sleeping. Insomnia had plagued the queen since her husband's untimely death fourteen years ago and it had grown worse with the losses of first Owain and then Prince Liahm one year past. This week, the anniversary of the prince succumbing to injuries sustained when a building scaffold collapsed on him, would be the worst for her.

The queen had insisted they attend the wedding nonetheless, and managed her grief long enough for them to support their daughter on such an important day. Once they returned, it had again fallen to Syl to help ease the monarch into sleep before finding rest of her own at her husband's side.

Sleep had eluded Ártur as well, keeping him from the bed even after Syl's return, as the unease that had crept over him earlier in the evening persisted throughout the night. East was where it originated, east where Kavan was. With the strong connections of heart, blood, and power between them, it took little effort for the healer to guess that the sensation within was rooted with his cousin.

Several times he almost talked himself into going to Alberni, to seek assurance in Kavan's well-being, but he did not give in to the temptation. He knew Kavan fretted over yet another child drawing away from his direct influence, as Madoc and Yóáná had done previously and others had done over the years. Not that Kavan had served as tutor for any of them in several years, but even Ártur felt a sense of loss at giving his daughter to a life without him in it as the primary male figure. For Kavan, who experienced such events as deep personal losses, Ártur imagined this night was torture.

"We could try for another." Syl's arms wrapped about his waist and her head rested between his shoulders. The breaking of dawn had brought a faint glow in the unlit room and the window, open since their return, gave the room a chill despite the hearth fire behind them. He had not noticed the cold until the warmth of his wife's soft form molded against his back.

"I thought we have been," he chuckled, covering her hands with his. They had never stopped trying, but conception was difficult for Elyri, nature's way, he believed, to counter their longevity and prevent the overpopulation it could create. Some Elyri marriages never produced children, some did not conceive until well past their hundredth year. He and Syl were blessed with two children at a young age, children who had both married young. Their adopted daughter,

Bianca, remained part of their lives, albeit a distant part from her home in Durham with her husband Wilred Dugan and their children. It was reasonable to believe there could be more children in their future, but there was no guarantee. What came next in their lives was up to them, and thankfully, with peace and calm reigning in Enesfel, Elyri again welcome, and their children building lives of their own in Bhryell, where Llucás too was engaged in harp making, Syl felt no reason to remain apart from her husband.

"Yes…well…we could try now."

Her playful tone was interrupted by a soft rapping on the bedroom door. He sighed in annoyance, having been prepared to give in to his wife's temptations, but as he turned in her arms and called "Enter," he recognized the presence on the other side of the wooden barrier.

The dark circles beneath Kavan's eyes spoke of no sleep and the traces on his white cheeks revealed tears that the bard had not bothered to wipe away. Or rather, Ártur noticed quickly, they were tears that silently fell, a sight that alarmed him as Kavan rarely wept, and even more rarely did so publically.

"sínréc…what has…?"

Kavan smoothed his black trousers with his palms, fidgeting to cover his emotional disintegration. The healer peeled from Syl's arms and crossed the room before the bard spoke again. Both men wore the clothing worn to the wedding the day before. Kavan did not make eye contact as he mumbled, "Come to Alberni with me, please."

"Of course. At once." Ártur did not ask why as he grabbed his medical bag from the desk. He glanced at Syl, who nodded approval of his departure. As healers, both understood the interruptions of emergencies better than most and had long ago learned to live with them. There would be time for expanding their family later.

"You will not need…"

"Not…?" Ártur's voice faltered. Rather than meet his gaze, Kavan looked at Syl before lowering his eyes again. Ártur scowled, feeling irrationally excluded when he knew there was no cause for petty jealousy. Syl would tease him for it later as this was not the first time he had felt jealous of those coming between him and his cousin during a shared moment.

The corners of Kavan's mouth twitched, twisted, and stretched as he struggled with words and the emotions behind them that brought another flush of tears. He had come to Rhidam directly from placing

Wortham on the bed prepared for him, and this separation, the first true one in what would be a permanent parting, was strangling and choking him. But the words had to be said. He would not allow them to be a silent passing through a touch of Ártur's hand. Ártur would come, preserve the corpse, and Syl would let the rest of Rhidam know.

The rest, that was, except for the copper-haired, bearded man who appeared in the corridor, drawn out of slumber, out of his room, by the tumult of power Kavan's arrival sent through the keep.

"Wortham is…gone."

Ártur took another step, bag dropping from his hand, to pull Kavan into an embrace. Just in time, he read his cousin's distress, the tensing and preparation for flight brought on by the impending intimacy of offered comfort, and Ártur lowered his arms in frustrated surrender.

"Are you sure?"

They were lame, pointless words, spoken out of disbelief rather than any doubt of Kavan's honesty. Kavan experienced the passing of souls in ways no one else did, the feeling of spirits crossing out of the world, seeing them gathered into the arms of the záryph who collected the deceased and escorted them into Ethenae. The trails of grief on Kavan's face spoke with unquestionable certainty. If Kavan said someone…Wortham…was gone…it had to be so.

"Preserve him." It was the only answer given to Ártur's question. Kavan turned, acknowledging Níkóá with fingers brushed over the back of the other man's hand, a gesture that brought a jerking of Ártur's shoulders and a refusal to look at the chamberlain as he passed.

The chamberlain, accustomed to that reaction from the healer when it came to Kavan, ignored the look and murmured, "Of course, my lord," before falling into step behind them.

Ártur wondered with frustration what task his cousin had given to the chamberlain. He heard his wife's grief-laden chuckle in his head rather than with his ears and quickly unknotted the jealous ribbon tightening within. Now more than ever, Kavan needed support, not petty bickering for attention. Kavan rarely asked for anything. Today, he had asked. From Ártur. From Syl. From Níkóá. Ártur was determined to set aside his feelings and help Kavan cope with his.

But Kavan did not go with him to Alberni, nor did Níkóá. Kavan only said there was something he needed to do.

Ártur suspected it would be hours before he saw Kavan again.

❧*❧

"k'gdhededhá Tusánt?"

Rhidam's only Elyri clergyman, the elected head of the Teren Faith despite his race, looked up from the scattered parchments and scrolls that cluttered his desk, bright-eyed despite the early hour. From the speed with which he had been writing, and the half-burned stubs of tallow candles in the stained brass desk sconce, Níkóá suspected the man had been awake since before dawn. Níkóá had been directed here by the gdhededhá preparing the náós for the first service of the day and it seemed, given the robes he wore, that Tusánt was scheduled to conduct the upcoming Gathering.

"Lord McCábhá; you're out early. What might I do for you?"

"Not for me. For Lord Cliáth." The Elyri's head popped up at the unexpected words. "There is no rush, but he has requested you to go to Alberni…to see to Lord Delamo's burial."

"Lord Del…" The writing quill dropped from Tusánt's hand and his fingers curled into fists.

When Kavan had long ago hinted that the position of k'gdhededhá could be his, Tusánt had not believed it possible, even though he had gone through the election process as if he had stood a chance of election. Only after k'gdhededhá Claide's death had Kavan revealed how close the selection had been between Tusánt and the Teren clergyman who had manipulated the vote with bribery, fear, and violence to tip the final count in his favor. During the second election, a necessity because Tusánt refused to step into the power vacuum without a fair vote amongst his peers, the decision had been nearly unanimous. Though the Teren Faithful had split from the Elyri leadership in Clarys, they had elected an Elyri as their leader.

In time, Tusánt believed there could be a reintegration of the Teren and Elyri Faithful, but it was not something he openly advocated. He did not mind the duties Faith heaped on him, the sometimes grim tasks he was asked to assume, but this was one of those times he wished someone else was responsible for the burden of tending the dead.

Then again, for Wortham, for Kavan, he would have felt slighted if anyone else had been asked.

"Yes, of course, blessed saints and záryph; when did this…"

"This morning…last night perhaps. I don't know." He had not attended the wedding in Bhryell, duty to the Crown and Enesfel taking precedent. The last time he had seen the aged captain over three weeks past, the man had looked worn and weary, every bit his seventy-three years. He had not, however, looked frail or on the precipice of death. If anything, Níkóá had expected Wortham to outlive many of the Teren around him out of sheer stubborn will to remain at Kavan's side. The love and devotion Wortham and Níkóá shared for the bard had made the two fast friends and the loss hit him hard. But not, he knew, as hard as it was hitting Kavan.

"He just brought the news; Ártur has gone to preserve the body." That much he knew from what he had seen and overheard through the healer's doorway and from Kavan's brief touch. Where the burial would be Níkóá could only speculate.

Tusánt gathered the pages of handwritten notes, his trembling hands making the task more awkward than it should be. It was too late to relegate the service to any of his fellow gdhededhá, though he was tempted to do so. This news, however, would significantly change the lesson he had intended to give.

Any comfort he could provide to Kavan would have to wait for another few hours, providing Ártur time to preserve the body and allowing the family the chance to begin to adjust to what he guessed was an unexpected shock. To his knowledge, the captain had not been ill, had been in good spirits the last time Tusánt had seen him, and he believed Kavan would have come to him requesting prayers if some ailment had been eating at the man's life.

"Are you going to them now?" It was no secret to those in the Lachlan inner circle, or Tusánt, that the chamberlain carried Elyri blood and was capable of using it. The man had his secrets, but in the Lachlan court, his racial heritage was not one of them.

"Aye; I will take them word of your arrival." Someone needed to be there to keep Kavan grounded, someone who would make few demands and carry few expectations. Someone who would not need the support Wortham's family would require and who could carry the weight of Kavan's grief without bias. Níkóá could think of no one better than himself for that responsibility.

"Tell them I shall be there as soon as the Gathering ends. An hour and a half…two at most. If there is anything they need, anything I can bring, they need only ask."

"I will tell them." Níkóá bowed and backed reverently from the man's chambers. The náós was filling as he crossed it; eyes followed him, the prickles of curious thought brushing across his skin as many tried to guess what business the chamberlain had in Hes á Redh so early in the day. He scowled, realizing he would have to avoid the Gate in order not to attract additional questions. He would have to walk to the keep and use a Gate there to reach Alberni. At least, he thought with a silent groan, the walk would give him time to assimilate this loss and prepare himself to aid Kavan as best he could.

❧*❧

The little boy with the mop of blonde hair squealed at the sight of the pale man who appeared in the center of the Hall and toddled as fast as his short legs would allow to wrap his arms tight around Kavan's knees. Prince Lorant was small for his age, the lingering effects of one childhood illness after another. He was healthy now and growing stronger under his parents' attentive care, but it was k'Ádhá's grace that allowed the boy to live. Without the miracles he allowed to pass through Kavan's hands, Enesfel's future king could have died at birth and several times thereafter. Kavan wondered often what forces were at work trying to take the child's life when the Sight had foretold his destiny, and he had sworn to the boy's father, Merrek Lachlan, the only child of his beloved lost Prince Muir, that he would do everything in his power to see that Lorant fulfilled providence. His efforts, and the amount of time spent with the boy in his short life thus far, had forged a strong bond between prince and bard, the same bond Kavan had shared with Muir and now shared with Merrek.

It was why the child's fervent greeting did not create a backlash of emotion. Lifting him into an embrace gave Kavan the chance to share a needed gesture of comfort with someone safe. He buried his face in the soft golden hair, took a deep, weeping breath to calm himself, and met the surprised gaze of the boy's father across the room.

"Lord Cliáth?"

Merrek had seen him the day before, at the wedding in Bhryell. He had grown up with Sóbhán as an older brother figure and refused to miss that wedding. While Kavan had come unannounced to Fiara many times, Merrek had not expected to see him today. Nor, it was obvious, had the woman behind him expected to have him appear out of the air through the exposed Gate.

Both Gabrielle and Merrek approached, one out of concern and one with the intent of prying the clingy child out of his arms. But

Kavan showed no inclination to release Lorant. Merrek saw that before he reached them and aborted his attempt.

While Merrek had known Wortham well, growing up beneath Kavan's roof and receiving discipline, instruction, and swordsmanship training from the former captain of the Káliel guard, it was Gabrielle Kavan had come to see. The woman's half-Elyri blood was failing, though sixty-five and appearing ten years younger, her robust health had gradually given way to frailty in the years since Owain's death. Her heart was strong and Kavan believed she would remain as mistress of her grandson's estate for another ten or more years before her strength failed. But it pained him to witness the toll of mortality. Especially today.

"My lady," he began in a choking voice as he shifted Lorant onto his hip. "I have come to bring you to Alberni, and you and your family as well, Merrek, if you wish to come…"

Gabrielle's thin hand clutched the bard's wrist. "Why?" she asked as Merrek said in protest, "This is an abrupt invitation…"

"Wortham is gone." It was no less painful to say those words again, but they found voice more easily than before. "Last evening, as the sun set. I ask you to…he would want you both there. All of you."

"Oh…Kavan…"

Gabrielle did not attempt to hide her tears. She had not been as close to Wortham as Kavan, indeed she had barely known the man on a personal level. But she had sent him to Enesfel with the conviction that he would be good for Kavan and she knew how close the two men were. This day had been inevitable, but she had prayed she would not be alive to endure it…or Kavan's pain.

"Of course we shall come," Merrek said emphatically. "All of us."

"All of us what, love?"

The heavily pregnant young woman looked so much like Queen Diona had when she had been younger that Kavan often had to look twice to be assured that this was not the queen. She had the same dark hair, the same pert nose and round face, but instead of her mother's blue eyes, she bore the nearly black ones of her father's family. The shading of her skin was also darker, the infusion of Hatuish blood into the Lachlan line lending a bronze cast to Diona's children and grandchildren.

Appearance, however, was the extent of similarities between the queen and her youngest child. Arlana enjoyed the fineries of silk and lace, of embroidery and the company of other ladies to gossip with in the warmth of the sun or at the hearth. She enjoyed laughing, dancing, and singing, and had little tolerance for matters of politics and diplomacy. All the girl had wanted since she was old enough to speak her mind was to be a wife and mother and at the age of thirteen, she had set her sights on Merrek. They shared the Lachlan name, though not Lachlan blood, and as Merrek's interest in Arlana began to reciprocate, it was a match the queen fervently welcomed and approved of. Arlana was the only member of the Lachlan family to marry into an Enesfel bloodline, and as deeply as Diona had adored Muir, there was no finer match, to her eyes, for her daughter.

The union had also lent itself to the appointment of Prince Merrek as the Heir to the Throne after Prince Liahm's death. Liahm's twin, Gamal, had already assumed the throne of Hatu, and Princess Inness had wed her cousin and de Corrmick heir in Neth, Prince Oska. Having no intention of bringing Enesfel under the rule of either Hatu or Neth, choosing to keep Enesfel as a sovereign kingdom and feeling strongly that Merrek's father, Muir, would have been Enesfel's greatest king if he had been born into the proper bloodline, Prince Merrek was the logical choice for the queen to select as her heir.

With Kavan's instruction and mentoring guiding him from infancy, Merrek was enough like his father that Diona was proud to honor him with the opportunity to rule Enesfel upon her death.

Arlana, Kavan could see again as she wrapped her arm around her husband's with a bright smile that showed no immediate notice of the mood in the room, did not have the head, or the heart, for ruling.

"Captain Delamo has passed," Merrek said, extracting his arm from hers to wrap it around her shoulders. He kissed her temple in response to her abrupt change of expression and quickly spoke again to address the words he knew would come next. "I'm sure Yóáná will be there...will want to see you...and Chethá and the MacLyrs. You need not fear the baby's care..."

"And he is not due for another two months," Gabrielle agreed warmly, her arm also wrapping around the younger woman's back. "You will be in the best company for care."

Arlana nodded, though her stricken expression did not change. "I know..." she whispered sorrowfully.

The memories of her problematic labor, her previous difficulties, and Lorant's frailty after birth, were strong in her mind. There had been healers aplenty when Lorant had been born in the Alberni estate, but as her eyes met Kavan's, she acknowledged her belief that it had been the White Bard's presence that had proven most valuable in keeping her son alive. She could think of nowhere better than Alberni, amongst a family of healers, to bear her second child, but still, the journey frightened her. She assumed they would travel by Gate, something she feared despite the number of times she had done it. That fear kept her mostly bound to Fiara, but this time, if she wanted to support her friends and family, she would be unable to avoid it. "I will ready some things for Lorant…and be with you shortly."

"And I will set affairs in order here until our return." Merrek clasped Kavan's shoulder with his free hand before leaving the bard in the Hall with his grandmother and son.

Gabrielle waited until they were gone, watching Lorant play with the pendants around Kavan's neck before speaking. "How are you?"

It was a question that, in the past, Kavan would have avoided. Gabrielle no longer intimidated him, having ceased pursuing him upon her marriage to Owain. They had known each other long enough for the relationship to be comfortable and he trusted her. "I am coping…" he admitted in a small voice.

"You're not thinking of leaving us, are you?"

He scowled and shook his head. "No. He would not forgive me for such a selfish act, and I have nowhere to go."

Owain's death had coincided with the need to undertake diplomatic talks with the Cordashian King Govert, an opportunity Kavan had accepted as it removed him briefly from the painful reminders in Enesfel. There were no crises now. King Gamal and his Cáner bride had cultural reformations in Hatu in hand. Cordash, enduring the lingering illness of their king, knew peace, and King Kjell and Asta Dugan-de Corrmick were guiding Neth through the most affluent period in the kingdom's remembered history. Káliel was celebrating an economic upsurge as Piran negotiated trade agreements and built the islands into a significant naval force. Elyriá remained Elyriá, quiet and peaceful, and thanks to the relationship Queen Diona fostered with the High Mother, there was more trade between the two lands than there had been since the days of King Innis. Even trade with the Cíbhóló had increased, a needed boon to Enesfel who was in desperate need during this time of foul weather that had ruined much of the harvests for the third year in a row.

There was nothing Kavan could do about the weather or poor harvests unless k'Ádhá saw fit to grant a miracle to restore the land to its bounty. The most Kavan could do was strive to keep the people of Alberni from starvation and thirst, a task that grew more difficult with each passing month. To abandon them because of Wortham's death would allow innocent people to die.

It would not bring Wortham back.

"I would never forgive myself."

Gabrielle gave him a weak smile and rubbed his arm. "For what it's worth, you know we would welcome you…and forgive you…but I am happy to hear you will stay." If Kavan felt strong enough not to run from his grief, then to her, everything would be alright. Or as right as it could be. "I'll get my things. Do you wish me to take him to…?"

"No. He will be buried in St. Kóráhm's. I want…I do not want…"

Gabrielle kissed his cheek, sparing him the need to say more. Of course Kavan wanted Wortham close. It would be his way of keeping his beloved friend in his life.

Lorant in his arms kept him grounded as he stood in what had once been Owain's home. Without the boy, Kavan knew he would feel lost in this place, in this moment, as he swallowed the strangling tangle of emotion. The prince pressed his forehead to Kavan's cheek in a gesture of comfort. If he had to wait for the others to join him, wallowing in remembrances of those he had lost, he preferred it to be with the child in his care, a focus on the living instead of the dead.

❧*❧

"I apologize for interrupting." Dhóri's smile was infectious, his natural mirth only marginally colored by the melancholy in his eyes. He loved Wortham as an uncle, a friend, but his faith was strong and he did not see death as something deserving of grief. Those few he knew who had died had been older, near a time of natural death, or in Prince Liahm's case, had suffered so debilitating an injury that death's release was a blessing. Death brought one into the realm of the divine and that, in Dhóri's youthful naiveté, was something to be welcomed. The loss of a loved one hurt, yes, but how could it be bad if that loved one now resided in Ethenae with Dhágdhuán and the záryph?

Sóbhán worried for the day his brother was disavowed of this notion, the day he suffered his first significant, inexplicable loss. He prayed he could be there for Dhóri when that day came. He did not think his brother would be able to bear such a loss alone.

"Something has happened?" Upstairs, they could hear Chethá singing as she moved about. Neither had eaten, but they felt no rush for that today. Barely wed, they had other things on their mind beyond food. Sugar-bread and milk left by family would suffice for their first meal on their first day as husband and wife.

"Captain Delamo is with k'Ádhá; bhydhá didn't want to tell you yet." A little warmth fell away from his expression but it returned quickly as he continued, "But I couldn't see keeping this from you, not even today." He did not see delivering this news as a bad thing with the potential to darken the newlyweds' moods, when a soul entering Ethenae was a blessing. "aendhá has preserved him and bhydhá's gone to tell Merrek, I presume. You will come, won't you?"

Sóbhán's mournful attempt to smile did not reach his eyes. The request for his return to Alberni was the true reason for Dhóri's visit. Kavan's son by blood adored their father, worshipped him in a way Sóbhán sometimes considered unhealthy, and Dhóri was concerned for Kavan's welfare after the loss of his dear friend. But he was equally attached to his older brother. When Sóbhán had begun to live in Bhryell, his apprenticeship blossoming into a position of employment, Dhóri had struggled to let him go. Since then, he took every opportunity to visit Bhryell, often using bhydáni Tíbhyan as an excuse that no one would question. Old enough to travel as he chose by then, he often did not tell Kavan about his visits unless he was asked.

Recently, however, Dhóri spent more time in St. Kóráhm's, his father's love of study and language and his religious fervor drawing him deeper into the books housed there and into the life of the gdhededhá. It appeared he would turn to a life in the Faith, though whether that was because it was an escape, a calling, or a means to please their father, Sóbhán did not know.

Dhóri played the pipes Bhyrhán Bhíncári had given him as a boy but he did not possess his father's musical skill or passion. He had no talent with his hands that lent itself to harp making and he expressed no interest in it. Nor would he be a healer as so many others in their extended family were. But he was good with numbers and languages and when Kavan arranged for the directionless young man to work with the scribes in the chellé hábhai, it had been the fit Dhóri needed. He assisted in monitoring donations, purchasing supplies and cataloging books and scrolls, and most recently in the distribution of resources to the Alberni community as they suffered through yet another poor harvest.

"Tell bhydhá we will be there as soon as we are able. You should speak with Bhen; he will want to be there." While Bhen MacLyr had not been close to Wortham, he was one of Kavan's staunchest supporters. Sóbhán understood the importance of moral support at a time like this, even if Dhóri did not.

"I will." Dhóri did not question his brother's request. If Sóbhán thought Bhen should come to Alberni, Dhóri would see that he came.

❧*❧

There were more people in the halls of the estate than there had been in many years, more than Kavan expected to see. He was not prone to entertaining, preferring privacy to balls and banquets. The events he had hosted in the past twenty years had been an extension of the Feast of Saint Kóráhm, when scores of musicians and artists were welcomed to the estate to share in creative communion. He bristled and felt a surge of panic when entering the hall and finding friends and kin gathered with somber expressions of comfort and condolences. Maybe he should have anticipated this. He had not.

Most were faces he expected; only the dark-haired man who came forward to embrace him despite his tension was a surprise. Bhríd Cáner had been to Alberni twice; in the past two decades, the two tended to see each other only in Rhidam when summoned by the queen for business or celebration. The birth of his daughters had removed Bhríd from life at court, a life he had chosen not to resume after the losses endured that same year. Instead, he had focused on Levonne, the vineyards, and his daughters, to the exclusion of nearly everything else, including his extended kin, whether in Enesfel or Elyriá.

But Bhríd had liked Wortham and understood the power of the loss his cousin suffered. In many ways, it mirrored the losses the Queen's Champion had suffered during so short a time, two sons and a wife he had never been able to replace.

If anyone possessed the right to embrace Kavan in comfort, respect, and understanding, the normally reserved Bhríd did.

Behind him, Editt stood with her hands clasped before her as if out of place in this gathering, her gown one of wealth above her status, her dirty blonde hair adorned with silver combs and pearls that she could not afford. Brought into the Levonne estate as barely more than a child who had suffered the loss of a child of her own, a woman who had served as nursemaid and nanny to the Cáner daughters, she had remained in Bhríd's employ in care of his household in the place where a wife would have been. She and Bhríd had never married, and while she went wherever Bhríd traveled, it had never been proven that their relationship was anything other than platonic. Speculation remained behind closed doors; none of those who knew Bhríd cared to ask. After the losses he had endured, the man deserved camaraderie and friendship where he could find it, and Editt's company appeared to do him good.

She was welcome wherever he went, even if she did not think so.

"You have my prayers," Bhríd mumbled, pressing a kiss to Kavan's ear before releasing him. Kavan nodded, unable to speak past the knot in his throat.

"The queen sends her regrets," Syl said sadly. "Ambassadors from Cordash arrived and she did not wish to delay their business. She did, however, request an audience with you and Prince Merrek as soon as you can arrange it. She says there are matters of utmost importance."

After meeting Merrek's gaze across the room, judging that the prince had already been presented with the summons, Kavan nodded. There was no wariness, no hesitation. His relationship with Diona had remained strained, business-like and proper, never the sort Kavan had shared with her father. The damage done to his trust and the need for most Elyri to keep sufficient distance from the Lachlan Crown for too many years had prevented them from rekindling the closeness that had existed during her childhood. He had tutored her children and provided music at any celebrations in the keep, but no longer did he live in Rhidam as a constant advisor to the throne. It had been safer, for Enesfel and himself, for Kavan to maintain that professional relationship as Diona fought to stabilize the kingdom. Afterward, there had been no compulsion for Kavan to resume life at court.

The only time he had considered doing so had been in the months after Espen's death, but his fear the Diona might seek comfort or affection from him as she had once done had kept him away.

As much as she had admired and respected Wortham, as much as she loved Kavan, it was little surprise to him that she would not come to see the man buried. Diona had buried too many. She would find some other way to honor the man's service.

Merrek, he knew, had been too long away from Rhidam, tending to his wife when he should have been tending to affairs of state. Other than convincing her to travel through the Gate again, there should be little difficulty in convincing Arlana to visit her mother. She had been complaining for weeks about wanting to go home before the new baby consumed her time and prevented her from visiting even longer.

"The meal is served," announced Rhyrdan from the back of the room at the dining hall entrance, dressed in a stately, somber fashion of white fit for such an occasion. His sweeping gesture invited the guests to the tables behind him covered with an assortment of dishes.

Both Zelenka and Emeria appeared weary but otherwise blank-faced at the opposite side of the room near the chair Kavan claimed as his own. The place beside it was set as well but the chair was draped in white with Wortham's sword resting where the man should be sitting. Zelenka looked uncomfortable with that setting, but judging from the tilt of Madoc's head, it had been the eldest son's decision and neither she, nor either of the other siblings, had the desire to go against Madoc's wishes. Only if Kavan objected would the sword be taken away but Kavan, seeing it there, found it oddly comforting.

Yóáná Delamo, the daughter of Gaelán Cáner and Asta Dugan, took Kavan's hand and accompanied him into the room. A healer like her father and so many others in the Cáner bloodline, she had been raised as part of Kavan's household until the age of three, when her healing gifts required training elsewhere. Her mother married Kjell de Corrmick that same year. Asta had been unable to rationalize rearing the girl in Neth and denying her the opportunity to develop her potential. She opted instead to provide her the best Elyri training as Gaelán would have wanted, even though it meant rarely seeing the only part of her late husband Asta would ever have. There was a hint of bitterness about the girl, giving the healer a harder edge than many in her profession, but she was skilled and determined and that edge allowed her to treat most patients without emotional investment.

Kavan was the only father Yóáná had known, Alberni her only home, and her choice to marry Wortham's oldest son bound her to this place even after Madoc was appointed Lord High Justice to the Crown and his subsequent appointment as Duke of Chantel. Rescuing Liahm when the scaffold had collapsed had earned Madoc both appointments, even though the prince later died of his injuries. That had not been

Madoc's fault; he had done what he could to save the prince and the queen had acknowledged his efforts accordingly.

Kavan was pleased to have them here. It was good for Wortham's family to be together.

The meal passed with tales of Wortham's life, stories told by others as Kavan listened, picking at a meal he could not eat. Many were tales he had never heard, tidbits from Wortham's interactions with others that Kavan had not been part of. They were shared, he realized, for his benefit. As many years as he and Wortham had spent together, not every moment had been in each other's company. Kavan valued those unfamiliar tales for they provided new moments and memories to treasure. If he had ever taken the captain's company for granted, he no longer did, and he prayed that Wortham had gone into peace knowing that any such slights had never been intentional.

It had been decided that Wortham would be buried the following dawn, which allowed the residents of St. Kóráhm's the opportunity to prepare a place for him, one of prominence that his children had selected together. Some of Kavan's guests, after more hours of talk and drink in front of the Hall hearth, retired to rooms their host provided while others lingered at the fire long into the night, talking more, drinking more than was healthy, while Kavan excused himself to keep watch over Wortham's still form one final time.

Zelenka would not see him. She had visited long enough to bathe his body and dress him in his favorite clothing and then left him under the watch of others. Her custom demanded the dead be attended to until left in a burial cave. With no cave nearby, she accepted the local custom of burial within the earth, but she could not stay with him despite her beliefs. It had been Wortham she had followed out of her distant homeland, Wortham who had given her children and a life she had never thought to have. Now that he was gone, she appeared as lost as Kavan felt.

He knew she would stay as the manager of his household and the servants. He would make sure she continued to know she was welcome, and with two of her children still here, she would go nowhere else. Kavan doubted she would be happy. Her children would give her solace, but Kavan suspected it would not be enough.

He had doubts about his happiness without Wortham as well.

Fingers tangled in the thick hair of wiry gray, Kavan sat beside the low cot on which Wortham rested and lay his head on the pillow, pressed against Wortham's for what comfort that would give. He no longer smelled like himself, smelled instead of the musky perfumed soap Zelenka had used, and there was no warmth, no gentle rise and fall of his chest, no snoring as if in slumber. No way to hear the music pushing through Kavan's head begging to be shared. If Wortham heard him, it was from somewhere far beyond Kavan's ability to touch him.

That did not stop his voice. Softly at first, then louder, with more conviction and passionate grief, Kavan sang from his soul, giving to Wortham, wherever he was, the gift of a farewell that proved his passing would not devastate the bard into eternal silence.

Throughout the Cliáth manor, heads lifted, eyes closed, and tears were shed to hear the offering to the dead that lasted until Kavan's voice could no longer push through his grief. Then the house was silent and Wortham's presence faded.

Captain Wortham Delamo was gone.

## ❧Chapter 3❧

K hwílen Kesábhá replaced every shovelful of dirt into the hole from whence it had come and oversaw the placement of the Kílyn cross marker Kavan had requisitioned at the head of the man's grave. Where the clay marred the white stone, he carefully cleaned it away with fingertips calloused by years spent scribing copies of books and scrolls brought to St. Kóráhm's for reproduction and safekeeping.

The vast library continued to expand as documents, both profane and sacred, arrived from every corner of the known realms to be copied, restored, housed, and redistributed into the hands of those who contributed to the library's upkeep. Kavan examined each document when it arrived to assess its content, and those he deemed of greatest significance, originals of ancient origin or tomes judged to be rarities, were copied and then housed in a room only he and Khwílen had access to. Even books forbidden by the Faith in Clarys were kept, not a single shred of history, philosophy, or secular enjoyment deemed worth destroying regardless of his feelings about the words or the nature of the imagery depicted within. The destruction of Kóráhm's books by the Faith hierarchy, and Kavan's subsequent discovery of how much of the man's history, life and beliefs had been lost, had taught him a valuable lesson. If there was a chance that any of these arcane, obscure tomes might prove useful to someone someday, Kavan believed it was a sin to destroy them.

Khwílen kept diligent watch over document after document, copying his share between periods of prayer and worship and service to the community both inside and outside of the chellé. It was a duty, an honor, he cherished, as was the responsibility for overseeing the dispensation of the dead.

The burial of a beloved patron was a service performed rarely, since so many in St. Kóráhm's were Elyri and thus likely to serve for decades. In the years since the chellé's opening, only five had been buried in this plot, the first having been k'gdhededhá Jermyn. The last was Wortham Delamo. Both men were dear to their benefactor and beloved by those who served within these walls. Neither had been part of the chellé community, but without Kavan, the abbey would not stand, so if the Duke chose to bury someone in this sacred ground, none of the adherents would complain. k'gdhededhá Jermyn had been an Alberni native, the leader of their faith in Enesfel, a member of the Order of Saint Kóráhm, making his interment here logical. Captain Delamo was welcome because he was beloved by Kavan.

No other reason was necessary.

At the foot of the upturned plot, having helped with the setting of the heavy marker but otherwise not interfering in the duty Khwílen had taken upon himself, Raenár Magk stood sentry with his sword in his hands, the sole soldier taking up the watch at Kavan's request. Wortham had been a soldier from the start, Kavan's protector, and had remained so after the anti-Elyri violence had robbed him of the sight in one eye. Together, Wortham and Raenár had trained each of the men serving the chellé as guards. The violence of two decades past had proven the need for protection, not only for the Elyri who served here but of others who came seeking shelter, solace, solitude, or something else. It was said that Kavan had placed other protections around the chellé, but Khwílen knew nothing about those things and so the three dozen men at arms were housed and fed in exchange for what they could offer. Not only did they serve a watch shift, they also participated in the daily life of the chellé, contributing to worship and work, many tending the Duke's private groves of fruit trees and fields of grain which lent considerable resources to the chellé's stores.

In these lean times, there was little successful growing, although the ground was tilled continuously so that, when the rain fell again, there might be the chance of planting and harvest. It was too late in the year for planting, the weather soon to turn frigid and bring possible of snow, so while his men mended walls and fences and prepared roofs for the winter, Raenár was here, watching over Wortham until Khwílen was done. He would remain until sunset as promised and then he would return to his primary duties with a heavy heart.

Wortham would be missed.

Khwílen did not know why Kavan had made this request of the Elyri captain, nor did he ask. Stone set, the ground once more in place, he straightened his stiff shoulders and wiped his hands on his trousers with a groan.

"Won't be the last I bury," he muttered, thinking of the people starving in the far north of Enesfel where too much rain had drowned the crops and in the southern quarter of the kingdom where a lack of rain had puckered the earth and kept crops from growing. People were dying there, or else leaving for the still fertile central regions of the kingdom, but even in those places, there was suffering. The less than average rainfall of the last three years, combined with the influx of population from north and south, took its toll on what resources the Crown and lords had managed to keep in reserve. If the weather did not improve, starvation and the rumors of northern and southern plague were going to overrun cities like Rhidam, Levonne, Chantel, and Alberni. Kingdom-wide devastation was not far away, and the residents of St. Kóráhm's would suffer with everyone else.

"Lord Cliáth will see to our welfare." Raenár did not know how, but he believed in the man he had come to Enesfel, to the chellé, to serve. His introduction to the bard had been through the miraculous appearance of St. Kóráhm in a cell where Kavan had been briefly imprisoned. Any man blessed enough to be granted the visitation of a saint was worth believing in.

"I pray you are right, Captain...but in case you're not, I ask you to pray for Enesfel and all the Sovereignties. I have a feeling we'll need those prayers more than a belief in miracles."

❧*❧

"You wished to see me?" Merrek found the queen in the dayroom brightly lit with both candles and a fire upon the hearth as well as the noonday sun that streamed through the open-curtained windows. He blinked at the brightness, noting at once the way the woman squinted at the book in her hands. He knew from his study of Lachlan history that she was the same age her father had been, give or take a handful of months, when he had passed the throne to her brother, but other than a scatter of white in her coal-black hair, she did not appear old to him.

She looked beautiful, as beautiful as his own bride, and he thanked k'Ádhá again for the blessing of Arlana in his life.

Diona looked at him, her welcoming smile erasing the frustration she felt more and more of late. She did not expect he would notice the look she had quickly hidden. Gesturing to the chair nearest her, she asked, "Has Kavan come with you?"

"Yes. He and Arlana both, as did Gabrielle, and Lorant of course." He smiled, hoping that news would please her. "They are settling him for a nap I believe, and then Arlana will be along to see you. I think Lord Cliáth is still in the oratory if you would like me to get him…"

Diona did want to see Kavan, to express her remorse and regret for the loss of Captain Delamo, offer the bard anything she had that might ease his suffering. This was the personal sort of loss she identified with, as personal as the loss of her husband and son had been, and though she knew there was little that would take away the pain, sometimes the offer was comfort enough. "No, not yet. I have matters to discuss with you first; there will be time to speak with him before the end of the day. Sit…please. Tell me how you are."

❧*❦

The corridors of the castle seemed oddly empty as Kavan exited the upper oratory in search of the queen. They were no emptier than they had been during his last visit here, but the absence of Wortham made everything seem emptier. He had no illusions that putting the man in the ground would ease his loneliness. Only time would bring solace and he had no hope that the day of finding it would come soon.

Without children to tend, to care for and mentor, without the company of those he had once served with, Kavan suspected the castle would continue to feel empty for quite some time.

He passed Fen Geli in the hall; the Inquisitor grinned and nodded but hurried about whatever business he was involved in and Kavan suspected he had not yet learned of Wortham's death. He was met by the same warmth from the passing servants, as if he had never been away, as if the day was like any other, and Kavan felt the tension in his body bleed away with each welcome he received.

Being in no hurry to face Diona, knowing she would be busy with Merrek and family, Kavan had paused for the opportunity to pray in a place he had once spent many hours. He mused that he should have brought his harp, but as he had no heart to perform, the thought had not occurred to him. His impression of Syl's request was of business to discuss, perhaps some desire to know the status of Alberni's food stores, his opinion of how to proceed through the struggle Enesfel faced, or that Diona wished to reminisce about her son and extend her condolences for Wortham in private. Kavan did not expect to be here more than a few hours. His harp would wait for his evening return when he again visited Wortham.

But prayers had now been spent and the memories of Wortham in this room, the miracles shared here, the comfort and company the man had selflessly offered again and again, scratched and burned through Kavan's concentration until he gave up on his efforts and left the altar in search of Diona. If not Diona, perhaps he would find Níkóá and share a few moments of friendly company. Ártur would no doubt appreciate his attention as well, but the force of the healer's concern for his well-being was more than Kavan wished to bear.

"Kavan."

Paying little attention to where his feet had led, his senses unconsciously following the aroma of the meal being set for the evening, Kavan paused outside the dayroom where Diona sat at the window. He blinked, unaware that so much of the day had passed. His prayers had found voice longer than he had intended.

"My apologies, My Queen. I did not see you there. I should have come sooner. My prayers are with your mourning on this day of remembrance…"

She stood and offered her hand, taking two hesitant and uncertain steps closer. Believing she thought him offended by her refusal to come to Wortham's burial, Kavan closed the distance and reached for her hand. She withdrew hers before he could touch it and inclined her head towards the nearest chair.

"This day is less about the past and more about what is now. Liahm," she sighed, "is long gone. You have reason to be distracted; this cannot be an easy day." She sighed and sat. "When Espen died, when Liahm died, I thought my life over. Not," she added with a slight twist of her lips, "that your friendship with Wortham was the same."

Feeling his cheeks flush at the implication of her words, Kavan lowered his head as he sat on the settee and made a show of arranging the pillows there. He and Wortham might not have shared physical intimacy, but Kavan could think of no one person as close in spirit and love as he had been with Wortham. Not even his parting with Orynn, for their brief time together, or with Myreth which had been briefer still, had burned with the flame of grief he carried for his friend. Whatever love was, it was surely what he felt for Wortham.

"But you endured," he murmured, thinking she was waiting for him to speak, to agree with her or not.

"There were children, other people, and the kingdom." She sighed. "Yes, I endured. I had to." Like her father before her, she had chosen not to remarry, but unlike her father, she refused to blame her children for Espen's death and refused to let his death define her. She had allowed suitors but had taken none of their attention to heart. Perhaps she was waiting for someone specific. Perhaps she felt that remarriage was not worth the risks. She was the Queen of Enesfel. She had no desire to share power with a man who would not appreciate her strengths.

Then had come the loss of Liahm, and Kavan believed any thoughts she had entertained about remarriage had been devoured by grief anew.

She closed the book she held and reached to place it on the table beside her. The volume teetered on the edge then fell to the floor with a thump. "I've gotten clumsy in my old age," she chuckled ruefully.

"You are not old." But something was wrong. Kavan could see it in the way she fumbled for the book, the way her eyes looked past it rather than at it, and he frowned. How had he not noticed these details before? "What is wrong, Diona?"

She winced but shrugged and laughed softly. "Why must something be wrong, Lord Harper?"

"You requested me here for a purpose." His gaze traveled up her arm as she lifted the book and watched her place it on the table, this time with more care. "I do not think it was to discuss Liahm or Wortham."

"You're wrong. I asked you here to express my sympathies and apologize for not being there when he was…"

Scowling, Kavan slid across the settee until he was at her side, noticing how she inched away and leaned towards the table as if to escape. "Duty makes demands of us at the worst times," he murmured, the dual meaning of his words fueling his actions as he caught her wrist. She stiffened but he did not release her. Though he was no healer, he had other skills and he knew she was hiding something.

Before he could voice his thoughts, Diona said, "I am bestowing the title of regent on Merrek."

Kavan's mouth snapped shut and he stared. Those were not the words he expected to hear from any Lachlan, particularly Diona.

She gently pulled free of his grasp and stood, moving to the window to put distance between them. Kavan saw it, hesitation in her steps, the way she gauged the distance around furniture, between herself and the window. "Are you ill?" he asked weakly, the sudden thought wrenching his already twisted gut into tighter knots. She was too young. Too vibrant. He could not lose her the way he had lost Arlan. Losing another Lachlan monarch was unthinkable.

"That would be preferable." Her tone was bitter, mirroring the clenching of her hands at her sides. "Do you know how frustrating it is to have all of my mental faculties…and yet being incapable of seeing the subjects I rule?"

Blind? The queen was blind…or growing so? The knowledge left him stunned and cold. "Has Ártur…?"

"There is nothing healers can do. They have tried, and you…" her gaze moved down to the wrist he had held and she sighed in defeat.

So she had called him here in hopes of a miracle and Kavan had failed her. "I am sorry," he whispered, though he knew it was no failing of his. He could not control the miracles k'Ádhá granted. If Kavan could spare her, he would. He held his hands before him, recalling a time when they had been as useless as the woman's eyes would soon be, remembering his helplessness and frustration vividly even after so many years. He understood her pain too well. "How long have you known?" he asked, wondering why his cousin had said nothing to him. Ártur had probably been ordered not to speak of it.

"Too long. I had hoped…" She sighed again and turned towards him. He could tell that she saw him, but not clearly, it seemed. "But I can ignore it no longer. Within six months, perhaps a year…perhaps less…it will be too late. I need his eyes, his ears…his feet and arms…to do the things I can no longer do."

Kavan stood and fretfully approached her. "Does Merrek know?"

"He does. I told him earlier today, and I will tell my advisors next, although I'm sure they suspect something is afoot. I choose to give Merrek the right of rule while I can still do so in a dignified manner, before I am forced aside. I can continue to rule outside of the public eye, but Merrek will be the face of the Lachlan monarchy. I trust

Merrek and know he will work with me. Two heads together will place Enesfel in competent hands without any regret." She paused and murmured, "Did your Sight ever predict this?"

He shook his head. The Sight had revealed she would be queen but never had he imagined the choice to pass on the throne would come while she remained alive.

"I am…" For the first time since Diona was a child, he drew her against him and hugged her, his hand on the back of her head, accepting the way she melted against him with gradual relief. There was nothing amorous about the way she clung to him. No attempt, as there had once been, to woo his love, only a little girl on the verge of losing herself to a physical failing she could not overcome. "I am sorry, Diona. I wish there was something I could do."

Shivering, not with desire but with the effort to control her sadness, she croaked, "You can pray. For me, for Merrek, for Enesfel." She tipped her head to look at his face. "There is plague in the south, plague in the north. Drought and dearth. It is only a matter of time before these things reach us. Some will accuse me of forsaking Enesfel…but it is precisely fear for Enesfel that forces me to rely on someone who can face these challenges sound in mind and body. I do not know if Merrek…if anyone…can pull Enesfel through this, but I do know I will not be able to do so alone, no matter how I wish it. k'Ádhá must take pity on us, Kavan, or else Enesfel will fall. Do not let Muir's son bear the burden of failure in the annals of history."

Kavan squeezed his eyes shut. "I'll do my best," he promised. There was little else he could do. Whether prayer would be enough to save Enesfel remained to be learned. "When will you…?"

"Two weeks. The news will be sent to the Lords in the morning. Those who will come will have to travel if they choose. Many might not, out of fear of plague, but they will be given time and opportunity. Arrangements must be made; Merrek must be brought up to date with the state of the kingdom, prepared for what he will face, given the chance to make appointments of his own staff if he chooses. You will…you will be here for him…if he needs you?"

Kavan looked at the half-crescent pendant Diona wore, the one that matched his own. It had originally belonged to Arlan, having been given to him by his father, and then passed to first Hagan and then Diona as each successor had stepped to the throne. He did not think she would give it to Merrek now.

"I will. I am bound to."

What would it mean if Diona kept the pendant? What would it mean if she chose to give it to Merrek? How would that transfer of power manifest itself? He was afraid to find out.

"If nothing else, Lorant needs me." He believed in Merrek's ability to rule without his direct counsel. He was less certain of Lorant's survival, despite his increasingly good health and the Sight that had shown Kavan the boy's future more than once. Someday, Lorant would claim Enesfel's throne too, but only if he remained alive. "Whatever his needs, Merrek has only to ask. He knows this, but I will, of course, reassure him."

Diona lay her head once more against the bard's broad chest. "Thank you, Kavan."

She remembered often sitting on his lap as a girl, ear pressed to his chest, listening to the beating of his heart as he told stories or plucked the buds of songs from the vines of brass harp strings. His warmth, his strength, the powerful beating of his life force, had been the most reassuring things in the world, next to her father. She had lost both men at nearly the same time in her life, something she had regretted ever since, and never had she thought to again be blessed with Kavan's steadfastness. How foolish she had been to let this go. How unfortunate to regain it only now with the gradual loss of her eyesight. Damned that fever last winter for robbing her. But she thanked the stars for this moment, his support given without fear or strings attached.

So long as Kavan persisted, the Lachlans, and Enesfel, could endure. She was certain of it.

In short order, every lord and lady in the farthest corners of the Sovereignty knew that due to health issues, the popular, strong, resourceful Queen of Enesfel, who had rescued the land from the scourge of the Corylliens and restored it to prosperity, was resigning some of the responsibilities of rule into the hands of Merrek Lachlan, son of a bastard, grandson of another, the husband of the princess, but a Lachlan nonetheless. Though Merrek had been present at every royal function since Liahm's death, and many others before that, he had not grown up in the public eye and most knew little about him. All that was known was that the queen had chosen him to share power in her time of need instead of giving Enesfel's throne to Hatu or Neth. Merrek was their best hope for fortune so long as the weather turned.

A change in the monarchy could not bring a change in weather, or an end to the plagues being jointly called the Yellow Sisters or the Yellow Death, but Merrek might bring other changes that would prove enough to save the kingdom from collapse.

Those recently gathered in Kavan's hall were unexpectedly summoned to Rhidam for the appointment of a prince-regent. Word was sent to Elyriá as well, so Kyne Mórne would know that, while the balance of power shifted in Rhidam, she was not losing an ally or a friend. Nobles and diplomats came from across the realms, and from Hatu, Kavan brought Gamal to be there for his mother when she needed her children most.

The message sent to Princess Inness, however, was tossed into the flames on the hearth as she sniffed in contempt, unopened and unread.

"You will not…?" started Prince Oska, prodding through the fire with the poker to rescue the message, hoping Inness would change her mind and read it. He already knew what the letter said, for the news had been delivered to his parents at the same hour, brought by the chamberlain of Enesfel himself, who had placed the written invitation in Oska's hands to give to his bristly bride. Oska had remained in the de Corrmick hall long enough to hear the reason for the change in leadership roles in Enesfel, not death but rather some debilitating ailment that left the queen unable to rule effectively alone.

Thinking about it again, he looked at his misshapen hand, his too-short leg, and sighed. If the great Queen of Enesfel, a woman he deeply admired, was forced to share her throne due to disability, what chance did Oska de Corrmick have of reigning? His mother assured him often that his mind was what mattered, and that with it, he could rule any lands he chose, but what if, he mused as he picked up the charred bit of parchment, she was wrong? What if Inness was right and his mother's words were lies?

"Watch her give away what should be mine?" Inness plopped onto the cushioned chair nearest the hearth and kicked a stray spark back into the fire with the toe of her boot. Unlike her sister, Inness preferred boots to slippers, trousers, or at least trousers beneath her dress when she was forced by decorum to wear one, to lace and velvet gowns. Her straight black hair was cut short to her neckline at the shoulder in a fashion that looked more boyish than princess-like, and she wore as little makeup and adornment as she could get away with. Her features, aristocratic and dark as her father's had been, gave her a regal air that none of her siblings shared and she was taller than her brothers or her parents. Next to Oska, she towered, but she had never made an issue of that height difference.

"Do you regret our marriage?" he asked, thinking that, perhaps if she had remained in Enesfel, unmarried, Inness would have the throne she coveted.

Inness shook her head. When the decision to marry had been made, Enesfel's throne had been promised to her brother Liahm. No one except Kavan could have foreseen the accident that had caused his death. No one except Kavan could have foreseen any situation that would force Queen Diona into the position she felt herself to be in now. Despite the decision that had removed her from Enesfel and the possibility of the right of rule at her mother's side, Inness would never regret her decision to marry Oska.

Oska was everything she needed him to be. His stature and physical impairments mattered not. Another princess would have resisted such a match, even though Oska was the heir to the Neth throne and a more-than-competent statesman. Inness had not cared. She had been the one to pursue him from a very early age. He accepted her as she was, just as she accepted him. It was a match that confounded their parents, but it had not been discouraged. Wedding the Lachlan and dc Corrmick bloodlines into such a tight pact would, both kingdoms hoped, cement a lasting peace between them where once there had been centuries of war.

Ignoring the pout that was a near-permanent feature on her face, Oska put the charred letter on the desk and began to rub her shoulders. His hand was not so malformed as to keep him from that. "You wouldn't go to share it with her, so why be angry?" There was enough estrangement between mother and daughter that Oska could not imagine any sharing of power between them. "What do you need them for? You have me. One day Neth will be ours."

"Will it?" she muttered, resting her head briefly against his arm. It was not the first time she had presented that question to him, nor would it be the last, but once again Oska chose to ignore it. His wife wanted so much more from life and he wanted desperately to give it to her.

"It will. I swear it. And when it is, we shall rule together." He would be monarch in name, but he trusted her judgment, her intellect, her shrewd strength that would empower his rule and lead Neth to a position of prominence once more. The land would be shed of its anti-Elyri stance, as that was the one thing he and his father agreed on when it came to Neth's future, but no longer would the kingdom suffer a deficit of military might, cowering beneath the shade of her neighbors to the east, west, and south.

Inness tilted her face to look at him with a smile. He was less handsome than some, his blond hair thin on top and cropped short against his skull to downplay its sparseness. His pale blue eyes were narrow and wide-set, his nose wide and flat. But his smile was warm, earnest, and intended only for her. She had long ago stopped noticing things that others called faults. Whatever fate k'Ádhá intended, Oska was hers and that would never change. "Thank you, husband."

That word, as always, made him beam.

"But I doubt we will attend, even your mother and father…or have you forgotten it will be your brother's birthday? Guests are due; even your sister should be here if Govert is healthy enough. I doubt your father will cancel such plans on so short notice, not when the lords will already be en route." If it had been Oska's birthday, she suspected an exception would have been made and his parents would have made the journey to Rhidam. But, she thought with a silent growl, such an exception would never be made for the preferred son Jerit.

"I haven't forgotten." His adoration of his baby brother was almost tangible and annoyed her enough that she sat forward, pulling away from him. Immediately regretting what he had said, or rather how he had said it, Oska sat on the arm of the chair and wrapped his arm around her shoulders. "He's a child. He's no threat to me, or us. He's more interested in being like Mother than being a king."

It was no secret in the de Corrmick castle that Asta Dugan de Corrmick, at one-time High Inquisitor of Enesfel, was teaching her youngest son the ways of the Association, the skills of a rogue, the life of a Dugan. Jerit had been the one to initiate the unconventional education, just as Asta had done from her father, and Kjell had agreed to it in the hopes that the knowledge could be employed in Neth as it had been so successfully in Enesfel. Time and again, Jerit promised Oska that, when his brother became king, Jerit would be the best inquisitor in the Sovereignties. The youngest de Corrmick was preparing himself for a life in which he would never rule on Neth's throne, despite his kingly name, would instead willingly serve his brother not as a prince at his side or a frivolous reveler, but as a useful member of court with skills a good king would need. Inness, however, refused to accept the almost eleven-year-old's intentions at face value.

Many things could change in three years. Jerit would mature and learn, and then Oska would see his brother for what he truly was.

Oska laughed off such nebulous threats, refusing to believe that his brother could mean anything other than what he said, that his position would ever change.

"He will not stay a child…and your father will see it."

"See what?" Inness shook her head and Oska frowned. "See what, Inness?" he prodded.

"That Jerit is better than you," she snapped.

"Better? Inness…how could you…?" He shrunk away from her, wounded by her words, bringing her to her knees before him, her arms wrapped lovingly around his wide body so that he could not escape.

"He's not better, husband," she purred pleadingly. "He could never be better. You will be the best king Neth has ever seen. You bear a hero's name and a hero you shall be. We will give Neth everything she deserves. Jerit cannot do that. He doesn't know how, will never know how, but your father will think the opposite…"

With her hands stroking his lower back, his upset was quickly soothed and he bent to kiss the top of her head in relief. Of course she meant his father would think Jerit was better. Inness would never insult Oska that way. She loved him as he was.

The look of relief on her face, buried as it was against his soft belly, went unseen, and the release of panic that tensed her shoulders and relaxed them again went unnoticed. She had not lost him.

In the dimness of their private chamber, Inness smiled.

The physician dried his hands on the cloth that hung from his waist as he stepped from the bedroom, his expression grim as he looked at the woman who twisted her fawn brown tresses around her fingers. Rarely did Bhetá Gabersdon appear vulnerable, her strength a gift from the man who had raised her intending that she should one day follow in his footsteps. But today, as they listened to the dry, labored coughing of the man in the room behind the physician, her distress and upset were understandable and expected.

"Do not go in, m'lady…the plague…"

It was the diagnosis she had expected as soon as the man once known as the youngest knight in Enesfel had taken to his bed. Balint was not a man to let sickness keep him from duty, and as the symptoms of the scourge had crept up on him, the shaking and uncoordinated movements, the general weakness and loss of short term memory, and now the difficulty breathing…with what breaths he could take exhaled with both mucus and blood, there had been very little else it could be. Most victims showed no symptoms until some three days after catching it. After that, it ran its course, resulting frequently in death within one to three weeks for the majority of people, sheep, and cattle who were infected. The symptoms had been long overdue and in the early stages, had been ignored so that Balint could carry on working amongst his needy subjects, without considering that he might be exposing them to death. By the time he was forced to bed, relenting against his wishes to the summoning of a physician, Bhetá knew it was too late to save him.

"If he's infected, I'm already exposed," she snapped. By the time symptoms began to appear, those around the victim were already tainted and her father, true to stubborn form, had been masking those symptoms for days as he pushed to keep his lands, his city, from collapsing beneath the weight of plague and drought. Nearly one-quarter of the city had succumbed to the ravaging disease, and to starvation and thirst, and many had fled, some north with the hopes of finding rain-kissed lands there, some south into Hatu. Nelori had not been the first city touched by disaster, as her proximity to the coast had meant moisture being carried in from the sea, but like Wexel and Jardin, it had not taken long to initiate a city-wide quarantine in the hopes of containing the spread. The quarantines had come too late, however, as it was known the plague had spread at least as far north as Seres and its surrounding territories, and from Hatu, reports of plague trickled back, telling of the spread there as well.

"I have news; I must see him. It cannot wait." It certainly would not wait for his death. Bhetá felt prepared to succeed him, to guide Nelori, but she did not feel prepared to lose her father. Without him, she would be alone, friendships and the quest for love having been set aside to become one of but a few female knights in the Sovereignties. She was also, according to the queen, the best knight, aside from Bhríd Cáner and her father, a distinction Bhetá proudly accepted.

Behind his mask of dried herbs and oil-soaked cloth, the physician nodded in reluctant agreement. He did not open the door, however, but stepped aside and allowed her to face her father and the plague on her own. Odds were, if she had been living with the man through the initial incubation period and first stages of decline, she was already a carrier. Since she had yet to show symptoms, perhaps she was one of the lucky few blessed to be immune.

She could, however, spread the contagion to others. With no idea how long the sickness remained active within a person's body, it was impossible to know how long she might be infected. How long she might need to stow herself away to protect others.

But at least she would be no threat to her father. And, the physician admitted as she entered the room lit by a single bedside candle, if she had already contracted it, symptomatic or not, her father was likely no threat to her nor she to him.

Balint stirred at the burst of cooler air that rushed in from the corridor and swirled around the room to be absorbed by the hearth fire and radiated back as warmth. "Bhetá…you should not be…"

"Too late for that, father," she said gently from the chair at his bedside. There was no accusation, only a gentle chastisement that he had continued to serve when he should have been resting and limiting the exposure, theirs and his, to sickness. "I'm not going to let some stodgy physician bring you this news…"

"What news?" From the note of hope, she knew he was hoping for some admission from her that she was to be married. He fretted about leaving her alone. But marriage meant children, and Bhetá would rather devote herself to the knighthood than be trapped in a home with squalling children. Besides, she carried Elyri blood. Other half-Elyri had married Teren spouses but Bhetá had no illusions about a Teren wanting to marry her when he learned the truth. The intimidation factor alone of being a superior swordsman and jouster kept most men from seriously pursuing her.

"The queen…Prince Merrek will be named regent in two weeks."

"Regent…we must go at once. She cannot…" He attempted to rise but Bhetá pushed him down with one hand.

"You are going nowhere."

"She may be dying…"

"She certainly will if you expose her to this." She pointed to the bloody cloths scattered around the bedside table. The physician should have taken those away. "The messenger stopped outside the walls to deliver the news without exposure…and I told another to relay our apologies for being unable to be there."

Balint groaned and sank into his pillows, his brow furrowed in consternation. "We should be…" After everything he had given to her father, her brother, to her, to fail his queen now was a dismal fate.

"I know." With the damp cloth from the washbasin, she dabbed his moist forehead, his neck, and upper chest in the hopes of easing his fever. "She will understand. It would be foolish for either of us to make the journey. We will not break isolation to put in an appearance. The Gabersdons are better than such political games."

Balint patted her hand as she grinned at him. "My wise girl."

In her gratitude for saving her life, the Elyri woman Dhybhé had agreed to marry him and gave him a single child before returning to Elyriá. There would be no shame in the unconventional union; she would outlive him, barring some unforeseen tragedy, and could afford to wait for that day to remarry, if she chose, without difficulty. Balint had never intended to marry, but the thought of an heir had been appealing, and so accepting Dhybhé's terms had been an easy choice. It had been better to have some of her, than none of her.

She had given him a daughter, had remained with him in Nelori until the child was weaned, and then, without a word of farewell, stepped out of his life as abruptly as she had fallen into it. Balint had been angry at first, denied the chance to say goodbye, but as years passed he had grown to accept her decision. He would have manipulated her with pleas, for himself and their daughter, into remaining in Nelori. It was not as if they had been deeply enamored with each other. There had been love and gratitude and respect, but it had not been, he knew, enough for her. Neither was their daughter.

He had never hidden the truth. When she grew old enough to inquire about her mother, Balint explained how the woman had been called home to Elyriá. That truth grew more elaborate and detailed as Bhetá matured, until the day she understood that her mother's leaving had nothing to do with a lack of love and more to do with needing to be where she belonged. She had left the girl with her father, as she had promised, knowing Bhetá would be adored and treasured.

If she resented her mother, Balint had never seen it. Instead, she had developed a close bond with him that resulted in her following his footsteps along a path Enesfel's queen had encouraged. With a woman inquisitor, Diona had no cause to discourage Bhetá's wish of knighthood, particularly when she proved herself more capable than many of those with whom she regularly competed in tournaments.

As Balint had grown older, more and more of the running of the Nelori estate was given into her hands, where she proved just as capable as she was on the tournament field. She would do well when he was gone, though Balint had not expected to leave her so soon.

"Rest, father." She ignored his coughing to kiss his forehead. "Get well, and then we shall journey to Rhidam together."

He nodded, coughing, knowing it was a journey he would likely never make.

❧Chapter 4❦

"Are you certain you wish to do this?"

Prince Merrek turned to see himself in the tall mirror brought into the stateroom where both he and his aunt, the queen, awaited their entrance cue. The week had been a flurry of conferences, business with dignitaries and advisors, of documents to sign, file, and record appropriately in preparation for the moment bearing down on them like a charging bull. The sharing of power was nearly complete, needing only the ceremonial dividing of the regalia between queen and prince, a practice that had not been done in several generations, and the pressing of the royal seal into already signed documents that would signal the act official. Until it was done, it was not too late for Diona to change her mind, to retain complete control as was her right, and Merrek, in the secret places of his heart, hoped she would do so. He believed in his capacity to rule, had been educated and prepared to take this step, and felt ready to do so, and sharing the obligation for Enesfel was not the same as being the king.

But he also believed in the queen's strengths, that her disability would not overly hinder her from leading Enesfel. There was no writ demanding she share power and her encroaching blindness did not affect her mind. His primary function would be as a figurehead, someone to be seen and heard on her behalf, someone who could read and sign documents she could not, someone who could judge visual clues she could no longer see. He was amicable to that arrangement, but Merrek cursed fate for trying to strip a good and strong ruler of what was legally hers.

He suspected that blindness, on top of the loss of her husband and son, had sapped her confidence, but he would never voice those thoughts. Perhaps if Kavan returned as her advisor, as the bard had once been for King Arlan, she would feel less need to share her crown.

Kavan would not take that step, whatever his reason, and so this was her judgment to make. It was her choice to step away before blindness forced her into inefficiency and she was determined to do it with the dignity of a true Lachlan. Her grace and determination made the prince respect her more.

"We could wait…"

"For the Yellow Death to take them all?" Her soft laugh was a false one, forced and hollow. "It is better for Enesfel that we do this while there are still lords and ladies to witness it. Little will fundamentally change. Or do you require time to consider…?"

He shook his head. "It is not that. But surely you acknowledge that you are fit and entitled to the throne; no one is asking you to…"

"I am not going to wait for them to do so. I will not be an object of ridicule, scorn, or pity at the end of pointed fingers. A robust leader is needed to guide Enesfel through what lies ahead, and I cannot do so effectively if I cannot see. Your father should have been where you are but I have faith and trust in your wisdom, just as the people shall."

The nerves he had kept appeased thus far overtook him and Merrek dropped to one knee, taking the woman's hand and pressing his lips to the royal ring. He had never known his father, but many had told him what sort of man Muir had been. There were only glowing tales of a man who had given his life for the islands of Káliel. His death had driven his mother mad, drove her to throw herself from the rooftop of the family villa when Merrek had been but a few weeks old. The decision was made to place the infant in the care of the man who had raised and trained his father, Lord Cliáth. His grandparents remained in his life, visiting him frequently in Alberni or bringing him to the island so he might never forget where he came from, might never feel abandoned. Merrek did not think he could have been more loved and regretted none of his youth. He believed himself uniquely groomed to face this day, but that belief made him no less nervous.

"I pray I live up to his memory…and your faith," he murmured.

"You shall," Diona whispered, cutting the threads of personal regret and trying to stuff them down into the cracks in her heart.

➦*➧

Unlike the majority of his ancestors, Kjell de Corrmick refused to fill the royal hall in Glevum with gaiety for the sake of merriment. He was not a glum or dour person; on the contrary, he was, even more so since his marriage, a good-natured, friendly man with a generous spirit who was proving to be the ruler Neth needed to pull itself together. Too long suppressed, burdened by selfish, brutal tyrants who had ruled with iron-fisted fear, Kjell was, to the surprise of most, everything that those before him had not been. Not the simpleton he had portrayed as a means of remaining alive in an atmosphere where de Corrmick killed de Corrmick out of paranoia and a quest for power. Kjell had proved with his survival that a king did not need brutality to rule.

Why host unending feasts to appease a handful of lords when that money could be put to better use? He invested in agriculture and trade ships, in building a standing army that was not only trained but housed and fed by the Crown. He increased access to education and Faith, areas which had been long denied to all but the wealthiest Nethites. He stored food and goods to provide to the people in times of distress and, when inclement weather began to slash at Enesfel's economy, he offered a trade of food in exchange for coin, for other goods, and the goodwill of his wife's homeland.

Joining the de Corrmick House to the Cordashian monarchy by the union of his only daughter to the king of Cordash, and joining his line further to the Lachlans through the marriage of his heir to Diona Lachlan's daughter served to strengthen Neth. The more secure the kingdom was in her relations with her neighbors, the more likely she would prosper.

If only he could arrange a marriage between his youngest son and one of the heirs of Kyne Mórne's House in Elyriá. That would be a coup unlike any the de Corrmicks had devised or had been willing to attempt. At a mere eleven years old, however, it would be several more years before Jerit was old enough to marry, and while Kjell had no issues with arranged marriages, the practice being customary throughout Neth's history, his strong-willed bride had other ideas. They had been fortunate to compromise, to be able to agree to arrange the marriages of their oldest children when those two, of their own initiative, expressed the desire for the spouses they now had. Jerit showed no such inclination yet, only an inclination towards his mother's mentoring in the ways of the Association, so Kjell saw no betrothal in Jerit's immediate future.

Besides, there were no Hatu brides available, as far as Kjell knew, and it was unlikely he could arrange introduction or marriage to any of the Kyne's many heirs. That might be pushing transformation in Neth too far too fast.

The celebration of the days of his children's births and various religious festivals, as befitting his throne, were welcome occasions for banquets, and so on this, Jerit's eleventh birthday, the de Corrmick halls would again ring with laughter and merriment. Deemed old enough to ride his new horse and old enough to participate in his first hunt, Jerit, his father, and brother had spent the morning darting across the nearby plains in search of scrub deer. Special care was taken to keep Oska on a horse. The elder prince was unable to manage either bow or spear to bring down game, but Kjell had taught him the skill of falconry and mastery of hunting hounds instead. While Kjell and Jerit focused on the deer, Oska brought in multiple rabbits, pheasants, and quail before they returned to Glevum at mid-day. The kitchen staff would set to preparing some of the kill for the evening's feast while father and sons rested and changed into appropriate clean clothes.

Delighted by an outing with his father and brother that he did not often have the chance to enjoy, Oska waved to Inness as she peered at him from the balcony outside their chamber window. She disappeared into the keep and for a moment, Oska scowled, fretting over her apparent coldness. Deciding that he had misread her actions as he was assisted from the horse, that she had either not seen his greeting or else was coming down to receive him, he shrugged away his concern and followed his brother inside. For the last several months, he and Jerit had been of similar height. Now, side by side, he noticed that Jerit was inching taller, knowledge that deepened his scowl. It would be difficult to continue to call himself big brother if Jerit outgrew him.

Inness did not come to welcome him as he hoped. Instead, Oska found her sulking in their room when he entered, muddy and disheveled but cheery from his ride in the crisp air and time spent with his father and brother.

"You know you were welcome to join us," he said warmly to soothe her ruffled nerves. The king knew how much Inness enjoyed the hunt; such invitations were always open-ended to the family.

"I would have been in the way," she grumped, watching him change out of his clothes but not offering to assist with the multiple buttons and clasps. Such things were cumbersome for him, but she knew he preferred to manage on his own most of the time.

"Nonsense."

He did not need to see her frown to know it was there.

"You see what he is doing, don't you?"

"Doing?" His tunic and vest were tossed on a chair and he leaned against the bedpost to yank off his boots with his good hand.

"Inviting you on Jerit's hunt, making you feel included, special…"

"They're my brother, my father. We're family; family is special. Of course I was included." Hearing her soft snort, he muttered, "I'm sorry your mother did not include you often in her…"

"Spare me." Inness rolled her eyes and got up to retrieve the trousers that were dropped, to add them to the collection of shirt and vest that were also in need of laundering.

Much of the exclusion she had experienced had been her own doing. For reasons she did not understand, she had not gotten along well with her mother as far back as her memories took her, but she had been close to her father. When he died, it had been easy to blame her mother, accurate or not, which had driven a deeper wedge into their relationship. Often when Diona tried to include her in activities shared with the twins, and later with Arlana as well, Inness had refused, feeling unwelcome and unimportant in the company of her brothers, both destined to be kings, and her bubbly, vivacious sister. In time, Diona had given up seeking her company, unless the occasion warranted the inclusion of all of the royal children, yet even then Inness had most often been inclined to refuse, leaving her place open to the inclusion of Merrek. It was partially Inness's fault that Diona chose Merrek as her regent, but the young woman firmly believed she should be the one appointed to the throne in Liahm's place. Merrek had, in her opinion, less of a claim to the throne than she had.

Voice cool, her tone as calculated as her words, she spoke without looking at him. "He's going to make Jerit heir to the throne. I can see it, even if you cannot."

"He will not…"

"If you do nothing about it, I will be left to rot in some remote manor without a thought as to my needs or welfare."

"Father would never do such a thing. Mother will not allow it."

"Oh no? Who do you think the favored son is? Does Kjell honor your birthdays with hunts?"

Indignant, Oska began to dress without looking at her. "No, but that's because I do not ask for a hunt. I would rather…"

"I saw you there, when you returned just now. You were happy."

"Not about the hunting, at least, that is not the…"

"Oh, I know. Your precious family time." With disgust in her voice and dirty clothes in her arms, she stopped in the doorway. "Don't seek my sympathy when Jerit is appointed to the throne. I've warned you."

She was gone before he could speak. Most often of late she seemed fixated on his father's relationship with Jerit, and the possibility of Oska being disinherited. There had never been cause to consider the validity of her fears and he had done his best to soothe them, to reassure her that their future would not be as bleak as she feared. Little by little, however, he was beginning to see the world as she did, noticing little details that suggested she could be correct. Though he continued to advocate belief in his father's judgment, to believe in the customs that favored the first-born son over all others, he was forced to admit that his father's breaking with established Neth tradition in other ways could hint that he would break the custom of inheritance as well and put the able-bodied Jerit on Glevum's throne.

Staring at himself in the mirror, he wondered if maybe his wife was right. Maybe she was not paranoid, not lying to gain sympathy or manipulate him. Maybe he was blind to his father's shortcomings out of familial loyalty and maybe, in the end, that would be his downfall.

Not his, he decided with a nod and grunt. He cared less about whether his future was altered than he did about Inness's. She deserved the best the world had to offer…and Oska was determined to prove himself man enough to provide it for her, imperfections and all.

࿊*࿊

The maple zerphánál burned on the way down, but it was a pleasant burn and one that the fiery-haired woman expected. Nothing else burned the way it did, but little else tasted as sweet or came with the blessing of the ágdháthé. It was often used for ceremonial purposes, feasts and special occasions, the wedding day being one of the most sacred. The joining of lives, of power, of eternity, and, in this instance, the joining of families whose combined resources and talents hinted at great things for the southern regions of the land. It had not been a marriage she sought, and at first, she had resisted it.

For her father, however, she relented. Ombhrís was strong of body and mind and together they would create healthy children and carry out the legacies of their bloodlines. It was in the ghísaer's best interest.

The burn of alcohol, weak though it was, landed in a hard knot in the pit of her stomach, creating dizziness she had not expected, had never experienced. She had tasted zerphánál before, at other high occasions and communal feasts, but something was different. Nerves perhaps? She could not put her finger on it, but it was noticeable enough that she turned on the stool to look at Ombhrís with alarm, turned in time to see a tall, broad shadow emerge from the wall behind him, arm raised, something in hand wielded to strike a deadly blow.

"Ombhrís!" she cried as the shadow arm came down and the man she had wed crumpled beneath the attack. Her scream was cut short by a hand clamped over her mouth, as she was lifted and dragged backward. The covering over her face cut the flow of air and consciousness quickly slipped away, but in those last waking moments, she dug deep into places she was only just beginning to learn to use, and struck out with everything she had.

Release came but could not stave off the darkness. The pain of her fall against the stone of the fire pit ring, a blow across her cheek, and the kick of a boot to her ribs were the last things she remembered.

❧*❧

Facing the people gathered in the Great Hall, less than she liked on Prince Merrek's behalf but more than enough for her own, the queen tried to find one face, any face, on which she could focus. But the edges of her vision were near crimson, and what shapes she could discern were blurred color distortions in the row nearest her. Eventually, she picked out what she believed to be the white hair and face of the Elyri harper, and latched on to that bit of familiarity. She decided it was wiser to sweep her gaze slowly across the crowd, however, to include all of her subjects in her words and give no indication of the nature of her predicament. She was determined to keep that secret as long as possible. Her advisors knew, her family, and if the servants did not suspect yet, they would soon enough as it became more difficult to hide. Despite the rumors circulating through Rhidam since the declaration two weeks previous, no one outside of the castle appeared to understand the reasons for her choice.

She unclasped the coronation mantle from around her shoulders and gave it to her chamberlain who officiated the ceremony together with k'gdhededhá Tusánt. He, in turn, placed it around Merrek's shoulders as Diona cleared her throat.

"This is not the typical state of affairs, but times such as these demand dire measures. Enesfel needs, deserves, leaders who can see beyond this darkness to the future." She chose her words carefully but doubted most would deduce her meaning until long after today. "It is with great joy that I bestow upon Prince Merrek the title of Prince-Regent, along with the sharing of responsibilities that the name and throne of Lachlan have bestowed upon me."

Kavan felt his breath catch as Diona's words hitched in her throat. On the day of her birth, the tingle of her touch had spoken of a long, full reign on Enesfel's throne. As devastating as Arlan's death had been, as unexpected and traumatic as Hagan's not long after, the day Diona had assumed the crown, Kavan had hoped it would be a long time before another Lachlan monarch was lost.

She was not lost, was still Enesfel's queen, but nothing would be the same.

Already hers had been a long reign by most standards, more than twenty years at the head of a kingdom she had helped to prosper and thrive. Few Lachlan kings, few monarchs in the Sovereignties, could claim so long a tenure. Thankfully, he was not losing her, not yet. Not as he had lost Arlan and Hagan. She would continue in Rhidam, queen in name if less so in daily function. Kavan could not imagine her content with this life, as she had always strived for something greater than a woman's life behind closed doors with gossip and sewing needles. Having tasted control, to relinquish it, to share it, would not be easy. She would dote on Lorant and any other grandchildren Merrek and Arlana gave her, but Kavan feared she would grow into isolation, feeling useless and alone, if she did not remain actively involved in Enesfel's rule. If that happened, she would sink into a shell of a person, wither, and give herself over to death.

Hopefully, he thought with a glance at the men who sat on either side of him, Merrek, Níkóá and Bhyrhán Bhíncári would make certain that did not happen. Bhyrhán had made the journey from Clarys on behalf of the High Mother to offer whatever support the queen required and he had hinted to Kavan that he would willingly remain in Enesfel if Diona and the new regent permitted it. It had been many years since Rhidam had enjoyed a resident bard at court. Kavan refused to resume that position after Arlan's death and Diona had never found anyone she considered worthy of that place.

Musicians had come and gone as they traveled through the city. Kavan hoped, for her sake and Bhyrhán's, that she would consider and accept the other bard's offer.

As Merrek knelt before the k'dedhá, the royal scepter and the ring were taken one by one from Diona and given over, each bestowing a degree of power. Diona's seal had already been pressed into place, signing the documents that permitted Merrek to rule beside her, and now, as Kavan watched in surprise, the half-moon pendant that hung around her neck was also removed and draped around Merrek's. The pendant passed on another binding that Merrek could not possibly understand and likely had not been told about.

It was something Kavan had not expected Diona to relinquish.

Kavan felt the power of the act pull and stretch between them, the threads of it still snared around Diona but now twisted to tearing to include Merrek. Until Kavan could touch the matching pendants together, until he could cement that new connection, he could not know if Diona would remain within that net of power. But he did understand that she meant for Kavan to guide and protect Merrek in his role as regent as Kavan guided and protected her.

It troubled him to think about what it might mean if she was detached from that binding power. It troubled him to think about what it might mean if she did.

He barely heard the oaths Merrek repeated before the assembly, for there was something else in that sensation of power, a crackling, a sizzle, a heaviness that dragged on his consciousness like thin cloth trying to support a too-dense stone. When the sensation broke, when the fabric gave way to the weight of that power, it was with a blinding discharge in his mind's eye, a surge of power that erupted throughout his body, into his limbs, his fingers and toes, set his physical self alight with energy and yet shut down every sense of psychic power within him. He blinked. He stared as he fought to remain upright, hands gripping the bench in front of him though he saw nothing of the room. What he did see, the dark shadows of an incense-filled chamber, was nothing he had seen before, a place filled with the clash and clatter of wood and steel, frightened cries both male and female…

…and then nothing.

It had to be the Sight, and yet, as the vision bled away, he was left psychically blind with an emptiness of power that frightened him more than anything had in many years. The sensation compelled him to flee, yet he could not will his body to move, and the certainty that he had to remain in this place for the queen and newly appointed prince-regent kept him from trying. Without turning his head, he eyed Bhyrhán, but the other Elyri bard showed no indication that he had experienced anything unusual, nor did Ártur or Syl who sat nearby. Níkóá too was relaxed, at ease, with those beyond him equally engrossed in the pageantry of the change of leadership.

That no one else felt anything was reassuring enough to allow Kavan to turn his thoughts inward to meditate, not on power or the lack of it but on the screaming voice of his inner self that needed to find calm. Music. Music would bring back the balance. Eyes closed, he gave focus over to the formation of notes inside his head, imagined them dancing into the midst of a melody he would set to harp strings later. Little by little, as he concentrated on music instead of the admonitions to the new regent that Tusánt was offering, Kavan could feel distant traces of power begin to sweep across the landscape of his soul, creeping towards his core with the slowness of honey on a chilly day. But the power was there, returning now, and though he knew no cause for such an experience, he felt relief as that power dripped into his center to fill him once more.

He needed to speak to Tíbhyan. Or Kóráhm. If anyone could explain what he had experienced, it would be one of those two men.

But he did not think he would have the strength to summon the Saint or manipulate the Gate to visit Bhryell for many more hours.

His greatest fear, at that moment, was that he might never have the power to do so again.

„*”

The venison was the best he had tasted, perhaps because he had been there for its kill, perhaps because he wanted it to be the best because it had been Jerit's first hunt though their father's kill. For all of that, however, for the joy of the music, the merriment of his doting mother who sat with her arm around his shoulders because no son of hers should sit alone at a birthday celebration, or the pride with which his father spoke of Oska's hunting accomplishments alongside Jerit's, the Nethite heir-apparent was unable to find enjoyment in an evening that he normally would have loved. Inness's warnings gnawed at him, making him suspicious of details he had never noticed before.

Was Jerit's bigger portion of venison due to his birthday…or was it favoritism? Were the bow and knife given, in addition to the horse earlier that day, equal to or more valuable than the collection of newly scribed books that had been commissioned and given to Oska on his eleventh birthday, books he had begged for just as his brother had begged for his own hunting bow and knife? Was the attentiveness of the staff given because it was Jerit's day, or had it been there all along and Oska was only now seeing it? Had his father made an equal number of toasts to his eldest's health, welfare and prosperity?

Oska could not remember. Too many years had passed since that particular birthday and memories could be tricky.

It did not help that after their squabble, Inness refused to join the celebration, claiming illness that may or may not have been real. Too often over the past few weeks, she had claimed illness, but whatever it was, it seemed to pass within hours, and then she was back to her usual moods that, while unpredictable, were at least understood by her husband. Now not only did her health concern him, a gnawing fear that perhaps this mystery ailment was the cause of her growing unrest, there was also the worry that they would be pulled apart by her fears and his inability or unwillingness to see things around them as she did. If she was wrong, how could he prove it when she resisted every argument he made?

Oska fidgeted. When his mother smiled at him, he managed a wan smile in return, fearful that she would detect his thoughts, know his fears, and confront him. Asta had always had a knack for reading people, especially her children. It had made typical childhood lies difficult to get past her and, he knew, helped to keep her husband honest in his dealings with family, friends, and the kingdom.

If she discerned Oska's troubled musings, she did not pursue them in this public setting. On her other side, at the head of the table, Kjell raised his glass in another toast, and Jerit, seated where his mother usually sat at the king's right hand…the same place Oska sat for his birthday banquets…followed suit. Asta turned from Kjell's eldest child, her second, and reached for her near-empty glass.

"Before we turn from feasting to dancing, join me in a final toast. To Jerit." Kjell, his long blonde hair tied back with a de Corrmick green ribbon, tendrils falling loose to frame his features, smiled at the boy beside him. "A fine man in the making, with all of the refinements required of a king. May your life never be wanting, your heart always full, your days long and blessed. Jerit."

"Jerit!" The toasts rose around the room as guests raised their glasses in honor of their host.

Every glass lifted except Oska's. His hand closed around the bowl of his glass but it refused to be lifted as if it was glued to the table or was too heavy for his good arm to hoist. All of the refinements required of a king. The words rang in his ears, repeating in a deafening echo that drove out every other sound in the room.

Inness was right.

Sweat beaded beneath the back of his collar and across his forehead. The hand around the glass began to tremble. Faster and shallower came his breathing until he believed he would faint from the effort. On the periphery of his vision, he vaguely noted guests rising to go into the Hall where musicians waited, the movement enough to allow him to push his stool backward for the intended escape. The effort was too abrupt; the stool toppled sideways and the jerking away from the wine glass caused it to tip and spill over his hand. He barely noticed as he staggered from the dining room, not looking back at his mother, his brother, and certainly not his father.

His father had betrayed him. It was as Inness said. Wise, learned Prince Oska had been a fool.

☙*❧

The harp felt good in his hands, comfortable in a place it did not seem to be enough of late, as he spent little time playing before people other than family or the residents of St. Kóráhm's. Wortham had been the last to hear brass strings, the last to enjoy the notes of a song in the throes of birthing, a song Kavan shared tonight without fanfare or mention of the man for whom it had been written. This day was about change, a beginning, not about what had been lost, despite how recently that loss had come.

The business of dealing with the dead, the estate left equally to his family, Kavan, and St. Kóráhm's, had consumed much of Kavan's time; the rest had been filled with aiding Merrek and Diona with the shuffling of power though they had not needed his help. Chamberlain McCábhá and Peter Dahl, Diona's former squire who accepted the post of chancellor upon Flannery McGranis's retirement, had carried the queen's business for many years and could have managed the details on their own. Volunteering his services kept Kavan traveling between Rhidam and Alberni, kept his life, his mind, occupied, so that there was little time to dwell on the emptiness Wortham's absence left. When he slept, it was in one of the many alcoves in the chellé, usually on a bench with a book at his side so that it appeared to any who found him as if he had fallen asleep reading or researching. Those who knew him best knew what he was doing, why he avoided home, but none had yet to pressure him to do otherwise.

Kavan's grief would be spent in the only ways he knew how to shed it, and life would move on. He would return to routine and home.

As the notes flowed, dancers drifted on and off the gallery floor, carrying conversation and occasional singing with them when some popular tune he played struck the hearts of the guests. Sometimes Bhyrhán was beside him, playing in unison, sometimes he was joined by Sóbhán and Dhóri to entertain the queen, her new regent, and guests with song. But mostly those men danced, Sóbhán with Chethá, Dhóri with any girl who accepted his requests, and Bhyrhán with Diona. It had taken many tries, and considerable cajoling, for the other bard to coax her, but eventually he convinced her that failing eyesight did not impede her ears and her feet. After that, she seemed unwilling to stop dancing except when someone else cut in to allow Bhyrhán to pick up his recorder to play another song with Kavan.

It was the first time, except for one or two dances given during her children's weddings and Gamal's coronation as Hatu's king, that the woman had allowed herself to publically celebrate since Espen's death. The shedding of responsibility seemed to be good for her. So too, it seemed, was Bhyrhán's attention. Whatever the sandy-haired bard had said to coax her to her feet, whatever he continued to say to her throughout the night, it appeared to have a positive effect.

It was good to see.

Arlana, in no condition to dance in her heavily pregnant state, remained seated as her husband gave his choice dances to his grandmother, his aunt, and the wives of his friends when they encouraged it. He spent most of his time conversing with lords and ladies, dukes and duchesses, generals and advisors, mixing politics with the festivities, intending to prove worthy of his appointment as regent. Halfway through the night's pleasures, Arlana excused herself to see to Prince Lorant's care, at which time Merrek set his mind to business in earnest, arranging meetings, setting appointments and audiences between advisors, himself, and the queen for the upcoming days, the party aspect of the evening set aside and mostly forgotten.

The guests would continue to eat and drink and dance as long as there was food, alcohol, and available music. The leanness of such commodities elsewhere in the kingdom at this time of growing hunger was forgotten in their zeal to indulge. Bhríd looked to be relaxed and enjoying himself, he and Editt laughing and talking the way the Elyri Duke of Levonne had once done with his wife. He was another Kavan was pleased to see had rediscovered joy after so many losses.

It gave Kavan hope that he would, someday, recover from Wortham's death. He did not know what it was to feel joy, as that was one emotion he did not believe he had ever experienced, or that he had failed to recognize as such if he had. But contentment and peace would be enough. Those were emotions he was familiar with, the only two he ever sought in his prayers.

Gradually the music allowed for the slow restoration of the energies in his center, his spirit filling with it until he believed he would not be left bereft as he had feared. The balance had been restored. He played until he was confident he had the strength to do the one thing he had promised himself he would do tonight, one thing he had not done since Wortham's death. It was one of but a few activities that invariably calmed him, if only temporarily, an expending of power that refreshed and invigorated him and helped bring his perspective back into focus.

Kavan wanted flight.

When the time came to excuse himself, with his harp returned safely to Alberni, flight was the refuge he sought. The white kestrel soared into the night with little thought for those left in celebration.

When he stumbled into his chambers, Oska spoke not a word. Nor did he light a candle, tend to the fire that had gone out during his absence, or even glance at his wife who lay on the bed with her arm over her eyes as if to shield them from non-existent light. She neither moved nor spoke as he threw open the balcony doors and let the evening air blast across his perspiring face. It chilled him but he barely noticed, and he was grateful that Inness did not immediately push him to speak, to explain himself. Her words would amount to, 'I told you so,' and Oska did not want to hear it. He only wanted to forget what he had heard and the way the realization made him feel.

If not for Inness, he might have been satisfied with being overlooked for the duty of kingship. He preferred research and books, languages and warm fires, to the stress of helping others with their mundane, petty, worldly problems. He could do it, and do it well. He could maintain the peace his father had won for Neth, could strengthen the military, and continue fostering relations with the other Sovereignties. He might do things differently than his father, but the goals and results would be similar.

But it would be a blow to his ego to have the throne yanked away, for no other reason than his physical limitations. Without the crown, he doubted he could convince Inness to remain at his side. He believed she cared for him, believed she loved him, but he was not foolish enough to have missed that the destined crown upon his head was the prize she wanted. If she could not be a monarch herself, she would be the wife of one, and Ethenae forbid if Oska lost that chance.

"Husband."

He had not heard her rise or cross the room, but suddenly her hands were on his shoulders, gently drawing him back against her with a tenderness she showed no one but him. "Are you feeling better?" he asked, hoping to keep the conversation far away from his sinking heart and the fury that nipped at his heels.

"It has passed," she reassured him, wondering if she dared reveal her suspicions. But his mood, the uncharacteristic anger she detected bubbling to the surface and disturbing his usual jovial calm, made her think better of addressing her troubles. He would not want to talk about her. He wanted to talk about himself.

"I spoke out of turn earlier," she began, thinking their quarrel the cause of his disjointed mood.

He shook his head. "No." He shook it again. "No, you were right to warn me, to be a dutiful wife and see to your husband, to our future."

Inness tensed, the stiffness radiating down her limbs and into his body through her hands. He glanced over his shoulder and though he could not see her well in the moonlight, he wagered she had lost color in her cheeks. The dutiful wife was one of the last things she wanted to be called. Her mouth twitched and her head cocked to the side as she closed her eyes and tried to suck in a deep breath.

"Apologies, Inness…that is not what I meant. It has not been done, but Jerit will be king. I no longer doubt my father's intentions. He will be king and I will be…we will be…"

Gaze narrowed, Inness stared across the city, watching the play of moonlight on the rooftops. Other than that narrowing and the pursing of her lips, Oska could not read what she must feel. Disappointment, he imagined. Fear. Anger and dismay. They were what he was feeling, so it made sense that she was as well.

Her words, when they came, were a hiss. "No. We will not. You will be the king you were born to be. I will not see you denied what was denied me."

"But…"

"You will be king. Together we will see it done. Kjell will not take this from you. I will not allow it." Seeing another protest about to begin, she put a finger to his lips. "What sort of wife would I be if I do not support my husband? Trust me, Oska. We will make this right."

He nodded, afraid to speak, not knowing what to say if he did, and welcomed her embrace when it came. He did trust Inness. Tonight, she was the only one he trusted in the entire world.

❧Chapter 5❧

Though approaching his fiftieth year, Kjell de Corrmick was still fit, owing in part to his resistance to the overindulgences of his predecessors and his enjoyment of running, wrestling, and any other physical activity he could find time and opportunity to participate in. His blonde hair was beginning to gray but the difference was barely noticeable to anyone except him and his wife. He watched as the woman on the edge of the bed unlaced her boots, which she wore most often instead of more lady-like slippers, and traced the curve of her back with his fingers.

So beautiful.

She was much younger than him and he felt blessed that she had agreed to marry him. She had lost her first husband before their child was born, leaving her free to remarry, but doing so, particularly marrying him, had meant giving up so much. She had been Enesfel's first woman inquisitor, the first in the Sovereignties, and a young mother, and yet for reasons that still bemused him, she had left that behind to come to Glevum as his queen.

She said it was because she loved him. He thought it was something more.

Her daughter from her first marriage carried enough Elyri blood to be a healer and so the girl had been fostered into the care of others, to be raised and trained where her gifts would not be feared and she would not be persecuted for the blood she carried. Kjell knew that Asta sometimes regretted that decision, felt she had betrayed her late husband, felt that she should have stayed with Yóáná to raise her and guide her education. But Kjell also knew that some sense of duty had brought Asta to Neth. The marriage of Lachlan and de Corrmick blood was a boon for both kingdoms and sometimes he feared Asta had married him more out of some sense of duty to the Lachlan Crown than anything else.

Maybe duty had been an escape from memory and pain.

But she loved him enough to stay, to bear him three children, and to remain faithfully at his side. She was one of his brightest advisors and used her time and talents to set up an information network in Glevum similar to what she had utilized in Rhidam. Between them, both with experience of watching people and noticing things that others would not, it had been easy to weed out corruption from the de Corrmick House, remove those who had ill-advised kings and led the kingdom through ruin, until Neth was at last free of the chokehold generations of de Corrmicks had held.

Kjell had never expected to marry. He was thankful every day that he had chosen wisely…and that Asta had accepted his proposal.

"You shouldn't have said that," she murmured, shoving her boots beneath the bed with her toes. Still small in stature, still sometimes mistaken for a younger girl by those who did not know her, she turned to face him on the edge of the bed. "You know how sensitive he is…"

"That wasn't what I meant. He's a smart man. He knows his future is secure."

"Is it?" She took Kjell's hands in hers and caressed his palms with her thumbs. "Things have changed, but do not think for a moment that there aren't those who look at him…who see his differences…and hope for someone else to rule in his stead."

Neither knew the cause of Oska's disabilities. Asta had suffered no more than the usual pregnancy sickness, had been careful with what she ate and drank, had done nothing that should have put her unborn child at risk, and yet he had been born less than sound in body. It had been a difficult labor, leaving Asta incapable of nursing him, and some blamed his disabilities on that without knowing that his afflictions had been with him at birth. Rika had been conceived almost immediately and she too had endured a problematic birth. The girl had difficulty with her hearing and vision but not enough to prevent her from living a normal life and not enough to prevent the king of Cordash from welcoming her as his queen.

The next three children conceived had been lost in the womb and Healer MacLyr had speculated that there was some incompatibility between Asta's blood and Kjell's that was the cause. He had seen such mismatches before. But then had come Jerit, a healthy child, an easy pregnancy, just as Asta had had with Yóáná. After his protracted birth, however, Asta had been unable to conceive again and the healers said she probably never would. Whatever fate Ethenae held for her and Kjell, it had given them all of the children they were destined to have.

She knew there were rumors, that some infidelity on her part was responsible for the heir's difficulties. That a match between de Corrmick and Lachlan should never have come to pass. That he, and every child save for Jerit, was tainted by poison in her body that had come from carrying a child with Elyri blood. She would never believe that, would never blame Gaelán for anything, not even his death. She had married Kjell out of duty and attraction as soon as it appeared that the Coryllien cult's threat was under control and in time had grown to love him. There were still moments, however, when she missed her childhood love and longed for him to live again.

That was a secret she never shared with anyone save for his child and, once, with Gaelán's father.

"His is the most brilliant mind in Neth; he will be our strongest king. People will see that," Kjell grunted stubbornly.

"If given the chance…if he is allowed to show them." She sighed. "Neth has, until you, never been good with patience or tolerance when it comes to leadership."

Considering that nearly every other de Corrmick king in the history books had been murdered and succeeded by the one most likely responsible for that murder, Kjell knew Asta's assertions were true. "Jerit would never…"

"Not Jerit, but someone who wants him to be king." Even now, despite everything Kjell had done, assassination was a threat they had to constantly be vigilant for. Just because Kjell was beloved, popular amongst the lords and nobles alike, respected by the military he was building, it did not mean that there were not those who longed for a return to the days when might equaled power.

Without speaking, Kjell paced the room while Asta, knowing not to interrupt his thoughts, prepared for bed. The party had lasted long into the night, and though they had not yet slept, it would be dawn soon. Kjell might not indulge his nobles with multiple, frivolous banquets, but when one was held, the food and wine flowed until the guests either retired or else fell asleep at tables and chairs within the dining and gathering halls. His habit was to remain until the end, encouragement for his subjects to enjoy as long as they wished, and Asta normally chose to remain with him, a united front between king and queen that Neth was not used to seeing. They would sleep now, as long as they wished, and then day-to-day life would resume.

"I will speak with him. We shall have a banquet in his honor, formally announcing his status as heir, and I will endeavor to include him in business more than I have so that the lords may perceive his competence and judge him by his merits." Kjell climbed into bed beside her and drew her against him.

Praying it would be enough to resolve the hurt she had read in Oska's flight from the revelry of the evening, Asta nodded and nestled her head against his shoulder. "Then we can discuss a trip to Rhidam?" Visiting her cousin, the queen, for an explanation of her actions was necessary and it would allow Asta to visit her eldest child. It had been too long since she had seen either one, and her husband owed a respectful visit to Enesfel's appointed prince-regent.

Peace must be kept.

Kjell smiled. "Yes. Oska first, then to Enesfel. I swear it."

Eyes closing with a yawn, Asta breathed, "I'll hold you to that."

᠗*᠗

"It is good to have you in Rhidam." Diona was not yet so blind that she could not admire the handsome Elyri piper, kin to the High Mother, who had spent several months in her court during the days of the Second Elyri Persecution. When he had been here then, it had been at great risk, and eventually, he had agreed with Kavan's assessment of removing the majority of Elyri influence from Rhidam to give the city, the land, a chance to heal. He looked no different than he had those many years ago, still looked to be a young man who could have been her son, if she were Elyri or had wed one. His dusty blonde hair was pulled away from his face, tied with a pale blue cord that matched the powdery color of his trousers and vest. Having grown up in the Kyne's court, he was no stranger to courtly dress and had a taste for fashion that neither Kavan nor Ártur cared to follow. "I did not think to see you again."

"Nonsense. You had only to ask and I would have come. I told you so before. I know your court is sadly lacking a minstrel." He sat on the bench beside her in the morning sun, soaking up the warmth that would soon be lost to the cast of winter. He wondered, as he stared across the sky from left to right, if Enesfel, the middle and southern portions at least, would know rain at last when winter came.

"I can remedy that lack…if you wish it."

Diona nodded, relaxed in his company. Seated in the courtyard alone, save for the pages and ladies in waiting who loitered beyond the perimeter of her vision, had been worrisome. His company lifted that stress and made her smile. "I was never certain when Rhidam would be safe enough for you; I did not want to put you at risk."

It was a risk he would have gladly taken if she had asked, but he kept that to himself. There were secrets he had taken to Clarys, never to be spoken, secrets that brought him back as soon as word of her abdication had reached the Kyne. "I came when I heard…"

"That was not necessary…"

"She could not be here; you know her health is failing." Mórne had ruled as Kyne longer than most, and all of Elyriá knew that in time she would leave them. There was talk for most of the last century about who would be elevated in her stead, talk carried on behind closed doors, for no one wanted to publically consider her mortality. For many, she had always been there, and would always remain.

"I wanted to come, have meant to for several years."

She covered his hand on his knee with hers. "I wish you had," she murmured. "To see me like…we shall never read together again."

Swallowing the lump in his throat, he coughed and shook his head, though she was not looking at him to see it. "On the contrary. I thought that, if you wish, I could read to you. For you. Poetry, books, ledgers, letters…anything you require or wish."

"You do not need…"

"Need, no…but I would be honored to do so, to serve as your eyes in whatever way I may. You are too young to live in a world of darkness." He hesitated then turned his hand over beneath hers, to intertwine their fingers. Without knowing if it would work, though assured by Kavan that such a thing should be possible, he opened a psychic link between them and concentrated on looking around the courtyard. He heard her gasp, felt her tense, and then slowly begin to relax as she realized that she was seeing the world more clearly than she had in over a year.

"How can you do that?" she murmured, turning her head to look to the side and finding that her vision failed until he had turned his head as well.

"An Elyri skill…courtesy of Lord Cliáth," he admitted. "I spoke of wanting to assist you and he suggested…" It embarrassed him to realize that Kavan might have known secrets he had kept hidden. Since Kavan had never spoken of them, however, Bhyrhán decided his secrets were safe. "It may not be enough to help you retain the throne I fear, for I doubt you would wish to spend every waking moment with me." He chuckled nervously. "But for now, if you find it helpful…"

Diona withdrew her hand and closed her eyes. No, such a solution to her loss of vision would never be practical for a queen. There were too many instances when private meetings were required. At those moments, she would be at the mercy of her blindness, unable to read the expressions of those with her, unable to make eye contact that would express innumerable thoughts without words. And though Elyri were once more safe in Enesfel, the people tolerant and accepting again, having one constantly at her side, physical contact required to allow her to see, would spread rumors of magic and potentially plant further seeds of discontent. It could not be done.

Despite his offer, she doubted he was suggesting an indefinite stay in Rhidam to serve her. To be given sight of any kind, and then lose it again, to more darkness than before, was a heartache she was not interested in.

"It is worth consideration," she said evasively, clasping her hands in her lap. Without looking at him, she could sense his surprising disappointment. Had he honestly thought to serve her? "But you are right…the court can use a musician of your talent. It will not be difficult to convince Merrek to bid you welcome for as long as you wish to stay. And," her tone softened, "if you're indeed interested in reading with me, I would enjoy that as well."

The palpable shift in his demeanor told her he was happy. His delight made her smile. "I am interested. You have but to send a servant for me and I shall come to you…"

She chuckled. "I do not mean later, I mean now, Lord Bhíncári."

"Bhyrhán, please."

It was not proper etiquette, perhaps, but he wanted no formality between them, though he did not dare call her by name.

"Bhyrhán. Come. Let us go in out of the sun." She got to her feet and with an outstretched hand, brought him up as well.

The clatter of horse's hooves across the lowered moat bridge, coming closer until they skittered on the stone courtyard, made her turn towards the sound. A palace soldier caught the animal's head and addressed the rider who spoke in haste as he dismounted. The stranger, plain in dress though with an expensive horse, recognized the queen across the distance that separated them, for he had barely begun to answer the soldier's questions before he shouted, "Your Majesty! A word! Lady Gabersdon has sent word!"

Diona glanced at Bhyrhán who, without spoken request, allowed her to take his arm so he could guide her towards the messenger without a faltering step. "What word from Nelori?" she asked.

The messenger bowed. "My lord, the Duke, has taken to bed with plague; the keep and city are besieged with it…"

Bhyrhán pulled Diona back and the soldier stepped swiftly between the stranger and his queen.

"Do not fear, Your Majesty," the stranger pleaded. "I am not from Nelori but from Hatu. I had trade goods meant for Nelori…but they would not permit entry into the city. I was not exposed to them. Word was shouted down from the wall and I left my wagon before their gates…alas without payment…"

Without addressing the matter of payment but still worried about the potential of exposure to one of the two plagues ravaging Enesfel, Diona said, "I am sorry to hear this news." She had once had a fond passion for Balint, but she had been a child, barely aware of such feelings towards men. Over time, those childhood fancies had given way to respect and more appropriate feelings that did not conflict with her love for Espen. Balint had served her father, her brother, and then her, with unwavering loyalty. To think him ravaged by an ailment claiming the lives of so many brought deep remorse.

"The lady sent me to express regrets for the events that necessitated a change in power." He spoke the words but showed no indication that he knew what they meant. He believed her to be the queen and addressed her thus. "She says if there is anything she can do, once the plague departs Nelori's gates, you have only to ask."

"Thank you, sir." Diona gestured to the soldier between them. "See to it that this man is given respite, that his horse is well-tended, and that both receive medical care if needed." If either horse or rider carried plague, which was possible from having traveled through the southern territories of Enesfel, she wanted to know. It had not occurred to her before today to shut the keep against such messengers, a precaution to keep the plague outside of the castle walls, but she realized she should have. It was a matter to bring up with Merrek, to make with him a decision that was no longer solely hers.

"A letter shall be drafted for you to take to Duke Gabersdon and his daughter," she assured the stranger as he was led beyond the walls where he could eat his fill at the Eagle's Nest Inn, rest, and have a physician see to his welfare. Diona did not move, only clutched tighter to Bhyrhán's arm as the messenger departed. When they were alone, she murmured, "He did not notice…"

The Elyri patted her hand. "Why should he? Your regal demeanor is beyond reproach. As dignified as ever."

"You, sir, are a flatterer."

"It is only flattery if it is not true," he corrected with a grin, turning towards the castle door.

Sensing the change in direction through his touch and movement, seeing the shadowing shape in the distance against the midday sun, she nodded. "I must speak with Merrek. He must know about the duke…that the Yellow Death may have come to Rhidam."

"As many days' ride as he has come from Nelori, he exhibits no sign of illness. I believe we are safe."

Diona shrugged. "It will take more than faith to save Enesfel." In truth, she sighed, the Yellow Death was likely already here.

∽*∽

The Rhidam castle was not home, but at one time it had been. Bhríd knew the halls, the rooms, the garden, and all of its secrets as well as he knew the estate in Levonne. He had never intended to stay away as long as he had; the estate should already have gone to one of Madalyn's daughters or to both of them if they wished to share it. But the eldest of the twins, Sylyhá, had married Prince Gamal before he had been crowned king of Hatu and had followed him south when providence gave him that crown. It had left the estate in the care of her twin Alyná, but she, in turn, had become Magistrate Piran Lachlan's second wife and had left Enesfel for Káliel. On that day, both of his daughters signed over the rights to the vineyard and the ruling of Levonne back to their father to keep it out of foreign hands.

By then, the pain of having lost both sons and their mother had faded enough that remaining in Levonne was no longer the arduous experience it had been when the girls were young. With Níkóá serving as chamberlain, and squire Peter having graduated to the office of chancellor, there had been no need for Bhríd to return to Rhidam. Nor was there any reason to go back to Elyriá as there was nothing there for him except for parents that he had not seen since he had married a Teren woman. At least in Rhidam there was Syl, and with no one else to manage them, he, as Levonne's duke, had a duty to the city, the region, and the vineyards left in his care. Madalyn had wed him to protect her estate. Serving Levonne and the estate were duties he felt honor-bound to obey.

"You slept long."

He did not ask where Editt had been when he awoke to find her gone, nor address her observation as she wrapped her arms around his waist and lay her head on his shoulder. Such shows of intimacy were shared in private, although their dances last evening might have spoken of a relationship they had never publically revealed. Editt, tall and slender, slightly boyish in figure, her hair already spun gray despite her relatively young age, had stayed on from nursing the girls to raising them, schooling them, caring for household matters for Bhríd as he tended to the needs of Levonne and the vineyards and the general upkeep of the estate. There had been respect and friendship between them for many years as the freshness of grief faded from Bhríd's eyes. Though she had been approached by more than one potential suitor during those years, she had refused each of them, a detail Bhríd eventually noticed. Marriage would have meant departing the duke's employ, and her big heart had been unable to leave him to endure his grief, his life, alone, nor leave the girls without a woman's guidance in their lives…or with some other woman's guidance.

Sometime after the girls' tenth birthday, the relationship with her cherished lord had blossomed into one of discrete, comfortable passion, hidden from the children, from the servants, from all of Levonne. Bhríd did not want to expose her to the anti-Elyri violence Madalyn had been subjected to and Editt did not want him to bear the embarrassment of an affair with a servant below his station.

But he had never seen her as a servant, and more than once had considered the subject of marriage. For the sake of the girls, however, so as not to interfere in the inheritance of the estate, and to avoid the threats of violence and perceived shame, they had chosen not to publically consummate their relationship. Neither felt a need for it. They were content with their lives as they were.

For reasons he had yet to account for, now that his daughters had married and left the estate to him, Bhríd was again considering marriage though he was reluctant to bring it up, to be rejected.

"I have news to share," she murmured, thankful he could not see her face, thankful he did not look at her now that she had spoken.

"If it is regarding the plague, I would rather not hear it until we are home." There had been infected ships come to port in Levonne, ships that had been turned back out to sea, their crews disallowed to embark, their cargos still in their holds. It had been a difficult choice to make, knowing that he might be damning the crews to death at sea, the ships to sinking, the cargos to loss at the bottom of the Bay of Phállá, but it was better than the risk of contaminating all of Levonne. If the Yellow Sisters had come to roost in his city, it would be a matter of a few days before it flooded the streets of Rhidam. He did not want to be responsible for so many lives lost should he allow one infected man, woman, or child to step off those ships.

"No…not the plague. Rather it is…"

When her arms tightened imperceptibly around him, her anxiety and tension radiating through her stance, he turned from the window to look at her. "It is what, Editt? Speak openly." She had never feared speaking to him before, except in the earliest days as a nursemaid when she barely knew him and he was snappish and rude with grief.

"I am with child."

The black-haired Elyri stared as if he had misheard her. After so many years together, without conception, she had assumed she was infertile, or else their Elyri-Teren mix of genes was discordant. It had been a relief of sorts to them both, for Bhríd could not bear the thought of further children after the loss of his sons, nor did he wish to expose them, or Editt, to the horrors his boys and wife had faced. They had taken every precaution they could devise. For Editt, though she had lost her child before he had met her, and that child's father with him, to a storm that had flooded the coastal fringes of Levonne and swept their home from beneath them, she had been content to raise Sylyhá and Alyná and care for someone else's home, keeping those two innocents safe. It had never occurred to her that she might conceive again, particularly when she was of an age when many women stopped bearing children.

"I do not…I did not want to tell you sooner, in case it was lost, but it has been nearly four months and the worst of that danger is past. Evidence will show soon…and I know you do not desire scandal…"

"With child…" His first reaction to the news was a sour sickness that made him pull away. "I…need to be…this cannot…are you…?"

"I have not seen a physician…for how could I explain myself?" She did not know what she had expected, but this reaction was not it. Yet, everything he had been striving to avoid was bound up in those words, in the possibility of another child, and she could not fault him for reacting badly.

It was too late to be done with the babe. If he rejected it, rejected her, her only choice would be to leave him.

"I need…" By now, he had retreated to the door, opened it, and paused with a hand clenched knuckle-white on the handle as he looked back at her. "Do not…please…wait for me. Stay here. I will return."

He needed air, needed to think somewhere alone, for she could read his face too easily and he did not want her to jump to conclusions before he had the chance to assimilate the news.

A child. A daughter? Or a son? His daughters had been easy to raise, neither possessing any noticeable degree of Elyri ability, and as twins, they remained close to one another as they matured. There had been none of the hatred that had come to exist between his sons, none of the rivalry that had resulted in the deaths of both boys.

Another daughter would be good.

There might yet be someone to bequeath the Levonne estate to.

It was not fair to stigmatize Editt with a child without a father. While he would not be the first man to sire a child outside of marriage, the first lord to have a child with a servant, leaving that child outside of marriage would condemn her to less than the life Bhríd wanted for her…or for any child of his. He could not be anything less than fair to child or mother, and Editt had given so much of herself without asking for anything in return.

Could he marry her? Could he shoulder that burden again, the eventual loss of another wife? Would she want that, or was she letting him know about the child as a courtesy? He knew it was no one else's, and he did not think she would keep the child from him once it was born, but would she accept publically claiming paternal rights when it might reflect badly on each of them?

Bhríd knew himself too well. Even as he asked those questions as his furiously whirling thoughts propelled him down one castle corridor after another, he knew what he would do, what he had to do. Not merely for propriety, not merely because it was right in the eyes of man, law, and k'Ádhá, but because it was honorable…and he cared too much about Editt, and this unborn child, to do anything else. He could not say he loved her; even his daughters had failed to hear those words as they grew up. He made sure the girls knew it without the words being said, however, and hoped that they, and Editt, knew the sincerity of his affections through his actions.

Those words had last been said to Madalyn and Bhríd had been unable to speak them again.

But he did not need to say them to do the right thing, so long as Editt would have him.

♺*♻

Merrek Lachlan, now prince-regent, a development of the day before that he found difficult to accommodate, had left his sleeping wife and brought Prince Lorant with him, allowing the boy to explore a home he was too young to remember from previous visits. Merrek had known this day would inevitably come, the day when the throne would be his, but he had not expected to share it with Diona. He was not aware of such a thing occurring in all of Enesfel's history. The nearest events to it had been an aged king whose protracted illness had lent itself to the need of his son ruling with him, and then the abdication of his grandfather to King Arlan. That event, as he had learned, had nothing to do with Owain Lachlan's fitness to rule and everything to do with who had been the rightful Lachlan heir.

There had been no sharing of power then.

Kavan had made certain Owain's son, raised as the king's son, was fit to be the king Owain could have been, and then likewise had done his best to prepare Merrek for it, just as he had done for Arlan, Hagan, and Diona. The skill, the goodness, the respectability of recent Lachlan monarchs had much to do with the mentoring of the White Bard and Merrek was determined to give the man his due in whatever way he could. Money Kavan did not want, property he already possessed, so Merrek did not know what he could offer that Kavan would accept, but he swore an oath to himself and k'Ádhá that he would find something befitting such a man.

He should have slept longer after a night spent getting to know the people of the Lachlan court more intimately than he had before. He had known most of them in passing, had spent enough time here as a child and younger man to know names and faces. Some of those people had watched him grow up or had grown up with him. He had sat at the queen's side during many meetings, many gatherings of nobles, and many days of hearing the peoples' petitions to the Crown. He knew the ways of court, of government, but none of those who were now his advisors too had experience with his decision-making skills, his views, or his confidence in leadership.

Last night, for him, had been more about business than merriment. Business, enjoying his wife's company, and watching Kavan with increasing concern.

Outwardly, it appeared that the bard was managing adequately since Wortham's death. Business as usual, things to take care of, work to be done, arrangements to be made. Anyone who knew him knew that Kavan kept his strongest feelings locked where no one, not even he, could see or experience them. Merrek's elders, particularly Healer MacLyr, claimed that Kavan was stronger than he had ever been, that he could and would survive this loss, but the prince was less certain. That loss was akin to losing a brother, a lover perhaps, part of one's self, and Merrek knew how he would feel if he lost such a person, lost Arlana, Lorant, or Kavan.

Perhaps what he needed to give Kavan, as his due for everything he had given the Lachlans and Enesfel, was the time to grieve and heal without responsibility to the Crown.

He was not prepared to do that now, the timing of events a critical, unfortunate thing that would hurt them all. Diona had brought the news about Duke Gabersdon, his daughter, and Nelori, and though Merrek had schooled his face to hide concern that Diona would not see, it bubbled within and he knew Diona sensed his disquiet. He was predominantly concerned about the boy he watched climbing over the dayroom furnishings. There was a chance, thanks to this messenger, as careful as he may have been, that the southern plague had come to Rhidam, to the keep…if it had not already done so via any other merchant or traveler who passed through in recent weeks. It took only moments for his initial anger to pass, eased by Bhyrhán's reassurance that the messenger had exhibited no symptoms to suggest infection.

Not everyone who carried it showed symptoms. It was impossible to know if the messenger was infected. The fearsome truth was that after so many months, with Rhidam the hub of the kingdom, the plagues were bound to reach them. Towns, villages, cities, and families confined themselves when the outbreaks came, but people passed through regardless. Without knowing how the scourges were transmitted, how could anyone know how long they would be safe?

Fear had brought trade to a trickle, filled the náós daily with those praying for miracles, signs of redemption, for cleansing rain. Some stood on street corners, giving cries of warning that the Yellow Sisters and inclement weather were Enesfel's punishment for the Elyri who had been slaughtered not so long ago. A handful of others dared to proclaim that they had not done enough to expel the Elyri, had allowed them to return, and thus the land was suffering.

Thankfully, the tide of public opinion quashed those dissidents before persecution reared its head again.

How many appeals had come before the Crown, or had been brought to k'gdhededhá Tusánt and Rankin begging for Elyri healers to be brought to Enesfel in the hopes of staunching the flow of death? But the Elyri were not immune to plague, it seemed, as there were reports that healers who had come were also dying from the suffering they were trying to treat. Had they successfully cured anyone? There were no reports of it. Once either plague was contracted, the victim either recovered or, most often, died in agony. What chance did anyone have if not even an Elyri healer could save a life?

One chance, and it was the reason Merrek feared allowing Kavan time to grieve his friend's passing. The talk on the streets, in the taverns, in the náós, was that only a miracle could save them, and there was only one man said to perform miracles. There had been reports of late, of visitors to k'gdhededhá Jermyn's burial site within St. Kóráhm's having been healed as they prayed to the martyred founder of the restored Faith in Enesfel. But that was an unconfirmed rumor.

What was not a rumor, what was a fact that Merrek had witnessed with his own eyes on more than one occasion, was that k'Ádhá blessed the world through Kavan's hands. If any miracle could end the Yellow Death spreading throughout Enesfel, northern Hatu, and southern Cordash and Neth, it would come through the White Bard.

What if, k'Ádhá forbid, the plague touched the royal House? His family? What if Diona, Merrek, or saints and záryph preserve them,

Lorant, became infected. Kavan had spared Lorant's life at birth, when the small infant had been too weak to breathe on his own, and then twice more during his first year of life when that weakness had made him susceptible to sickness in his lungs and there had been no healer near enough to save him. Kavan's assurance that Lorant would be king did little to ease Merrek's worry for his small, but very active, son. With the plagues to come and Kavan not near enough to save Lorant one more time, what hope would the child, the kingdom, have?

Yet, he sighed as he stared out the window, Lorant, now curled up on the settee with his arms wrapped around a cushion, even if Kavan could miraculously vanquish plagues, there was surely nothing he could do about the weather, and without an improvement, the suffering would continue to rise. Kavan could not bring rain to the parched southern plains nor staunch the falling of it that had flooded too much of the arable land in the north. Artificial conduits and reservoirs had been dug to drain the floodwaters, making some of the lands at the fringes of the floodplains into the agricultural center of the kingdom, the best lands suitable for growing. Many from the suffering stretches of Enesfel had traveled there, for work, for food, for an attempt at a new life, pulling the region's resources to the breaking point. For they brought death with them, and the mixing of northern plague and southern guaranteed that many who settled in those places died within a month or two of arrival.

It gave other pilgrims a chance, but how much of a chance was it, when death seemed all but guaranteed?

Choosing to allow Lorant to sleep where he was, the prince took a book from the shelf the queen kept filled and sat at the window to read, hoping to clear his head of what-ifs. Kavan could not change the weather, could not control miracles. Whatever k'Ádhá intended for the future, fretting would not change anything. Queen and regent would see that every precaution was taken to protect those within the keep, particularly their family, but the rest was out of their hands.

## ⋙ Chapter 6 ⋙

With no agenda or intent to his escape, the kestrel flew for hours across the vast Enesfel's sky until the first traces of dawn began to creep above the Llaethlágárá. As was true so often of late, the sky was clear of clouds, its blanket of stars spread in all directions, pinpoints of light blinking out as daylight overtook each one and erased them. It was no surprise that instinct brought him to the lakeside grove he had discovered as a child and had visited often throughout his life. It had been a long time since he had been here, responsibilities, duties and his contentment with what he had been given creating no cause to stray far from Alberni. But the quest to appease his troubled spirit this night invariably brought him to the place he had often sought solace before.

A figure lying in shadow, appearing to have crawled from the lake and collapsed, invading his refuge, made him wary as he arrived with the intent to enjoy a swim and a short period of rest in nature's embrace. He made several circles of the shrinking lake, seeking danger or a trap in the unusual residual trace of power that tingled in the air. Unable to identify it, unable to get a clear view of whoever was here through the branches, he knew only that the intruder was a woman.

Sensing no threat in her or in the surrounding burn of power, he swooped down into the cover of the parched forest and emerged into sunlight not as a kestrel but as a man wearing the clothing he had worn during the coronation banquet the night before. Not a ghost, though some might think him such with his white skin and silver-white hair, he cautiously approached the twisted form at the water's edge. His wary eyes quickly read the scene, the lack of trampled autumn grass that suggested she had neither wandered here nor been brought and deposited by whoever her attackers had been.

No, he deduced as he knelt beside the woman dressed in a delicate gown of pale blue, the gown cut to expose one shoulder, what had brought her here had been a great surge of energy, maybe the same surge that had drained him of power the night before. There was a strong sense of residual force throbbing in the ground beneath her, as though a Gate had been opened and then closed again. There had never been a Gate in this clearing, yet the closer he came to that place, the more certain he was that there was one here now. Or there had been. When he reached for her, touching her arm to roll her towards him to learn if she breathed, if she lived, he gasped. His grasp on her shoulder tightened and his mouth opened to take in the breath sucked from him that he now struggled for.

She was power. Raw, unfocused, virgin power underutilized, contained within a shell, behind a face, that he recognized though had forgotten about until now.

They had never met, but long ago the Sight had shown him a series of glimpses of this moment, a woman by his lake, a woman with the deepest red hair he had ever seen. She was not kin, not even distantly, of the woman he had loved, not his unmet daughter, for this woman, bruised and beaten as she was, was older than Dhóri by many years. Twice as old, perhaps.

He knew she was Elyri, though her power lacked training and containment.

Her shallow breath felt warm on his hand, making him shiver as he sought signs of life. There were dark splotches across her face and around her neck, a split lip and abrasions on her cheeks and exposed shoulder, a gash over her brow that had left a trail of blood down her skin to kiss her swollen eye. She needed medical attention, perhaps healing, but he was no healer. Of all of the gifts Kavan was blessed with, healing was not one of them unless k'Ádhá granted a miracle.

He felt no familiar signs to precipitate a miraculous event. Given the state of her injuries and the tears in her gown, he was afraid to move her, afraid to cause more harm, but he could not leave her alone while he sought help. The shadow of a Gate he could feel was too weak to use. His only option was the one he took. Reaching within and across the miles, he called to the one person who could best provide the assistance she needed. Contact made, request given, he pulled off his silk tunic, ripping it down the front so that it was wide enough to cover her upper body and shoulders, and then he set about building a fire to stave off the air's chill.

He would not leave her alone, no matter how uncomfortable her proximity made him. He had forgotten those visions, had forgotten the panic he had experienced with each of those short moments of Sight. Now she was here, after so many years, and he was certain her arrival would turn his existence upside down. A woman this beautiful, this strong of power, could do nothing else.

Though he followed his cousin's directions to the Gate in the village ruins he had not used since the days of rescuing Prince Arlan from the attempts on his life, it had taken nearly two hours for the healer to find the bard, having to track his aura on foot through the forest. Unlike Kavan, he was not adept at shapechanging and disliked doing so, and so he moved in his own form between trees and thorny brush until he caught the faint sweetness of a cedar fire ahead. Not a forest fire; there was not enough smoke for that. He hastened his steps and found his way to the lakeside where the flicker and crackle of fire could be detected through the underbrush.

"sínréc?" he called, announcing his arrival before emerging into the clearing. He felt Kavan's life force always ahead but did not breathe easy until he saw him seated, shirtless, beside the fire he had made, with a woman lying on the other side of the heat.

"She appears to have been beaten," Kavan murmured to stave off questions. "I dared not move her." As the healer descended the embankment, he added, "It took you too long…"

Ártur shrugged. "Your summons did not sound urgent."

It was a poor excuse; Kavan rarely made a request that was not important, but without the sense of urgency, Ártur had felt no need to resort to the speed of flight. He knelt at the woman's side and drew Kavan's torn shirt away to examine her. "Who is she?" he asked, noting the unusual fabric of a tattered gown that was hardly suitable for early autumn's fading warmth. The thin material was bloody and muddy, sticking to her in many places, and though he could heal her with the gown in place, it would be easier to do so, to clean her and make her comfortable, if she was free of fabric that barely offered decent covering. As he began to peel the gown away, Kavan got to his feet and moved to the water's edge to wash his hands in the lake. There was no need for it, but he was no less comfortable with nudity, save for that of children, than he had been as a younger man.

"I do not know. The Sight…" His shoulders twitched as if to shrug. "There was a shift, a surge, a sucking of power last evening that led me here, but I know no more. I do not believe she was dumped here."

"She's in no condition to have walked here…too many bones cracked beneath the bruises…as if she's been kicked…"

Kavan's head bobbed in agreement though he did not look at his cousin. "I believe she came via Gate, but I don't know how that is possible. There is energy here…as if there was one…but it is gone now." Detectable still, but not a Gate he could use. "I don't think she is trained enough to have created, and destroyed, a Gate to deposit her here. Even I cannot do that."

That was one skill Kavan had yet to learn, though it was one he frequently wished he had and scoured every Elyri manuscript he located in the hopes of learning. Whoever had once created the Gates, whatever knowledge had existed regarding the process, had been lost.

By the time he forced himself to turn, Ártur had the woman covered with both the torn tunic and the cloak the healer had been wearing, her destroyed clothing tossed aside, useless. His hands were splayed across her upper chest, below her throat and shoulders, above her covered breasts, his eyes closed in concentration. There were the wide bruises of choking hands about her throat and Kavan scowled to see them. She was lucky to be alive.

"Will she live?"

"Hush, sínréc…let me work." She had not been so badly injured as to be at the brink of death, but he continued to assess her condition as he mended broken bones and internal damage.

Hating to be useless and idle, Kavan tore strips from her gown and with water from the lake began to delicately bathe the blood from her face and neck. The sun was nearing its zenith, the heat of the day no longer requiring the fire, but he let it burn in case her damp skin was cold. With sunlight free of the shadowing trees, it enabled him to better see her features, to notice the differences and similarities in her face, not just to Orynn but to other Elyri. Until she could speak, he would have no answers about who she was, where she came from, how she had come to be here in this condition, unless he read her.

The notion of touching her thoughts, however, of such intimate sharing between them, knotted his stomach and discolored his face. He was grateful for the damp cloth between his skin and hers.

By the time Ártur rocked back on his heels and pulled his hands away, the fire had spluttered out and Kavan, having finished with the cursory bathing, had moved far enough away that he could not easily give in to the temptation to touch her.

"She'll live. None of her injuries were life-threatening, whatever sleep agent she had been given is nearly out of her blood, but she will be uncomfortable for a week or more as the bruising heals. We should get her indoors, to warmth, find her something to wear…"

"Not Rhidam." Moving her there might afford her the constant care of several healers, should she require it, but it would take her too far away when Kavan had questions she needed to answer. He was not ready to spend that much time in Rhidam. She must not go to Rhidam. Not until he knew what the Sight intended to show him. "Alberni."

Used to the oddities of Kavan's suggestions, not perplexed by this one given Alberni's nearness, the healer asked, "Your house? Or…?"

"My house," he confirmed, ignoring his cousin's expression.

Yawning, the lack of sleep and expenditure of energy taking its toll, Ártur muttered, "We will have to walk to the ruins from here…and I do not have the strength to carry her."

He nearly laughed at Kavan's expected reaction, an alarmed, horror-stricken expression that spoke of discomfort Ártur felt Kavan should be well past by now. He supposed that the many years that had passed since Dhóri's conception with a woman Kavan would not talk about had allowed Kavan's awkward shyness to resurface. Or maybe it had never left. Kavan was unlike any man Ártur knew, and some things, he imagined, would never change.

Though terrified of touching her, Kavan stared at the unconscious form beneath his torn shirt and sighed with a shiver. Ártur was right. Healing expended a great amount of energy, even for someone as adept and experienced as Ártur. Having to trek back to the ruins would be tiring enough. Expecting him to carry the injured, unconscious woman as well, to appease Kavan's conscience, was unfair.

"You will leave your cloak around her?" he squeaked.

Chuckling, Ártur replied, "Of course." It was either that or leaving her nude, and even Ártur would not want to risk embarrassment should she wake, or leave her open to public scrutiny. He helped tuck the heavy yellow fabric of his cloak around her so there was no risk of touching her in an unseemly way, and then adjusted the cloth as Kavan lifted her. So long as she remained covered and he did not touch her skin, Kavan would have less of a problem carrying her.

Neither man spoke as they trudged through the trees. What city the ruins had once been, Kavan had never investigated, nor had he ever discovered what disaster had caused its abandonment. In the ensuing centuries, the buildings collapsed, many of the stones were taken away, and most usable material had become the bounty for scavengers. It had changed little since Ártur first found it, since Kavan had first been here, beyond the falling of more partial walls as the clay and mortar between the stones disintegrated and loosened, allowing for collapse. Coming back to where a period of great change in Enesfel's history had begun gave the healer the sense that some other significant change was upon them.

He wondered what it would be.

With the bard's arms full, unable to take Ártur's hands when they reached the Gate in what Kavan assured him had once been a náós or other place of worship, the healer curled his hands around his cousin's wrists and made the power connection between where they stood and the Gate within Kavan's home. Though he established that link, he allowed Kavan to transport them because it was easier and the bard enjoyed the use of power. The mist that formed was cool in contrast to the warm air of day; it enveloped them swiftly, and after a brief sense of floating, of disassociation between mind and body, they were deposited in the Alberni estate, a journey that would have taken a day or more on foot or horseback, completed in the span of a few breaths.

The woman in Kavan's arms did not stir except to turn her face more tightly to his chest and murmur in a small, frightened, hoarse whisper, "Ombhrís."

❧*❧

"Who is she?"

Dhóri bounded into the dining hall where Rhyrdan discussed household needs with his mother. Rhyrdan had seen Kavan carry a woman into a room upstairs, the room next to the Duke's, with Ártur following close behind, and had been there when Emeria was asked for warm water. Rhyrdan had not seen Kavan since, and though he doubted the bard had remained in the room as Emeria tended the woman's needs, the bard could have retreated to his chamber through the door that joined the two suites and remained there until Emeria finished. That, or perhaps he had gone out again. Kavan was prone to disappearing for hours or days when he was troubled, and Rhyrdan understood that few things would trouble the Duke more than the loss of his best friend.

But Rhyrdan wished Kavan would stay long enough for a discussion he needed to have. There was no one else, not the lively Dhóri, not his absent brother or wife, not his sister, not the prince-regent, and assuredly not his sullen, withdrawn mother, with whom he could talk about the man he too missed dearly. He and Emeria were barely managing to maintain the day-to-day running of the estate as well as their grief and their mother's.

How had his father managed the details so efficiently?

"A stranger. I don't know. I only got a glimpse of her and I did not have the chance to speak with your father. I have not seen them since their arrival." Rhyrdan watched his mother slip into the kitchen, again wondering how he might help her, or if he could.

"Is she Elyri? Perhaps we should introduce ourselves and…"

"She is injured, in no condition for introductions or small talk. Your father will present her, should she live. We will not accost her…"

Though Dhóri frowned, the look of disappointment passed quickly. "No more dying. I will pray in the oratory until dinner is ready, unless bhydhá looks for me…"

"You're not returning to…" Dhóri spent most of his days in St. Kórahm's, scribing, aiding the gdhededhásur with whatever the abbey needed. At this hour, when there was still sunlight remaining in which to work, it was unusual for Dhóri to choose to do anything else.

Bouncing on his toes, the dark-haired young man said, "There was power last night, Rhyrdan. I felt it…and I know bhydhá did too. He had to. It has to do with her…it must…and I want to know why. Why else would he have found her and brought her here?"

"He found her when he was out; there needs be no more to it than that. He brought her here because there was nowhere else to…"

"St. Kórahm's," Dhóri interrupted as if the other options were obvious. "Or St. Maicel's…or to a healer…"

"Ártur is with them…she has the best healer there is." Dhóri's prying insistence on answers about their guest rubbed Rhyrdan wrong. He was curious too; everyone in the house was. But most were wiser than to pry into the Duke's business. Father and son or not, Rhyrdan did not believe that Dhóri should be snooping. "They brought her where it seemed best. Waiting in the oratory for news is not going to gain you answers faster."

Except that the oratory was on the other side of Kavan's room and thus nearer where the stranger was being cared for than St. Kóráhm's. There was a strategy to Dhóri's choice, that Rhyrdan grumpily wished he did not recognize. No good was going to come of Dhóri interfering in his father's affairs. Wortham would have said the same thing.

The evening passed, the night and following day with it, and though Ártur departed before dinner was served that first day, Kavan did not come to the dining room to partake with his family. If he left his rooms, it was while the household slept, and while Rhyrdan chose not to fret, hoping that having someone, something, to tend to was helping Kavan cope with his recent loss, Dhóri was less forgiving. He fretted about the likelihood that his father had brought plague into the house, that he chose to remain locked in his rooms so as not to infect anyone. Why else would he avoid his son? Despite Rhyrdan's efforts to reassure him, to remind him that Kavan was prone to extended periods of solitude, sometimes in the estate, sometimes in St. Kóráhm's, sometimes elsewhere, Dhóri continued to take his distance, and his hiding their guest, as a personal affront.

In the barred rooms, entered only by Emeria when she brought food for the stranger in the hopes that she and Kavan would eat, though Kavan ate little himself, the bard watched over his guest, seated at her bedside with his harp, or a book, always busying himself so as not to look at her but unable to leave her. Ártur's return the second evening to examine her proved that she was on the mend, needing only to recover from the blows to her head and the bruising she had suffered. There was no cause for concern. She would awaken on her own, with no need for Kavan to keep watch.

No need, that was, except for his desire to know who she was, where she had come from, and why the pull of her untrained power lured him as a horse to the reins. Only once had he given in to the temptation to touch her, to try to read her with fingertips pressed to her temples. Instead of answers, Kavan encountered a wall of power around her thoughts as firmly in place as his own was.

Not untrained then, or else she had taught herself to block others, to keep herself hidden, as Kavan had done when he was a child first discovering his gifts. Was she hiding? From those who had hurt her? Could she have been the source of the drain on his power? Had she created and dismantled a Gate to reach the lake, and if so why?

From where?

The inability to find answers, the draw of her power, as well as the allure of her face, the color of her hair, the curves beneath the blankets, the sound of her breathing, frightened him.

His fear was not enough to propel him to leave.

❧*❧

"What do you mean he cannot come?" Still possessed of an impertinent streak that sometimes surfaced when she could not get her way, Diona stopped short of stomping her foot in frustration and uttering unrealistic demands. She could not order Kavan to come to Rhidam without exerting royal prerogative, but it did not prevent her from wishing she could.

"He has guests." It was not precisely accurate, and under other circumstances, Kavan might have left guests to entertain themselves for a few hours or put them in Wortham's care to be attended to. But Wortham could not see to this duty, and even if he had been there to do so, this was a duty Kavan would give to no one else. Ártur had never seen Kavan react to anyone as he reacted to the enigmatic woman who had seemingly dropped from the sky. Such a puzzle was cause enough for Kavan's focus, and while Ártur was curious to watch the developments unfold, he was not going to tell anyone in Rhidam, particularly Diona, that Kavan's guest was a woman.

"It must be someone of import if he will not come for a few hours," she snorted. Bhyrhán had returned to Clarys, intending to put his affairs in order with the Kyne and gather some of his personal belongings for a stay of indeterminate length in the Lachlan court. Without him to distract and soothe her, without his voice and the use of his eyes to help her see, or his pipes to fill her days with music, Diona was seeking anyone, anything, to fill barren hours with purpose. She had never been one for sewing with her ladies, for gossip and idle chatter. She was accustomed to the responsibilities of sovereignty.

As Merrek took up one duty after another, Diona was gradually discovering the benefits of gossip, for it gave her tidbits of news she did not always get from her advisors. Merrek welcomed her input and attendance to all matters of business, and he consulted her on every matter of importance that came to his attention, but she chose not to devote every hour of her day focused on duties that would eventually fall entirely on Merrek's shoulders. He had to learn the art of ruling. Unlike most previous kings, he had the opportunity to learn such things in practice while the queen was there to guide and advise him. He was an intelligent man; he did not need her looming over him as he sought the respect of the people and his advisers.

Ártur bowed. "I believe it must be."

"You have not met them?"

Aware of the slip of his tongue, the healer shrugged. "I have been in Alberni only long enough to see to his state of mind. I fear he is not himself and wanted to see his welfare with my own eyes. That is when I learned he has guests."

Sighing, Diona let her shoulders sag. "Yes…you should see to him. He did not speak of Wortham when he was here. My efforts to engage him in conversation failed. You are sure there are guests…that he is not avoiding you…avoiding us?"

"I am. Rhyrdan has assured me of it."

The mention of the youngest Delamo's name made Diona smile wistfully. "I'm glad he has Rhyrdan." Rhyrdan was so much like his father, in appearance, in temperament, in devotion, if not in worldly experience and training, that she imagined his company would be particularly soothing. Or else it would be a too painful reminder.

Her smile faded. She wished she could speak to Kavan to determine which it was. "When will you see him next?"

"Tomorrow evening." Ártur had just returned from Alberni when he encountered the queen in the corridor, but he did not tell her where he had been. "I will convey your desire for music when I see him." Perhaps the opportunity to make music before a familiar audience would be enough to draw the bard away from the stranger. "When is Bhyrhán returning?" He did not know about their agreement, that Bhyrhán was sharing his eyesight with her, he only knew that the two spent many hours together and that it had brought a carefree air back to the woman's mood that had not been there since Espen's death.

"The end of the week…so long as Kyne does not forbid it."

"She's not like that." Ártur did not know the woman the way Kavan did, but he knew her by reputation, and he knew she was fond of Diona. So long as Rhidam was safe as it could be, and Bhyrhán knew the risks, her kinsman was allowed to follow his own path. The male heirs of the High Mother had fewer restrictions than did the females, for any one of the women could be appointed in the Kyne's place, should she die or pass out of the world as Elyri-kind did at the end of their days. "If he promised his return, I'm sure he will hold to it. It will be good to have him here. I miss the constant ring of music."

"As do I."

"May I escort you somewhere?" Though she still had eyesight enough to find her way, the lack of light in the corridors would not be easy to navigate.

Diona shook her head. "I know the way to my rooms." Her voice was more clipped than intended and she immediately muttered, "I am sorry, Ártur."

He bowed. "No offense taken. I will see you in the morning?"

"Indeed. Goodnight, Lord Healer."

"Good night, My Queen." He was relieved, as he watched her pass, that she had not pressed for more details about Kavan. He did not know how long he should hide the truth, or if he even should.

Edging towards cognizance, a process that felt like slogging through the bog her parents had warned her away from as a child, brought with it an awareness of music, soft, sweet, melodic notes on metal strings. The tinkling reminded her of the rocking of a boat on the sea, bringing with it memories of her brother, of colorful ribbons of light reflected across the glassy water, the smell of brine and wet canvas, and the chill of the wind blowing across the bow, propelling them towards the shore. It was a pleasant memory, distant but fresh, and for the longest time, she listened, hovering between wakefulness and sleep, not certain that the sound was real. It hurt to think, to focus, so she allowed the sound to lull her, carry her driftingly on the calming tones, taking comfort in the pictures in her mind that warred with the increasing awareness of pain points throughout her body.

Gradually she grew in the assurance that the experience of her ears was real, for the nearer she drew towards waking, the louder and more persistent the notes became, as if the music was played upon the ever-nearing shore. Memories of ocean breezes gave way to the warmth and the security of comfortable bedding, and the aroma of a wood fire burning on a hearth, though she could not see or hear its crackle.

With the smell of smoke, however, came other memories, a shadow, an arm raised to strike, arms pinning her, covering her mouth…kicks and blows…and before darkness took her, the lowering of that arm, its weapon aiming directly for the head of…

She sat up with a scream, lashing out with a blast of power to force her assailants away, her eyes wide, her heart thumping as if it would explode from her chest. Someone was immediately there, hands closed around hers. Sensing no one, the touch surprised her, and she yanked her hands back to be free of the hold. Simultaneously thinking the masculine presence to be Ombhrís, she followed another instinct and buried her face against the man's chest. Tremors ran in shockwaves through her. Arms around her shoulders, tentative and stiff, conveyed a sense of calm and assurance that allowed her to push her fear aside as other smells, herbal incense with faint, earthy floral undertones, filled her nostrils and sank into her agitated center.

A nightmare. That's what it had to be. No such crime had been committed across the land in generations. Surely no one would have tried to kill her and Ombhrís on their wedding night. There was no reason for such an act.

Relaxation, however, brought with it the returned awareness of pain, as though she had tumbled down a mountain and lived to tell of her fall. The music that had accompanied her waking had stopped, and there came a pounding on wood, the rattle of loose metal hinges, and an unfamiliar voice speaking phrases she did not understand.

"bhydhá…are you well?"

She opened her eyes and pulled back in confusion.

She stared.

Kavan sighed, the sound tremulous and nervous, as he was both relieved to have her pull away and unexpectedly disappointed that she had. Unable to break from the gaze that held his as a second knock came, he managed to say, "All is well, Dhóri."

The breath on the other side of the door caught, held, and when it released, Kavan could hear his son's frustration.

Dhóri deserved the truth.

But the truth was still unknown and would have to wait, as now he was caught in the warmth of sand-gold eyes, the color of which he had never seen in a person. He opened his mouth to speak again but the search for words of reassurance or welcome failed.

He was a spirit, surely. White. Flawless like the stone effigies the márbhyndhánis sometimes displayed. Fragile in its fineness, and yet bearing the strength of the sea, the mountains, the moon, the stars in the sky. She had never seen another like him…and yet it felt as if she had known him all of her life.

Mesmerized, confused by that unreasonable familiarity, she reached for his face, to test his reality. The twitch at the corners of his mouth and eyes made her pause. A spirit made flesh…for he had been solid, real, moments before when she had sought comfort against him. He was as the freshly fallen snow, his hair the silver blue-white of moonlight upon the winter-mountain peaks, his eyes…his green eyes reflections of the spring grass in the fields at home.

Ignoring his distress this time, her outstretched hand continued nearer to his thick hair. He stiffened but did not draw away, frozen in place, until she caught the strands between her fingers. He was real…and she was here…wherever here was. On the stand beside him, a small black harp, carved in the shape of a kestrel in flight. Seeing it made her pull back abruptly. She shook her head. Not…

It could not be.

"bhir phehonís phaern Gálínphel …" she whispered, her voice a dry cracked croaking sound of amazement and disbelief.

Her voice broke the hold her eyes held over him and Kavan stood, crossing the room to fill a cup with water from the tray Emeria had left. His head throbbing from that blast of power she had cast upon waking, he intended to take the water to her, but the echoes of her words blared in his ears, the words and how she had spoken them.

Not Enesi or Trade. Not Cíbhóló, Hatuish, Nethic, or Cordashian. Not the language of the far south that Zelenka and Wortham had helped him learn over the last twenty years.

High Elyri. But not. A similarity of words, of context and structure and syntax…and yet not the same. A dialect, perhaps, though he had never encountered variations within the High Elyri form taught by the bhydáni and gdhededhá to those students desiring to learn it.

A dialect in which the word bhir she had used for white had been transposed for the term phyr, for blue, with which he was familiar.

How simple it was, he knew, for words to change in sound and meaning over time. How easy it was for a mishearing of a song to result in mistranslation. The song he knew spoke of a bird far from home. Nothing more. Kavan was not a bird.

Resorting to High Elyri in the hopes that the language would be similar enough for her to understand, he said, "Do not speak yet…" He had to keep her from saying more as he put the cup in her hands, stiffening again, through every fiber of his being, into the places he would rather not think about, when her fingers brushed his. "You are in Alberni, my home." She stared, either not understanding or choosing not to speak in favor of quickly draining the water she had been given. "I found you in the forest, near a lake, you were beaten."

He watched her face, her body language, paying close attention to the subtleties of the power shifts in her aura, seeking clues that might tell him how he could help her.


She heard his words, marking their differences and finding him peculiar for it. The language was similar enough that she understood the gist of what he was saying, but the words made little sense. Where was Alberni? A new ghís…although the room she was in was like no home she had seen and was too old, she determined, to be part of a new ghís. Perhaps this was néósag…but he had said his home, and though she had felt deep power in him when he had held her, power that had been the first clue that he was not Ombhrís, she did not think he was márbhyndhánis.

So where was she, she wondered again, and how had she come to be here? Had he abducted her, been part of a plot against her and Ombhrís? Though she shrank against the headboard, she dismissed that thought as soon as it came. There was nothing violent in him and his tale of finding her was a truthful one. His thoughts might be blocked, but if he was lying, she believed she would know.

She looked at her arms, not bare now but covered in comfortable white fabric, the softest she had ever touched. Stroking it, she looked at her host, willing him to continue.

Kavan, thinking the look in her eyes to be a question he was embarrassed to answer, flushed and stepped back from the bed, shaking his head apologetically. "My cousin, Ártur MacLyr, tended you, dressed you. He is ílMairós…I would never…" The thought of undressing her filled him with a familiar uncomfortable throbbing.

"MacLyr." She could hear the disbelief in her voice. There had been no Llyrs in the lands in innumerable centuries. They had been banished long ago for acts of treason and defiance against authority. To be the son of a Llyr meant that she too had been banished, sent away not on a ship but through a Gate. It also meant she could never return, never go home, never see her brother again…never know what had become of Ombhrís…never see that justice was done for this act without the chance to prove herself. Someone must have learned the truth…but who? Why had she not been afforded the customary trial?

Staring as if bitten, Kavan wondered if she knew Ártur, or if Ártur knew her. Ártur had shown no hint of it, but Kavan had paid less attention to his cousin than he had to the injured woman. Or perhaps not Ártur. Perhaps Bhen, or Sámel, or other kin in Bhryell. His expression softened as unshed tears rose in her eyes and when the empty metal cup dropped from her trembling hand, he retrieved it. Thinking his reaction upset her, he quickly asked, "Are you hungry? Shall I send for water so you may bathe? Is there anything…?"

"I…" she sniffed and rolled away, finding his words clearer as she curled into a ball. "I would like to be alone. Please."

Alone. Leave her. Not many of her words made sense; Kavan understood that one, but he did not think he could do it, leave her alone and unguarded. What if she fled? What if she needed help and he was not here to see that she got it? What if she needed him?

A voice in the back of his head screamed 'fool', which allowed him to take a faltering step towards the door. Now that she was awake, of course she did not need him. His desire to be needed, to have his company wanted, was selfish, irrational, and unwarranted. She owed him nothing for saving her life and if she felt well enough to leave, or if she wished to be alone, it was his place to accommodate her.

Hearing her weep as he backed through the door and closed it between them was one of the hardest things he had ever had to bear.


Relieved to be alone, she rolled again, this time to her back, before sitting up and drying her cheeks of unwanted tears. Crying was not going to solve anything. It hurt unbearably to be banished without trial or notice, sent away from her home for unspecified crimes, but she had known the risks of following the veiled path. Her beliefs, and those of her father, had been kept hidden, secret, for a reason. Only a few others had known, and she had faith that none of them would have spoken betrayal. There were other ways, however, more invasive and frightening ways, for the márbhyndhánis to gain information, and such ways might have been employed against her brother, who did not have the knowledge or ability to withstand such methods.

Or maybe they, whoever they were, had no proof of crimes and had acted on rumor alone, a preemptive strike against someone or something that threatened hánag, the natural order of life. She supposed she had been lucky to be spared the kylldrenai. To have been spared whatever fate had befallen Ombhrís.

Her frown began to quiver at the corners and she stood to distract herself from grief, an act that caused the room to sway. Surely Ombhrís was dead. The blow of a heavy smith's hammer, the blow she had seen fall, would have been enough to crush a man's skull. While she could admit to a degree of relief at not having consummated a marriage she had not been entirely committed to, she had no desire for Ombhrís to be dead and had not wanted out of the marriage badly enough to have considered such an action herself.

He had been talked into their match for the same reasons she had been. Trade between ghís, ties between powerful families, the unification of power between two of the wealthiest ghísaer. The good of the people, her father had said. The honor of the family. The benefit of the ghís and the ghísaer.

Ombhrís did not deserve to die for that.

It was his death, however, that twisted the reality of her situation and distorted its logic. If she had been taken, banished by the márbhyndhánis for anarchic beliefs, Ombhrís would have been left unharmed. Brought in for questioning, held until it was discovered that he was guiltless of his bride's beliefs, but not killed. Murder was nearly unheard of amongst their kind, execution rarer still. If not the márbhyndhánis, then who was responsible for these terrible crimes? Who had killed Ombhrís and sent her into the forbidden lands? Why?

And how had they done it without the márbhyndhánis' skills?

It was a puzzle she would likely never solve. None of the banished returned to the land of the dhóbhaen, at least none of those expelled through the rynlagne. Lacking the knowledge to create or use one herself, unsure they existed in this land of exile, she would have to begin again, make the most of the life she had been permitted to keep, learn the ways of the local people, find a way to be of service.

The best place to begin, she thought with a sigh of resignation, was apologizing to her benefactor and making use of whatever knowledge and aid he could provide. He spoke her tongue, or a form near enough to it that they should be able to converse. If he was, indeed, the one the ancient stories foretold, then her coming here might have been preordained. Assuming he would speak with her in the morning, as long as she had not offended him or broken some law or taboo in her first interaction with him, she would face him when the sun broke a new day.

She staggered to the full-length mirror that hung near a second door she had not noticed earlier. The silken shirt, not long enough to be the gown she had first thought it to be, swished and swayed against her skin like a caress, lighting the nerves of the bruised skin beneath. It hung loosely from her shoulders to below her knees, the fit suggesting it belonged to someone taller with broader shoulders. Was it his, she mused, the thought an unexpectedly warming one that made her feel more at ease.

In the mirror, she studied her reflection, the mottled skin that made her into a horrid shade of herself. Her dark swollen eye and lip and the cut on her forehead pink from recent healing but not yet faded. Pushing up the sleeves, pulling open the V neckline, lifting the hem to expose her thighs, she saw that there was hardly an inch of her that was not similarly discolored. She had no recollection of being beaten enough to warrant her appearance, so perhaps the bruising was a result of the banishment through the rynlagne. She had never been through one. Few had. What did she know about how such travel worked?

A knock on the door prompted the hasty dropping of the shirt to cover herself, hoping that her host had returned. His disquiet with physical contact, perhaps with her company, had been obvious; she could imagine how he would react to the sight of her exposed body. Even the thought of his healer cousin dressing her had embarrassed him. When, she wondered, had nudity become taboo?

Was it just him?

But the voice that called, "M'lady?" from the other side of the door was female, knowledge that made her relax as she tottered back to the bed. "May we fill your tub?"

It took several moments to piece together what the woman had asked. If not for her father's efforts to teach her taerén, and the still difficult practice of reading the thoughts of another, she would know none of the woman's words. She barely understood the ones she did recognize, the accent being different, the intonation of syllables an unusual cadence that she struggled to make sense of. Scowling, realizing she had not noticed any sort of bathing facilities in the room she repositioned the blankets over her lap and said, "du, please…enter." Maybe, she thought as she eyed the door near the mirror, there was a bathing area there.

She did not think the other woman would understand her words, but she hoped her intent would be recognized.

The woman who entered appeared old, despite the relative youth of her body, and bone-tired. Her features were on the dowdy side, a woman without the glow of vitality, but she was friendly in appearance, though upon seeing her, the only thought again racing through the stranger's head was 'taeré'. It was known that the kairénté, the taeré, lived across the channel; their small fishing or trade boats sometimes braved the tumultuous northern sea using the largely inhospitable Hínesur as stepping stones when they dared approach the dhóbhaen homeland. It should not surprise her to find the taeré in the place of banishment too, but it did. It was especially surprising to find one living with a dhóbhaen, even if it was in servitude.

She was followed by a cherub of a girl and three boys carrying buckets of steaming water. The girl was the mirror image of the older woman, but the boys showed kinship only to one another. They paused inside the room and bowed or curtsied in address.

"I am Zelenka…I manage this house for Lord Cliáth."

The stranger's breath caught and she shook her head. She barely understood most of the words but that one word was spoken as clearly as a bird call. No, she told herself. It could not be possible.

That name, too, had died out generations ago.

"M'lady? Should I send for a physician?"

She shook her head no, sensing the woman's concern without knowing her words. She hurt all over, an ache she knew would be soothed by heated water that would awaken the sting of abrasions, but she did not need a healer for those things. She was hungry, thirsty, and tired, but most of all she wanted answers. She did not need a healer's care. Not anymore.

"Lord Cliáth commands you have everything you require. This is Emeria, my daughter." She nudged the young woman forward. "She will tend you as long as you remain with us."

"It is not…" Servitude was not unheard of. People entered into service to pay off debts or to acquire something they needed or wanted for which there was no adequate payment available. Service was as tradable as any material commodity. Servitude aboard fishing and trade ships was often the best way to acquire a vessel of one's own. Perhaps that was the case here. Not willing to believe her host would subjugate another into service, she decided to treat these people as equals, whatever their breeding.

After a look passed between mother and daughter, Zelenka waved her hand, trying to be cheerful, but it was a strained mood unsustained by emotion. "A fine lady such as you should lack for nothing and my lord's generosity is well known…"

There was a note to the words that the stranger did not understand, an emotional quality that suggested she might not be wanted here despite the lord's choice. Casting a sidelong glance at the harp left behind in the man's haste to depart, she frowned, not wanting to take advantage of hospitality not wanting to appear greedy or rude.

Emeria came to the bedside and took her hand, unknowingly providing, in that skin-to-skin contact, a means for understanding. Diplomacy and trade with the taeré made learning this skill a necessity, even though it was a skill she had needed to hide at all times. With a link between their thoughts, it allowed her to know the intent of Emeria's words more easily without struggling to comprehend and would allow the serving girl to understand her in a similar fashion. It was too difficult to manage the skill with more than a single individual at a time and required significant concentration, but until she learned the local languages, it would be a necessity.

"Accepting what is offered freely is not taking advantage," Emeria said more warmly than her mother, apparently more accepting of the disruption of a stranger's arrival. She curtseyed again and drew back the folded screen adorned with pastoral scenery woven on filmy Káliel silk as the others went out for more water. "Can you get in on your own?" she asked as she emptied the buckets into the wooden tub lined with a thin sheen of hammered copper.

Marveling at the sight, the stranger rose from the bed and shuffled nearer to study the tub more closely. There was nothing like this at home. Bathing was a thing done in a bowl or in nature, most often in the cold rivers and lakes that abounded, unless one lived near one of the numerous hot springs that bubbled from beneath the frozen landscape. Some had dug into the earth to free such springs and built rooms around them for communal bathing chambers but this did not look to be such a spring.

"Perhaps…" She watched Emeria add one bucket of cooler water to the hot, and then another, until putting her hand into it proved the temperature to be bearable.

"There will be more soon," Emeria assured her, adding a fragrant floral oil to the water, a pleasing scent her charge did not recognize.

"Raebhá…please."

The R rolled on her tongue in a foreign way but Emeria did her best to imitate the sound. "Lady Raebhá," she said. "Suits you. Come, in with you before the boys return and see what they shouldn't."

The words confirmed that nudity was not something these people shared and so Raebhá tried to be careful as she slipped out of the nightshirt and climbed into the tub with one hand on the side to steady herself. Emeria kept her head politely turned, bending instead to pick up the discarded gown. With a clucking of her tongue, she said, "He should have asked for one of mine, or mother's, not given you his," as if scolding the absent lord.

So it was his. From what little Raebhá had perceived in their first encounter, it seemed an uncharacteristic gesture to make, an intimate one that made her flush. Thankfully, the steamy water and the bruises across her skin masked that response. "It is comfortable," she said, trying to sound both casual and sincere. "I like it. If he gave it, I should make use of it, don't you think? Wouldn't it be rude to reject it?"

"Hmmph," Emeria sniffed, hanging the shirt over the back of a nearby chair. Their guest had a point, but it did not seem proper to her. Women did not wear men's clothing…at least proper women did not unless riding…or unless one was Gabrielle Dilyn, Asta Dugan de Corrmick, or the female knight Bhetá Gabersdon. No one else, as far as Emeria was concerned, should wear such things. "We will see that you have proper dresses come the morrow…a tailor, seamstress, and shoemaker will come if you are well enough. The clothing you were found in was not…serviceable."

More water arrived, allowing Raebhá to sit decently covered in warm water made cloudy by bath oils and petals. The tray of food that had been near the door before was taken away when Zelenka and the boys left the first time, and another with fresh food, hot bread and cheese, and slabs of what smelled like waterfowl, was set within

Raebhá's reach. She did not know how long it had been since she had last eaten but she realized now how hungry she was.

"I am afraid," Emeria said as she delicately sponged water over Raebhá's mottled skin, "there was little dinner left. We eat after the lord, or sometimes with him, and the men leave little to pick over. Boys and men, you know. We did not anticipate you waking...."

Raebhá smiled at the reference. She had seen virile young men and older, sedentary ones alike, feasting as if they had never eaten or would never eat again. She knew how they could be.

"If this is not enough, I will find more..."

"No, this is acceptable. My gratitude. Eating too much before sleep will bring nightmares." She anticipated nightmares regardless, as her subconscious continued making sense of how she had come to be in this unfamiliar place.

"Happens to me too." Having pulled the stool close to the tub now that everyone else was gone, Emeria asked, "Shall I wash your hair?"

Though she wanted to be alone, Raebhá did not think it polite to send Emeria away when the woman had been instructed by the lord to serve her. She nodded and picked at her food as Emeria bathed her. The boys returned with firewood, and Zelenka brought fresh linens to change the bedding as they tidied the room, the cloth screen preventing Raebhá from watching them and allowing her to bathe uninterrupted. Only when the dirty bedding was removed and the woman and boys had gone did Emeria help her from the tub and aid in drying her before the warmth of the newly stoked fire.

Emeria reluctantly helped her put on the shirt the lord had provided and brushed out her hair. No one touched the harp. Little speaking was done except for an occasional idle question from Emeria to make Raebhá feel at ease.

"They will empty the water in the morning," Emeria eventually explained, moving the tray to the bedside table so that their guest could reach it without rising if she chose to eat more or fill her cup with water. She did not share what a rare luxury a bath in this time of drought was. The water would be put to good use. "You've had enough interruptions; you need your sleep. If you require anything, you have only to summon me..." The girl gestured to a braided green cord hanging in one corner of the room, a system Kavan had borrowed from Káliel to allow guests privacy and aid all at once. "I will hear it wherever I am."

Not understanding how, Raebhá nodded as if she did and settled against the headboard. Emeria adjusted the blankets over her, still smiling as she had done all evening, as if she was happy to serve.

"Thank you…for all of this…" Raebhá murmured.

"It is good to have a woman here…one who is not a minstrel. You're not…are you?"

Raebhá shook her head, silently contemplating Emeria's statement as the girl lit the new candle in the bedside sconce and then retreated from the room.

Was he a bard? Was the song more accurate than she had at first thought? She dared to reverently run her fingers over the glistening black wood of the harp, surprised to find that, while it looked wet, it was not. Its intricate design was the work of an expert craftsman. Her memory of its tone, as she had come to wakefulness, was of a finely pitched instrument. The harps of legend were said to have been magnificent things, the best in the world. The dhóbhaen had lost much when the last of the Cliáths had been banished from the land.

Maybe, she thought, the craft had not been lost. Not if her host was, indeed, of that ancient bloodline.

She tried unsuccessfully to find Ombhrís inside her head, within her heart, but he was not there, too far from her in distance, separated by marriage bonds not yet initiated, or else dead and beyond reach. Nor could she find her brother, but he was untrained, his power unhoned and weak. She doubted she could reach him even if she were capable of the feat.

Too weary, too disheartened to do anything more than she had, she drew the blankets around her like a cocoon, wondering if this was the lord's room, wondering where he had gone, wondering, with another glance at the harp, if he would play for her again if she asked.

When she awoke in the morning, the instrument was gone.

## ❧Chapter 7❦

"Who is she, bhydhá?"

Kavan should have expected that the oratory would be no place to hide, not from his staff who would know where to seek him, and not from his son who had recently spent his share of time in this room. Kavan felt the young man's presence when he came in, but he had not considered that he might return tonight.

He recognized Rhyrdan's footsteps behind Dhóri's without turning, recognized that, like his father, he was always reluctant to enter, to interrupt Kavan at prayer, without invitation. Dhóri, however, felt no such reluctance. Kavan lifted his eyes to the image of Dhágdhuán the Intercessor hanging on the wall behind the dark wood altar and then shifted on his knees to face the pair, his gaze first meeting Rhyrdan's and then Dhóri's. Rhyrdan remained near the door while Dhóri reached the altar steps and sat beside his father, his expression lit with curiosity that would not be easily appeased.

"I do not know."

"You spoke with her. You brought her here. You must…"

"I don't." During those prayers, Kavan realized he had not introduced himself or asked her name, and as she had seemed weary and distraught, had asked to be alone, he had not had the opportunity to do so. "I found her near the lake." The boys would know which lake, as Kavan had taken them there as children, particularly Dhóri, Sóbhán and Yóáná, when they had been learning to shapechange. "She has suffered an accident or an attack, and needs time to…"

"Ártur has healed her, yes?" It was the first time Rhyrdan had spoken. He would rather know that the healer had been here to tend to the woman than think that he had been here to tend some unrevealed condition in Kavan.

"He has," Kavan murmured, inclining his head to Rhyrdan's unspoken concern, "and I am well."

Dhóri inched nearer. "Will we meet her? Will she stay with us?"

The hairs across the back of Kavan's neck prickled as the muscles there, and along his shoulders, arms, and back, tensed. "For the time being, I imagine so." He willed away that burst of negativity and continued, "She may wish to return home, she may require legal aid or sanctuary. She is welcome to stay as she recovers, as long as necessary. After that…"

He shrugged. He had no hold over her, beyond finding her and assuring that she recovered. But he hoped she would stay long enough to answer his questions, long enough to allow him to help her. It felt important that he do so, though he could not rationalize that feeling.

"When she is ready, she may require a horse. Rhyrdan, if you see to one for her…"

"Is she Elyri?"

Both Rhyrdan and Kavan stared at Dhóri, his interruption unappreciated but expected. While normally polite, Kavan had never been able to instill in Dhóri the value of patience, of not interrupting when others were speaking. If a thought came into Dhóri's head, a question or comment, it often burst out unhindered.

"She is…kin." Elyri but not Elyri, though he did not know how it could be. Her use of language was unlike any he had encountered in Elyriá, so unless she was from some remote village that clung to a nearly dead form, she had to have come from somewhere else. But that possibility seemed absurd, leaving him at a loss for an explanation.

But the word kin felt oddly appropriate.

The word deflated some of Dhóri's boisterous mood and Kavan deduced why Dhóri was so interested in this guest. Most of those who had grown up beneath Kavan's care were wed, save for Rhyrdan and Dhóri. Rhyrdan could be, was old enough for it, but he had yet to show an interest in the pursuit of a wife. Dhóri, while young for an Elyri, appeared to be feeling left out of the life his friends, and especially his brother, were pursuing. He too, Kavan recognized, wanted a wife.

That interest suggested that there would be no lifelong commitment to the Faith as he had begun to believe was his son's future. There were ways to serve while married, but the life of a gdhededhá, which Dhóri had been pursuing, meant abstinence, chastity, never marrying.

Maybe Dhóri wanted to explore his options before making a final commitment. There was nothing wrong with that.

The choice was not Kavan's. Dhóri must forge his path and live it.

"You will likely meet her soon, as she is now awake. Perhaps in the morning if she is comfortable and willing. But remember, she has been through a great trauma. Do not press her with unending questions and prying. Allow her time to adjust and settle."

The reminder was as much for himself as for Dhóri.

"We will see that she has what she requires," Rhyrdan promised. Whatever she needed, whatever Kavan wanted to provide, Rhyrdan would see that it happened. His father would have done the same thing.

❧*❧

Wace Elotti was an old man. He had to remind himself that every time someone came to him with a job, had to weigh his physical capabilities against the likely demands of any given duty. Whatever Elyri was in his blood, a detail Kavan had verified for him years ago, allowed him to perform as a man perhaps twenty years younger, but even that, in his line of business, was an age beyond prime. His actions were slower, his hearing and eyesight less acute, and while he would still beat many in combat, he had no doubts that each job he took brought him nearer to a violent end. Such an end might be fitting, but he did not want his life to end in defeat. He did not want his death to be the highlight of someone else's career.

Expert bounty hunter that he was, he much preferred to disappear into anonymity, to disappear into myth and speculative tales and mystery. He would prefer that no one was ever sure what had become of the once-fierce Cíbhóló hunter.

It was what had brought him to Rhidam. He would not retire here, of course. His face was too well known to be anonymous. But he knew people in this city, or he had once. Feeling nostalgic of late, he wanted to see many of them again before fading into obscurity, particularly Lord Cliáth. Maybe, while he was here, he could earn himself one or two more commissions before disappearing from the world. He had coin enough to live frugally for many years, but his intent was something much different.

"Mr. Elotti." Rouvyn Talis was the one to greet the hunter at the closely guarded castle gates. Now that the command was in place to inspect all visitors for symptoms of the Yellow Sisters, one of the physicians had to be available at all hours to do so. It had been many years since he had seen the man before him, enough time to give him wisdom and confidence he had not possessed when Wace had first crossed his path. They were young men no longer. Rouvyn had grown rounder, his blonde hair sparse but long enough to tie at the neck, while Wace's hair was growing white, his face etched with the deep crags of age and combat, his shoulders beginning to stoop. To Physician Talis, however, the man was still imposing enough to make him uncomfortable as he held forth a gloved hand and gave the man a quick, visual inspection. "What brings you to Rhidam?"

Elotti smiled, admiring Rouvyn's poise. At one time it had been a much-rumored fact that Wace preferred the company of suggestible younger men. Rouvyn had been such a man, but his association with Kavan had changed him, and by the time Wace found him again, Rouvyn had become a more assertive person. There were no regrets at the time. Wace had gone on to other companions but he felt a twinge of regret that he had not gotten to know Rouvyn better.

"I come seeking Lord Cliáth…or Agis." He knew that Asta Dugan was the queen of Neth but he had not visited there and did not know if he would take the time to do so. He knew Prince Owain had died several years past after multiple missed opportunities to reconnect. It left fewer and fewer living within the Lachlan keep who would remember him. The queen, most likely, as he had worked for her in clearing Kavan of murder charges, finding King Hagan's killer, and had helped erase the Coryllien stain from the land. The same held for Healer MacLyr. He had known Fen before the merchant had become Enesfel's Inquisitor and he had already crossed paths with the man the night before in the Eagle's Nest Tavern where both had shared drink.

Other than the bard and general, there were few he cared to see.

"I'm sorry…the general succumbed to sickness early last spring."

"He lived a life of honor. I regret to hear he is gone." Fen had not shared that detail; Wace had not thought to inquire. He had not known the general intimately, but as two of only a few Cíbhóló living in or frequently visiting Rhidam, they had shared drinks on occasion, games of chance, and news of their homeland that Wace delivered when his business brought him to town. "I pray not Lord Cliáth as well?" Unless

Rouvyn would drink with him, the hunter feared he had wasted his time in coming here.

"Lord Cliáth is well. I have not seen him recently, but he comes and goes between Rhidam and Alberni at his whim. If you would like a room, would care to wait for him…"

"No," Wace chortled. "No room in a castle for me. I've got a place in the Eagle's Nest." He thumbed over his shoulder towards the inn and tavern nearest to the keep. "I'll be there for the foreseeable future…so if you would tell him I'm here, that I'd like to speak with him, I would be indebted."

Rouvyn smiled and offered his hand again. "No debts, Wace," he dared to use the man's name. "I will tell Healer MacLyr; he will certainly see Lord Cliáth before I do. Perhaps it will spur his return. It is good to see you."

"And you." Deciding he had nothing to lose by asking, Wace offered, "When duty permits, come, join me for a drink. I think you and I should have a proper conversation."

The physician caught his breath, eyed the other man warily, but seeing and sensing no dark motive, he eventually bobbed his head. "I will see to it that I do," he agreed. If nothing else, there was history to put behind them. Rouvyn, like Wace, recognized this might be their only opportunity to do that.

❧*❧

It was a late morning meal brought to her room, for by the time Raebhá awoke, the sun's position through the only window in the chamber appeared quite high. She ate as Emeria and her mother puttered around the room and the serving boys emptied the bathing basin in silence. The food was unfamiliar and she wanted to take her time eating it, to study the flavors, the textures. But it seemed she would not be left alone until she finished, and so she ate quickly in order to set the tray aside. Zelenka nodded and left with it as Raebhá expected, at which time Emeria provided a gown of dark green and crème, a dress too loose across the bust but otherwise fitting well enough to service her needs for this day.

Raebhá studied herself in the mirror, noticing that the cut of the dress covered the majority of her bruises as Emeria pinned her rich auburn hair away from her ears with silver combs. The cinch-waisted cut of the gown was awkward and uncomfortable, the hairstyle unfamiliar, yet both were pleasing, to the eye, and as she turned from side to side to see herself more fully, she wondered what Ombhrís would think.

The question was quickly followed by the thought of whether her host would approve.

After helping her don the unfamiliar styles but failing to find shoes that fit comfortably, the serving woman escorted her barefoot into a bright room on the first floor of the manor where several clothiers had gathered, their wares spread for perusal with the hopes that she would select from them. Instruction had been left for the purchase of a formal gown and seven days of the clothing of her choice. Raebhá gaped at the collection, running her fingers over the diverse, unfamiliar fabrics in colors and styles she did not recognize. She had never seen so many articles, so many gowns, shoes, and accessories, in one place. Unlike most of the styles of home, everything appeared intricate, costly, and well-made yet just as functional, of the finest materials and artistry. It embarrassed her that her host intended to give so much after her questionable initial treatment of him. Perhaps he thought to buy her approval and smooth any tensions between them.

With all of the pieces unfamiliar, her afternoon filled with the trying on of one gown after another, she eventually grew frustrated with the choices and weary of the effort to stand, to ignore the pain of bruises and abraded skin, the energy it took to understand so much foreign speech. To satisfy Emeria, however, and because she believed she should dress according to local custom if she was to stay here, she selected a kirtle, two long skirts in shades of green along with three peasant blouses in assorted shades, an embroidered ebony bodice, and a vest in emerald green. The greens accentuated the flecks in her sand-gold eyes and had always been her favorite color to wear.

That it mirrored her host's eyes as well was something she refused to consider too deeply.

A heavy cloak lined with fur, a style which reminded her of home, was added to the purchases despite the day's warmth, as Emeria assured her the weather would be cold soon. There were silver cloth slippers for the formal gown but she opted for a pair of boots and argued for a pair of leather breeches from one of the tailors which would be brought the following evening. Thinking that she should have one of her own, she also requested a sleeping chemise, although she had no intention of returning her host's to him until he asked for it or the staff took it for cleaning and did not return it.

Wearing it had afforded her a more fitful rest than expected. If wearing it kept the nightmares at bay, she would never take it off.

There was no need for more clothing, except for a pair of gloves that the leatherworker included without charge. She had no intention of remaining at her host's expense longer than necessary to start life anew. These items would suffice.

Just because none of the banished had ever returned to the land of the dhóbhaen did not mean there was no way back. The thought had come to her upon waking and persisted throughout the ordeal of acquiring a wardrobe. She might be able to find a pony and wagon, or a ship. If nothing else, she could set off on foot and seek a way home. Such a quest might take all of her days and might seem ungrateful to the man who had saved her life.

But the offense burning within her demanded appeasement. She was determined to return home and learn who had done this to her and Ombhrís and why.

Though there had been no opportunity to talk to her host about such things, to learn if the journey was possible, Raebhá felt confident that if anyone could help her, her host could.

But would he?

She did not see him that day, although several times during her fittings she had felt the presence of another outside the room, one eager to enter and introduce himself but who was consistently shooed away. Raebhá did not think it was her host, and Emeria confirmed that the Lord often spent many hours in the neighboring chellé, amongst the people he lauded over, or in the city of Rhidam with the queen. Sometimes he was away for days. Barely understanding what she was told, Raebhá wondered, after ejecting him from her room, after the way she had touched him without permission, if he was avoiding her.

Avoidance was something she suspected he was very adept at.

What she also learned from Emeria, however, was that she had been asleep for most of three days after being found, and that, while the healer had come each evening to be sure she was well, Lord Cliáth had remained with her nearly every moment of each of those days. Emeria seemed to believe his attention was significant. Having no experience with the man, Raebhá did not agree, thinking it merely the sort of concern anyone would express for one in their care. Such attention would, if he was the lord of many lands, warrant a need to be away to attend to business now that she had recovered. Maybe this evening, or tomorrow, he would return, show her his sprawling, magnificent fortress, and answer every question she had.

She might be able to answer those she knew he had as well.

❧*❧

"Be reasonable, Oska. Father loves you. Nothing's changed."

Oska paced away from his brother, refusing to look at him. "You're wrong, Jerit. Everything has changed. You heard the toast."

Unsure how to respond to the brother he idolized, the youngest de Corrmick kicked at a stone on the ground with frustration. "Drunken toasts don't prove anything," he muttered. "He didn't mean 'when'; he meant 'if'…and you know I don't want to be king. I want to work with you as your inquisitor."

"It doesn't matter what either of us wants." Oska shoved his hands into the pockets of his cloak and pulled the fabric closer to banish the day's offshore chill. "You'll see. But I won't let it happen. I won't."

"Yes, talk to father. That will help. He'll understand." At eleven years old, having lived a life sheltered from many of the darker corners of the world despite his mother's teachings, and knowing that his brother had a gift for talking, debating, stating his case, it made sense that a talk with their father was what his brother intended. So far, both of their parents had been unable to speak with their eldest son, as he had steadfastly avoided them since the birthday banquet. It was why Jerit had sought him out and come to him now. If Oska would not speak with their mother, only Jerit had a chance of reaching him.

"Shall I bring them? Or tell them?"

"I will see to it when I'm ready." Oska did not want this confrontation. He would prefer to avoid his parents. But Inness said he must face his father and had promised that she would help him prepare for that clash. He was not ready yet. Together with his wife, he would know when the time was right, know what to say and do to secure his place on Neth's throne. So long as it did not mean harming his brother, Oska was willing to try almost anything.

❧*❧

"I would not call this being a gracious host," Ártur said with a wry grin when he entered the room the bard usually utilized when circumstances brought him for extended stays in Rhidam. He found his cousin staring out the window towards the east, towards Alberni, and it took no effort to guess where his thoughts were bent. He had avoided speaking of his cousin's guest, but he was beginning to wonder about Kavan's state of mind with his obvious refusal to acknowledge or address his preoccupation.

"I should be here."

The healer leaned on the sill beside him, staring absent into the courtyard. "To what end? Bhyrhán is here, and Lorant is the healthiest he has ever been."

"Merrek…"

"Has more advisors than he needs. He has the Queen to guide him. I know you feel responsible…but he's not Arlan. You have schooled him to the best of your ability and made certain he is surrounded by the best people. He's more prepared for this than Arlan was when we went to war. And Diona is not going anywhere."

Kavan knew that to be true. Arlan had been young, an idealistic boy with no worldly experience, dreams of glorious battles, and a notion of ruling in grandeur. Death in battle, his brush with it, had tempered him and convinced him that he needed to heed Kavan's counsel more than he had if he was to succeed as ruler. Kavan had been his most steadfast advisor, absent only twice during the years of his reign. With his death, the distance between the Lachlan monarchs and Kavan had stretched and thinned. Hagan had not had the chance to benefit from Kavan's counsel, though Kavan continued to believe that if he had been here, the young king might have lived longer. Diona was headstrong enough, as well as mortified by the way she had treated him, that she only sought Kavan's advice for the weightiest matters. Kavan was closer to Merrek, but there was no reason to believe that the prince would need to rely on Kavan the way Arlan had.

When Kavan did not speak, Ártur continued, "She has been alone long enough…provided she is still there."

Kavan bristled, ignoring the twisting in his chest as he muttered, "She is not alone."

"Oh yes, she has the servants. Zelenka, Emeria…Rhyrdan and Dhóri…but I imagine she has questions they cannot answer, or that should be answered by you and no one else."

"She knows your name."

The healer cocked his head and waited. When no more was said, he shrugged. "Many in the Sovereignties know it, including many who have never met me…"

"She is not of the Sovereignties." Before Ártur could ask what he meant, Kavan continued, "She should not know…"

"Perhaps she awoke long enough to hear us talking, or heard my name spoken by the staff?"

Kavan shook his head. "When I said she was in Alberni, the look she gave…and knowing the name MacLyr… she knows who I am."

"That's less of a surprise than knowing my name."

"Not me precisely," Kavan countered. "She called me the White Bard of Gallínphel."

Ártur started to speak but words failed him. It was a bastardization of the song many Elyri knew, but it was possible she had misheard it as a child and thus learned the words differently. "With the legends around your name," he eventually sighed, "it should not surprise you that someone twisted the words of a song to honor you…"

"That's not it."

"sínréc…you're the one person in all the lands that anyone would know by sight and reputation, even if they had never crossed paths with you. Her knowing of you means nothing."

"Perhaps." The healer could be right, but Kavan believed differently. Believed that there was more to her than he had seen, beyond the alarmingly pleasing nature of her face, her hair, her hands, that he could not banish from his thoughts. "I saw her many years ago, flashes of Sight told me I would find her by the lake. I forgot it until I saw her. The Sight foretold change. I can feel it…and it troubles me."

"Does it trouble you because she reminds you of someone else?"

Kavan rarely spoke of Dhóri's mother. Ártur knew she had been a redhead, as Gabrielle was in her youth. He knew she had been a seeress, that she carried Teren, Elyri, and Phae in her blood as well as something unidentified. He knew there was power involved in Dhóri's conception, a lack of physical consummation that should not have resulted in children but had given Kavan both a son and a daughter, a daughter he was never likely to meet. He knew that Orynn had been a sword wielder, a speaker of many tongues, and had, in Kavan's darkest hour, been there for him with Wortham when others could not be.

Beyond the red hair, however, he did not know if the stranger bore any similarities to the mother of Kavan's son.

His words made Kavan scowl. Gabrielle was loved, but not enough for him to wish to marry her. He had never felt that compulsion, as if he had known she was destined for someone else. His initial feelings for her had confused and frightened him and he had fled from what could have been a glorious thing. There were fewer doubts about his feelings for Orynn. He had admitted his love without shame although the dream at the foot of Kóráhm's shrine continued to be an occasional source of discomfiture. Sometimes he wondered if his love for Orynn had been born out of depression, because she was someone to latch on to when he felt the most lost and desperate.

But this woman, whose name he did not know…was different. This was no first-time attraction, nor the result of depression and a need for understanding, despite the painful burden of Wortham's death. Kavan had, over the years, grown to acknowledge beautiful women when he saw them, but this one possessed something everyone else, except Orynn, had lacked.

A strength of psychic power that, as Ártur had once explained, could be enough to draw Elyri together. Kavan felt ensnared by her as soon as he had touched her untrained power, as soon as he had touched her and found her thoughts blocked. As soon as her weak efforts of self-defense had slammed against his shields. The strength of power that lay beneath served to enhance her allure so that he could not keep her out of his head.

The mystery she represented, how she had gotten to the lake, the differences in her speech, her words, pulled him in deeper.

None of that, he argued, was the same as love.

He chose not to answer the question but imagined that was answer enough when he saw the healer's head bob out of the corner of his eye.

"At least consider this; if she is not from the Sovereignties, as you say…she should be told the way of things here, the dangers she might face, from someone who understands those things and will not embellish them or hide the implications of the choices available to her. You have taken her into your home, sínréc. You owe her that."

"Very well," Kavan sighed with more vexation than he felt. He had been talking himself into returning to Alberni when Ártur entered the room. The healer had done nothing more than argue in support of a choice Kavan knew to be best. "After dinner, I will return and see to my obligation as host. But if Merrek needs me…"

Ártur clasped Kavan's shoulder. "I will summon you at once as I always have." Sometimes it was like twisting a knife in a wound to convince Kavan to act, even in moments where he knew action was prudent, but the bard always did what was needed. It would be no different now, and the healer wished he could be there to listen to the conversation to come.

❧ * ❦

Boredom, restlessness, and loneliness gradually took their toll until Raebhá began to wander the house from room to room, endeavoring to memorize the incomprehensible vastness of this fortress. She could think of no néósag or dhó dónáré that equaled its size or opulence. Sleeping rooms furnished with dark-wood four-post beds, rooms with cushioned chairs wide enough for two or three to sit on or for one to sit and stretch out their legs upon in a reclining position. Shelves with books, rare commodities seemingly in abundance here, or else he was a collector of such things. Paintings, sculptures, and tapestries, not so many to be tasteless yet enough to speak of the prominence of their owner, most picturing unfamiliar scenes she guessed to be hallowed. She wondered, as she pushed open another door on the third floor of this wing of the manor, what sort of faith these people had.

She was not comfortable enough to ask questions of the taeré, and wanted none asked of her, and so she did her best to avoid others in her quest through corridors lit by oil lamps in iron sconces on the walls. A deep-throated bell had called some time ago, followed not long after by the ringing of one through the halls of the manor, summoning those who lived here to dine though she did not know that was what the sound meant. Though hungry, she felt uncomfortable with the thought of being surrounded by people who would pry and ask questions she did not think she could answer. The effort to break the language barrier of so many would be overwhelming and she was weary enough to wish to avoid that for as long as she could.

She avoided the kitchen, the larder, and washroom, where the staff gathered. There had been one locked door on the first floor, and one on the third, and she had not gathered the courage to see what was beyond the second door in her room. Most sleeping rooms on the third floor appeared unused, and of those she opened, she found only one that appeared to belong, judging by the furnishings covered with white cloth, to someone no longer there. Not her host, however, and so she guessed that his room lay behind the locked door beside hers, beyond the second door in her chamber.

It was logical that he should keep her where he could conveniently assist her recovery, but if he was uncomfortable with her proximity, perhaps she should request to move to another.

Or perhaps she should do nothing and await his return.

Her exploration brought her to the last unexplored door on this level, an unlit corner chamber, a place she understood to be holy as soon as she pushed the door soundlessly open. The air within was heavy with the perfume of incense, the same scent she had smelled on his clothes when he had offered her comfort. It carried an almost tangible sense of faith, of hope, of peace, stronger than she had experienced elsewhere. Wondering why that was, she brought forth a small tongue of flame in her palm, one of the few gifts dhóbhaen were permitted to practice, intending to find either candles she could light or a wall lamp to illuminate the chamber.

The search for better lighting was set aside in favor of the carved wooden image above the altar at the front of the room. Confident she was alone, she inched forward, feeling welcome here despite the holiness, until she could touch the feet of the burning form.

Though she could not be certain, and she found the idea surprising and illogical all at once, instinct told her who this suffering figure represented. Nothing happened when her fingers brushed over the wood but she had not expected it to. The time of miracles had passed when her people killed the divine messenger. Emotions whirling, she hung her head as though unworthy to stand before him.

She wondered if she dared leave this house alone. There was little reason to believe that her host would want to see her, and yet it was his home; sooner or later he would come back to it. With each hour he was away, she wondered if he would be relieved to return and find her gone. He might have spared her life, but the company of a stranger, a woman, in his home seemed to unsettle him. Her demand to be left alone had not helped.

When asked, Emeria had indicated that there were maps to be found in the neighboring chellé hábhai of St. Kóráhm's. Raebhá did not know who St. Kóráhm was, or why land charts might be accumulated there, but it might be worth approaching someone in that place to discover a path home. At least she might be able to judge where she was and how far from home she had been sent. Once a route was determined, she would need food, a knife, a bow for hunting, some means of protection in a land where she understood few and would be understood by even fewer. She would need clothing suitable for travel and something with which to barter for shelter and additional food along the way. It might be a long journey, a year or more, but she believed she could make it.

Her host might help her. Or he might talk her out of such a futile endeavor. She half hoped he would, but with each passing hour, his absence enabled her to talk herself into inevitable departure.

On the wall to her right, a large tapestry hung, floor to ceiling, depicting the man from the pyre behind her appearing in the sky, surrounded by winged beings said to accompany and protect the divine, appearing to a shepherd harper with a lame foot. The scene meant nothing, but in tracing the heavy wool threads from which the image was woven, she could feel the significance it had to its owner. He spent many hours in this room; Raebhá could feel it in the charged air. Reflex compelled her to her knees in reverence, but a surge of power behind her told her she was no longer alone. She turned towards the source, not the door but a small curtained room on the other side, not knowing what she would see, but not expecting her white-skinned host to emerge from that chamber.

She was certain he had not been there before.

Nor had he expected to find her in his private place. Sometimes Wortham had joined him here, sometimes the children, but mostly his privacy was respected in this room. Not that she could be expected to know she was trespassing. If no one had seen fit to tell her not to enter, curious exploration would have brought her here eventually.

He realized he did not mind.

"You know of St. Kóráhm?" he asked in response to her reverence, forcing his voice to cooperate rather than continue to gape at her. The green of her skirt was darker than his eyes, but he wondered if the color had been selected, by her or his staff, on his behalf. That seemed absurd and so, distracting himself from the embarrassment of staring at the curve of her waist, he opted for speaking of religious matters.

It was safer. Having two rows of wooden benches between them, separated by a narrow aisle, was a safe thing as well.

"Forgive my intrusion, lásánai." She bowed her head apologetically but his sharp intake of breath made her look up again. "Do I misspeak?"

"I am not lásánai." He was not comfortable with that title, of having voluntary power over another's life. It frightened him to think that anyone held him in such esteem, although he knew that many across the Sovereignties did. They did not, however, use that term.

She sighed. "Very well." Maybe it meant something different to him than it did to her, given the differences in their languages. After a glance at the tapestry, she replied to his previous question with a shake of her head. "I do not know this story, but the work is beautiful." Attention once more on her host, she continued, "Emeria calls you Lord Cliáth. May I…or shall I…or would you prefer lord?"

"I prefer Kavan; I am not your lord." He was nothing to her beyond the man who had found her and provided shelter as she recovered. She did not owe him the courtesy of a title. "How is it you have power? You are Elyri…yet not…"

"Elyri?" She blinked, staring, his confirmation of what she believed still shocking. "Why would I be…?"

"Teren cannot use the power." His gaze flickered down to the handlight still burning in her palm. "Yet you are not from Elyriá. Your use of the High Language is different from the form I know." It seemed a good place to open a dialog, an easy place devoid of religious or sexual tension. He went to the front of the room, placed the harp he carried on the altar, and then lit two oil lamps on the wall at the sides of the altar with his handlight, a brighter, more powerful flame than any Raebhá had seen.

His voice, gentle, androgynous, yet powerful in tone, was like the flame to a moth, drawing her to the front-most bench, but she kept her distance so as not to unsettle him. Blessed k'ágdhá, she thought, how did anyone resist him? He could rule kingdoms if he chose, although from Emeria she already knew he was no ruler.

"I am from the land of the dhóbhaen."

Kindred? Kavan frowned. He sat on the same short bench she did, at the opposite end, his body turned towards her with interest. Seated together, the fact that she was a head shorter than him was less obvious. "I do not know where that is."

"Nor do I know where I am," she admitted, holding out a hand in greeting the way she had seen the staff do to others. "Raebhá."

Though he hesitated in anticipation of what might happen, Kavan could not resist the lure of her offering, the need to connect with the power she possessed too commanding to ignore. Though he did not try to breach it, as their hands clasped together, he once again found the barrier in place that barred him from her thoughts. "Raebhá."

Her name rolled easily off his tongue, the intonation and rolling R coming easily to him, the sound like a prayer, in such a sweet manner that it made her shiver and lower her gaze. Feeling the rise of her body heat, more than seeing her flush in the lambent light, combined with the way her head bowed pushed Kavan as far towards the edge of the bench as he could get and still be seated on it, attempting to put more distance between himself and a danger he was struggling to resist.

Despite his intent to escape, however, he failed to release her hand. "You shield your thoughts and yet are hwonághk…"

"hwonag? Of course I am. Only the márbhyndhánis may be trained. But," she smiled sheepishly, enjoying the warmth of his hand in hers as well as the warmth in her belly that told her that whatever this meeting was, it was not casual. "It has not been for lack of trying." Admitting this could be dangerous, but she believed she could trust him. "My father did his best to instruct me, but it is difficult when there are spies everywhere."

She chose not to attempt a communication link, preferring instead to attempt to speak in the strangely similar yet different language they both knew. She suspected his thoughts, his power, were more heavily guarded and shielded than her own and such a link would be impossible to establish because of it.

Kavan nodded, seeing but not seeing, her hand released so that his could clench together in his lap. "This is Alberni…in Enesfel…"

"Not Elyriá of which you spoke?"

"No. I am…unable…to return to my home there." He did not risk revealing more.

Raebhá sighed and nodded. "Then we are both outcasts."

"Is that how you…?"

"I believe so. It was my wedding night…" She saw him blanch and regretted, for the first time, that morsel of truth. She had never expected to feel regret; marriage was supposed to be a good and special thing. "The feasting was complete; Ombhrís and I returned to our home…but there were shadows…they struck him. A hand came over my mouth, an arm around my throat. I fought, but then came the darkness, and I awoke in your home."

Talking about it brought frustrated tears to her eyes which she swiped away with the back of her hand and a stubbornly defiant scowl. "I do not know why, unless they learned I was practicing…unless they knew of my faith. But they would not have killed Ombhrís for my choices. It is never done. At the most, he would have been offered kylldrenai…as I should have been if I had been permitted an inquest."

However unfair it had been, Kavan, at least, had been allowed a lopsided sort of hearing before excommunication. Whatever debate had occurred amongst the gdhededhá in Clarys, k'gdhededhá Tumm had overruled everyone and sanctioned the excommunication with an executive writ. Raebhá had not been permitted that much, if that was indeed why she had been abducted and sent away.

"Were you in a position of leadership? Power? Wealth?"

"Wealth is having what you need and beauty around you to enjoy." She tried to smile, her eyes roving the room to admire the splendor, the artistry of the hardwood altar, the carved wooden benches, the iron oil sconces, the sacred figure hanging behind the dais. Kavan had simple tastes, his wealth was not in the elaborate but in carefully selected bits of art purposely placed. She had already seen that. "I was chosen to be kymyhé of Gálinphel upon my father's passing. Ombhrís is, was…the son of the kydhé of Werem, from the ghís of Nyrau. We were chosen to wed to strengthen trade ties between our ghísaer."

So many words he did not know, so many that sounded like words he knew and yet whose meanings were different. It was one word she had spoken before, however, that again snagged his focus. "Gallínphel…is a real place?"

"Of course. The full name is gál yllínphel, meaning place of birth; it is one of the most fertile ghísaer on Dhóbhaen. It is…" She paused, thinking of the word to describe it, and asked, "Alberni…is a smaller part of Enesfel?" The names sounded foreign as she spoke them.

"Alberni is my city. I am duke, its leader, and answer to the Queen of Enesfel. Enesfel is a kingdom of many cities, towns, and villages."

"Then the ghísaer of Gálínphel is as the kingdom of Enesfel and I am its…queen?"

"Queen…yes, as you are a woman."

She smiled, feeling unexpectedly flattered to hear him say that. "Queen then. Yes. And as your queen lives in a…city…"

"Rhidam."

"I live within the ghís of Curnydhá…"

Kavan jerked back so abruptly that he tumbled off the bench to the floor and crabbed backward until he bumped into the bench across the aisle. Kóráhm, his thoughts screamed. Sósáná…the land across the sea…the prince who had taken her away…

It was all true.

Of course it was true. The old woman who had long ago told him the tale, and Kóráhm's confession afterward, had confirmed it. Kavan had never thought either of them to be lying. But a 'land across the sea' was vague, like a fairytale with nothing to substantiate it, and so Kavan had given the matter little further thought in the years since learning the truth. With no books, no scrolls, no recorded history to support the notion of a land across the sea, it was only that.

A story.

He knew Elyri had not always lived in the land called Elyriá. He knew they had migrated from the southern lands, through Hatu, settling all of the Five Sovereignties, eventually abandoning most of them in favor of the protected territory behind the Llaethlágárá. They had lived in the lands south of Hatu, for Kóráhm had been there, and others too, known to the people in those places as…

"…k'elyryhánag…"

The word was a gasp, a sickening sound that squeezed out of his too-tight throat. That it was the word from which Elyri derived, Kavan had deduced when he first heard it, but he had never thought, in all of his years of study, to find its meaning.

Raebhá knew. In that moment of panic, floored by the implications of revelations, particularly the fact that she was connected to Kóráhm, the only thing he wanted was to escape and quiet his head.

"Kavan?" She could not guess the reasons for his state, although she surmised from the frantic darting of his gaze that it had something to do with the tapestry on the wall behind her…and the word he had spoken in disbelief that she had not heard outside of history lessons.

"I…no." He fought to his feet and staggered, using the back of the benches to steady himself, to the door. "Do not…this cannot…how?"

Each aborted question dangled until he disappeared into the corridor. Dismayed, disheartened that she had again caused offense without intending to do so, and not knowing how, Raebhá watched the door bounce closed between them.

When his shock wore off, perhaps he would speak with her again. He did not strike her as the sort of man to shy away from the truth, no matter how troublesome that truth might be. He would return and he would want to know more, and maybe then he would answer questions for her as well. For now, the hour was late and she, still aching from her ordeal, desired sleep, though she doubted her thoughts, like ponies galloping in her head, would be easily lulled to rest.

When she opened the oratory door, she came face to face with a younger man, barely beyond adolescence, a man with ink-black hair and gray-blue eyes who looked otherwise, save for the color of his skin and hair, much like her host. A younger brother, perhaps, or son, although he had not said he was married and there had been no indication of a woman of the house, only Zelenka and Emeria and other staff she had witnessed bustling in and out of rooms throughout the day. Or perhaps the room adorned in drapings had belonged to his wife. It appeared that if he had been married, he was no longer.

"What have you done to bhydhá?" the young man demanded before the door was all the way open. Her tentative smile caught him off guard and drained some of the annoyance from his tirade while his words simultaneously bled some of the light from her weary eyes.

"I have done nothing," she replied, chin tipped in defiance. That might not be true, but he did not need to know that. When she realized he did not understand her, she casually brushed her fingers across his hand on the door to establish a link between them. Unlike Kavan, whatever their kinship, this man's thoughts were not guarded. "We were speaking and…" She sighed and her shoulders drooped. "I must have said something I should not have but I do not know what it was."

Having never seen his father distressed, Dhóri did not believe her. He had never known words to have such an effect on his father. "We will see what he says when he returns."

"He has gone?" Again, she wondered sadly?

"He often flies when he needs to think, or else he prays." He glanced over her shoulder through the door she held open into the oratory where the oil lamps still burned. If he could not pray here, he might have gone to Rhidam, or, since he fled from the only Gate Dhóri knew of in their home, he might have gone to St. Kóráhm's. Those and the lake were the only retreats he was aware of. "I am Dhóri."

"His son?"

"Yes." It pleased him when strangers identified him with his father. Most, not knowing there had ever been a woman in the White Bard's life, assumed they were siblings or cousins or saw no relationship between them.

"I am Raebhá. Perhaps…" She glanced backward as well. "Can you tell me about that man…the shepherd?"

"Saint. Kóráhm? He is my father's patron. It is said he appears to my father, that they talk face to face, although I have never seen him to know if that's true." He sounded disappointed.

"Saint?" Though the conversation was interpreted through the link, she was unable to translate the word.

"Someone blessed by k'Ádhá, given dispensation and recognition by Clarys to serve as a mediator between people and Dhágdhuán."

"Why a mediator? Why pray to Dhágdhuán? He was only…"

"A man, yes." He chuckled and reached for the door so that she did not have to hold it. Gesturing into the oratory, he waited for her to follow to where the tapestry hung. "You sound like my father." He saw the arch of her brow, an indication of interest that prompted him to continue. She was Elyri, kin his father said, but if she did not know of Kóráhm perhaps she did not know the true Faith as he did.

"Dhágdhuán was the first among the Faithful, the one who appeared to Kóráhm and others…to bring us to the true Faith. As the first, he has the place of distinction in Ethenae with k'Ádhá." He talked as if explaining to a child, assuming that she knew none of what he spoke about. If she did not know who Kóráhm was, then his father was right. She could not be from Elyriá.

"Saints are men and women, often martyrs for the Faith…often people who performed miracles during their lives or who appeared after their deaths to aid others."

He considered mentioning that someday he expected his father would be among those names for the miracles he was said to perform, but he neither wanted to brag nor admit that, in comparison to his father, he would likely never have a place within history books. He wanted to be important, wanted to be someone of note and merit, but he did not know how to make that happen.

None of this, however, explained Kavan's flight from the house.

"Kóráhm was a great man then…of miracles?" The last word sounded awkward on her tongue.

"There were none recorded during his life; he lived during a time of great persecution…many of our kind were murdered by Teren for our differences. Kóráhm sought peace, wrote treatises exposing what he saw as the failings of the Faith which could have contributed to persecution. After his martyrdom by fire, as Dhágdhuán died, he appeared to many people, bringing miracles, too many for the gdhededhá to ignore. So they declared him a saint despite his writings. Many call him the Heretic Saint. My father bears his name, as aendhá Ártur says Kóráhm came to his mother the night she bore him and said my father would be blessed."

Despite his efforts to hide it, Raebhá noted the hint of bitterness in the young man's voice. It would be difficult for anyone to live beneath such a shadow, whether the tales were true or not.

"And now he is heretic too." Dhóri shrugged. "Perhaps we're kin after all. But bhydhá is right. I find no fault in his positions, nor do those in the chellé. Such beliefs can be dangerous and he does not wish to disenchant the Faithful." Often of late, Dhóri questioned whether he should take up his father's stance and proclaim it to all corners of the world. Perhaps then he would be remembered in much the same way his father would be.

"Walking a dissident path is not easy. People die for such things."

"That is so," Dhóri agreed, stumbling on the one argument that had thus far prevented him from taking up his father's path of Faith. "But sometimes it needs to be done. He will bring change, whether he wishes it or not. It is already happening, in little ways. If I can make some contribution to…"

"I am sure he has no desire for your life to be in danger."

The young man shrugged. Whatever had upset his father was pushed from conscious thought. "He cannot protect me forever."

"It is a father's position to try." Raebhá chose not to ask about his mother or other family. She was curious but believed such details should come from Kavan, not his son. "I am to bed; if you see him, will you tell him I wish to continue our discussion on the morrow?"

"I will." Dhóri looked disappointed at losing her company, but trusting she was not due to depart Alberni, he hoped for a second chance to talk, even if it was about religious matters. That, at least, was a topic he knew enough about to sound educated and wise.

❧*❧

Arms draped over the stone that marked where Wortham lay, Kavan clung to it as if to the man himself, noting that the upturned earth still bore witness to the too-recent burial. He wept, wishing the man was here to listen to him, to provide bits of wisdom that Kavan sometimes overlooked in his more emotional moments. Only at the man's bedside, as he awaited the burial, had Kavan allowed himself to mourn, but a single instance would never be enough to purge his grief. Such episodes of sadness had come often during the first year after Muir's death, after Owain's, and Kavan suspected it would come similarly for Wortham if he allowed it. It was crucial. It was healthy, Ártur said. Important. But it would never be easy, and whereas he had then had Wortham's shoulder to weep upon, now he had no one. Some would be willing, but the only one he might have felt comfortable sharing his pain with was himself grieving this same man.

Or should have been, although, in his insistence in forging ahead with the care of the estate in his father's stead, Rhyrdan seemed to have buried his grief as deeply as Kavan.

Maybe soon Kavan would approach him, encourage Rhyrdan to let go of some of his pain and share his own.

Eventually, he turned and slid to the ground, sitting with his back to the stone, wondering if anyone in St. Kóráhm's had seen him. This had not been his intended destination, but in his upset, he instinctively sought the comfort of the one who had always been able to offer it.

Maybe he should go to Ártur. He would find a listening heart in his cousin. But this was a topic he did not feel comfortable sharing with the healer, not when it made so little sense to him.

"It won't if you do not go back to her."

It had been many months since Kóráhm had sat beside him, sharing the comfort of a solid hand on his knee. Most often, since the cleansing of the temple and altar beneath Rhidam's castle, when Kóráhm came it was in insubstantial form, a presence only. It was always comforting, regardless of his form, but it was not always enough. When Kavan felt the most in need of seeing him, however, the Heretic-Saint seemed to know and came to share his company in tangible form.

In relief, Kavan leaned against him, his head on the man's gray-cloaked shoulder. Kóráhm obliged with an arm around him.

"I will appear a fool." He had fled her twice. What sort of weak man must she think him to be?

"Hardly a fool, átaelás mai," chuckled the copper-haired man. "Only one confused and overwhelmed by unexpected knowledge."

"What does it mean? How can she…?"

The saint shook his head. "I may not speak of this. These are not my secrets, my story, to tell, beyond what you already know. Even if I could, you would not believe me without going…seeing for yourself."

"Going? To her land? But we do not…there is no way…"

Lips pressed to the top of his head. "There is always a way."

The feel of the kiss against his hair remained, the feel of the solid form beside him, the shoulder beneath his cheek, but Kavan knew that Kóráhm was no longer there, at least no longer present in physical form, which meant there would be no further words of advice or comfort. But the energy of his spirit was comfort enough and so Kavan continued to lean there as the darkness gradually gave way to dawn.

There is always a way.

He clung to those words as he stood, listening to the early risers within the buildings, people preparing for the first Gathering of the day and their routine after that. There might be no maps, no known roads to follow to where she called home, but perhaps he did not need one. He had found his way to Gorbesh and home again. If there was a way to help her return home, a way to return her to her family, to help her learn who had accosted her and sent her here, Kavan had to try.

It was the only way, if he wanted the answers she held.

❧Chapter 8❧

"My apologies for last evening."

The words should have been easier to say, for they were heartfelt and Kavan rarely had difficulty apologizing for his mistakes. Claiming responsibility for things, even things that were not his fault, was something he was prone to doing even after nearly twenty-two years of trying to break free of the proclivity. Finding her in the Hall, dressed in leather breeches and a white tunic tucked at the waist caught him off guard, her appearance reminding him so much of Gabrielle the first time he had met her that her allure, the beauty of the morning sun streaming through the window onto the copper of her hair, robbed him of breath and clarity of thought. With Gabrielle, those accompanying feelings had been new and frightening. Now he understood the tightening in his body, the throb and ache she inspired.

But she was married, and so long as there was doubt as to her husband's fate, so long as there was the slimmest chance she might be able to return to him, Kavan had no right to her. These were feelings he must bury and ignore, even though they, and the effort to hide them, made his voice sound peculiar to his ears.

"Lord Cli…Kavan." Raebhá corrected as she faced him, noting at once that he wore the same clothes he had worn the night before and knowing that he had spent some of his time outdoors by the smudges of dry soil on the legs of his trousers. "You do not owe me; I should…"

"Lord Cliáth." The woman who entered was young, blonde, and Elyri, and, if Raebhá gauged correctly by the yellow ribbon adorning the edges of her blouse and the yellow of her vest, a healer, was hastening down the stairs into the Hall with concern on her face.

"Yóáná?"

"You are needed in Rhidam…Prince Lorant…"

Though the interruption annoyed him, an emergency involving the child was a duty he must tend immediately. Kavan had reached the bottom of the stairs where the blonde had already begun descending, before he looked back at Raebhá with disappointment. He had anticipated their conversation since Kóráhm suggested he might be able to help her, that she held the answers he sought and that he need not fear. He had been anticipating her company.

But it would not be.

"I will return as soon as I am able," he promised, not expecting her to believe him but hoping she would.

He was no healer, but if there was someone in need, and he could indeed perform miracles as his son claimed, then duty must be obeyed. "Go," she murmured, masking her disappointment. He had come back. Raebhá believed him when he said he would return again.

❧*❧

Prince Merrek tried to soothe his inconsolable wife as she wailed and reached for their child while the two healers fussed over the boy. A tumble from the platform in the Hall, where the prince had been playing on the throne as his father spoke with the chancellor and chamberlain about the morning's report from Wexel, had resulted in a fractured arm and a bump on his head from which he had yet to wake. Brain injuries were tricky, as even an Elyri healer could not anticipate how an individual might recover, or if they would, no matter how quickly healing was offered. Healer Delamo, Gaelán and Asta's only child, happened through the Hall as the fall occurred, and though she had done everything possible, and the older healers had arrived shortly thereafter to verify for the prince-regent she had done all she could, the boy had yet to move on his own save for the even rise and fall of his chest. The prince demanded Kavan's attendance in the hopes that some miracle might again spare his son, but it had taken nearly ten minutes to bring the bard running into the room the prince shared with his mother. There was little opportunity for Kavan to ask what had happened, but he had read the details from Yóáná's open thoughts as the two took the Gate to Rhidam.

Kavan had no sooner entered the room when Merrek cried, "Do something, Kavan!"

Attributing his frantic demand to Arlana's hysterics, since Merrek was normally more composed, Kavan said nothing. An exchange of glances between Kavan and Ártur told the bard all he wanted to know and the healers stepped aside to make room for him. Kavan sat on the bed and gathered the child into his arms to clasp him to his chest, one hand cradling the back of his curly blonde head. Gently Kavan rocked side to side and began to sing.

Ten minutes passed. Twenty. Thirty. No change came save for the calming of the adults in the room. There was no showering of power, no discharge of energy through his hands, nothing that seemed to affect the prince in either a positive or negative way. When Kavan paused his stream of songs to rest his voice, the small hand splayed against his chest flexed into a fist, crumpling the fabric beneath, and the boy's small voice demanded, "Sing more," in the silent room.

"Lorant!" Arlana lurched towards the bed but Syl blocked her way as Ártur sat beside Kavan and held the child's head between his hands. Moments later, he drew back with a relieved smile.

"You did it, Kavan! You saved my…"

"I've done nothing," Kavan assured him as Ártur pried the boy from Kavan's arms and handed him to his mother to soothe the pregnant woman's fears. "There was no…"

"He would have awoken on his own," the healer assured them. "It happens with head injuries. We will observe him for a few days, look for any significant changes in his behavior, and then we will know his condition. Yóáná will stay with him…"

"I want him with me," the princess demanded, clutching Lorant tightly as if expecting someone to take him. The boy struggled to be free of his mother's overprotective embrace.

Yóáná, one of the young women Arlana had spent extensive time with while growing up, smiled and put her arms around the princess's shoulders. "Of course he is staying with you. I shall too, in case he needs anything." She was not the only one in the room to be concerned that, after her hysterics, the princess too might require care. There was a possibility that she and the child she carried could have been harmed by her distress.

"Kavan. A word. Come with me."

Another exchange of glances was shared between cousins and Kavan followed the prince out of his wife's chamber into his own. Exhausted from Arlana's distress and his own fears, the prince collapsed into the first chair he reached and slung his arm over his eyes to block out the sunlight.

"I want you to stay in Rhidam."

"My Prince…"

"I came too close to losing my son…again. Without you here…"

"I did nothing for him…except sing. This time there was no miracle, and I cannot…"

"This time. But what about the next time?" He peered out at Kavan from beneath his slightly lifted arm. "He needs you."

"Merrek." Having raised the prince from infancy, Kavan felt at ease calling him by name. He knelt before the sprawled man and touched his knee. "I cannot control miracles. What happened before was k'Ádhá's will, not mine, not yours. If k'Ádhá has plans for Lorant, which I believe he does, he will see that Lorant survives…whether I am here or not. He will be king one day."

"The portent, on the day he was born? You've had it before? Did you have it with me? With others? You know it to be accurate?"

"I did not feel it with you but I think that is because…"

"I do not bear Lachlan blood." He had the name, courtesy of his bastard father and bastard grandfather, both of whom were reared as Lachlans without the bond of blood. Kavan had never said it and Merrek did not want him to now. Not being Lachlan by blood would make him a placeholder monarch until a rightful blood Lachlan could take the throne. A rightful Lachlan like Lorant.

"With Arlan, Hagan, Diona, Gamal…the premonition was that each would take the throne." There was another that Kavan never spoke of, for the idea of it worried him like a puzzle he could not solve. "I do not doubt Lorant will be king." From the strength of that spark at their first touch, Kavan expected the boy would have a long, successful reign.

"I would feel better if you…"

"Is this a command then, My Prince?"

The humble tone brought Merrek's arm down and his head up at last. The bard's head remained bowed as he awaited an answer. Despite Merrek's passionate reaction, he recalled the promise made to himself not many days past. He needed to repay Kavan for everything the bard had already done for him, raising him, training him, guiding him, saving Lorant's life multiple times. Making such a command when it was not necessary was no way to repay such kindness.

"No," he sighed. "It is not a command. A hope, yes…but not…"

"I am a Gate away. You can send for me any time you have need. You know I will do anything in my power for you." As he had loved the father, so too Kavan loved the son, this boy he had raised as his own, the only shred, save Lorant, that he had left of Owain and Muir. Kavan would never stop loving him.

Merrek's hand closed around Kavan's. "I know." Arching his neck to relieve its stiffness, he said, "Have you heard the news? There has been rain in Wexel! Not enough to stimulate crops, but enough in rain barrels, I am told, to provide fresh water to the people."

"That is good news." After two years of drought, the southern portion of the kingdom needed more such rains before recovery could begin, but a single storm might be a precursor of more to follow as the normally wet season of the year began to creep across the kingdom.

"Indeed, Peter was sharing the news when Lorant…" He shook his head to wipe away that memory. "Oh, and Physician Talis announced a visitor for you yesterday. I believe he is staying at the Eagle's Nest; we could not risk the possibility of his being a carrier."

Kavan cocked his head. If concern for the plague had reached Merrek and Diona, how much longer would travel via the Gate be permitted? Rhidam had been fortunate thus far, as both plagues had yet to creep into the heart of the land, but few expected their fortune to persist. Once it reached Rhidam, protecting the queen and her family would be enough to close the gates, inside and out, and force those within to live as though under siege until it passed.

"I will go now." He was intrigued by this nameless visitor. A traveling minstrel, perhaps, for they were the sort who most often came looking for him. "I have duties in Alberni to return to, but I will see the prince again before I depart to be sure he is well."

With the bard's hand in his, Merrek rose and pulled Kavan to his feet. "Thank you. For coming, for everything."

"It is my honor and privilege to serve, My Prince." The twinkle in his eyes, a look Merrek did not expect to see so soon after Wortham's death, an expression that indicated the bard was teasing, made Merrek smile in return. It also assured him that everything would be all right.

Kavan was met at the main castle door by a kinsman he had not expected to find still in Rhidam. His business the day before had prevented him and Bhríd from crossing paths and Kavan had assumed the former chamberlain had returned to Levonne as soon as the coronation was over. Thinking that he remained out of kindness on Diona's behalf, or that Merrek had asked him to remain on some business matter, Kavan smiled and accepted the handshake which was as much of a greeting as Bhríd typically allowed anyone.

"I was hoping to see you. I missed you yesterday."

"If I had known you sought me, I would have made time for you. What has kept you in Rhidam? Waiting for me?"

"Yes. Mostly. I could have gone to you but..." Bhríd shrugged with a grin. "Please, if you have a moment, would you come?"

Curious though not concerned, hearing no suffering in his kinsman's voice although there was a stressful note there, Kavan nodded and followed. "How are things in Levonne?"

"The grapes are poor...for winemaking at least." Perched on the coast, Levonne enjoyed a constant influx of moisture blown in from the sea, but it was not enough to quench thirsty vines. "We are finding other uses for them, drying them for consumption so as not to waste what the harvest did provide. The southern plague has been reported on the docks; we have been forced to halt incoming ships...and for now, there will be no outgoing ones either. We are left to store what we have...and I fear it will not outlast the drought and plague."

"Perhaps a trade can be made...Alberni still has grain to spare." It would not be much, but supplementing Alberni's stores with dried grapes while augmenting Levonne's with grain would be an appropriate trade.

"We will see to it. Thank you."

"You have heard of the recent rain in Wexel?"

"Aye, I hope it reaches all of the south and stops short of Dorshur."

Rhidam fell into the region of the kingdom that had suffered too much rain for the past two years but was located on the fringes of the hardest hit lands. They had suffered little from the rainfall itself and Levonne had fallen under the influence of too little rain. But both cities suffered the results of the northern storms as the banks of the Tegid too frequently burst, flooding all riverside businesses, residences, and farmland and forest. They and Alberni were the cities to have suffered the least, but they would not be spared indefinitely.

Bhríd led Kavan to the morning room where Editt was reading in the early light. The woman glanced at Bhríd, put her book down, and rose to greet them. "Lord Cliáth, it is good to see you." She, like Bhríd, extended her hand, not in the greeting of a servant but as one of equal station. Kavan, not standing on formality, did not think the gesture unusual, particularly given the relationship he suspected between her and Bhríd. He took her hand, intending to bring it to his lips, but stopped before the action was completed. He blinked several times until the surprise subsided and then he glanced at Bhríd.

"No one else knows," Bhríd said, satisfied to see confirmation in Kavan's eyes. Her condition could have been confirmed by any of the healers, but Bhríd had not wanted a fuss made. He only wanted to be certain before he did what he felt honor-bound to do next.

He trusted Kavan's discretion.

"How do you…?"

Sighing, Bhríd continued to look at Editt as he replied. He had already said these words to her, but felt them worth repeating. "I am uncertain. I am excited. I am terrified. I do not want a repeat of…and if the child carries Elyri traits…"

He felt lucky that his daughters had not. Both had a talent for anticipating the acts and words of others, for being able to say and do the right things to discreetly resolve situations they found themselves in, but how much of that was Elyri power and how much was the natural intuition of twins, Bhríd did not know. Only one of his children had shown significant ability and that child had suffered greatly for it.

"Persecution is past…and I do not believe the girls will wish harm upon a sibling." Neither had reason to do so, as both were married and about to begin families of their own. Both worried about their father's welfare and urged him often to start life again, find a wife and raise a new family, whether with Editt or someone else.

"You should not worry for this child or any others."

Relieved to hear those words, satisfied to know that seeking Kavan had been the right thing to do, Bhríd's shoulders relaxed and he squeezed Editt's hand. "Then you will do us the honor of attending our wedding?"

Kavan bowed his head. "I shall be honored to do so. You know I will be there. When do you expect to be wed?"

"Within weeks, perhaps days, as soon as k'gdhededhá Tusánt is available and I put things in order. You, Ártur, Syl; we do not ask anyone else to attend. No one will be told, just as they will not know of the child until after. There is no need for spectacle or for them to know the circumstances."

Understanding the need to keep appearances, particularly for Editt's sake since she would be the one to suffer the most public scorn or ridicule if the truth was widely known, Kavan murmured, "Of course. You will let me know? I am anticipating a journey, but I will not take it until after you are joined and you," he kissed Editt's knuckles, "are made kin."

"A journey no one else knows of?" Kavan had rarely traveled beyond the Sovereignties in over twenty years and Bhríd did not think this sounded to be the sort of travel taken to Elyria or Neth. To Hatu, perhaps, to St. Kóráhm's shrine, as it was known he made that pilgrimage at least once a year. He was due to make that visit soon.

"No one. It has not been confirmed and until I am certain of the details, I prefer it to remain that way."

"On my honor," Bhríd promised. Wherever Kavan intended to go, it was not whimsy. Kavan rarely acted on a whim. It must be a grave matter, one Bhríd hoped did not reflect danger for the Sovereignties.

Heart full, of joy, worry, and sorrow, Kavan left the keep under the watchful eyes of the sentries, crossed the moat, and walked to the Eagle's Nest, his steps sure and no longer concerned about anti-Elyri violence. He rarely passed through Rhidam's streets, choosing the Gates instead to travel between castle and náós, but it was not out of fear. It was convenient and bypassed the sense that the people of Rhidam would want more from him than he could give if they saw him. It had been too long since he had played outside of the walls of either the keep, his own home, or the walls of the Faith, but his legend persisted, stronger than before the Persecution, as if he had never left. The story of his mangled hands and their miraculous healing had been added to his mythos, as well as a host of miracles he had never performed. Often he wished he could pass among them as any other man, but he had accepted at last that he would never be ordinary.

At this hour of the day, the tavern was sparsely populated when he entered, wondering how he would find whoever was waiting to see him. The noon meal had been cleared and people had gone off about their business. His wondering was short-lived, as the large man leaning against the bar, the only patron drinking, turned to see who had come in…and smiled.

"Had a feeling you'd turn up today. Expected to stand here until you did." It seemed he had already drunk his share, but the bartender appeared ill-inclined to encourage the big man to go elsewhere. Rather than offer to shake his hand, the hunter embraced Kavan in a grip that reminded him of Wortham.

"Wace." It had been so long since he had seen the bounty hunter that he had expected to hear he was dead. Despite his graying hair and the lines on his face, he did not look ready to die any time soon. "It is good to see you." His voice quavered as he spoke.

Wace tugged him to a barstool and nudged him onto it. "I've heard about the Captain," he said, his hand squeezing the bard's shoulder. "I'm sorry to hear it. He was an honorable man and a good friend. I admit to some envy of what you and he shared." He grinned, the only time Kavan had ever seen the intimidating man look sheepish. "Not that I begrudge you that."

Appreciating the supportive gesture but unwilling to talk about Wortham, Kavan nodded his gratitude. "What brings you to Rhidam?"

"Making the last rounds…thinking it may be time to give up hunting before a target slits my throat or puts an arrow through my eye. Not ashamed to say I'm not the hunter I use to be." He tapped the counter and the bartender hesitantly put another mug of ale in front of him. The man eyed Kavan but the bard shook his head. Water was too precious a commodity to ask for when he was not thirsty.

"I suspect you're capable enough."

"Maybe, but I'm less inclined these days to find out if it's true. Figure if I hang around Rhidam long enough, something should come up, one or two or three last jobs…then I'm thinking of disappearing where no one can find me…where no one would think to look."

"Is there such a place?"

Chugging half of his drink, he waited for the bartender to move away. His voice dropped and he replied, "St. Kóráhm's." He grinned at Kavan's surprise. "Quiet, no fighting, a little gardening…"

"It would not be the life you're accustomed to."

"That's the point. It is either that or return to the desert, and I've been away so long I no longer feel I belong there. The heat and sand would be the death of me. From what I've heard, if I get an itch to pick up a sword again, I could serve with the sentry staff…or maybe train a few lads…" He paused, shrugged, and added, "That is if you could make room for one less than noble bounty hunter with a dubious past."

Kavan did not know where the man's religious beliefs lay. General Agis, also a Cíbhóló, had practiced the Faith with his counterparts in

Rhidam, but he had also followed many prayer rituals and practices shared by his native people, and Kavan had never explored the man's private beliefs. He knew less about Wace's beliefs, but he did know that the man had lived a dark, bloody life filled with questionable deeds and relationships. But many came to Faith late in life, if they were not born and raised in it, and it was not Kavan's place to deny anyone the pursuit of their soul's desire. If Wace wanted peace, if he wanted a new beginning, he would find it in St. Kóráhm's. If he found Faith while there, then his coming would be a blessed thing indeed.

"You will be welcome, I assure you. I will inform k'gdhededhá Khwílen and Captain Magk that you may be arriving…so that they will not be surprised if you do." Not when. Kavan would not pressure Wace's decision. Wace would not respond well to pressure and Kavan did not have the heart to try.

"Thank you." Having Kavan's approval for that choice mattered more than the choice itself. Knowing there was a place to retire, if he chose it, eased Wace's mind. "Got plans for today?"

Kavan nodded. "I do; there is something in Alberni that requires my attention." The devotion in the man's dark eyes was another thing Kavan had not noticed before. He weighed his promise to Raebhá against this moment. The nerves that again jangled at the thought of being in her company reminded him that while he had promised to return, he had not indicated how quickly that return would be. Duty had already kept him in Rhidam long enough that it was now the cusp of mid-day. What harm would there be in lingering a little longer? "But we can dine together now, if you wish. There is time for that."

Wace's fist pounding on the counter again got the bartender's attention as he gave Kavan the wide, feral grin with which the bard was familiar. "Dine we shall! You'll tell me everything I have missed!"

That, Kavan suspected, would take longer than time spent eating.

❧Chapter 9❧

Rhyrdan scowled as the two horses trotted out of the courtyard on the path towards the heart of Alberni. He could not blame the woman for being weary of remaining trapped within the confines of the manor, even if she was still recovering from what Kavan had suggested had been a severe beating and looked uncomfortable on the back of the horse provided to her. With her scarlet hair and eyes the pale gold of the sand along Alberni's shore, there was something wild about her, something far removed from the life of nobility and privilege Dhóri knew. Not that Dhóri was spoiled; he had been brought up no differently than Rhyrdan or any of the other children Kavan had raised, mentored, or tutored. None of them had suffered a lack of necessities, but Kavan had made sure they knew how to work for what they wanted. It was not, however, the sort of life Rhyrdan believed their guest was accustomed to.

Still, they could have settled for a walk around the grounds, in the orchards or the gardens, rather than ride into Alberni.

It should be Kavan's duty and privilege to provide such a tour. But some obligation had summoned him to Rhidam, leaving Raebhá to her own amusements, and while Rhyrdan had considered it acceptable politeness to offer a tour of the grounds, he came to do so too late. Dhóri was already spiriting her away for a ride through the city, despite the growing dangers of the Yellow Death.

Only a single incident had been reported in Alberni thus far, two weeks prior, that person kept isolated in a solitary room to eventually succumb to his affliction. No cases had been reported since but what, Rhyrdan wondered, did they know about the length of time it took to show infection? What did they know of how it was passed? The few who had been exposed to the dead man had also been quarantined in a house at the edge of Alberni and to date had not fallen ill.

But what did that mean?

Unlike Dhóri, Rhyrdan did not believe it meant that Alberni would be spared. Kavan might be blessed by the hand of k'Ádhá, but he was not divine. Why risk the woman's health for a jaunt?

Dhóri swore he had explained the risks, that she accepted them and wanted the ride. Rhyrdan had not had the opportunity to ask her for verification. Duties had called him away long enough for the pair to make their escape. Knowing no reason for Dhóri to lie, when Dhóri, like his father, was a truthful man, Rhyrdan chose to believe him.

What he did not trust was the look on Dhóri's face, the change in his demeanor, every time he spoke of their guest, or to her. There was interest there that, as far as Rhyrdan could see, she did not share. It was an interest, however, that Rhyrdan had seen in Kavan. If his perception was accurate, such feelings were a very rare thing for Kavan and Rhyrdan did not think a rivalry between father and son would end well. Having just lost Wortham, Rhyrdan worried for Kavan should the situation turn troublesome.

Dhóri felt no such concern as he pointed out landmarks, giving his companion every tidbit of historical significance he had learned about his city. She did not seem particularly comfortable on the tall horse, suggesting she was not accustomed to riding, but she fared well enough at their slow pace through town. He was determined to do right by her, make an impression after noticing his father's apparent lack of interest and determination to be elsewhere. Unaware that Kavan had returned that morning, he worried that his father was suffering a bout of madness or melancholia borne of whatever she had said to him and Wortham's death before that. Dhóri felt it was his duty, therefore, to learn what he could, determine her motives for coming to Alberni, for remaining in their home, what her intentions and plans were for the future. If she meant to harm his father, Dhóri would see to it that she was not allowed to carry those intentions out.

He was intrigued by her. She was older than him, but in years he thought her nearer his age than his father's. Elyri or not, what woman would be interested in a man so much older, even if that man was still in his prime? Unaware that she was married, for she wore no symbol of that match, Dhóri believed he stood a chance as a suitor. He could offer her little, but that would change if she proved interested in him, would change enough to make a future worth pursuing.

Raebhá, unaware of his interest, agreed to the ride for the opportunity of open sky and crisp air. The change in the leaves, from summer green to crimson and gold, told her it was autumn though to her the weather seemed mild and warm, pleasant enough that she had resisted the need for a cloak. Dhóri insisted, reminding her that she was recovering and should be careful with her health. Though she did not appreciate being coddled, she did accept that she would need her health when she chose to leave, and so she gave in to his persistence.

It was with that upcoming journey in mind that she asked questions about language, commerce, and custom, about geography and climate and the distance between Alberni and the nearest cities. She inquired about the unfamiliar ships in the harbor when Dhóri took her to see them, ships that might, perhaps, for the right price, be chartered to carry her home…once she determined where home was from where she stood. It was a price she could not pay, and if she offered the promise of goods for trade upon reaching home, there was no guarantee that, should she survive the journey, her brother or anyone else would be willing to honor her agreement.

As leery as dhóbhaen were of outsiders, that trip might turn into a waste of the sailors' time, or turn hostile and possibly fatal.

dhóbhaen were not violent, but abandoning foreign sailors to the mercy of unfamiliar seas rather than provide them anything of worth was a distinct possibility.

Buildings two and sometimes three levels tall lined the streets, buildings of a fashion she did not recognize. There were unfamiliar animals, unfamiliar smells, clothing of such finery she was amazed that people chose to wear it as they went about their day-to-day affairs. Goods on display, visible in open windows and on carts in front of open doors, a variety of bread and cheeses, meats and vegetables, and sticky sweet treats not available at home. The supply was short, Dhóri claimed, due to years of poor harvest, but to Raebhá, the bounty she saw was an astounding thing.

There were tools and weapons and housewares similar and yet different than those she used. The sounds of life were the same, clanging metal, the squeals of animals awaiting sale or slaughter, the laughter of children and the calls of neighbors with greetings and insults differentiated by the tone of voice and expression on the face of the speakers. There was a noticeable difference between those laboring with their hands and the young man who rode beside her, to whom many bowed or otherwise gave reverence as they passed. When they rode by a man on a street corner, leaning on a crutch, one arm wrapped in dirty bandages, a leg missing from some accident, injury, or ailment, she stopped her horse to stare at him. He held out a wooden bowl, rattling it at passersby as if asking for something.

"Who is this man? What is he doing?"

"A beggar," Dhóri replied with a note of indifference. "Possibly Association…although they aren't active in Alberni."

"Association? What is a beggar?"

"You know…the poor who cannot provide for themselves…who cannot work…seeking coin and food from any who will give it."

"Has he no family to care for him?"

Seeing her dismay, he replied, "Likely not, or they may be unable to do so. You have no…?"

"We care for our disadvantaged. It is the way of things."

That sounded like disdain and Dhóri huffed, "As do we. Alberni is unlike other cities in Enesfel. There are shelters to see to their needs, run by the gdhededhá, funded by the Faith and donations of others…like my father. But…" He sighed and fished in his vest pocket for what coins he carried. "The drought in the south and floods in the north are making times harder. Harvests have been poor. Many come to the places that still offer hope…Alberni, Levonne, Rhidam, until our streets overflow with them. Our resources are stretched. While he may be lame," he leaned over, dropped the coins into the man's bowl, and straightened in the saddle, "he may be better off than he appears. If he's Association, he could be here on business. Out of respect for my family, the Association does not cause trouble here, but they are everywhere…spies, thieves, killers."

He shook his head, wondering again about his father's connections to such people. Kavan did not tolerate crime in Alberni, but those caught and arrested were rarely Association. Dhóri knew of them, but he had yet to meet anyone in Alberni who might be members of that elite group.

Surprised that an organized band of criminals could exist, could be allowed to exist, Raebhá nudged her horse to follow Dhóri, silent with her thoughts, her mount closer behind his now. Such a thing could not happen at home. Those left without families were taken in by another if they were too young, too old, or unfit to provide for their own needs. With the threat of kylldrenai ever-present, when the márbhyndhánis could read one's thoughts and know the most secret of crimes, few dared to commit questionable acts.

Except to her and Ombhrís, someone had dared.

But these were not dhóbhaen…or Elyri as Kavan had called his people. These people could neither shield their thoughts nor read those of others. Could Kavan? Did he use the threat of it to rule, or did he give his subjects his trust and direct them without threat? She was curious to ask him at the end of the day, expecting him to have returned home by the time she and Dhóri arrived.

"Come…let me show you St. Maicel's; you must see it." He grinned, a wide, boyish look that brightened his face and made his eyes sparkle. The quaint but ornate náós was something that must be seen, Dhóri thought as he turned his horse down a side street, because it would wipe the darkness of crime and poverty from her thoughts. He did not want her to associate Alberni with darkness. He wanted her to like it here. Like it enough to stay.

❧*❧

As soon as Kavan stepped from the oratory Gate into the room, he knew Raebhá was not there. Not in the oratory, not in the manor, not within easy reach of his senses. He frowned, struggling with the panic that snapped at his chest, making it difficult to breathe. There was enough of her lingering in the air to set his nerves to tingling, enough of her scent to tickle his nose and awaken feelings he did not want to think about. They were inappropriate, but so long as he did not act on them, they were forgivable. He was only a man, after all.

He passed her room and hesitated, considering entering with his hand on the latch. But she was not there and if, by chance, her belongings still were, it would be embarrassing to be caught there, even if this was his home. Choosing not to invade her privacy, he descended to the first level, expecting to find Rhyrdan, Emeria, or Zelenka to inquire about their guest's whereabouts, hoping he could do so without appearing desperate to find her.

At the bottom of the stairs in the entrance hall where he had left her earlier, he was greeted with the sound of scraping boots. Rhyrdan, with his back to him, bent at the waist as he worked to avoid carrying too much dust into the house; he looked enough like his father to cause Kavan to grip the railing and stop midstep, his heart seizing again.

This repeated distress would be his death. How much could his heart take before he stopped breathing or his heart ceased pounding?

Rhyrdan glanced at him and straightened with a welcoming smile. "You are home. Mother asked how many to expect for dinner. I could not give her a number…"

"Prince Lorant suffered a fall," Kavan explained. "Nothing serious but Merrek and Arlana wanted my assurance that he is well." He came down the final two steps, eyeing the door behind Rhyrdan and then both large windows directly to either side. "Where is…?" he began in as neutral of a tone as he could muster.

Rhyrdan noted what he had heard in the man's voice before, an unexpected note of interest after a lifetime of solitude. At times, Rhyrdan had thought Kavan and his father were more a married couple than anyone else he knew. "She is with Dhóri, in the city. She wanted to be outdoors and Dhóri volunteered to show her Alberni."

The bard's frown deepened but he hid it with a turn of his head towards the dining hall door. Escorting her through Alberni should have been his responsibility as duke and her host, but a combination of factors had prevented him from fulfilling an obligation he had actively avoided. He was a negligent host, as Ártur had said. Of course she would want fresh air, and if she were to remain with them for an indeterminate amount of time, as Kavan hoped, she would need to learn her way about the city as well as learn customs he suspected were different from hers.

If he was indisposed or duty-bound to be away, then Dhóri was in his right as son and heir to fulfill such duties. It should not irritate Kavan to be displaced by his son; he should be proud of Dhóri for stepping up to the task and fulfilling his responsibilities. But Kavan's words, when they came, expressed frustration and regret despite his effort to quash those emotions. "Good. She should learn our customs, our city…and it is not healthy to be confined." Immediately feeling petty and foolish, he added. "I will be in…"

Where, he wondered, his words interrupted by a crash in the dining hall and Zelenka's angry shout following hard upon to chastise whoever was behind the mistake. Petulantly, Kavan's first response to his own question was to consider leaving again, without a word of his whereabouts or his plans, punishment for Raebhá not being here when he returned, for accepting the tour without him. Punishment for Dhóri's acting on his behalf. Punishment to everyone purely for irritating him when it was no one's fault but his own.

In the softer corners of his heart, he knew he would only be punishing himself. He would not chastise Zelenka or anyone else. He would not berate his son for fulfilling his role as heir to the estate. If Raebhá returned to find him gone again, he expected she would leave without a farewell, without a word or trace or the answers he needed.

"I'll be in my study," he concluded. "I've work to do and do not wish to be disturbed." He took a few steps towards the corridor to his right, hesitated, and then added, "But I do wish to know when they return. Send word, if you will…and tell your mother that if I dine it will be late. If she will save a plate, I will be in her debt."

Rhyrdan could not read Kavan's thoughts, could not guess the nature of the turmoil in the man's eyes, but he could read in Kavan's body language that he was troubled and perplexed. Rhyrdan bowed, a slight gesture his father sometimes used, and said, "I shall do both." Preventing Kavan from continuing he asked, "The prince?"

"Healthy, praise k'Ádhá. Yóáná tended him promptly, he suffers no more than a bump on his head."

"Praise be," Rhyrdan sighed with relief. With the recent shift in leadership, and plague and drought reaping the land of souls, the last thing Enesfel needed was to suffer the loss of the child prince.

Books, tablets, parchments, and scrolls were taken from the shelves in his study and placed on the mahogany desk where Kavan spent hours perusing them, alternating between them as his research pulled him deeper into the enigma of history. Some of the documents were originals, some were copies made by the scribes in the chellé, others were copies brought to him from across the Sovereignties, many sent by Asta and Kjell from Neth, others by Inquisitor Geli when his travels took him across the realms. Kavan kept several on hand until he had the chance to read them, study them, before passing them into the care of k'dedhá Khwílen and the scribes. Documents Kavan considered the most valuable were taken directly to the vault, where only three people had access to them.

Two, Kavan thought grimly, now that Wortham was gone.

Perhaps it would be wise to reveal those secrets to Rhyrdan as he had to Wortham.

Blank sheets of parchment, his favorite quills and styluses, and an ample supply of ink had also been set in place before he settled and began his hunt, seeking clues as to who Raebhá was, where she had come from, and how she had come to be in a place where no Gate existed. Rather than think about the quest as a means of helping her get home, as he realized more and more that he did not want her to leave, Kavan tailored his research around seeking the truth about where St. Kóráhm had come from.

Not in Ergothé or Clarys. That much Kavan knew. If Raebhá's clues were accurate, the saint had been born somewhere far from the lands Kavan knew. Learning the truth, finding that land, those people, to set the record of Kóráhm's life in order was a goal Kavan was far more comfortable pursuing.

The evening tolling of St. Kóráhm's carillons, echoed by the pealing of St. Maicel's throatier chimes on the opposite side of Alberni, went unmarked as hours passed, bringing the darkness with them. Barely noticing the time, not thinking about it, Kavan absently lit the oil lamp at the edge of his desk with his handlight and continued to read, making notes of morsels of knowledge that might be significant. Nor did he note or acknowledge the call of Zelenka's dinner bell which was followed soon after by the clatter of horses' hooves on the gravel outside the study window. Such noises were commonplace, expected, and not the sort of things to disrupt Kavan's concentration when he was focused on study or music.

It was Dhóri's boisterous, infectious laughter in the corridors outside of the room that lifted Kavan's head from the pages, his son's merriment and the sense of her that seeped through the cracks around the door and slipped over his skin like Káliel silk. He stiffened and sat straight in the high-backed chair, using willpower to remain where he was instead of rushing into the hall to greet her, using it to push the memories of the vision of her from that morning out of his thoughts. The desire to see her, speak with her, to apologize for his behavior was a temptation best resisted. She would be hungry, weary from her outing, and likely desire a bath and rest and a change of clothing.

Nothing Kavan wanted should interfere with that.

Judging by his son's good humor and the sound of her voice, she enjoyed his company. Neither would welcome his intrusion.

Kavan threw his focus back into research, although now with less attention than before as his senses were half tuned to following her aura. Expecting Rhyrdan to interrupt with news of their return, as Kavan had asked of him, kept him from focusing as well.

The distraction would pass, he thought with annoyance, as soon as Rhyrdan brought him word.

But the flame of her in his home that shifted and moved in and out of the range of his perceptions ultimately forced him to acknowledge that focus was not going to be possible until he spoke with her, put his mind at ease that she was not angry. His mind would not settle until she put to rest the myriad of questions galloping through his head.

Wrestling with the demons of temptation and the effort to concentrate, he did not notice the soft rapping on the wooden door. When it pushed open with a creak, he jumped, scattering the books at his elbow, and then stared at the woman who entered wearing the same attire she had worn that morning.

"aeyrudgh…I did not mean to startle you…"

"No, it is…please, come in." He retrieved the fallen tomes and arranged them on his desk as she closed the door. "Was your tour of Alberni informative? I apologize I was unable to accompany you."

Apologize and regretted it, but there was nothing to be done.

"Duty called. I understand." Her easy smile as she sat across the desk from him was a welcome sight. "The emergency has passed?"

"It has."

Again, she smiled. "I'm pleased to hear it. Rhyrdan said you wished to know of my return. I wanted to tell you myself, and to apologize for whatever I said last evening that offended you."

"Misunderstandings are to be expected." Similarities in language or not, until they understood one another, there would be more such confusion. "I was not offended. I was shocked." He leaned back in his chair, hands clasped before him to prevent nervous fidgeting as he ordered his thoughts, hoping she would have time to speak with him now and not assume that his hesitation was indicative of wanting her to leave. "k'elyryhánag. You know what it means?"

"You don't?" There were enough differences in the forms of their words that he might not, and enough generations had gone between the use of that word and the present that its meaning, its use, might have changed or disappeared altogether.

"The word does not exist in standard Elyri or High Elyri…not in any documents or records I have found. The only place I encountered it was far to the south, in a land few in the Five Sovereignties know.

Zelenka's mother used it; I believe it is the word from which Elyri is derived, a previous form of our collective name perhaps, but she died before she could tell me what it means…if she even knew. I met another who might have known, but he would not speak of it and now he too is gone. If you know…pray tell me."

Returning his gaze with sympathy, Raebhá sucked in a breath and exhaled slowly. "I…are you sure…?"

"I must know," he replied in a pleading whisper. He would not flee her again. That decision had been made.

She nodded in acceptance of his request, hoping she would not regret giving in to his demand. "It has not been used amongst my people in more generations than anyone I know has lived. Generations upon generations have passed…and it is barely uttered save in lessons of history. If I tell you…"

If she told him the truth, she feared he would hate and blame her for those events long past.

Kavan pushed the parchment he had been writing on aside and leaned his elbows on his desk. "Too much of the history of my people has been lost, never spoken if it is known…and there are things that I know which do not make sense…"

"Such as Gálínphel?"

"Yes. And Curnydhá. I asked about St. Kóráhm because…he is di Curnydhá."

"Kóráhm of Curnydhá?" Equally intrigued, she inched the chair nearer to the desk so that she could lean her elbows on it. "I do not know that name."

He nodded. "His mother was said to have been a princess, or married to a prince from across the sea. Kóráhm grew up in the lands south of Hatu, but I do not believe he was born there." And the Heretic-Saint will not tell me, he thought with frustration. "When he was grown, his mother, Sósáná, disappeared; the legends claim that her prince came on a great ship during a storm to take her home, but Kóráhm and his brother were left behind."

"There was…" Kavan watched thoughts dance behind her eyes, play across her face, until she murmured, "One of the last to be banished was the daughter of the kydhé of Curnydhá…she bore that name. He took a ship and went in search of her not long after she was banished, but neither was ever seen again. Perhaps it was the same woman? Perhaps she was with child at the time of her banishment and this child could be the man you know?"

It made sense, although without proof it was only speculation. A father instead of a husband made little difference to the base facts of the tale. Kavan wondered if there were written records in the place she called home, if they would fill in any of the gaps of Kóráhm's story.

What had become of that ship after she had left her sons behind? Why had she left her sons in favor of her father?

"Why was she expelled? What crime had she…?"

"She was k'elyryhánag." There was a heavy sound in her throat revealing her discomfort with what she was telling him. "As am I." She silenced his questions with a raised hand. "hánag is the natural order of things, custom…the way things have been and must remain. elyry…is defiant, disobedient…"

And the k before them together, Kavan deduced, meant that the epitaph applied to a specific group of people who were traitors, heretics, insurrectionists, or some combination of the three things. Such a title would have served as a derogatory one for outsiders.

He rose from the chair and turned towards the window to stare at the sky, letting his thoughts weave through the threads she presented. There was a whistle outside, the sound of increasing wind, and he wondered absently if a storm was brewing out to sea. Why a banished sect, branded with such a name, would have kept any part of that name for themselves made no sense unless…

"They were proud of their disobedience?"

Not knowing what he was thinking, she nodded. "They deserved to be. Without them, the truth of k'ágdhá would never have come to the dhóbhaen."

When he turned, it was to kneel beside her, leaning against the arm of her chair, eager to learn, the intimacy of the position lost as he asked, "You share the Faith? You know its origins? Of Dhágdhuán?"

"Origins?" She faced him, her leg pressed to his. "I don't know…"

He did not notice the contact in his excitement, attributing the pounding of his heart to the thrill of lost knowledge so close at hand. "Tell me what you do know, how one comes to be k'elyryhánag…how so many came to be banished." For there had to be many to account for the spread of the Elyri throughout the Sovereignties before coming together behind the mountains. "Tell me the truth. All of it."

For a moment, her hand lifted, her fingers itching to brush a tendril of hair from his face, but she aborted the gesture and instead toyed with her hair. "You are a seeker of truth." Few people she knew wanted such honesty, preferring the security of myth and custom to the discomfort of uncovering the unknown. This man, despite the disquiet he knew it might bring, preferred the unknown to be known, a trait, she realized that meant a great deal to her.

"It was long ago. Generations between, like I said. The story is told that Dhedec di Curnydhá and his crew traveled through the Hínesur to a land unexplored by the dhóbhaen. His ship was caught in a mighty storm, dashed on the rocks as ships often are in the Hínesur. He was left for dead by the ágdháthé. Only Dhedec and his master builder, Gaed di Cliáth survived..." She paused, expecting him to react to the use of his surname, but despite the excited twinkle in his eyes, he merely nodded and gestured for her to continue.

"They were saved by the taeré, by a fisherman known as Dhágdhuán. As he nursed their wounds and restored their health, he told them of k'ágdhá's love and mercy, spoke of divinity not distant from creation but part of it, one who oversees, interacts, participates in the lives of those who revere him instead of hiding in the mists of the unknown. Such divine interaction was...the dhóbhaen believe that the ágdháthé created the world and then left it to its ways. Believing that one is above the others...or that there is only one as many came to believe, was unacceptable."

"Heresy." Kavan understood that condition well.

She nodded, grateful he understood despite the language struggle between them. "But there was more, for during those years another fracture developed. All dhóbhaen are born with gifts; we are taught to make light, to be warm or cool as weather requires, but only phemárógdh and márbhyndhánis are permitted additional training."

"phemárógdh?"

Raebhá paused, seeking the best way to explain, then replied, "Ones who tend the sick and injured."

"Healers." Now that she defined it, he could hear the relationship between words in their separate tongues and he wanted to know more. For now, however, he encouraged her to continue the history lesson.

"Healers. Yes. As far back as the dhóbhaen have been, the gifts have been viewed as outside of the order...for nothing else...not the taeré or birds or beasts can do such things. For most, learning to use them is outside of custom and natural order. There were three, kin of Dhedec, from the ghísaer of Cliáth and Bhíncári…”

Raebhá hesitated as Kavan's breath caught but he did not interrupt.

“When Dhedec and Gaed returned with Dhágdhuán, they went first to their kin, Drebhoti di Cliáth and cousins Llyr and Zythán di Bhíncári.”

There was more of a strangled sound this time as Kavan dropped back to sit on the floor, breaking physical contact, staring at her with fire in his eyes. Dhedec and Gaed were unfamiliar names, but the others were names he had encountered in his quest to cleanse the subterranean chapel beneath the Lachlan keep and, perhaps, save the Faith from itself.

“Llyr? Drebhoti? Who were they? Were they metallurgists? Blacksmiths? Weaponsmiths?”

Curious that Kavan should know so little about their history and yet know those names, Raebhá leaned on the arm of the chair, closing the distance between them. “It is said that Llyr was phemárógdh, but his family crafted cups, platters…utensils for eating…sometimes ritual tools and objects for the márbhyndhánis. Drebhoti was márbhyndhánis, as was Zythán.”

And Zythán was Bhíncári. Kavan wondered if Kyne Mórne knew. He wondered if that was the connection that had prompted her to send him to Bhórdh in search of answers. He wondered how much more the ancient woman knew. If this Zythán was the same one.

He wondered if he would have the opportunity to ask.

“There was…I had use of the Chalice of Llyr…and the Staff of Drebhoti…for a short time…” Kavan's small voice echoed behind the nervous clenching and unclenching of his fists. He still possessed those items and wondered if she would recognize them if he showed them. As long ago as they had been created, however, he guessed she would not. “They are items of great power…but their origins were unknown…only their names…”

“Those chosen as márbhyndhánis are born with great ability, taken from their families and trained in its use. If anyone could give power to a material object, it would have been Drebhoti for it is said he did great things before his fall. Unlike others, he and Zythán believed all dhóbhaen should be taught to use the gifts we carry. Together with Llyr, they taught in secret, Gaed and Dhedec first, and then after

Dhágdhuán's arrival, more came…for he too espoused the notion that gifts given at birth should be used to the glory of the divine."

She paused for a breath and to let him absorb what she had said thus far. "Dhágdhuán spoke of zethenaer…somewhere beyond life that the living do not need to fear…taught that the bhur, the spirit of the dead, does not linger to torment the living but passes to life with the divinity of nature. These things, the acceptable use of power, a belief in k'ágdhá overall, the assurance that death of the body was not the end but something else, they were as frowned upon then as they are now."

Raebhá shrugged and tucked her hair behind her ear. "Because there could be no acceptance of these things, the márbhyndhánis decided to send the adherents of these beliefs away, particularly when Dhágdhuán's execution resulted not in the disbanding of his devotees but the increase of them. So many, and it was unthinkable to execute them all. Dhágdhuán was the first, the only, execution in our history. Most were sent out to sea, but some were sent through the rynlagne…as it seems I was."

Her voice wavered, cracked, and she closed her eyes, seeking solace she did not expect to find. Then a touch, and when she looked, a white hand covered hers, the contact strong and sure, bringing serenity only felt when staring across the dark sea, or into the night sky, or across a landscape of fresh snow beneath the moonlight. The unanticipated gesture, one she knew he did not make easily, tugged the corners of her mouth into a ghosting smile of gratitude.

For his sake, she forced herself to continue despite the desire to weep for what she had lost. "I don't know how many ships were sent…how many people were on them…how many people were sent away. Whole ghís were emptied, men, women, children…including the ghís of Cliáth. A few escaped into other ghís, most did not. All the ghís were since renamed or abandoned, and no one speaks those names in conversation. No one knows what became of the outcasts. There were rumors that some found their way back only to be banished again, or returned and reintegrated into sympathetic ghís. Over the centuries, expeditions have gone west seeking the truth; those who return bring riches and tales of the taeré and wildlands…but none spoke of k'elyryhánag…as if they were erased."

She stared at their hands again; doing so brought his attention to his unconscious action and he abruptly withdrew his touch.

"The men you spoke of…they were on those ships?" It had to be true, but Kavan needed to hear her say it.

"They were…which is why so many attempted the impossible and sailed to find proof, in the hopes that they lived. Much was lost in those years…great minds, great talent, great power. When I saw your harp, heard your name…" Her expression softened. "Not a single Cliáthan harp has been made since those times. The few that remain are priceless. Those who have attempted imitations fall short. To find you here…to know that not everything we were was lost to the world…but only to the dhóbhaen…it is a blessed thing."

Kavan flushed and looked at his lap. "I am no harp maker. My father, my uncle, my son…others of my kin…" His shoulders rose and fell. "I play them, but I lack the skill of my forbearers to craft them."

"But the skill exists still. That is enough. And the name. You spoke of di Curnydhá…MacLyr…are there Bhíncári as well?"

"Yes…many of them." As he lifted his head, he shook his hair from his eyes. "Our history, as much as we know, begins within the Five Sovereignties, where we lived for many generations until persecution by the Teren in the time of Kóráhm forced the majority of my people behind the Llaethlágárá Mountains, where the Teren did not follow. To most, there is no history beyond that, though there are paintings and tapestries of tall, broad ships…and songs such as the Blue Bird of Gallínphel…"

He chose not to argue the semantics of the translation as he wondered how many other poems and songs spoke of places and people not mythological but very real in a world that had been lost to them. The years, the times of the tales, did not match. Elyri had lived behind the Llaethlágárá when Kóráhm first traveled there, and in the other Sovereignties as well, but if some had found their way to those places on the head of the spear of banishment, there was no reason to think that others could not have come before them, or that the period of banishment had been carried out over numerous generations…for purposes that perhaps Raebhá knew nothing about.

"My travels south, in search of the staff and chalice, taught me that our history stretched there, but I have found no hints as to how we came to be there, how long we lived there, what became of those who had. The story of Sósáná and the ship from beyond the sea was more myth than truth…until now."

Now there was much more he wanted to know, needed to know, so much history to explore and uncover…but only if he went to the source, as Kóráhm suggested. While the thought of returning Raebhá to her home, finding her husband if he lived, tore through Kavan with a force he did not believe he could bear, the possibility of that truth, learning the forgotten history of his people, his Faith, was too strong of a siren to resist. The need to know had been his weakness even as a boy standing before k'gdhededhá Dórímyr. It would, he knew, be one of his primary weaknesses until the day he died.

Interpreting his silence as deep thought and perhaps fatigue, Raebhá leaned back, her mien as neutral as she could manage. "I should retire; I have taken advantage of your company for too long."

"You have taken advantage of nothing. My house is yours, its shelter and all within freely given." His voice trailed off in amazement at the words so easily spoken without previous intention or plan.

Raebhá bowed her head, her hair tumbling around her face to shield it from view. She did not believe the offer was an easy one. Hospitality and kindness were expected. This was different. "Your offer touches me and I thank you for it, but I cannot stay. Whether Ombhrís is alive or dead," she swallowed, "my people need me. They deserve to know the truth as you do. I deserve to know it too."

At the mention of her husband's name, his shoulders knotted and he got to his feet, jaw clenched to avoid saying things he should not.

"I do not know how I will find my way," she continued without looking at him, "but I believe I must."

"Of course." The words were ground out and Kavan retreated to his chair to put the desk between them. His hand swept across the clutter there. "I am looking for information about where you come from, but I regret I have found nothing helpful yet." Without looking at her, he felt her disappointment, and behind that, a conflicting coloring of regret of a different nature. "How do you propose to…?"

"A ship, perhaps. A pony. On foot, if need be. I can protect myself, survive the wilds. I will find the way. I ask for nothing more of you than my life you have already saved…except perhaps a few coins to start me on my way if that is the customary manner of trade…"

"You have not healed…"

"Not fully, not yet," she agreed.

"I can show you what has become of the banished, if you wish…"

"And risk your safety by returning to Elyriá?" She shook her head grimly. "Dhóri spoke of the matter when he offered the same. I will not allow you to risk your freedom for my enlightenment…as tempting as it is. Written histories, if they exist, will suffice. I would like to take one with me when I go."

Reading it would not be easy, but she would study every nuanced word until she understood what was said. She was not eager to depart, despite her words, and she was already planning for the future. If she could find her way home, she would be able to find her way back to Alberni. Perhaps, by then, a trip to Elyriá might be possible.

Kavan sighed. "At least allow me…" His palm smoothed over the parchment that lay unwrinkled before him. "Tomorrow, and as many days as it might take, we will study the records in St. Kóráhm's for the answers you seek, for a tale or a map that might serve as a guide to your travels. Once it is found, I will charter a ship if I can."

"If you cannot? If no map exists…or no ship is willing to make a journey into the unknown?"

He locked his gaze on hers, answering her question without conscious consideration. "I swear to you, my lady, I will return you to your people." He did not know how, but he would strive towards that promise until his last breath was stolen away. Kóráhm had said it was possible, therefore It must be.

"I cannot…" Her heart soared. Such a noble promise, such sincerity in his eyes, his voice. But she could not hold him to it. "You do not owe me…"

"I do this for me."

More than getting her home, doing this was to satisfy his own needs. The need to see to her safety, the need to see her land for himself and prove its reality. The need to learn the fullness of the tale she told. The need to not let her go without a fight. He had pushed Gabrielle out of his life and had lost Orynn to the duties of her calling. If there was a chance that Raebhá's husband had been killed, as crass as that admission was so soon after her loss, Kavan would not give up on the possibility that she might grow to feel for him the way he was beginning to believe he felt for her.

Not love at first sight, but the intense power bond of two Elyri souls, that he did not think he could fight against.

Nor did he want to.

"How else to learn so many truths," he added when she did not speak, "then to see them for myself?"

"Truth and knowledge at all costs? What of your family? Your duties? Your queen?"

"I will address those in time." There was no guarantee, after all, that he would find what they needed in the chellé's vast library. "If we must, we will search for clues in the halls of the Faith, in the house of the Kyne, in Clarys." Those were the only libraries he knew of that rivaled his own in St. Kóráhm's. "Tomorrow we search, and every day after, until you are recovered and we find the way." He sat, determined now to spend the rest of his evening buried in ancient and obscure texts in search of what she needed. "Sleep assured, my lady, that I will not break faith with you. You will see your home again."

She believed he meant what he said, as he said it, but would that promise hold? Could he keep it? As she reached the door, intending to take his advice and sleep if her thoughts would allow, Raebhá hesitated long enough to look over her shoulder at him, his head bowed so that his face was hidden behind his white hair. A beautiful vision in the light of the single lamp, a beautiful vision with an equally beautiful soul and an equally beautiful fount of power.

"Kavan?"

The tremor in her voice sent a shiver up his spine; he forced himself not to look at her lest she notice the flush it caused. "Yes?"

"Might I…there is something I would like to ask …" Something more precious than history to her, more precious than coins, more precious than the possibility of going home.

Kavan tensed, recalling a similar moment with Gabrielle, and the quill dropped from his hand. The dread of what she might ask stole his words, though his mouth opened to speak.

Not understanding the fear rolling off of him, Raebhá shook her head with a sigh. She did not want him to fear her, though she did not know why he did. "I am sorry…"

"No," he squeaked. "You may ask me anything." Whatever she wanted he would give, so long as it meant she was happy and might remain with him a little while longer.

"There is great power in you; I feel it. Dhóri calls you the most powerful ágdháni to have ever lived…perhaps greater than the legends of Drebhoti and Llyr and Zythán. Unlike my people, though you are not márbhyndhánis, you are trained. I beseech you to teach me…if only a little…while we may…anything, any skill, that I might use to my advantage when I face those who sent me here against my will."

Teach her.

Touch her mind.

Touch her knowledge, her power.

Touch her.

Despite the warnings shouted in the wariest corners of himself, Kavan nodded once. "I will teach you what I can, Raebhá. Come to me in the morning. I will be here."

To refuse that request, he was sure, would be the death of him…or at least the death of the parts of his heart Wortham's passing had not already destroyed.

She smiled and allowed the door to close between them. Did she, she wondered as she leaned her back against the door and rested her hand on her giddily fluttering stomach, want him to find her a way home? Did she honestly want him to keep his promise?

If he did, would she be able to bid him farewell?

She had only known him a short time but already Raebhá was beginning to have her doubts.

❧*152*❧

❧Chapter 10❧

The storm Kavan hoped would blow in from the sea failed to materialize, but the wind brought with it a drastic drop in temperature that kept many huddled before fires when there was no work to be done. A restful night's sleep brought Raebhá back to the study, to where Kavan remained buried in research, his stack of books and parchments having grown smaller during those long night hours. She thought he would be exhausted, but as she studied him from the doorway, his eyes were bright, his demeanor upbeat and bursting with energy when she looked in on him. He motioned her in, any residual awkwardness or tension from the night before erased or buried. He did not look up from his efforts until Rhyrdan came to tend the fire, at which time Kavan closed the finished books and gestured for her to join him on the hearth.

He knew from his first contact with her that there was power there, more than most Elyri but not as strong as his own. He did not expect to ever find an equal. She claimed that she could produce a handlight and regulate her body temperature, and she had learned to block her thoughts and to bridge a communication gap with a touch…a skill Kavan had never learned. How useful it would have been when traveling the lands south of Hatu. How useful it might be if he traveled with her to her land.

"Sit…please…" He sat cross-legged on the hearth and turned his palms face-up on his knees. "Give me your hands."

Raebhá eyed him skeptically, reluctant to prompt another retreat by physical contact. But the offer was made, and if this was how he chose to teach, if this was the way it was done, she would not wait for him to ask twice or withdraw the offer.

She sat as he did, legs crossed, near enough to hesitantly put her hands on his, near enough that their knees pressed together. She felt the shudder, though whether it was his or hers she could not say. With the opening of his core of power, however, the physical was gone.

Only the power remained.

"I will show you…and you will follow."

"Yes," she whispered breathlessly.

He chose not to begin with new skills but rather with honing her power through exercises meant to strengthen it, contain and control it, expend it more efficiently. Such skills would allow her extended use of any ability, allow her to communicate with more than a single individual at a time, protect her thoughts with a reduced expenditure of power. It also prepared her for the skills he intended to teach later. The foundation was important, particularly for adults who lacked the groundwork of Elyri power. He had gone over these trails of power with Níkóá.

Teaching was a place of comfort for him.

Contact with her would allow him to discover how to communicate as she did, so that he could practice that skill himself.

A knock eventually broke Raebhá's concentration and forced Kavan to pull his power into himself long enough to call, "Enter," to the familiar presence beyond the door. He would have been content to ignore the interruption as he often did when deeply involved in study or meditation, but Dhóri's arrival brought with it the aromas of the morning meal and Kavan relented to the necessity of nourishment, particularly for his new pupil.

A shadow crossed the younger man's face when he saw the intimacy of their position on the hearth. But having sat thus with his father, alert to the tingle of power in the air that tickled across his skin, he understood that what he saw was the intimacy of shared power, nothing more.

"I brought you something; Rhyrdan said you were both here." He sat with them and put the tray on the floor in front of him where they could reach it.

"Thank you," Raebhá said with a gratified grin as she picked up a warm slice of buttered barley bread and took a bite, hungrier than she expected. Kavan took a slice as well but his gratitude was relayed in a simple nod.

It was enough to make Dhóri smile.

Rhyrdan had told him not to interrupt his father.

That his father was not angry proved Rhyrdan wrong.

"I intend to go to St. Kóráhm's this morning…if you would care for a tour," Dhóri offered eagerly. "We'll be spared the wind and…"

Though Kavan uttered no sound and his expression remained neutral, the residual power bond between them transmitted something akin to a choking sound of annoyance. Discreetly, without looking at Kavan to suggest she had detected that reaction to his son's request and without tipping Dhóri to it as well, Raebhá shook her head with enough regret in her expression to hopefully soothe both men's nerves. "I plan to avail myself of this educational opportunity while I can. Your praise of his prowess made me curious, Dhóri. What better opportunity will I have?"

Dhóri started to frown, realizing he had set himself up for this moment and was now unable to take back his words without offending his father. Nor would he take back claims he believed to be true.

He knew his father's skill. Claiming anything other than mastery would be, in his opinion, an absurd lie.

Instead, he looked at Kavan with a smile and asked, "Is there room for another? May I join?"

He did not need physical contact for instruction, having had more than his share of education already, but he would not pass up a chance to practice, to pick up new skills, and be in Raebhá's company.

Kavan sucked in a breath around the second mouthful of bread, the bite and the chewing masking his response. Unable to concoct a rejection that was not either rude or failed to hide his desire to be alone with Raebhá, he eventually nodded and said, "Very well." To Raebhá he murmured, "When you are ready, we shall begin again."

Dhóri's eagerness was obvious. Kavan did not believe, when his son grinned with a playful wink that made her giggle, that his eagerness had anything to do with the chance for further education.

More than once, as the day became absorbed with power play at the most basic levels, Dhóri's infectious laughter brought similar sounds of amusement from her.

By the time Dhóri grew bored with the simplistic exercises being taught, lessons he interrupted too often to make the morning hours productive, and bowed out of the too-easy lessons, Kavan was struggling to control his annoyance and the compulsion to ask his son to find amusement elsewhere. He was relieved when Dhóri departed for St. Kóráhm's as he had intended, but on the reverse of that relief was a troubling annoyance that Kavan could not shake.

Why did she not laugh for him?

Was he so stern, so stoic, so reserved? Was he lacking, an unworthy companion desired only for the teaching he could provide?

Teaching kept her here, however. And he liked to teach.

The remainder of that day passed. A second. A third. Hunkered before the fire out of the gale, Elyri power became the center of their existence. Meals were brought to them but Dhóri did not join them again. The quest for a route to the land of the dhóbhaen was set aside in favor of this new sharing of knowledge, a shift in focus that she seemed not to mind in her excitement to learn more of the forbidden.

Kavan was happy simply that she had ceased seeking a way home. There were moments when he felt guilty, but when she retreated to a night of exhausted sleep, he drew on the surplus of energy to enable him to turn to the books. Each morning she came, each morning sought more, without asking if he had slept, without inquiring about his studies, without questioning what further information he had gained.

He hoped she had changed her mind. Hoped that the allure of what he had to teach was enough to make her want to stay.

On the evening of the fourth day, after Raebhá retired for the night, when the manor was still except for the dying wheeze of the passing rainless storm, Kavan, having finished as much research as his home library permitted, returned the books and scrolls to their shelves and retreated to the oratory to pray, to beseech k'Ádhá and Kóráhm for some sign as to what the future held, what he was meant to do next.

As much as he hoped she would choose to stay, as his student if nothing more, he could feel the moment approaching when her heart would again bend towards what she had been forced to leave against her will. If she had been legally sent away, given an explanation of the crimes levied against her, perhaps she would have accepted her fate as Kavan had accepted excommunication from the Clarys Faith. Being abducted, seeing her husband struck down from the shadows, sent here by an unidentified means, left too many open questions, left her people without their legitimate ruler, driving her to make things right. If the same fate had befallen Diona, Kavan had no doubts she too would have fought to return to her rightful place. It was in her Lachlan blood.

Raebhá, being of St. Kóráhm's bloodline as Kavan was, would never give up easily.

A sound, a quiet easing whisper of power, and then a visitor emerged from the k'rylag, a man who had only been in his home a handful of times by Kavan's memory. Kavan got to his feet to greet him and clasped the man's strong hand in welcome.

"Bhríd. It is an honor to have you here." He frowned for a moment before asking, "Have you come with news? Prince Lorant? Arlana?"

If the healers were occupied in the care of the prince, the prince-regent, or if Princess Arlana was giving birth, then Bhríd might be the one sent for him.

Returning the greeting, Bhríd took a moment to observe the similarities of this room to the oratory in Rhidam where Kavan had spent so many hours of his life. The Kóráhm tapestry hung there instead of in his chambers and the image of Dhágdhuán above this alter was more abstract, less life-like than Rhidam's, but beyond that, the room appeared to be a smaller version of the other.

"The prince is as if nothing happened. He runs, he screams, he plays like any child his age. The prince-regent is seeking suitable playmates. Inquisitor Geli's youngest is but two years older and has already been introduced but the princess is fretful over the influence the boy might have."

He cleared his throat, knowing that Kavan would understand his inference. Nearly a year after Fen's wife had passed of a fever, Enesfel's inquisitor had begun a long-term relationship with the young woman Marta who had served as Asta's Association contact during her time as inquisitor. She continued to do the same for Fen after Asta's marriage and departure for Neth. Marta had no desire for a life in the castle and Fen did not have the heart to remarry after the loss of his wife, thus their relationship remained as it was, through many years and five healthy children. Marta's continued connection to the Association meant an atmosphere where her children were less the sort Princess Arlana approved of, but Arlana liked Fen and he was the royal inquisitor. Thus she would, Kavan knew, give the child a chance to be a suitable playmate for Lorant.

The bigger threat, however, was more reports of the Yellow Death brought into Rhidam, and it was worrisome that the exposure to a companion residing in the city rather than inside the keep would open the prince to illness and death.

"The countryside is rife with plague," Bhríd continued. "It will be days, weeks at most, before it spreads through Levonne, Rhidam…"

And through Alberni. He did not need to say it for Kavan to hear the words. It was not the sort of news he wanted to hear.

At least Lorant had survived his fall without lasting harm. That was relief enough for the moment.

Bhríd shrugged. "On a brighter note, I come to inform you that my wedding will be in four days, in the castle oratory if you allow…"

"It is not my place to…"

"Perhaps not," Bhríd grinned, "but that room is more yours than anyone else's. Everyone in the keep knows it. k'dedhá Tusánt is arranging his schedule to allow time. Ártur, Syl, Queen Diona…Prince Merrek…they will all attend. Bhyrhán too. I have spoken with Sóbhán already to invite him and Chethá…and Yóáná and Madoc of course. The girls cannot be there, though they have given me their joy and blessing…and my parents will not…"

His and Syl's parents had never traveled out of Elyriá and had little approval to offer their son for marrying his second Teren wife. They may not have disowned him as Ártur's father would likely have done, but they had been vocal in their opposition to Bhríd's first wife the last time he had seen them. He did not want to hear those words again.

"I would be honored if you will come…and Dhóri…and Rhyrdan, Emeria, and their mother if they would like to be there." In Bhríd's eyes, Rhyrdan was as Wortham had been, Kavan's right hand, even if the bard had yet to accept it and make it so. He could not invite the son without the mother and sister. Nor did he want to exclude them.

"And a guest?" Kavan asked without considering the discomfort such an invitation might present Raebhá or himself. He wanted her there, wanted her to meet the progeny of those who had brought their worlds together through a thread of names from a distant past.

Bhríd's only reaction was a slightly arched brow. "If you wish," he replied warmly. Such a guest must be of import to Kavan if he wished them to be included, and that made them important to Bhríd. "I must return now, as I promised Editt I would not be long. Tomorrow we choose a gown…I suspect it will make for a long day."

His lips curled in amusement. Such domestic duties were beneath many men, barely tolerated by others, but Bhríd had enjoyed accommodating his first wife in such ways and it was little surprise he would do so for Editt. Seeing it was a good thing. Bhríd needed joy in his life. Kavan was happy he had found it again.

"What time shall we arrive?"

"I will let you know as soon as k'dedhá Tusánt gives me word. Thank you, cousin."

"You are welcome."

Bhríd's news proved a welcome distraction from Kavan's troubled thoughts and allowed promising, positive prayers to fill the remainder of his night. When the chellé's bells announced that morning had arrived, Kavan returned to the study, expecting Raebhá to be there but not expecting his son. The way Dhóri rocked back and forth on the balls and heels of his feet, with an exasperated expression and his hands clasped behind his back, suggested that he had been impatiently awaiting his father's arrival longer than Raebhá had.

The woman, again dressed in trousers as she seemed to prefer, much to Emeria's dismay, greeted Kavan with a smile and the curtsey she had learned from Emeria some days ago. Her easy expression revealed her comfort in his home and to Kavan, that ease fed into the growing hope that she would choose to remain in Alberni.

"Kavan," she murmured warmly.

Not 'my lord'. His skin flushed with prickles of delight.

"bhydhá." Dhóri, after spending so many days excluded…by his own choice…from the company of his father and their guest, had gotten up the nerve to make another attempt to woo her into a pastime that did not involve his father, only to have the duties of the estate intrude on his plans. "Rhyrdan asks permission, and my assistance, in repairing the broken window in Zelenka's room, with your approval. He cannot do it alone and there is no one else to aid him."

Dhóri suspected, without proof, that Rhyrdan had made no effort to enlist the help of anyone else.

Unaware that there was such a repair to be made, but trusting Rhyrdan's judgment that repairs were needed, Kavan nodded. Perhaps the need was less than pressing but likely Rhyrdan, as his father would have done, had chosen to lure Dhóri away to permit Kavan privacy with their guest.

"Very well. Before you go, there is news. Bhríd is to wed four days hence and requests our attendance. It will be a small gathering in the Lachlan oratory, but if you, Emeria, Rhyrdan, and Zelenka will join us, the six of us will go together."

"Of course we will!" He could not speak on behalf of the others, but Kavan was not surprised that he did so. "Shall I tell them?"

"If you would, please. Thank you."

Assuming that the count of the invitation meant that Raebhá would be joining them, Dhóri offered her a florid bow with a smooth, "My lady," making her smile and giggle at his antics before he left. Her response again brought Kavan a flash of annoyance, driving the sliver of resentment he sought to ignore a little further into his heart.

Without looking at her, turning instead to the tidying of his mostly empty desk, Kavan murmured, "You shall be my guest…if you wish to attend with us." He slid the inkwell back into place. "It will allow you to meet descendants of Bhíncári, Cáner…and Llyr…since I am unable to take you to Elyriá to do so."

"I would like to be witness to your customs…to see how they vary from my own." There was honest interest but also dismay as it brought her marriage to the forefront of her thoughts. It had been nearly two weeks since she had wed and been ripped from her husband's side, but it felt to have been much longer. Though she knew the legalities of it, she did not feel married.

The glance at the back of her hand revealed the absence of the marriage mark. Failure to consummate the joining, to unite in body and power, had denied her that. There was some disappointment because of it, but also a degree of relief that she had begun to feel and was not yet prepared to acknowledge. Those events, her marriage and abduction, felt like they belonged in another lifetime, someone else's lifetime. Not hers.

Still, there was duty to consider, duties she had willfully, stubbornly neglected in favor of the skills she had learned over the past few days. It was duty that reluctantly prompted her now.

"You spoke of maps…in St. Kóráhm's?"

Her words, hesitant and meek, plucked the hope from Kavan's heart. "I do not know if any will be of use, but perhaps they will reveal something that will help…and teach you about the Sovereignties where you are now." He stared into the hearth fire and forced himself to utter the next words. "Do you wish to go to the chellé today?" It was not the way he wished to spend his time with her. What he longed for, however, did not matter.

She heard his remorse and sighed. "I think I must." It was nothing to do with wishing. It was duty and duty alone.

"Come then; let us go." A tour of the chellé would postpone research, keep her at his side a little longer, though it would not put off the inevitable. He should not have spoken of a wedding.

That had been his mistake.

๑Chapter 11๑

There were numerous alcoves scattered throughout St. Kóráhm's, some with benches, some with tables, some with kneelers or without furnishings, some with only the floor, carpeted or not, on which to kneel or prostrate oneself before a work of religious art or framed scripture or holy saying meant to provide inspiration or motivate reflection. The alcove nearest the library contained a long table and a wide window that opened to overlook the burial plot, providing a view of Wortham's grave marker though Kavan endeavored not to look at it.

It was to this alcove Kavan habitually gravitated when he came to the chellé to study, even before Wortham's death, and it was where, after escorting Raebhá around the complex, the two ended up, a selection of maps in hand that Kavan thought might prove useful. He had viewed them before, had studied them often in his efforts to better learn Kóráhm's history; if any map might offer a clue as to where he had been born, these rolled maps were a good place to start.

Thanks to Raebhá's input, Kavan had small clues to work with, but as she helped to roll out the first map to view the vastness of his world for the first time, he did not think those clues would be enough to find an uncharted land an any of the Five Sovereignties maps.

He left her alone to study the first, to return minutes later with several texts obtained from the southern lands thanks to Fen's masterful trading over the years. He recalled descriptions of harsh, arid mountains east of Hatu and of a vast wasteland beyond that where few dared to travel and from where fewer returned. They were details supported by the nearly mythological sailor Dóhn Bhlethan who was said to have followed the coast beyond Hatu's eastern border. His ship journeyed along the edge of that endless wasteland before being caught in a sea storm of such force that his ship was damaged and forced to limpingly return to its home harbor. Many of his crew died, and his own end came within weeks of his return to Elyriá's shores.

The myth Kavan recalled blamed the death of the crew on sea swells taller than the masts, on beasts of a size capable of swallowing whole ships, of a spell cast by a sorcerer that caught the ship unmoving on a glassy sea for weeks. The ship was lost long enough for many of the crew to suffer thirst delirium and the pangs of starvation.

The myth, as far as Kavan could ascertain, had arisen in the earliest days of the founding of Elyriá, and he wondered if perhaps the story was more historical than mythological. Perhaps it had been twisted into a tale of horror to discourage seafarers, Elyri and Teren alike, from venturing too far east. If so, the effort had worked, for while Elyriá's few ships crossed the Bay of Phállá to trade with Káliel or Hatu, and rounded the northern coast to trade with Cordash to the west, none had, to Kavan's knowledge, gone further east or west.

Perhaps the early Elyri settlers wished to protect themselves from those who had banished them or desired to keep an unbreachable distance between them and those who shunned them.

If so, sailing east from Hatu, remaining within sight of the shore, might bring a ship to the destination Raebhá sought, provided they could avoid the creatures, the storms, the doldrums, the madness, hunger, and thirst that were said to have decimated Bhlethán's crew.

There was little else of benefit to be found in the chellé's vaults. The world, to all available resources, stopped at the mountains east of Hatu and stretched into unending badlands.

Leaving Raebhá in the capable hands of the chellé's residents, to browse the books and treasures to her heart's content, with the instructions to see her to the manor when she wished to depart, Kavan returned the maps and books to their places for safekeeping and ventured to Alberni's docks in search of a captain who might be willing to undertake such an adventurous journey.

But the tale of Captain Bhlethan had long ago been merged into the Teren mythos too, making even the least superstitious sailor reluctant to push east. As with those who refused to travel by land south of Hatu, or to attempt to cross the vast Cíbhóló desert, most felt little need to make the dangerous effort when they had everything they needed within the boundaries of the Five Sovereignties. Why brave the unknowns of hostile environments, behemoths, and barbarians when there were dangers enough within familiar territory?

No promise of payment, of riches to be found along the way, was enough to entice the captains Kavan found, and though many promised to spread the offer to others, Kavan suspected his efforts had failed. The too real threat of plague had moored too many ships as it was. There were not likely to be any arrivals soon, and those that came would be, he suspected, unlikely to dock and just as unlikely to willingly take the risk he offered.

It left the possibility of manning a small sailing vessel of their own along the coast, or a trek through mountains and wastelands and unknown territories on foot or horseback, a prospect he did not relish but could undertake. They could go to King Gamal and receive adequate supplies for such a journey, but what was the likelihood, he wondered as he lay down to sleep that night for the first time in days, that the two of them alone could survive such a journey? How long would it take?

Was there proof that traveling east was the direction to go?

His journey south of Hatu had taken nine months to complete. A journey of this magnitude would take much longer. Could he leave Alberni so long? Was Khyrdan prepared for the duty of managing the estate without his father, without Kavan? Was Dhóri? Could he abandon his family, his friends, his people, at a time of plague? How would his sons, his queen and prince, and Enesfel, fare without him?

Was the success or failure of Enesfel and the Lachlans his responsibility?

Though he retired early without eating, after depositing the gift he had purchased in Raebhá's room, the weight of the questions that had driven him to seek the solitude of his bed, the pressure of so many unknowns, refused to allow him to sleep. In addition, the day spent confined in that alcove with the heat of her presence, her scent, her aura of power, had rubbed all of his senses raw. Escaping to be alone did nothing to soothe him. For several hours he tossed and turned, the fever in his soul raging until he was forced to open the window wider in the hopes that the brisk night air would soothe his burning thoughts. It did nothing more than make him shiver in his nightshirt, the cold adding to the trembling his nerves had been subjected to all day.

How could she not have noticed?

He needed flight. It was the only exercise that would both empty his spirit and perhaps leave him exhausted enough for sleep or else leave him refreshed to face the rising sun of a new day. He pushed the panes open, preparing for the change from man to kestrel…

…and aborted his plan when the sound of the door opening and closing again in the adjacent room cut through his concentration. Her light footsteps passed. He listened, but the oratory door did not open. Curious as to where she was going at such a late hour when he thought her asleep, he crept into the corridor and followed, waiting until he would not be seen, tracing her agitated aura to the stairs. Down. He was relieved she was not seeking Dhóri though he could think of no reason why she would be.

The stone steps were cold on his feet but he neither noticed that or the darkness; he was only aware of the wafting trail left by the energy of her handlight. He slowed as he neared the bottom, the glow brighter for a moment and then extinguished with a blast of frigid air that blew through the Hall.

She stood at the threshold, the double doors thrown open, staring to her left, towards the east, her arms wrapped around herself though he doubted she was cold, even in the long thin shirt she wore. His shirt.

Had she worn it every night?

Why did that please him?

Her gesture appeared to be one of seeking comfort and seeing it, guessing that she was staring in the direction she believed her homeland to be, made him sad.

He stopped behind her, close enough that he could embrace her if his arms did not feel bound to his side by the flood of emotion within. He had never been good at offering comfort to anyone except children, though he knew others found peace in his touch. If he touched her, however, he feared he would break.

"I am sorry I have found no ship…but I will find a way to make the journey possible. I swear it."

"Don't," she sighed, every sense alive with his nearness. She could not decide between pulling away from it or moving closer. Despite the expected nervousness she had felt when alone with Ombhrís the night her world had collapsed, she had never felt the excitement she felt with Kavan. There was no rightness or wrongness of the feeling, only a noticeable difference that she felt no shame acknowledging.

"Do not make promises you cannot keep. It is enough that you are willing to try." She tugged her hair back with one hand, pulled it down to one side of her head, and twisted it around her fingers. "After studying the charts today…I think it must be an unreasonable journey to make on foot, through mountains and desert and…without food and water…" She shook her head. "There are reasons the banished never returned. They could not survive the journey…"

"They did not return because they were not welcome."

Some might have died during their voyage; some might have been too ill or weary to try. Others might have borne the cumbersome burden of despair. But the primary reason they did not go back, he believed, had been the certainty that they had little or nothing to return to. Their people had betrayed them over a difference in belief, over an argument of power. Why go back and risk further punishment when they could begin life anew and follow the mandates of their hearts?

He had faced those same dilemmas when he considered returning to Elyriá. Eventually, he had set the possibility aside in favor of making do with the life he had. He was content where he was.

"Maybe." It was a reluctant admission devoid of hope.

Hand on her shoulder, he turned her towards him, his fear of contact temporarily pushed aside. "There is always a way, Raebhá," he murmured. "I will find it. I always do." He was not a man prone to giving up until a problem was solved or was proven to be unsolvable. "Trust me. Give me time."

Her head cocked, her cheek nuzzling against his wrist as his hand rested on her shoulder, and she closed her eyes with a susurrating sigh. Something in his words, his tone, or perhaps in the emerald of his eyes made her want to believe. Made her stomach flutter and her knees grow weak. Leaning her head against his arm gave her time to find the strength to stand steady but once she did, she did not want to move.

Her father had spoken about love long before her betrothal, how two people connected and bonded in ways rooted in the soul and the heart, not merely in the head or the eyes. To have all four roots entwine was the ideal one could strive for, but most were lucky if they found someone with only a single root or perhaps two. She shared one, possibly two, with Ombhrís, as he was handsome to look upon and was intellectually compatible.

With Kavan, it was different. It did not take much consideration to believe that all four roots of bonding had entwined through every corner of her being. It was necessary to return home to see if Ombhrís might, by some miracle, be alive, but she believed she would never find another who fulfilled every part of her soul, with whom every binding root was tangled and knotted.

The pale man beside her was the one her father had spoken about.

What a cruel trick of fate k'ágdhá had played upon them both.

When she looked into his face with sadness and whispered, "I do trust you," the spark in her eyes, a spark that mirrored what already burned within him, caused him to step abruptly, awkwardly back, putting a safe distance between them. He did not want to repel her with inappropriate actions and such actions seemed harder to resist every time they touched.

Her grief moved him. Hand rotating inward to cup her face, he wondered how he could ease her pain. He would do anything she asked but was afraid to say so. The need to do something prompted a strained whispered question that sprang from his heart without consciously choosing the offer. "Would you care for a diversion?"

It was a small thing, but at the moment it was the only thing that came to mind that did not involve kissing her trembling mouth.

"Diversion?" This time she understood the nature of his retreat; it was the flare of heat and power between them. He was not afraid of her. He was afraid of himself.

Kavan stepped outside, a few feet from the door, and spoke without looking back. "It's been too long without using power. I need it. I may be able to show you how to…" He stopped in the center of the stony path and looked at her. "Not many know how, and few of those who do are willing to practice it, but it is my weakness."

She watched without speaking until it seemed he wanted her to follow. "It makes you irritable not to practice?"

"Akin to a child having eaten and napped and wanting to run, to play, but being told they must be still and quiet." He grinned sheepishly, a rare sight that filled her with warmth. "I hold so much and it returns so quickly, that to go for days without using it can be…"

"It sounds unbearable."

"Unbearable…and wonderful…and frustrating…and comforting all at once." He studied the sky for a moment, then glanced north towards the forest. Should he run or should he fly? Unable to decide, wanting to accommodate her, he said, "Choose an animal."

When there was no immediate reply, he looked to see her staring at him in bewilderment. Realizing she was gawking, she coughed to allow the words out of her breathless throat. "You can change?"

"You know of it?" It was not an unreasonable expectation, but in a culture of suppressed power, he had not thought such a rare talent would be common knowledge.

"There is an epic…Bhrán the Adventurer…who used the guises of animals to escape his misfortunes. As a child, I often thought how wonderful such a gift would be, but never imagined it possible…until Mánd showed me how…"

"You can shift?" The revelation was surprising enough that he did not question the name she had spoken.

"I learned only a single form, and never managed it for long…but there were times when he and I…before Ombhrís…"

He was thankful she did not finish the statement. If she had been with another man before her husband, he preferred not to know the details. His fleeting imagination was unsettling enough.

Though she could not see his flushed face she could sense his mood and giggled as she reached his side. "He was márbhyndhánis, a friend of my father's…selected to teach the veiled things my father could not. Sometimes my father joined us…but he had responsibilities as kydhé and it was difficult for him to escape them. Anyone might seek him without notice and he could not risk being caught."

She imagined now that he had been watched, that they both had been, for how else would anyone have learned she was practicing?

"What form?"

Both Dhóri and Sóbhán had joined him as children, but as Sóbhán spent more and more time in Bhryell as his internship blossomed and his relationship with Chethá grew, those shared moments became fewer. Dhóri had no fondness for shapechanging and had done it primarily to be included in the time Sóbhán spent with Kavan. As the time with Sóbhán decreased, so too did Dhóri's participation. Kavan was left to practice that skill alone, and though solitude was often the purpose of flight or runs through forest and field as the White Hart, he sometimes craved having someone to share those jaunts with.

"A wolf. Wolves are bountiful, revered and protected so long as they do not raid the flocks or attack people, and so Mánd chose that form to teach me."

"Then wolves it shall be." He pointed to the tree line. "I know places that are safe to run, if you wish to…"

Beginning to peel her nightshirt from her shoulders, she eagerly replied, "I do." Such a run would tire her enough that she hoped to finally be able to sleep when they were done. She stopped undressing, however, beneath his mortified, embarrassed stare. "One must undress to change," she said matter-of-factly. "Surely you have…"

Kavan shook his head no, then yes, and finally no again. He had seen the bodies of men and women prepared for burial, bodies of the dead. The bodies of children. He had seen Orynn's nude bathing shadow behind a tent wall. But even in his dreams, of Orynn, of Gabrielle, when he had been younger, neither appeared nude, not even in that odd 'dream' instance when Dhóri and his sister were conceived.

To avoid an uncomfortable conversation, not wanting to explain himself if she asked, he changed without word or effort. To Raebhá, it was as if she blinked and a moonlight silver wolf devoured Kavan to stand in his place. There had been no shedding of clothes, no rending of fabric, as Mánd had told her was part of the process if one did not undress beforehand, and unlike any change she had witnessed with her father or Mánd that often took up to a minute to complete, Kavan's change had happened in the span of a single heartbeat.

She crouched and extended a hand, wanting to touch him, to assure herself that this was her host contained in the body of a wolf. The color of the pelt beneath her hand, the green of its eyes, told her he was real.

He seemed less resistant to her touch in that form than he was as a man. The feel of his fur made her grin.

"I will try," she decided out loud. If he could change while clothed, so could she. There was no reason, beyond a lack of experience, that she should not be able to do as he had done. "I want to see your land as the wolf sees."

The white wolf backed up a few paces, giving her room to change without the interference of his power. He monitored her focus, her gathering of energy, her channeling efforts, the skills he had taught her and helped hone, until a crimson wolf materialized from the air and claimed the place where she had been standing. The smaller wolf shook out its fur as an animal would if covered with rain, and then yipped her eagerness to follow him. He returned the audible signal and broke into a run, determined to reach trees before anyone within the nearby structures chose to hunt them.

They ran, chasing through the forest, under the brush, baying at the moon in response to a distant pack's call, bumping and rubbing past one another when abrupt shifts in direction called for it. In a form other than his own, Kavan had few qualms about touching her, instinctively communicating intentions as a wolf might, through sound and touch and scent. He showed her every secret place he knew, thickets that only animals could enter, caves and clearings and creeks that fed into rivers, many dry or nearly so. There was joy in the run, joy in the sharing, joy in being with her. Joy in not needing words to understand and be understood.

He felt the same joy in her playful nips, in her intentional drops before him that caused him to leap over her, in the landing rolls and the rapid sweeping of her tail.

There had to be a way to make this last.

By the time he brought her to the edge of a pond amid a forest clearing, he could read her weariness, the stress that holding the change caused. She had learned much from him but she was not prepared for the sort of extended shift Kavan was accustomed to. His energy was far from depleted but she needed a safe place to rest, to recharge dwindling power if they were to make it home to the manor before dawn, which was still two or three hours from breaking.

"We shall rest here," he explained, resuming his form, the reversion taking no longer than the initial change had. The red wolf loped to his side, panting but looking pleased, and after several seconds of power transfer and focus, Raebhá reappeared. Unsteady on her feet, exhaustion and the expenditure of so much energy having drained her, she stumbled as her knees buckled. Kavan caught her and held her up. She slipped one arm around his waist to steady herself, her head resting against his shoulder, her other hand pressed to his chest with his nightshirt balled in her fist.

Her rapid breathing and the thundering of her heart suggested exertion, exhaustion; believing her too weak to stand, he continued to hold her, pretending to ignore the way she molded against him. He closed his eyes, intending to meditate on anything to erase the awareness of her. His efforts were greeted with the shift and tipping of her head against his shoulder, the caress of air against his throat.

His breath caught and he struggled to expel it as hers feathered over his skin. He knew that feeling from dreams, but this was very real and sent a shudder through him that knotted his belly and drove away thoughts of anything else. The arm around her tightened in reflex and he moved, an act borne of instinct rather than intent, until his mouth lowered and met hers.

Kavan groaned, hunger and fire devouring him, and brought her down on the mossy earth. Rather than resist as he thought she would, she met his kiss with passionate force, raking her fingers along the white skin beneath the fabric of the nightshirt that was quickly shed and cast aside to lie abandoned with hers. A man prone to self-control, the need of her, something he had never sought with another, the need to be hers, binding them in a way that would never be lost, burned away every awareness of his surroundings and mortified him with its overpowering compulsion. He could not fight it. There was only her, the sweet floral scent of the bath oils she had used enmeshed with the warmth and taste of salt exertion on her skin. Everywhere her hands roamed burned hot with the tingle of power and arousal. Everywhere his fingers passed left trembling in their wake.

When she welcomed him into her secret embrace, an impulse that came without thought, that came on the waves of need for something more, he whimpered, shuddered, and lay still to cry softly with both physical, mental, and spiritual relief into her tangled hair. Her arms around him, a hand behind his head gently cradling, a feeling of home and belonging he had believed forever beyond his grasp, beyond his wildest imaginings of how this moment should be…could be.

How could anything so pure be wrong?

They lay entwined in the forest's embrace, her soothing kisses and soft murmurs bringing him to a sleep that she quickly joined. Bird song and autumn insect hums wove with the gentle rustle of leaves and her heartbeat beneath his ear gradually growing calm again. There was nothing else, no outside world to intrude on the contentment Kavan had found.

The rising of the sun, its heat on the arm wrapped possessively around her body as she burrowed against him brought a second unplanned union, longer but no less ardent, a sliding of sweat-soaked skin against skin that this time brought her to tears too. After another short sleep, roused this time by the cracking of twigs that announced the arrival of a lynx seeking water from the pond, a third joining, slow and tender, awkward and hesitant in its exploration, brought them to the apex of noon and a third much-needed slumber.

When Kavan awoke again, the sun was setting beneath the treetops in the west and the beautiful woman was still beside him, her hair mussed, her skin still flushed with passion. His own felt both hot and cold against hers. The rawness of nerve endings meant he detected everything, the breeze, the minute changes of temperature as branches swayed and moved the shadows and sun over his body, the movement of the wind, the tickle of insects. The ease of her breathing and the natural rise and fall of power as it ebbed and flowed in her contented slumber. His muscles ached in a host of unusual places but none were unpleasant and not one of them, nor the reason for it, gave him cause for regret. He could trace her sun-kissed softness, the swell of her breasts, the arch of her hip, the flat of her stomach, without blushing. He looked upon her without any of the expected sense of shame and realized he felt none of it for his nudity either, even as she shifted into his warmth, awakening further need in his belly.

As tempting as it was to rouse her, to claim her again, to satiate the unending hunger, now that his brain had re-engaged, now that he could think of the world beyond this mossy clearing and their tangled limbs, he was aware of the rumble in his belly, aware of his thirst and the passage of time, aware that, come dawn, he must be in Rhidam for Bhríd's wedding. If he did not go, there would be questions, and this was not a secret he wished to divulge. Rhyrdan and Dhóri were surely looking for them, worried and troubled.

Duty called. There was no choice but to return to the estate.

But blessed Kóráhm, he thought with a moan as he disentangled from her embrace and moved to the water's edge, quenched his thirst with cupped palms, and then stood with his arms wrapped around himself, he did not want to go back.

Raebhá rolled, her hands seeking the assurance of Kavan's presence, but found herself alone and sat with a languid start. There was no misremembering where she was, why she was here, and no regret. The movement of nearby shadow proved he had not abandoned her out of some afterglow of guilt as she feared, but stood with his back to her, no more than ten feet away, his white skin gleaming beneath the late afternoon sun. He looked relaxed, at one with the universe, with nature, with himself in ways he had not looked before.

She had never seen a more beautiful person in her life. His beauty had as much to do with the purity of his complexion as it did his shape, his comportment, the definition of each line of his form. If she had learned one thing during these last hours together, it was that he had no idea how beautiful he was.

When he had wept, she recognized not tears of pain or sorrow but tears of relief in knowing that he was every bit the man he had feared he could never be.

Raebhá did not understand how he could ever have believed otherwise.

This had not been planned. zethenaer, she thought, the possibility of foregoing her promises and taking another who was not her husband, had not crossed her mind. It was as if power had compelled them and they had been helpless against it.

Or maybe they had not been so helpless to resist and had rather chosen to allow nature and power to run its course.

She felt no regret. This was, as her father had explained, the way it was meant to be. She understood what he meant now. Being with Ombhrís would have been duty. Being with Kavan was right and good, free and pure. She had found herself here, with him, more fully than she ever had before, a gift of understanding she could not repay. And she had given Kavan something equally priceless, the gift of knowing, finding himself that meant more than any vows she could have made.

He was content there, silhouetted by the setting sun.

It would not last. They would have to leave this place. This could not happen again. Not until she knew the truth about Ombhrís. Maybe not even then.

Thinking music, focused on the notes inside his head to drive everything else away, Kavan absorbed nature's energy to replenish what had been spent loving the woman who owned his heart and soul. He did not notice her movement until Raebhá's arms wrapped around his waist, her hands on his stomach pulling him back against her. This time when he shivered, it was not out of fear.

In her touch, with mental barriers torn down between them, he could feel that last lingering thought, a thought that pierced his heart and made his breath hitch. She was right, but knowing it did not lessen the sting. "We should go back," he whispered, covering her hands with his without looking at her. Her breath on his shoulder and neck was warm in the cooling air and he could feel the beating of her heart.

It was safer to focus on the ripples of dying sunlight on the water than to focus on her. Despite his words, however, he did not move.

"We should." She kissed the nape of his neck, along his spine between his shoulders, and smiled at the pulses that tickled through him in response. She chose not to say anything else that might spoil this moment. He already knew those thoughts, already knew that this brief intimacy would be over too soon.

"There will be a dinner in the evening; the Lachlans will insist on it." Bhríd had served the Lachlans for so many years, as chancellor, chamberlain, and King and Queen's champion, a title he continued to hold regardless of the rarity of his visits to Rhidam or participation in tournaments. Queen Diona and Prince Merrek would honor him because it was the right and noble thing to do. Kavan would be expected to play. Having spent too many days without his harp, he looked forward to turning his attention to music. Raebhá was eager to hear him, he knew, and music would ease the longing to have her in his arms that he did not expect to ever leave him.

He did not believe he would ever hold her that way again. That she would ever hold him and welcome him into her soul's embrace. Not while the thought lingered that her husband could be alive.

Maybe not even when she knew the truth.

He scowled but the look was gone before he withdrew from her hold and picked up his nightshirt from where it had been discarded. Raebhá did not need to see his expression to imagine his moment of regret. Before she could question him, seek his thoughts, every level of mental protection he possessed was once more in place.

She could no longer reach him.

"Afterward, the following morning, we will resume our search. If need be, we will go to Clarys. We will find what you seek."

The clipped edge of his words was unintended but the abrupt surge of sorrow sharpened their edges and took away the last of his comfort.

There was no going back. What was done, was done. He was hers, and soon enough, she would be ripped out of his life.

k'Ádhá help me, he prayed before the pair of wolves began their race back through the forest in the direction of the estate. I do not believe I can endure this.

❧*❧

Prince Oska watched the setting sun from the room that looked over the courtyard, a room where he had often played as a boy because so few adults rarely came to it. The servants kept it cleaned, rearranged the sofas and settees and chairs periodically to keep it usable, but there were other lounges, libraries, meeting rooms, and dayrooms that his father and mother and brother preferred to use. There had been a time when his mother had been here with him, and his sister, but that had been before Jerit was born. In small ways, Oska was relieved that his mother had never brought Jerit here, had kept this as his secret place. It became his place to retreat when his little brother grew bothersome or when he simply wanted to be alone with his books.

After eleven years Jerit had yet to find him here and Rika was no longer in Glevum to share it. If his mother considered that he still came here, she did not come either, leaving it his special place.

Or perhaps, as Inness suggested, his mother no longer cared enough to pursue her eldest son or spend time with him here.

He shook his head with a scowl before closing the window against the night's chill. Regardless of his father's perceived contempt, Oska refused to believe that his mother shared it. Asta accepted and welcomed everyone. Asta loved her children unconditionally. Asta would never turn on him, scorn him for his differences, or deny him what was his by the order of his birthright.

What Inness suggested, the plan she had initiated on his behalf, was for the best. He knew it. It would guarantee his right to the throne without the need for anyone to be hurt, would force his father to decree that, only in the event of Oska's death without an heir, could Jerit sit upon Neth's throne. Not because Jerit would be a bad king, but because Oska was the rightful heir. It was as simple as that.

There were a few more details to arrange, Inness had said, a few more guarantees to secure before they could approach Kjell with demands. When those things were done, when everything was ready, she would guide Oska through the steps required if he wanted to stake his rightful claim to Neth. Though he could admit his anxiety to himself, he would not admit it to his wife. Nor would he regret what had to be done. The future of Neth was too important to leave it up to the prejudicial whims of his father.

❧Chapter 12❧

Spending his night in the oratory, not in repentant prayer but rather in the composing of passion-colored songs for Bhríd's wedding, Kavan managed to avoid everyone after he and Raebhá returned to the manor. It had been difficult leaving her at her bedroom doorway, difficult forcing a separation that neither of them felt, but it needed to be done. It would not do for family and staff to know the reason for their absence. It was enough that they would know both were home. Rhyrdan had stopped outside of the oratory to listen to the music for several minutes before returning to his rest, but no one interrupted Kavan. Not even Raebhá.

Her absence stung but came as no surprise. He had overstepped the boundaries of being a kind and honorable host, had allowed something to happen that should not have. Whatever the reasons, whatever excuses he made, the logical thing to do was allow distance to come between them.

Otherwise, it would happen again.

He bathed after their return, mourning the loss of her scent on his skin, brushed the evidence of the forest floor from his hair, and then escaped to the altar steps with his harp. When his awareness of time, and the tolling of St. Kóráhm's bells, told him that others would soon join him, the instrument fell quiet in his hands. The cessation of music left his mind vulnerable to unwanted, whirling thoughts and he was grateful when the door opened.

"You should have had breakfast with us," Rhyrdan scolded lightly.

"I was not hungry." He was very hungry, not having eaten in over a day, and the agitated churning of his stomach belied his words, but

Rhyrdan understood. Not hungry meant he had not wanted to eat, not that his body did not want nourishment.

But Kavan felt unable to associate with anyone who might question where he had been, for anyone noticing his absence would have noticed Raebhá's as well, and he was certain the reason for it would be written all over his face. Everyone would know.

What would Wortham have thought of him now?

How could they not know? How could he discreetly indicate his whereabouts without either lying or besmirching her reputation as a lady? How could anyone looking at him not see the truth?

Footsteps on the corridor stones. A flare in his core as he felt Raebhá draw near that made the tightness of his breeches in his kneeling position uncomfortable. The formal gown of green and silver had a purpose at last and with the fit of it accentuating her curves, it was hard for Kavan to look away when she entered, her steps slightly awkward in the unfamiliar slippers.

At the hollow of her throat, the topaz-yellow stone, the color of her eyes, in its silver floral setting, that he had found during his excursion through Alberni seeking transport home for her, glowed warmly against her skin on the pale crème ribbon that displayed it. He was pleased that she wore it and read in her eyes that she knew he had been the one to gift it to her.

"We are ready for Rhidam," said Dhóri as he entered, following her as closely as decency allowed, grinning to catch her eye though she was looking at the tapestry on the wall to avoid maintaining eye contact with Kavan. If Dhóri had noticed the expensive adorning gift at her throat, he did not question it. "I can take Raebhá."

With a gentle laugh and the continuing avoidance of anyone's gaze, Raebhá said, "I can ride my own horse, thank you."

Kavan rose, tucked his harp under his arm, and gestured to the curtained chamber. "There will be no horses. It will be tight, but we will go together. Rhyrdan? Emeria? Your mother?"

The young man shook his head. It was no surprise Zelenka would avoid this public event without her husband. Not even the lure of Diona's company could sway her. Her choice made, it was also no surprise that Emeria chose to stay dutifully with her mother.

Dhóri pouted but followed his father into the chamber, tugging Raebhá's arm so that, once Rhyrdan joined them, they were crowded into the small space.

Confused, finding herself between the two younger men with one hand in Dhóri's and the other in Rhyrdan's, there came a moment of panic when Kavan closed his eyes and the aura of energy crept up around her ankles like vines out of a mist. Having never traveled through a Gate, save for the one that had sent her to this land, she did not know that was where she stood. Since she could not recall the beating her bruises indicated she had suffered, she believed that the Gate had been the cause of her injuries.

She would not have entered this one willingly if she had known what was to transpire.

Neither young man seemed concerned. They squeezed her hands in response to her anxiety as her vision filled with hazy gray fog. Moments later, the sensation of floating passed, bringing with it no trace of pain, and she dared follow Rhyrdan's gentle guidance out from behind a curtain she did not remember being closed. She frowned as he pushed it aside and together they stepped out of the chamber.

The room was much the same, but larger, and no tapestry hung on the opposite wall. The image of Dhágdhuán above the alter was more life-like, stained with traces of rust-red, and the altar here was stone rather than wood.

She choked on her surprise as Kavan emerged from the chamber. "k'rylag," he murmured to her unasked question. The name was different but she understood it. Perhaps, she mused in amazement and turmoil, the Gate had not been the cause of her injuries, if it had been a Gate that had brought her to Kavan.

It was the first moment that Kavan considered the possibility that perhaps a Gate could get Raebhá home.

"sínréc."

Ártur came through the door as if he had expected Kavan's arrival, or had felt it or heard his voice. It turned Kavan's thoughts from the direction they had begun to circle. The healer's grin was welcoming, though it faltered when the sweep of his gaze landed on the woman whose life he had helped save. Of course Kavan would invite her as he had mentioned petitioning the prince-regent on her behalf should she wish or choose to seek retribution for the abuse she had suffered.

Though she stood apart from Kavan, the distance created by the two younger men with them, Ártur sensed a change in his cousin. He could not account for it, but he could attribute it to her easily enough.

"It is good to see you. Dhóri, Rhyrdan, welcome back."

"Thank you, aendhá," Dhóri replied, again tugging the woman after him. "You have met Lady Raebhá?"

Ártur was not the only one to note the tension across Kavan's shoulders. The woman pried herself politely from Dhóri's grasp and offered the healer an awkward bow and Rhyrdan stepped into the opening her gesture created to throw his arm around Dhóri's shoulders in a brotherly fashion. By easing Dhóri away from her, it allowed Kavan to relax.

"We should find Sóbhán, Yóáná, and Madoc," Rhyrdan cheerfully said to Dhóri. "Let them know we're here." Yóáná was like a sister to both of them and Madoc was as much brother in spirit to Dhóri as he was by blood to Rhyrdan. Sóbhán, likewise, was a brother to them all.

Dhóri, however, was not interested in leaving Raebhá.

"Ártur MacLyr." She recognized him from the aura of power that set healers apart. His face was familiar enough to suggest she had awakened briefly under his care. "I owe you my life. Thank you."

"I'm pleased to see you strong," Ártur chuckled with a bow. He had stopped checking on her condition once Kavan said she was awake but he had not stopped worrying about her. "My cousin is an acceptable host, I hope."

The teasing nature of the question made her smile and made Kavan move away to place his harp on the altar. The intimacy of mind, body, and spirit shared with Kavan allowed her to understand Ártur's words with minimal difficulty and allowed her to communicate with him in kind. "Exceedingly so," she assured them both. "I could ask for no more than he has given. I appreciate his care and generosity."

Ártur heard the nuances in her tone and accent that revealed that Trade was not her normal language, but he could not place them. It did not concern him. Kavan's behavior, the way he focused on dusting the altar's top with his hand, as if ignoring her, contradicting her assertion of hospitality, did.

"Why don't you…?" he began, hoping for a moment alone with his cousin by suggesting the younger men give their guest a tour.

"I am to introduce her to the queen and prince," Kavan said abruptly, quick steps bringing him to her side. "And to Bhríd and Bhyrhán if he is here."

"He returned last night." There was no obvious reason for Kavan to intend hasty introductions, but he often did things Ártur did not understand for reasons he chose not to explain. Until he had the opportunity to speak privately with his cousin, his curiosity and concern would remain unappeased.

"Good." In an uncharacteristic gesture, Kavan offered Raebhá his arm and murmured, "My lady?" If he noted his cousin's surprise or Rhyrdan's small smirk, he did not acknowledge them. Dhóri's flash of disappointment as the woman curled her hand around Kavan's arm, was met with the drawing back of the bard's shoulders, a tilt of his chin, and a slight puffing of his chest that was unlike any action Ártur had seen him make.

Dhóri scowled, pulled free from Rhyrdan, and stalked out of the oratory past his father, his elbow catching the taller man in the ribs. Kavan almost retorted, was about to demand deference from his normally respectful son, but he realized quickly, as the young man threw open the oratory door and went out, that his behavior was as out of character as Dhóri's. They were permitting Raebhá to drive a rift between them.

Or rather Kavan was.

He would be forced to give her up soon enough. He was not ready to lose her to anyone, especially not his son, before that day came.

He mulled over what he should do without letting go of the hand resting on his arm. Rhyrdan had gone after Dhóri, Kavan imagined, but Ártur continued to follow and was there to open the library chamber where the regent and Arlana shared breakfast with Queen Diona, Prince Lorant, and Bhyrhán.

"Kavan. Welcome."

Though there was no need for it, as his station demanded no such courtesy from the prince, Merrek stood to embrace the bard affectionately. Only then did Kavan withdraw from Raebhá's hand. Prince Lorant, playing on the floor with a collection of carved wooden shapes Sóbhán had made for him, dropped the toys in favor of scooting towards Raebhá to demand Raebhá's attention. Merrek looked at his wife in surprise. The prince rarely approached strangers on his own. Arlana, nervous about him doing so, hurried to catch him.

"My lady, this is Queen Diona, Prince-regent Merrek, his wife Princess Arlana." There was no need to explain the politics that had created the recent shift in leadership. "That," Kavan said as Raebhá touched the boy's suppliant hands, "is Prince Lorant." Once Arlana had the child in her arms with an awkward expression, Kavan shifted Raebhá's attention to the other man in the room. "Bhyrhán Bhíncári."

"Bhíncári." She smiled as she clasped the blonde's hands. He was regal of dress and manner, suggesting a noble upbringing, but he was amicable and polite in his curiosity as he returned her greeting. "It is a privilege to meet all of you; Kavan speaks highly of you."

"This," Kavan said, pushing off the nervous flutter that tried to nest in the back of his throat, "is Raebhá di Curnydhá."

The silent reverent reaction to her name made Raebhá laugh awkwardly to dispel it. She had not considered that others would react to her name as Kavan had. She had not realized how well-known Kóráhm might be. "A distant relation, several generations removed I assure you. Kin by blood, but not descent."

"Then it is we who are honored." The regent's bow was as sincere as his greeting to Kavan had been. "You are from the south then?" Not knowing where Curnydhá was, but knowing the stories of how Kavan had traveled beyond Hatu's borders to learn of the saint's origins, it seemed logical that this woman too hailed from the lands from whence Kóráhm had come.

Diona spoke before Kavan or Raebhá had the opportunity to do so, grateful for once that she could not see clearly. "I assume you are the guest Ártur spoke of? Have the perpetrators of your attack been found?" The Alberni providence was one of the safest in Enesfel; if someone had attacked a descendant or relative of his patron, and a defenseless woman at that, Diona could not imagine such a crime going unpunished. A crime against the saint's kin was a crime against the saint; Kavan would never allow that to be unanswered.

"They are being sought. I wished to present her before…" Kavan cleared his throat, knowing that his words would raise questions, principally from Ártur, "I ask leave to escort her safely home."

It was a peculiar request. That sort of consent was rarely necessary since Kavan could travel within the Sovereignties through the Gates and be back before anyone realized he was gone. But perhaps, Ártur pensively mused at the rear of the gathering, more determined now for private words with his cousin, Kavan's guest hailed from the province where Zelenka had come from. It might account for the peculiarities in her speech. Perhaps there were few Gates in the region she called home or there was some other reason he intended to go there.

That journey had taken Kavan many months. This one might take the same, through a countryside rife with the Yellow Death. The Queen frowned. The opening door kept her from speaking as a page entered to announce the arrival of k'gdhededhá Tusánt who was on his way to the oratory. Diona sniffed as Merrek grasped Kavan's wrist in a firm, cordial grip and she said, "We shall speak of this later."

"Indeed we shall," Merrek agreed, a cooler, sterner note in his voice than the queen's held.

So prolonged an absence from the man who had saved his son's life so many times did not sit well with the prince but having made an unspoken promise to the bard, the prince would need to hear Kavan's request before denying it. Both Diona and Merrek knew that if they did deny the request, and Kavan deemed the journey important enough, he would do as he saw fit regardless of their admonition. His request was a polite formality.

The political undertones of the short exchange told Raebhá as much about those in the room as any lengthy conversation could. The queen had the ultimate and final say, but the indirectness of her gaze hinted at some ailment that might have prompted her to share power with the prince. The woman Arlana was the queen's daughter, bypassed for power by some relationship Raebhá did not understand or perhaps because of her uneasy temperament. Bhyrhán was some manner of advisor or attaché, possessing a place of importance for the queen that was not immediately obvious.

Kavan was bound to these people, beholden to them, but in truth, they seemed as indebted to him, and more reliant on the services Kavan provided than he was on them. Kavan might not be the ruler of this land, but his word, his opinion, his judgment held more sway with the Lachlans than he, or they, might admit to.

"I will tell Editt," Arlana murmured. There was no need for it, as the servants would already have done so, but with Prince Lorant struggling in her arms to reach the foreign woman, the princess wanted to remove the child from the room. Kavan might trust this stranger, but Arlana, in her overprotectiveness, was not ready to do so.

"Let us go up." Diona, one arm curled around Bhyrhán's, was the first to reach the door, the first to go through it, smiling at Kavan as she passed, her eyes seeking answers from his face that she could only see clearly when she was near to him. She saw nothing there.

To the page, Kavan said, "Please tell the others it is time."

"Yes, m'lord," the boy said with a bow before sprinting away.

In the oratory again, where Bhríd waited at the altar, speaking with Tusánt, the attendees took their places. Kavan cast a short look at Ártur and left Raebhá in his care when Tusánt motioned the bard forward. There was no one in Rhidam to harm her, there was no threat here. The only threat was to Kavan, and the healer, deciding it prudent not to create a scene when Dhóri and the younger family members entered, sat their guest between him and Syl, introducing her as they took their places. Dhóri frowned at the arrangement but since he did not think the choice was an intentional affront, he squeezed her shoulder lightly as he sat behind her, announcing his return, that he was there for her.

The attention Dhóri would draw was not worth asking his cousin to move. When Sóbhán sat beside him, unaccompanied by Chethá as her healing duties had prevented her attendance, there was nowhere else for Dhóri to go.

Lacking the time for a proper introduction, Sóbhán nodded at the woman between the healers and smiled.

Words exchanged at the altar, Kavan took up his harp and sat on the steps to one side of the chamber. Tusánt and Bhríd waited until the bride, the queen, and Yóáná entered.

Raebhá, unaware that the healer had manipulated her into a protected position until Dhóri touched her shoulder, swallowed the unsettled burn at the back of her throat. The impending confrontation between father and son was impossible to ignore. She liked Dhóri, admired his quick mind and bright outlook, and she did not want to force that confrontation by being distant or rude.

Thankful for the interruption of the women's arrival, Raebhá turned her focus to the marriage ceremony, admiring the royal blue of the bride's gown that matched the color and fabric worn by the dark-haired man at the altar. She had not met the groom yet, but he was undoubtedly Elyri.

The bride was taeré.

Such things were permitted here? She supposed the intermingling of Elyri and taeré would inevitably allow for romantic attachments, but the prospect of intermarriage had not occurred to her. In Dhóbhaen, it was never done.

Could they have children? Were there laws regulating the dispensation of property and name and title?

Curious, she leaned forward as if to see more clearly as Princess Arlana joined her husband on the front bench opposite where Raebhá sat. The other two women, one also a healer as was the woman seated on Raebhá's other side, waited for some cue to proceed.

Harp on his knees, Kavan swallowed, closed his eyes, and touched his fingers to the strings, forcing away awareness of everything save for the notes. Praying that no one could see the flush he felt when the first notes brought Raebhá's focus away from the bride to the man whose face she caressed with her eyes, he let the music flow.

They were not the songs he had written that morning, however, but something that grew and formed in response to the energy in the room. Delicate, somber notes that spoke of grace and forgiveness, of love and joy and the sense of redemption he could feel in Bhríd's aura. It had taken more than twenty years for the Lachlan Champion to find himself after the loss of his sons and his wife; now in this new family, with the promise of new life awaiting him, he felt redeemed for whatever transgressions had cost him so much.

Kavan allowed the music to next follow Editt, notes of calm and joy and grounding that she had been for Bhríd since their first meeting. This was not a union born of fire but one born of the everlasting earth, solid as the unshakable mountains, a union that would endure until years took her from Bhríd's side. There would be no loss in childbirth. Kavan was certain. Nor did he foresee any upheaval of persecution to come between them and rip this child away. Kavan believed, as Tusánt wrapped the velvet joining cord around their clasped hands to begin the ceremony, that Bhríd had found the peace he longed for, that would allow him to live, not merely exist day to day.

Thoughts shifting to Raebhá's energy, though he refused to look at her, he wondered fleetingly if he might have found the same thing…except for the unfortunate detail of her marriage.

No elaborate vows were spoken. There was no ringing of bells or chanting lessons, no letting of blood or laying blessings on the couple from the small gathering. Though Kavan had spoken of persecution, of prejudice and periodic hatred, none of those in this room seemed divided by such things. These kindred willingly served the taeré rulers, who in turn showed them the deepest respect, admiration, and affection. This simple ceremony, complete after an exchange of verbal promises between husband and wife and a kiss to seal their life-pact, was among the most hopeful ceremonies Raebhá had witnessed.

Less complicated in many ways, free of superstition, than her wedding had been.

Facing their guests, Editt's hand in his, still united though no longer bound by the cord he had tied into a belt about her waist, Bhríd bent his head in gratitude. "Thank you for being here. The Queen has provided a banquet in the Hall; we would be honored if you join us. Others will be there…and my lord," he bowed to Kavan, "I hope you will see fit to attend us with further music."

Kavan accepted the request with a bowed head; it was a role he expected whenever he came to Rhidam and one he welcomed for it was the most comfortable for him to fill. Though he briefly considered dances with Raebhá, he knew he would not do so. A public display, the spell she would weave around him if he touched her, would raise questions, draw attention and reveal details about his feelings to too many. He had admitted those feelings to himself on the altar steps in Alberni, but he had not spoken them to her. While he believed she knew, he was not ready for anyone else to know how he felt about another man's wife.

He lingered at the altar as the others began to file out, but when he realized Ártur was intent on staying, that Syl's company at Raebhá's side would not be enough to deter Dhóri, Kavan got to his feet and hastily joined them.

He could not avoid his cousin's questions indefinitely, but he intended to do so as long as possible.

Curved wooden tables in the Hall were filled with an array of delicacies and treats, enough to feed the collection of lords, ladies, advisors, and other guests. Most were aware that they were there to celebrate the Duke of Levonne's marriage, though they assumed it had taken place in Levonne some time ago and was now being honored by the Lachlans he served. Most did not care if they had been included in a ceremony. After so many years away from the Lachlan House, most of those Bhríd had been close to were no longer present, no longer living. Guests were here to drink and eat of the royal bounty before dearth robbed the royal house too. Many hoped to score moments of the queen or regent's precious time. They would feast for any reason the Lachlans gave, or for no reason at all, so long as it was at the Lachlans' expense.

The advantage of Kavan's position on the throne's platform with Bhyrhán sometimes beside him meant that he could watch Raebhá's movements as she wove through the crowd with a statesman's ease, speaking most often to those with influence, to those with information or knowledge that she could take home when she left. How better to learn the ways of an unfamiliar land and unfamiliar people? He worried that she might reveal too much about her origins, so that people would think her mad, or would say too much about their relationship, whatever that relationship was. But Kavan sensed no negativity or undue distress in the room and no one looked at her, or him, with disdain, or concern. No one paid her unusual attention, other than Ártur Sóbhán, the prince, and Dhóri whenever he succeeded in coaxing her into a dance.

Dhóri seemed to take a perverse joy in wooing her into dances Kavan could not give, but Kavan refused to be baited. Her reluctance each time Dhóri asked, as if deferring to Kavan in some way, the distance she kept between herself and the younger Cliáth, her irregular refusal in favor of whatever dialogue she was engaged in, was enough to reassure Kavan that she was not favoring Dhóri.

She was a diplomat. A queen in a foreign land. She understood the gracious discretion of obliging her hosts while preserving her dignity. She deserved to enjoy herself, deserved to learn what she could of her kindred and the Teren they were allied with. She deserved things Kavan could not give. He would not dance, not in front of these people he knew so well, not when he believed they would harshly judge him, and her, for his involvement with a married woman.

Not that any of them except perhaps Dhóri knew that truth.

Dhóri would not be judged for it; he was young, impulsive, and did not have the burden of public history Kavan carried. There were expectations on the White Bard, expectations that would keep him far from Raebhá until the evening ended.

Two hours into the revelry, a group of minstrels entered the Hall, a group Kavan recognized who often performed for the revelries Diona hosted. Local men and women who were not a permanent part of the court. They played for events when Kavan was unavailable, filled in the stretches of silence when he took pause during those events where he was, and continued into the nights whenever he quietly excused himself. After an exchange of greetings, the ensemble relieved the playing pair of their duties. While Bhyrhán returned to the queen's side, preventing her from pestering the bard for answers Kavan would not give, Kavan was swept into the State Room by the regent before he reached the bottom of the platform steps.

"Lady Raebhá is a good match for you," Merrek began after closing the door and draining the goblet he carried. His crimson cape was slung over one shoulder, revealing the royal colors of his attire, the black vest with the amber tunic beneath. His cheeks were ruddy with drink but thus far he maintained his head and his composure and when Kavan glanced into the goblet now set upon the table, he could tell that whatever had been in it was no longer alcohol. Merrek had never been one to lose his head to drink.

"We are not…" Kavan began, feeling the blood drain from his face and his hands tighten around the harp he refused to leave in the Hall.

Merrek chuckled as Kavan took two hasty steps back as if retreating from an accusation. "I meant you are like-minded, learned, of similar ideologies. It is little wonder she finds your company stimulating." He perched on the edge of the table after pushing the goblet aside so it did not fall. "She's not the only one who does, of course; I'm never surprised when strangers fall under your spell. She's equally elusive too, for she would not speak of her home…"

Sensing that Merrek was fishing for details, Kavan murmured, "That is complicated."

"So I guessed. It is far from here, that much is certain…and you want to escort her there."

Kavan sighed at the question in that statement. "She does not know how to get there from here. Enesfel is unfamiliar to her, our languages, our customs, foreign. Expecting her to make such a journey alone…I could not allow a lady to make such a perilous trip without escort, nor would I ask any man to go if I am not willing to go myself."

"Perilous…?" Merrek scowled.

"Possibly. For others at least. For her, certainly. Someone tried to kill her. I would be remiss to send her into harm's way without defense."

"There are no Gates? You expect to make this journey on foot?"

"Perhaps." Kavan sensed his cousin's presence outside the door, the healer listening to the conversation. It was just as well, for it would spare Kavan the need to answer the questions again. "She does not know how to use the Gates. She has told me there are very few near her home and she could not direct me to one if any are near enough. Using a Gate to an unfamiliar destination can be difficult…and dangerous." Difficult and dangerous for most Elyri, but less so, Kavan believed, for him. If he could pinpoint any Gate in her land, using it might be simple enough, but he had no idea yet how to locate one.

There were certain Gates scattered throughout the Sovereignties, like the one in Fiara, that connected to unknown, unfamiliar locations, specks of light linked to destinations Kavan could not identify and had never investigated. Were any of those near her home? Could he reach her land from such a Gate?

Did he dare try and risk ending up in the sea?

"I have not ruled out a Gate. By foot is not ideal, and we've found no ship willing to risk the Yellow Sisters. I did not save her life to send her on such a journey without protection, not if some seek her death."

Merrek squeezed Kavan's shoulder. "If you do this…who will protect you? Who will protect Lorant?"

"The Prince is healthy and strong."

"He is a child, small and…"

"Growing stronger each day. There are three healers and a physician to see to his care. I cannot control miracles, My Prince, but I promise you he will live to be king. Perhaps that does not dispel your fears, but I pray you believe me."

Merrek's hand fell. "You would not say it if you did not believe it to be so, if the signs did not reveal his future, but trust, in this instance…" He shook his head. "Arlana fears for him more than I."

"You love your son. Worry is natural."

"I love and worry for you as well, Kavan," he murmured, "as did my father and grandfather. As does the Queen. Without Captain Delamo to…" He stopped at the flash of pain burned across Kavan's eyes and hung his head. "I'm sorry…"

"No, you are right. He will not be at my side. Not this time."

"Rhyrdan would…"

"No." Kavan took a breath, knowing the word was said hastily, released it to calm himself, and then shook his head. "Not this time. I can protect myself. If I make this journey, Dhóri will need Rhyrdan to help manage Alberni while I am gone. I must do this alone."

"If? Do you think the trip may be unnecessary?"

Kavan regretted the moment of hope he had inadvertently given, even though it mirrored the hope he carried. "Only if she chooses to remain in Enesfel, which I do not foresee. She is nobility, a queen to her people. She needs to find her way back. If there is a way…"

"She must return." The duty of rule was something Merrek grew to understand more each day now that he shared the crown with Diona. Kavan had helped Arlan reclaim the Lachlan throne; of course he would help Raebhá too. "I cannot say I'm pleased about you not being here if I need you. Enesfel has relied on your council for so long…"

Merrek straightened and tugged on his vest as he stood. "I have all of the knowledge and wisdom you could bestow. I have faith and I have men and women of good council. I can rule without you…and perhaps doing so will prove to the naysayers that no Lachlan requires Elyri guidance to rule fair and wise. You have no more obligation to me, to us, than what you have freely given…no more than any other lord in Enesfel. In truth, I believe Enesfel must repay you for the services you selflessly tender. If you see to Alberni's care, arrange with Níkóá to provide your people, your house, what they need…and you swear that you will come to me as soon as you return, swear that you will return…I shall not prevent you from going…and I will do my best to sway the queen."

He held out his hand, seeking to clasp Kavan's rather than seeking a promising kiss to the Lachlan ring, but it was the kiss that Kavan gave from one bended knee, his head bowed in respect. "I will do as you ask, My Prince. Thank you."

Both relieved and disappointed, Kavan realized that some part of him had expected to be denied the opportunity. That he had hoped to be refused so that he might use that refusal to convince Raebhá to remain, at least until the plague had passed. In time, she might even grow to no longer desire leaving. But he suspected she would instead be inclined to undertake the journey without him. She did not expect Kavan, or anyone else, to travel with her, so long as he could point her way and offer her enough support to begin her voyage.

"You will not leave before the end of the evening, will you?" At mid-afternoon now, the revelry was likely to last as long as people were sober enough to remain on their feet.

"Until she wishes to return to Alberni, I will be here." Kavan did not anticipate travel within the next few days, unless using a Gate became a viable option. At the moment, he was not interested in investigating the possibility.

Merrek squeezed the bard's hand, relishing the contact with the man who had raised and schooled him, been to him the father he had never been able to know. "Good. I shall see you in the Hall."

Ártur stumbled backward as the prince opened the door and sheepishly attempted to look as if he had just arrived and reached for the handle. "My apologies, Your Majesty," he murmured with a bow that covered his embarrassment.

"You may speak with him now, Lord Healer," Merrek chuckled, brushing past to return to the Hall where the merry sound of raucous singing rose from both minstrels and guests. Ártur waited until the prince was out of sight before rising from his bow to see Kavan staring at him expectantly.

"It is true then? What Rhyrdan says?"

One brow raised, Kavan said, "I don't know what Rhyrdan says."

"That you and she are…"

Kavan cleared his throat to avoid what he thought Ártur was about to say. "She is a married woman."

"Whose husband has been killed…"

"Presumably so." Rhyrdan must have heard that news from Dhóri. Or else Raebhá had told him. "Perhaps he survived the…"

"And you intend to return her home to learn the truth? What if he is dead? Do you intend to remain with her? Convince her to give up her throne to return to Alberni?"

"I…"

"What if he is alive?"

Though he was used to Ártur pushing for answers, these were questions Kavan had not answered for himself. No matter what scenario he concocted, he could not foresee or foretell the outcome. The Sight showed him nothing. The future was hidden from his efforts to plan for it.

"I know only that she should not make this journey alone. If anything were to…" He opened the window and looked across the courtyard into the cloudless blue sky so as not to look at Ártur. "I would never forgive myself."

"You would never know."

"I would know." She was in his soul now, rooted so deeply that he knew he would never be free of her, no matter the distance between them. Nor did he want to be.

Ártur scowled, opened his mouth to protest, and then clamped it closed with wide-eyed amazement. Kavan had close bonds with others, with the Lachlan monarchs through the pendant pieces they shared, with friends he was closest to, with some of his kin. This woman was not kin, was no Lachlan. From the way Kavan spoke those words, the healer did not think this was a matter of friendship. There was only one certain way she could be so bound to his cousin, and it was something Ártur had doubted Kavan would find.

Hoped, yes, but like Kavan, he had given up on the belief that such a bond, except with Wortham perhaps, was likely to happen.

"You've…" he stammered.

The bard's shoulders tensed. He swallowed, relaxed, and they slumped again but the stance of defeat did not last long. Only Wortham or Ártur would have been able to divine this truth. That the healer could see it, sense it, did not surprise Kavan. "I should feel shame, Ártur…I should regret this…but I do not. k'Ádhá knows…the guilt I feel is because I do not regret it." He felt ashamed for not feeling guiltier, a conundrum he did not know how to resolve. "Wherever she is, whatever the future…she is…" It seemed premature to call her the other half of his soul, the way he had called Wortham such, but it was how he viewed her. More fully his other half than anyone he had ever known. Similar to Wortham…but not the same.

She was the piece he had been missing. She filled the vacancy Wortham had left and overflowed it. How could he regret that?

"What about Dhóri?"

"I don't know. He hopes, he wants…but she is not…does not want what he does."

Ártur nodded and pulled a chair from the long oak table and sank into it. He had watched her reluctant accommodation of Dhóri's attentions, had watched the young man's unabashed infatuation from the moment they arrived in Rhidam. "She should tell him, not you…but I wasn't thinking about…I meant…" He took a breath and shrugged. "If you do this, if you leave with her, what becomes of Dhóri? Sóbhán? Rhyrdan? Alberni and St. Kóráhm's? Have you considered them?" He did not speak his name but believed his inclusion was implied.

"St. Kóráhm's is in good hands." Kavan was not involved in the daily management of the chellé, only served as its benefactor and worked to procure books and manuscripts for the library. Others did that as well, however, and the payments from his estate would not cease if Kavan was not there to see it done. "Rhyrdan is capable of managing the estate."

"Don't you think he would rather serve beside you as Wortham…"

The way Kavan flinched made Ártur regret the suggestion.

"He would…but I cannot…" Kavan's voice broke and his grip on the sill tightened. "Someday…he will. I need him there. But not yet. Not now. He reminds me too much of…and I am not prepared to shoulder that reminder. I want him there because of who he is…not because of who he reminds me of."

"That is fair." Ártur paused, waiting for his cousin to regain his composure, wanting to hug Kavan and allow him to weep but knowing Kavan would not permit such a gesture. "Dhóri and Sóbhán?"

"Sóbhán has no need of me now."

"That is not true…"

"He has his own family. His own life. I have given him everything I can, my eternal love…which he will never lack for. Dhóri…"

Dhóri presented problems Kavan did not have answers for. He would be acting lord of Alberni during the expected short absence, and he had the head for numbers and organization that would allow him to keep the estate running efficiently. But Kavan was less certain that he could be a leader, a ruler, especially since he was prone to seeing the good in everyone instead of bearing a realistic view of the world that would allow him to make good decisions. Sometimes he seemed to Kavan too naïve for a position of leadership.

Though Dhóri was not spiteful or vindictive by nature, with the strain between them now, Kavan feared he would deliberately make poor choices to destroy what his father had worked to build.

"I cannot bring him with me, should I do this. It would serve no useful purpose."

"Time spent with you might be beneficial for him…"

"With me and with her," Kavan reminded with a shake of his head. "I do not foresee that being beneficial for anyone."

"Nor will abandoning him."

"I would never abandon him."

"Not even to remain with her…wherever your travels take you?"

Kavan swallowed a gulp of air and scowled.

"You don't know how long you'll be gone…where you are going."

Closing the window, Kavan pulled a chair to sit across from Ártur, put his elbows on his knees his fists beneath his chin and said, "She hails from the city of Curnydhá, in the realm of Gálínphel, somewhere across the sea. It is where Kóráhm was born, where the Faith was born. Where Dhágdhuán died…the land from which all Elyri come."

The healer blinked rapidly as he stared. "Gallin…how can…how do you know this?"

Grabbing Ártur's hand, debating the logic of dumping what little he knew into the healer's head and deciding against it, Kavan begged, "Please, do not speak of these things to anyone. So much of what we have been taught, told, is but a shadow of the truth. There is so much…and I do not want you accused of heresy too."

"Heresy?"

"I know only what history Raebhá has shared thus far…but there is much more to the truth than we know."

"Which is why you wish to make this journey."

He had few doubts Kavan loved Raebhá, even if he was unable to say the words or unwilling to identify the attachment for what it was. But since the day Ártur had found Kavan his first book, a forbidden volume of Kóráhm's teachings, Kavan had been on a quest for the sort of knowledge most people avoided. A quest to know why he was different, why Elyri believed as they did. Where they had come from and where they went when the old ones wandered into the wilderness for the last time. The more hidden and forbidden the knowledge, the more eagerly Kavan sought it.

If there was a chance that Raebhá's tales were true, that the details might ingratiate him into the good graces of the Faith or help him be content apart from it, Kavan would chase that knowledge to the ends of the world.

"I need to know." Perhaps if he knew, his life would make sense. All he needed was knowledge, truth, music, his children…and Raebhá at his side.

It was Ártur's turn to sigh. "I do not like it…but I understand." He had hated the months Kavan had been away during the quest to restore his hands and to seek a way to purge Enesfel of the cancerous persecution of violence that had been devouring it. He had not liked knowing that Kavan might never return.

This time Kavan would not be running from something but his return, to Ártur, felt no less certain. With the lure of love at the other end, Kavan's return felt highly unlikely.

"I will keep faith with you, hold your secrets…but when you come home, I want you to tell me everything you learn. Everything, no matter what it is. Heresy or not."

Kavan bobbed his head. "I will tell you, I swear."

The promise was enough for Ártur to believe that Kavan would come back to him. Perhaps not soon, perhaps not for years to come, but he would return.

"When do you intend to…?"

"I don't know. But I promise I will not leave without a farewell." Not like last time. No matter how he chose to make this journey, he would not abandon those dearest to him without the courtesy of a goodbye. He had done that once.

This time would be different.

❧*196*☙

## ⁊Chapter 13

Lords and ladies lay around the Lachlans' Great Hall, some at tables littered with the remnants of feasting or on side benches where they had collapsed when weary of dancing, or propped against one another in corners where they had drunk themselves into a stupor over cordial conversation. Servants and palace guards had helped some into billeting rooms throughout the evening while others staggered there on their own. Some, despite their intentions to reach comfortable beds, were found in alcoves, on the stairs, or in the corridors, wherever they happened to land when overconsumption overtook them. It would take the staff several hours to get everyone to private rooms and strip the Hall of the evidence of the all-day affair, but at least they, and those they tended, had been afforded the luxury, even if only for a few hours, of a distraction from the suffering world. For feasts in the time of dearth, of which the servants were allowed to partake from what remained, were rare, and though this one had been sparser than a typical Lachlan banquet, it was more than many, noble and low-born alike, could look forward to after the celebration ended.

Bhríd and Editt had been the first to retire, returning to Levonne before the bells of Hes á Redh rung the compline hour. If any but his kin and the royal family, whom they had made sure to thank for this honor when bidding them farewell, noticed their absence, no one inquired. Ártur, Syl, Yóáná, and Rouvyn remained available should any over-indulgent guest require a healer's remedies and Madoc, the Lord High Justice, remained for his wife's safety as well as to put down inebriated squabbles before they got out of hand. He also remained to speak with his brother about how their mother and sister faired since their father's passing. Rhyrdan's distraction meant that Kavan lingered as well, long after he normally would have, though he knew that Ártur could have brought Rhyrdan to Alberni if need be.

But Kavan wanted Rhyrdan with him, wanted him there in the Gate when he departed, to serve as a buffer between him, Dhóri, and Raebhá. Kavan did not trust himself alone with either of them. He did not trust himself alone with both.

For Dhóri had taken every opportunity to be as alone with Raebhá as the hall full of revelers would allow and he made certain that his father saw them together. The moment the young man noticed her not engaged in conversation with some lord or lady, dignitary or servant, musician or gdhededhá, Dhóri was there, taking her hand, urging her to dance. She did not always relent, appeared grateful when Merrek, Rhyrdan, Sóbhán, Bhyrhán, Níkóá, and even Ártur intervened with dialogue or dances or the opportunity to see or try something new. Dhóri resented the intrusions but continued to try.

Kavan never did.

He remembered how easily he had lost himself to dancing with Orynn, how the world had ceased to exist in those joyous hours together. Such abandon could not be risked here. There were moments when Raebhá, across the room or dancing past him, caught his eye, moments when she wished to approach him. Kavan, afraid of a request he could not fill, not trusting himself to hold her and still troubled by his earlier admission to Ártur, looked away. Stolen glances revealed her regret, a look that stabbed like a dagger into his heart.

It was no wonder she accepted Dhóri's company when it was offered and there was no one else to come between them. Eventually, she ceased trying to win Kavan's attention. It was no wonder that Dhóri, witnessing this, made the effort to take advantage of the woman's company when his father would not.

As soon as she wearied of the game the two were playing, wearied of being a pawn, as soon as the number of those with whom she could hold coherent conversation dropped too low, she sought Rhyrdan and asked to be taken back to Alberni. Since he could not accommodate her request, they jointly approached Kavan and she unsuccessfully hid her disappointment by refusing to look him in the eye. The awkwardness he felt in her presence melted into guilt for hurting her and shame for abandoning her to strangers. She deserved better.

He had failed her.

The four, since Dhóri was not far behind, took leave of the regent and queen. Diona, sensing the tension between the bard and Merrek, was determined to get to the heart of the matter, but it would not happen this night, as Merrek had already retired to his rooms and his sleeping wife, and Kavan had left the hall for the nearest Gate.

Once in Alberni, Rhyrdan forcibly dragged Dhóri out of the oratory to aid in securing the house for the night. The young Elyri was not pleased to be separated from the woman he was attempting to court, but the hour was late and she would likely retire to sleep as his father knelt before the altar in prayer as he often did late in the night.

So long as his father was in prayer and Raebhá was asleep, Kavan would be no threat.

Raebhá, however, was in no rush to leave the oratory and stood with the green velvet curtain of the Purification Chamber at her back, watching Kavan kneel with his hands clenched in his lap. Prayer was an uncommon thing in her land, but reverence was something she recognized. His effort appeared unproductive; he was anxious, fidgety, and unfocused. She guessed he wanted to be alone, that he was trying to shut her out, shut out the world.

The tension between his shoulders, however, and the cocking of his head so that he could monitor her movement as she stepped away from the curtain, suggested otherwise and caused her to stop, to stand still and look at the back of his bowed head.

"My lord," she finally murmured, cautiously moving forward, monitoring the shifting strain in his body until she judged she should go no nearer. "I do not know what has happened, what I have done, what has changed, why you shun me. But know this," she sighed and looked at the figure of Dhágdhuán. She believed she knew the reasons, but claiming ignorance meant that he might voice his thoughts and allow them to clear the air. "Give me what I require for my journey and I will depart as soon as I am able. I do not wish to trouble you, to be a burden or cause disquiet…"

The heaviness, the pain, in her voice made him sigh, a sound that was almost a groan. "You are no burden." Kavan's whisper sounded louder than he expected in the silence of the stone room.

"But there is discomfort and disquiet…"

Kavan's jaw clenched, his hands twisted around each other, but he forced his voice to begin. "It is…before you…I have never…" He felt she should know the truth, should understand if she did not already, but how could he explain? How could she believe him when Dhóri's existence would disprove his claim?

Behind him, her head cocked, she listened to the struggle in his voice, uncertain what he was trying to say. Why should he be embarrassed? Nothing he had done, as far as she knew, warranted that. "Kavan…"

Hurrying on to another subject, one more preferable and easier to discuss, he continued. "I have spoken with Ártur and with Prince Merrek of my intentions to travel…"

"You have duties here…"

"Duties can be managed by others for a time. I made a promise."

She sat on the step and was not surprised when he inched slightly away. "While I appreciate the sentiment, I do not hold you to…"

"I do." He shifted on his knees to face her and directly regretted it, for seeing the hurt and confusion in her eyes only added to his own.

"I do not ask you to honor your word when it makes you uncomfortable to be near me. The duration of the journey would be unbearable, for both of us, and I will not have it." It was not what she wanted, but she would accept the inevitable if she had to.

"There might be another way, a safer and faster way." Not that he wanted faster, but she was right in saying that a prolonged journey would be intolerable for them unless Kavan swallowed his pride and shared his secrets. When she did not ask what he meant, he continued, "I believe I may be able to use the k'rylag."

Her face lost color and her hands clenched in her laps. "How? The one that sent me here did not…you said there was no rynlagne where you found me."

Hearing the trepidation in her voice, he tried to reassure her. "There was none. But there was power, power that suggested the use of one. I believe the nearest Gate was too far for you to have walked to the lake, with no memory of getting there, but there was power in the earth…beneath you. The day you arrived I felt it."

Worried about what she would think of him, he cleared his throat and looked at his hands before continuing. "There was a great sucking of power, something that ripped all of mine from me. I believe it was taken to…that it was the power needed to open the k'rylag that brought you here, to a place no gate existed. I do not know how such could be possible, but it happened and so possible it is. Likely the same power is used to create a k'rylag, but the knowledge of how to do that has been long lost. I am limited to those Gates that already exist, but I think it possible to use one…to take you back."

Unconsciously he stroked the harp with one hand, the strings silent beneath his fingers although it appeared he was listening to the sounds they should have made. "I know of Gates that exit to a single place, a place without a Gate to return. I know of others…" His eyes fluttered closed as if he would see what he spoke of behind his lids. "When using a Gate there are lights, points of power reflecting every other Gate to which one may connect. The pattern is unchanging. I know many of them, but there are some Gates through which others are visible, destinations I do not recognize…that I have never tried to access. It is possible…" He met her gaze, hoping the sight of her and the joy such news should bring her, would east the sting of his offering. "If my people came from your land, if they built the Gates when they arrived here, it makes sense that they could have built Gates that could take them home, even if they never used them."

"If that is so…why did they not return?" The question was as much for herself, for the ancestors who had gone before her, as it was for him.

"Fear? Contentment with their new lives? The quest for adventure? Perhaps some did go back but chose not to stay or hid."

Raebhá scowled at the suggestion that there could be history she did not know, history kept hidden. Many in the tales of expulsion had been forced to leave their families; might they have come back for them? Had some of the rumored disappearances been people taken through the Gates by banished families desiring reunification? What else were the márbhyndhánis hiding? "I cannot use these…Gates. Only the márbhyndhánis…"

"But I can."

"Wouldn't it be dangerous?" The journey to Rhidam and back had seemed safe and easy, but without knowing how the Gates worked, Raebhá could not imagine how distance might affect their use.

"No more than an extended journey by land or sea." He expected travel by Gate to be much safer. Whatever energy he had to expend to manipulate such a Gate would likely not kill him and he would protect her from any power pushback. He believed he could control the Gates. The sea, the elements, were out of his control. "The primary risk…I would not know where such a Gate would take us. It could be anywhere in your lands…or somewhere else entirely. We could emerge in a building, in the wilds, on a vessel."

He had never found a Gate on a ship, but Elyria had few ships, and if, as Raebhá indicated during their research, hers were people of the sea, it might not be unreasonable for a Gate to be built on a ship.

"I do not know where they are; the márbhyndhánis protect them as fiercely as they protect the knowledge and power. I think they must be within a néósag, a dhó dónáré, or perhaps the sacred places in the mountains. As winter sets, it will be colder than you're accustomed to…and such places are many days' travel from any ghísaer."

"Then we plan accordingly. Clothing, food, weapons, supplies, anything you think we might need."

"Kavan." She reached for his hand, clenching it so that he could not pull away. She was happy when he did not try. What he suggested frightened her but she trusted him. He would not have saved her life, cared for her, if he meant to kill her now. Nor would he risk his own life if he did not think he could keep her safe. "If you can get me through a rynlagne, that will be enough."

"I cannot send you without going myself." Someone had done so in sending her here, but sending someone without making the journey himself was a skill Kavan had never imagined possible. Or perhaps someone had come with her and then gone back, abandoning her. There had never been a need for Kavan to try, and he would not practice by putting her life at risk.

"What happens after I take you through," his hand began to tremble in hers, "will depend on where we end up. I will see you safely home. That is my promise to you."

He would not leave her alone in a place of hostile land and weather. Wherever he took her, he would need to know she was safe, that she was home, before he would be satisfied to leave her. He needed to know she was married still, whatever came next. Bringing her hands to his lips, he kissed her knuckles, taking the time to breathe in the scent of her before rising and drawing her to her feet.

Her head bobbed tentatively as she stared at their joined hands.

"Make a list of requirements for a journey through your land at this time of year. Get it to me when you can. I will set my affairs in order so that travel will not disrupt the estate or the city. Such preparations may take a few days, and I will need time to locate the sort of Gate we require…but I promise that when it is done, I will take you…if you still wish to go."

Still holding his hand, she cautiously leaned forward and kissed his mouth in gratitude, prompting a groan in his chest that made her warm and giddy. It also made her sad to say what came next. "It is not my wish, but I must." She needed to know if Ombhrís lived, to know how much of her heart she could give to this man. "You understand?"

He nodded, not trusting his voice, not trusting the igniting fires throughout his body. He needed to know that truth too to be free of the conflicting guilt that dogged him.

How much worse would he feel, he wondered, when he told Dhóri his plans?

❧*❧

"You will be away indefinitely?"

Raenár Magk had, at one time, served the Faith in Clarys as a soldier and captain, had served and done the bidding of the Faith leaders without question or reserve, until Saint Kóráhm the Heretic appeared before him and led him to question everything he believed. Unable to complete the commission he had been given, finding no evidence of the crimes of which Kavan had been accused, and unable to continue, in good conscience, serving the organization which had later stripped Kavan of his rights within that Faith, Raenár had been left with no choice. He followed the White Bard to Enesfel to serve him as Captain of the Guard within St. Kóráhm's chellé hábhai. His force was small, thirty-nine men plus himself, but with the fortifications Kavan assured him were in place, that squad should be adequate to hold off all but the largest of armies. If any army that large ever had cause to storm St. Kóráhm's, Raenár thought that would be a very grim day for Enesfel, Alberni, and the Faith.

Having spoken with Khwílen already to assure the man that his contributions to the abbey would continue during his absence, the easiest task before him today, Kavan glanced at the man who walked in step beside him. There were few soldiers in Elyriá; those there were, were intended for the protection of the Kyne or were ceremonial soldiers for the Faith who at most had the duty of hunting and arresting heretics. As that was a rare occurrence and with crimes against the Kyne's House rarer still, Elyri soldiers were seldom trained for full combat. Many had above-average training with Power, but those were not the skills Kavan required. Upon coming to Enesfel, Raenár had thrown himself into every training regimen he could, spending hours with Wortham, Bhríd, Duke Gabersdon, and General Agis, to become a more well-rounded, capable soldier. Kavan awarded his efforts with trust and friendship, treasures the captain knew were rare.

"I pray not," Kavan admitted. In his head, his wishes were that they would Gate close enough to Raebhá's home to discover her husband dead, to see the criminals swiftly brought to justice, and that she would leave someone else in charge to return to Alberni with him. It was a hope he clung to despite how unrealistic it was. Why expect her to give up things that he would not? "I am hopeful that a Gate will deliver us close to her home so that I may return quickly...days, perhaps weeks at most."

He had not told Khwílen his destination, when he would depart, only of his intent to see the lady safely home and see that justice was done for the attempt on her life. He was optimistic about his chances with a Gate. He was less optimistic about his future with Raebhá.

"Rhyrdan and Dhóri and Zelenka will manage the estate...but I ask that you aid them." Neither young man had borne such obligation before, and with the threat of plague looming and the stores of food in the region continuing to dwindle, Kavan did not expect their task to be easy. It was those threats that would draw Kavan home. He could not leave the future of his province in unskilled hands for long. "Do what must be done for the survival of our people, but do not abuse anyone unnecessarily."

"You know I will not. You have discussed this with…"

"Not yet. I will speak with them nearer to my departure. There is still much to do. I do not intend to leave for several more days."

He expected it would take the majority of a week to set the estate in order, to make arrangements, acquire what they might need for this venture and to say his farewells to friends. Not having seen Raebhá's list, not having seen her yet today as he had left before daybreak to pray at Wortham's grave in the hopes of communion not only with him but with Kóráhm, Kavan did not know what supplies she wanted. He could only guess how long preparations would take. "I am off to speak with Sheriff Groff, and will tell him to interface with you on any matters of security that arise."

"I will call on him this evening to discuss it so that we are of a mind as to how to manage Alberni. Shall we include Master Rhyrdan and Master Dhóri?"

"Not until I have expressed my expectations to them." He did not expect that dialogue to be an easy one, and wondered if he should request Sóbhán and Madoc's presence to facilitate a productive discourse. But both had their own lives, responsibilities of their own, and Alberni's care was not among them.

"Very well. If my sword will be of use to your travels, you have but to ask." He smiled and shook Kavan's hand. He did not expect to be included in what sounded to be a short trip, but he felt honor-bound to offer. "If I do not see you beforehand, safe travels, my lord."

"Best wishes and safety to you, Captain."

Sheriff Groff, a brash, brawl-scarred man, absent two fingers on his left hand and several teeth, was nevertheless a respected and well-liked sheriff, a man known to be fair but tough, not prone to putting up with dissidents and criminals. Most knew him to be unafraid of stepping into a fight to resolve it with powerful punches and thus they usually backed down from disagreements as soon as he entered the fray. Wortham had first met him in a tavern where the two shared several drinks during the stressful hours before Madoc's birth, and it had been Wortham's recommendation that had gotten Groff his job. For all of his brashness, he respected Kavan's authority and prided himself in making Alberni one of the safest provinces, for Teren and Elyri alike, in Enesfel.

As this was not the first journey Kavan had taken, the bard being known to spend weeks at a time in Rhidam, Fiara, or Káliel, Groff thought nothing of the Duke's admonitions and instructions. The only differences were famine and plague, and the leaving of the reins of power in the hands of two young men, barely older than boys, instead of Wortham. That would put more responsibility on Groff's shoulders but he considered himself up to the task, no matter how dire the situation became.

By the time Kavan returned to the manor, Zelenka and Emeria had the evening meal set, stew and bread, a portent of the dwindling food stores. Kavan had cut the house to the meagerest of meals as soon as the food shortage had begun, to extend the stores as long as possible, but the effects were felt. If not for fish and mussels brought in from the sea, Alberni and Levonne might have succumbed to hunger as early as much of the rest of Enesfel had.

Raebhá was seated in the chair near the head of the table where Rhyrdan placed her, with him seated at her side to shield her from Dhóri's attention. She looked uneasy, uncomfortable, while stoically trying to appear calm as Dhóri took the chair across from her, the seat that had once been Wortham's. He might not be able to touch her but he could smile and engage her in conversation, which was what he wanted. It did not occur to him to leave Wortham's chair unoccupied.

Zelenka, Emeria, and the other servants, Darys by birth or marriage, joined them as Kavan had asked, and though it was not uncommon for him to draw them together for meals, it suggested to Rhyrdan that Kavan had summoned them for a purpose. When the bard's countenance brightened upon seeing Raebhá, after a scowl of annoyance at his son, but not speaking or making eye contact with her, Rhyrdan was sure of it.

Waiting for everyone to be served and for Dhóri to offer the blessing over the meal as he often did, doing his best to ignore his son's presumptive assuming of that seat at the table, Kavan fingered his cup as he absorbed the powerful aura of the woman beside him. Despite his focus on her mission throughout the day, he had felt anxious without her company, as if what he was preparing to do was not real. Seeing her, however, strengthened the uneasy resolve to do what he had dreaded since late last night.

"Rhyrdan, Dhóri, I must ask a favor of you." He had intended to put this dialogue off but he knew both young men were bright enough to realize something was afoot. This was not the sort of news he should lay on their shoulders at the last minute.

"Anything." The tone, the timbre, the word itself sounded so much like Wortham that tears filled Kavan's eyes and he felt himself shrivel inside. Perhaps his choice was wrong. Perhaps he should bring Rhyrdan with him. Perhaps instead of pushing the young man away during these painful days, he should embrace him and hold him closer. But Dhóri and Alberni would need Rhyrdan more, dictating Kavan's final decision.

"I must be away from Alberni for a time. While I am gone, the running of the estate and province will fall to you both. Captain Magk and Sheriff Groff will aid in overseeing Alberni and assist as necessary, and Níkóá will be available if you need him, but the two of you will serve as authority in my stead."

"I will see that everything is taken care of, Father," Dhóri exclaimed, his gaze shifting to Raebhá where he expected to do most of his caring. She was their guest, after all. If his father was leaving, she became his responsibility.

Rather than flinch from the young man's gaze, Raebhá, regretting the words that came next for the pain they would cause both father and son, looked at Dhóri sympathetically and murmured, "Lord Cliáth is taking me home."

"Taking you…" For several moments, the words seemed not to register. Dhóri stared back and forth between her and his father as his expression morphed through a range of emotions before finally settling into the one Kavan expected.

Betrayal.

"How can you…? I don't want you to leave! I thought we were…"

"Dhóri," Kavan interrupted, preferring his son's ire be directed at him. "She is married." The words pained him to say, pained him to admit. "She is the ruler of many lands, banished here. Now that she is recovered, it's time for her to root out her enemies and resume…"

"Married…?" Though he had been told that truth, Dhóri said it as if he had never believed it. "How could you mislead…?"

She blinked several times, surprised, before replying, "I have never lied to you, Dhóri…and I am sorry if you believe I have. It was not my intent…"

"You took advantage of my hospitality and my…" He rose from the table, slamming his fist upon it in a rare fit of pique.

"Dhóri." The single interrupting word was spoken in a tone Kavan had never used with his son, or with anyone as far as Rhyrdan recalled.

Not hearing the note of threat, or choosing to ignore it, Dhóri barked, "You are taking her away from me! You cannot bear that I might have something you do not!"

"While the lady is under my roof," Kavan growled, emphasizing his claim on the estate, "she is afforded the hospitality of this house; there is nothing to take advantage of." He ignored the rest of the comment, as the issue was more complicated than he wanted to publically discuss, or discuss at all with his son. His feelings, his affairs, the matters of his heart, were private and would remain that way until the day came to speak of them.

"Go if you want! I will not be responsible for the estate! It is never going to be mine!"

Without touching his meal, Dhóri stormed from the dining hall, leaving a wake of slamming doors and clattering chairs and benches as he tipped things over on his way. No one followed and no one spoke. Servants busied their attention with their meals, although Zelenka looked anxiously after the young man she had cared for as her own child, wondering if she should go after him. Emeria's hand on her arm kept her from rising and when Kavan began to eat, to return the room to a normal humor, Zelenka did as well.

Raebhá, face flushed with mortification, toyed with her spoon and picked at her bread. While she had been aware of Dhóri's interest, she had not believed it strong enough to lead to such an outburst, that it was interest enough to cause a rift between father and son. The outburst robbed her of her appetite and gave her cause to reconsider sneaking away during the night.

Although he had not spoken during the argument, Rhyrdan listened and made notes of details he had not noticed before. While he had been told that Raebhá was married, he had been acutely aware of Kavan's growing interest in her, attachment the bard unsuccessfully hid. After Kavan's efforts to keep distance between them the day before in Rhidam, Rhyrdan now decided that the man hoped to cut emotional ties before her inevitable departure. If she was intent on leaving despite her feelings, feelings Rhyrdan could see in the way she picked at her meal and resisted looking at Kavan, leaving for a husband and world from which she had been expelled, of course Kavan would want to see her safely on her way…and would be crumbling inside because of it.

Having just lost his best friend, how could he not be devastated?

Rhyrdan's eyes softened with tears.

He waited for what seemed a respectable amount of time, allowing people to eat without interruption, before setting down his spoon and saying, "I will go with you, if you wish. You may need…"

"I need you here." Kavan's words were more clipped than intended.

"If my father was here…"

Eyes narrowed, his tone cooler than he liked, Kavan growled, "You are not your father." He immediately regretted those words and his tone and sighed. "Rhyrdan, even if he…this is something I would undertake without him. We will journey by Gate. I'll see her home and return." Each time he said it, it became another nail sealing his future closed, for unless he convinced her to come back, he would return to Alberni alone. "There will be no need of your sword. But..." He looked towards the door where Dhóri had gone. "I do need you here."

Rhyrdan was younger than Dhóri, but Kavan felt him more sensible and, unfortunately, more practical, just as his father had been.

Rhyrdan did not hide his disappointment and instead nodded. "Very well," he muttered with a glum expression. "Everything will be in order upon your return. I swear it."

"I trust you, Rhyrdan. I would not ask this of you if I did not." Kavan was thankful Rhyrdan did not fight him as Dhóri had, although the young man's frustration troubled him. Wortham had been much more than a sword arm. He had been the man on whom Kavan could depend for anything: an arm to fight for him, a shoulder to lean on, a head to manage Alberni, a heart to protect Kavan's children. He had been Kavan's heart and soul. Wortham would have been disappointed to be disallowed to travel with him, but he would have accepted the duty with honor. Kavan did not think Rhyrdan yet shared that sense of honor, as if anything other than proving his sword skill was somehow an inferior duty. Hopefully, upon his return, Kavan would be able to prove differently to both Rhyrdan and his son.

One by one, after several more minutes of silence punctuated by an occasional question by his staff on how the estate should be run during his absence, many of the questions flitting around the edges of their concerns for hunger and plague, the room emptied, leaving Kavan and Raebhá alone. She pulled a scrap of parchment from the pocket at her waist and slid it over the table. Her hand paused halfway; she took a breath and reached across.

"Emeria helped me write it."

Kavan took it, his fingers brushing hers as she hesitated to release it, and then unfolded it to read without looking at her or speaking.

Most items on the list were expected. Outerwear suitable for extreme winter temperatures, weaponry suitable for both protection and for hunting, food that traveled well, and extra clothing. Some of it he could easily acquire, although he did not think he could find suitable winter clothing in Alberni where the weather rarely became unbearably frigid. Some, in this time of dwindling food and a reduction of trade goods, might take longer to obtain. He would have to consider where to acquire such items with relative haste.

The longer he put this off, the more difficult it would be to leave.

"Does he resent me for replacing his mother?" It seemed absurd as she asked, but she had seen such emotion before in children enduring the remarriages of their parents.

Kavan shook his head. "He has always been a passionate young man, prone to speaking his heart without reservation, without thinking about his words before speaking. Never before has he shown interest in women, but after his brother's recent marriage, I think he believes it is expected. Or he expects it of himself." His voice and breath lodged in the back of his throat and he coughed to clear it. "As for…he never knew his mother, save for a few minutes after his birth."

Thinking he meant that Dhóri's mother had died in childbirth, Raebhá covered his hand and squeezed gently. "I am sorry."

"It wasn't like that." He showed no inclination to speak more about Dhóri's mother and was visibly grateful that Raebhá did not press for details. "Tomorrow I will go to Rhidam, speak to the prince and Ártur…and bring back what I can. Ask Emeria to set aside food…and I will speak to Sóbhán. I will give you coin so that you may purchase requirements if you wish. If we succeed in securing what we need, we could depart for Fiara the following morning and pray the Gate there, and k'Ádhá, are kind to us. If not that day, then as soon after as can be arranged. If Fiara's Gate does not afford us passage, we will try others."

Situated further north, where the winters were colder than in Alberni, it was possible they could acquire some items from the list in Fiara. It, and Gabrielle, were the other reasons to try there first.

Pouting, hit by a strangling ache around her heart, she whispered, "I am sure you want me away so that your life can return to normal." There was no reasonable cause for her to blame herself but she felt responsible nonetheless.

"Raebhá…I swear to you." He pressed her palm against his cheek and closed his eyes as he held it there before grazing his lips over the heel of her hand. He shivered as the tremor of fire ran through him. "I do not want you to leave. Me. Here. Ever. If there was anything I could do to make you stay, I would. Long ago…"

Fumbling for words, he dared not look at her as he said them. "I Saw you, in that clearing where I found you. I knew nothing about you, who you were, why you were there, but in that glimpse, I knew that finding you would change my life. Whatever the future holds, nothing will ever be normal for me. Or perhaps…" The corners of his lips tugged up into the beginnings of a smile. "Perhaps it will become normal at last."

Orynn had taught his heart that he could love without shame, but Raebhá had taught him that on a much deeper level. He had sought to be a man like any other, to love and be loved, and now that seeking had borne fruit. Now he knew and believed those things. Whether she left him or remained, that knowledge had changed everything.

Raebhá understood then that, for all of his openness during those hours in the forest, there were still secrets he kept buried, details that shamed and embarrassed him. She marveled at his control. She had yet to touch the stories of his life, to learn what made him the man she was just beginning to know, just as she had been given no time to reveal herself, and as the time of departure drew nigh, she knew she might never know him in the way she wished to. "I will speak to him if you think it will…"

"I do not believe it will help," he sighed, shaking his head so that his cheek rubbed against her hand. "I don't forbid it, but I don't think it will be of use."

She nodded. Kavan knew him best. Perhaps it would be wisest to wait until Dhóri's temper had lessened and his rage calmed. The younger man could be as volatile as his father was serene. "I will retire, if I may?" She longed to be begged to stay, to continue to touch him, to be held and lie with him until the sun kissed the new day, but that, she decided, was a risky thing. It would be difficult enough to explain herself to Ombhrís if she found him alive. Judging by the shudder that passed through Kavan as he released her hand, further intimacy would make their parting, when it came, much more difficult for them both. The probability of hurting him was already tearing her apart.

He released her hand and did not watch her go, only closed his eyes as she ran her fingers affectionately over his shoulder, leaving a lingering trail of warmth. Such a simple gesture, yet one that settled into the deepest corners of his soul and made him warm all over.

Again she mused as she glanced at him, perhaps leaving on her own, on foot, would be the most humane gesture she could make. Cut the ties before either of them had the chance to prevent it from happening. It was not, however, a choice she could make. For just as he did not want to lose her, she did not want to say goodbye.

꘠*꘠

Kavan's visit to the prince and his cousin was put off as long as he could justifiably do so. Careful to avoid areas of the city where the Yellow Death was rumored to be, seeking the best supplies he could obtain regardless of cost, had taken longer than he hoped but it effectively allowed him to put off the inevitable departure from Alberni, the inexorable loss of her.

A brief drink and farewell shared with Wace in the Eagle's Nest likewise postponed the inevitable.

But facing those in Rhidam needed to be done and when he went, it was at an hour that allowed him to elude the queen and avoid the questions about Raebhá he expected her to ask. Both men attempted in vain to dissuade his plans, but there was no better way, in Kavan's opinion, for Raebhá to get home. He was the only man who might be able to travel by Gate into the unknown. If he failed, if she was forced to journey by land or by sea, Kavan could not, in good conscience, allow her to undertake the trip alone.

Reluctantly accepting his arguments while demanding his promise to return as soon as he was able, Both Merrek and Ártur were compelled to acknowledge his decision and let him go.

The visit ended with Níkóá coming to Alberni, his offered assistance to manage the province with Dhóri and Rhyrdan something he wanted to discuss in depth over the last sharing they would enjoy for the foreseeable future. Sóbhán was there when they arrived, relaxing at the hearth in Kavan's study, a cup of water in his hands.

"You thought to be away without a farewell," Sóbhán teased, setting the cup aside and rising to greet Kavan as he entered. He shook Níkóá's hand but his smile remained on his father.

Kavan scowled. "Did Dhóri…?"

"Tell me you are leaving? No…though from what Emeria says I'm surprised he did not." His brother's propensity for sharing everything with Sóbhán appeared to have faltered in this case of anger and resentment against their father.

"Ártur then…I told him not to…"

"Being newly married does not preclude me from being family. You should have come to me and…"

"I do not intend to be away long. There is no need to…"

"Intention or not, I would hate to learn of something happening while you're away that means we never said farewell."

Kavan understood the melancholy note in the young man's voice and bowed his head apologetically. Too many people had disappeared from Sóbhán's life; he did not want Kavan to disappear as well.

"I am sorry…I intended to come tonight…I did not think…did not want to interfere…"

"It's alright, bhydhá. You're never an interference." Sóbhán embraced him, erasing any hard feelings between them. "This has nothing to do with Wortham, does it?"

Kavan pushed down the grief the utterance brought with it and shook his head. "This is no flight of depression, though the timing may make it seem so. I must see to the lady's safety; I owe her that much…"

"I believe it is the lady who owes you." But he knew Kavan well. The man's sense of propriety would not simply cease with a guest's recovery. He would do everything in his power to accommodate someone he cared about, and if what Ártur and Emeria said was true, if what he had seen in Rhidam was correct, if his perceptions were accurate, Kavan did care about this woman. It was comforting to see.

"Emeria told me about Dhóri…I intend to see him while I'm here, speak to him on your behalf…and perhaps talk to the woman who has sparked such drama…"

"Raebhá has done nothing…"

"Oh yes, she has," chuckled Níkóá as he sat in the chair where Sóbhán had been and propped his feet on the stool.

The twitches at the corners of Kavan's mouth and eyes as he struggled to find something fitting to say, the movements of his fingers as if over harp strings as he attempted to soothe his nervousness, were familiar tells to Sóbhán and made him smile. Only two other people had elicited those tells in the bard, Dhóri's mother, on the rare occasions when Kavan spoke of her, and Wortham. Having so recently married, Sóbhán recognized the flush on the bard's skin, the softening of his voice when he spoke of Raebhá, the sparkle in his eyes when he looked at her. His father more than cared for this stranger. He was smitten, and so too, Sóbhán understood, was Dhóri.

It was the reason Sóbhán was eager to speak with her more intimately than he had in Rhidam. He wanted to be sure she was worth the heartbreak Kavan stood to suffer, worth the upset between his father and brother. He wanted to get a better sense of her so that he might help smooth his family's unsettled nerves before their relationships fell apart. Unlike Dhóri, Sóbhán could see this relationship as a positive thing for their father…if only Raebhá chose to remain in Alberni. If she did not, could not, if Kavan had lost his heart and was losing her as he had lost Wortham, Sóbhán worried for his father's state of mind.

He wanted assurances that what his father faced was worth the heartache. He wanted assurances that his brother was overreacting before he tried to talk Dhóri out of his outrage.

"Is she here?"

"I presume so." Kavan had just returned, had not yet seen her, but at this hour he knew of nowhere else she would be. "But there is business I must…"

The clop-clop of hooves in the courtyard and Rhyrdan's shout to someone nearby announced his return to the manor and was enough of an interruption to prevent Kavan from making awkward, nervous excuses. Only one horse, and thus Rhyrdan had not accompanied Raebhá into Alberni. Respecting his father's discomfort and whatever business he had to conduct with the chamberlain, Sóbhán bowed his head with a smile and chose to make his retreat.

"I'm going to say hello to Rhyrdan," he said warmly, "but you and I will speak later…you will not leave before we do."

"I will not." Kavan's audible sigh of relief made Sóbhán's smile wider. Rhyrdan's timely return spared him an awkward conversation, but only for a short time.

"Good." He embraced Kavan again. "I'll see you later, and talk sense to Dhóri if I can."

Kavan did not believe it would be that easy, but perhaps the older brother could offer solace to the younger that Kavan could not give.

Níkóá nursed a glass of apple brandy he had poured as Kavan withdrew behind the desk, listening to the retreating thud of steps in the hall and gauging the unspoken thoughts behind the bard's eyes.

"You are certain about this journey? That this is wise…given the state of the kingdom…and your family?"

"I'm not certain of anything," Kavan admitted wearily, "but the state of Enesfel and Alberni will not be affected by my staying or going." The state of his family, however, would be in flux whether

Raebhá stayed or left…whether he went with her or not. The nature of that flux was the only matter in question.

"If the plague comes to Alberni?"

Kavan sighed. That was his primary fear, that he would be gone when the plague rooted, that he would lose someone he loved when he was unable to be with them. "I don't plan to be away long. I don't know where the Gate will take us, how near to her home we shall be, but once I am certain she is safe in her land, I will come home." He had made promises to too many people and his ties to Alberni, St. Kóráhm's, and those living around him guaranteed his return.

"If there are Gates," Níkóá said, draining the cup and rising to refill it, "then there is nothing to stop you from traveling back and forth between her home and here, is there?" He laughed at Kavan's expression. "Come now; you cannot say you have not considered it. And yes, your intentions are transparent, my friend, at least to me."

"Having had three wives and untold mistresses does not make you an expert," Kavan muttered without looking at him.

"What does it make me?" the chamberlain asked, still laughing.

His first wife had died in childbirth, costing him the child as well but leaving him with a substantial dowry of land and coin. His second wife had been an older widow, the wife of a lord killed during the years of anti-Elyri violence. Some accused Níkóá of marrying for money, for she died in her sleep after eight months of marriage, supplying him with a reasonable sized estate beyond the eastern fringes of Rhidam and again, an income with it that, when combined with his income from the Lachlans and his gains from his first wife, set him well for the future. There had been accusations of murder, but the healers and Lord Justice had cleared him of wrongdoing both times and those who knew him best had witnessed his tender attentiveness to both women and knew him to have been loyal to each. Many of the years after were filled with one mistress after another, gaining him a reputation for womanizing not unlike his father. He was careful not to father children, wanting no string of bastards to grow up penniless as he had, and when one young woman of whom he had seemed particularly fond did conceive, he married her at once.

She too had died in childbirth after two miscarriages, leaving Níkóá with a beloved daughter nearly a year older than Prince Lorant.

Having promised to educate the girl when she was old enough, promising to test her gifts, if she had any, and train her to use and hide them, it was yet another reason for Kavan to return to Enesfel.

"I recognize lovesickness when I see it. I've suffered it often enough," he chuckled.

Kavan frowned. "She is married…"

"It doesn't stop the heart from wanting. You also said he was struck down in the attack that sent her here, that he might be dead."

"I'll not wish such a fate on him so that I may…"

"Wishing or not will not change facts. When you know the truth, you will be able to decide. And if her people are kin…they will have much to offer. Knowledge, history, language." Again he chuckled at the bard's expression. "Aside from her name, there are too many clues to hint at her obvious kinship. I don't know Elyriá as you do, am not as proficient in the High Language, but I know enough to listen and observe. Maybe she could walk through Clarys unrecognized as foreign, but there would be those who would know…and be as threatened by her as they are by you."

Kavan knew what he meant. What Kavan knew of history, of Kóráhm and the First Persecution, of the Zythánite connection to the Faith, had been enough to bring charges of heresy on his head. He wondered what the Kyne, the political elders, the heads of the Faith, would think of the things he had already learned from Raebhá. He could not guess what he would think and conclude as further truths unfolded, but he felt compelled to discover them. Kóráhm had encouraged him towards the pursuit of this trip, this knowledge, the last time they spoke. The Heretic-Saint apparently deemed him ready to learn secrets previously hidden.

"She is not a threat."

"She was to someone, or she wouldn't have been banished." With his second glass of brandy drained, Níkóá stood and waited for Kavan to do the same. "You'll leave tomorrow?"

"In the evening, perhaps…or the day after. There are supplies to gather still, details to see to here. Then I must go to Fiara, for the Gate I believe I need is there."

"Which will mean a visit to Gabrielle." He grinned. Níkóá had tried to win her after Owain's death and the death of his third wife, thinking that they would be a well-suited pair of compatible blood, but Gabrielle had no interest in remarriage. The only man she might have married stood with Níkóá now and she knew, as did everyone else, that such a union would never happen. "Perhaps I should go with you." It was an offer to ease potential awkwardness as well as see Gabrielle again, but he was not surprised when Kavan refused.

"I can do this...but thank you." Kavan was both curious and anxious about what the two women would think of one another but he did not think Gabrielle would suspect the truth.

"Very well. I will come every other day, check with Rhyrdan and Dhóri; they have only to send for me any other time. I will do my best to bring Dhóri to reason, or at least settle his mind if Sóbhán fails."

"He respects you both; I pray you are successful." Kavan had already received a similar promise from Khwílen, the other man Dhóri admired and respected. If there was any hope of regaining his son's love and esteem, Kavan prayed that those men, and time apart, would be enough to find it.

Níkóá gripped the bard's arms and pulled him into an embrace, the same sort Kavan had gotten from Merrek and Ártur. Few, except for his sons and Ártur, dared such physical displays, knowing how uncomfortable they made Kavan, but Níkóá, like the others, cared only for the expression of love it gave, and so Kavan endured it. "Be careful, brother." He kissed the side of Kavan's face.

"You are not staying?"

"I may return, but I wish to speak with Raenár and Groff before the hour grows too late. If I have not returned when you start dinner, do not wait for me. As for the boys, I'll watch over them as if they are my own...but don't leave me as the only father they have."

"I could ask for none better." Níkóá might be half-Teren by birth, a Lachlan by blood though his secret remained hidden, but to Kavan, Níkóá was the brother he had never had. As the chamberlain never failed to express when they were together, brother was exactly the way he saw Kavan. Ártur was his cousin. Owain had been his friend. Wortham something more intimate. But Níkóá was brother, and that made him unique.

❧*❧

"A matter of power; I don't understand it, but I know it to be true."

Sóbhán walked beside the woman through the rear garden, where autumn had robbed the trees of leaves so that only the pines showed green against the sky's fading blue. The lack of decent rain caused the leaves to crunch beneath their feet on the stony path.

He did not know what he had expected Raebhá to be like. Having enjoyed her company at the wedding banquet, dancing with her and doing his best to engage her in convivial conversation to rescue her from his brother's overbearing attention, they had not waded into serious conversation then so he was pleased to do so now. If she was what Kavan expected her to be, needed her to be, it was enough. He certainly found her striking, intelligent, and possessing enough mysteries to keep Kavan enthralled for a lifetime.

She paused to look at him, not sure how they had stumbled into this topic, or why Sóbhán felt it important that she know this truth. When Rhyrdan had brought him to her, as she assisted Emeria in the inventorying of food to determine what could be spared for the lord's journey, Raebhá had been surprised. Emeria encouraged her to go, to speak with Kavan's adopted son before she was deprived of the opportunity to know him better, and they had chosen to walk here, in the garden, where there was little chance of interruption.

From an upper window, she was aware that Dhóri watched her, but beyond eliciting a promise from Sóbhán that he would do his utmost to temper his brother's anger, they chose not to talk about him.

They talked at length about Bhryell, about harps and the Cliáthan tradition, about his new wife and Kavan's home where they resided. They discussed how he had come to be in Kavan's care, the years of persecution that Kavan had told her little about, until gradually their exchange shifted to the young man's glowing assessment of the bard who had accepted him into his heart without an obligation to do so.

She supposed that had led to what she heard now. But it was still a peculiar thing for a son to say about his father.

"I don't know how it was accomplished…he does not speak of her much," Sóbhán continued with a trace of melancholy as they resumed walking. "Dhóri has a sister…a twin…born of the same power, raised by their mother's people to be trained in the power that conceived and bore them. I don't think we shall ever meet or know her."

Conceived in power. The question that arose from that was one she did not speak but it was, she realized, answered by words Kavan had failed to say the evening after Bhríd's marriage. He had fathered children, but had never given himself to a woman…or had a woman give themselves to him. It was no wonder the strength of the ties between them were so powerful. It was no wonder he had wept, that he struggled so with his heart, his desires, his soul.

It was no wonder, in the face of his Faith, his sense of duty and morality, that he felt guilt.

It was no wonder her impending departure was tearing him apart.

This was knowledge that should have come from him, not his son, but she was glad to know it, even though knowing broke her heart.

She wiped her eyes, her cheeks, and realized she had stopped walking again to stare in the direction of the pond, the clearing, where Kavan's world had been inexplicably changed because of her and hers changed because of him. Would she have allowed it to happen if she had known this truth?

Being frank with herself, she doubted she would have changed a thing. She did not believe she could have if she had wanted to.

A sound, like a distant door opening, made her start, guilty, and glance towards the manor. No one was there, the door was closed and she prayed that Kavan had not been there to hear Sóbhán's words, or to read her thoughts, the tangled emotions of her swelling heart. If he had, he would flee her again.

"He has not sought them?" she whispered, turning the dialogue from such an intimate revelation to something equally personal and yet less delicate. A daughter was a safer topic and would, she hoped, allow her to regain composure before they returned to the house.

"Orynn has passed…or so he says. As for…" Sóbhán wrapped a comforting arm around her shoulders, acknowledging her shift in mood but not making obvious notice of her tears. "I do not think he knows where to begin…or he is respecting their mother's wishes." Or he is afraid to look, to find her, he thought with a sigh. "Maybe he will, one day." One day when Raebhá was gone, when Dhóri no longer needed him, when there were no children to tutor and no crises to solve. One day when that need for knowing demanded to be filled.

"To lose a child…"

"It is less difficult to lose what one has never had or known than it is to lose what is close to our hearts…."

Raebhá's gaze fell.

Believing his point made, judging her sincerity in the reaction to his words, Sóbhán said softly, "You will take care of him, wherever you are going? He is strong in spirit…ágdháni…but there is fragility he does not allow most to see. Does not want us to see…but it is there. I pray you see it too, that you will protect him as he will protect you."

Sóbhán did not want Kavan to return a broken, demoralized, shattered shell of a man.

She nodded, a persistent determination to defend Kavan at all costs now lodging in her breast. She had done this thing; she was responsible for him now. She gladly accepted that charge and every potential risk that came with it "I'll do everything in my power, Sóbhán. I swear that to you."

She did not want to see Kavan broken. Whatever their future, she did not want to be the one responsible for destroying him. She would do what she could, what she must, whether Kavan wished it or not.

## ❧ Chapter 14 ❧

I t took too long to acquire the winter clothing Raebhá recommended and to find a bow and knife suitable for the quest they were undertaking. He did not second-guess her, assuming she would not request such things if she did not know how to use them, but for himself, he brought only the knife the Zabin villagers had given him, crafted of the same peculiar silver-white metal that two of his pendants were made from. Weapons for him were a last resort, but a knife could have practical uses should they find themselves in the wilds.

He hoped those things would be unnecessary, that they would pass through the Gate to a place of civilization, if not the place where she lived, somewhere where gaining transport for further travel would be simple. While he was in no hurry to be parted from her, the news that morning of plague on a ship in the port disturbed him enough to consider postponing their departure. If plague had come to Alberni, how could he in good conscience leave Rhyrdan and Dhóri to face it alone? Nor did he relish the possibility of carrying the Yellow Death to Raebhá's people.

But Sheriff Groff assured him that the matter was in hand, that the unfortunate souls were quarantined to the ship, that they had enough food and water to sustain them for a week or more, and that no goods or personnel had been brought ashore. So long as the Yellow Sisters did not travel through the air, Alberni was safe. One physician and a gdhededhá from St. Maicel's had gone aboard to care for the afflicted crew with the knowledge that they would not be allowed to leave that ship until there were assurances that the plague had passed.

"I can manage Alberni." Rhyrdan did not sound confident, but he did sound resolved, and determination was often the key to success. His father had served as Kavan's most faithful and stalwart steward and his son was determined to prove himself likewise equal to the task. "Lord McCábhá and the others will provide what we need…and I expect you to be home soon." His grip around Kavan's hand with both of his was tight enough to transmit the plea behind his words.

"As soon as I am able, I swear it. If you need me, even to hear my voice…" Kavan shifted the power until his words echoed within the seventeen-year-old's head, 'you need only to go to Ártur, Khwílen or Níkóá. They may be able to reach me.'

It was the first time such psychic intimacy had been shared between them. Kavan had often shared it with Wortham, for Wortham's trust had encouraged such sharing. He held his breath as he waited for Rhyrdan's reaction, expecting shock and rejection as often happened the first time Teren experienced such a sharing. Instead, Rhyrdan grinned after an initial look of surprise and hugged the bard tightly.

"That is good to know," he murmured, saying the words aloud against the older man's neck. The size of him, the feel of his bearlike arms, the scent of his dark curly hair was so much like Wortham it was as if his friend had returned to embrace him one more time. Kavan held fast, struggling with the tearing that rose in his chest, and might have given in to weeping if the oratory door had not opened.

Hoping it would be Dhóri come to see him off, Kavan stepped away, his back to the door, to hide the emotion he knew was on his face. Rhyrdan kept his hand on the bard's back, a gesture of comfort, as Raebhá, not Dhóri, joined them at the front of the room where their packs waited at Kavan's feet.

"Is it time?" Rhyrdan had not spent as much time with Raebhá as Dhóri or Kavan, but he liked her, and he knew she made Kavan happy in a melancholy sort of way. The bard deserved happiness, though it seemed that lasting joy was not for him to have.

Raebhá could not answer his question, her heart heavy from the goodbyes she had shared with Emeria, Zelenka, and the others who had been so kind to her during her stay. Kavan had said his farewells earlier, having come here to share parting words with Sóbhán before the young man returned to Bhryell, but Raebhá had waited until the last minute to do so, finding the parting more difficult than expected.

If she was to travel by Gate, she would again be at Kavan's mercy, and judging by the sadness filling the room, she feared he had changed his mind. She almost wished he had. Understanding the state of his house, his relationships, the dangers threatening his province, she would not blame him if he had, or if he had decided to postpone this attempt until some later time. Even if they left tonight, and succeeded, she expected no more than an escort through the Gate and his immediate return home.

Her secret hope was that he would change his mind and stay with her, drawn by the wonders of history he was hungry to learn. If he stayed with her, they would have many more days together. But they would be days filled with temptation that would cause them both to suffer so long as there was any chance she was legally wed.

Kavan squared his shoulders, wiped his eyes, and said, "It is." He could not put this off. Duty and honor. The sooner it was done, the sooner he would return to duty and honor here too. "I will be in Fiara for the evening, should you need anything."

"I will be well, Kavan…záryph and St. Kóráhm travel with you…and bring you home safely."

"I would rather they remain and protect you and Dhóri, but I believe they can do both." Picking up the pack that contained the red wood kestrel harp that had once belonged to the young bard Eridel, a change of clothes, and the collection of heavy winterwear Raebhá had advised, a round iron cooking bowl, and a sheet of canvas for shelter, along with his share of food and water, he gestured to the Purification Chamber. His knife was sheathed at his hip. "Shall we?"

Raebhá hesitated long enough to embrace the young man with them. His was a strong body, broad and more powerful than Kavan's, but young and gentle in its returned warmth. "Thank you, Lord Delamo, for your generosity and hospitality, when I cannot have made your lives easy. Please, relay my gratitude and appreciation to Dhóri, and my regrets…"

She wished Kavan would speak of the young taeré's father, the one whose loss weighed so heavily on the house but whom Kavan had locked deep into secret places where no one would ever expose those memories. What she knew of Wortham came from his son and daughter, from Dhóri, from people she had spoken with in Rhidam. Never once had Kavan even spoken the man's name.

She had been told Rhyrdan was much like him. She wished she could have met the man Kavan had held so dear.

She hoped in time that wound would heal, that her departure did not compound it, and that Rhyrdan, the resolute young man in her embrace, would grow to fill the emptiness she was about to leave.

"Give him my wishes and love as well." Kavan continued to hope Dhóri would come, but the window of opportunity to bid farewell was nearly closed and it pained him to leave things the way they were.

"I will see it done." Rhyrdan watched the pair disappear behind the curtain and draw it closed. He could not see their feet in the shadows and had no power with which to know when the Gate was activated, but moments later, he knew he was alone.

The room was still.

His fists balled at his sides, his frustration and disappointment seeking an outlet. Despite Kavan's assurances, he believed the bard would have taken him if he had been a proven man of responsibility and combat. Once Kavan returned, Rhyrdan was determined to be the mirror image of his father, to be everything Kavan needed him to be. Never again would Rhyrdan be left behind for not being good enough.

Kjell de Corrmick was a king unlike any other Neth had known, a man of peace who had worked hard to bring prosperity to his land after centuries of suppression, abuse, cruelty, and violence perpetrated by the de Corrmick's who had gone before. Unlike the majority of those kings, he had become regent through the accident that had claimed his drunken brother's life and had then become king when his nephew, barely six years old, had choked on a fruit pit and suffocated before it could be dislodged. Kjell believed he, or someone else, could have saved the child, but the youngster's mother would not allow Kjell to touch him, certain that the ruling prince intended to kill her son. The choking boy had been taken from the hall and nearly thirty minutes later the news had come that, though the pit had been dislodged, Prince Hesl had suffered for lack of air for too long and had died.

Sometimes Kjell wondered if the boy had been killed by someone wanting to keep Kjell on the throne. But the hefty child had been prone to stuffing too much in his mouth at once, to swallowing food without chewing it properly, and so his death had appeared neither shocking nor suspicious. Kjell had sworn he would never kill to gain Neth's throne and the fates had seen to it that it was an oath kept.

There had been other promises kept as well, offering education to anyone who desired it, permitting the ownership of weapons and the training of a proper military that consisted not of men forced into service but of men paid, housed, and taught the ways of combat. Agricultural skills he had gleaned from Neth's neighbors on all sides, renovations in building and business that he had learned from books, Faith he had gained on his own and the acceptance of Elyri that had come with it. All of these things he had given to his kingdom, resulting in new prosperity and security that Neth badly needed. He was a man, a king, of the people and Neth rewarded him for it with the longest, most successful reign of any king in Neth's history.

But Kjell was no fool, though some had considered him such when he had been younger. His tendency to watch, to listen, to keep his fingers on the pulse of his adversaries, had continued after he was crowned regent and then king. Some longed for the reunification of Neth with the portion of land that had been stripped from them and granted to Enesfel. Some wanted a return to the days when Neth had been a kingdom to fear, a kingdom with strength, with the capacity to raid, to fight, to cast shadows of dismay into the hearts of their enemies. Those who could not see that being allies with Cordash, Enesfel, and Elyriá was better than being the enemy. Such men had a right to their opinions and Kjell did not want to keep his hard-won peace by suppressing those who opposed his policies. He encouraged dialogues with those of dissenting opinions, but few offers were accepted. Men could talk, men could believe what they wished, so long as they did not disrupt the kingdom.

It was that vigilance that had him more on edge since his youngest son's banquet. Something was not right within the House de Corrmick. It was not in words spoken, not in actions taken, but something that he felt in the looks of some around him, house servants, guards, and royal attendants. Not by all, not even by most, but by enough that it made the hairs on his neck and arms stand on edge whenever he entered or left a room. In response, he tightened security and directed General Stone to see to his family's safety. As days passed, he fretted more and more that they were not safe, that something was coming, and he needed to see to it that his family was safely tucked away so that he could turn his full attention to whatever was afoot.

"You should go," he repeated to his wife across the small table where they dined. Jerit had already finished and gone off to his room and Oska and Inness had chosen not to join them as was usually the case. The young couple often chose to dine alone and Kjell suspected they would soon demand a home of their own. With that in mind, he had begun scouting suitable duchies near Glevum that would provide them with income. Neither was satisfied living in the king's shadow. They needed a home. "As you say, your cousin will benefit from your kindness, and we should offer support to her and Merrek. You should see Yóáná. A girl needs her mother. Go; take Jerit with you…"

"What about you? You should come…"

"I should…and I shall…but there are matters I need to tend to before I will be free to follow."

Asta scowled. "What matters?" She was unaware of anything pressing that required his immediate attention. Normally he shared everything with her, trusting her judgment and the experience she had gained as Enesfel's inquisitor during the kingdom's darkest time.

He smiled and kissed her palm. "Nothing like that," he assured her. "Mundane duties of a king. I've been pondering your request and think it best you travel before the weather turns. Things have settled now that the celebration is past so it's a good time for that visit. Soon winter will be upon us, the turn of the year, and you'll lose the opportunity if you don't take it. That is, if you still wish to go…"

"I do." Diona's decision to share the responsibilities of ruling was unexpected, and Asta worried for her cousin's health and state of mind. If Diona was ailing, Asta wanted to be there for her. And she missed her eldest daughter, was eager to see how marriage was treating her since she had not seen Yóáná since the young woman had become a full healer within the Lachlan court alongside Ártur and Syl two years ago. It had been too long between visits and the fault, Asta believed, was entirely her own.

"Good. I shall have a carriage ready in the morning."

"So soon?" Asta chuckled. "Who is this new mistress you are so eager to trade me for?"

"No mistress…aside from a mountain of documents to be signed and advisors needs to address," he laughed, getting up to kiss the top of her head. "Why delay when the weather is agreeable?"

"Hmmm…" Feigning suspicion, she turned her head and kissed his stomach. "I should see to packing for the journey…but I suggest you complete your evening's affairs quickly. I intend to share one more night with you before you expel me from our bed."

"I shall make haste and prepare gifts for Diona and the new regent, and for Lady Gabrielle if you will see it delivered on your way?"

"Only if you hurry as promised," she teased. "Dally and you will find yourself barred from our bed…and I may leave without waiting for your gifts."

After kissing her mouth, satisfied that she did not suspect his fears, Kjell strode from the room to see to the carriage and gifts…and to again discuss his concerns with General Stone. If trouble was brewing, he hoped his general had been able to ferret out some nugget of evidence to either prove him right or prove him paranoid. The sooner trouble was extinguished, the sooner he could unite with his wife and son in Rhidam, the sooner he would be satisfied for their safety and the security of Neth.

Though she had hoped to be instructed in the use of the rynlagne, Kavan took them through it so swiftly that Raebhá barely had time to take a breath and notice the connecting points of light he had spoken of before finding herself in the center of an expansive entry hall of a building that felt older to her than the Alberni estate. The hall was adorned with crimson, cobalt, and amber, the colors Merrek had adopted upon his inheritance of the Fiara estate from his grandfather. She and Kavan stood in the open, upon a blood-red sun of marble inlaid on the floor, not in some small chamber or cupboard where she had come to expect Gates to be.

This was a richer home than Kavan's. Expensively adorned, richly constructed. Kavan looked at home here, and yet out of place at the same time as they paused to look and listen to the evening sounds around them.

Being just past the hour of the evening meal, there were noises from the dining room and the crackling evidence of a hearth fire to the side beyond a partially open door. There was no one to greet them, no one to surprise with their abrupt appearance in the room, but being suddenly exposed as they were, Raebhá grasped Kavan's arm with an unexpected rush of anxiety. He glanced at her with a reassuring nod and then led her into the room where the fire burned.

She was there. Kavan knew it. He worried for Gabrielle living alone, now that her grandson resided in Rhidam with his wife and son. Perhaps, Kavan mused as he stepped into the doorway to see her squatting upon the hearth tending the fire, he should invite her to Alberni, or encourage her to join Merrek in Rhidam or Piran on Káliel. The change was likely to do her, and Diona, much good, and seeing her youngest son would likewise be a balm.

He did not speak from the doorway until she realized she was not alone and looked up from the fire to see him in her home where he had not been in many weeks.

"Kavan. This is a surprise." Her smile faltered when she noted the woman behind him, someone unfamiliar whose hand was wrapped around his arm. Seeing the stranger was less surprising than the anxious handhold that Kavan seemed not to object to.

"I apologize for the late hour," he said with a bow, stepping away from Raebhá's hand when he realized Gabrielle had made note of it.

Raebhá side-eyed him curiously.

"You know you never need to apologize for coming here. Owain and Merrek both made you welcome…as do I. And it is not so late. Come. Sit by the fire and warm yourselves."

It was a tempting invitation, but one Kavan was not comfortable accepting now that he was here. "We have not come to infringe on your hospitality. We need your Gate…but I did not want to use it without visiting first." She looked weary, older than he thought she should, than she had when he had last seen her weeks before. Teren with Elyri blood were affected differently, some exhibiting strong Elyri traits, others exhibiting none. Gabrielle's gifts had faded with age, and now Elyri longevity appeared to be failing. "Are you well?"

"Always worrying, Kavan." Since he had not come into the sitting room, she went to him. "Who is your friend?" The woman had to be a friend, possibly something more, though Gabrielle expected Kavan to deny that if she asked.

"Apologies." He bowed again, his voice shaky, embarrassed that he had not already made that introduction. "This is Lady di Curnydhá. Raebhá, this is Gabrielle Dilyn-Lachlan, a longtime friend."

Both women made note of the last name of the other and Kavan shuddered as they visually assessed one another. "My lady," Raebhá murmured, giving the woman a bow, acknowledging whatever status her name conferred while hiding both the question, and the understanding, of what this woman was, or had been, to Kavan.

"Welcome."

"I am escorting her home…"

"That requires use of my Gate? Not yours?" His hasty interruption made Gabrielle smile as it supported her suspicion that this was a relationship he did not want to be known, one he was not entirely comfortable with. He was no stranger to passion, he could not be if he had fathered a son, but Gabrielle had seen often how expressions of passion and affection made the bard uncomfortable.

Confirming his embarrassment, Kavan lowered his gaze. "There are…this Gate is one of a few that have access to places that most others do not," he explained.

"Places beyond the Sovereignties?" She assumed he meant the southern lands, or perhaps somewhere within the great Cíbhóló desert, though the other copper-haired woman did not appear native to the Cíbhóló tribes. But there were cities rumored to be beyond the desert, so she might have come from there, if such places existed.

"Yes." It was the most he was willing to reveal.

"Surely you have time to share a drink…raisin pudding perhaps? Rooms for the night? It is too dark to travel…"

"It will be dark whatever hour we choose," Raebhá said without explaining. It was a detail she had not considered relevant before now.

The disclosure made Kavan frown but not as much as when she said, "I would like to try this pudding. Surely we have time?" If home was on the other side of this Gate, a short delay for this visit, another hour or two in Kavan's company, would be worth sharing the offered hospitality.

Against his better judgment, Kavan sighed. He did not understand the argument of darkness, realized now the awkwardness that being caught between these women would cause, but as it had been his choice to announce their arrival to Gabrielle, it was his burden to honor her hospitality. If he had not considered staying in this house overnight, if the Gate failed, he knew he should have waited to depart Alberni in the morning.

That Gabrielle avoided his questions regarding her welfare was another cause that bid him return to the sitting room and take a place before the fire as she had originally offered, leaving his pack with Raebhá's at the threshold.

Servants were summoned and returned moments later with bowls of savory bread sweetened with raisins and drenched with sugared cream. Gabrielle added a splash of rum to hers from a bottle kept on the mantle, where Owain had always kept his favorite liquor, but she did not offer any to her guests. Elyri did not drink, and she was confident this stranger was also Elyri.

Raebhá brought the spoon of sweets to her lips, tasted it, and smiled. Kavan smiled too.

"How fares Merrek?" Gabrielle asked, turning the silence to a topic of conversation that Kavan would not avoid.

"He is well, as are Arlana and Lorant. Being regent suits him."

She smiled. "We knew it would. How could it not? His blood and upbringing guarantee his success."

"Thank you." It was a compliment he felt worth acknowledging, though he did not think Merrek's success would be solely due to the years he had mentored Muir's son. "He has many good voices to guide him." He did not need Kavan's amongst them to succeed.

"Lady Raebhá? Have you come from business in Rhidam?"

The question was innocent on the surface, and not so innocent underneath, and Gabrielle's smile was neutral and friendly despite Kavan's scowl. Her intentions rarely slipped past him. Nor did Raebhá misinterpret her interest or intent and Gabrielle could not help but smile more sincerely when the woman replied, "An accident stranded me in Alberni, but I am recovered and fit to travel home."

"Lord Cliáth's generosity to those in need is well known. His is the most generous soul in the Sovereignties. You could have found no better benefactor to see to your recovery."

"He found me," Raebhá said just as warmly, confident that at one time Lady Dilyn had loved Kavan. Perhaps she still did, although Kavan did not appear to share her affection. He cherished Gabrielle, considered her a dear friend, but Gabrielle was no threat in the way Ombhrís would be if he lived. "I was indeed fortunate, and am all the more so that he is willing to spare me a too-long journey home."

"You did not travel by Gate then?"

Raebhá shook her head. "That is one skill I have not learned, but I pray he will teach me before we part ways." She turned her beseeching eyes onto Kavan but quickly looked back at Gabrielle with a more neutral expression.

"He is the best teacher in Enesfel, regardless of the matter." Gabrielle had seen it with Diona, with Muir, with Merrek, with Yóáná and all of those Kavan had mentored. Amused by his discomfiture, she smiled. "He'll never admit it, but if anyone can teach you, it is him." Before he could interrupt, she continued, "Have you brought your harp? Would you be willing to share a song or two before you go?'

The shift from flattery, from the two women talking about him as if he was not in the room, was welcome. "I did. I will play if you wish." Doing so would prevent further awkward conversation, he hoped, and so he retrieved the red kestrel harp and returned to the cushioned stool where he had been.

Seeing him play in this more intimate setting instead of the oratory or the Great Hall of the Lachlan Castle was a gift Raebhá had longed for since waking to the notes of his harp. This instrument was exquisite too, a replica or duplicate of the black one; the sound of the brass strings was much the same. The notes beneath his fingers were delicate, tender and warm, coming as if of their own choice without thought or planning by the man responsible for them.

With his eyes closed, he surrendered to the muses, giving them, and his deepest thoughts and feelings, a voice that only he could give. His calm serenity, the procession of notes melding one tune seamlessly into another, the underscoring of passion, were things Raebhá felt as well as heard and it birthed a need to give him herself and never withdraw. The tales of a Cliáthan's quality were well-founded, but this beauty was not created by the harp alone. This beauty that filled her senses so that she was drowning in it was all Kavan's, and the love and sorrow in her breast swelled until it spilled into tears on her cheeks.

Gabrielle, though keenly aware of the effect Kavan's music could have, was unprepared for the fire it lit within her, a longing she had not felt since before Owain had fallen too ill to fill it. It did not surprise her to witness the music's effect on Raebhá, for what listener had not been moved to tears by the notes Kavan offered? Those notes, the realization that the voice of passion and longing was Kavan's, were an astonishing admission of feelings he could not otherwise confess, and as Gabrielle watched first his face, and then Raebhá's, she understood. This was a shared, forbidden passion. After so many years of life alone save for the great love he had born Wortham, Kavan had finally found one with whom he could share his soul…but for whatever reason, it was a sharing that could never be fulfilled or sustained. He had lost Wortham. He expected to lose this too.

Gabrielle's heart broke for him.

That he was able to deliver Raebhá somewhere against his heart's wishes explained the underlying melancholy that gave rise to the droplets clinging to his lashes. His pain fed hers but Gabrielle stubbornly wiped her tears away with a hand to her damp cheeks. Eventually, she closed her eyes to witness his private pain no longer, except through the notes he played.

Soon, however, she opened them again when a hand covered hers. The music still played, Kavan singlehandedly producing notes while he offered the comfort of his touch, seeking the cause of her sadness, understanding the loss of Owain, the loss of a child, in a way that others might not. She forced a smile as she withdrew her hand but the moment of touch was enough to tell Kavan things she had not said.

There was no illness here, no creeping advance of age, but for the first time in their years of acquaintance, she was accepting that when he left, she might not see him again. He had always come back to her, time after time over the years, but this time felt different. She believed it, and through that belief, Kavan believed it as well.

The music faltered. He stopped playing and stared into the dying fire, both hands unmoving on the strings when Raebhá opened her eyes to look at him. With no knowledge of what had passed between Kavan and Gabrielle, she was still certain that the impending weight of another farewell was crushing his tender spirit.

With the fire nearly out, Gabrielle knew more time had passed in music than Kavan had expected to give. It was nearing midnight she judged, and the servants had collected the empty bowls and taken her glass away without interruption. His music had entranced them all, and despite the sadness she carried, she felt content. It was the sort of parting gift that only the White Bard could give.

He remembered tales of this city, tales Kavan had told during their too brief time together, tales of a grandeur outmatched only by the Elyri capital of Clarys where he had yet to go. Though the darkness robbed Rhidam of some of the majestic impressions he might have had of her, the flicker of candlelight behind the colored glass windows of the náos before him was remarkable enough to suggest what the rest of the city must be like. Kavan had found such grandeur cold and unsettling, preferring instead the simplicity of the massive structure Myreth had called home. Since leaving Gorbesh, since traveling the lands in search of the man who had opened his eyes and impacted his soul, Myreth had grown to love the complexities of a world he had never known existed. How could Kavan prefer simplicity to this? How could anyone think that k'Ádhá wanted man to live in poverty, isolation, and simplicity when the world offered so much more?

Why had Qol denied him this for so many years?

In the glow of the full moon, he glanced at the rolled parchment she had given him, reading the directions again though he did not need to. He knew them by heart now, knew where he was to room and await his benefactor's instructions. Faith had led him here, faith and the certainty that what he was to do was necessary. k'Ádhá would never stand for such an artifact falling into the hands of the unfaithful. He had been charged with securing it, making certain it was delivered to where it would be safeguarded for all time. The prospect of finding the White Bard again, after so many years of near despair in seeking him, lit a fire in Myreth's soul and turned him away from the naós in search of the establishment known as the Eagle's Nest. There would be a bed there, a warm meal despite the hour, and money with which to survive until further instruction arrived.

But if Kavan was here, as so many voices on his journey suggested he should be, that was all the payment Myreth needed.

He missed his pale twin too dearly to need anything more than seeing him again.

❧*❧

"Do not risk your life heedlessly," Kavan murmured, he and Raebhá again standing at the center of the crimson sun, the tingle of the Gate's energy beneath his feet pricking his senses. Both were dressed in every layer of clothing they had brought, though it was not cold enough in Fiara to warrant it, and Gabrielle wondered where they expected to go that required such protection. Kavan read the questions on her face as she handed him an additional bundle of food from her larder, food he hoped he would not need. He would return it to her, if he could, knowing that she, like every other person in Enesfel, was rationing what they had until the dearth was behind them. He would not, however, attempt to answer her questions since he did not understand the need for such protection.

He could have gleaned glimpses of their destination from Raebhá's mind but he refused to try. The less he knew, the less real the inevitable moment of parting would be.

"They are my people now; Fiara is my home. I do no more than you would, if you were in my place," Gabrielle responded with a dismissive wave. "Every precaution is being taken, I assure you."

"I do not want to return and learn that plague has taken you."

Gabrielle, her most persuasive smile in place, one that had once made Kavan cower and blush with awkward desire, said, "No plague will claim me. I will not permit it. Raebhá, I pray we meet again when we shall have more time to talk."

Her words, rather than her smile, brought a deeper flush to Kavan's face. Raebhá grinned, understanding the teasing, and replied, "I welcome that day, Gabrielle. Please, see to your welfare until we meet once more. I shall pray for your health." Plague was a danger she understood, and if Gabrielle was exposing herself to it for the care of her people, prayers for her safety were necessary, whether the ágdháthé listened or not.

"And I will pray for yours." She kissed Kavan's cheek, a lingering kiss of farewell that again caused the bard to lower his gaze. "Thank you, Kavan, for coming tonight."

"Thank you for welcoming us…and for your amity." Their long-held friendship, despite its initial awkwardness, was one Kavan would always cherish. So much would have been different without her in his life. Without her, Arlan might not have become king. Without her, there would have been no Wortham. Both Kavan and Enesfel owed her a debt that no evening of music could repay. He prayed that his gratitude was enough for her.

As she smiled and stepped out of the circle of power that was Fiara's only Gate, Kavan took Raebhá's hands, his eyes locked on Gabrielle's, and sent a heartfelt request to Kóráhm that the saint would protect her while Kavan was gone.

He had every intention of seeing her again.

❧*❧

A noise, distant and out of place, the sound of boots on stone and the drawing of metal from leather, brought Kjell abruptly awake. The jarring of the bed roused Asta, but before she could question him, he pressed his fingers to her lips. Though he did not hear the sound again, nor any other night sound that was unusual for the castle and the city outside, the heaviness of dread and expectation would not leave him.

"Go," he hissed. "Take our sons…get them out of Glevum."

"Kjell?" Asta understood the warning and was moving without further explanation. She had not heard whatever had startled him, but she felt the danger in the charged air as soon as she awoke. It was a skill her father had been unable to teach, a sense that each person had to develop on their own, but it was one that any member of the Association, or anyone in league with them, developed quickly to survive. If they did not, they died. For the Dugans from Durham, it was a sense and skill that seemed as innate to them as breathing. She snagged her cloak from the bedpost and wrapped it around herself. "I will not leave you…"

"Keep our sons safe. I will join you…send word when it's clear."

The war between instincts swayed her in favor of his instruction, in favor of her sons. Moving to Neth, even with Kjell as king, had come with inherent risks. Perhaps, she often mused, it was those risks as much as their mutual affection and desire for family that had drawn her here. After all, once the Corylliens were purged from Rhidam and peace was restored, the day-to-day life of Inquisitor had offered considerably less excitement than Asta had become accustomed to.

She would rather stay and fight this unknown with her husband, but Jerit was too young to defend himself. Oska would have Inness and his personal guards, as well as his own skill, as limited as that might be, to keep him safe. Like Asta, Inness knew the feel of a sword in her hand. The two could fight together in defense of their family. Jerit was not old enough to do likewise. Asta would gather them and get them to safety and trust that Kjell would see to his own.

Oska and Inness were not in their chambers and she could not spare the time to look for them. In the main corridors of the castle, she could hear shouting, running, the clamor of weapons as she crept hastily through the secret passages Kjell had shown her. Before making it to Jerit's room, the boy appeared in the passage before her, visibly shaken in the light of the candle he carried.

"Mother…?"

She grabbed his free hand. "Stay quiet." She wondered if the carriage was packed for the morning's departure as Kjell had intended and if she could reach it before the chaos overtook them.

Sword in hand, Kjell threw open his door to come face to face with his eldest son and a handful of men, Oska's personal guard, familiar faces but not part of his inner circle of guards. The men who should have been keeping watch at his door lay bleeding on the stones at the threshold. Expecting that Oska was there to warn him, help him, he cried, "What is happening?" before the young man and the guards pushed him back into his bed-chamber. The commotion further down the corridor, men in arms locked in combat, suggested an invasion or some assault upon the royal family being handled by his loyal forces. His glimpse of them was brief, the push causing him to stumble. His effort to right his balance was met by a knife thrust into his belly.

The face twisted by anger and now horror at his own actions hissed, "I am taking what you seek to deny me…father."

Down stairs, through more dark hidden passages, and always the sounds of fighting in the rooms and corridors they fled past. So many combatants suggested an uprising and the growing distance between her and Kjell filled Asta with a burgeoning fear for his safety. But it was Jerit she had to think about, and when they reached the door that would bring them out of the castle not far from the stables, Asta forced herself not to turn back. Jerit was a good horseman but he would never survive on his own in the night, not if there were forces intent on taking the de Corrmick throne.

She had to believe that the fighting she heard was loyalists putting an uprising in its place.

She listened with the door cracked open and heard no combat nearby. "When I open the door…run to the stable. As fast as you can. We will take a horse…" There was no time to fuss with the carriage. A single horse would be faster.

"Father…Oska…?"

"Your father is taking care of Oska. They will join us in Fiara."

That would be the best place to meet, although Kjell had not said it. It was many days ride from Glevum, but it would be a haven. Part of Enesfel now, it was beyond the reach of anyone in Neth who wished them harm. "They'll be fine. Now…ready…run!"

She threw open the door and sprinted towards the stable, Jerit's hand clutched in hers, the candle he had been holding dropped on the stone floor in the passage that she slammed closed behind them.

"Oska?" Confused, gasping in agony, Kjell sank to the floor, staring wide-eyed at the face of a son he no longer knew. The young man stepped back, struck by the betrayal on Kjell's face, the betrayal of love, the revulsion of the blood on his hands.

His father's blood.

Sickened by what he had done, Oska bumped into someone behind him and breathed with a flash of relief to find his wife there. She would know what to do to fix this.

The relief lasted only as long as it took to make note of her dispassionate regard as she stared at the man at their feet. "Away, husband. I will take care of this."

Oska did not give thought to what she meant. The stain on the front of his father's shirt was spreading and with the bile surging into his throat, Oska pushed back through the guards gathered around him and ran as fast as his uneven legs would allow, back to his room where he could be sick in private.

Asta swung open the stall with one hand and untied the roan's halter with the other as Jerit climbed onto the animal's broad back. He was barely settled before his mother was behind him, kicking the horse into motion. Voices rose after them but Asta made no effort to determine if they were friendly, whether they were pursuing her or urging her to safety. The horse galloped through the open palace gates, into Glevum's streets, and towards the open countryside south of Neth's seat of power. She shut the tumult within the castle out of her ears, out of her thoughts, and focused on one thing, getting Jerit away. Only when that was done would she look back…and wonder about the family she was leaving behind.

What he saw in her eyes, a cold, calculated lust for dominance, was something Kjell knew he should have long ago expected from her. Inness was no Lachlan. Not in her heart, not in her soul. If anything, Inness was more de Corrmick in the fashion of the old kings, more than Kjell, or Oska, would ever be.

"I should have known it would be you," he croaked, struggling to rise, determined to meet this woman on his feet.

Inness swung, something heavy in her hand that he did not see until too late, and with a blinding eruption of pain above his ear, Kjell crumbled to the floor and did not move.

*

The connection came more easily than expected, those unexplored points of contact brighter this night as though Raebhá's hands in his were magnifying them. Certain that their brilliance meant his suspicions were correct, that success would shortly be his, he reached through an unexpected chaotic burst of static power at his center, for the brightest point, hoping that such brilliance implied a Gate most often, or most recently, used.

The darkness of that static, the chaos behind it, revealed a horror that pulled against Kavan as he caught the connection and pulled towards it, dragging like an anchor in the mud against a powerful current. It took all of his strength to complete the process, leaving nothing to shield himself from a gnashing pain in his belly and head that made him scream and collapse into Raebhá's arms.

❧239❧

# Part 2

❧Chapter 15❧

The scream was ripped from his lips by the force of frigid wind when the Gate deposited Kavan and Raebhá in a snow-filled basin crested on three sides by jagged peaks raking the black sky with ice-encrusted fingers. Those were details Kavan could not absorb as the psychic pain piercing his head and clawing through his abdomen continued despite the now-distant origin of the event that precipitated it. The intensity was enough to blur both physical and psychic vision, to rob his legs of strength, so that he was only capable of clinging to the woman with him and gasping for gulps of glacial air.

"Kavan!" With his arms around her neck and one of hers around his body, Raebhá struggled to keep them both from falling into the deep snow or sliding down the embankment as she brushed his hair from his face and tried to read his thoughts, ascertain what was wrong. There were too many layers of clothing to see any injuries, but his agony was visible in his twisted, distorted features.

Believing his condition to be the result of the Gate, remembering how long he believed she had been unconscious when he found her, she scanned the horizon for anywhere that could provide decent shelter. There was little to be seen, only a rocky outcropping to the north that could protect them from the northern gale and the high eastern slope of the bowl, should snow and ice break free and slide.

Half dragging the stumbling man towards shelter took longer than she wanted and her lungs ached from the effort to breathe the too-thin, icy oxygen. She should cover her mouth and nose, should cover his, but her focus was getting him to shelter. There were no timbers to burn for a fire at this altitude and she could not judge if he was conscious enough, capable enough, to regulate his body temperature. She did not know if it was a skill he knew. Her best option was to move as far back into the sheltering outcropping as possible, kick away the snowdrift from the rocky ground, and pull him against her. With the canvas sheet they had brought and long folds of both multilayered cloaks wrapped around them, their heads covered in fur-lined hoods, she turned her core temperature as high as she dared. Willing to hold him that way for as long as it took, willing to expend her limited energy to keep him alive, she watched him fight through whatever he was enduring and wished she could take it away.

Where in the name of Dhágdhuán were they?

At Princess Arlana's bedside, Ártur's knees buckled, throwing him to the floor. He hit the corner of the nightstand, clutching his head between his hands, grimacing and growling at the unexpected burst of pain and fiery power that came down like a hammer behind his eyes. Syl yelped in surprise and turned to help him, leaving Yóáná and Physician Talis to ease the woman's labor. The lady healer's fingers brushed against her husband's bloody temple but he swept her hand away, though not before she healed the gash there. Her efforts did not ease the pain, but as the seconds rushed past, the threads between the source of it and the healer stretched until they snapped, leaving him briefly blind with the flash of power released in that severing.

"What is it?"

Ártur shook his head and allowed Syl to help him up. The source was Kavan. Something bad had happened. To his cousin? To someone near his cousin? From the distance between them, a distance along the binding threads too great to gauge, he guessed that Kavan had gone through the Gate to a place no Elyri living had ever been, and he prayed that agony was not the result of some horrible death met on the other side of it. For the moment, he believed Kavan lived. Until he learned otherwise, the princess and the child she was about to bring into the world were more important. There was nothing he could do for Kavan, but he could help Princess Arlana.

❧*❦

Kavan rolled towards the warmth. It smelled pleasant, of almond blossoms and the sea and fragrant pines like those rimming the Alberni estate. Burying his face in that scent soothed him, soothed the screaming in his skull and the slicing ache in his stomach. Wortham. It had to be Wortham. He could not yet think, could not adequately gauge his surroundings, but he was warming now, the chill in the air melting away, and that helped center the power that had burst and been sucked from him minutes before.

❧*❦

Asta kept the horse off the main road, intending not to be seen as the animal slowed, its heaving sides speaking of impending collapse if she pushed on. They were not far enough from Glevum, had not yet reached the outskirts of Gorea where she hoped she would be safe long enough to rest and find her son food and drink. Jerit, frightened and weary, clung to her, silently shaking against her. They would need rest and succor, but they could not dally in any one place for long if they were to reach Fiara in a timely manner. Not knowing what had happened behind them, Asta was leery of relying on those she normally trusted and leery of stopping too long. But the horse could not continue without rest and their current crawling pace would be a detriment if they had been followed.

A little further, she decided, patting the animal's neck reassuringly, choosing to accept a slow pace for now while being extra diligent to the noises of the night. With luck, the horse would get its second wind by the time flight was again necessary. A little further to Gorea and she would seek the only shelter she believed she could make use of. If anyone was going to protect the Queen of Neth and her son, it would be the Association. The name Dugan would guarantee it.

❧*❦

Wiping his hands on a cloth stained with a collection of bodily fluids, Ártur emerged from Arlana's chamber, weary but with a satisfied light in his eyes that masked his lingering pain. The prince stopped pacing and took the healer tightly by both arms while behind him, near the window, Diona sat on a bench with her back against the wall and Bhyrhán at her side clutching her hand. Níkóá rocked on his heels, hands behind his back near the door into the corridor, doing his best to patiently wait for news.

"How…?"

"The princess and child are well, My Prince. Both are resting. There were no complications…you have a son."

"A son!" he spun and pulled Diona up into his embrace, spinning her around with delight. "A son!"

"You are blessed," the woman said, kissing his cheeks, smiling with equal joy that her daughter was well. Having lost her mother to childbirth complications, having been with Arlana through miscarriages and the loss of another child during birth, the ordeal was always terrifying for Diona. She wondered how she had lived through the births of two sons and two daughters, and how her youngest had successfully survived to have children of her own. Sometimes she attributed that survival to Kavan, but realistically, he had nothing to do with it. Nor had he been here this time to secure Arlana's life and that of the newborn prince.

"He is to be christened Conroy Owain in two days. His name is already decided. Lord Chamberlain, you will see to the details? Take the news to k'dedhá Tusánt so the people will know."

"Isn't that premature, My Lord?" the healer began.

"You said he is healthy and well. He is, isn't he?"

"He is."

"Then it is hardly premature. With the goodwill of the people behind him, he will live a long, healthy life. I wish to see them."

"As soon as…"

The door between chambers opened and Syl, ignoring her husband's scowl, motioned the monarch into the room where his wife held their tawny-haired son. The infant flexed his fingers and yawned, smacking his lips and trying to wiggle free of the binding blankets. Physician Talis and Yóáná directed the midwives in the gathering of soiled towels and bowls of dirty water to dispose of.

"Ártur needs his rest." Syl hooked her arm around her husband's and bowed to the queen without explanation. There was a trace of bruising and blood on the side of his head though she noticed that he kept that injury to the side so that no one in the room could see it. She did not expect him to speak of the mishap, but she did want him to have some quiet rest to recover. Such an episode was not like him.

Odds were, it hinged on Kavan, k'Ádhá protect him, wherever the bard happened to be. "Summon us if we are needed."

"Thank you, Syl…we shall." With three healers and a physician at court, there was always healing available and everyone knew that Yóáná, as Arlana's friend, would stay with her through the night and the next few days as she recovered and the child learned to nurse. If Prince Conroy survived, it would be Yóáná's doing.

❧*❧

Despite the pounding in his head, Kavan forced his eyes open and rolled onto his back, realizing that the embracing warmth he recalled had either been imagined or else was now gone. Despite his hazy memory, he knew now it had not been Wortham at his side. The world was dark, the only evidence he had of the passage of time was the stillness in his core and the stable power within. He struggled to sit, his belly burning with the memory of a blade's cut, but analysis of his clothing and then the skin beneath revealed no wound.

The Sight then, or else something passing through the bond that held him to the Lachlan monarchs. He had not yet, he realized, bonded his pendant, his force, to Prince Merrek, so there was no way to know, to guess, whether Diona or Merrek had been the one injured. It was either that, feeling some wound experienced by one of them, or else the Sight revealing a glimpse of something that had happened, or would happen, but not enough of a glimpse to tell him who was injured or where it had occurred. He believed the moment had been intensified by accessing the power needed to operate this Gate, greater power than typically necessary to make a connection and travel through. He felt no Gate now and detected none within the range of his senses, but he did not recall having moved far from their arrival point. Any Gate, even one with a single point of exit should have a signature of power, but he felt nothing.

Had he unwittingly created one or was he too weak to feel it?

"Where are…?" he mumbled to the air, rubbing his eyes, assuming without testing that he was not alone.

"Kavan." The nearby silhouette against a wall of white snow returned to kneel beside him. When she brushed his hair from his face, he pressed his cheek against her hand without thinking. "Judging by the stars, we are where we should be…within reason. It is morning…"

"It is…"

"The northland ghísaer know darkness most of the winter. The sun shows over the horizon near midday for an hour or so and then sinks again. The moon is out; it and the stars will guide us when you're ready to travel." Raebhá pressed her hand to his forehead as if seeking a fever; he fought to rise but found that, while his core was stronger, his body was not. "What happened?"

"llánec."

"llán…you mean llónec." She blinked and fell back to sit on the ground. "You are a Seer?"

"I…" He disliked being called that, but there were few other appropriate words to use. He made note of the variation in the word before speaking again. "I am sometimes shown things…know them before they happen, or as they happen…the way I knew I would find you at the lake. Someone is injured…" He fingered his stomach through his many layers of clothing. "I don't know who…whether it was here…or there…I do not know if it was a fatal wound…but I felt as if it happened to me. That often implies the other individual is someone I know…someone I am close to."

Once it had been Arlan whose injuries he had felt. It could now be Prince Merrek or the queen. Or perhaps Ártur. Speculation, however, was not going to help. He did not know. He had to hope, assume, that whoever it had been, they lived.

He looked at her, expecting disbelief or the sort of awe and reverence that often came when others learned how different Kavan was. Instead, her fingers followed his, testing the soundness of his flesh, seeking bleeding she did not find. He shivered and caught her hand, holding it there rather than removing it.

"You seem whole," she murmured, relieved to find him so, relieved that he seemed to have no memory of the night spent in her arms. Whatever he had experienced, it had left no physical trace. "How will you know…will you need to return…to help…?"

"I am no healer; there will be nothing I can do." Enough time had passed that if the injury had happened at the same time he had felt it, if it had been a fatal one, the recipient was beyond his help.

"You want to be there, to know." She would want it if she was in his place. "When you are ready, we will go, find a Gate and…"

"Are we near your home?"

She shook her head. "We're too far north. By the stars, I think we'll have to go north to find the nearest ghís; north should be the shortest path out of the mountains. When we reach the coast, we'll find a vessel to take us south to Gálínphel, unless you find another Gate."

Dreading the thought of a sea journey more than a trek through the cold and snow, Kavan closed his eyes, focused on the power inside, and reached outward, seeking any point that might indicate a Gate. What he found, after many minutes of concentration, did not feel like the signature power of a Gate but it was power nonetheless. He could not be certain of the source, but it would serve as a beacon to guide them north, using the hope that power also meant civilization.

"There is something…northeast of us. I don't believe it is a Gate, but it might be of use…might be a dwelling and people." It might be the one they had recently traveled through, as he remembered little of their arrival except for pain.

"Northeast." She scowled. He did likewise. Offering her hand as she stood, she murmured, "Come. See."

With her assistance, Kavan made it to his feet and stiffly trudged to the edge of their sheltered outcropping. The wind was biting cold and he impulsively wrapped his arms around himself. Turning in the direction of the power source revealed a foreboding peak that stretched several hundred feet above them. Slowly he turned his head, then his body, drawing his senses in an arc to study where they were.

Like the Llaethlágárá that served as the border separating Elyria from Enesfel and Neth, these crags, the ones on three sides of them and the range that spread east and south as far as he could see in the moonlight, were sharp, uneven, unfriendly, the sort not easily passed on foot and impossible to pass with a wagon or most pack animals. The bowl upon whose edge they stood spread to the east and looked to be the only direction they could travel without climbing gear.

"Where did we…?"

Raebhá pointed into the snowy bowl; he followed the direction with outstretched power but detected nothing there. If there had been a Gate there before, it was there no longer. How that could be possible was a mystery he did not have the time to investigate.

Survival meant getting out of the mountains. Mysteries of power would have to wait.

"Can you fly?"

After a moment of deciphering his intention, she shook her head. She had only ever taken the shape of a wolf. "I have never tried…and my reserves were spent keeping you warm." The last was added sheepishly and she did not look at him as she said it.

"I can warm myself…"

"You were in no state to do anything last night."

From what Kavan recalled of the emergence through the Gate, of stumbling through snow, and from the general weakness of his body, he knew she spoke the truth. If he was honest, flight would not yet be easy for him either. He would have to regain strength before he could consider flight to be an option.

"Then we eat…and walk." They could wait here until he recovered, but that could be many hours away and Kavan preferred to reach that power source before the weather turned foul. He had never been in a place as cold as where he stood, had never imagined a place where the sun failed to shine, where there was no day. What kind of world did she live in, he mused, digging through the pack Gabrielle had given them to present now-frozen bread and cheese?

He cupped first the bread, and then the cheese, in his palms, warming the meal until it was soft enough to break and eat, and then gave portions to her and took some for himself.

What kind of world was this that the k'elyryhánag had been forced to leave behind?

He conserved strength by not speaking, and when they had eaten enough to dull the pangs of hunger, they began the awkward hike over the frozen snow towards the bowl's edge. It was not a difficult trek thus far, but Kavan suspected the journey would grow more treacherous, more dangerous, when they were forced to climb, up or down, to proceed.

Kóráhm, stay with us, he thought, wrapping the scarf around his face as Raebhá had done and studying the stars as he followed her. It would do him well to memorize their positions if he was to rely on them for direction and the telling of time. Should anything happen to Raebhá before they were free of these mountains, Kavan would have to find their way on his own.

᠀*᠀

"Come, Jerit." Asta slid off the horse and caught her son as he dropped sleepily into her arms. They were still dressed in their nightclothes and were barefoot beneath the cloaks both had been wise enough to grab when the commotion descended on the de Corrmick castle. They had no coin, only the horse and Asta's sword. The horse might provide enough bartering wealth to purchase clothes and have money for a few meals, but they would need the animal if they were to reach Fiara. It was too far from Gorea to walk.

Giving up their only means of protection was out of the question.

The seaside city's sleepy streets had yet to stir, but the hopes that they would find someone who could help kept Asta moving, guiding the horse with one hand on its reins, the other arm around Jerit's shoulders. Keen eyes, use to the clues of the street, sought details that could keep them safe, and in time, as they trudged, she found the tavern she sought, the golden light of a fire and the aroma of baking bread spilling into the pre-dawn street.

The North Star.

The Association frequented here.

"We're not open," called the woman behind the counter without looking up from her early morning duties.

"Please…my son needs somewhere to sit by the warmth of a fire…we have ridden all night…may we…?"

The pale, round woman, her hair as pasty as her complexion, looked up, took stock of what little they wore, and scowled. She seemed disinclined to allow them to enter, until she caught Asta's discreet hand gesture that prompted her to open the door. "Ethenae, no one should travel at night like that," she said, making a show of her words and actions in case anyone nearby questioned her generosity. "Come…to the fire with you both."

She shooed them towards the center of the room where a fire pit provided warmth. They sat on the raised stone hearth where Asta could keep an eye on the tethered horse, and several minutes later, the woman brought bread on a thin metal plate stained and dented from extensive use and warm tea in equally battered metal cups.

"Looking for the Three-Eyed Urchin," Asta murmured.

"Not in yet…but might be later. What happened?"

"Trouble…in Glevum." It was true enough, while vague, to suffice as an answer.

Thankfully, she did not seem to recognize Asta, nor the prince, nor their royal status, only the Association signals and codes she used, which Asta decided was a blessing. If the de Corrmicks were at risk, it was wise to remain anonymous. Within the ranks of the Association, so long as one did not double-cross or betray another member, Asta expected to be safe.

She had contacts in Glevum but there had not been time to seek any of them, not when it had been necessary to get as far from the castle as she could before they were discovered. Asta shrugged, her expression wary, and their hostess decided not to push for details.

Asta knew Neth's history. Anyone storming the castle was after the king and his heirs. Unless his supporters, his soldiers, had repelled the attack, Kjell was dead, or soon would be. Most often when a Nethite king was deposed, his family was slaughtered to prevent a challenging claim to the throne and an attack on the usurper in return. She did not know of any others with valid claims, but that did not mean someone would not try to make one.

Her heart tried to seize in her breast and she fought to keep breathing as the worry for her family crowded around her more rational thoughts. It took all of her willpower to resist curling into a ball and giving in to distraught weeping.

She could not do that. Not with Jerit to protect. It was not her way.

She had to believe Kjell's forces were strong enough to protect him. If, by some horrible stroke of fate, they were not, Asta would find Oska and do whatever it took to put him on the throne in his father's place. She would do likewise for Jerit if that was her only option, if the traitors had gotten to Oska too.

Too tired to devour the offered meal, they nibbled and sipped, Jerit fighting to stay awake while Asta watched the early morning patrons trickle in. The weather had been kinder to Neth than to Enesfel, and so food had continued to be plentiful enough to send grain to aid the cities of northern Enesfel. It meant the people who came to eat were not yet lacking food and there was abundance enough to serve them.

Asta was grateful for that.

Most people ignored them, others looked at them with curiosity or suspicion, some with pity or loathing and some, thinking them beggars, left coins on the hearth between them. Though tempted to return the offerings, feeling above such charity, Asta decided not to. If the Association could not help them and they continued to hide their identities, they would need those coins to reach Fiara.

A balding man with scarred features and three fingers missing on his left hand dropped coins between them and put his hand on Asta's shoulder. When she met his gaze, she realized who he was with a start.

He pulled her up by the arm, a show for the guests who would surely think the fellow was buying her services. She managed to scoop up the coins and Jerit snatched both the sword and food she left behind. The man pushed her down at an empty corner table and by the time Jerit reached them, the balding man had dropped onto the bench opposite her with the table between them.

"Wallace…you got my message."

"Didn't expect a Dugan in a place like this…especially you," he muttered in a quiet voice. "What you doing here?" He looked her over, aware that her sword was aimed at his belly beneath the table. She had asked to see him, not the other way around, but he supposed being manhandled to the table was enough to make her cautious.

Wallace had served as one of her contacts sporadically during her years in Neth, bringing word, as a fence, of illegal merchandise, typically slaves, animals, or poisons, being smuggled in and out of Neth. Originally from Cordash, the man's career brought him to Glevum early in life and he had stayed for the opportunities it afforded. With both Gorea and Glevum being port cities, he spent a fair deal of time traveling between the two, wherever the demand for his talents, or the requests of Onea Pantel, took him.

When in Gorea, the North Star was his haven.

"We need clothes…a fresh horse…supplies to reach Fiara. Can you help us?"

He continued to study them and bobbed his head at the portly woman who came to serve him, a different woman than the one who had brought Asta and Jerit inside. He shooed her away after putting coins in her plump palm and smiled.

"Wallace," she growled.

"Yes, yes, I can do that. You a place to stay while I prepare?"

"No, this is an unexpected turn."

"So I see." He bobbed his head. "Need to get word to Glevum?"

"I need clothes, somewhere to sleep, provisions, and a horse," she hissed. She trusted him more than she trusted most other Association contacts, believed he would not betray her, but Wallace had never been the most punctual, straightforward of fellows. As an afterthought, not wanting to discourage any generosity he might provide, her expression and tone softened. "It has been a long, difficult night. If you can get me word from Glevum…let me know how things are there…"

Whether she wanted anyone to know she and Jerit were alive and safe would depend on the state of affairs in the castle.

"I'll send a runner. You can rest till they're back." He drank the watery ale he had ordered directly from the pitcher in several noisy gulps and then staggered to his feet, motioning for Asta to follow. "I know a place…not here, too many have seen you, but close."

If there was trouble in Glevum, she would want to stay hidden. The Association might be loyal to the Dugan name, but if anyone recognized her, one wrong word to one wrong person would mean trouble. Going underground was her best chance. "Come." The sun had risen and it was time to get out of sight. Wallace knew the place.

❧*❧

In a world of perpetual night, unsure of how long he had slept, Kavan's internal clock had no sense of how much time had passed. The trail the stars made across the sky, assuming they traveled at the same speed he was accustomed to, suggested the passage of the better part of a day. The moon had been visible when they started but disappeared not long after, just as the sun had done at the midday hour. It created a peculiar mauve and amber glow that faded directly into an orange and azure twilight before the world settled into black again.

As striking as the vision was, as fond as he was of the night, Kavan did not think he could get used to a world without a day.

He wondered what Wortham would have thought of this place.

Wortham should be here with him.

He and Raebhá journeyed east, leaving a trudging trail in the snow of the mountain bowl, until she pointed to a pass between peaks that looked as if it could lead them over the rim in the direction they wanted to go. They paused at the base of the pass to eat, to drink snow water melted in their hands, during that short period of partial daylight, and then they began their ascent, doing their best to ignore the painful ache of blisters and cramping muscles. Raebhá led, following the stars and Kavan's directions towards the source of distant power in the hopes that it would be a promising destination.

More familiar with this sort of travel than he was, she paused often, expecting to give him the chance to catch up to her relentless pace. But he was always close behind, more sure-footed than she expected, nearly matching her agility over rocks and snow. His determination compensated for his lack of familiarity with the terrain, and her show of high spirits encouraged him to press on, but after his recent collapse, she believed if he continued to push himself, he would be susceptible to another one.

They had to find shelter.

She smiled behind the scarf as her feet slipped and he caught her, offering a helpful hand. Alone, their chances of survival were slim. Together, she believed they could accomplish anything. He would continue with her until they found a Gate, or found civilization, until she was safe, and maybe even after that. She should encourage him to return to whoever had been hurt enough to cause him physical torment. She should encourage him to leave her. Someone needed him.

But as they struggled together through the snow up the steep, incline, she was grateful he was with her and admitted that, promises or no, his company was preferable to solitude and kept her thoughts focused forward instead of behind. Someone needed him, but she needed him too.

Fatigue and the strain of the unfamiliar altitude caught up to them and when she found a tunneled-out cave in the snow, still a long way from the summit of the pass, they took shelter within it. The wind blew harder, the sound it made as it pushed past the cave entrance was like an extended moan of pain and made them both shudder.

Kavan sank to the ground with a groan, pulled down the scarf, and rubbed his face to encourage feeling in his cheeks and forehead.

"You know these mountains?" They had not spoken since the hike began, had communicated via touch and hand gestures. Now he wanted to talk, to fill the intimate silence with something other than the longing to hold her.

How else was he to learn of this place if he did not ask?

Removing food from her pack, she handed it to him for thawing and then shoved her pack into place beside his. The bow clattered against the stones, unused thus far, as they had seen no animals. "Not this far north, but yes. Each of us, except the physically or mentally unable, undergoes a survival test when we come of age. The land is wild, the forests and mountains filled with beasts and other dangers; the knowledge to survive is needed if we are to prosper."

"Everyone? Surely there are some who never leave their villages, who do not brave the wilderness?" He flipped over the morsel of cheese in his hands to continue warming it.

"We often travel between ghísaer…for trade, for family, for festivals. Life is too long to remain confined to one place."

The corners of Kavan's mouth twisted in amusement. The majority of Elyri rarely traveled beyond the village, town, or city of their birth unless marriage compelled them. Some traveled to the major urban centers such as Clarys, or to neighboring centers of inhabitation, for trade or festivals, as Raebhá said, but they were a relatively small percentage of the population. Paths through their kingdom were ancient and well worn. Bandits were practically unheard of and assault by animals was equally rare. Few would brave those paths, however, preferring the comforts of civilization and familiar neighbors.

It was another reason why there was so little travel for Elyri across the Llaethlágárá. It was safer, easier, to stay home.

Perhaps after having journeyed so far to reach that new land, the desire to never travel again had become deeply ingrained in those ancient settlers who were their ancestors, and subsequent generations had taken the sedentary life to heart.

"You underwent the trial?" He handed her half of the meal and began to eat his own.

"Of course. Men undertake it in their twentieth year…women between their twentieth and thirtieth…when fertility begins. There are rituals beyond the test, measures to try our readiness to join the world of our elders. It's complicated, dangerous and stressful…but every year we look forward to the new initiates…to welcoming those who can provide into the embrace of adulthood."

"What if someone does not pass?

"Assuming they do not perish or aren't badly injured, they may undertake it the next year, and every year after until they do. The most tests I ever heard of were five. Most of us complete it on the first try as we are prepared for it from the time we stop being children." Seated across from him, legs outstretched so that her feet pressed against his knees, she took a bite and asked, "You don't have such challenges?"

One hand on her boot, an absent gesture of amity, he shook his head. "Children are taught to read, write, and count, to know history, from the age of six or seven; it usually lasts about seven years or until they enter an apprenticeship for a craft. Some become apprentices earlier and stop studying. Some continue to study for much longer."

"Do all children learn to use the power?" Dhóri and Sóbhán obviously had, but of the other Elyri she had met, she did not know if any but the healers had trained.

"Most are taught the basics; it's considered too dangerous not to be marginally trained. To remain untrained is considered a grave threat to others, although some refuse to train their children. It starts as we begin learning to read and write and count. Training can last as few as three years but most continue until they cease formal education. Some are fortunate to continue training as long as they wish, even past the age of needing their parents' permission."

Kavan, she presumed, was one of those fortunate few. "You had your parents' permission to…"

"My parents were lost when I was an infant…fire and plague. My aunt and uncle, Ártur's parents, served as guardians until I was old enough to take guardianship of myself. I trained and studied until there was nothing more for the bhydáni to teach me."

Thinking that meant his teacher had been of limited knowledge, not knowing how old he had been at that time and the alternative being too amazing to consider, she nodded. "Now you are the teacher, the scholar, a minstrel and advisor to the queen, and a duke."

Kavan started to speak and then scowled. "The last not by choice, but it affords me the freedom from worry about hunger or shelter for myself and my family."

"You're a man of many talents." Raebhá grinned, warmed by his embarrassment, and shifted to lie beside him, her belly satisfied with the meager meal. "We should sleep if we're to go on in the morning."

Was it night now? Would it be morning when they started again?

He had only her word to judge by.

He hesitated to lay beside her, her proximity unsettling now that his blush had settled low in his body. But the sharing of heat would make survival more certain; he had no desire to die here or to allow her to do so. He settled back, his pack beneath his head, and although he flinched when she snuggled closer, one arm over his stomach, he did not retreat. The comfort and welcome of her nearness, her offered warmth, were stronger than his awkwardness, and so with one arm, he pulled her closer while the other pushed beneath her until she was wrapped in his embrace where his heart felt certain she belonged.

❧Chapter 16❧

Saul Peado, a man of the sword who had come to serve Hes á Redh as protector to Rhidam's only Elyri gdhededhá, had remained on in the Faith, as had his fellow bodyguard Edward, to become gdhededhá themselves under Tusánt's leadership. With Rankin serving as primary dedhá now that Tusánt had been elevated to k'gdhededhá of all Enesfel, and a recently initiated gdhededhá named Caldar Cates, the Faith in Rhidam had thrived since the cessation of Coryllien violence. Many had come to serve as adjuncts, a need that increased as the onset of hunger brought misery to everyone in the kingdom. Together, Saul and Edward oversaw the choir and the management of festival Gatherings while Rankin managed the coffers and scheduled visits to sick parishioners throughout the náós' sphere of influence. It left Tusánt to the day-to-day running's, the business of Faith, and the relationships with other sees, particularly the one in Clarys with whom he struggled to find a bond, a door, for reunification.

But k'gdhededhá Tumm had no desire for reconciliation without concessions made by the Teren Faithful, the first among them being the expulsion of the White Bard from the Teren Faith. Tusánt could not, in good conscience, agree to that, but he continued to seek a way around that stipulation, believing that a unified Faith was best for all of the Sovereignties.

Many Faith leaders in Clarys were less convinced that this was so.

Saul and others stood behind their leader and few in Enesfel thought ill of the man fairly elected by a near-unanimous vote to lead them, and like the others who served in Rhidam, none found fault with

Lord Cliáth. The man had given too much of himself to the Faith, and to the Lachlans to deserve excommunication.

The morning service was over, leaving the Gathering Hall to be swept, the benches to be polished, the candles in the sconces to be replaced by a trio of adjuncts while Saul cleaned the holy chalice and refilled the sacred serbháló in preparation for the next Gathering. The sounds of the others working were comforting, normal and familiar, and he noticed at once when another set of footsteps joined the cacophony of chatter, moving benches, and shuffling feet. He closed the cabinet door and turned as the stranger, a blonde fellow carrying a large box covered with a cloth, reached the altar steps. His smile expressed no threat.

"Good day, dedhá. Might I have a word with k'dedhá Tusánt? I'm told he serves here still?"

"He does, but he is occupied. May I ask your name and purpose?"

"Cedric O'Grady…son of the late duke and brother of the current one," the stranger said with a bow made awkward by the item he carried. "Not that they know I'm here or care aught of my travels. My business is a private matter for the k'gdhededhá so I can wait for him. Do you think he'll be long?"

"I'll ask. Please, sit if you wish, Mr. O'Grady."

"Thank you." Cedric bowed.

When Saul returned several minutes later, he was not surprised to find the blonde standing where he had left him. Saul smiled and motioned for him to follow into the thóres. They passed several closed doors, wooden and plain in construction compared to the Gathering Hall they had left, all bearing locks that were deemed necessary in response to the violence of the Persecution. When they stopped before a partially open door, the sounds of movement behind it ceased as Saul raised his hand to announce his return.

"No need for that," the Elyri called with a chuckle before the knock came. "Please…come in."

Saul pushed the door with one hand but did not enter as he motioned Cedric through. Cedric passed, murmured his thanks, and cocked his head at the surprise of the door closing behind him. With so many anti-persecution precautions in place, he had not expected to be left alone in the room with the k'gdhededhá. After the martyrdom of Jermyn Tythilius, he had not expected to be trusted here.

No one had yet asked what he carried.

"Do you wish to sit, Mr. O'Grady? Saul says you have business?"

Tall and thin, the k'dedhá's face looked barely older than a boy's, with only his eyes revealing his age, wisdom, and a guarded sense of wariness as he adjusted the robe he had changed into and smoothed down his hair with one hand while studying his visitor and the covered box he carried. Cedric bowed at the question and nodded.

"I'm to deliver this to Alberni, to Lord Cliáth if he'll have it, or to St. Kóráhm's if he will not. I wish to pay my respects to the queen while I am here and believe Hes á Redh is the safest place to keep this while I do." He offered the covered box to the other man, holding it as if it was the most fragile, beloved item he possessed.

"What is it? May I?"

Cedric nodded and Tusánt lifted the cloth to peek beneath it. The box was glass on all sides except the bottom, its edges bound with gold seaming, the lid latched with a heavy iron lock. Inside, folded into multiple layers, was a charcoal gray bundle of fabric that looked of little import. It showed scorch marks along some of its edges, as if it had escaped a fire, and Tusánt guessed that there was other evidence of damage he could not see. There were no visible markings of identification, leaving Tusánt puzzled as to why the cloth was being treated with such caution.

"You are skeptical. I don't blame you. I was skeptical when I was asked to deliver this to Lord Cliáth. The fellow assured me of its authenticity, and with the miracles that have followed on my journey here from the desert, I believe this to be as claimed."

"A relic?" Making no effort to read the glass, Tusánt turned the box from side to side and raised it to look at the bottom.

"Healing mostly…water brought up from the rocks in a place that had not seen groundwater in years…the calming of a wild horse that crippled several who attempted to break it. I saw many of these things with my own eyes. There's no other explanation for them save miracles…and Lord Cliáth was nowhere nearby to have been the cause of such things. If anything were to cause such wonders, surely the mantle of Saint Kóráhm would."

Tusánt gaped. Stories of the Heretic-Saint's martyrdom told of his escape from the pyre on which he had been set alight. His followers had saved the mantle from the flames and spirited it, and his body, away. No one had seen the mantle, or the saint, again, although rumors of its existence and location had persisted. If anyone could verify its authenticity, it would surely be the man most closely associated with the Heretic-Saint.

"Lord Cliáth is not here," he whispered. His hands began to tremble so he put the box on his desk so he would not drop it.

"In Rhidam? Yes, I thought as much. I expect to find him in Alberni after I pay respects to the queen…"

"I am told Kavan is away on business of an indefinite nature…I do not know when he will return. But k'gdhededhá Khwílen will certainly keep it secure in the interim. I'm told there are many precious relics housed in St. Kóráhm's. Does anyone know what you…?"

Cedric shook his head with a grin, satisfied to be believed. "I've told no one as I've had no desire to create a pilgrimage of followers all the way to Alberni. Nor could I risk it being damaged or stolen."

"Indeed. I swear to you I will secure it while you call upon the queen, if that is your wish."

He wondered if he dared take it to Clarys for authentication. Given k'gdhededhá Tumm's opinions of Kavan and his patron, Tusánt thought it best not to. The mantle would likely be seized and then hidden away in one of Clarys' many vaults or else destroyed.

No, the best place for it, for now, was St. Kóráhm's.

"We can take it there this evening if you wish."

Patting the pipe at his hip, Cedric grinned and said, "I hope my visit will not be as short as that. I could use the coin."

That the man was a bard, and the son of a duke, explained his acquaintance with Kavan. He was not so acquainted, however, as to know about Gates. "Then I wish you good fortune, my lord. This will remain safe until your return."

No one except the laundress came into his room unannounced, and she had served Hes á Redh for so long that there was no reason to mistrust her. Tusánt put the box upon his dresser, covered it with the embroidered cloth that had shielded it before, and followed Cedric out, making sure to lock his door on the way. Just because he trusted those he lived with did not mean Tusánt was willing to risk such an artifact. If it was genuine, it was the most precious piece of his Faith he had ever encountered. He wanted to take no chance with its safety.

❧*❧

Raebhá claimed it was morning but Kavan could not be certain with the continued absence of sunlight when they emerged from their shelter and began their ascent once more. Only the position of the stars had changed, but the increasing cover of blowing snow and clouds that the howling wind drove in from the east obscured them. By the time the storm peaked, it was too late to return to their previous cover, and since limited visibility made each step more treacherous, they kept watch for viable shelter as Kavan followed the psychic beacon that pulsed brighter despite the foul weather. They often traveled hand in hand, or hand to back, assisting each other up the narrow pass, and made no stop to eat or rest.

If the wind and clouds brought a blizzard, they might be lost in the snow forever.

The world was white, devoid of smell save for his breath into the fabric protecting his face, devoid of most sounds except the whistling wind and the snow crunch beneath their boots.

It was impossible to judge the passage of time without the movement of the stars to guide them.

Sometime after the faint glow of noon brightened the snow-blown white horizon and faded again, they reached what they judged to be the crest of the pass and paused for the first time to catch their breath and gain their bearings. The source of that power signature was nearer, should be within Kavan's line of sight, but he could see only the wind-driven snow. Using his inner senses instead of his eyes, he turned his face, and then his body, in the direction of the power, thinking it the direction they should travel.

The shift of his weight on the uneven, icy ground pulled a foot out from under him. Instinctively, his hand sought Raebhá's to steady himself. She slipped from his grasp and he careened down the northern slope, his pack clutched to his chest with one hand to avoid losing it as he fell. Raebhá's squawk as she jerked from his unexpected reach unbalanced her and she too tumbled down the incline. A barrier of stone, flat and smooth as if eroded after part of the mountain sheared away, broke their descent. His surprise at the abrupt stop was cut short when Raebhá rolled into him. Her dropped pack came behind, the steepness of the incline enough to deposit the bundle beside her rather than leaving it somewhere back up the path.

He met her gaze, asking if she was good without words, and she nodded that she was as he fought to his feet and helped her up, pausing to brush snow from her lashes. Satisfied with her welfare, confident of his own, forehead touched briefly to hers to convey his relief, he turned to inspect the stone surface that had broken their descent.

This was it. He knew it before he pressed his hand to the stone. Even with the thick layers of leather and cloth and knitted woolen mittens between his skin and the rock, there was a strong enough shock of power, a jolt of the sort he recognized now that he was near enough to touch it. There was an entrance here, warded and sealed, not with physical locks but with the energy of an ancient and powerful source. The ward and lock system was similar to what he used to protect the contents of St. Kóráhm's hidden vaults. Such a thing should not exist here. Few Elyri could create, manipulate, or destroy such wards; Kavan knew of only one other who could do so, one of Bhryell's bhydáni whom Tíbhyan had coerced into teaching the skill to Kavan. It was both surprising and amazing and one of the last things he expected to encounter so far up amongst these craggy peaks.

Excited, he ripped off his gloves, exposing his hands not just to the cold but to the power in the stone despite Raebhá's inhaled breath of concern and confusion. Kavan was surprised she did not feel it too. If he could find the entrance, if he could break the wards, it would gain them a secure shelter in which to wait out the moaning wind.

If they were lucky, there might be a Gate inside.

Raebhá watched through the blowing snow as Kavan moved along the wall, following so as not to lose sight of him, following to prevent him from falling again. They might each be able to survive the mountains alone, keep themselves warm, but eventually, even his power would wane and the loss of visibility and shelter would result in freezing to death or a fall more harmful than this last one had been.

To Kavan, the wards were less sophisticated than those he had created in St. Kóráhm's and thus he found them easy to dismantle. He located the power pressure points, untangled the threads that wove through them, pulled back the pin of power that bound them, and then swallowed hard as the energy flashed back into him like a shockwave. His lids fluttered as tremors rumbled beneath his hands and under their feet and then the stone began to groan as the slab retracted into the mountain on one side just far enough for them to enter one at a time. The movement of stone and earth brought with it a collapse of snow from above that was thankfully not enough to bury them.

It slid over them, angled to the edge of the ledge on which they stood, and piled against the mountainside at their back.

The stale stench of death blasted them as the passage was exposed, an old smell detectable behind their scarf coverings before mingling with the snowy gale and being swept away by the storm. Holding his breath against it, Kavan created a tongue of flame in one hand, intense enough in the darkness that Raebhá shielded her eyes and relied on his guiding grip to lead her inside. They each took a single step, hers more hesitant than his, to pass the threshold between the storm and security. An echoing cracking sound, the depression and release of a spring, revealed a pressure plate hidden beneath centuries of dust, the activation of which caused the stone door to slide back into place more quickly than it had opened. Kavan jerked Raebhá inside as the closing stone cut them off from the howling wind.

Startled, Raebhá slid from Kavan's grasp and fell to her knees, yanking the scarf from her face to breathe more easily and voicing a question he would have no answer for.

"What is this place?"

Kavan, startled by the closing of the door, lost his handlight; he too pulled his scarf down as he willed warmth into his hands. Relieved she was safe, his gaze, his other senses, darted around in the total darkness but he detected no threat, only decades, or perhaps centuries, of emptiness below the power contained here. "You don't know?"

If she knew, she would tell him. As remote as this place was, as stale, foul, and musty as the expulsion of air had been, he sensed that no one had been here in years. Perhaps it had been forgotten. There was no reason she should know, no reason except that, to Kavan, it held an air of significance that contradicted its abandoned aura.

Handlight reignited, he raised it above his head and began to turn, visually examining details long hidden from mortal eyes. The shape of the cavern appeared natural, but its concave walls were smoothed to a polished sheen, as if the room had been intended for ritualistic use. Across from the now-closed door, a tunnel pushed deeper into the earth, a passage that, when he stood at its entrance, was blocked by a heap of crumbled rock and broken timbers at the farthest edge of the light's penetration. Despite its long disuse, power was still strong here, stronger than he believed it should be, particularly further down the passage, and he was curious to investigate.

"Can we get out?"

Raebhá shifted on her knees, watching the glow of his handlight as it tracked over the walls, her assessment of the room's age and prior usage mirroring his. Unless this was an ancient holy place, nothing she had learned or studied could explain this place, but if it was a peculiarity of the northern people, there was no reason for her to know about it. The smell of death, the obvious knowledge that something unnatural to the dhóbhaen had happened here, turned her stomach. From where she knelt, she could not see into the passage but she did not need to see into it to read the curiosity that prevented him from answering her. "What is it?"

When he again did not reply, she got to her feet and came to his side to see the corridor and the blockage beyond the edge of his handlight. She saw the recesses of doorways but could not determine what held Kavan's interest. "Kavan?"

Hearing the distress in her tone though not understanding it, he absently took her hand in his, using his touch to soothe her. "If there is a way in, there is a way out." Even if he could not see it. Even if he had to force the door open, or destroy it, they would not be trapped in this place. "For now, we're free from the storm…there are timbers there, wood for a fire."

The wood, likely ceiling braces that might have collapsed with age or with the natural movement of the earth, was old enough that it might not burn well, but burning it was worth the attempt. "Only if we're careful," she whispered. "We do not want to bring the ceiling down."

He scowled, unaware of why a fire should cause such a collapse. He could feel a slight push of air over his face, suggesting the structure was not tightly sealed, so he believed it would be safe enough to build a fire for periodic warmth and to heat the dried meat in their pack.

For any other need, their ability to regulate their body heat and their handlights would suffice.

Air coming from behind the collapse might suggest a way out but he was in no hurry to go back into the storm. He wanted to eat, to rest, to sleep. He wanted to know the secrets this place held.

Pointing to the doorways visible in the glow of the handlight, he murmured, "We should make sure we're alone. Perhaps the nature of this place will be revealed."

He did not sense any other life, not people, not animals, but the strong source of power might, he knew, mask something.

Or someone.

If there was a Gate here, he should know that too.

Raebhá tentatively nodded in agreement though with less compulsion to uncover the unknown. Darkness was as natural as light, as air and earth and every other part of the world and she was not afraid of it. Nor was she typically afraid of the unknown, often finding it exhilarating to uncover something new. Something in this place, however, the trapped feeling she could not shake, the smell of long-dead things, was disconcerting, and she stayed as close to Kavan as she could as he moved forward, watching his step this time in case there were other traps in store.

The corridor did not appear to be a mineshaft, although perhaps it had begun as one. There was a natural inherent power here that might have led those in the past to convert this place from a mine to a place with other uses. The walls were planed smooth as the entrance had been, meeting the floor at straight angles. Foot traffic had worn a path in the center of the passage, suggesting this place had once been extensively used, but it was not the roughly rounded channel into the earth Kavan had seen in mines.

Nor did mines contain doors to either side of a shaft, locked doors into rooms that required keys to open. There were no keys that Kavan could find, only his hand on the frozen latch beneath the keyhole. Prompted by the absence of his handlight when he shifted power to this new problem, Raebhá created one for them both to see what he was doing. It would also allow them, if the door opened, to see whatever waited in the silence beyond the windowless wooden barrier.

The metal grew hot beneath his hand as he forced power into the lock so that the rusted, frozen pins would turn beneath the strength of his determination. At last they snapped, the fatigued metal giving way so that the latch tongue depressed and the door groaned on squealing hinges. There was the renewed reek of death, stronger than it had been at the outer door. Handlight springing to life in his palm, supplementing Raebhá's, Kavan glanced at her over his shoulder and then stepped into the frigid room.

His stomach lurched. He stared. Behind him, Raebhá's voice was a stolen squeak of horror. Chained to the walls so that they could neither sit nor recline, the corpses of more than two dozen men and women, sickly ruddy and gray, hung emaciated, their sunken flesh having succumbed to cold, to thirst, to starvation in the darkness that had been their prison. The cold had hindered decay, had kept each preserved in whatever state fate had stolen their lives and had molded flesh to bone, leaving them a terrifying sight. Some bore wounds, traces of blades or beatings, open mouths without tongues, or discolored cuts across their throats through which their lives had seeped down their necks and the front of their clothing to form iced-over stains at their feet.

Raebhá's feet refused to move. "This…cannot be; this is not possible." Shaking her head from side to side, she struggled to make sense of what she saw. There were no stories in all of their histories, in the myths and legends of ages past, to explain this.

It was obviously possible, or else the most elaborate illusion or vision Kavan had ever seen. He started forward, determined to have answers, but Raebhá grabbed his hand and yanked him back.

Fraught to explain herself, so frightened she could not move, Raebhá hissed, "You don't understand; this is not possible! The law forbids death as punishment! The only man to ever suffer execution was Dhágdhuán. Who are these people? How did they get here? Why…did this happen?"

Maybe they were taeré, condemned for some crime against the dhóbhaen, or other taeré had imprisoned them here, but that neither explained nor excused their execution.

Kavan understood the power such a revelation could exert on a person, the effect of shattered beliefs and disillusionment. Hearing that it was her people, his kin and blood, who had executed the voice of their Faith, the first among k'Ádhá's children, was a shock itself and something he would seek clarification for later. This was the second time Raebhá had said it, but it was the first time the words sank past the porches of his ears. The Faith taught Dhágdhuán's execution but never identified those responsible, as if his killers had been nameless, faceless others without significance. Or else his death was placed at the feet of the Teren, making Dhágdhuán the first of his race and Faith to die at Teren hands.

What if that story, like so many others, was wrong?

He gently pried his hand from hers with a soft kiss on her forehead. "I will learn the truth…give me the chance to…"

"No." Again she shook her head in adamant defiance. Seeing the evidence was gruesome enough; knowing the truth was a frightening concept she did not want to face.

Kavan might be the seeker of truth. She admired him for it. In this instance, however, her curiosity was at odds with the certainty that she would rather not know what lies she had been told.

He cupped her chin and kissed her mouth, hoping to ease her anxieties as well as his own. Rather than still his heart, the kiss birthed a fire that warmed his flesh and forced him to back away before he could be further tempted. "They cannot hurt us…but the truth must be known. For their sake. It is the only way to honor them, to give their suffering voice. Whatever their crimes, they did not deserve to be abandoned to history and forgotten."

Hands wrapped around his wrists, she pressed her forehead to his and willed herself to breathe slower, finding calm in his presence, his touch, the nearness of his scent, the strength of his power.

He spoke the truth. Never in their taught histories had the punishment of criminals been so harsh. Thieves repaid their debts with servitude or goods in equal portion to what was taken. Physical disputes were punished through public shaming and, if deemed necessary, a period of kylldrenai. On the very rare occasion where one was proven guilty of the intentional death of another, either more extensive kylldrenai was demanded by the márbhyndhánis or else the guilty was banished to the land of the taeré with strict instructions to never return to the land of the dhóbhaen.

Even the followers of Dhágdhuán and those who believed in the right to use their natural born power had been sent away on ships or through Gates instead of enduring the burning death Dhágdhuán had suffered. Death was a curse, an unnatural end to the dhóbhaen, an interruption to the flow of energy through nature, into their lives, and back into the world when the Ceasing arrived. The death of the dhóbhaen caused a restless energy and created all manner of negative things for the living. No dhóbhaen would knowingly bring another here to kill them or leave them to perish in the dark.

If someone had done so, as was obviously the case given the evidence of her eyes, if there was some terrible secret in the history of the dhóbhaen that the people were prevented from knowing, or if the taeré had been here, done this, without the dhóbhaen's knowledge, then Kavan was right. Someone had to know; the truth had to be told.

The verse about the White Bard of Gálínphel shining light into the darkness might come to pass as the portents foretold…but not in the way Raebhá or anyone else expected. She held her breath, nodded with determination, and let go of his wrists. If the curse of death was contained in this place, she had already been exposed to it.

If she was to suffer the bhur, if Kavan was to suffer, they deserved to know why.

Kavan did not touch the dead, choosing instead to study their shriveled forms, seeking some remnant of identity. Although the faded scraps of clothing hanging from their desiccated frames suggested people of means, none wore items of value. They did not wear enough clothing to keep warm, but at least none had been stripped nude as part of their punishment. They were dressed similarly enough to indicate they had lived in a similar age, to hint that they had come from a similar region and background, but it was no longer possible, by looking at them, to determine their age or kinship or if they had been brought here together or at separate times.

Not possible unless Kavan touched them and he did not have the stomach to read each of the more than two dozen bodies hanging here. Curiosity compelled him back into the passage to open the door across the hall in the same manner as he had the first, revealing a second cell as he suspected. This one was smaller and contained a single individual, a man twisted sideways in his shackles as though he had strained against them, fighting to reach the others until his breath and heart gave out. The residue of power was strongest here, absorbed into the walls, into the floor, as if the captive had used what he had in a vain attempt to escape.

It was this man Kavan chose to touch, a man of enough import to imprison alone, a man whose long hair, now the color of his emaciated skin, hung in a queue over his shoulder, bound by a faded metallic thread. A man whose facial features were forever twisted in an agonized visage of despair.

Kavan gently pressed his fingertips to the man's forehead, a touch meant to be much longer but which ended abruptly as he was thrown against the opposite wall by unseen hands. Raebhá ran to his side and knelt there, the crack as he impacted the wall frightening her.

The shackled corpse crumbled and fell in a shower of dust the color of dried mushrooms onto the floor. The power that held him upright was released by Kavan's touch, expended to force away someone the captive had likely anticipated being his jailors. A final, desperate attempt at freedom or revenge that had ended in neither.

"Cliáth." The name echoed in his head, into his bones, filling him with a dread and wonder that had no voice, only a long, low, "Gaed."

She had said that name before.

Raebhá shook her head as if it would cleanse the name from her ears, as if it would erase the revelations that erupted with its utterance. The stories, the legends, the myths. The records of history the márbhyndhánis taught every generation of children, portraying Gaed Cliáth and his companions as heretics and traitors, claiming they had been banished on a ship of outcasts, expelled from the land, from history, as nothing but blemishes, minute dark stains on the glorious history of the dhóbhaen.

Not just Gaed, but his family. His sister, his mother, his sons, all sent away, never heard from again. Friends and compatriots. Fellow believers. Only his wife was spared, allowed to remain behind for reasons never revealed in any history Raebhá had been taught.

Had Gaed come back for his wife? Was he not placed on a ship but sent to languish here, to suffer and die in the dark? Perhaps he and those like him, Dhedec and Zythán and all of the others had been walled up in these rooms and any beyond the collapse in the hall, to endure agonizing deaths at the hands of those forbidden to kill?

If so, how had there come to be Cliáths, MacLyrs, Bhíncáris or Curnydhás from whom Kavan, Kóráhm, and others had sprung, in the lands of the west?

Why was this man here?

Who were the others?

With a groan, Raebhá sat with defeat and buried her face against Kavan's shoulder. "What does this mean?" she whispered, her voice cracking and raw. He was battling his own demons, his own questions, but it did not prevent her from voicing hers.

"I…don't know."

What he did know was that, except for those whose throats had been slit, the others had died at this man's hand, or rather, died at the mercy of his mind, an eruption of power thrust out with enough force to kill them instantly, a mercy killing intended to spare further agony. sídysá, that self-defense ability that Kavan carried without the need of training in its use, had stopped their hearts. The power of the act, amplified by the cavern's natural energy, explained the residual power here, explained the agony the man had shouldered in that final act, the responsibility for so many lives that he could not save and had been forced to extinguish instead.

Had he died then, or had he lingered long after beneath the weight of what he had done? If he could do all of this, why had he not freed them rather than take their lives?

Why? How? Kavan did not think he could ever know.

There was nothing left of the man except dust and fragments of bone scattered beneath the manacles. Perhaps Kavan could learn something from the stone, from the bindings, or from the power that clung to the walls and floor around them. Perhaps he could learn more from the dead across the hall. But the heaviness in his head, in his chest, combined with Raebhá's disjointed sobbing against his neck, left Kavan too weak-willed to pursue answers.

He wished Wortham was here to help ease his heart's burden.

Without Wortham, Kavan instead wanted Kóráhm to come and take this burden of knowledge long enough to give him the peace of sleep. Perhaps sleep would be enough to allow him to forget.

❧Chapter 17❧

Too much excitement had jangled his nerves, twisted his stomach, and sapped him of the strength to rise from his bed. Time and again the nightmares came, and in his fever-induced delirium, he could not be sure where the line between dream and reality existed. He remembered things, flashes of sight and sound, blood on his hands, the smell and feel of it that never left him whether awake or asleep. Thinking that his wife could clear his head of the webs of tangled thought, that she would know the truth and reassure him of it, he called for her repeatedly.

Yet she did not come, or if she did, it was during periods of hallucination so that he could not recall her company.

When the moment of clarity returned, when he felt no fever in his body and no fog in his brain, he opened his eyes and struggled to sit. He was in his own room, his own bed, and from the weakness of the glow at the open window, he guessed it was midafternoon. The light silhouetted a figure there, and after a moment of panic that he was not alone, that someone had come to claim his life, he breathed a sigh of relief and recognition.

"Inness…by the gods you gave me a fright!"

"You should rise, Oska…there are things we must do. The kingdom awaits your attention."

"Kingdom?" he yawned as he rubbed his sticky eyes. "That's father's duty…"

She faced him, a candle in her hand illuminating the angles of her jaw and cheeks, lending a sinister pall to her features as she regarded him coolly. "How is he to do that when you stabbed him?"

"I…?" The memories came back in a hammering rush between his eyes, causing him to wince and frantically wipe his hands on the bedding before staring at them to see there was no blood there. "That cannot…he's my…is he dead?"

"He's no longer an obstacle, husband. The throne is yours, as I promised it would be."

"Mother? Jerit?"

"Fled like the cowards they are." Inness sniffed and tipped up her chin. "There is no one to oppose you."

"I will be executed as a traitor!"

"By who? No one knows the truth. Captain Fraen reports that a faction loyal to Jerit undertook the uprising, executed the king, intended to execute you. Jerit and your mother were driven into hiding when loyalist forces united to stop them. The perpetrators have been arrested and await execution." She took a step closer, intentionally softening her features to express the sympathy she knew Oska expected. "Nothing prevents you from assuming your place, Oska. I promised he would never deny you what was rightfully yours. The throne is…"

"But I killed my father!" Oska wailed, collapsing back onto the bed and drawing the blankets over his head to stifle the moaning. Lies, all lies…but that much was true.

"Come now." Inness stared at him, surprised by his reaction, wondering how much of the truth she dared tell him. She suspected that the truth would cause him to unravel everything she had planned, and so decided it was best to tell him nothing, help him cope with the moment. He would improve in time.

"The kingdom needs a statement." When she tried to pull the blankets away, he clutched them more tightly, like a turtle refusing to emerge from its shell.

"I can't. I won't. I don't know anything. You do it, Inness."

"I am not the king."

Neither am I, Oska's inner voice screamed. Aloud he croaked, "You are my wife. I don't feel…I cannot…speak for me. This time. Find my brother!"

There was a sound. He thought it was a sigh of sadness but as he was unable to see her, it could have been a sound of exasperation or a sound of conquest. She stroked the back of his head, also hidden beneath the blankets, and then he felt the press of her mouth at his temple. "Very well, husband. I shall speak for you. Rest, and when you wake again, we'll greet your kingdom together."

He nodded but did not emerge. This was not his kingdom. He was no king, despite his desire to be one and his belief in his ability. He had killed his father, a man who had done nothing but love him despite his imperfections, and had ruled Neth with more compassion, fairness, and wisdom than any before him.

Jerit had to be found. Jerit had to be safe.

Oska was a traitor to Neth…and was surely damned for it.

❧*❧

"I need do no such thing." Dhóri's arms crossed his chest, a shield that put a barrier between him and Rhyrdan, a shield to hide his bruised ego. "You cannot force me to…"

"Someday Alberni and its titles will be yours. Such decisions should be…"

"Should be made by the man responsible for its upkeep…"

"He is not here to…"

"He should be! He left us to…"

"To prove our capabilities and worth by carrying out the duties he has given us," Rhyrdan snarled with exasperation. He understood Dhóri's feelings, felt his rejection, although he did not share the added burden of jealousy over a woman. Kavan had not taken Raebhá from him, and no woman had taken Kavan away. Rhyrdan took the bard at his word when the man said he would return as soon as he was able. If he brought Raebhá back after the completion of her business, that would be something Rhyrdan would face when it happened. His father would have been happy that Kavan had found someone. Rhyrdan was doing his best to feel that same happiness.

Dhóri's face twisted with annoyance. "I am responsible and…"

"Prove it. Saying it is not enough. Words cannot prove ability, only action can…"

But Dhóri had heard enough and chose to stalk through the manor gates towards the chellé from where he had come some hours earlier. Since Kavan's departure, Dhóri spent the majority of his time there, returning home at erratic hours as if expecting to find his father returned without announcing his arrival. Finding Kavan absent, he invariably returned to the chellé, usually without a word to anyone.

Rhyrdan catching him this time was chance.

Dawn today had brought dark clouds over the sea's distant horizon. With a steady wind blowing from the south, there was hope that those clouds would bring rain before the day was over and so Rhyrdan had set the staff to putting out barrels and pails, anything with which to catch the rain if they were so blessed. It was too late in the year for planting, but Rhyrdan had directed workmen to plow up the cracked, stagnant fields so that rain could be absorbed more easily by the freshly turned soil. Others were inspecting the roofing of each manor building, the windows and doors too, for soundness. Rhyrdan helped where he could, when he was not directing others in their work, and he believed that Dhóri should be by his side, working with him.

Wortham would have done the same. Kavan would have been in the fields, on the roof, alongside his people.

Dhóri was not Kavan, was not Wortham. With his brother out of sight, Rhyrdan grudgingly accepted that such help would not come.

A scent on the breeze rushed across his skin and he tilted his face into it, closing his eyes to focus on the smell. It smelled of salt, of rain, and a faint trace of something else carried upon a distant rumble.

Lightning.

Kóráhm no, he thought, throwing himself back into the work. After so long without precipitation, though they needed the rain, lightning was something the dried regions of Enesfel could not afford.

Praise be, Captain Magk and people from the chellé were due to arrive soon. Rhyrdan was not sure he could finish what needed to be done on his own.

❧*❧

A solid night's rest, for Jerit at least, brought the creak of wheels to the door of the structure in whose basement Wallace had hidden Asta and her son. A covered merchant wagon, pulled by two sturdy bay drafts, would carry them at a strong, steady pace towards the Neth Enesfel border, hidden amidst crates and trunks and bolts of cloth destined for trade, protected from anyone who might be looking for them. The horse ridden from Glevum was tethered to the back and followed behind without resistance. There would be no need to change mounts every few hours or be forced to stop for extended periods to allow the animals to rest. Riding inside the coach would be easier on both of them and might afford Asta the sleep she had not yet found.

She had spent the night holding Jerit with one arm, her other hand clutching the sword on the off chance that Wallace sold them out or that someone had followed them to the basement and done so. Now she stayed attentive to the sounds of the night, using the clop-clop of the horses' hooves and the creaking of the wheels to distract her thoughts from the darker paths they seemed determined to follow.

She could not know what had happened in Glevum. She could not know who had instigated the attack or why. She picked at the bits she could recall, this person or that who had opposed Kjell at one time or another, who had worked to undermine his progressive changes to turn the hands of history ahead. But those threads were mere theories, guesses, and all her efforts did was provide a host of potential enemies to watch for as she traveled further from her husband's side.

By the time the wagon departed Gorea, there had been no word from Glevum though Wallace swore that he had spies there who would bring word, intercepting the wagon along its journey, as soon as anything was learned. So far, there had been nothing. It could take days, she knew, if they came at all, and speculating in the interim would only distract her from the necessities of survival. She had a child to think about. She had to protect them both.

Jerit shifted again, his head lolling in her lap, the narrowness of their hiding place barely allowing for his movement. They had been in this cramped place for so long now, stopping only to eat and take care of other physical needs before climbing back in again. She hated not being able to see. She hated feeling trapped.

For the first time in many years, Asta wished her father was here to help and advise her.

❧*❧

"I regret Lord Cliáth is not here; he has spoken of you fondly."

Bhyrhán smiled at the other man, finally having the opportunity to spend a few moments alone with the minstrel who had come to call on the Lachlan House. Upon Cedric's arrival, he had been spirited away by the queen and prince to discuss the conditions of the lands the older man had passed through on his travels, as well as to share any information he might have on the state of things in Cordash. News was difficult to come by now that so many towns and villages had quarantined in response to the Yellow Death.

Any visitor to the keep, particularly one as well-traveled as Cedric O'Grady, was a welcomed source of information.

But the minstrel had spent too long outside of the Sovereignties and knew only of the plague and famine from the roads he had journeyed on to cross Enesfel from the desert. Thus far, neither of the Yellow Sisters had taken root amongst the desert tribesmen and they had limited their trade to keep it that way. Their economy, too, was suffering, but they were not suffering as much as the people of Enesfel.

"I knew my chances of finding him were slim, but the visit is obligatory nonetheless. Perhaps he'll be in Alberni by the time I arrive, for I long to see his face when he receives what I bring."

"If you bring books or items of a musical nature, I guarantee they will be well received."

"Something better." Cedric stretched his legs in front of the fire to ease their stiffness. Some days he wondered if he should give up his wandering, should return to Cordash and settle on his family's estate. But there was little affection or closeness between him and his brothers and it had been so long since he had been in Cordash it no longer felt like home. He did not know what he would do if he stopped traveling, unless he acquired a patron to feed him, house him, and support his performing skills. Maybe, he mused over the rim of his wine glass, he had come to Rhidam with that hope in mind.

"What could be better?" Bhyrhán had known his kinsman for many years, though not as well as some, and he could think of nothing Kavan treasured more than old texts and unusual, rare instruments.

"The mantle of St. Kóráhm."

Bhyrhán was only the second person Cedric had told, and the other bard's expression did not disappoint. "The people who entrusted it to me swear to its authenticity, and they knew enough of Lord Cliáth to ask that he receives it. It has left healing in its wake as I traveled, so I have faith it is what I was told. If anyone can validate the claim, I'd wager Lord Cliáth can."

"Aye; if it is so, no one will value it more. Where is it now?"

"In safekeeping in the náós. I considered bringing it here but thought it best to leave it on holy ground. The queen has extended her hospitality for as long as I wish to remain in Rhidam…and I admit I am weary of travel. A few days more here, I think, sharing with you and any other minstrels I can find, will be a welcome respite." Like all traveling musicians, the opportunity to share new songs and tales with others of his ilk was an oft sought-after way to pass the time.

"You are most welcome." And if Cedric's claims were true, if a fount of healing miracles was at hand, perhaps a miracle was just what was needed. Diona, at least, could use one. It was a gift greater than anything else Bhyrhán could give her.

❧*❧

Such an artifact should not be hidden from the public.

gdhededhá Caldar, having grown up on the outskirts of the town of Theron, had a healthy respect for miracles and saints. Saint Eada, the patroness of forgiveness and those who hungered, had hailed from Caldar's city, leaving behind a collection of relics, pieces of her life considered sacred and blessed and were known to have fostered uncountable miracles in the centuries they had been enshrined in the náós there. Most of the items, except for her entombed body, had long ago been claimed by Clarys and transported there, to be housed with relics belonging to other saints on display. The Faith venerated twelve saints, one celebrated each month of the year, but since the contention of Kóráhm, whom the ruling gdhededhá could not decide if he was saint or heretic, there had been thirteen.

Caldar venerated them all with fanatical reverence, even Kóráhm, and he followed Kavan's career of reported miracles closely in the belief that the White Bard would one day be elevated as the highest saint of all…even if he was currently excommunicated by the Elyri Faith leadership. Kavan's ascension, he believed, would solidify Kóráhm's place in the pantheon, and for the first time, there would be more than the official twelve. Caldar could not foresee any of the current saints being displaced. Each had been venerated for too long, and was too beloved by the Faithful, to be discarded.

To overhear mention of the mantel through Tusánt's closed door, to learn that it had been found and was now within the walls of Hes á Redh, even temporarily, was an honor and blessing beyond any Caldar could have hoped to see. Hiding the sacred mantle from the Faithful, to him, was a grievous sin, one he took upon himself to rectify.

With his own hands, he built a wooden shrine upon which to display the holy relic in its case. He installed the structure at the front of the Gathering Hall without a word to anyone. k'gdhededhá was out, the business of visiting the housebound Faithful something Tusánt took seriously despite his elevation to the highest religious post in the land. With the holy season not far off, Edward and Saul were preoccupied with the choir and arranging the succession of Gatherings ahead. Rankin, unaware of the holy relic they housed, paid Caldar's business no attention, not even when he installed the crude but serviceable platform where it could be easily viewed.

Having once apprenticed as a locksmith and blacksmith, it took Caldar little effort to get into Tusánt's room where he fell on his knees before the soot marred, gray fabric folded with care in its gold and glass encasement. He did not need to touch it to believe it was authentic. He had only to see it. There was nothing else that folded cloth could be.

Carefully, not desiring to harm either the housing or the fabric it contained, Caldar carried it into the Gathering Hall and positioned it on its display shelf. If it remained in Rhidam longer than he had overheard it might, or if k'gdhededhá Tusánt chose to keep it here rather than allow Cedric to deliver it to St. Kóráhm's as intended, Caldar would see to a more permanent, more befitting display. He imagined that Tusánt, however, and Kóráhm himself, would prefer the sacred cloth to be stationed in the chellé that bore his name in Alberni. Now that he saw the transparent box displayed on the work of his own hands, he believed that a man such as Kóráhm would prefer a display such as this over one fashioned of precious metals and elaborate carvings that Clarys would bestow if the relic went there instead.

He had never been to Alberni. He had no idea the nature of display or storage that awaited the mantle there. He trusted Lord Cliáth would do what was best. For now, this would do.

Caught in his reverence of this sanctified gift, Caldar did not hear the approach of parishioners. He did not notice them beside him until a woman's gasp and shriek spun him sideways in alarm. The man with her appeared old, stooped, his skin jaundiced and sporting a collection of pustules the color of old bruises on each side of his jaw, below his ears, and on the naked skin near his armpits. As Caldar stared, the fellow, gazing upon the mantle with no idea what it was, knowing it to be holy only because of its prominent display, dropped the twisted forked stick he had been using as a crutch, straightened his posture, and took several steps forward to touch the glass.

It appeared he moved unaided for the first time in many years, his steps faltering and unsteady. The dirty woman who had screamed, someone Caldar presumed to be the man's daughter or granddaughter, began to babble, speaking so fast and so toothlessly incoherent that Caldar could not understand her. The man stood at the box, stroking the glass and weeping, only agreeing to be pulled away from it when the woman dragged him towards the door, leaving the crutch discarded on the altar steps, whatever they had come to see a gdhededhá about having been forgotten.

A miracle, Caldar thought with ecstasy. He had, for the first time in his life, witnessed a miracle. Kóráhm had helped the lame to walk, and soon others from around Rhidam would come for healing too. He needed to set up a donation box. He needed to provide candles for visitors to use in the holy stations, candles for prayer, penance, and praise. He ran off, not thinking to cover the relic, feeling no need to hide it now that he had witnessed what it could do.

It was not until many hours later, after another dozen or so of Rhidam's needy had come for Kóráhm's blessing, that Caldar realized that the first man, whose crutch he had picked up and put away, had sported the symptoms of the northern plague, the boils, the jaundice, the rheumy eyes. Caldar, having touched that crutch, had exposed himself, and in turn others, to the scourge.

He was unworried. Hes á Redh housed the mantle of Saint Kóráhm and Kóráhm was healing the sick. No one, himself included, would contract the plague so long as the mantle was here. Kóráhm's mantle would ensure that the people of Rhidam were safe and in time, every trace of the Yellow Death in the city would be cleansed away.

Kóráhm's mantle would assure that no one would die.

❧*❧

Hours passed into days as the storm wailed outside of their shelter, waxing and waning, unrelenting in its power, trapping them where they were in little danger of freezing or being buried or lost in avalanches or the furious flurries. Raebhá worried about the snow's depth, whether the way would be passable when they chose to go out, if they would run out of food before they were able to safely leave. If Kavan dreaded the same, he kept his fears to himself as he continued to inspect the details of their shelter.

They did not discuss the bodies in the room that he had resealed and not entered again. The dead could not escape, but sealing the door had given Raebhá peace of mind, as if it would seal in the memories of what they had seen and learned. As determined as she was in her denial, Kavan decided it would be of little use to ask questions. She did not have the answers he wanted. She was as puzzled as he was.

Some of the long hours were spent in prayer and contemplation, in remembrances of those he had lost, and in occasional escapes into brass-strung songs offered to the saint he wished would come. They found warmth in front of fires built of power intended to conserve the collapsed timbers Raebhá gathered as she sought any small items they might be able to use amongst the fallen debris. With the doors sealed, she was able to pretend that what lay behind them had only been a dream. Gradually, as if her picking through the debris was opening a passage big enough for air and power to seep through, Kavan grew aware of a familiar but weak energy signature that lay somewhere beyond the collapse. He knew that trace, as faint as it was.

An abandoned Gate.

He considered clearing more of the corridor every time he and Raebhá freed another broken bit of timber. The possibility that there might be other rooms, more dead abandoned to the ravages of time, as upsetting for Raebhá as it was, discouraged him from trying. Timbers here, inside of a mountain where no trees grew, meant they had been transported from a lower altitude, and if Raebhá was correct, they could not be far from a ghís. Locating a Gate, risking further collapse of the structure, was not worth disturbing the dead, though Kavan would prefer a Gate to further travel in the snowy darkness.

When the storm passed, provided they could get out through the door they had come in through, they would continue down the mountain towards civilization.

If the door would not succumb to his efforts to break through, digging out the Gate would be reconsidered.

Instead, in the hopes of distracting Raebhá from their predicament, Kavan offered additional training when she was clearheaded enough for it. They spoke of customs, of the evolution of their languages, of the things that made Elyri and dhóbhaen the same or different. Each morsel of information was locked into memory so that Kavan could record it as soon as he had the opportunity to do so.

The journal he had intended to bring for noting such details had been left in favor of additional food and the history books Raebhá had asked for, a decision he knew was a good one as he awoke one more time to a rumble in his belly and an unusual silence inside the chamber that he had not noticed in several days.

He tilted his head and listened.

"The wind has stopped," he murmured, more to himself than to the woman he suspected was still asleep. Sharing one another's body warmth was a necessity as it conserved energy that Kavan felt was better used to suppress hunger and feign a fire's warmth. Huddled side by side beneath cloaks and blankets, he grew more comfortable with her presence, her company, her touch, and began to fear what he must face when the day came she was no longer beside him. Secretly, he hoped that the bond would grow strong enough to be unbreakable, strong enough to overpower the forces determined to pull them apart.

That hope was a slippery, tenuous thing.

Raebhá stirred, rolled towards him, and listened without opening her eyes. She had been dreaming before he spoke, of her fields, her family, the life she had known before. The remembrances evaporated on the tails of his words; all she heard was Kavan's heart against her ear, heard his breathing, and with her hand on his arm felt the faint, constant rumbling hum of power that resonated inside of him. Like the dream, those things were comforting, welcome and endearing.

There were no sounds outside their shelter.

Sighing, realizing their time together in this hidden place may have reached its inevitable end, she opened her eyes to blink at the light of the crackling fire. In its amber glow, his pale skin looked vaguely sinister, a thought that made her grin despite her dashed hopes. Kavan did not have a sinister bone in his body.

"Do we dare?" They had previously discussed what opening that doorway might entail. If forced to destroy the stone, it would no longer block the wind or protect them from the cold. If they were forced to remain here after that, they would have to retreat to one of the cell rooms to hold out the wind.

Raebhá dreaded that possibility.

She preferred the safety here, the solitude away from the cares behind or ahead of them. It had been too easy, in this hidden place, to pretend the burdens they carried did not exist. Here it was only the two of them. Here, nothing else mattered.

Toeing the pack at his feet, Kavan stretched as he sat, feeling the same but forcing himself to be practical. "I think we must." They had another week of food if they continued to conserve it, but the water skins they had brought were nearly empty. Outside there would be snow to slake their thirst, but only if they opened the door. Food, without crossing paths with animals they could hunt or plants they could consume, he did not believe they would easily find.

He pushed the tangle of 'what ifs' out of his thoughts and began to stuff things back into his pack, storing them carefully around the harp to protect it from a fall or the elements.

Reluctantly agreeing without speaking, Raebhá too began to repack her bag, dressing again in her extra layers of clothing, as Kavan did, expecting the fire to be blown out as soon as the door opened and exposed them to the colder air. When the packs were secured, she picked them both up as Kavan brushed his hand against her cheek and motioned her back to the farthest side of the chamber.

Not knowing what to anticipate, shivering with the dark tunnel, the closed doors, and the rubble at her back, she watched Kavan spread his hands against the stone as he had done before. She expected the stone to slide open as Kavan's hands moved across the surface as if hoping for a button, a latch, or something else she could not see.

Nothing happened for several minutes. Kavan's probing fingers and senses found no trigger in the stone and no power bindings to unlock. He stepped back, consternation on his face, pressed on the floor plate that had closed the door before, and then reinvestigated the door and both sides of the entry. With no opening mechanism and no wards to break, he concluded that the only way out for anyone who had come here would have been the barely detectable Gate…or some trigger elsewhere that they had not taken the time to look for. There was too much wall, floor, and ceiling to investigate, including that which they could not access, and he did not want to spend the time necessary when their supplies were running low.

He scolded himself for not searching before.

It was less time-consuming, however, and a much-needed release of pent-up power, to spread his hands upon the rock again. He pushed tendrils of energy around the razor-thin edges of the door, and after wrapping the stone with it and throwing up a shield to protect himself and Raebhá from the blast, compressed the power, drew it in towards his center, and collapsed the energy in on itself. The effort crushed stone to dust with an ear-popping burst of force, leaving a shoulder-high drift of snow and the clear black sky beyond in its place.

"How did you…?" Raebhá came cautiously forward, curious and awed by the increasingly greater depths of power and skill he continued to reveal. It was reassuring to see the sky, to peek at stars above the rim of the snowdrift, to hear none of the howling wind that had blasted past them for the last several days. If she had been alone, she would not have gotten out.

She had few doubts that Kavan was the one prophecies spoke of, for no other man contained and controlled such power.

Kavan did it with ease.

He shrugged, holding one hand back to keep her from coming closer. "Something I learned long ago. It's proven useful."

The power was drawn back into himself, gathered as his other hand tightened into a fist, and when his hand flared open, the snow wall blocking the entrance blasted outwards into the dark and spread across the silvery mountain landscape. Raebhá felt the gathering, felt the release, felt the following gratification and relief that Kavan experienced with the expenditure of power. He made the act look effortless, but she knew it was not. His satisfaction made her smile.

Only when both hands came down did she take that as the signal to join him; she paused to kiss the side of his neck as if to reassure both him and herself. Kavan shivered and kissed her forehead, realizing how easily that action came to him.

"I could study with you for a lifetime and never master the gifts," she murmured. She doubted anyone could.

Again he shrugged, this time sheepishly, and took his pack to sling over his shoulder. He never intended to make anyone feel inferior; he only desired to learn everything he could, master the power he had been given, for whatever purpose k'Ádhá had blessed him. There was always a need to know more. It was an obligation he took seriously.

Stars glimmered above them, and along the horizon, the faint glow suggested the rising or setting of the sun at the midday hour. The barely visible orange sheen did not affect the air temperature but the sky was clear of clouds and wind. Their tumble had taken them off the path they had previously followed, and the way out of this wide chasm would be hazardous, but there was no reason not to press on.

To find civilization, they had to continue north.

With an offered hand, he drew Raebhá up from their shelter back into the world and followed the wall and the ledge in the direction they needed to go.

On into the dark.

Not once did he stop to consider that this day of rebirth into the world coincided with the day of his birth.

❞*❝

"I did not know!" Caldar wrung his hands, struggling not to pace the width of the altar steps beneath his superiors' stares. "It heals people! I swear it! I saw it! I believe all will be well…"

"Will be?" Caldar was young, but not so young as to warrant the foolhardy risk he had taken with the line of Faithful queued from the altar to náós door, winding through the burial markers to the gate at the street. Tusánt had been away from the náós longer than intended, tending the sick, the dying, the housebound, those worried about plague, only to return to the sight now before him. From the number gathered, he guested the youngest dedhá had put the mantle on display many hours ago. It would have taken several hours for word of its existence, and the rumors of miracles granted, to spread, to account so many gathered to see it.

Finding the discarded crutch surrounded by abandoned remnants of clothing, rags, and other evidence of disease and disability left by those claiming to be cured, Rankin fretted at what awaited them. The dark crusty stain along the top of the crutch concerned him but Caldar had not been present then to ask. The young dedhá's return coincided with Tusánt's notice of a woman with alarming yellowish-brown boils beneath her ears. Edward and Saul were attempting to banish the crowd but the visitors were reluctant to leave. Tusánt did not believe in locking the náós at night, but what he saw alarmed him enough that the decision was an easy one to make.

"It's plague, Caldar!"

"But Kóráhm…"

"The miracle of healing does not mean we foolishly expose them…and ourselves," interjected Rankin, saying what he knew Tusánt would not. The k'gdhededhá did not like to use such words as foolish, did not want to belittle or degrade people, but Rankin could see this risk in no way but foolish, and he was unafraid to say so.

"You'll see all of this burned," Tusánt grunted, pointing at the items in front of the altar, "and the Gathering Hall scrubbed. We cannot afford plague here. I must get word to the queen, tell her of this before an outbreak begins…tell her Hes á Redh may not be safe for any in the keep…that we may not be safe any longer. The mantle is off-limits, Caldar. Master O'Grady is taking it to Saint Kóráhm's and that will be that. You should have consulted me instead of breaking into my room…"

Caldar pouted and bowed his head, accepting the rebuke while feeling justified in sharing such a relic with the people of Rhidam. While he believed Saint Kóráhm would never permit an outbreak while his mantle remained in Rhidam, the reminder that the artifact would soon be taken to its resting place suggested that the exposure of so many to the Yellow Death might already be on his shoulders.

"I will pray for mercy." Not for himself but for everyone he might have endangered. He would also pray for the miracle that would keep the holy mantle in Rhidam until the Yellow Sisters had passed.

❧*❧

The bells of Hes Dhágdhuán began to toll with the setting of the sun and all of Clarys stopped its toil. Conversations silenced, meals were abandoned, revelers gathered in Clarys for the Festival of St. Kóráhm laid aside their merrymaking to stare in silence towards the sound, some going into the streets to face the great ivory tower visible from every corner of the city. Weeks had passed with the old man's aging afflictions pulling him further and further from duty. A great force of will had kept him in Clarys, at his post, in his office, despite the call that drew his kind away to some unknown, frightening end.

Hwensen wondered, as he closed his eyes and let the tolling reverberate into his bones, if it had been piety of office that had kept k'gdhededhá Tumm here or if it had been fear of that other end that kept him at the mercy of his failing body. It was a form of suicide as surely as k'gdhededhá Dórímyr had endured, if not an outright act of it, committed by those of their kind who were unwilling to face the other unknown, but equally natural, end of Elyri life.

How could that other end, so common to Elyri, be more terrifying than the end Dhágdhuán promised awaited after death?

Having prepared for this day, candidates had come from throughout Elyriá, gathering over the last two weeks, some weeping and bemoaning the loss of their leader while others hovered like carrion waiting to pick over what remained after Tumm's passing. Within a week or two, the election process would begin, but Hwensen, like many others, believed the selection of the Faith's next leader had already been decided. gdhededhá Ylár had been acting on Tumm's behalf for most of the last year, the man's son and caregiver being in the ideal position to share his thoughts, to be his voice, to play his role when Tumm's failing health kept him from his duties. Ylár had always been a popular choice amongst gdhededhá and the people alike, losing last time, some believed, simply due to the veneration of Tumm's age and Tumm's close relationship to Dórímyr.

The rules had to be followed, the process completed according to centuries of practice, before any change of leadership could be official. Hwensen would be there, just as he had been for the last election. On his desk, already drawn up and signed, according to those same rules, by every gdhededhá in Elyriá he had been able to convince to sign it, a petition to undo one of the worst injustices he had ever witnessed.

k'Ádhá, Dhágdhuán, záryph, and all the saints be with the old man's spirit in his rest…and give guidance and wisdom to whoever was elected to take his place.

The tolling of the bell faded. Hwensen sighed again, pondering the irony of Tumm's death coinciding with St. Kóráhm's feast day.

❧*❧

Most of the lights in Hes á Redh had been extinguished early, an effort made to discourage those who continued to gather in the náós yard and at the front door, men and women who refused to leave. Some reluctantly shuffled off, intending, no doubt, to return in the morning when the náós was expected to open its doors again. Others ignored the cold night air's effect on aching joints and stiff muscles and sat wherever they could find a reasonably sheltered spot in the yard.

The dark-haired man, his hair tied at the nape of his neck with a black ribbon, had succeeded in getting inside before the doors had been locked and had hidden in the choir loft awaiting a quieter hour when he would be able to do as he intended.

She had been right to send him here. Kavan was not in Rhidam as he had hoped, but his true purpose in coming had been to rescue the holy mantle of Saint Kóráhm from those who could not appreciate what they had. Not that he doubted the piety or sanctity of the Faith leaders, as the k'gdhededhá had seen fit to finally close the doors to keep the mantle from being a continued public spectacle. But gleaning such adoration was not the function of holy relics, nor should they be displayed to rake donations from the ones its' healing benefited.

It should never have been brought here. Should never have been left here. The mantle belonged to St. Kóráhm's, in Kavan's hands, and he intended to see that was where it ended up. Now that the náos was still, he could claim it and be gone, through one of the thóres doors he had scoped earlier in the day, without disturbing anyone. She had set him on this path and it was one he followed with a glad and willing heart. Kavan, he believed, would agree with his choices.

Silent streets embraced him but he held no fear of the dark. He would have come earlier, but other business had detained him, keeping him from this duty longer than he intended. He was a friendly, jovial, respectful man, not one to break with company without pressing cause or need, and visiting the mantle again, making sure it was intact and safe, had seemed a responsibility that could wait a little while longer.

It was safe where it was.

He saw the crowd outside of the náos, shadow figures huddled beneath blankets around small fires or oil pots for warmth against the air's chill. He first thought it was a holy day that he had forgotten. Saint Kóráhm's day, wasn't it? That made sense. Then he wondered if someone of importance, a townsman or one of the dedhá, was sick or had died to warrant this show of devotion and veneration. When a shade propped on crutches hobbled off towards a side street, however, he understood why they had gathered.

Word had spread about the mantle. Tales of healing had taken root. Perhaps someone, as he carried the treasure into the city, had been healed and followed him to Hes á Redh, spreading the news, bringing miracle seekers in his wake. It did not surprise him, but he did wonder, pausing in the street far enough from the crowd to be unnoticed, how he could get inside to reassure himself of the mantle's safety if the náos doors were locked.

Perhaps he did not need to. The crowd's presence suggested the mantle was inside and the barred doors meant that no one had access to it that should not. He trusted the k'gdhededhá. He would come again after the sun rose.

"Tomorrow," he murmured to himself. "I will come."

"No…you won't."

Startled, he froze, the split second all it took for someone to swing. Something cold and piercing struck the side of his neck. He reeled, one hand clutching his throat, coming away wet with blood as the other flailed about seeking something to grab, someone to strike.

One staggering step.

Another.

Then nothing.

# &Chapter 18&

"For the love of all things holy!" shouted the prince, having looked in on the pasty corpse brought to the keep so that those who had met him could confirm the deceased was indeed Cedric O'Grady as the sheriff claimed. "Who in the name of k'Ádhá would want to…? Where was he? When did this happen?"

Inquisitor Geli, his frame nearly as broad as he was tall, circled the table on which the body lay, poking, prodding, moving limbs or turning them in his quest for clues to answer the prince's queries. His square face looked harsh in its concentration and he said nothing, leaving the chamberlain to soothe the prince's agitation.

"He had no purse, no rings…and you can see where something was pulled from around his neck…"

"Robbery then?"

Most of the Crown avoided dealings with the Association, an uneasy truce that existed thanks to the late Caol Dugan. Criminal investigations and punishment were left in the hands of Lord High Justice Madoc Delamo or the hands of one of Rhidam's sheriffs. If the Association ran afoul of either authority, so be it. The Inquisitor relied on the Association for information, and those informants were paid well for their cooperation, with the awareness that the Crown could not turn a blind eye to all of their activities.

Something such as this, a high-profile murder or significant theft, was treated with care and would, regardless of the perpetrator, be handled accordingly. While the murder and robbery of a minstrel might seem like a small thing, O'Grady had been both a friend of Lord Cliáth's and the brother of a duke.

Whoever had done this, whatever the reason, would be held accountable.

"The man likes his drink…he was found not far from the Boar and Sow…perhaps he had been there to play and…" offered Níkóá, his eyes following Geli's movements and investigation. The chamberlain had spent one evening drinking with Cedric in the Eagle's Nest and knew how fond of drink he was. Níkóá suspected O'Grady had been making the rounds of the city taverns to play, drink, and gather coin in preparation to move on to his next destination.

"I smell no alcohol," Fen said as he tilted the man's head, opened his mouth, and sniffed. "If he had his pipe, the thieves took that too…"

"Thieves? More than one?"

"Conjecture," the Inquisitor said with a shrug. Someone to strike, another to grab his belongings. The area where the body was found was too exposed for a single person to have spent time pilfering the body of a man just killed. "But there is this…"

He indicated the three punctures on Cedric's neck.

"Coryllien dagger?" Merrek asked. He had never seen the triple-edged dagger, or the sort of damage it caused, but he had heard tales surrounding it as a child in the aftermath of the Second Elyri Persecution.

"Knuckle-biter," Fen corrected. "Common among thieves and cutthroats. Sometimes poisoned…but I don't see any trace of that. It's little, easily concealed in a closed fist. Can hide the blades inside," he held up his hand to demonstrate the blades concealed against the palm used with an open-handed slapping gesture, "or can line the knuckles of a closed fist like so…" He again demonstrated, this time of an object with blades protruding outward between the fingers of a clenched fist.

"So it could have belonged to anyone." Merrek scowled deeper.

"Someone who knew where to strike, but yes. From the location of the blow, I'd say it was a bleed out, a punctured artery. If I may speak with Madoc…question the tavern's patrons and owners…search his room in the Eagle's Nest…"

"Do it. Robbery or not, that," the prince pointed at the bruising at the side of the man's neck and the three punctures in the center, "is excessive. You don't need to kill a man to steal from him…and I don't remember him having anything of value when he was here."

"Doesn't mean there wasn't anything." Fen wiped his hands on his trousers. "Might I make use of Wace Elotti's expertise?"

The prince frowned. "Do you think that's necessary?"

"No…but he's available…and he produces results. He's staying at the Eagle's Nest too. Might be able to track down anyone who favors the knuckle biter. Together we should make short work of this matter."

Though he knew little of the infamous bounty hunter beyond rumors and stories told around dinner tables and at hearth gatherings, Merrek understood that many in Rhidam, Kavan included, respected the man's skill. "Get to it," he decided, "and let me know when the killer is caught. I want to see his face before he's hung."

Chamberlain and inquisitor looked at one another without a word. It was rare that a monarch passed judgment before a criminal was caught and tried. But Cedric, for all of his newness to court, had been a link to the most respected man in Enesfel. If there was even a small possibility that this act was connected to Kavan, a threat to him, Merrek wanted to see the crime punished before it devolved into another period of persecution. He believed Diona would concur.

❧*❦

The naós and thóres were searched top to bottom, every room scoured, every resident questioned, but the glass case stood open and empty on the stand Caldar had made for it and no one had any inkling of how it had been opened. Where its contents were. Why it had not been removed from the naós at the end of the evening as Tusánt had instructed. Preferring to take the other gdhededhá at their word rather than believe they would lie to him, Tusánt elected not to read them, even when none claimed to have seen the relic since the previous evening. None had touched the case other than Caldar, nor had he dared try to open the locked and sealed box for which he had no key.

Someone had. In a frantic hope for evidence, Tusánt placed his fingers to the glass, opened his senses, and attempted to read the case. It was a skill he rarely used, preferring to leave that messy duty to anyone the Lachlans might appoint when the situation called for it. But in matters of Faith, Tusánt was the only Elyri in Rhidam, one of the few Elyri outside of St. Kóráhm's to serve the Faith in Enesfel, and that made this theft against the Faith his responsibility. No matter how hard he tried, however, how far he pushed his senses, he gained nothing from the case except Caldar's touch when he had set the case on the stand, the touch of the first man in Rhidam healed by it, his brief contact when he had taken it from Cedric and put it on his dresser…and several prolonged contacts with Cedric before that.

Cedric had never opened the box. Although Tusánt suspected Caldar, in his zeal, to be the only one likely to take the mantle so that it would not be removed from Rhidam, whoever had done so left no passing trace. Gloves could have protected a thief's identity. Or else the thief was Elyri. Tusánt guessed the former, for he could think of no Elyri he knew in Rhidam who would do such a thing.

Nor did he believe that anyone from Hes Dhágdhuán would have confiscated the mantle in secret, if word had somehow managed to reach Clarys. But anything connected to the Heretic-Saint had the potential of raising the Elyri leaders' ire. Perhaps they had done just that, to keep the already muddy waters around Kóráhm from further agitated stirring.

Tusánt frowned and sent Saul to the keep with the news about the mantle and the news about the plague. Cedric should know what had become of his precious artifact. It was right and fair that he knew the truth, that Tusánt had failed in his duty to protect Kóráhm's mantle.

He, meanwhile, would call upon Clarys on the off chance he was wrong. If the mantle had been confiscated, he wanted to know why. He wanted it back.

❧*☙

"Drop your shoulder. Shift your weight." Raenár used his hands on the younger man's hips to help him achieve a better fighting stance. Rhyrdan had trained with his father since he was old enough to pick up a toy sword. He spent considerable time practicing with any other swordsmen of note as well, including Captain Magk. He lacked neither skill nor strength and bested his older brother in mock combat continuously since the age of twelve.

But Kavan leaving him behind had fueled the belief that he was not good enough, and so he had come to the captain in search of anything he could learn which might, in turn, impress Alberni's duke.

Raenár assured him that further training was unnecessary, but he had time to fill and Rhyrdan insisted. The captain arranged a series of tests to be completed with some of the soldiers serving the chellé, allowing him to study the young man's strengths and faults from a distance, looking for any details that could be improved on.

The primary thing Rhyrdan lacked was experience, but there were matters of form and balance that could be polished, so Raenár began his lessons with those.

"Why the need for such honing?" the captain asked after several passes between them proved that Rhyrdan had taken the morning's instruction to heart. "Is there war in the offing of which I'm unaware?"

"No." Rhyrdan wiped his brow, sheathing the sword to shake Raenár's hand. "I want to be as my father was, to prove I am worthy."

"Of being a Delamo? Or being Lord Cliáth's man?"

Back to the captain now as he stooped to retrieve the shield he had earlier discarded, his embarrassment could not be seen. "I know it is too soon after…and I am not my father…perhaps I can never be…as he was…to Kavan…but I would appreciate the opportunity to try."

"Many of us would," Raenár admitted with a sigh. "He will choose a right hand in time; it will happen naturally, as it should, if it is to be. You cannot force yourself into that position, no matter how you train, or how like your father you are. If Lord Cliáth needs…"

"He needs someone beside him to…"

"He needs respect more than he needs a protector. He needs someone to tend to the mundane when his head is filled with music and loftier thoughts. He needs understanding and acceptance. He needs security. He needs love."

"I can give him those things." In Rhyrdan's eyes, he already gave Kavan all of those, had been giving them since he had moved from boy to young man. Assuming responsibility for the manor's upkeep was new, but he had been aiding his father in those duties for several years, taking on more and more responsibilities as his father aged, he matured, and Madoc left Alberni to pursue a life in Rhidam. Rhyrdan had picked up the reins after his father's passing and he was determined to be as effective as Wortham had been. He was the head of the Delamo family now. He would prove that he could do everything asked and required of him.

"Then he shall see it and reward you accordingly," Raenár smiled. Kavan always rewarded those he deemed worthy. It was why Raenár had a post in Saint Kóráhm's and had not had to face punishment in Clarys after his failure to deliver the bard to the Council. Having been the one to arrest and oversee his brief incarceration, Raenár would not have blamed Kavan for mistrusting or hating him. What he had received from the bard had been the opposite.

How Kavan might reward Rhyrdan, Raenár could not say, but he knew the bard would do so.

Sheriff Groff stumbled through the courtyard gates, red-faced and panting with a look of panic flashing in his eyes. "My Lord Delamo, it has happened…it is here, as we feared…"

"What is here?" Rhyrdan asked though only one possibility came to mind.

"Plague, my lord, three families in the western farms…I have posted men for quarantine but…"

"But it's only a matter of days." The Yellow Death spread quickly, particularly since it had yet to be determined how either variety passed between people. It had been found on ships at the harbor, quarantined ships that no one had boarded or left. It was unlikely the cases were related, being on opposite sides of the city as they were, but now the threat was doubled and they could not afford to be idle about the risks. Rhyrdan looked to Raenár for suggestions. Overseeing the estate, the town, his family were quite different from managing a plague. Rhyrdan did not feel adequately prepared for this.

He doubted anyone was.

His hope that Kavan would be here to control this situation when it arose was now a futile one.

"Clean the streets of debris. Gather stray animals and quarantine them away from people. Inspect all remaining food stores, inspect the water," the captain grunted. There was little food left, and k'Ádhá help them if contaminated food proved to be the cause of the Yellow Death. "I will send people to assist; we close the roads into the city and send messengers to surrounding regions that it is not safe here. Post warnings on the roads at our borders."

"Aye, Captain," Groff said with a salute and a bow.

"Do we send word to Rhidam?" Rhyrdan was concerned about his brother. Madoc should know that his family was at risk, should know that he should not come to Alberni.

Raenár shook his head. "These are precautions, my lord. Let us assess the situation before we panic. Perhaps these will prove to be isolated cases and no further action will be necessary."

Groff was already running off, making haste to see to the safety of the city. Feeling certain that it was too late for isolated cases, Rhyrdan shifted his shield and muttered, "Do you think they will be, Captain?"

No, Raenár thought with a groan. These cases were likely the harbinger of horror, as such things had been for other communities. Their city had been spared longer than most. It was their time to suffer.

His groan was the only answer Rhyrdan needed. "I must tell Dhóri…and Sóbhán." And despite Raenár's suggestion, he would find some way to get word to Madoc and Yóáná.

If only there was a way to get this news to Kavan.

❧*❧

The wagon bouncing along at full speed up the path that led to Fiara's ruling estate was an unexpected sight, bringing Gabrielle from the upstairs window to the front door in haste, thinking it was some follow-up message to the declaration that another great-grandson had been born. She was fearful that the visitors bore bad news on the heels of the prior announcement, and the guards standing protectively at the door would not let her pass until they verified the intent of the arrivals. If the charging cart was the precursor to an attack, the guards would not allow her to rush blindly into it. She was about to order them aside when the horses and wagon stopped, the driver hopped down and helped a woman and boy from the back.

Other than the driver, the two were alone and carried no trunks, no belongings other than the sword the woman carried. Their clothes, nondescript trousers and tunics, were unkempt as if worn for several days, their hair wild, and their weary faces were marred by sunken circles beneath their eyes. Their cloaks, however, were expensive, and though it had been several years since Gabrielle had seen the other woman, she recognized her at once.

She pushed her guards aside. "Asta. Come in." To a servant behind her, she said, "Broth and wine." When Asta was near enough, her arm protectively around her son as she warily eyed the men with swords who lined her approach, Gabrielle tenderly caught her hand and encouraged her to come in. "You must sit. Rest."

"Jerit needs a bed." It was morning, but the nonstop travel had not been conducive to restful sleep for either of them.

"I'm fine, mother," the boy said with a yawn, trying to appear more confident and well off than he felt.

"You are no such thing. You will fall ill if you don't rest." She had seen fires in the outlying countryside, people dressed in tatters, sickly people burning their dead with rags tied over their faces. The driver

❧*295❧*

had avoided stopping in such places for fear of the plague Asta had only heard about in Glevum, but they might have been exposed despite their efforts. As weary as they were, she feared they were susceptible to contagion but trusted they would be safe here.

"You will both eat and then rest."

Gabrielle set them before the fire in the sitting room as servants brought the requested broth, bread, and wine. Giving them leave to eat without bombarding them with questions, Gabrielle busied herself with the fire. This was no social call. This was something darker.

Asta picked at her meal while making sure Jerit ate every bit of his, and then after a shared look with their hostess, followed a servant upstairs to see that her son was bathed and settled into the provided bed. It was nearly an hour later before she returned, by which time her meal was cold and had been taken away.

She was more interested in the wine, or something stronger, and spoke only after she had drained her glass a third time.

"We require sanctuary."

Gabrielle's breath hitched as she settled on the stool before Asta. "You have it. You know you do. What has…where is…?"

"Kjell will join us…when he can." Asta chose not to voice her fears that her husband would not join her though she knew they colored the strained tone of her voice. "Some faction stormed the castle…an inside job…Jerit and I barely made it out…"

"By k'Ádhá." If there had been a coup in Glevum, what were the odds that Kjell, Oska, and Inness had survived? The king had the backing of the military, of the people, but Gabrielle had learned over years of association with Owain how politics in Neth often operated. More than one king had been deposed by uprisings and assassinations and though Asta had not said it, there was the possibility that Kjell would never join or send for her.

"We should tell Merrek. He will send troops if you…"

Asta shook her head. "I don't think that's…Kjell has either bested his assailants or…"

Or he had not and someone else controlled Neth. Jerit was not old enough to secure and hold the throne. Weakened by plague and hunger, Asta did not know if Enesfel could afford to send soldiers into what might be the precursor to a war they were not fit to win.

She needed to know more first. She needed to know how things stood in Glevum.

"Word follows; I should know more soon. Kjell asked me to wait for him here…if that is…?"

"It is no inconvenience; you are welcome." Family by marriage, bound through the de Corrmicks and Lachlans, Owain had always welcomed his nephew's family. Caol Dugan's family. "You may stay as long as necessary. Whatever resources I have are at your disposal. Now please, Asta…you should rest too. You're safe here, I swear it."

Owain and Merrek had made certain the Fiara estate was well protected and the Lachlan Crown had garrisoned men in Fiara when the prince had made this his home. All would be on alert for trouble and would not hesitate to act if trouble had followed them.

Though Asta thought to refuse, still anxious for her son's safety and worried about her husband and other son, there was little she could do. No need to be vigilant, no need for action until she received word from Wallace or Kjell. She could only wait. Sleep might not come easily, or at all, but it was worth the effort to try.

Whatever lay ahead, she would need rest and a clear head.

She stopped at the foot of the stairs and looked back at the sitting-room door where Gabrielle watched her. For a woman who had never felt much need for religious faith, it felt like a peculiar thing to ask, but she murmured, "Will you pray for them?" If there was anyone in the universe watching over them, this seemed the ideal time to come to terms with that and seek whatever help could be offered.

"I will," Gabrielle promised. She wanted to offer assurance but there was little she could give. Asta would not believe that everything would be alright until she saw that they were with her own eyes.

❧*❧

"k'gdhededhá Tumm is…?"

Hwensen nodded as he slid the glass of water across the carved oak table towards his unexpected guest. He had not served the k'gdhededhá in the same capacity as he had served Dórímyr, as those responsibilities had fallen instead on Ylár who already served Tumm as caregiver and aide. Hwensen had, instead, worked with Kluín in his efforts to support Kavan's reinstatement into the Faith, to strive for the reunification of the Elyri and Teren sects, and to seek out the pockets of Zythánites exposed because of Dórímyr's involvement with them.

"Last night. I should have sent word but, as you can imagine, there's been much to do. He'd been ailing for weeks, you know. I'm surprised he did not pass sooner or go his way…"

Tusánt snorted and cupped the glass in his hands. "Like Dórímyr, he was too stubborn to go easily. Elections?"

"Soon. Most of the candidates have lingered in Clarys since he took ill." His bitterness was swallowed with a gulp of water. "But you did not come because of Tumm."

"No, I came on other business." The Faith was divided by politics and race, but to Tusánt, they were still one entity, an entity that shared business regardless of their differences. "Have you heard of any relics coming into store here? One recently arrived in Hes á Redh…but it has been stolen from its locked box, from the locked náós, suggesting the thief may have used the Gates."

Shaking his head, Hwensen shuffled through the documents on his desk. The duties of the k'gdhededhá may have been assumed by Ylár, but much of the paperwork had fallen to Hwensen as before because he knew those avenues of bureaucracy better than anyone in Clarys. "No…not unless it has not been reported yet…or has been confiscated without lawful notice."

Tusánt rubbed his temples in frustration. "I thought…hoped…that the k'phóredhet had confiscated it. Not that I want them to, but at least that would make sense. If we must seek a thief outside of the Faith, I do not know where to begin."

"I was not aware Hes á Redh housed relics…"

"We didn't until this one came to us on its way to Lord Cliáth."

Hwensen's brow crept up in surprise. Holy relics, in the eyes of the Faith, were never to be kept in the hands of private citizens. Only in rare cases where the items in question were family treasures and heirlooms and the descendants of the original owner still had possession of them, was that unwritten law sometimes overlooked. The k'phóredhet continued to hound those families in the hopes that the items would be relinquished. Such things were kept in a secure vault, to be brought out for viewing at the k'phóredhet's and k'gdhededhá's discretion, though that rarely happened.

Sometimes Hwensen wondered if it was a means of erasing the claims of 'miracle' from the public's minds.

"Lord Cliáth? Why would…?"

Tusánt gave a little smile. "What better place for Saint Kóráhm's mantle?"

Even amongst the top authorities of the Faith, the tales of the Heretic-Saint's involvement in the White Bard's life flourished, making Kavan's standing in the Faith all the more precarious. If Heretic Kóráhm was influential on Kavan, did not that mark Kavan for heresy? If not, if the miracle-working bard was as blessed as it appeared, was Kóráhm a heretic?

"The mantle? By the saints…it has surfaced?" The mantle had been a rumor since the day it had been taken from the site of Kóráhm's martyrdom several generations earlier. "Where has it…?"

"I do not know. The gentleman who brought it mentioned crossing from the desert…giving rise to miraculous healing on its journey. I have not seen the miracles he spoke of, though there are those in Rhidam already making claims…but I have seen the mantle. I dared not touch it, but if anyone can verify its authenticity…"

"Lord Cliáth can," Hwensen agreed. "I assure you, if word of it had reached Clarys, the halls would be buzzing. At least Ylár or I would have been told. If it has been confiscated…"

Only Tumm could have called for such an act or a k'phóredhet vote. Tumm had been too ill to do so and the council had not convened in more than a week.

"I will listen for rumors. If anyone here knows of it…has taken it without permission, they will be dealt with accordingly."

❧*❧

Rankin was left with the duty of overseeing further investigation within Hes á Redh, although he did not expect to find anything. Belongings and rooms were searched more than once, every room cleaned to limit contamination by death-infected articles that had lingered too long at the altar and by those people who had passed through the náós the day before.

If plague now infested Rhidam, efforts to clean the náós were futile. Only barring entry would keep contamination out and that was not yet an option worth considering. People needed their faith during such trying times and every gdhededhá within these walls had a sacred duty and calling to provide comfort and counseling as it was needed. Prayer was the only protection they had, now that the healing mantle of Saint Kóráhm was gone.

"gdhededhá Rankin."

He looked up from his absent rearranging of the prayer candles in their sconces at the young man who had entered. He knew Madoc from his childhood and saw him more frequently now that he was positioned as Lord High Justice. He was young for the title, but he seemed well-suited to the task and took his duties seriously.

"What may I do for you, Lord Justice?"

"I was told there has been a theft?" The rumor had come to him through Fen's Association contacts, but it had not indicated the nature of the theft. As it was known that O'Grady had left something with the gdhededhásur for safekeeping, and now the minstrel had been killed, the two incidences hardly seemed coincidental.

Rankin nodded his head. He was not surprised that word had reached the justice so quickly, given the importance of what had been taken. "Aye, a holy artifact destined for St. Kóráhm's. It was here." He gestured towards the glass case which had previously housed the mantle. "The case was locked, but as you can see…"

It was locked no longer. The lock was open, as with a key, showing no indication of breakage.

Rankin continued, "The náós doors were locked too, to protect it, and now…" He shrugged.

Madoc lifted the box carefully to inspect the bottom. "Who had the key?" he asked, finding nothing amiss on the box.

"Mr. O'Grady, we assume, who delivered the relic to us and is to take it to St. Kóráhm's when his business in Rhidam is complete."

"Unfortunately that will no longer be possible." Even if the item had not been stolen. Madoc did not believe the missing article to be truly sacred; too many false artifacts appeared over the years for him to believe in genuine ones, and with Enesfel in the grips of starvation and plague, it was of little surprise that such an object would appear in Rhidam to offer comfort to the gullible.

"Mister O'Grady has been murdered." The Inquisitor had not indicated finding a key, but since the minstrel had apparently been robbed of his valuables, perhaps the killer had taken it.

Rankin's shoulder's sagged with dismay. "When? How?"

"Last night. It appears to have been a robbery, as his purse and belongings were missing. Inquisitor Geli and Hunter Elotti are investigating. It appears he might have been robbed of this key…" If the thief had known about this relic, had been looking for a key, it offered a motive for theft and possibly murder.

But, Madoc mused as he glanced back at the door, neither explained how a thief had entered through a locked door unnoticed.

As if reading the justice's thoughts, Rankin shook his head. "We've questioned everyone here. No one saw anything, heard anything. No one was allowed to enter after the doors were sealed."

"You noticed nothing unusual yesterday?"

"Not unless you consider a line of Faithful hoping for miracles to be unusual. dedhá Caldar took it upon himself to display the relic, and once the rumor of miracles began…"

"Miracles?" Madoc scoffed. He had never been present during the life-saving miracles that had spared Prince Lorant's life. Madoc had never witnessed anything remotely miraculous, and though his father and wife claimed to have seen things, and Kavan was said to perform them, Madoc could not believe it. He was a man who preferred proof over hearsay and was inclined to seek other explanations for the miraculous, including the possibility that Kavan carried some amount of the healing gifts without realizing it. Why would he not when he was said to be the most powerful Elyri to have ever lived?

"Indeed. It would not surprise me if any one of them would want to make off with the mantle, to sell it or demand payment from others for the privilege of healing, but I pray that is not the case. k'dedhá Tusánt will be gravely disappointed to hear this news."

"I'll share this with the Inquisitor; perhaps he will find it useful. Maybe someone managed to hide inside before the doors were locked." How the doors could have locked again behind the escaping thief was a separate mystery. "Keep everyone here…I'm sure the Inquisitor will want to question…"

"k'gdhededhá Tusánt has already…"

"And we have not. Nor have we searched the grounds, but we shall. Mr. Elotti as well. The queen has made this our highest priority."

Rankin frowned but nodded his reluctant agreement. They could not deny the Crown the right to investigate; perhaps the skilled eyes of the bounty hunter, inquisitor, and justice would find something Rankin and Tusánt failed to see.

It would make little difference. By now the relic was well on its way out of Rhidam, disappearing from history once more.

❧302❧

❧Chapter 19❦

Inness watched her husband stagger drunkenly out of the dining room where he had finally deigned to eat with the rest of the household and the lords and advisors she had gathered that night. It was important to discuss the necessary changes to the regime, what would be expected of the men sharing the king's table. But Oska was unable to carry out the most basic conversation without resorting to muttered, incoherent phrases. Since the hour he emerged from his chambers, he had done so in nothing but his sleeping gown, his short hair mussed, his face unshaven, his limp more pronounced. Blaming his condition on drunken grief, Inness worked to convince the staff and royal advisors that the shock of his beloved father's death at the hands of Prince Jerit's supporters had been great. In time he would settle, would come to terms with his father's death and his brother and mother's betrayal, and would rise to the weight of rule as was expected.

At her request, the staff removed all traces of wine from his chambers and once he began wandering the castle barefoot and wild-eyed, calling his brother's name, they removed it from other rooms as well. With no alcohol to imbibe, Inness expected he would come to his senses quicker and regain his peace of mind. The wine was kept out of his hands as they ate, so when he staggered out of the room this time, Inness was forced to contemplate the possibility that his behavior was fueled not by alcohol but by something more serious.

She had always known that his was not a strong constitution, that he was a politician, a philosopher, a planner, thinker, and poet…not a warrior. Not a man of fierce heart and action. He had sworn that he could, and would, be the one to confront his father. She had provided the knife, suggested that it might be needed as a threat. He had followed through on that act, but she had not thought he would use the blade. She had expected to do the deed herself if it became necessary. The cost of the act for Oska may have been his wits.

Inness could solve many problems, but healing her husband's mind was not one of them.

A physician was needed, she decided, perhaps even an Elyri healer if she could find one who would keep their secrets. For now, she turned her focus to the guests with a polite, apologetic, and slightly sad smile. A physician could heal the troubled king's body while she kept Neth running and soothed the fears of those seated with her. She knew her husband. She could rule the kingdom until the day he was ready to do so and she would remain by his side until then, the dutiful queen.

A wailing sing-song cry of Jerit's name rose from the corridor, far away from the dining hall but audible to all seated there. Servants ran to attend their king, but Inness remained where she was. Oska needed her, but Neth needed her more. This was the way things had to be.

⇛*⇝

Kavan's internal clock had lost track of the days and nights that had passed since his arrival in this place. They climbed and walked when they had the energy and found suitable shelter from the wind and snow, to sleep when exhaustion and cold overtook them. Attempts to count the brief periods of sunlight became futile when the orb stopped topping the horizon and the mountain peaks and faces blocked their view. Climbing down, then up, and then down again allowed little energy for talk or the practice of power skills; everything they had went towards northward movement and survival. The food had grown sparser, their bellies now constantly arumble with hunger, and only the distant lure of a hoped-for Gate and the promise to see Raebhá safely home served as the impetus to keep Kavan moving through bouts of occasional dismay when yet one more peak appeared in their path. But they had dropped lower in altitude, their struggle to breathe lessened, and Kavan prayed constantly, beseeching Ethenae for a sign that the road they traveled would bring them to shelter before they collapsed.

He again considered flight, but Raebhá did not know how and he would not leave her. Even when she encouraged him to use it to pinpoint their location, to seek a suitable destination, he tried to refuse. Only thrice did he resort to flight to help select a path through or around obstacles, but he never lost sight of her, fearing that if he did, they would become separated and one or both of them would die.

Each time she waited for his return and greeted him with a warm embrace through the bulk of their protective attire. A new path laid, they would begin again. Sometimes she was ahead of him. Sometimes behind. Sometimes beside. When his spirits flagged, she encouraged him with a touch that found its way into his soul and filled him with joy and a sense of ease that warmed him more than any protective layer of clothing could. She never seemed disheartened or discouraged and Kavan found strength in that. He trusted she would bring them both to civilization, that her sense of direction in these mountains, beneath these stars, would not fail.

He was watching his feet push through a light layer of drifted snow as he picked his way along the narrow incline they had chosen this day when Raebhá tugged on his arm the way she often did to get his attention. His gaze followed her pointing finger towards the sky to their right, past the stone overhang that protected them from the occasional slide of ice and snow. His breath caught and he stopped climbing, unable to believe what he beheld to the east.

The darkness was cut with ribbons of green and purple, undulating curtains of colored light bleeding from one shade to the other, stretching from the eastern mountaintops as far up as he could see. Eyes on the display, he clambered along the path, covering the last several yards of the incline with renewed vigor, until he reached the peak where no overhang or mountain face blocked his view. The display crossed the entire sky, the pattern shifting and changing hue as though a living, growing thing.

Never in his life had he seen or imagined such a vision, a dance of light arced all around them. Absently he slid down the scarf that protected his mouth and nose from cold and whispered, "What is this?" Not magic, not power as he knew it, but a spectacle worth studying, understanding, naming.

"We know it by many names…but most call it l/óph phaern ágdháthé…ribs of the gods…or chyrt ghymaemis…sky ribbons…or thai phemár…blessed lights. We see it in the late autumn to the early spring every year. Sometimes it shines for hours…days. Sometimes it is there for a few moments and then is gone. Blue, green, purple…red, pink, yellow…pale or bright or deep. It's never the same. Sometimes we see it in Gálínphel, but it is more common in the north. I'm surprised we have not seen it before now, but perhaps the conditions were not right."

"Conditions?"

"No one knows why they come…or how. They just appear. Some say they are the souls of those lost at sea…or what becomes of those who have ceased. Many say that, though the ágdháthé do not interact with us, they send the chyrt ghymaemis to remind us they are there."

A sign from k'Ádhá. Was this, Kavan mused, the sign he sought? Kóráhm had not come, the záryph remained distant, but perhaps the saint could not show himself here, and Kavan had not spent time enough in prayer and meditation with his harp to draw the záryph. Perhaps this was the only means they had to give him direction and remind him he was not alone.

Raebhá smiled at the awe and reverence in his voice and on his face as he turned, head thrown back to watch the tapestry of undulating color. Similar rapture was usually seen on the faces of children when they saw the lights for the first time, when the myths were told and the night of fire and music commenced to allow each child to experience the beauty before it faded.

Most adults Raebhá knew lost interest in the phenomenon, became jaded to the yearly ritualistic beauty on display. Many barely noticed their appearance in the sky. She and her father and brother had marked each appearance with celebration and remembrance for those in their family who were no longer with them. Kavan was the first man, apart from her father and brother and her brother's best friend, to openly marvel at the lights, the first to unabashedly express the child-like wonder at a thing of beauty that could not be explained.

"I never tire of watching them," she murmured, slipping her hand into his, hoping to see this sight through his eyes. "We…my family, we use to watch together, our ritual…when they came…one I hope to instill in my children someday."

Ignoring the uncomfortable twist in his belly at the mention of the children she would have with her husband if, by k'Ádhá's blessing he still lived, Kavan nodded but said nothing. Only the twitch at the corner of his mouth and eyes showed he had heard her, but as she was not looking at him, she did not see it.

With no wind, the air was calm, unbroken by sound except for a soft melodic hum that began in the back of his throat without his awareness. When he did realize he was humming, that the melody was born of childhood memories from a time when most recalled nothing, he opened his mouth, thinking of his mother, about to remark in wonder that some remnant of this majesty existed in Elyri memory still, even if only in a child's lullaby. There were words there, words he should not remember, but words that he knew were a reflection of the colorful ribbons of light glimmering off of the pristine snow that his mother, or no Elyri alive today, had ever seen.

> *maimís kyryth keh nís*
> *íth k'bhekalomár*
> *zugdhu dhe ubé ghlaebh*
> *yó hne íth agdhár ebh cónyses*

From far away, carried uninterrupted on the night air, another sound undercut his song, the harmonic chanting of multiple voices, the sort men gave up to lend a rhythm to heavy manual labor. It was faint, almost unnoticeable as the rise and fall gave volume to some notes and stole it from others. The gleeful spark in Raebhá's eyes indicated she heard it as well. Any question she had been about to ask about Kavan's song, any comment he might have made about the same, was lost in unexpected elation.

The revelation did not need to be spoken to be real. It was difficult to ascertain the direction the chanting came from, but both believed, based on the position of the stars and their direction of travel, that the sound rose neither from the west nor the south. North once again seemed promising; for as long as the song continued, they had a beacon to follow.

"We should go." Kavan would have preferred to remain where he was, basking in what he believed was a sign meant for him, a sign that had forced him to stand still and listen to the night. If they had been walking, he might not have heard the chanting over the crunch of their feet on the snow, his breathing, his pounding heart. He thanked k'Ádhá for the moment of stillness and kept his eyes on the ribbons of light, both of which had blessed him with an answer to his prayers.

Wortham, he thought warmly, would have loved this sight as much as he did.

❧*❧

Sometimes, duplicating effort was a productive thing, particularly when it came to the investigation of a crime. No two investigators conducted a search in the same way, and so Wace went over every detail of the scenes himself, searching the place Cedric's body had been found, studying the surrounding buildings, comparing the position of the man's head and body, for any clue as to what he had seen when he had fallen, what his last moments might have been. The blood he had shed was now scattered into the dust of the dry street, trampled by passing feet, hooves, and wheels, but that meant not lying in blood when Wace lay on the spot where Cedric would have been. Passersby gawked at him, some recognizing him and edging away in fear, some giving him and the inquisitor a wide berth as they presumed business was underway. The bounty hunter did not care if they stared, did not care if people were afraid of him or thought him mad. He barely noticed. What he did notice were the glances he received from the royal guardsmen as Fen helped him to his feet.

The stiffness in his body reminded him again why he had decided to make this his final job for the Lachlan Crown.

None of the nearby business people had witnessed anything unusual the evening of the murder and Wace heard no hint of fallacy in their statements, no lies or deceit. The minstrel had dropped in sight of the náós and, Wace judged from the position of the fallen body, had been going towards it rather than coming away. It seemed likely he had not been carrying the missing relic when struck down, despite ample evidence that someone had taken hidden refuge in Hes á Redh before the doors were locked. Someone had been there…but not Cedric. They were the only details the inquiry had thus far offered.

Instinct told him the killer had been following O'Grady for a long time. May have followed him to Rhidam. He needed to retrace the minstrel's journey, needed to learn where he had traveled from. Discover where he had come into possession of the mantle, who had given it to him and why. He would have to go back to the beginning. Back to the source.

Back to the desert.

Wace would not find the killer in Rhidam. By now, he suspected he would not find the killer in Enesfel.

It had been a long time since he had been in his homeland, and as he had told Kavan, he felt little desire to return there. As he bid farewell to Inquisitor Geli with the promise of visiting the villages and farms surrounding Rhidam before making a journey west to follow the route O'Grady had traveled, a promise of reporting every detail he learned, Wace understood he had no choice. He knew the rumors, knew the stories, knew the long-held oral traditions of the Cíbhóló. Going to St. Kóráhm's would have to wait. Going home had, perhaps, been his destiny all along.

❧*❦

Without a horse, having never learned to ride and having few coins with which to buy one if he had known how, Myreth had been forced out of Rhidam on foot, fleeing to avoid the charges he knew would be levied should he be caught with that which he carried. He did not consider the act theft, but rather a furthering of the effort to get this precious object into the hands of the man it belonged to. He did not know the previous courier's intent. He only knew his instructions, his desire to see a man again that he had not seen in far too long.

His heart swelled with longing.

Had Kavan gone back for him as promised, when his need for the Chalice and Staff were sated? Myreth berated himself often for not waiting, argued that he should have stayed when the doors of the order opened and his community was freed to step into the world if they wished. Qol had wanted him to stay, had begged it of him, but for the first time in his life, believing in his stubborn heart that he could find the Elyri bard within a matter of days, Myreth took destiny into his own hands, setting out the moment he was permitted to leave.

Surely the pull of the light inside Kavan would draw them together and they would never be separated.

Reality proved a harsh teacher, and the charity of others in return for his singing or a day's labor proved to be the only way he could accommodate his basic needs. His unfamiliarity with customs and languages had brought him afoul of the law more than once despite his desire to do right. Kavan's presence gradually dimmed, never disappearing but fading enough that it became more difficult to follow. Only the stories and rumors about the White Bard guided him, sometimes leading him astray, until his journey eventually brought him to the southern fringes of the land called Hatu.

It was there he met her, the dark-haired, enigmatic beauty who looked as though she could have been his kin, his twin. A woman who went only by the name Bhás, who promised what he wanted most in return for his aid in her quest. Though tall, Bhás was a thin, spritely, frail-looking creature in need of a man's strength and voice in a land where women were the lesser of the sexes. Expecting it to be a simple thing that would be accomplished quickly, that he would be once more on the certain path of finding Kavan, Myreth agreed.

One quest turned into two, into five, until the years and miles took him deep into the desert, into the rolling hills of Cordash, the forests of Neth, and back to the Cíbhóló again. She tempted him with coin, with knowledge, with trinkets and jewels he intended to deliver to Kavan, and with enough of her affections to keep him interested without pushing too much against decades of indoctrination. She tempted him with the assurance that she knew Kavan, that she would help find the bard, that she would see them reunited as he wished.

Believing her claims of sightings in one place or another, Myreth had followed her directions, even when time after time her information proved inaccurate. Time held little meaning for a man who could live for centuries, except for the continuing ache of Kavan's absence, until he grew weary of being led astray too often and repeatedly duped. Though they never traveled together, and Bhás's contact with him had become increasingly through letters or messengers sent to wherever he happened to be, Myreth had finally chosen to cut ties with her.

He ignored her last dozen or so messages in favor of traveling a path that he believed brought him nearer to Kavan. When he was certain of his direction at last, she showed herself again. He was satisfied with the chance to tell her to her face that he would no longer do her bidding. Too many years had been wasted. He needed Kavan.

But her friendly company, her beautiful face, the charm of her touch were seductive. She brought with her the promise of Saint Kóráhm's mantle and the opportunity to deliver it into Kavan's hands. It was a lure Myreth was unable to refuse. Kóráhm, as sacred as the saint was to Myreth, was even more so to Kavan. The White Bard possessed the saint's ring, was graced with his company and favor in often tangible ways. If the mantle existed, it belonged to Kavan.

Myreth had agreed to this one last task.

For two years he and Bhás followed every rumor that surfaced, sometimes working and traveling together in their quest for it. The mantle had finally come within reach when it was delivered to the blonde minstrel. Myreth was prepared to take it, but Bhás bid him stay his hand, follow Cedric, and learn where the man was taking it.

Frustrated, Myreth only agreed because the minstrel was traveling into Enesfel, in the direction Myreth believed Kavan to be.

He lost contact with Bhás, aside from periodic messages delivered when his travels paused for more than a few days due to lack of coin or because the minstrel's journey also paused. The jewels, the trinkets he had been given, had been long ago traded for coin, leaving him with nothing. Not knowing Cedric's intended destination, when he left the mantle in Hes á Redh in favor of visiting the Rhidam castle and making a too-long circuit of local taverns, Myreth had believed that the mantle had been delivered to where Cedric intended it to stay. His belief was more certain when he viewed the mantle on display at the front of the Gathering Hall.

He could not abide the thought of it remaining there, not when it should be with Kavan, and Bhás insisted that Saint Kóráhm had appeared to her in a dream and told her the mantle must be delivered to Lord Cliáth.

The harper was not in Rhidam. He was the Duke of Alberni. That meant traveling to Alberni. It meant taking the mantle on the last leg of its saint-approved journey.

That was not theft but the virtuous act of imparting a priceless item into the custody of the most decent, holy man Myreth had ever known.

A week on foot at most, less if he ran along the main road, more if he was forced to travel through the cover of the forests that lined much of the east road between Rhidam and Alberni. Compared to the more than twenty years he had spent seeking Kavan, enduring the desperate longing to be at the man's side, a week was nothing.

As long as he avoided arrest for this sacred duty, there was nothing more in the world he wanted.

❧*❧

Gabrielle closed the door behind the messenger who had delivered the rolled parchment held in her hand, a parchment sealed with brown wax, an insignia she did not recognize stamped upon it, and a dirty strip of twine knotted so that it was set into the hardened wax. None would be able to untie it without breaking the seal or cutting the cord, and it was not Gabrielle's place to do so. Her hands trembled; her stomach twisted into a tight, acidic ball. She knew what this had to be, the news Asta was waiting for, news she hoped was good.

Asta's footsteps on the stairs caused Gabrielle to fear the news would not be what they hoped.

Hearing the voices, Asta descended in time to see the door close and Gabrielle turn from it with the parchment in her hand. "For me?"

She sounded less afraid than she felt.

Though reluctant to turn it over, Gabrielle extended the offering, her breath catching when Asta took the scroll.

The seal was barely noticed as she broke it open, recognized as an Association mark but unremarkable in any other way. She began walking towards the sitting room as she read it. Gabrielle followed. When Asta stopped and the parchment slid from her fingers, Gabrielle was there to catch it and to grasp the younger woman's shoulder supportively. Though her face lost color and her eyes lost what little spark of life had remained over the past several days, she showed no other trace of emotion as she murmured, "Oska has the throne."

"Oska…does that mean…?"

"Kjell is…" He had to be dead. Or seriously injured. How else could Oska have the crown?

"But if Oska…then it's a good thing? It should be safe for you and Jerit to…?"

Asta shook her head. "The claim is that loyalists to Jerit, to me, led a revolt to make him king, to bring Neth under Enesfel's rule."

"That's absurd!" Gabrielle began to read the scroll, but Asta snatched it away. Only four words jumped off the page and caught her eye.

Presumed to be dead.

Who?

"We should have foreseen this." But how could they have predicted such a turn of events? Oska was not the sort of man to turn on his family. He was the sort, however, to assume leadership to contain the chaos while the details were sorted out and guilt was determined. Perhaps, Asta mused, she should go back, plead Jerit's case. But she did not dare leave her youngest son. Not until she was certain he would be safe.

"What will you do?"

Asta did not reply at first, instead stared at the words on the parchment without actually seeing them, those four words burning like a brand deeper and deeper into her heart. Kjell. Dead. A king with so much promise…died for what? Not that Neth's fanatical factions ever needed a reason. The fear of change might have been enough for some. Or the fear of her.

She was a Lachlan after all. The Lachlans had stripped territory from Neth. Maybe her marriage to Kjell had been all that was needed to spark this catastrophe.

But Inness was a Lachlan too…and she was still there as far as Asta knew. Perhaps there was hope.

"Rhidam," she eventually whispered, defeat dragging at the end of the word. "I go home."

Her father was not there. Her brother was not there. Her husband and two of her children were not there. But her cousin was. Yóáná was. The Lachlan keep was where she had grown up. Rhidam was, for now, the only home Asta had, and she believed Jerit would be protected there while she decided what to do next.

&*&

It was a risk, but a risk he believed Kavan would take if he was home to face the Yellow Sisters sinking their fangs into Alberni's population. Rhyrdan had been prepared to take the risk alone, ride through the starving, ailing masses, assess the situation, and perhaps offer comfort with his presence. But Captain Magk would not allow it. With Dhóri throwing what the captain considered an unnecessary and inappropriate tantrum, refusing to accept responsibility for his family's estate as if it would somehow punish his father, Rhyrdan was the closest thing Alberni had to a lord. Thanks to his father's steadfastness, the Delamo name was respected and trusted and no one questioned Rhyrdan's authority.

Respect, was of little benefit when the suffering barely lifted their heads to note who was passing through the much-needed cold autumn shower. The Yellow Death was thus far contained to four outlying streets, but no one expected the containment to last. How could it, when those outside of the confinement came to deliver food, water, and words of comfort, when the extended drizzling storm caused the streets to run dark with mud, blood, and the waste of the dying?

No contact was permitted, as Rhyrdan could not be sure the containment rules were upheld, and with no certainty of the method of spread, that precaution, and the covering of mouths and noses, might not be enough to protect anyone. With the dead accumulating in those streets, where the dogs and rats and crows made an effort to pick over the corpses waiting to be gathered by volunteers for burning in a burial pit at the northern edge of the city, how could anyone remain safe? Fires did not burn well beneath the much-needed rain and the pits gathered water as they were dug and Rhyrdan feared the run-off might wash the contagion over the earth, into the river or the sea, into wells and underground cisterns where the community water pooled.

But the dead could not remain where they fell, so they were dealt with as best they could be in the hopes that the sickness they carried would not poison anyone else.

"We need to release more stores," Rhyrdan muttered beneath the collar he had turned up against the rain as he turned his horse towards the manor. Rain dripped from the brim of his hat and the horse again shook its head to rid its mane and eyes of the heaviness of moisture.

The captain's frown did not change. He saw little hope for those already infected, and as a realist, a man prone more to pessimism than optimism, he did not think food was the solution. If there was a solution, it was in the hands of k'Ádhá since Kavan was not here to offer it. "I don't think that will help. The suffering are beyond the need for more food; it would be a waste of..."

"Not for them," the younger man hesitantly agreed. "For the others, those most at risk, to give them strength to remain healthy."

Though not convinced such a measure would be beneficial, the captain nodded. It was a sound enough precaution, and if the rain continued as it had for the last week, there was hope for a crop in the spring, provided there was anyone left to plant and harvest it. He wondered if the rain fell in other drought-ridden regions of Enesfel. "I will speak with Groff, determine what remains that we can distribute."

"Encourage the fishermen to increase production. We are low on grain and the livestock is at risk, but the fish are not." At least, he did not believe the taint of the plague had affected the creatures of the sea. "Have Groff appoint someone to oversee distribution of the catch as evenly as possible. No one is to be favored, not even my family."

Many the captain had known and served over the years would have demanded differently, claiming shares as their right because of their status, as if they were needed to rule and hence deserved more. Clarys had known little dearth in his lifetime, but any shortage of commodity was often met by men of power in the same way. Kavan, he knew, would be proud that Rhyrdan was not such a man.

"Aye, I will see to it."

They were near enough to the house now that he trusted Rhyrdan's safety and so he peeled off to seek Sheriff Groff and visit the docks as instructed. The day's directives, the state of the city, would be passed on to k'gdhededhá Khwílen as well upon his return to St. Kóráhm's. There was discussion among the gdhededhá as to how best to help the afflicted. The memory of the last plague, one which had also begun amongst Teren and spread into Elyriá and had proven just as deadly to them, was still fresh in the minds of the Elyri old enough to have lived through it or whose parents had done so. There was no such memory amongst the Teren, only stories a few generations old. The desire to help, to follow their faith, warred with their fears. The captain understood it. Many Teren did not.

In time, he trusted faith would win. Raenár knew it. Rhyrdan and Khwílen knew it. Every man and woman in the chellé hábhai knew it.

It was less certain if those living in Alberni would win as well.

The rain that bathed Alberni fell harder in Rhidam, the relentless pounding flooding low-lying streets and fields, seeping into the bottom levels of some structures despite the efforts to keep the water at bay. It rushed into the Tegid, diverted there from flooded streets when possible, swelling the banks again. Since an abundance of rain in the northern reaches of Enesfel meant a too high level in the Tegid for the past three years, many of the foundations of businesses located on the river's banks had become unstable, left unusable.

No one knew if it rained in the north. No one knew how far inland the storm's reach extended. Rhidam's first significant rain in three years was creating a similar deluge, however, and the city was ill-prepared for it. Even the castle moat threatened to overflow despite the trenches dug to allow the water to recede towards the river. Similar trenches throughout Rhidam clogged with leaves and debris, creating overspills of water and mud into the streets. Residents dug constantly to clear them, to create new channels, to protect homes and structures threatened by the desperately needed rain.

With the mud and water came plague. Nearest the Tegid's bank, where the moisture accumulated and bred mold and mildew on the interior walls and in the straw used to line floors or thatch roofs, the sickness took hold and spread, rushing like the flow of water, reaching from the northern edges of Rhidam and the southern to collide in the center and create a swelling bubble of death on either side of the river.

With more people residing on the east side of the Tegid, the collection of victims of one or both Sisters grew more rapidly there, pushing deeper into the heart of Rhidam. Soldiers, both royal guard and those conscripted by the lord justice and sheriff, did their best to cordon off the infected streets, to halt traffic between the plague zones and those areas still untouched but the contagion found its way around every effort made to contain it until even the soldiers and the clergy sent to assist the afflicted became victims.

Ártur wrung his hands, scrubbed a hand through his hair, and then wrung them again as he listened, his back turned to reports of death inundating them from one source after another. He remembered the last plague, the one that had taken Donal Lachlan's daughters, had taken Ártur's sister and had robbed Kavan of his mother. So many had perished, Teren and Elyri alike, but that scourge felt as if it was dwarfed by what the Sovereignties faced now. Years of hunger had weakened them, left many too feeble in body and spirit to fight the assault of two different sources of disease. Some would survive; they always did. Some would be unaffected. But there would likely be no pattern to their survival, thus no way to successfully care for anyone.

News had come the day before of the death of Balint Gabersdon. If a strong man could not defeat this stroke of death, what hope did anyone else have?

"I want Arlana and the boys away from here," Merrek growled.

"There is nowhere to send them, My Liege," Níkóá sighed. "The scourge has spread into Fiara, likely into Neth. All of Enesfel is…"

"Cordash. Hatu. They can go to my brother's…or Káliel."

Fen cracked his knuckles, a frustrated habit that he was often unaware of. "They are afflicted as we are. Nowhere is safe."

"Then Elyriá. The mountains will protect them," Merrek snapped.

"We don't know that, Sire." Ártur turned at last, his expression grim. "None of us has been there…they may be as infected…"

With Elyri travel no longer restricted or discouraged, merchants, artists, performers, and healers had resumed traveling into Teren lands and any of them could have carried the contagion back with them. The influx of healers into Rhidam over the last several days suggested that news of the Yellow Death had passed east. How likely was it that the diseases themselves had done the same?

"Find out. If it is safe, if my family is not already infected, I want them where they will be out of harm's way. The children cannot be…"

Baby Conroy was too young to survive a plague, and Prince Lorant was not the strongest of children. The prince had to think about the future of Enesfel rather than his wife's desire to stay at his side or his own to keep them near. The princes had to survive.

Ártur sighed. It was not that he disagreed with the prince. He and Syl had argued upon waking about the issue, when he had tried to convince her to return to Bhryell to wait out the plagues, to remain away from the possibility of suffering and death that Ártur could not bear. As he would not leave the Lachlans, however, seeing it as his duty to remain with the royal family to aide them, should any become infected, Syl chose to remain as well. She had fled the violence more than twenty years ago to protect their young children, but now those children were grown, married, and she was less afraid of the Yellow Death than she had been of uncontrolled violence.

Besides, as long as Elyriá remained plague-free, Syl felt she could do more to benefit the people of Enesfel than she could do for her own kind. Chethá was there already, one of eight healers in the regions nearest Bhryell, three in the village itself. Syl would not be needed there as she was here and she chose not to leave her husband's side again. If he was staying in Rhidam, so would she.

At the moment, she argued, they did not know if either Yellow Sister would affect Elyri. Some human illnesses did. Others did not.

"Yes, My Liege. Very well." Perhaps by convincing Syl to visit their daughter, to learn of the safety of Elyriá first hand, his wife would be prompted to remain there as he wished.

❧*❧

The mountains sloped into a valley dense with craggy pines, spruce, yew, and a frozen lake that gave way to a river winding towards the lights of the coastal settlement. As they descended the mountain, Kavan recognized a cluster of buildings gathered at the edge of the sea, their rooftops covered with the snow that had begun to fall hours before and which continued as they reached the foot of the pass. The distance between them and the lights, the fact that the settlement appeared like no city Kavan had ever seen, and the heavy snowfall that slowed them, did little to discourage his increased pace. Foul weather or no, miles of forest and open white flatland, by the time the stars' position indicated nightfall, he hoped they would have reached shelter and civilization, people he was eager to meet.

At least they would reach the cover of the forest.

The valley stretched south but there were no lights there, only endless white to the horizon of sea black in the unending night.

If everything Raebhá told him was true, these people were kin. It was proof of kinship that Kavan wanted as strongly as he desired shelter, proof that he wanted more than the possibility of a usable Gate.

They reached a portion of the forest where trees had been recently felled and followed the dragging paths of logs towards the river. The cuts in the snow disappeared at the river's edge, where Raebhá squatted and tested the depth of the snow with her hand.

She looked at him with a nod.

"I'd say we were hearing the woodsmen. The ponies and sleds took the logs in." It had taken them two days after the chanting ceased to reach the end of the mountain pass and another day to make their way down the final mountain face to the forest's edge. The woodsmen were gone, no trace left of their passing thanks to the snowfall, but here at the river's edge, he accepted her assessment. She knew these people, their habits and practices. She knew this climate. He did not.

"If we follow the river we may reach the ghís soon if the weather remains in our favor." She stood slowly, seeming to Kavan to suffer a weary ache, and he steadied her with both hands.

They had traveled too many days with little food. She needed rest and warmth. "Do you wish to stop?" Though they had not come far today, the trees would offer shelter, the broken branches a decent fire.

Raebhá shook her head and tugged free with a forced smile. "Why rest here when we can rest in the shelter of a home, with a hearth, warm food, and soft bedding? Or would you rather…?"

Only as she spoke did she consider that he might wish to avoid civilization a while longer. Civilization meant the chance of a Gate, and a Gate meant inevitable separation. "We can rest if you prefer…"

Scanning the flow of the ice-covered river, using the light of the stars reflecting off the fresh snow, Kavan was able to follow the river's path until it turned through the trees taking it beyond their line of sight. He heard her words but could not find the voice to answer her. Instead, he stepped onto the ice, confident it would hold them if it had held fallen trees and the ponies used to drag them. The river's path would be more level than the thick growth of vegetation at its edges.

He considered taking the wolf shape as they could pass over the snow faster and easier, but she seemed too weary for the change and as she had surmised, he was reluctant to hasten their journey towards its end. They would be forced to part soon enough.

One hour after another they trudged, the snow preventing them from slipping on the ice, neither speaking as anticipation and trepidation built. The forest thinned, exposing more of the snowy sky, until the river broke away from the trees and the forest gave way to land that Kavan guessed served as growing fields when the snow melted enough for planting. The warmth of light through distant windows was joined by curls of white smoke through roof vents, its sweet scent beckoning them forward.

With no cover to shield them, they could not retreat when a group of dark shapes armed with spears and long, hooked poles emerged from the edge of the settlement, approaching with a determination that Kavan did not interpret as friendly. The nearly two dozen individuals shouted; Kavan could not understand them but when Raebhá stopped walking and held up her arms as if to show she was no threat, he did likewise. He could not understand most of her words as he had been gradually learning to do, and it frustrated him not to know what was being said. A regional dialect, perhaps, guttural and harsh, made harsher by what he decided were demands made.

He wanted to touch her, to access their conversation. He could not.

Whatever Raebhá said went unheeded. The strangers, bundled in furs and skins so that only their eyes were visible, surrounded them and with barked commands herded them with the points of their poles towards the settlement. Raebhá caught Kavan's eye, offering a silent, confused apology, but other than her unfruitful attempts to question the welcome party, she chose not to speak until they reached the outlying cluster of similarly constructed round structures. Only two were standard four-sided buildings, one oblong and bursting with loud voices, tantalizing smells, and boisterous music.

Half of the group peeled away, ushering Kavan into the first building they reached. He did not have the chance to inspect the others. The rest of the group pushed Raebhá further along.

"Raebhá!" Kavan shouted, reaching for her as someone struck him with the blunt end of a fishing tool. The blow was hard enough to cause him to stumble. Someone scooped up the pack that slid from his shoulder as another opened the door and shoved him inside. There was the distinct click of a lock, words barked that he did not understand, followed by the crunch of boots through snow that left him alone in what appeared to be a storeroom filled with blocks of ice, empty crates, bales of grasses, and thick furry skins suspended from hooks. There was no means for a fire unless he burned the crates, no food unless he resorted to dried grass and hides, and no water except for the snow that blew through the crack beneath the door.

Peculiar behavior for non-violent people. But perhaps things had changed with Raebhá's abduction. Or maybe they were nowhere near her people, her lands, as she believed and these people were other than those she expected them to be. Kavan chastised himself for making no effort to read them, but the idea had not come until too late.

Choosing to believe that they thought him to be her abductor, that they had taken her for care and questioning, that he would be released as soon as her identity was revealed and the situation explained and resolved to the settlers' satisfaction, Kavan decided not to free himself. That might raise the ire of the villagers and he did not want enemies. He moved the bundles of grasses so that they served as a three-sided warming shelter and then sat between them, his back to the bales, one of the thick white pelts taken down from the wall to keep him warm. He was cold without Raebhá's warmth at his side, but this solitude would have been bearable if he could be certain she was alright.

❧Chapter 20❧

The rider refused to stop when the palace sentries tried to stay the horse at the gates. When she threw back the hood of her cloak, most recognized her pale red hair and the features that marked her as both Lachlan and Dugan. There were unspoken questions, curiosity about why the Queen of Neth and one of her sons had come on a single horse without escort, but Asta had refused attendants when Gabrielle offered. In Enesfel she was safe and could travel faster on her own. She doubted any murdering factions had followed her out of Neth.

She had sent word to Oska, demanding information, wanting to know he was well, wanting to know what had happened to Kjell. If Oska was king, Kjell was either incapacitated or dead, murdered…but had he been given a proper burial? What had happened? And how? How was Oska's health? How was Inness? Asta instructed that a reply was to be sent to Rhidam but it would be a long time in coming, two weeks or more she presumed. She would petition her queen-cousin for aid if Oska required it, even if that aid came in the form of a meager handful of men not overcome by plague.

"Where is the queen?" she demanded as she swung from the horse and pulled Jerit down with her. "I must see her."

Having witnessed the initial courtyard turmoil from the guardhouse where he had been conducting business, Níkóá strode across the yard to greet her. "Lady de Corrmick; this is unexpected…"

"I need to see Diona. I demand it."

That was a strong term to use, and out of character unless there was a matter of grave import, and so he escorted her and the boy into the keep with a wave to dismiss the sentries to their duties and the palace staff to care for the weary horse. As Asta and her son carried few belongings, Níkóá's first assumption was that they had been robbed on the road and it was her purpose for being here.

Maybe the rest of her party had been killed.

As she marched ahead at a pace that he struggled to keep up with, she did not see his scowl. "Where is she? Merrek? Where is Yóáná?"

"I left the Prince-Regent in the morning room over an hour ago…"

Asta turned without direction towards that room. Níkóá caught up with her in time to open the morning room door where Merrek sat with Diona. Both looked up in annoyance at the intrusion, but when they saw the woman and child behind Níkóá, and the mixed expression of relief, dismay, and anxiety on Asta's face, the annoyance evaporated.

"Asta!" Diona ignored decorum to stand and welcome her cousin in an embrace. "We were not expecting…"

"My trip was unforeseen." Her voice cracked as she fought to maintain composure while seeking signs of her daughter.

Merrek lay a hand on her shoulder. At the door, Níkóá began to back out of the room, assuming the queen and her kin would want privacy, but a glance from Merrek bid him stay.

"What has happened?" Diona asked.

"I…" Sensing Merrek's movement, Asta looked over her shoulder and softly asked, "Lord Chamberlain, will you take Jerit to Yóáná, tell her I wish to see her?"

Though annoyed at being relegated to the role of babysitter, Níkóá looked at the prince, questioning the conflicting order, and Merrek waved him on. "Yes, my lady," he said in a tone so neutral that it masked his annoyance. If the topic of discussion concerned him, he would be told soon enough. If Yóáná was where he had last seen her, he should not miss much of this conversation.

"Mother," Jerit whined, scowling, annoyed to be treated like a child. Some news had come regarding his father and brother that had prompted their departure from Fiara, that much he guessed, but his mother refused to speak of it.

"Rest, son. I shall come to you when my business with the queen is complete. Say hello to your sister."

Yóáná had been present for Jerit's birth, as she had been for Oska and Rika's, and had visited her siblings on a couple of rare occasions, but they did not know one another well enough to be on intimate terms.

Maybe, for as long as Asta was forced to stay in Rhidam, the siblings could grow accustomed to one another.

Though his frown did not fall away, Jerit left with the Chamberlain he had met only twice before. When the door closed, Asta stepped back from her cousin to study her, noticing a difference in her eyes that had not been there before. "Now tell me…what has caused you to give up the throne? Not," she managed a weak smile at Merrek despite the haunting shadows in her eyes, "that I doubt your qualifications."

Merrek was so much like his father in face, comportment, and attitude that Asta could not imagine him being less than capable.

"I've not given up anything. As for…it was time." Diona shrugged, resuming her seat as if weary. "Enesfel needs someone who can see the future, whose vision can lead the kingdom through this crisis. A queen without eyesight can only do so much…"

"Nonsense," Merrek scolded lightly without turning his attention from Asta. "You can do whatever you set your mind to. The Crown is yours. I am only here to assist…"

"You are…?" Kneeling before her cousin, Asta clutched her hands.

Diona interrupted before Asta could say the word. "Not yet, but I will be. That last fever has taken it little by little, until I can no longer hide it or pretend it is not a hindrance. Bhyrhán has been of great help and comfort, allowing me to see yet a little longer the things I will miss when my eyes are gone…but it would not do for him to stand at the throne at my side. I will not risk his life that way."

"I am sorry. There is nothing the healers can do?"

"Ártur has tried…and there has been no miracle." Her light tone was meant to mask her regret and disappointment. "But you…tell us why you have come? Not merely because of this?"

"I meant to be here for the ceremony…but duties would not permit it." It was true, though it was not the reason Asta was here. She got up from her knees and took a nearby chair before continuing. "We intended to make the journey together, in support of you both." She sighed and looked at her hands. "But not like this."

Giving neither of them a chance to question her, Asta added, "There has been an insurrection in Glevum."

Merrek leaned forward, his posture alert as if ready to fight while Diona's wide eyes expressed horror and concern.

"I'm told it was carried out by a faction intending to put Jerit on the throne, that Kjell has been killed…"

"Asta!"

"The uprising was put down," she hastily continued, avoiding lingering on Kjell or his fate, "and Oska has assumed the throne, but until I know it is safe for Jerit to return to Glevum, we seek sanctuary."

"You have it," Diona said without hesitation as Merrek asked, "Why would anyone…?"

"There are some who desire a return to the old ways…who have opposed Kjell from the start because they perceive him as weak, regardless of the benefits Neth has reaped. I imagine they think Jerit, being young enough to require regents, would be easily manipulated. Oska is lucky they did not kill him as well."

"And Inness? Is she…?"

It was not a marriage match Diona would have chosen for her eldest daughter, as much as she loved her nephew, but it was the match Inness had chosen and one that Diona therefore supported. Further joining the Lachlan House with Neth, the joining of bloodlines and political like-mindedness, should be in the best interest of the Sovereignties. Despite any disparities between herself and her second cousin, Inness had attached herself to Oska at an early age, writing letters to him when they were apart, favoring his company when the de Corrmicks and Lachlans came together. Inness had been his best friend and confidant for so long that Asta believed her sensitive son would be too devastated to rule if he had lost her.

"I have no word of her death; I believe her to be well. Oska needs her more than ever. Jerit does not know…Kjell insisted we escape, that I keep Jerit safe…but I have not had the heart to tell him more."

"He deserves to know…"

Asta nodded. "I know he does…but I want to be certain. I want word from Oska. Once I know the details, I will tell Jerit everything. Please, do not speak of this."

"We will not," the prince promised.

"I also request men for Oska, should he require it to restore order."

"There are few men to spare; plague and hunger are draining our ranks. Others have returned home to family and lands ravaged by the weather. But we will send what we can, if Oska needs them. I will speak to the general and see what can be done, if you will excuse me."

Protecting family and the allegiance forged with Neth these past twenty years was important. Merrek did not need his aunt's advice to know that and see it done.

"Thank you." Asta watched him leave the room and groaned; her cousin took her hand. Having military backing brought Asta comfort as she had expected it would, but it did nothing to bring Kjell back.

❧*❧

As Hwensen anticipated, it took less than two weeks to gather the remaining stray candidates to Clarys and conduct the vote that would install a new k'gdhededhá at the head of the Elyri Faith. Tusánt chose to leave matters in Rhidam on Rankin's shoulders to sit in on the election process and, he hoped, have the opportunity to provide input should the vote appear to be leaning in an unfavorable direction. Some did not approve of the Teren Faith taking part in the proceedings, but the vote to permit him to stay was swayed in his favor and he remained despite the smattering of harsh glares directed at him.

There was little need for concern as the pre-vote dialogue favored one man above the rest, as Hwensen had anticipated. When the election bells announced the appointment, it was Ylár who stepped onto the balcony in the dark blue robes of leadership, the sapphire and silver ring on the middle finger of his left hand, and the silver and gold gilded staff held in his right. Seeing him, the purple scarring over his scalp and the hawkish appearance of his features made no less intimidating by the change in attire, gave Tusánt hope for the future of the Faith. Ylár was a young man by comparison to other candidates and his two predecessors. If fate was with him, he could hold the post for over a hundred years, likely longer, plenty of time, Tusánt believed, to reconcile the Elyri and Teren churches under one banner of Faith.

He assumed that was what the new k'gdhededhá wished to discuss when Ylár's emissaries, Hwensen and two other men with apostolic weapons of office, summoned him to a meeting before Ylár had even finished his inauguration Lesson. Tusánt had nearly thirty minutes to collect his thoughts, prepare an argument for reunification, and nervously pace before the tall man with intimidating features strode into the room. Tusánt scrambled to his feet, having just settled onto a cushioned settee when the door opened, and crossed to offer the customary bow and kiss the man's ring. Ylár, however, did not offer his hand for that greeting.

"Regardless of custom, Tusánt, you and I are equals…leaders of the Faith in our prospective homes. I see no need for formality, do you?" His tone was warm, belying his daunting visage, and he smiled with relief now that the first part of the ritual day was over. There would be a banquet later, followed by a High Gathering where the masses would pay homage to their Faith leader, but as such things took time to prepare, Ylár had an opportunity to relax. While he had eased his stance and given the staff to Hwensen who had closed the door to leave the two leaders alone, Ylár's thoughts were on business.

"You are k'gdhededhá to me. Only politics makes us equal."

"Sometimes politics separate those who should be equal into factions where there is no reason for it. There should be more equality between Elyri and Teren, I think, and less division."

Tusánt smiled with relief. "That is what you have asked me here to discuss? Healing this division of the Faithful?"

Shaking his head, Ylár sat and gestured for the other man to sit as well. "It is on my agenda, but it will take time, Tusánt. There are too many variances of opinion, too many strained tempers, too much tempest between our peoples. It will take time to soothe wounds and bring others to accept and welcome reconciliation. I intend to make it happen, but it will require patience, my friend."

Were they friends? Tusánt had not considered it, since they barely knew each other, but perhaps in Ylár's eyes, they knew each other well enough. "I will do everything I can to facilitate it."

"Good. I do not think a reunion is possible on the terms we once knew, but we will see what the future brings. Since you are here, I have a favor to ask. As you know, upon appointment it is the k'gdhededhá's right to grant pardon. Some push to extend pardon to Lláhy, to honor Dórímyr's memory but I do not believe that an appropriate use of prerogative. He was influential in his father's death. Such a crime cannot be easily set aside, and I see it as no honor for the father to forgive the son. But there is another wrong I wish to see righted and none will challenge me when I do, now that Tumm is gone."

"Another wrong?" Tusánt felt tension race through his shoulders and up his neck so that his head began to throb.

"I'm sure you know of Kluín and Hwensen's petition. I'm sure you signed it. Bring Lord Cliáth to me. I will lift excommunication and welcome him into the Faith."

Ylár's words bled away the abrupt accumulation of tension and Tusánt breathed a heavy sigh of relief. Ylár smiled slightly to see it.

"While there are some who are afraid or uncomfortable with the ambiguities Lord Cliáth embodies, most agree that excommunication was a personal vendetta for Dórímyr and Tumm. He has been apart from the Faith too long." He sighed and toyed with his sleeve. "Kyne Mórne is fading…and she desires to see him again, hear him again…a privilege impossible while excommunication is upon him."

The news brought tears to Tusánt's eyes. Mórne had been Kyne for so many years, centuries it had been, there when Tusánt had been born and all of the years since. It was difficult to imagine Elyriá without her. He opened his mouth to speak but Ylár shook his head.

"It is not publically known, though it likely soon will be. Right now, only the family knows." Although Tusánt was unaware of it, Ylár, being the father to several of the Kyne's great-grandchildren, was amongst those family members. There had been a single gdhededhá chosen to serve the Kyne's family over the years, a confessor and confidant and one to bless each new child, each state event, a liaison between the Faith and the secular world. Ylár could have been that man. It would explain his confidential knowledge. "He should not be kept from his family, his Faith, for a private vendetta. I will not stand for it. Bring him to me so that I might…"

"I cannot."

"Cannot?" Ylár frowned.

"He is away, escorting a dignitary home. I am unable to reach him." He could hear the unspoken questions: why not use the Gates, where could he have traveled to that put him beyond the reach of communication, why did Tusánt's words sound so final? Tusánt shrugged. "I do not know where he has gone, to be honest. I believe far south of Hatu. I do not know when he will return."

Ylár snorted and steepled his hands under his chin. "He does not need to be here, of course, to put the reversal into effect, but I prefer him to sign the writ as proof that he is aware of the change…and I desire to tell him this news in person. When you see him, will you send him to me? Without announcing the cause?"

"It might be difficult, given that he knows he faces arrest should he return to Elyriá, but I will do my utmost to bring him to you. I…thank you for this. Kluín, Hwensen, and Khwílen will likewise wish to express…"

"Not until Lord Cliáth knows. None must know before him. Swear to me, Tusánt."

"Not even his family?"

"Not even his family."

Though he frowned, Tusánt nodded in acceptance of the terms. Whatever requirements were necessary to clear Kavan's name, his soul, of the stain Dórímyr and Tumm had cast upon it, Tusánt was willing to fulfill them.

"Thank you." Ylár's smile was relieved. He stood; Tusánt did likewise. "I will send Hwensen as often as I can, keep you abreast of business and summon you to discussions we hold on matters of Faith law and reunification. I want you here. You need to be part of the efforts if we are to reach an accord…and as the representative of the Teren Faith, you should have a voice in our deliberations."

"I will come as I can; thank you." He clasped the offered hand and Ylár put his other hand over the three joined ones. This was a man capable of bringing amity and stability to the Faith. Tusánt prayed he could match the other man's strength of character to facilitate peace.

❧*❧

"I am sorry."

Yóáná did not know what else to say. She loved her mother, was grateful for the life the woman had provided for her by allowing for training she could not have received in Neth, but as very little of her life had been spent in Asta's care, neither could claim closeness to the other. It had been a surprise to learn Asta was here unannounced, and then a horror to learn the reason behind her arrival.

Yóáná did not know Kjell well either, but he seemed a good man of honest intent and character, a man who had provided the first taste of greatness to Neth that had not come at the end of a sword or a rope.

He did not deserve such a death.

She looked at her mother's hand clutched in hers and wondered how she could help. She felt Asta's turmoil, her fear, but also the comfort she found in her daughter's hands. Somehow, the contact reminded Asta of the father Yóáná had never known, and that pleased the younger woman and filled her with unexpected melancholy.

Having wandered the keep for hours after she visited Diona and Merrick, after a weeping visit to Gaelán's burial marker in the Lachlan garden to tell him her troubles, as if he would have answers for her,

Asta had come back inside in search of her son, in search of her daughter, in search of her absent peace of mind. There had been panic at first to find they were not together, but the reassurance that Jerit was secure in the company of the MacLyrs, Prince Lorant, and the chamberlain's daughter Seren, allowed Asta the opportunity to speak with Yóáná at length. They had talked of Rhidam, of her marriage, of plague, before the conversation eventually shifted to the reason for Asta's presence here, the reason she could not go back to Glevum.

Throughout their time together, despite their open and honest sharing, Asta could feel the distance between them, something she had never experienced with her father, a distance that should not exist between her and Gaelán's daughter. Yóáná's father had been good and honorable too, a bright spot in Asta's heart that had never burned out despite a life cut off too soon. Asta should have done more for Yóáná, should have stayed with her, should have given her everything she had been unable to give to Gaelán.

In a way she had. She had given Yóáná a healer's life. But she had failed to give her enough of a mother's love.

Perhaps that had come as a product of the loss of her own mother that had given Asta so little motherly experience to draw from.

"It will be an adjustment for Jerit…he does not yet know…but he will…and I fear he will not understand. He will need you…" The way you needed me, the way I failed to give.

The hand around Asta's tightened. "He will be safe with me…and if today was any indicator, it will do Prince Lorant good to have him here." There was a nine years difference in their ages, but the little prince had already taken to following Jerit through the castle halls, and Jerit, without a younger sibling of his own, seemed eager for the company of someone he could teach and interact with.

"I'm glad to hear it. He will need friends." Uprooted from Glevum, losing Oska, Jerit would need the support of others, whatever the future held.

As would Asta.

Though Yóáná did not say it, the bond shared in their clasped hands proved to Asta that she could count on her daughter despite her failures. For as long as she was here, Asta would do her best to make up for those disappointments.

❧*❧

"If you do not believe me, test me!"

Raebhá's plea and demand again went unanswered, just as it had every day since being thrust into this small, locked room. Her captors continued to ask the same questions: who was she? Why had she come from the mountains with the ghostly stranger? Who was he and why was he here? Could she prove her identity? They listened but seemed not to believe her. They never spoke other than to ask those questions, and then left her alone again. Though they refused to answer her, she was able to glean, through conversations heard through the walls, that she and Kavan had made it to the ghísaer of Ghené, to the ghís of Phaurd. She deduced that none of those interrogating her were márbhyndhánis. It was likely none of them knew about the Gate in the mountains or could tell her what it meant.

A lack of training explained why none sought to read her. None would know how. Without a leader's direction, none would feel permitted to take action against her or Kavan. Instead, they settled for repetitive questions while they waited for instruction and guidance.

She wondered how long that would be. By her calculations and the tick marks made on the wall, she had been questioned twenty-two times, always early in the morning. There was a small shuttered window through which she could watch the positions of the stars as the hours passed which helped confirm her calculations. She was well-fed, given adequate furs for the cot she was allowed, a fire in the central pit offered warmth, and a single whale tallow candle came with each meal to provide light, but her belongings had been confiscated and she remained alone, seeing only those who questioned her.

She worried about Kavan but lacked the skill to seek his presence or determine his welfare. Many times, as she tried to sleep, she believed she felt him with her, a soothing comfort in the darkness. It calmed her to find, each time the sensation came, that he seemed unharmed, but she had no idea where he was. Was he being questioned as well? Did he understand their captors and did his answers coincide with hers? Did their captors understand him or were they frightened by his differences, his language, dialect, and appearance?

If he could blast them free of stone and snow, why had he not freed himself and her?

She sank heavily onto the cot and lay back, weary of pacing and tempted to sleep again. With a hand on her abdomen, she spread the other on the frozen mud-brick wall, closed her eyes, and tried to seek

Kavan's presence. It was easy to imagine that he did not act out of respect for a culture he was unfamiliar with, his curiosity about their captors equal to their curiosity about him. Maybe he feared retribution if he acted. Maybe he was afraid they would hurt her. Maybe he was being better treated than she was, not a captive but a pampered guest.

He would have won her release if that was so. Or perhaps it was his influence that allowed her the basic luxuries she enjoyed. If he was free to move about, she was certain he would have come for her, come to her. If she knew, she would feel better about her predicament.

Instead, she fretted, for with each passing day she became more certain of an unexpected turn she had not thought possible, or likely, before. Actions, no matter how big or small, always had consequences. Now she was presented with one she did not know how to handle.

The matter might be moot, however, if she and Kavan were not released soon. They would not be killed, but what other fate they might face concerned her.

Particularly now.

Elsewhere, denied a bed or the warmth of a fire but given additional furs for protection against the cold and two meals each day at regular intervals, Kavan did not believe he was in danger of execution. Those who brought his meals never spoke. After an initial period of sleep that first day, he sought Raebhá's presence within, traced the threads across the seaside town, and reassured himself then, and each day since, that she was well and unharmed. He could read her loneliness, her confusion, her consternation with their quandary, but he did not intrude on her thoughts. So long as she was unharmed and alive, he was satisfied.

More often than not, his troubled musings stretched back to the Sovereignties, to his cousin, his sons, his friends whom he had abandoned in the face of hunger and plague. And for what? To freeze or live as a captive in this perpetually dark world? He needed to be free, to get Raebhá home, to find a Gate that would take him back to his. He had promised Rhyrdan a swift return and he had, by his best calculations, been away for nearly a month and a half. Kóráhm's feast day, his birthday, had passed. Yet here in this place, he had been unable to summon Kóráhm, and his efforts to touch the thoughts of anyone in Rhidam, Bhryell, or Alberni was of little comfort. He could brush fingers of power over their minds but communication with any so far away was going to take more effort.

He was conserving his energy in case the day came that he needed it to escape this place and get Raebhá out alive.

With little else to do, however, it was an effort he began to practice, reaching from one beloved heart to another, drawing power, draining himself nearly to exhaustion, pushing, stretching, always seeking to reach further, longer, looking for the moment when the effort to communicate with Ártur or any one of the others came as easily to him as a handlight did.

His well of power and command of it were increasing.

The focus helped untangle his thoughts from the man he felt guilty of leaving behind, a dead man who should have been here with him.

Kavan had no notion of how far away he was from the lands he knew. He only knew that it had to be further in miles than he had been during his sojourn south of Hatu, further than the south most cities he had visited of Gorbesh and Pa'aliaka. He longed for a map, a means of constructing an image of the world that would fulfill his curiosity. The hindrance of the great mountains had forced Raebhá's people to become a sea-faring lot. Surely they had mapping abilities that they could offer. How far had they traveled? How much of the world might they have mapped?

If he ever got out of this room, Kavan intended to find out.

None of the corridors looked familiar though he had lived here his entire life. Everything existed in shadows, each figure a shuffling corpse bathed in blood. There was a constant chatter in his head, voices both strange and familiar, shouting and screeching, gasping and whispering, never normal conversation but always muffled through a heavy veil or blaring so that the pain of them shot through his temples and between his eyes, causing him to squint and wince. Efforts made to cover his ears, bits of cloth stuck into them to block out external sound which compounded the internal chaos, were futile, most often resulting in aborted attempts by others to communicate with him. If he heard them, was aware of people around him, it did not show. He trudged or fled from one room to the next, driven by ghosts no one else could see, looking for his brother. Many shook their heads, scratched their chins, clucked their tongues, and more than one eyed Inness with suspicion.

What was she doing to their king to drive him mad?

Those closest, however, knew how she sat with him during the nights of screaming terror, how she held him and talked to him into the stillness of restless sleep, only to endure waking some short time later to more thrashing and wailing, always the same names on his tongue, names that told the House de Corrmick that the uprising, the loss of his brother, and the death of his father had deeply traumatized the new king.

Inness saw it too and bitterly tried to find a way to help her husband. She had believed his fortitude strong enough to do what needed to be done, had pushed that notion onto his shoulders for as long as they had known one another, scolding and reassuring him every time he claimed weakness that he was a man of strength, the man Neth needed if she was to regain glory. When the time for action had come, sensing his wavering faith, she offered to be the one to act. It had been an insincere offer, one whose tone and phrasing revealed his struggling weakness and bolstered his resolve to follow through, if for no other reason than to prove to his wife that he was the man she believed him to be.

She would have done the deed herself if she had known this would be the result.

As she watched him balancing on the parapet, hands tight against his chest so that she could not see them, staring into the clouds that had brought night over Glevum hours earlier, unable to tell if his eyes were open or closed from where she stood, Inness realized her folly in pushing Oska too far. Still, she believed there was strength in him, that all he needed to do was move past the death of his father and then they could rule Neth together as they had always intended to do. She was strong enough for both of them. All she needed to do was regain his faith, his trust, and help him regain his presence of mind.

"Oska, husband; please. Come down. Come before the fire. Sit with me. The weather turns foul and you must sleep."

He seemed not to hear. Perhaps he was sleepwalking as he sometimes did. He did not react to her words or her company. She watched his arms move and his head tip back slightly and then, slowly, one arm fell to his side. His fingers uncurled from around the metal chalice he held and it clattered to the balcony behind the parapet.

Perplexed, Inness took a step forward, wondering where he had gotten the alcohol she had so carefully hidden, intending to pick it up, but when Oska unsteadily teetered upon the ledge as if in response to her movement, she froze.

"It should have been me."

"No," she scolded, having heard those words too many times. "You are where you are meant to be; you are king, as I promised."

Oska's eyes closed. He shook his head, the hand that had held the chalice flexing to the memory of the blade it had wielded, the blade that had ended his father's reign. And for what?

"He was a grand king."

Kjell had ended centuries of barbaric infighting and iron-fisted rule, had provided the people of Neth with education and the chance to serve the military with honor instead of forced conscription that pointlessly claimed the lives of so many and left too few to tend the land and provide the commodities the kingdom needed to thrive. Kjell had provided a stability that no Nethite could remember.

Oska had brought that dream to an ugly, brutal end for what? So that he could sit on that throne? The throne that was destined to have been his anyhow? How could he further the man's legacy when his were the actions of the de Corrmicks of olde?

"He was a good king."

Inness snorted. "He was a coward, hiding behind a Lachlan wife, stripping Neth of power and…"

Slowly Oska's head turned, and though he did not open his eyes, he seemed to stare at her with an expression of perplexed bitterness. "How am I any different?"

It was the most rational thing he had said, the most rational he had sounded, since the uprising. Hoping for a clearheaded conversation, Inness picked up the chalice. "You are smarter than…"

"Smarter, but not wiser." He seemed to look at the ground far beneath his feet. Inness took the opportunity to step closer. He did not flinch, not even when she set the chalice on the wide lip of the parapet and took his hand.

"Wise enough to…"

A tremor ran through him. Inness felt it through their joined hands.

"It should have been me. Jerit is gone. We could not even bury him."

"That is unreasonable…"

"I'm going to tell them…"

"Oska, come down; we will talk this through."

"…everything."

"They'll kill us both!"

"No, they won't. Tell Jerit…it'll only be…"

His too-short leg shifted on the sloping stone ledge. He convulsed. She reached for his leg but came up empty-handed as he squawked and tumbled headlong from the height of the third-floor balcony.

"Oska!"

The reply that came back was the crack and thud of flesh and bone impacting the stone of the courtyard.

<br>

## ❧Chapter 21❦

<br>

Sentries and staff ran from all directions to come to the side of their fallen young king, but Inness did not linger on the balcony to witness the outcome. Nor did she go to the courtyard to be with him, choosing instead to retreat into the room. Not content there, knowing there would be questions about why she had not stopped him from climbing onto the parapet if she was in the chamber with him, she retreated to her private adjoining room and forced herself to lie in bed as though asleep, to await the inevitable pounding on her door.

Afterward was a whirlwind, expressing shock and grief over her husband's death, staving off unavoidable questions by advisors who wanted to ascertain her exact location at the time of the fall, people asking how she wished to proceed with the care of his broken body. The physicians determined that the contents of the chalice, the deep red Glevum ale that Oska favored, had been laced with some foreign substance, possibly poison, possibly a sleeping aid, possibly some other residue left when the cup had been cleaned, but whether that had contributed to his fall could not be determined.

With all of the alcohol hidden from his reach, how had he come upon enough to fill his cup…and how had it come to be tainted?

Inness was too numb for grief; shock she did not have to feign. This was not supposed to happen. How had her calculations gone so awry? All of her planning, all of their scheming, their intent to rule together, was gone in one fatal instant. Suicide? Accident? Murder? No one knew and as the advisors and counselors gathered to discuss the future of Neth, who was to rule now that two kings had died in so short a span and the other prince remained unaccounted for, Inness knew she had to act quickly. She had to subvert anger and lingering shock and secure her place, her future before blame turned against her.

She refused to be cast aside, sent to Rhidam in disgrace, castoff as unnecessary in the land she had adopted as her own. In Rhidam, she would be no one. There would be no future for her. Here, she had one card yet to play but she did not know if it would be enough to overcome monarchical bias and the need for someone to blame.

Standing before them, chin lifted proudly though her rounded shoulders and hands clasped before her spoke of the grief and mourning they wanted to see, she cleared her throat. "Sirs, if I may." She waited for them to settle before starting again. "What options do we have? Prince Jerit is still unfound and by your own investigation and admissions, it was his supporters who assassinated King…"

Voices rose in dissent. "Supporters! Not the Prince! He's a child! There is no proof that he either knew of or plotted…"

"He fled!"

"With his mother! He's a boy! To plan such a thing at his age is unheard of!"

"His mother then. She is a Lachlan!"

"She is a Dugan…"

"Of Lachlan blood…

"She was our queen! She was a good and faithful wife!"

Inness gave the men time to fight amongst themselves, content to allow their discord until the mention of Lachlan ancestry arose. Afraid that those arguments would be turned against her, she pounded the table once with the flat of her hand, an unexpected sound that drew the men's attention from arguing.

"Must I remind you, I carry Lachlan blood?" The men squirmed in their chairs. "I agree with Lord Lumel. Prince Jerit lacks the maturity to plan such an uprising, but whether it was Queen Asta or someone else who formulated the plot, we cannot know until we find her or find someone who will expose the guilty. Regardless, Prince Jerit is not here. We can turn to Princess Rika, accept Cordashian rule and lose our sovereignty, or we can intensify the search for Prince Jerit and remain without leadership until he is found, vulnerable to Cordash, Enesfel, and Elyriá. We can bicker, create factions and fight each other. King Kjell left us weak. We cannot afford this chaos."

Iden Stone, general of Neth's forces and staunch supporter of Kjell's, a friend since before Kjell's crowning and a man who believed in the changes the late monarch had sought to bring, eyed the woman skeptically. "You are suggesting we make you queen?"

He had not been able to reach Kjell's room during that night of violence. He had been forced, by the happenstance of his presence in the sentry bunkhouse settling a now trivial dispute between two of his men, to fight his way into the castle, through dozens of faceless men behind unmarked armor. Nearly all of the opposing force was killed in the incursion but by the time he reached the royal chambers, the king, his wife, and youngest son were gone.

The body he had later seen alongside other royal advisors and lords was no more King Kjell than Stone was. But others, less intimately familiar with Kjell, saw the royal signet on the bloody, mangled hand of a blonde man whose face had been caved in, and accepted the claim of his identity without argument.

Stone did not accept it. He clung to the hope that the king and his family were alive. Until he could prove it, until he could find them, he was a smart enough man, experienced in the ways of the de Corrmick royal court, to play the game and stay alive. Doing so, however, did not mean he could not cautiously question the motives of the ambitious woman before them.

Dissension echoed around the table, as Inness had expected. Women did not rule in Neth. Women held no power, publically or within the home. de Corrmick princes married kin or else noblewomen of no consequence with no claim to the throne by birth or blood. de Corrmick princesses were married to noblemen or wealthy merchants or officers within the army. By decree and practice, the children of a princess were never in line for the throne, but some de Corrmicks in the past who had either attempted to assassinate their way into power or who had successfully done so, had been exactly that…children of the matriarchal line.

"I am of royal blood. I am de Corrmick by marriage. This is my home, my family, my land. My actions since King Kjell's death, my support of my husband, prove this. I am the only one here to…"

"No woman may…"

"I know Nethite law. Nethite history. Did I not serve in King Oska's stead during his madness? Did I not prove myself capable?"

"Absolutely not!"

"Neth will never…"

"Regent then, until either Prince Jerit is found and brought back or King Oska's son is born and comes of age."

"Son?"

Eyes narrowed around the table, scrutinizing her. Her marriage to Oska had been long enough that it should have produced multiple children by now but there had been none. She was aware of the rumors claiming Oska to be incapable of fathering children because he was a cripple…or that Inness refused his bed because of his deformities.

Of late she had heard talk that her refusal had contributed to his madness.

Tipping her chin again, she stared at General Stone. "I am carrying his son." Her eyes swept the faces around the table, seeking a swaying of their perception, their mood, but she determined nothing certain. "Send the physicians. Send for any midwife you care to ask. Confirm it if you must." She paused for a breath before continuing. "Neth needs power consolidated in one voice if we are to survive. Someone strong enough to put down civil discord, to prevent factions from tearing the kingdom apart, to keep other kingdoms from devouring us. As long as I hold the throne, as regent or otherwise, neither Cordash nor Enesfel will attempt to overthrow and annex us. Rika loved her brother…and my mother would not dare…"

"Your mother is no longer the ruling…"

"I guarantee her voice is heard through Prince Merrek. So long as she lives and I am here, Neth is safe. This is the most reasonable…"

"Leave us." Captain Fraen the Elder barked and waved his hand at her dismissively. Though the late King Merkar had killed his father, the son had survived and climbed the ranks to captain as quickly as he had been able. His name was the only thing that hindered him from becoming general, as the reminder that his father had attempted to assassinate Kjell had never been far from the king's thoughts. His bitterness over the constant denial of promotion had led to a peculiar bond of sorts between him and Inness, and he was the only man of power in the room she respected. He was a man she trusted, as much as she did anyone, to act in her best interest.

She hesitated after the demand long enough to express that she would not be bullied or ordered about, that she would depart only when she was ready to do so, and then went to the door where she paused and looked back.

"Consider our course, gentlemen. This is in Neth's best interest. I swear on my life, and that of Oska's son, that I will restore Neth's eminence if allowed to do so. We will again be strong and feared."

Just as she intended she would be.


She left them then, retreating as far as the corridor to consider her options. She could not linger like an over-eager pup seeking to please its master or like a beggar awaiting handouts. Nor would she retreat to her private chambers like a timid mouse. While Neth's advisors and lords deliberated, there was business to attend, matters within Neth that could not wait. Continuing as she had been, she increased the number of men seeking Jerit and Asta, believing them to have taken refuge in the streets of Glevum, believing that Asta would never have gone far without her husband and eldest son. Asta would have remained to right the injustice of Kjell's, and now Oska's, death and would seek retribution for both.

Inness was confident that Asta would make a mistake and that she and the prince would be found. What Inness would do when that happened, she had not yet decided.

Her actions would hinge upon the fate being decided for her by a collection of men she had no desire to be beholden to.

Preliminary plans were set into play that would call for the shutdown of the education venues Kjell had instituted so that the funds for such efforts could be diverted into creating a once more powerful military force. Decrees were refined which would recall all capable men who had received training during Kjell's reign, to Glevum, to strengthen her core force. The common man would again be denied the right to bear weapons; the right would again be restricted to those who served the Crown. Should she gain the throne, an outcome she believed inevitable, whether as queen or as regent, she would give the people of Neth no opportunity to rise against her or undermine her intentions of increasing Neth's might.

The hours of deliberation dragged. Inness's indignation bloomed. Seeking an outlet for her frustration, she climbed the tower stairs, passed the pair of hand-picked sentries who served here during the day, snatching the keys from one of them as she strode to the thick wooden door strengthened with iron bands, a room without bars, with only a single high window for air and periodic light. With a torch taken from the wall to light her way, she unlocked the door and kicked it open with the toe of her boot. The grating of chain on stone joined the wheezing effort of a man determined to stand, bringing her face to face, as the door closed behind her, with the visage covered with dried blood and grime. Remaining out of his reach, she stared him in the eye, the flickering glow of the torchlight twisting his features into a distorted caricature. The stench in the room caused her nose to wrinkle but it was not enough to force her to retreat.

"You did this to him," she spat, daggers of fire and ice shooting within her voice. This was the first time she had seen him since sending him here. Seeing him now, injured, weak, but still defiant in posture and expression, fueled her outrage. "You robbed him of strength, sought to deprive him of the throne that was his birthright."

Kjell said nothing and asked no questions. Maybe he could not speak. Other than the wound his son had inflicted and the blow that had robbed him of consciousness, Inness did not know what other injuries he might have sustained when her men brutally hoisted him to the tower. The blood left at the scene of the crime, the destruction of the room, the forged letter claiming responsibility for the king's death and the mutilated corpse later left at the palace gates had been enough to convince Oska of his father's fate, enough to convince the royal advisors and the people of Glevum, all while the man was kept here.

Inness had no good reason for keeping the former king alive. She argued with herself that she might still need him as a pawn or guarantee, but she worried that he was a threat to her, and to Oska, as long as he lived. As her husband's mental and emotional state had deteriorated, she often considered bringing him here, proving that he had not killed his father, that the man lived, and that the guilt driving Oska mad was baseless. But as he had said in those moments before his death, Oska had already reached the point of confession. If he had known his father lived, Inness had no doubt Oska would have recanted his claim to the throne and returned it to Kjell's hands regardless of the consequences to himself or his wife.

No, she thought with a touch of remorse. Oska would have shouldered all of the blame for the uprising and attack. He would never have sacrificed his beloved wife. He would have protected her. That was the sort of man he had been.

He was nothing like his wife.

"You made him a coward. You filled him with guilt! You drove him mad! And now he's gone!"

She shoved, knocking him back off his feet. "Do not think this is the end of it. Neth will rise from the ashes of ruin you burned her to…and I will dance beneath your swinging corpse."

From his place on the floor, Kjell shed silent tears and watched her flee, not from the room, not from him, but, he thought, from herself. For if Oska was dead, however it had come to pass, then Inness blamed herself. As much as the idea appalled him, he realized she might have even had a hand in Oska's death, as she had a hand in Kjell's overthrow.

For his son's innocent, tortured, too pure for the world soul, the captive king wept.

❧*❧

Ylár did not expect his inaugural act to be popular with his fellow gdhededhá when they learned about his decision. Whatever each one's private opinions were of the White Bard, many respected Ylár's antecedents, and the reversal of excommunication was even rarer than excommunication itself. Kavan had been the first to endure that fate since the height of the Zythánites activity, and no one could name, without resorting to Faith archives, men or women who had been barred from the Faith or were later accepted back into it.

But Ylár too was respected and better liked than either Tumm or Dórímyr and it was his right to make this choice as he set to task at the start of his term without the approval of anyone else. He signed the parchment carefully, stamped it with his seal of office, and when the ink was dry, he rolled it and secured it in a storage tube. On the other side of the desk, Hwensen held out his hand when the tube was offered, his eyes wide at the reversal. The writ was signed in secret, not out of fear but because Ylár wanted none to give Kavan the news before he could do so. Outside of the council chambers, Hwensen was only one of two men who knew and they had both been sworn to secrecy.

Others believed the writ awaited Kavan's attendance, an interview to learn his position after so long outside of the Elyri Faith. Some would bemoan Ylár's apparent reluctance to make use of his inaugural prerogative. None knew the act had already been completed, that the declaration of clemency was already in effect.

Hiding his smile with his bow at the k'gdhededhá's nod of dismissal, Hwensen backed from the room, his mission now to file the writ where all important Faith documents were stored. For now, this was a secret he would gladly keep despite the bubbling temptation to go to Bhryell and share the welcome news with Kavan's family.

❧*❧

"Well?"

The two physicians and the midwife sent to verify Inness's claim looked at one another, one of the two men wiping his clean hands nervously on the smock he most often wore. He did not look at those with him, however, reluctant to show any weakness beyond the reflex he had been unable to control. As the chosen spokesman of the trio, he bowed before the host of advisors and nobles and stammered, "The signs are there. She is with child."

Several faces frowned.

"You are certain?"

"We all concur," the second physician added.

"A son?" someone else asked.

The midwife scowled. "There is no way to know that before birth, my lord. A woman's intuition is often the best indicator; if she believes it is a son, it may be so, but we will not know until the child is here."

Captain Fraen shooed the trio out of the room to allow deliberation to continue. No one thanked them.

No one was sure how they felt about the news.

As the door closed, the woman at the end of the corridor, who had followed her examiners here, hoping for swift good news, watched with the most dispassionate expression she could muster as they passed with barely a bow. She had not expected those three to have news, as those behind the closed door would have revealed nothing outright and would waste more time in talk. But she was hopeful and willing to wait, if necessary, to take further action to secure her place.

❧*❧

Fen frowned as he watched the woman at the window staring absently at something in the courtyard, or perhaps at nothing as even from his side angle he could see the vacancy in her. Though she had shared her news only with Merrek and Diona, such news could not remain secret for long.

Out of political necessity, it had been shared with Lord General Garran Declan, a young, ambitious knight who had proven himself often in tournaments and the breaking up of brawls and street fights. He had come to Diona's attention through her husband but he had not been elevated to the status of general until the past winter's bout of pneumonia robbed Enesfel of General Agis.

In turn, Asta's news had been shared with both Fen, in the hopes that more details might be gleaned through his network of informants, and to Chamberlain McCábhá, who had the responsibility of overseeing day-to-day matters within the keep and who found himself shadowed by the young de Corrmick prince, answering a multitude of questions about his work and in turn being told what little Jerit knew about the events that had expelled him from his home.

As days turned into weeks, with rumors slowly trickling from Neth into Rhidam, bringing no concrete news but further stories that supported the likelihood that King Kjell had been killed in a coup, many in Rhidam's castle endeavored to draw Asta out of herself, make her smile, offer her hope. Bhyrhán came closest, his easygoing mannerisms seeming to soothe her nerves as much as they did Diona's. But those moments of levity were short-lived and Asta slipped again into melancholic stoicism.

She tended her son morning and evening, and spent unspeaking hours with her daughter, an effort, Fen believed, to reassure herself that her youngest and oldest children had not been taken from her as well. The rest of the time, however, the de Corrmick prince was left to fend for himself. He spent his time with the chamberlain, with Chancellor Dahl, or with Prince Lorant, the only other royal child, other than the infant Prince Conroy, in the keep.

Something had to change. Asta's focus on silence and darkness was not healthy, and many worried about her state of mind. Last evening, when Elotti returned to the castle from his tour of nearby villages as he continued seeking details about the theft of the mantle from Hes á Redh and the murder of Cedric, Yóáná had presented an idea that Fen had not considered. He berated himself much of the night for not having come up with the possibility on his own.

He knew Asta. He liked her. He respected her talents. This suggestion should have been his.

He was here to offer it, after gaining approval from the queen, but had spent the last several minutes watching her, realizing more and more how far away she was that she failed to notice him there. As former inquisitor, she should be alert to her surroundings.

She appeared not to notice he was in the room.

When he opened his mouth to speak, she asked quietly, "How long will you stand there?" suggesting her unresponsiveness to his presence was a matter of apathy, not blankness or inattention.

"Someone's come to see you."

Her shoulders tensed and her jaw twitched but she expressed no intention of moving or speaking for several moments. Gradually the tension bled away and she got up, smoothing her tunic with absent gestures. She followed when Fen led the way and he wondered if she feared news about her husband or about her son on Neth's throne…the son who had yet to reply to her messages. Her face was devoid of emotion, her steps even and normal, until Fen opened the stateroom and allowed her to pass. The light on her face when she saw the bounty hunter was the first positive expression he had seen since her arrival.

"Wace." She hurried in and clasped his hands, refraining from an undignified embrace. "It has been a long time."

"It has." His enthusiastic smile brought more of hers to the surface. "Has Geli explained our situation?" He could have expressed his regret for recent events and support for what she was going through, but he believed he knew the woman better than that. She did not want pity. Asta needed a purpose, a distraction, and he and Fen intended to give it to her.

"Situation?"

Fen pulled out a chair and the three of them sat. "There was a bard here, Cedric O'Grady…brother of the duke and friend of Lord Cliáth's. He was traveling through Rhidam on his way to Alberni, conveying what he alleged to be the mantle of Saint Kóráhm. He left it for safekeeping with the gdhededhá at Hes á Redh, but it was stolen…and Mr. O'Grady was murdered that same night."

Wace slid a collection of pages towards her, notes he had made for the queen's benefit which he felt would be more useful in Asta's hands. "There's no proof that the theft and murder are connected, except for his relationship to the mantle and the approximate hour of each incident. We've been searching locally, interrogating everyone who prefers the knuckle biter, everyone who has been in the náós but have made no progress. I intend to follow O'Grady's trail backward to determine if he was followed, targeted, from the desert where his journey presumably originated."

"Presumably?" Asta asked as she began scanning the pages.

"There are numerous legends in Cíbhóló lore of the mantle's existence…of it being possessed by one tribe or another, of the healing it is said to bestow. If it has been in the desert since being taken from the site of his martyrdom…and if O'Grady crossed from the desert as Prince Merrek claims, then someone knows how he obtained it. If it was stolen, someone may have gone to great lengths to retrieve it."

Frowning, Asta leaned back in her chair. Tracking such a rumor could take a lifetime, even for an experienced hunter like Wace. She did not know what he hoped to learn from that backward quest, but she trusted his judgment if he thought the trail worth pursuing. "Do you know it was here? That it was real or is it…?"

"It was in Hes á Redh," Fen assured her. "k'dedhá Tusánt saw it, as did the other gdhededhá and several dozen townsfolk who swarmed the náós to be healed."

"Healed?" she scoffed. Asta did not believe in the healing abilities of relics or objects. Elyri could heal, Kavan had been known to do so through k'Ádhá-granted miracles, but for an object to do so merely by being looked at or touched was absurd.

"We have interviewed those who experienced it…and people who knew them before healing. The effect appears genuine. dedhá Tusánt fears whoever stole it has done so for monetary gain, either to use it or to sell its power in this time of plague."

"At least," Wace nodded, "it's the motive some believe most likely. I believe the original keepers followed to take it back…and punish the perceived thief."

"Believe…but there have been no reports of anyone else being healed. Either the person who has it has gone into hiding until suspicion fades or else it has been removed from Rhidam. Wace could be right, that it may be on its way back to the desert, as none of my contacts," Fen grunted sourly, "have found a trail or provided clues."

"Which is why we need you." Wace smirked as Asta side-eyed him. "Your expertise."

"I am no longer…"

Fen propped his feet on the table and steepled his fingers beneath his chin. "You can work with me. Your name, the Dugan reputation, your former post…it's kept you in good standing in Rhidam and the provinces. I have a hunch you'll have more luck with the Association than I've had." He smiled. "I have no doubt you'll consider angles I've failed to see. Between the two of us…three of us," he corrected with a nod at Wace, "and the justice and sheriff, we should be able to find the murderer and recover the mantle before it leaves Enesfel."

"If it hasn't already," the bounty hunter added.

Asta looked back and forth between the two with measured skepticism. Both were strong and capable, well-versed in their duties and successful. Given time, they would likely find what they sought. Yet time was not on their side with a theft such as this. If the mantle was genuine, miracles or not, it should be in the hands of the Faith, either at Hes á Redh or St. Kóráhm's.

Wace's assessment might be an accurate one; the mantle might already have traveled beyond their reach. Another skilled set of eyes and ears might be the key to solving both crimes. But asking for her help, she realized, was as much for her benefit as it was for theirs, an effort to focus her quick, active mind on something other than recent events and the unknown fate of her family.

A scowl tugged at the corners of her lips. She could waste effort on resenting what they were asking, resenting why. She could resume those darker thoughts that had taken too much of her attention away from Jerit and kept her wallowing in self-pity. Or she could do something, resume duties she had carried before marriage had taken her to Neth. Perhaps at the same time, she could put the Association's resources to work in the hopes of learning what had happened in Glevum that night and what had happened since.

Eventually, she bobbed her head.

"Take me to the crime scenes…tell me everything you know…tell me who you have spoken with and point me to them. I'll do my best, Fen. I can't guarantee success, but I'll try."

Both men smiled and Fen offered his hand. "None of us can, but between the three of us, we stand a better chance."

Ꝉ*ꝋ

Awakened from one of his periods of sleep by the jangle of keys at the door, Kavan was instantly alert though he did not move from his huddle beneath the protective furs of his bedding. He had enough energy to warm himself without them, but before coming here, he had never had to do so for a prolonged period against such extremes. The practice was good, vital, but the additional comfort of the layers of pelts was appreciated. He wanted to conserve as much power as he could in case the moment arrived that he needed to initiate an escape.

It was not the usual hour for a meal. From the sounds of the movement beyond the walls of his prison, he judged the hour to be mid-day and through the doorway, when it opened, he could see heavy snowfall obscuring the structures he was accustomed to seeing across the footpath. A steady wind blew the snow sideways rather than straight to the ground and the three figures at the door were covered with a fine, clinging layer of it. Having abandoned their efforts to speak to him since he either did not understand them or refused to talk, they motioned for him to come with them. Intrigued and perplexed, his brow twitched; when he did not move fast enough, hands reached to pull him to his feet. A look, steely and measured in warning, made the two draw back, uncomfortable in his presence for the first time. Gone was their bravado and the superiority they had shown before as they realized Kavan might be more dangerous than he appeared.

They did not touch him as they escorted him, armed only with fishing spears and knives, to a structure atop a steep snowy hillock with stone steps set, or perhaps carved, into the ground. The building was different than most, an elaborate long-house of stone and earth and thatch. A ceremonial venue, he guessed, whereas most of the others, similar on the outside in design and fabrication, appeared to be homes or other storage buildings like the one in which he had been detained. Despite their proximity to the eastern sea, those smells were weak, diluted, perhaps, by the more domestic smells around him.

Smoke curled through stacks on the roof and light clawed around the cracks of the plank-shuttered windows. Voices rose and fell within, calm and pleasant, expressing no traces of the hostility or fear he expected. In their midst, a familiar presence grew stronger as he and his escorts trudged up the steps and neared the wooden double doors.

His heart hammered. His breath caught and held until the door pushed open and he was able to lock eyes with Raebhá for the first time in more than a month. She looked pale, drawn and weary, but unharmed and though she did not smile, keeping her visible emotions in check in front of their captors, he believed her relief mirrored his. The two men seated to one side of the room, near the warmth of one of the central fire pits, were unfamiliar, but their position and the demeanor of the others with them suggested they were men of import.

A trial, he wondered with brief trepidation. Raebhá expressed no concern; if she felt it she hid it from them, and Kavan too. Banter in the room stopped when Kavan's escort propelled him deeper into the ghís kelyhag to stand at Raebhá's side in front of the pair of men.

They scrutinized him, the sort of study he was used to from people seeing his unusual appearance for the first time. The man wearing embroidered ceremonial robes stood and began to circle him at a safe distance. There was a prick of energy prying against his defenses, the man growing frustrated at being unable to dig beyond them.

Having much to protect, however, prevented Kavan from submitting to the stranger's curiosity.

"Who are you?"

This time, Kavan understood the words. He scanned the room before speaking, faces he saw for the first time since the room was warm enough for the villagers to have their heads, faces, and hands exposed. Many sat or stood at the tables in the rooms without the bulky layers of pelts and fabrics and furs to warm them. Leather and wool and some unknown fabric, most in plain tunics and trousers, with only some of the women in dresses with no visible waistline or gathered to the body beneath their busts. They looked at ease, eating, drinking, watching the newcomers with a mix of curiosity and wariness.

Most were shorter than Kavan and those in Elyriá. Broader of shoulder and hip from a life of physical toil, they were still thin and slight of build, perhaps from a scarcity of food. Like Elyri, everyone in the room had light hair, blondes and pale browns and a variety of reds. Those whose eyes he could see bore the Elyri hallmark blues and greens, hazels and greys, with not a single brown or black among them. And like those back home, not one bore facial hair.

None he saw bore eyes the color of Raebhá's.

The women's hair was long, most wearing it coiled and braided into elaborate patterns on their heads. A host of young men clustered at the far end of the room wore their hair short, as if it had been shorn and was now growing back. The older men, however, wore their hair longer, many also with it plated or otherwise styled so as not to be an encumbrance. The youngest in the room, boys and girls, dressed in similar breeches and long-sleeved tunics, had similar shaggy hair so that they were indistinguishable by gender.

None looked as wizened with age as Tíbhyan and Kavan imagined that, whatever differences in longevity existed, the harshness of their environment played a significant factor in it.

He did not doubt that these people shared a common lineage with Elyri. Kavan wondered, as they studied him, if they could see it too.

Having shown no indication that he could communicate with them before, Kavan glanced at Raebhá, seeking some prompt, some verification that doing so now would be the right thing. He considered touching her thoughts, connecting with her enough to gain an accurate translation of what was being said, but he knew, from what she had previously told him, the use of such abilities by anyone other than the márbhyndhánis was forbidden. It would be bad enough that his thoughts were protected too thoroughly for the inspector to access.

But the words were near enough to High Elyri, as Raebhá's were, that Kavan had little difficulty translating that simple question.

"Kavan Cliáth, Duke of Alberni." He hesitated, squared his shoulders as he swallowed the trepidation at the back of his throat, and added, "the White Bard of Bhryell."

His title would mean nothing to them, though his surname might. Kavan never used the moniker others throughout the Sovereignties had saddled him with, but by speaking it in High Elyri, the words would sound similar enough to their captors' language that White Bard would attract their attention and, he hoped, prompt them to release him and Raebhá without any negative, devastating effect.

Heads turned, attention more fully on him now. His accent was peculiar, his words awkward and unfamiliar, but Cliáth was a name they knew from history and the sounds of his words were close enough to their tongue for them to recognize a kinship of language. The reference to their mythos, the audacity of a man suggesting he was the incarnation of myth, was enough to make everyone take notice.

The leaders looked at one another before the robed individual circled back around and slowly approached, gaze narrowed and cool in challenge. He took one of Kavan's hands between his and asked, "Where is Bhryell.? Where is Alberni?"

Knowing what the man intended, the opening of communication between them the way Raebhá had shown him could be done, Kavan struggled with himself for a moment, weighing the pros and cons of answering, gauging how much access to give, how much he dare share about himself.

He decided to allow just enough access for easier communication but not enough to permit a glimpse into his thoughts. Before he could answer or explain, Raebhá replied in a steady defiant voice as if challenging their disbelief. "The lands of the elyryhánag."

Faces scowled. Some in the room gasped or muttered. The stories were known, men and women banished, heretics and traitors, but few believed it was likely, or possible, that those ancient outcasts had survived the exile, could have prospered so that someday one of their ancestors could return and stand before them. It was likely they had perished as penance for their blasphemies and disobedience.

If Kavan was indeed from those unknown, distant places, how many more of the banished had lived?

In the face of the seated man, Kavan read the fear that many like him would come and bring back the chaos of those troubled days.

Raebhá continued in an agreeable, even tone, with the sort of calm and ease that someone born into a political structure would master at a young age. Since no one tested her assertion nor spoke against her, she must have deemed it safe to continue and Kavan was content to allow her to speak.

These were more her kin than his. She should be the one to negotiate with them. "kydhé is escorting me home from where I was sent. He is no harm or threat to us."

Some conversation must have occurred between Raebhá and these two men before Kavan joined them, revealing his identity and the events that had sent her away from her home. It seemed to temper the scowl on the seated man's face but the man standing in front of Kavan looked no less agitated. He stepped to one side, however, for the kydhé to see him, his eyes never leaving Kavan as if he believed him to be more of a threat now than he had been before.

Whatever her words had been, whatever his visual assessment of Kavan was, the man without robes appeared satisfied with his conclusion. "kydhé Kavan, welcome to Phaurd" He addressed Kavan as an equal, interpreting the man's spoken title as an admission of a position of power, leadership, and respect. "kymyhé Raebhá has spoken of the dark and amazing events that cast her far from home, brought her to you…and of the care you provided to a stranger. As you made her welcome in your land, so you are welcome here."

He ignored the heated side-eyed glance of the robed man and continued. "We ask apology for the treatment you received. It was not our intent to hold you captive. As márbhyndhánis Phínc and I were away; it was decided to contain you until we could decide what should be done. Rumors of the assault have swept Dhóbhaen and brought with it an uncommon fear. Such calculated violence is unheard of. Someone emerging from the mountains, particularly one such as you," he nodded to Kavan, his eyes sweeping over him from head to toe, "is rare. It is a treacherous journey, particularly at this time of year."

"So I discovered," Kavan bowed, accepting the apology. He might have done as these people did, with a peculiar stranger in their midst, without a means of communicating or learning that stranger's intent. Anyone who did not know her, hearing of Raebhá's vanishing, would have been reluctant to believe her identity without a way to prove it.

From the kydhé's words, he guessed that few knew of the Gate far up in those mountains. Maybe they did not know that cavern existed either. Of those few who might detect the power of it, fewer still would know what it was, how to gain entrance to the cavern, or how to work a Gate if they found it. It raised questions of how Kavan had come from a far-off land to be in those mountains outside of the snowy, seaside town, questions he did not know how to answer.

Perhaps they feared that the banished had not gone far away after all. Perhaps they feared that the heretics continued to live in secret places in the mountains and would descend to exact revenge.

Such belief would explain the sharp, wary gaze of márbhyndhánis Phínc and the uncertainty on the faces of others.

"It is a benevolent gesture to escort the kymyhé home, but you will have to wait for the ice to break before you journey south."

Sensing Kavan's bristling tension without looking at him, Raebhá explained, "It happens in the north, once or twice a year. The water in the bay, at the mouth of the river, along the shore, freezes, locking ships into place." The ice had been partially responsible for their imprisonment. Such things in the north could not be helped.

"We must wait until spring?" From the amount of snow in the mountains, on the rooftops, still lining the village streets, falling from the sky, spring seemed to be months away, and while it would mean more time spent in Raebhá's company, they would not be able to spend it in ways Kavan would prefer, and he had a family, a province, a queen, a kingdom that needed him.

Perhaps he should consider breaking the ice but doing so without raising the ire of their hosts would be tricky.

Without knowing the reasons behind Kavan's frustration, assuming that it was the bonds of duty that drove him, the kydhé chuckled. "Until the sea unlocks the cove, until a warmer current sweeps the ice to the deep. Weeks at most. Fear not; you will not be captives any longer. Now you are honored guests."

Both were of the same status as he was and such hospitality was expected. If Kavan was the fulfillment of myth and prophecy as he appeared, though they had no proof of this beyond his ghostly visage, then treating him as an enemy could result in curses on their ghís that the kydhé wanted no responsibility for.

márbhyndhánis Phínc, dismissing the prospect that Kavan was anything more than a stranger from a people once rejected, did not attempt to hide his disapproval. "He is elyryhánag."

"I am Elyri," Kavan corrected, proud of his heritage, though here it made him an outcast of a different sort. It set him apart in this land more than it ever had in Enesfel, and while the admission might give rise to fear and prejudice, it might also protect him and allow him to prove that the use of their innate power was no threat unless one chose to use it as such. "But by k'Ádhá, I mean no harm."

He realized too late his mistake in setting one of the ágdháthé above the others, but thankfully the kydhé appeared less offended by the slip than Phínc did. Kavan hurriedly continued, hoping his words might be understood as a result of their language differences, even while he bore no shame for his beliefs. "I wish to see Raebhá to her rightful place," whether that rightful place was here in the land of the dhóbhaen or at his side in Alberni.

"We cannot…"

"Phínc," the kydhé chuckled again. "kydhé Kavan has come far to see this duty done, at great risk to himself, you must admit. If kymyhé Raebhá wishes to proceed with his escort, it is not for us to interfere. Inhospitality to a traveler is a grave injustice; they have endured enough of that."

The nerves at the back of Kavan's neck prickled with disquiet and he forced himself not to express his doubts. This welcome could be a ruse, a trap, not just for him but for Raebhá. She did not know who had come for her on her wedding night, who had attacked her and her new husband and sent her to a land from which they presumed she would not return. Her beliefs, her secret training with the power, could have spread with the tales of her abduction. Other márbhyndhánis might have shared accusations of heresy to abort a rise of radical beliefs. Kavan knew such fear firsthand. If other holy men feared her, this one might as well.

Someone with training and skill had used the Gate to banish her.

"Thank you, Dhóláhr," Raebhá said with a bow, foregoing his title to address him on a personal level. So, Kavan thought with an unexpected twinge of jealousy, this kydhé and Raebhá knew one another. Perhaps that meant they were safe.

Kavan's fears and suspicions were not assuaged.

"Your belongings await you." Dhóláhr gestured to the packs spread on a nearby bench, the contents of each emptied and examined but seemingly undamaged. Dhóláhr ran his hand over the red wood of the harp with admiration. "No instrument of such quality has existed here in centuries. If they do, they are hidden as the unimaginable treasures they are. Is this the work of your hands?"

"My kin…my ancestors, are the artisans who fashion such works. My talent lies in music, not in drawing instruments from wood."

Dhóláhr nodded in appreciation of Kavan's honesty. Whatever else Kavan might be, Dhóláhr judged him to be an honest man. "I have permitted no one to touch it, but I pray you will play for us this evening. Allow us to hear her beauty?"

Taken aback by the request, Kavan bowed. They, like Raebhá, equated him with their mythical prophesied White Bard of Gálínphel without the titled claim he had made. The opportunity to prove the tale true, the chance to hear an instrument that existed only in their legends of the long banished Cliáthan makers, was a difficult thing to resist.

It had been a long time since Kavan had played. Thinking about it made the ends of his fingers tingle with anticipation. If accepting the invitation contributed to preferential treatment and the use of a ship south when the ice broke, Kavan would gladly do it.

"I would be honored, kydhé."

"Good." Dhóláhr, his face bright now like a child expecting favors, motioned two men forward. They might have been the guards at Kavan's cell. They might have been anyone else. "Show our guests to quarters and see their needs are met. Give them what they require. We will gather this evening. kydhé, I look forward to your gift."

"I look forward to sharing it." An ally in a position of power might be in their favor, if Raebhá considered the man trustworthy. Having served kings and lords and others of wealth and influence, Kavan believed he could negotiate between these two men, so long as neither deemed him a threat or threatened Raebhá.

márbhyndhánis Phínc's stabbing gaze followed as they gathered their belongings and were escorted from the ghís kelyhag to an empty structure not far from it. Close enough, Kavan deduced, that the few armed men at the ghís kelyhag door would monitor their activities should they leave the shelter for any reason. They might be free, they might no longer be detained against their will, but they would be watched until they either proved themselves or else left this place.

Or at least, Kavan would be watched. He was the one these people did not trust, a foreigner of power even if they had not seen it, a residual outcast of a time when their society splintered, fractured, and threatened to crumble. Kavan would be considered a threat to the natural order, elyryhánag, whether he behaved as one or not.

Once inside the building that was to be temporarily theirs, a place he concluded was an unused home, he was able to relax, able to study where he was when the door closed. The lower level of the wood, stone, and thatch construct contained a circular fire-pit with a dwindling fire, a table and chairs carved of rough wood, and had ample open space with ladders on four sides leading up to sleeping lofts which reminded Kavan of Zelenka's home in Gorbesh. The fire cast off the chill and there was a faint aroma of something having been cooked, or perhaps added to the fire to make the room more inviting.

The door had barely shut, closing out the frigid wind, when Raebhá dropped her pack and wrapped her arms around Kavan's waist, burying her face in the crook of his neck so that her breath seeped through the fabric to warm his skin. She trembled in his returned embrace, afraid he would not return it. She welcomed his kisses on her head, across her temples and cheeks, and gifted him with soft sighs and whimpers with each stroke of his hand through her hair. The sounds lit a fire in his blood that longed to be quenched by her kisses. It had been an eternity since he held her, long icy days of worry for them both, longer nights of trying to sleep alone with their fears.

Kavan felt no shame or embarrassment in her greeting, or what he freely offered in return.

His desire was met with the tipping of her face until their mouths met and he groaned, knowing at once that no kiss would satiate the raging in his belly. He wanted so much more, but it was more that he could not have. Her reluctant pulling out of the kiss, though she remained in his arms, pressed against him with her head on his chest, put her mouth out of reach, reminding him of their circumstances. This time his groan was one of frustration but he did not try to force capitulation. She was right to resist when his willpower was waning. Until they knew certain inevitable truths, she could not succumb to her heart's wishes, or his, particularly if they were at risk of discovery from people Kavan did not trust.

"I feared for your life," she whispered, blinking away tears. "I did not know what they wanted of me, of you…why they would not believe me when I answered their questions. They were right to be cautious while Dhóláhr was away, but it wasn't caution I sensed. It was fear. I did not believe they would harm me…but you?" She sniffed and wiped her eyes on the heel of her hand. "We may be non-violent people, but fear could give rise to the unimaginable."

"My existence is a threat…not only to them but to many in Elyriá," Kavan muttered with a sigh, attempting to pull away but unable to do so with her arms tight around his waist. He did not try again. "I will do my best to prove myself. There is fear, but also curiosity. I will be cautious. I will see that you are safe, that you reach your home as I promised."

She risked a kiss of gratitude before letting him go and tossing two bits of wood onto the fire. As she stoked it with the metal prod lying nearby, she listened to his movement behind her. He took the packs and put them on the table, drew out his harp, and began a slow circle of the room. A glance told her he was studying the construction technique, the details of everything that might connect him to the people who had given birth to his. "Is there a rynlagne here?"

Kavan shook his head but continued his perusal without looking at her. "The nearest one is the one we left behind. If there is one here, it has been so long unused it no longer bears a noticeable energy signature." Or it was hidden. He might be able to detect one if he stood on it, or near it, but going door to door in search of one was risky.

Wherever the márbhyndhánis and kydhé had been, they had either traveled on foot or they had returned by boat before the sea locked the bay to boat traffic.

"Then we wait…and pray the sea breaks soon." If she could remain here safe with Kavan, build a life with him, she would happily do so. But each faced too many obstacles to make that a realistic dream and the people of Phaurd were too suspicious to make their life an easy one. "Perhaps your Saint Kóráhm will grant us the passage we seek."

She smiled though he could not see it as the fire flared and additional warmth spilled into the room. It was as much the hope of which she spoke that warmed him as it was the heat of the fire.

"I will continue to pray he will hear me," Kavan agreed. It had been so long since he had felt Kóráhm's company he doubted the saint could hear or reach him in this land. It seemed a peculiar limitation, so perhaps Kóráhm's absence had less to do with his inability as his choice not to come. Whatever Kóráhm knew of this land, whatever he had kept from Kavan during the years of their acquaintance, they were truths he had said Kavan needed to learn on his own.

Maybe, if Kavan prayed earnestly, the Saint would give him the comfort of his presence if not his voice, his physical form, answers to his pleas, or an answer to Raebhá's request. Perhaps he could dispel the ice. Whatever their desires, duty called each of them home.

## ❧Chapter 22❦

The mud-brick inn was nearly abandoned as visitors and townsfolk ceased patronage. Most from outside Alberni no longer traveled into the heart of the city and those in the city were afraid to mingle for fear of the Yellow Death. The increasing scarcity of food meant most such establishments had little to offer except increasingly watered ale, hardtack bread, and watery gruels or soups scavenged from whatever their larders contained.

Despite the quarantines and precautions put in place by the council, by those in St. Kóráhm's and by Rhyrdan on behalf of the absent duke and his son, within eight weeks of Myreth's arrival in Alberni, almost half of the city was afflicted with plague. Myreth had chosen this inn for its proximity to the manor, for its distance from the worst of the contagion, but the symptoms had steadily crept throughout the city, first signs of the northern plague and then the southern, until nowhere was safe. Myreth tried to gain an audience with Kavan only to learn from the staff that the bard was not in Alberni and no one could offer a reasonable expectation of when he was due.

With the owners of the inn fled, as so many other businessmen and peasants had in the hopes of outrunning the Yellow Sisters, there was only one barkeep still at hand and three other guests with rooms on the building's second floor. There was no one to collect more payment for the room Myreth had spent every coin he had to reserve. Without coin and with the scarcity of food that added to Alberni's woes, Myreth wondered how long he could afford to wait for Kavan's return.

Not that he had anywhere to go. Nor was there anywhere else he wanted to be.

He fretted that the staff was lying, that he was being kept from the pale man, but surely if Kavan was near, unless he too was afflicted with plague, he would sense Myreth's presence and come to him. Or the young lord seen leaving the manor more than once in the company of an armed guard would have sent word as Myreth had begged of the girl spoken with at the manor's gate. Thus far, no one had come, no summons sent, instilling a deeper certainty that it was as claimed.

Try as he did, Myreth only felt a residual hint of the bard, something fading more as time passed. Kavan was not here.

Last night's death of merchants in the adjacent shop must have been the final straw for the barkeep, as there was no trace of him when Myreth descended the stairs in the pre-dawn hours when the fellow was typically preparing the day's meager offerings. His room had been cold and he came down in the hopes of kindling or taking advantage of the tavern's fire, but only embers glowed on the hearth. One of the remaining patrons sprawled on a bench at the counter, drinking his way through a keg of diluted ale. The other two had not yet come down or else had left much earlier.

The drunken man ignored Myreth as he poked through the pantries and came up with two loaves of stale bread, a couple of small, pasty apples, and a handful of salted pork carefully rationed for the daily stews. A few turnips, a bunch of shriveled carrots, and a small sack of dried grapes were added to the stash. He wondered if he should prepare a stew, share it with the man at the counter, but as the fellow seemed oblivious to his presence and Myreth had no desire to remain and be accused of looting, he tucked his pack under his arm and went to the hearth in the hopes of stoking enough heat from what remained to warm his hands.

His patron had been long out of touch, paying no further coin for following through on her wishes, for getting this far on his quest. Without coin, without food, without warm shelter, he might not survive long enough to get the treasure into Kavan's hands. The bard might not be here, but Myreth had sworn to this sacred duty.

He rubbed his palms together and glanced to his right across the mostly empty tavern, musing that his duty might best be served by delivering his precious possession to St. Kóráhm's, particularly now that he had fallen to the notice of hidden eyes beneath a wide-brimmed hat across the room, a fellow Myreth had not noticed before.

Maybe he had come in while Myreth scoured the pantry. Maybe he had been here all along.

Whoever the stranger was, he was pretending not to show interest in Myreth or the drunkard at the counter. Myreth, however, felt his interest like needles pricking across the back of his neck. Having no training in combat or defense and having not the smallest shred of violence in his heart, he chose flight over fight and decided it was time to leave. He would make his delivery as close to its destination as he could and then decide where to go afterward.

His pack, always close to avoid theft, was slung over his shoulder as he tucked his food bundle beneath his arm. He stared through the open doorway at the gray morning sky, senses partially attuned to the figure in the corner. The last several mornings had promised rain, yet the clouds gave little more than a misting, enough to leave a damp sheen over buildings and streets but not enough to replenish depleted stores. The previous rain had helped, but it would not be enough to break the cycle of drought.

The young lord, out on his early excursion at the same hour that he came every day, wore a heavy brown canvas cloak designed to keep the moisture out, giving Myreth the hope for more rain…and his timely appearance offered some security from the threat he felt from the stranger rising from the corner.

There was no time to take the mantle to St. Kóráhm's. He had to take the opportunity presenting itself now.

As if in tune with his thoughts and intentions, the clouds opened and the rain began to fall.

Tightening his grip on the packs, he rushed into the street, his face tipped into the moisture with a laugh that made his emergence into the path of the duo from the manor look more accidental than it was. Inside the inn, the other came as far as the doorway, but as people emerged one by one or in small groups from the nearby structures to greet the lord, there was no chance for him to pursue.

The distraction of others allowed Myreth to weave through the clusters until he reached the young man. The stranger followed for a short way but dropped back as Myreth approached one he assumed to be an agent of the duke. The mounted man pushed his hood back to enjoy the rain too, his dark curls collecting the moisture, droplets appearing along his bearded chin and jaw. As he passed through the thin crowd, he drew something from the basket he carried and pressed it into one open hand after another, greeting people with a smile, a kind word, showing little fear of either the people or the potential of plague that came with the brush of each hand. The rider beside him was less welcoming of such touches and scowled at those who clung too long on the lord's hand but his objections remained unheeded.

When he reached Myreth, he pressed a handful of dried dates into his outstretched palm and murmured, "Bless you."

"My lord." Myreth covered the man's hand with his empty one and shook his head. "I…give this to some more needy than me." He did not think this to be Kavan's son, although he had heard there was an heir whom Myreth had not yet seen. The thought of the bard married twisted Myreth's stomach into uncomfortable knots. The beard, and the flashes of details that passed in the touch of their hands spoke of Teren blood, a man who had recently lost a father and who served Kavan not out of obligation but out of abiding respect and love. Not a lord then, but a friend, someone who adored the bard as much as Myreth did, someone the bard trusted.

That was a relief and comfort.

Rhyrdan cocked his head at the man's peculiar accent, noting the packs he carried and the red of an apple visible through a slit in the wrapped cloth he carried. "Are you a traveler? A pilgrim?"

He passed the dates to another individual with the same smile and greeting. Travel between cities had nearly ceased, the dwindling of commerce doing as much to hurt the city as the shortages of food and water. There were rumors of pilgrims in the south, people flocking to holy sites in the hopes of healing, seeking penance for sins ranging from the mundane to the Second Persecution that had cost the land so many lives. Fanatics abounded and while this man did not look like a religious fanatic, he also did not appear to be a migrant merchant.

"I came in search of Lord Cliáth, to deliver something to him." He shifted his packs and opened one, causing the soldier to grasp for his sword and prepare to draw it. "I mean no harm…he and I met many years ago. He may not remember me," Myreth added with a sad note in his quavering voice, "but I remember him."

"He is a difficult man to forget, aye." Rhyrdan stayed Raenár's sword with a gesture, studying the handsome fellow more closely. Odds were, few forgot this fellow's face or name either. "He has a remarkable memory for those who pass through his life. I would wager he would consider you a man not easily forgotten."

He could not pinpoint what there was about this stranger with the black hair and russet brown eyes that prompted his words, but he believed Kavan would have found this man intriguing enough to leave a lasting impression. "What do you have for him?"

Myreth's gaze shifted with embarrassment, unused to flattery, and he bent at the waist in a bow. The man following him was gradually drifting nearer as if to listen to their conversation and Myreth's tone dropped in response. "I would hope he has not forgotten," he admitted. It had taken longer than intended to travel this far; if Kavan had forgotten him, there would be no one but himself to blame.

The item he withdrew from his pack was wrapped in several layers of protective waxed canvas, fabric, and burlap because he wanted to be sure no damage was done to it. He held the bundle towards the young man but did not unwrap it. "This is my sacred charge. I swore an oath to see this into his hands, but as he is not here…" He shrugged and withdrew it when Rhyrdan reached for it. "It must be protected, kept safe, opened by no one but him…for only he should possess such a treasure. If he has not returned, is not expected…"

Sighing, Rhyrdan straightened in his saddle. "I do not know when he is due. Duty took him far and until that duty is complete…" He struggled daily to have faith in the bard's safety and his eventual return, but fear dogged him every moment of his day as the Yellow Sisters ravaged Alberni and Kavan's absence stretched longer. Seeing the stranger's regret, Rhyrdan forced a hopeful smile. "You are welcome to bring it to the keep and leave it, if you wish…or if you desire security Captain Magk can deliver it to k'gdhededhá Khwílen in the chellé for safekeeping."

Myreth bowed again. "No offense, my lord, but I would deliver it to the chellé myself, to this k'gdhededhá Khwílen if he is the man to speak to, if you believe him honest and in the lord's confidence, if you will escort me…"

Raenár grunted, relaxing his stance, but kept his hand on his sword. A soldier's instincts, even when not tempered by war, alerted him to the proximity of someone in the crowd watching with too much interest. The curious often watched Rhyrdan's actions, but this felt too intense, too focused, to be casual.

"We shall escort you," offered Rhyrdan. "And if you require lodging or shelter, I'll see that the gdhededhá grants it."

He briefly considered receiving the stranger into Kavan's home, but caution ruled against it. Rhyrdan might have invited his delivery but that was different than offering him shelter in the manor. Plague and hunger could drive anyone to a lord's door with a claim of familiarity, and Kavan was widely known and recognized throughout the lands. Some might even be able to offer 'proof' that they knew him, but without verification, Rhyrdan did not want to endanger his mother, sister, or the rest of the staff.

In the chellé hábhai, there were armed men to see to his trustworthiness, and Khwílen had the means to identify the man's intentions and honesty if he chose.

"That would be…thank you." Staying within the walls of St. Kóráhm would be both a blessing and a curse, as it would bring back melancholy memories of the life Myreth had escaped in Gorbesh and the memories of the one who had encouraged him to leave that place and spread his wings in the world. He feared he might fall into the familiar pattern of safe and comfortable behavior should he linger more than a handful of nights in such a place while awaiting Kavan's return, that he might choose to never leave.

His heart was torn by conflicting desires.

There was no harm in going to see it, however, in visiting the shrine Kavan had founded in honor of his patron, of meeting the man chosen to lead the Faithful in that place. It might even serve as a haven against the Yellow Death, as those who had chosen to aid the ailing kept themselves outside of the walls to avoid exposing those inside. Then again, he sighed as he fell into step beside the young man's horse, everyone in Alberni was likely already exposed. If he, or any inside that holy place, was infected, it was only a matter of time before the symptoms appeared.

Taking refuge there would, he hoped, protect him from whoever was following him. If it was the mantle the stranger wanted, bestowing it into the hands of the k'gdhededhá and St. Kóráhm's was the best thing Myreth could do.

Even the man at his side appeared to know there was no hiding from the plague, since Rhyrdan made no effort to cover his face when passing the ailing or the dead. Myreth wondered if Rhyrdan's faith was enough to protect him. He wondered if his own would protect him too, not only from the Yellow Death but also from whoever stalked him.

He prayed, for both his and Rhyrdan's sake, that faith was enough.

Myreth's footsteps faltered when another young man met them at the opening of the chellé gates, a youth whose waves of black hair were as dark as his own, whose blue-gray eyes stared as if they should know each other from some other time or place. His features were similar enough to Kavan's that there was no doubt that this was the bard's son. The similarities brought remembrances so powerful that Myreth's knees knocked and he was thankful they stopped walking so that he could lock them and remain standing.

"Brother." Rhyrdan was happy to see him; it had been over two weeks since Dhóri had come to the house and manorial duties kept Rhyrdan too busy to allow visits to St. Kóráhm's in search of his surrogate brother. Only Raenár's daily updates told Rhyrdan where Dhóri was and how he was faring. Without Dhóri, without Kavan, the manor felt lonely and empty. "It is good to see you."

Without looking at Rhyrdan the 'brother' who had supplanted him in his father's favor he believed, Dhóri grunted, "What brings you here? Come to spy on me?" as he stared at the stranger with him.

Bristling with lines of sadness around his eyes and mouth, Rhyrdan shook his head. "You will do what you will. I did not come for you." Maybe, he realized once the words were uttered and he noticed the ripple of tension across Dhóri's face and shoulders, having someone come to look in on him was what Dhóri wanted, despite the protest. Maybe he believed Rhyrdan did not care.

Shifting in his saddle, he decided he would make more effort to communicate with Dhóri himself rather than through Raenár. "This gentleman is here to see k'gdhededhá Kesábhá."

"So find him; I have duties." Dhóri patted the bulging satchel hanging at his side and pointed at the quartet of gdhededhá who had come to the gate with him and were now pulling away, heading into the heart of the city. They elbowed politely past the man who continued to follow from the inn but now loitered in the shadows of the last city building some distance behind.

He was too far away to be a threat to Myreth.

"You are tending the…"

"It's no different than what you are doing," Dhóri huffed.

"It's quite different. My contact is fleeting with…"

"It's contact and that's enough. Besides, Elyri are immune. I don't fear dying."

Rhyrdan scowled. It was true that, in Alberni at least, none of the Elyri in the chellé had yet shown symptoms of either plague. But neither had any of the Teren gdhededhá, and there were rumors that Elyri elsewhere in Enesfel had fallen victim to the sickness. There seemed little connection thus far between those who contracted the Yellow Death and those who did not, who died and who survived, and Rhyrdan worried about what Kavan would do if he returned to find any of those he loved dying or dead.

Would Kavan's blood, the blood rumored to have survived one of the most virulent poisons in the Sovereignties, be capable of withstanding the Yellow Death? Would it be enough to protect Dhóri?

"I don't fear death either, but I do fear…"

Raenár cleared his throat, disrupting the impending argument. Dhóri had Rhyrdan on the defensive and he would continue to pick at Rhyrdan's weaknesses until the younger man bled in frustration. "If I may, sir, I will find k'gdhededhá Kesábhá and bring him…"

"Yes." Rhyrdan took a breath, grateful for the interference. "Do that, Captain. Thank you."

With the argument aborted, Dhóri drew back his shoulders and stalked away, not caring to linger for either a lecture or the awkward silence he expected to follow. He gave one look back at the stranger but did not speak to him.

Despite the jealousy he felt for Rhyrdan assuming care of the estate, a duty Dhóri knew was expected of him, it was a duty he felt ill-equipped to shoulder. He had a good head for numbers and finances, but being responsible for the lives of others, judging them, directing them, was not something he felt comfortable undertaking. He wanted his father to be proud of him but he did not believe he could live up to the responsibility of ruling the province.

Helping the sick and the dying, however, were things Dhóri could do, duties he felt comfortable and happy undertaking, and he struggled to believe that Kavan would be just as proud of him for that as he would be if Dhóri managed the province as acting duke.

If he died in the service of holy duty, in the service of the people, then his father would either memorialize him or forever carry the regret and blame of the day he had taken Raebhá away, the day he had pushed Dhóri out of his life and refused to take him with him, out of Enesfel, out of harm's way when he had left to take Raebhá home.

Though tempted to say something, having questions but feeling they were ones best asked of Kavan, Myreth glanced at Rhyrdan and kept his mouth closed as he watched the soldier cross the courtyard with a blonde Elyri in pale green ceremonial robes. The man had the sweet, handsome, angelic face of someone content in his divine calling, a look Myreth had once been told he too carried. Myreth was less certain of that now, his holy calling shed upon the secular altar at the opening of the monastery's gates when he escaped into the world. He clung to the beliefs in which he was raised, refused to succumb to the irreligious nature of most people, but he had no doubt he had changed. His faith had been stretched over the last twenty years.

This man coming towards him showed no wearing of belief.

His rapt, content expression left Myreth pondering if it was possible to return to that solid foundation of belief…and if that was what he wanted.

"k'gdhededhá." He dropped to one knee, a reflex that appeared overly dramatic to Raenár but felt right and respectful to Myreth. The bundle was offered with beseeching, hopeful eyes as in the distance, the shadow he could not see felt to grow agitated. "This is intended for Lord Cliáth, but as he is not available to receive it, may it reside here until he returns? There is nowhere more fitting for it to be."

Khwílen accepted the reverent gesture with a smile and a hand laid upon the dark head of hair. Despite the man's youthful appearance, that touch revealed great age and some degree of Elyri in his blood, as well as something more ancient and powerful than Khwílen was accustomed to finding. Through the touch, he also felt a connection to Kavan, a kinship of spirit that made his heart soar to touch it. "May I ask what you bring?" he murmured as the blessing hand withdrew.

Myreth shook his head. He wanted to tell the truth, but he knew he was being hunted, a thief who had broken into Hes á Redh and stolen this priceless relic, even though the mantle had been taken to the destination its previous carrier had intended. Still uncertain as to why his patroness had not allowed the minstrel to complete his delivery, had believed the man had motives other than those he claimed, Myreth had acted in what he believed to be the mantle's best interest. To reveal its nature might end badly for him.

He hoped that getting the mantle behind the protective walls of St. Kóráhm's would shield it, and him, and call off those seeking a thief.

"It is for Lord Cliáth to learn the truth," he murmured. "It may not be as claimed, though I believe it is, and his eyes alone should have the privilege of revelation before anyone else views it."

Over his bowed head and bent back, Khwílen, Rhyrdan, and Raenár shared a quizzical look, but the cryptic words and prohibition did not stop Khwílen from taking the offered package. He flinched, startled by the power that pulsed through the layers of containment; it did not reveal the nature of the contents but it did explain why the stranger believed it should be in Kavan's hands. Any item of power such as this should be in the possession of someone equal in power to contain, control, and protect it.

"This is…" he stammered. "I will see he gets this, that it is kept secure until his return. I swear to its safety, sir. You have my word."

A weight lifted from Myreth's shoulders that he had not realized he carried. If it was the mantle his pursuer wanted, he did not think they would be able to spirit it out of the chellé. With the mantle out of his hands, he believed he would be safe, although lingering in Alberni might no longer be wise.

It might be days, or weeks, until Kavan's return. Myreth's primary business was complete. These people had seen his face. If those looking for him followed his delivery here, his hunters would have a face to put to the crime. But he did not know where he could go to stay out of the public eye, where he could wait for either his patroness to beckon him or for the White Bard's return.

"Thank you, k'gdhededhá. And please…" His gaze passed back and forth among the men. "When the lord returns…tell him 'hábhai áti nhwaethár dhe; aiónag naibhíth ebh'."

Khwílen blinked, surprised, the only one who seemed to understand the High Elyri the stranger used. It heightened his belief that the fellow shared an acquaintance with the bard. He offered a solemn bow and watched the man depart, wishing he could spend more time with him or had gotten the man's name. Hopefully, his description, the phrase, and the mysterious package in his hands would be enough to answer Kavan's inevitable questions.

❧ * ❧

It was gone.

She had followed its power across the desert, across Enesfel, guiding it into Myreth's hands so that her beautiful pawn could, in turn, deliver it into the hands of the bhedhuaethag.

There had been a brief dimming.

Then it was gone.

Not knowing what it meant, how a relic of such power could cease to be, there was only one logical, feasible explanation.

He had done it. Destroyed it. Again.

Why would he do such a thing?

Not that she cared about the relic. The fragment of an enemy's life meant nothing, a means to an end. But that lure should have been enough to pull him to her, enough to entice him into Myreth's orbit and draw him into her snare.

Perhaps Myreth needed more time.

Time she could grant, despite the irritation of waiting.

If the lure of the mantle, of Myreth, failed, she would have to fall back on another plan.

Either way, in time, he would be hers. Kóráhm's mantle, Myreth's life, or something else. Sooner or later, she would have what was hers.

She had seen the fires.

She could wait.

❧*❦

Four weeks. Massive blocks of blue-white ice, each seemingly larger than the other, floated in from the endless black sea to the north and east, locking the mouth of the river and the coast until it was possible to walk on it from the land to the edge of the sea as if walking on water. Kavan stood on the eastern-most point where the ice field stopped and the dark water began, where the northern edge of the shore ceased to extend east and instead turned north. The pink and green lights snaked in translucent ribbons across the perpetual night sky, temporarily allaying his longing for the sun, the longing for home.

So many days spent in this ice-locked town where it was impossible to study the architecture behind mountains of drifted snow. So many weeks offering music and historic tales of Elyriá and the Sovereignties in exchange for housing, meals, and the warmth of a fire. There were many more he could tell, but there were equally as many he did not believe it prudent to share. The town's elders, even márbhyndhánis Phínc wanted to know everything, thirsted for stories of those who had once lived in the land of the dhóbhaen, but Kavan felt a darker motive in Phínc's desire for tales of the outcasts.

It proved difficult to glean history from the villagers. His questions were typically directed to the márbhyndhánis or the kydhé. Kavan did not believe the people lacked knowledge, as Raebhá held a wealth of historical information and was eager and willing to share it. While she might be better educated, either from a more affluent population center or else as a product of her position and status, Kavan guessed that for many in this town, education was less important than survival skills. It was just as likely, he mused when contemplating the way Phínc avoided most of his questions or redirected them into more banal topics, that the power establishment, or this particular man, cast a far-reaching, intimidating shadow that kept those beneath him from speaking of anything potentially embarrassing or dangerous.

kydhé Dhóláhr was neither intimidated by Phínc nor reluctant to speak, but doing so in a public forum had proven impossible and it was difficult to gain a private conversation with him. Phínc was always there, always nearby, his gray eyes constantly watching, his ears and other senses always listening.

Kavan decided it was best not to challenge his authority.

It mattered not the hour of the day; the villagers with less work to do in the endless frozen night flocked to Kavan, men and women who sensed unfamiliar power, who hungered and thirsted for something that Kavan gave to those around him without effort…just as it had been in the Five Sovereignties.

Were there miracles, he wondered, thinking of the hands that sought to touch him, hands reaching for his, bowed heads begging for the blessing of a single touch. No tales of past miracles could have spread here and Kavan had not experienced the congregation of záryph, the flow of power through him, or the presence of Kóráhm since coming out of the mountains. That did not mean that those for whom he played, those he spoke to, touched, sang for, had not felt something. It did not mean they had not experienced power, Elyri or divine, and taken it home with them at the end of each day.

It brought them back to him with the tolling of every morning's chime. If the leaders suspected anything, if there had been rumors of miracles, they had yet to seem any more suspicious than they had upon Kavan's arrival. Dhóláhr, instead, grew more interested in his company, lingering often to watch his people with fascination instead of suspicion. That state of affairs, Kavan believed, could not last. The too public attention and the desire to keep any use of power out of their eyes, had kept him from attempting to rid the bay of its barricade. How long would it be before he was rejected as Dhágdhuán had been rejected? How long before he faced the same fate?

He had no desire to die a martyr's death, either in the Five Sovereignties or in this remote, snowy place.

The crunch of frozen snow brought a welcome distraction from a turn of thought Kavan did not want to follow. Raebhá stopped beside him, sliding her hand into his, an intimate touch they could share only because here, at this late hour, at the edge of the world, they were alone. Her warmth, her reassurance, and her recent growing anxiety, coupled with unconsummated longing and the joy of her company, combined to fill his heart each hour of each day. In moments such as this, he struggled with the thought that she was the cause, or his love for her was the cause, of the absence of Kóráhm and the familiar holy presences. Every time the thought reared up, it drove a spike of guilt through him, which in turn brought a pang of different guilt, the reminder that he was prone to deny himself joy if it meant the perception of righteous, religious suffering.

He could not have it both ways.

A spark of that reminiscent pain, of their use lost and regained, ghosted through his hands. The one she held tightened around hers and she brought it to her lips to kiss the back of his knuckles.

Both the pain and guilt evaporated and he looked at her with a small, relieved smile.

"The sea is breaking," she murmured, pointing to the southern edge of the ice blockade where an immense slab of ice was grating against the rocky promontory to push out to sea. The air was still, the sky cloudless without the threat of further snow. Only the soft slap of the sea on the ice and the occasional squawk of the flightless black birds that huddled on the rocky shore undercut her words. Kavan had not noticed the movement of the ice, having been too preoccupied with the colored light ribbons and the eastern edge of the ice field which appeared unaffected by whatever current flowed beneath their feet.

He watched, gauging its movement, trying to interpret what he saw without the experience to understand it. "How long?"

"If it continues, if nothing changes, a few weeks. Perhaps days, if fortune is with us." If not for the constant tension, the pull between

Kavan and the kydhé and márbhyndhánis, Raebhá believed she would be content to remain in this place. It was impossible not to see the way people flocked to Kavan, however, impossible not to draw comparisons, accurate or not, to the histories of Dhágdhuán she had learned as a child. Her association with him might put her as much at risk as he was if, when, the backlash came, but she, like so many others, was unable to stay away. She had no desire to.

Kavan had done no wrong. His heart was pure.

And she loved him. She was comfortable in that knowledge, regardless of what the future held but certain facts might still come between them, each one a burden in a different way.

Sensing her change in mood, Kavan scowled. "What is it?"

Raebhá shook her head. She wanted to discuss those burdens but could not utter them. Not if it was likely to cause him pain. Other matters needed to be resolved first. "It is nothing…wondering how things are at home, for both of us."

"I wonder the same." The pull of worry for family and friends was the only true threat to his happiness, the only thing except for the knowledge that she was married to another. So long as that was true, he had no future here. He could go back to where he belonged, but without a Gate, doing so was not yet an option.

There was no guarantee that any Gate he found would take him home. There was no guarantee he would see Alberni, Bhryell, Rhidam…or his sons and kin and friends again.

A gust of salty breeze wafted off the sea, lifting his hair from his face, causing him to shiver despite the layers of clothing he wore and his automatic internal temperature regulation. Raebhá shivered too, and his concern for her overrode the wish to remain here alone.

"We should go back."

"du…we should," she agreed with a melancholy sigh. The sounds of villagers milling about the town, after he had put down his harp and left them to be alone, had ceased, people finally retreating to homes and beds, for a few hours of sleep. There was no risk of further interaction tonight.

Risk or no, she released his hand as they crossed from ice to shore and approached the core of the village side by side without touching. No one could know the truth of their relationship, nor could she risk letting him in. Not if she was to protect the position she had lost and hoped to regain upon her return to Gálínphel. Not if she was to protect Kavan as she had promised Sóbhán she would do.

❧*❦

Her crowning as regent was anticlimactic, a behind-closed-doors bestowing of power that allowed Neth to continue functioning with the least amount of disturbance to the people. No formal proclamation was made, and people assumed she would be regent until Prince Jerit was found and returned. But from the changes creeping across the land, changes that harkened to the days when Neth was a more powerful, more insular kingdom, even the lowliest of peasants in the fields knew the truth.

The time of prosperity and change heralded by the anointing of Kjell de Corrmick had ended. A 'true' de Corrmick, albeit one by marriage instead of blood, had returned to the throne in Glevum. Any chance the royal family name had possessed of shedding its heavy-handed history evaporated with Kjell and Oska's deaths.

## ❧Chapter 23❧

The volley of fire arrows rained down on the unsuspecting boat from the cliffs as it sailed towards the wide, shallow bay that was its destination. There was no reason for the vessel's captain to think there would be no welcome here. Never in recorded history had a ship been turned away. Never had anyone on this shore launched what could only be an act of war, without provocation.

The crew tried to row away from the threat, but there were not enough to man the oars as too many were rushing to douse fires eating at her wooden hull or were flailing with screams as burning pitch ignited their clothes, setting men and ship alike ablaze. A few jumped into the turbulent sea, struggling towards the shore with the hopes that the water would save them from the flames. None from the coast offered aid. Perhaps the shouts could not be heard over the storm. There were few onlookers beyond the assailants, no cries of concern or offered help.

There was only a second shower of arrows intended to finish what the first round had not.

The screams in the night gave way to the roar of the sea, the rumble of the wind, and the crackle of burning timber. By the first hint of the new day, all that remained of the boat was wreckage that sank slowly beneath the water and the few corpses that washed onto the beach and wedged between the rocks.

Those were quickly found and removed before others saw them. The night's events would remain the secret of a few, the secret of men who could not afford to be unveiled by anyone sailing beneath the banner of a family vanquished. The territory belonged to new blood; until revealed otherwise, those under that command would obey.

*

"There is no choice, Lord Healer. We both know it." The prince wiped his nose, pulled up the collar of his cloak, and buttoned the topmost button beneath his throat to hide the discoloration, the bruise-yellow pustules that heralded the arrival of the Yellow Death within Enesfel's seat of power. "They cannot be allowed to see me. They must be sent away."

Ártur groaned and scrubbed his hand through his hair. "By now, odds are they have also been exposed. We all have…"

"Lorant must live. You said he shows no symptoms…"

"You didn't either before this morning. That does not mean…"

"I will not risk it. They must be removed from Rhidam at once."

"And taken where? Nowhere in Enesfel is…"

"Take them to Elyriá. They will be safe there."

It took effort not to scowl. There was a chance that the prince was right, that Lorant, his mother, and infant brother, kept isolated as they had been, had not been exposed. They had contact with no one except the healers and immediate family, but even those individuals interacted with staff, and in some cases visitors from outside. The chance of exposure remained. Did it come in the water? The air? On the dogs, cats, mice, and rats? On the horses? In the food they ate?

The prince was the third to show symptoms today, a soldier and a member of the kitchen staff were quarantined only an hour before Merrek sent for Ártur.

Which meant every healer and physician in the keep was now exposed if they had not been before.

"It could spread to…"

"Ártur." Merrek clutched the healer's hands. With the excuse of feeling cold, no one had questioned Ártur's choice to wear gloves, but though it reduced physical contact, it might not be enough to protect anyone. "How many times have you or Syl or Yóáná been to Bhryell since the onset? Has it spread there yet?"

"Not that I…"

"It is said Elyri are immune…"

"Resistant is not the same as immune."

"But it is also true that there have been no reports from Elyriá of plague, despite merchants and healers traveling there and back. There is risk, I know…and in faith, I do not ask this lightly. I know what I ask. If Enesfel is to lose…"

"You're not dying."

Merrek grunted. "The odds are not in my favor. Sir Gabersdon…"

"Was an old man. You are not. It is primarily the young, the frail, the infirm, the elderly…those already weak…"

"All the more reason to see Lorant and Conroy to safety. With my future uncertain, they must be protected. Enesfel cannot lose them."

The logic was irrefutable, and though the risk was great, Ártur too could see no better way. He did not like it, however, and wished that Kavan was here to present them with a miracle or another option.

"I will speak with Chethá, see if she and Sóbhán will care for Lorant and Conroy for a time." The young couple was a better option than Ártur's parents. Bhen would be his second choice, but having taken on more duties within the family business, proving to be an apt mentor for a handful of apprentices, his time was limited.

"And Arlana…she must go…"

"I have no authority to command her, My Liege…and you know that if she learns of your illness, the princess will refuse to leave."

"She will not," Merrek growled and took several steps towards the door. "Not if I command her to…"

"You must not go to her…to expose them…"

Frustrated, Merrek stopped with his hand on the latch and groaned. Ártur was right. The risk would be foolish. "I…you will take a message to her. I will write it and you will read it so she does not touch the page, and then you will go to Bhryell and secure a haven for them. Today. At once. We will not waste time. I may have days, a few weeks at most…and I want them far away before then. Sit and wait for me, and then be on your way."

It might mean never seeing his wife and sons again, but better that than watching everyone around him suffer and die.


❧*❧


The steadily falling snow had brought with it small white peeks of choppy water, which, as fortune held, cleared enough ice from the cove to make passage possible. A small vessel, just over fifty feet long, with no discernable bow or stern, was put into the water three days after the ice began to break. It differed only in its size from the three others moored there during the duration of Kavan's stay. When the danger of ice had come, the smaller boats had been hauled onto land to avoid potential damage from the sharp edges of the frozen sea. Most were stored upturned so their hull served as a shelter for supplies, while a few very small ones hung on the sides of homes.

Eight sets of oars were supplemented by a rectangular sail that flapped in the wind, scattering the drifting snow. The boat was wide but shallow, designed not only for the sea but for the movement of people or goods up the numerous rivers Dhóbhaen contained, allowing them to sail in as little as three feet of water if not overburdened. The design left no room for a hold, for a below deck, meaning they would be exposed to the elements.

For short journeys, with the communal practice of temperature regulation and an abundance of pelts and furs to protect goods and people alike, such exposure was of little concern.

He and Raebhá were provided with outer cloaks made from the pelts of creatures Kavan had yet to see, a smooth textured material that naturally repelled water, lined with fur that aided in the retention of body heat. Voluminous and hooded, they were made more waterproof by the application of animal tallow that, while not pleasing to smell, made moisture bead and roll away like rain on glass. Worn over their other clothing, he expected they would remain dry unless they were met with a severe storm or high waves.

Water-tight crates and barrels were stored at one end of the boat, containing food, water, and zerphánál for their journey. Seats with oars lined the middle. The boat's captain would stand primarily on a raised platform near what, for this journey at least, looked to be the rear of the craft.

Reluctant to drink the local alcohol, despite noting that none of these people suffered the ill effects he expected, Kavan hoped he could accumulate enough falling snow to keep his water skin full. Expecting the sea-sickness that tended to plague him, he did not expect to eat or drink much for the duration of their journey.

"You are welcome to remain until spring, kydhé Cliáth," Dhóláhr said, both hands gripping the bard's shoulders. If not for his smile, Kavan would have interpreted the gesture as a threat or an attempt to restrain him.

Thanks to Raebhá's continued coaching, Kavan had less difficulty with the language differences. He bowed his head. "I appreciate the offer and your hospitality, but duty beckons."

"I am sure Raebhá's ghís needs her." Raebhá, already at the other end of the boat in the place designated for her and Kavan to sit, looked at them as if she heard her name. She nodded, but Kavan thought the gesture to be to the kydhé rather than to him. She had grown more distant, spending much of her time with the village leaders conducting business Kavan was not invited to attend. She joined him for the communal evening meals, returned to the house with him, continued to instruct him in the language of the dhóbhaen, and then retired to her chosen sleeping loft with no fanfare or expressed affection.

If she was eager to be free of him or was forcing distance to make their eventual parting easier, this journey would be unbearable.

Dhóláhr gestured to the men preparing the boat for launch. One stood at the prow with a stone held up to his eye through which he appeared to be studying the sky. "They will take you to Curnydhá. If the current is auspicious, it shall take no more than two weeks to reach Gíldyágh, where you can restock supplies in Maras. Curnydhá is another two weeks of favorable seas to the south. I pray that what is found there is not…" He shook his head. "I have no news, but events such as she describes must not be overlooked. These people will provide what safety they can for both of you."

Though the dhóbhaen did not learn combat, beyond wrestling skills taught to children as part of their survival training, the twenty-five people now finished loading the boat and preparing for sail were trained to the hunt and all manner of hard labor. They ought to be enough for protection against wild creatures or whatever troubles awaited Raebhá in Curnydhá. Only if the whole of her territory was against her might the twenty-five fail to be enough.

What they could not know was that Kavan had an arsenal of ways to protect her, to protect all of them. "They will suffice. Thank you."

"íts hílylám márist dhes agk íts ágdháthé hwábhi kremh kelem."

None of these people believed in gods active in their lives. The gods gave life but they had not remained to oversee what they had done and had little regard for those placed on the earth. It made the ritualized farewell a strange thing to hear. It was no wonder, thought Kavan as he boarded the swaying vessel and steadied himself, that these people had latched onto the notion of one deity above all others who cared and wanted to be an active part of their lives.

He settled beside Raebhá, the narrowness of the bench providing little room so that their legs pressed together. The layers of protective clothing offered only a muted sense of each other through the fabric. It was more than she had allowed recently, enough to make his heart pound. She made no effort to retreat, having nowhere else to go, but he refused to take any action that would elicit questions from the crew.

"He bids us a safe and swift journey," he murmured. "A few more weeks and you will be home."

"du," she sighed in acknowledgment.

He could not guess if her disappointed tone was the result of having to leave him or if it came at the expense of their forced proximity. Rather than ask, he stared at the diminishing village as the boat moved away from the dock and along the coastline south.

He did not want to know the truth.

❧ * ❦

Ártur could hear Arlana's wailing accompanied by shouted profanities in Merrek's deeper voice the moment he emerged from the oratory Gate. His soul, then his body, grew cold. The sensation briefly overcame him, froze his feet to the floor, making him unable to will his muscles to cooperate and take him to the sound's point of origin.

Not the children, he prayed, the fear of it punching through his panic and allowing him to hasten to the princess's chamber. The door stood open and a gaggle of servants was clustered around it by the time he reached it.

"Out! All of you!" The prince's command scattered the servants. Ártur's steps faltered, thinking perhaps the prince did not want him there either. When Merrek saw him, he beckoned him into the room with rapid hand motions. "I told you to…"

"I went to Bhryell as asked, My Lord; I have just returned…"

The prince grabbed his arm and yanked him closer. Ártur could have scolded him for exposing Arlana and their new son to his symptoms, but with one look at her, and the infant at her breast, he knew the cause of the man's outrage. It would not have mattered if he had gone to Bhryell today or yesterday.

"I wanted them…" It had been less than an hour since the prince's message had been delivered to his wife, demanding that she and the children leave Rhidam. Ártur had not entered the sleeping woman's chamber to give her the message but had left it with one of her ladies to be delivered when she awoke. It lay open and curled on the bedside table. "What of…?"

"Syl is seeing to him," Arlana sobbed through choking breath. "If he shows no symptoms, you will take him to Elyriá."

"Very well." There was no reason or cause to deny their request save for the chance that Lorant too was afflicted. The damage was done. He gestured to Prince Conroy. "You should not be nursing him. It will expose him further…"

"What more harm can it do? Who will nurse him? No one else will touch him…and I will not watch as he wastes and starves."

She had a valid point, so he nodded grimly. Nursing would, at least, offer the child some small degree of comfort and affection in his suffering. In the doorway behind him, both Yóáná and Syl appeared, though Syl remained slightly to one side in an attempt to protect the boy tugging at her skirts behind her. Syl murmured, "I will take him to Bhryell…if that is your wish."

She knew what her husband had done to secure that right and had heard enough from the raised voices to know the issue at hand. Chethá, like any healer, would not consider the risk; she would protect the prince as surely as his parents would.

"Do it. Yóáná, see to my wife and child, keep them comfortable, help them sleep, heal them if you can. Ártur, with me. There is one thing I must do before I place myself under lock; I want your help."

"Aye, My Lord."

Ártur did not know what Merrek wanted, but as the Yellow Sisters strangled them, he would do anything he could to help…including giving his life if he thought it would save the Lachlan regent.

❧*☙

The young prince did not understand what was happening, why he was in this unfamiliar house full of strangers, how he had gotten here, why his mother, father, and new brother were not with him. He had vague remembrances of Sóbhán and it was to him Lorant clung when Syl managed to pry his small arms from around her neck.

"But why?" he whined, rubbing his eyes, having been roused from his nap for this unexpected adventure.

"Your mother and father do not want you sick," Syl replied, stroking his head, evading his grasp again. "Too many in Rhidam are sick, and you must stay healthy. They'll send for you as soon as it's safe." It might be an empty promise, and there was no guarantee what sort of world he would find when he did return to Rhidam, but it was the closest she could get to the truth without frightening him further.

"You and I shall have great fun," Sóbhán promised. "I'll show you how I make harps. We shall ride in the forest. I will introduce you to other children. And if you are very good we might even visit Clarys."

Only one of those temptations made the small face brighten. "Other children?" Lorant had so few playmates in Rhidam that the opportunity to meet others his age was exciting. "Will Jerit come?"

"Perhaps. First, you must finish your rest; it will not do for you to be tired." Chethá leveled a scolding look at her husband who shrugged as he carried the boy to the room upstairs where Dhóri had slept as an infant. They might have been hastily made promises, but having never been a parent, it was the first thing he thought of to help the prince feel unafraid in this unfamiliar place.

Once they were out of sight, Sóbhán singing as he and Lorant went up the stairs, Chethá hugged her mother. "You'll be safe?"

"Elyri occurrences are rare…I have heard of only two cases. Both healers survived."

"How many others might you not have heard of? Which plague did they have? There aren't many Elyri healers in…"

"There are enough." Syl pulled back to look her daughter in the eye. "Would you rather I take him?"

Sighing, Chethá shook her head. "It would be of little use. Sóbhán and I…you and father…Kavan and Dhóri…come and go through the Gate often; any one of us, or those who trade, may have brought the Yellow Death to Bhryell already. I trust your assessment, Father's assessment, that Prince Lorant is healthy. I will watch over him to be certain it remains that way. Plague is either here…or it isn't."

"I pray it isn't." They walked onto the porch where the rain dripped from the wood-shingled overhang. Syl hoped the reports of rain in southern Enesfel were accurate and that the Llaethlágárá captured enough of this storm so that the northern reaches of Enesfel stayed dry enough for the land to begin to heal. It might do little against the ravages of the Yellow Sisters, but if the weather balanced and crop growth resumed, it would be a blessing.

"I may not come for some time to limit the transfer of sickness, but if there is news, I shall leave it in the Gate. Check there as you can. It is already arranged with your father."

Chethá's lips quivered, fear swelling that she might never see her mother or father again. There was no guarantee with plague, but she would do her utmost to believe all would be well. "We will see each other soon…and Prince Lorant too. I swear it."

Kissing Chethá farewell before raising the hood of her cloak to cross Bhryell to make the one visit she had promised her husband she would make, Syl besought every saint and záryph, and Dhágdhuán and k'Ádhá themselves, that her daughter's promise held true.

❧*❧

Asta crouched at the highest point on the outside of the náos, peering down at Inquisitor Geli who stood at the place where Cedric had been found, rain running in rivulets from the brim of her hat. It was a peculiar position from which to investigate a street murder, but she had spoken to everyone in the homes and businesses surrounding that spot, had examined the now-trampled intersection, and had crept through every alley from where an attacker could have lunged. All she found was a torn bit of a cloak, but as so many others traveled through that passage, it was unlikely this belonged to the killer or the thief. She would save it for one of the Elyri to read. Too many days had been spent seeking a killer they might never find, and she saw no reason to believe they would find his identity today.

Of those in Rhidam most familiar with the knuckle biter, none, to Asta's eye, was the killer they sought.

The search was proving futile, but as Fen had gambled, it was enough to distract Asta from the cavern of dark thoughts to which she had nearly succumbed.

Little in the náos spoke of clues either. With no broken latches or doors, it seemed that the thief had either been let in by someone inside or had been hiding and possessed enough skill with locks to be able to get out without breaking a door or a window.

Unless the thief was Elyri. Use of a Gate would have permitted an Elyri to get in and out without detection.

Asta did not think an Elyri thief to be a likely murderer.

Her perch offered her nothing except an escape from the growing stench of damp, plague-ridden streets. Death was here now. Would she and her son be lucky enough to escape it again?

❧*❦

Bhyrhán continued to squeeze Diona's hand long after Merrek and Ártur left them alone in the library, just as she clung to his. He could hear her struggles to breathe, feel the pounding of her pulse and the desperate need to say something meaningful though the words refused to come. The news, while expected, was the sort she had never wanted to hear, the realization of nightmares brought to life that thrust her back into a position she did not feel fit to fulfill.

"I cannot reclaim my full duties; without your eyes, I cannot…"

"My eyes are yours, my lady, for as long as you require them."

"They will know…"

"Merrek needs you. Enesfel needs you."

"I am exposed. There is no telling…Enesfel needs a strong…"

"You are one of the strongest people I know. Right now, Merrek is not, and his son is not of age. You are the queen; the right of rule is still yours and for now, you are fit and healthy. You are the only person to carry this weight unless you want to designate Gamal or Inness in Merrek's stead."

Her raised hand silenced him but she did not draw away. If she had not brought Merrek and his family to Rhidam, none of this would be happening. Perhaps they would have been exposed in Fiara, especially to the northern plague, which would have caused Diona to blame herself for not bringing them here. None of this was her fault.

Bhyrhán was right. She was the queen, and thus the one responsible to shoulder Enesfel's burdens until Merrek was well enough to return to help her. She had to prepare for the possibility that the worst might come to pass. She would not put Enesfel under Hatu's or Neth's control, as much as she loved her son and daughter. Enesfel needed to retain its sovereignty and could only do that if she took back the full reins of leadership.

If she did not, there would be chaos of a sort that Enesfel had not experienced in hundreds of years.

For several minutes, she stared at the Lachlan portraits on the wall, blurry images with which she was very familiar. The Lachlan kings, stretching back to the grandfather she had never known, all there, even the vile King Bowen. Except for Owain. He had accepted his portrait from Asta's mother and hung it in the Hall of the Fiara estate. Before his death, Diona had tried to commission a new one, asked to have a replica made of the original, but Owain refused. Whatever secret had led him to abdicate the throne to Arlan was one that, to Diona's knowledge, had been taken with him to his grave. Perhaps Kavan and Gabrielle knew, but Diona doubted they would tell her.

One by one, she studied each image as best she could, from the most recent to the oldest, from her portrait to the one of her grandfather, reflecting on each long enough to consider how they might have managed this situation. She only knew most of them via story and reputation, but it was enough to cement her decision.

For the first time, she saw something she had not noticed before.

Thinking it a trick of her failing sight, she crossed the room, careful to avoid furnishings with a hand outstretched. She traced the lines of that face with her fingers. It was a flat image, not like examining a face, but close up, she could see it without the aid of her fingers, without Bhyrhán's eyes. Her own did not deceive her.

What did it mean?

From the bench where he remained, watching her in case she stumbled, Bhyrhán observed her actions, perplexed by them though he imagined she was weighing her options the way any good queen would. "My Lady?" he asked, sensing her disquiet but attributing it to the burden she carried.

"It is nothing." She shook her head and turned to face him with a weak smile. When her hand reached for his, he came without a word. There was relief in that contact, even though he still found sharing his vision to be a strain on his gifts at times.

"If your intentions are true," Diona added, "I will do as Enesfel bids. If anyone inquires about your constancy in my company," she forced a grin that she only partially felt, "we shall let them wonder."

She would pray he did not pay the price for standing at her side.

❧*❧

"The regent cannot see you," Ártur murmured, his voice strained and quiet. "You should take your findings to the queen."

"It was you I came to see, Lord Healer…but why may I not see Merrek? What has happened?"

Asta was not one to be put off when she wanted answers. If she did not hear the truth from Ártur, she would seek it from someone else. Swallowing the groan of despair, he muttered, "Plague. Merrek, Arlana, Prince Conroy…"

"All?" Asta's brow furrowed as she frowned.

"Different strains. The prince-regent has contracted the northern, Arlana and the prince the southern. They are quarantined, the castle as well; I am surprised the guards allowed you entry."

"They cannot keep me out," the Queen of Neth snorted. If they tried, Asta had skills that would allow her to get inside…or out again. "Fen either. We cannot work if…"

"Aye…but the risk…"

"Appears no greater in here than out there…and my son is here." From her vest pocket, she drew out a scrap of dull brown cloth stained by rain and dust and held it to him. "This was found near the scene of Mr. O'Grady's murder. It is unlikely to be of value, snagged too recently, but I am hoping you can garner a face from it, any information at all…even if it serves only to rule this clue out."

She placed the scrap in his outstretched palm, watched his eyes flutter closed, and held her breath as she waited. Footsteps at the end of the corridor made her look over her shoulder to see Elotti joining them. With a closed leather satchel hanging off one shoulder, he bobbed his head once but did not speak as the healer sought answers in the most innocuous of details.

"He waited in the alley for someone, watching the naós, expecting someone to come out…"

Asta and Wace looked at each other. An accessory? Someone planning to take the stolen relic? There was little proof but the chance of either was high. "Can you draw him?" she asked, trying not to break his focus but still seeking answers. "Can you see him?"

Ártur blinked and refocused on those in the hall. "I shall endeavor to do so," he agreed. Drawing would take his mind temporarily off the looming threat of death. "I will get to it soon as I may."

"Thank you." Asta returned his half-bow, allowing him to retreat on whatever business she had interrupted. To Wace, she asked, "You are leaving?"

"I will be of more use tracking the mantle, finding its origins, discovering who sought to steal it then I shall be here. You and Fen have Rhidam in hand…and may soon have a suspect it appears."

"It may be nothing. A man waiting for another in an alley could be anyone, mean anything. But I'm hopeful enough to pursue it."

"I wish you success." His secret wish, though not a man prone to prayer, particularly to the god of the Five Sovereignties, was that Asta's husband lived and she would have the opportunity to reunite her family. He did not say so as he saw no need to upset her with reminders. "I wish you and your son health in these difficult times."

"You likewise, Wace. May your horse fly north like the geese and leave plague and starvation behind."

The reminder of plague and the news of the ill health of the royal family sent her in search of her son, praying as she climbed towards the chamber she and Jerit shared, that he was there and not infected too. With no word from her eldest son, Asta did not dare lose this one.

❧*❦

"Sit, Lord Chamberlain. Drink with me." Diona gestured to the chair across from her where a poured glass of sherry waited. He would know she had not poured it herself, as her eyesight did not permit such things any longer, but her usual Elyri companion and collection of ladies were conspicuously absent. She was prone to meeting with her advisors alone and so Níkóá felt at ease accepting the invitation. With the prince-regent struggling with the plague, isolated from his wife, his infant son, and everyone else, too early to know if he would recover, the queen was forced to meet Enesfel's needs. To protect her health, many of those needs were passed into the chamberlain's hands. It kept Níkóá busy, too busy to contemplate his own exposure. He had not shared a private audience with the queen, as she too had limited her contact to anyone beyond the healers, but she communicated with her chamberlain multiple times a day.

When she called, he dared not refuse. He hoped for good news.

"Does the prince fare better today?" he asked as he sat and reached for the glass. Alcohol did not affect him as it did full-blood Elyri, which was fortunate since he enjoyed it more than he thought he should. Waving the glass beneath his nose, he recognized the bouquet of his favorite sherry and smiled.

"I do not know. Ártur believes he will improve, but I will only believe in his good health when I see him myself. It is unlikely he will resume as regent any time soon." Not while his wife and son fought for life. Not until the symptoms of Yellow Death were behind them.

Níkóá's strained smile faded. "k'dedhá Tusánt wishes to come, to offer his blessing to each, but only if you approve."

"It is wiser he offers prayers from the naós," she sighed. Her family could use those prayers, but the risk of laying on hands was too great, for both the Lachlan sick and the as yet un-inflicted clergy.

"At least Prince Lorant is safe…and if Ártur believes there is hope for recovery, I shall likewise have hope and praise k'Ádhá that the toll on us has not yet been more grave."

"Indeed." The growing number of Enesfel's people lost would prove difficult to recover from, but if the prince-regent was lost, Enesfel would struggle. If he lost his wife or his sons, the kingdom would suffer along with their queen and prince-regent. She traced her fingers absently over the carved edge of the tabletop between them, the pause long enough to allow the formulation of the words she said next. "As long as the Yellow Death lingers, there is risk to them, to me, which is why I intend to recommend to Merrek that we name you regent in our stead, should I, or Prince Lorant require one, or name you heir to the throne if we are all taken."

Níkóá's sun-browned face lost color. He had come into the room expecting some manner of duty but he had not expected this. "My lady…I am hardly worthy of…there must be a better choice…"

"There is none. Arlana will never be right for the throne; she knows it as well as I do. Inness is in Neth, Gamal in Hatu. You are the only other of Lachlan blood worthy to claim the crown."

The empty glass dropped from Níkóá's hand. There were other Lachlans, Asta, her brother and nephews and nieces in Durham, even Prince Jerit had a distant claim. But the Dugans had given up their nobility for lives as merchants, landowners, lords, and members of the Association as their ancestors had been before them. One might accept the responsibility of kingship, but none Níkóá had met had the desire for it. Prince Jerit stood to inherit the throne of Neth, if both father and brother were lost, and he was still too young to rule. Asta would stand with him if that was his destiny; until the situation in Neth was resolved, she could not claim Enesfel's throne. Too many in Neth and Enesfel would resist the merging of the two kingdoms.

Níkóá's claim, bastard son of a former king, was the strongest, regardless of the Elyri blood he carried.

"How long have you…?"

"Known you are kin to Farrell? Not long. Not until it occurred to me that you and he share a near-identical face. Not before now." She gestured to the portraits on the wall. Níkóá was familiar with them, had come often to study the face of the father he had never met. Often he wondered why no one else noticed that likeness. Until Diona, it seemed no one had paid enough attention to see it.

"I am…a bastard son born of an Elyri mother," he confirmed, voice low and thin, "and Farrell the First. I never knew him, but I know of him through my mother. You cannot…promise me you will not reveal this, My Queen. I have no wish for such notoriety."

"I must share the truth with Merrek. He will question my endorsement and deserves to know. If it comes that you are required to sit on our throne, the people of Enesfel will need to know too."

"They will turn on me…to think there is Elyri blood on Enesfel's throne…as I hardly look old enough to be his son…"

"Then his grandson by decree…do not fret, Níkóá…we well do what is right by Enesfel, and by you. Lord Cliáth knew, didn't he?"

The way she spoke of the bard in the past tense made the hairs over Níkóá's body stand on end. "He knows, yes," he replied, correcting her tense to show that he believed Kavan was alive and would return home. "He has known since we met, before he recommended me as chamberlain. Lord Owain, Lord MacLyr, likewise know…"

"Of course they do." They had each known Farrell. Recognizing his son was to be expected. In those days of persecution, Diona believed Kavan's efforts to bring Níkóá under the banner of the Lachlan House had been as much for Níkóá's protection as it had been for whatever scheme they had plotted to bring k'gdhededhá Claide to justice. Whatever that plan had been, bringing Níkóá into the royal sphere had proven a positive choice. Afterward, with no one suitable to serve as chamberlain, Diona was grateful Níkóá agreed to stay. She had never asked questions but had trusted Kavan's recommendation, as she hoped Merrek would accept hers now.

"You have the blood," possibly more than Merrek, she mused, "and you have the experience at court, the head for it, the gentility and demeanor. You are well-liked and popular…"

"I will not remain so when it is learned that my mother was…" he fretted, despite her reassurance.

She patted his wrist. "Do not invite those troubles before they come. k'Ádhá willing, Prince Lorant will grow into a fine king and Merrek will rule long and well before him when I am gone. But we must know we have an option in you, if it is needed."

Níkóá bowed his head. He did not believe he had either the right or experience for such a duty. He had lived anonymously for so long that the thought of wearing the crown was uncomfortable, as was introducing further Elyri blood into the Lachlan line. He had gone so long unrecognized that he had begun to believe his familial ties would never be known, but it had been, he sighed, only a matter of time. By exposing the truth to Kavan, revelation had become inevitable. There was no hiding. If he had to throw off the cloak of common man, at least within the walls of the keep, he would do so. It was throwing that cloak off before the rest of the world that he was afraid of.

Though feeble and unsteady, Merrek was deemed healthier, or as healthy as he could be so soon after exposure, by every healer in the keep. The discoloration of his skin, the boils, the fever, were gradually passing and he was eating and drinking again and tonight slept fitfully for the first time, without coughing blood or wrestling with fever and the dreams it inspired. Syl was with the princess who was likewise improving but considerably weaker, considerably sicklier, than her husband was. Yóáná tended Prince Conroy, seeing to his care so that his mother could sleep except when he needed to nurse or his mother wanted him with her for comfort.

For the first night since the Yellow Sisters had entered the Lachlan castle, Ártur was able to retreat to his room, grateful to try to sleep in his own bed. He listened to the welcome sound of rain outside his cracked open window, watching forks of lightning streak from one corner of the opening to another. Lightning brought the fear of fire through the land further south and the farmlands surrounding Rhidam, but as this was the fourth storm in two weeks, the deluge was welcome there and worth the risk. Maybe, if the rain stretched far to the north, the Tegid would overflow its banks again, but the region to the south needed the moisture. Many hoped the southern drought might be over.

The Yellow Sisters had brought death to the palace staff, more than a dozen men and women had succumbed, and nearly two dozen soldiers as well, exposed through their ongoing collection of corpses.

The majority of deaths had come at the hands of the northern plague, but Merrek had thankfully survived. The effort made to keep Diona isolated, with only Bhyrhán and three of her ladies for company, in the hopes that she would be spared, appeared to be working. She developed a cough with the onset of rain; Ártur was treating it, watching for other symptoms, but so far, she was safe.

The newest case in the keep was Physician Talis, one of those who, like the prince, suffered from the northern plague, but it was too early to know if he would recover. The royal staff of healers and nurses were driven to exhaustion, caring for so many others inside the castle, making them susceptible, and it was no surprise when Rouvyn announced his suffering.

Prince Conroy, lacking a lifetime of antibodies, continued to fight for his life. Ártur was surprised the infant had lived this long but he did not expect the prince's good fortune to last. There was only so much Yóáná could do to keep his tiny body strong. She could not fight his battle for life forever.

It was why, when the knock came as Ártur tossed beneath his blankets, he felt no surprise to see the young healer there, her damp cheeks and grief-stricken eyes telling as much of the news as the lump wrapped in a blanket in her hands.

"I cannot tell her," Yóáná mumbled, her normal detachment from her patients failing. "The prince…he was choking on blood. When I turned him to his side, saw the same on the bedding, I had not the heart to stop it, to allow his unending suffering. I let him…"

Ártur, climbing out of bed, wrapped his arm around the young woman's shoulders and guided her into his room. At this early hour, before the sun crested the horizon, there should be no one in the corridor, but he did not want to risk anyone else reporting this news to the prince or his wife. It would be best if such words came from Ártur.

Yóáná had not been a healer for long. Her training had consisted of common ailments and conditions, cuts, bruises, broken bones, a few limbs and digits severed in accidents, pregnancies, and childbirth. She had been spared the trauma of battle that Ártur had known and this was, to his knowledge, the first time a patient had died in her care, the first time when the choice of living or dying had been placed before her. Some would question her choice, but not Ártur. Conroy's death had been an inevitable shadow over the castle. Letting him go had been the humane thing to do. Ártur trusted her judgment.

"You did not fail him…or his parents. He had too little blood to give, too little life to cling to," he murmured around the sob at the back of his throat as he peeled back the blanket to press his fingers to the tiny pale face. "You gave his suffering an end. You gave him peace."

"But we are sworn to…"

"Allowing inevitable death to end suffering is not killing. It is accepting k'Ádhá's will, giving what is his into his hands. The prince was too young to survive; it is a miracle he lived as long as he did. That is a testament to your skill and effort more than anything else."

"If I was skilled," she allowed him to take the infant and wiped her cheeks and eyes on her sleeves, "I could have saved him, be able to save them all."

Ártur sighed. The only one he knew who could do such a thing was Kavan, and Ártur had no idea where his cousin was, if he was alive, if he was ever returning to Enesfel. "No healer, no matter how skilled, can stem plague. Believe me; I have tried. Every healer facing this is trying. With time, we may be able to slow its spread, but that is not the same. People will die, sometimes despite what we do, sometimes because what we do isn't enough. Sometimes a choice has to be made to let death win. It is rarely an easy decision, but you will learn to trust when it is the right one."

She wiped her eyes again. "The bedding should be burned, the room cleaned. Will you…?"

"I have preserved him." It was one skill Yóáná had not yet mastered, but one Ártur was well-experienced with. "Take him to the oratory; tell Syl what has happened so that she may tell the princess. I will go to the prince." The two women could console Arlana, he hoped. He knew she would be devastated.

The queen's and prince's reactions would be harder to judge.

Merrek was in his room where he had stayed since his symptoms first appeared, seated at the window with a lantern to read by what little early morning light the storm gave. Ártur was the only person allowed into the room as Merrek continued to push through his recovery. Merrek had known the healer all of his life; there was little ceremony between them any longer.

"I thought you were sleeping." Merrek placed a strip of ribbon in the crease between pages and beckoned him nearer.

"I tried to, but my restless head had other intentions." He attempted to force a smile but the prince saw through the effort.

"What weighs on you, Ártur?"

Seeing no need to couch the bad news in platitudes, for Merrek preferred candor to fancy speech, Ártur took a breath and said, "Prince Conroy has died, Your Majesty. I am sorry."

On the table, the prince's hand clenched, his knuckles turning white with the pressure although his expression did not change beyond the flicker of pain that crossed his eyes and a twitch at the corners of his mouth. There was no need to seek details. Though he had not seen his son in two weeks, he had heard enough about those who had suffered the southern plague to know his son had been in agony. He did not know how the boy had lived as long as he had. More than once Merrek had come close to asking Ártur to end the babe's suffering. He had felt from the onset that Conroy could not survive, not without Kavan's help, and though he had tried to hope, he had been unable to bear the thought of his child suffering.

If not for Arlana's insistence on doing everything possible to keep the prince alive, Merrek would have released him into the eternal hands of the záryph days ago.

He gave one long, slow breath and unclenched his hands. Conroy's suffering was over. He bowed his head, closed his eyes, and gave a silent prayer for the babe's soul before whispering, "Lorant?"

"Healthy at last report. If you wish me to go to Bhryell…"

"Please." It had been less than two days since word had come from Chethá, but it was two days too long. As the sole Lachlan heir, Lorant needed to survive. "Arlana?"

"Mending, but frail. Yóáná and Syl are relaying the news."

"I should be with her."

Ártur stifled his rash refusal. There were moments when one did not disagree with royalty and this, he believed, was one of them. Both Merrek and Arlana were improving; so long as they did not pass their varying ailments to each other, there seemed little harm in allowing them to grieve this loss together. It was the compassionate thing to do.

Tying his robe about his waist, Merrek paused at the door. "Ask Níkóá to arrange for interment…and send word to k'dedhá Tusánt." He looked sternly at the healer, expecting a protest. No one had been permitted into or out of the castle in weeks. The invitation would mark a significant break in plague protocol, particularly when none knew how the rest of Rhidam was fairing. "He will be buried properly…by a man of the Faith…with every Lachlan who has gone before. If not

Tusánt one of the others. And bring me word of Lorant as soon as that is done. I need to know he is well."

"Yes, Your Majesty."

Ártur did not follow him. He had his own duties, and facing a wailing woman was not one of them. He would grieve Conroy later, hopefully in his wife's arms so that they could mourn together.

## ❧Chapter 24❧

The wooden craft pushed through the falling snow, trying to remain within sight of the craggy shore and the occasional collection of structures making up one village after another, but finding that the snowfall often obscured their vision, masking even the stars by which they navigated. The oarsmen slowed, sometimes ceasing their efforts, allowing the current to sweep from the north in the direction they meant to travel. They steered enough to avoid the coastline, guided by the ghrískáy, the sunstone they used for navigation, and when visibility returned, allowing them to reposition themselves, the oarsmen brought the boat parallel with the land again and begin rowing fiercely to make up for any delay the weather and the lack of visibility created.

None seemed concerned, as if they were accustomed to this occurrence. Growing up in a land of darkness, mountains, snow, and water would bestow many skills with which Kavan was unfamiliar. He accepted that they knew what they were doing and chose not to worry about either the delay or their position and destination.

Wortham would have been at home here, on this sea. Kavan tried to see the world through the late captain's eyes, but doing so compounded the heartache of memory and so he pushed those thoughts aside to focus on more immediate things.

He considered once, during the first heavy snowfall, pushing the boat through the current to propel them forward. Without knowing the lay of the not-so-distant shore or the topography beneath the waves, he decided not to risk running aground. He put his trust in the mariners and in Raebhá's comfort with their smooth sailing.

Thrice, however, when the lead sailor chose to force the boat ashore, either to camp with the hull serving as a windbreak or else in a fishing village, Kavan despaired that they might never be free of the snow and the cold, would never again know the warmth and security of hearth and home.

The fourteen-day journey to the Gíldyágh ghís of Maras stretched to twenty, the darkness giving way to longer and longer periods of daylight the further south they traveled. When the lanterns on the shore again announced the nearness of docks and a village the size of the one where they had begun, Kavan stood with a rush of elation and relief. He had not been seasick, the slow-moving nature of their journey upon a glassy sea and his inability to see the surrounding expanse of water had lessened those usually troublesome symptoms. The few times they made landfall to wait out the heaviest of the snow were not enough to steady his legs when he climbed stiffly out of the boat onto the wooden dock.

He turned to offer his hand to Raebhá, to assist her from the boat despite his unsteady stance. For a moment it looked as if she would refuse but instead, she accepted the gesture with downcast eyes. It was another indicator of the growing wedge between them and he scowled, deciding they must speak privately at the first opportunity. The journey surrounded by others afforded no occasion to talk. He hoped that now that they had reached their resupply stop that would change.

A portly man, or one who seemed so beneath layers of clothing, skins, and fur, barreled down the dock, his huffing heard long before he reached them. For the first time in more than twenty days, Raebhá's face lit with something akin to joy, and Kavan was forced to refrain from stepping in the way when the man and his retainers reached them.

She clasped the man's hands. "Bhregdh; it is good to see you."

"Raebhá? By the chyrt ghymaemis! It is you. Welcome to Maras! When I heard you were taken, I despaired…but you look well?" He embraced her, proving he was not as short as his girth suggested.

"I was fortunate," she admitted without offering details of where she had been and why, or how she had gotten there. "These people from Ghené are my escort. This is Kavan Cliáth."

"Cliáth!" Any more introduction Raebhá might have made was truncated by the surprise and enthusiasm that long-extinct name brought with it. "Come. Into the Hall. We will speak in warmth over zerphánál and mutton."

"We are to restock and we would like to…" she began. Bhregdh shook his head and tugged her along with his arm curled around hers and a wave of his other hand that beckoned Kavan to follow.

"Supplies you shall have; there is time for that once you are warm and rested. Everyone will be given quarters for tonight…but first, there is someone you will want to see."

Beneath the light of the nearly full moon that did its best to pierce the falling snow, Raebhá appeared to lose color as she looked at Kavan with anxious eyes. What Kavan saw was mirrored in the knot that sank lower in his belly and the strangling pressure that rose in his throat. Was he here? Had the man Kavan irrationally struggled not to hate survived and sought refuge in this ghísaer, escaping those who had attacked him and his wife?

His jaw twitched and he tore his gaze away, refusing to look at her, not wanting to reveal his thoughts, pushing emotion down to where he hoped he could control it as their walk took them up a slippery often-tread path of mud and ice into the middle of this town. It was easier to focus on the path, the buildings around him less snowbound than those in Phaurd, than it was to dwell on the impending end of their journey.

If she wanted to be free, the moment of escape felt imminent.

The style of the structures was much the same as those in Phaurd save for the variation in color of stone, lumber, and clay and the carved adornments etched into the wood over doorways, into frames, into the posts that made up the supports of each building. They were similarly tall enough for the typical sleeping lofts in the round dwellings but here, one of the two oblong structures was taller still, a full two levels with a wooden balcony wrapping the entire upper floor. Kavan wondered what was housed there, why the distinction in construct, but he did not have the opportunity yet to inquire.

Maras was a bigger village than Phaurd, the cluster of homes and farms spreading out from the shore to the forest's edge to the west and stretched as far south along the sea as he could see through the falling snow. Their path twisted back on itself, bringing them east again after several hundred yards, to a ghís kelyhag on a promontory overlooking the sea, a ghís kelyhag with a lookout tower from which the lights of lanterns and torches reached out as a beacon to those on the water.

The sailors of Ghené remained near their charges, ready to act if Raebhá was threatened as they had promised they would, but Bhregdh seemed less threatening than anyone in Phaurd had seemed. None of the villagers gawked or followed to discover who their visitors were. Many recognized the ship's sigil and assumed the visitors accompanied by their kydhé were dignitaries on business.

Bound in warm clothing as he was, Kavan's features were hidden from view.

Despite his efforts to locate a Gate, a necessity that helped direct his focus away from what awaited, he detected no power signature within reach of the ghís. Perhaps in the forests around the village's perimeter or the snowbound mounts beyond, but he could not feel one from where he walked. If none was found, he would be forced to travel west on foot to find his way home. There was little likelihood, he mused sullenly as Bhregdh threw open the ghís kelyhag doors, that he would be given a ship and crew to sail home to Enesfel.

There were few people inside at this early morning hour, only a dozen or so, dressed as those in Phaurd had been, many of whom were tending the fire pits or cleaning away debris from the previous evening's communal meal. There were five, however, four men in the robes of the márbhyndhánis that Phínc had worn and one in the plainer style of a man well-off but not burdened with too much wealth. In the warmth of the long room, even with the dying fires that were being rebuilt for the day, the people here did not need bulky layers that hid their faces. When the five turned to see who was entering, Raebhá gave a squeaking gasp, dropped her pack, and threw off her outer cloak before dashing across the room.

"Iólán!"

Not her husband, Kavan realized too late to prevent the jealous flare in his center. His efforts to swallow the possessive growl produced an awkward sound that stuck in the back of his mouth in a painful knot. His feet stopped, unable to propel him forward as he watched and fought, at this safe distance, to shut down the ball of destruction forming in his core. There was no threat, he scolded himself. His life was not in danger. Nor was Raebhá's.

The energy he understood. The impulse to release it with impunity, out of jealousy, he did not. Not understanding it, barely able to contain it, frightened him enough that he forced a step back, balled his fists, and began a silent count as he forced the power to dissipate.

The one named Iólán, one eye sand-gold like hers and the other a pale blue, hugged her and buried his face in her hair as she kissed his cheek and clung to him. "taeásne! You live! How?"

Through an elated sob, she kissed his other cheek and said, "It is a long tale." Her fears, while in Alberni, had been about Ombhrís' fate and what it would mean, but as the boat had pushed south from Phaurd, she had begun to consider what her brother's fate had been as well, whether those who had turned against her had turned on him too. A friendly, outgoing, respectable man, she did not think anyone would have cause to punish her brother for anything they thought her guilty of, but there was no way to be certain until she saw him.

Now that she did, in Maras of all places, she thanked the stars he was safe.

Looking over her shoulder in that embrace, noting the collection of Ghené sailors that had scattered towards the fire pits, passing around Kavan as if he was a fixed point in the current, Iólán tried to distinguish the face beneath the hood and wraps of the individual who radiated power without moving or speaking. He did not need training to feel it. Anyone around them should be able to feel it, he surmised, and many did, judging by the way they shied away from the stranger or fidgeted nervously wherever they were in the room.

The only one who showed no fear in the presence of that power was Raebhá, who turned with an arm still around Iólán's shoulders and eagerly beckoned the bard forward.

Bhregdh and the márbhyndhánis were uncomfortable too, sliding away when Kavan, after relenting to the summons, reached them and lowered his hood and the cloth wrappings around his face. They were afraid, but Iólán judged, also intrigued.

"You have time to tell it," he said, drawing strength from Raebhá's calm while noticing her awkwardness as Kavan drew near. She did not fear him, but she did fear something.

"Kavan Cliáth…my brother, Iólán."

"There are no…" grunted one of the márbhyndhánis.

"You know that is not true," she teased affectionately, looking away from Kavan's intensity now that he had joined them. kydhé Bhregdh steered them to the nearest roaring fire and sat on one of the curved benches there, with Raebhá between him and Iólán. The márbhyndhánis did not sit, instead remained standing shoulder to shoulder, blocking the fire's light and warmth, prompting Kavan to remain standing as well. He wanted to pace, to be free of the nervous energy pinging around inside of him, but he compromised by taking a stance where he could easily watch each of the others. Someone took his cloak, to hang it on a peg on the wall where others hung throughout the ghís kelyhag, but he kept his pack in his arms, close to his chest like a shield.

"Tell us what happened. Iólán's tale is sorely lacking details," encouraged Bhregdh, who again gestured for Kavan to sit. When Kavan did not move, the older man barked a command to someone across the room who quickly brought a stool to place behind Kavan.

Kavan inclined his head gratefully but did not yet sit. The perceived threat of the márbhyndhánis would not permit it.

The telling of the story was no easier as she struggled between the truth and how much she thought her brother and the others should know. "Someone was there, waiting for us to arrive perhaps, I don't know. They struck Ombhrís, hit me, banished me to the lands where the elyryhánag thrive…"

"He is…?"

More than one in the room reacted with similar distress. Rather than hang his head in some contrived gesture of meekness, Kavan drew back his shoulders but Raebhá did not allow him the opportunity to defend himself.

"He saved my life." The weight of her gratitude, the debt she felt she owed him, brightened her words. "When they…whoever they were… sent me through a rynlagne to a place where none should have found me, I might have died if not for Kavan." She looked at him fondly with an affectionate nod and smile of respect before adding, "Without him, I would not be here."

A different márbhyndhánis, muttered "That's absurd. No one else can…"

Raebhá's face again lost color, as if the implications he stumbled over had just occurred to her as well. The possibility that the márbhyndhánis here, in Ghené, and elsewhere might be in collusion or contact with those in Curnydhá who intended her harm had also not crossed her mind before. Reflexively she drew closer to her brother, although he would be unable to protect her if the márbhyndhánis intended her ill.

Only one person could, but she feared for him as well. Kavan could do extraordinary things but he was only one man. The márbhyndhánis were many.

"Or one of the elyryhánag," said another with a haughty sniff, his expression and tone suggesting he understood the implications of being one of the limited few who could have committed such an act. He sounded eager to deflect suspicion. "They could have ripped you from your home to…"

One of his fellow márbhyndhánis looked at him with horror. "Those banished centuries ago? Come here? Take one of our…" as another rebutted, "No elyryhánag could have the knowledge to use…"

Raebhá shook her head and squeezed her brother's hand, wishing it was Kavan's but thankful he was beyond her reach. Politically, the physical distance between them was for the best. "I have met them…MacLyrs and Cáners, Bhíncári and Cliáths. di Curnydhás." She had not met Kóráhm but knew of him and that was enough to imply familiarity. "Many of those sent away lived, thrived…a vast nation far from here, shoulder to shoulder with the taeré. I would have been stranded in that place if not for Kavan…"

"Your ship brought you to Phaurd?"

"No ship, a rynlagne," Raebhá repeated, realizing as she said it that Kavan's ability to use the Gates suggested a possibility of elyryhánag attacking her, abducting her, though it was a possibility that made little sense. They would have had to know who she was, where she was.

There were surely more important targets on the island.

The márbhyndhánis looked at one another with narrowed eyes before one muttered, "How do we know he did not assault you and Ombhrís, intend to kill you both, take you with the intent…?"

"Kill?" The questions went unanswered. She did not look at Kavan despite the unintended surge of hope that she pushed down so that only her anxiety squeaked out. How could she feel both hope and shock and grief at the same time? "He is dead?"

Iólán glowered at the márbhyndhánis and tightened his arm around his sister's shoulders. "We don't know. Audh dragged me to a boat, said my life was in danger. There was shouting, sounds of an assault but I couldn't see anything. He said they were after me too…but there was no time to ask who they were, who was their target…whether you were safe. I've talked with only one fellow from

Curnydhá since coming here, a man who fled the same night on another boat. He told tales…that you and Ombhrís were taken, killed…that he was injured and lived in a state of dreams from which he will not wake. Following so hard upon my flight, there's no way he could know. There's no proof and the weather has not permitted travel. No one comes from Curnydhá and the ship we sent many weeks past has not come back. I would go myself, but…"

"But I could not risk the only living member of your family to such dangers if the threat is real. If someone aimed to destroy your line," Bhregdh said with a stern shake of his head and a suspicious glance at the márbhyndhánis, "returning alone would not be wise."

"I am going back." Raebhá lifted her chin. Iólán's tale suggested a larger threat than retaliation for her illicit activities. ghís-wide chaos was a horror to consider.

Despite the bravado of her words, she shared a brief, worried glance with Kavan as the older man began, "kymyhé…"

She shook her head. "It must be done, Bhregdh. They are my people, my ghís, my ghísaer. My father would expect it. I need to know who has done this, who sought to destroy me, Iólán, whether Ombhrís lives. I owe them that. Lord Cliáth will see me safely there."

"This man is no fighter," sneered one of the márbhyndhánis.

"Neither are any of ours," Iólán reminded him.

Kavan's skin crawled with the negativity in the room, the doubt and suspicion, and his jaw twitched.

"This man," Raebhá hissed, "has skills you will only dream of."

The boast was rash, but she felt the assertion must be made. From Kavan's frown, she was certain he would have said the same thing.

From the look in his eyes when he again met her gaze, however, he was proud of her fortitude, even while being afraid for her life.

There had been no outlet for power during the weeks at sea, beyond keeping himself warm, and Kavan appeared to be seeking an excuse to use it. That itch, combined with emotions he was having difficulty controlling, might have prompted a response but knowing how the dhóbhaen viewed uses of power, he refrained from doing so.

He felt no regret or fear connected to Raebhá's assertion of his abilities, only pride and certainty that it was true and a willingness to prove it. The márbhyndhánis controlled power, a degree of learning and training, more than the collection of hwonag in the room, but none of them, Kavan believed, could match him.

No one could.

"I have sworn to see her safely home," he said tightly, reining in his darker feelings. "I will not break that oath. Anyone seeking to challenge me, stop me…" His words trailed off, the threat not needing to be completed. His intentions were understood.

Iólán did not believe the threat was directed at him. Rather he heard an invitation and stood, offering his hands to the bard in a ritual greeting, his expression eager and determined. "I will journey with you to support my sister," he exclaimed, charging the márbhyndhánis to challenge him. When the offered sealing of the pact was accepted, Iólán nodded and said, "Tonight we feast in celebration, and tomorrow, when the ships are full, we journey south."

"Pardon, kydhé," began the Ghené captain who had remained nearby at a respectful distance. The rest of the crew had scattered about the long room, dropping their belongings anywhere that looked to be a suitable place for eventual sleep. "We are charged with the duty of returning her home. We go south to Curnydhá as well."

"You are welcome to do so. I value your honor. If someone wishes her ill," someone with the power to send Raebhá through a rynlagne, "you shall discharge your duties and keep my sister safe. Sailing beneath the sigil of Ghené will be safer than any other."

"I do not need a host…" There was no word for army in their tongue, as there had never been war or a significant outbreak of violence except during the era of Dhágdhuán's death. Raebhá did not believe she needed to threaten those she ruled. The prospect of violence on her behalf sickened her. If someone perceived her as dangerous, her presence would be threat enough and no collection of men and women armed with fishing, lumbering, farming, and mountaineering implements would protect her.

Iólán growled. "The threat's only to those who threatened you, taeásne, if they are still in Curnydhá. I will keep you safe until you are once more kymyhé. It's your right by birth, right by law, and any who has taken hands against that right deserves to be met in kind."

He looked at Kavan as if seeking agreement and the bard was pleased to find that not only did they agree, he also liked this fellow he had come close to killing. He was doubly relieved he had not.

"Your brother is right; you must be protected." Because if anything else happened to her, there would be a rash of destruction and death in this land unlike anything the dhóbhaen could imagine.

Iólán smiled. "It's settled. Raebhá, come, tell me of your journey, and later we feast, with kydhé Bhregdh's blessing, of course."

"Yes! Yes! We shall feast," Bhregdh reiterated his earlier offer, regardless of the judgmental, suspicious scowls of the márbhyndhánis.

There were questions Iólán desired to ask his sister, to ask Kavan, but not in this public place. Duty and gratitude prompted him to invite the white-skinned man to his home as well, but he first intended to speak to his sister privately, to wring from her the tale of her abduction and depart things that were for her ears alone. He trusted Bhregdh would see to Kavan's comforts and those of the sailors. The sister he had believed dead was his priority.

❧*❦

Chethá sank onto the edge of the chair, scrubbing her face with her hands the way her father often did, listening to Sóbhán tell a story to Prince Lorant by the hearth where they were protected from the cold. She did not blame the child for what Bhryell faced, for coming here had not been his fault or choice. Truthfully, there were nearly a dozen people in Bhryell, herself and her husband included, who could have brought this horror from Enesfel. Perhaps even Chethá's mother or father had innocently carried death with them. There was, as far as she knew, no way to determine a carrier until they exhibited symptoms and thus far, Prince Lorant was exhibiting no signs of illness. Nor were she or Sóbhán.

Five of Bhryell's oldest citizens, three men who had returned from trading in Enesfel, a pregnant woman, and seven children were thus far afflicted, and while none had yet to die, Chethá expected half to do so before the end of the week…most of them children. Symptoms had sprung up in the village within a week of Lorant's arrival and had run their course in two people already, a pair of sisters who exhibited symptoms the day after the prince's arrival yet had outlasted the illness and were now in recovery. Both were siblings of one of the infected merchants, the pregnant woman the wife of another, and so Chethá believed it likely that one of those three men, or all of them, was responsible for bringing death to Bhryell. The perceived timing, however, led some to blame the child prince, particularly since one of the afflicted children had played with Lorant before spreading the ailment to his siblings and cousins.

Little more than a week had passed between the exposure and the presentation of symptoms.

The prince, so far, remained healthy. To keep it that way, Chethá was forced to consider temporarily abandoning her healer duties.

He should have been asleep hours ago but he was homesick and fussy. Sóbhán brought him downstairs to the fire to share stories and a cup of warm milk in the hopes that it would settle him into sleep. Chethá was surprised to see them when she returned. She had considered staying away, resisting further exposure, but both were already exposed and she had nowhere else to go. Perhaps they would be spared, perhaps k'Ádhá would continue to protect them as he had done with the rest of her family.

She lurched in the chair when hands settled on her shoulders; blinking, she realized that Sóbhán was no longer at the hearth but rather behind her. He smiled when she looked sheepishly at him and then bent to kiss the top of her head. The prince was not there.

"Need anything? There is soup in the kettle…bread still…"

She shook her head. "I don't think I could eat." He came around the chair and sat on the stool in front of her. "Lorant looks well."

"Not a cough or a sniffle. You?"

Her head shook wearily from side to side. "Only tired." It had been days since she had sat with him, seen him more than through an open doorway, and she wanted more than her hands in his. Exhaustion kept her slouched in the high-backed chair. "I'm losing Bhront…and his sister…and more will die within days without some miracle."

"It's not your fault."

"I know…but I feel there should be something I can do to ease their suffering, more than I do."

"You could kill them."

For a moment she looked aghast until she realized he was not serious. Not so far-fetched of a notion, she thought grimly. For those on the path towards death, was it not kinder to help them avoid an agonizing end? At what point did a patient go from hope to incurable?

She had yet to learn that truth.

"Enough will die as it is. Bhryell is small; we cannot afford more."

"If k'Ádhá favors us, fewer will die than the last time." Nearly half of the village's population had succumbed to the plague that had swept the Sovereignties nearly seventy-five years ago. As slowly as Elyri populations grew, Bhryell was just beginning to recover from that loss. Another devastating period like that would leave Bhryell nearly abandoned. "I am going to bed. Will you join me?" He got up and offered his hand.

She shook her head. "Not yet. I want to sit here for a bit."

"Alright." He kissed her again, knowing she would doze in the chair instead of coming upstairs. He would not blame her if she did.

❧*❦

"You must tell him. He deserves to know."

"Know what?" It was the only part of the conversation Kavan overheard as he returned to the ghís kelyhag where people gathered for the evening meal. The custom of shared meals was meant to strengthen the community. Children wrestled and played, weaving among the adults as they ran. People stood or sat in clusters, conversing in animated voices as they collected around the fire pits. A sheep turned on a spit, one of the animals that, along with fish and waterfowl, was a staple of their diet, especially during winter months when there was no growing to be done. This repast was intended for Raebhá's benefit. Those Kavan saw were not malnourished or suffering. There was no want for food, shelter, or clothing even in the clutches of winter. No want for daily needs. The villagers took care of their own, a custom his people had grown away from outside of the náós walls.

It made Kavan again feel pleased about the inclusion of his staff at mealtimes, about including them in other aspects of his life. Not lesser. Only different. It reminded him of the pious society in Gorbesh.

That in turn reminded him of Myreth.

Raebhá opened her mouth, her expression one of awkward discomfort, but Iólán clasped Kavan's shoulders as people here did in greeting, and smiled. Kavan had been supplied clean clothing in the local fashion, with soft undergarments to protect his skin from scratchy woolen overclothes. There had been hot water in a bowl to bathe and an empty home in which to rest, but he had been unable to remain still, uncomfortable in a place he did not feel welcome. Iólán's greeting eased that disquiet only enough to counterbalance the feeling created by Raebhá's countenance.

"kydhé Cliáth, you appear rested."

"I am." Time spent off of the sea had done much for his state of mind and his physical comfort.

"Good. There's someone in Curnydhá who will be overjoyed to meet you but not if we take abuse in your care. He's spoken often of you, but I didn't believe his tales. None of us did until…"

"kydhé, come. Sit at my side."

Bhregdh's interruption disallowed the continuation of Iólán's excited ramblings, but Raebhá's relief did not go unnoticed. Assuming he was the one meant to be told something, it was easy to believe the interrupted discussion concerned Raebhá's husband. Despite Iólán's assertion that Ombhrís' fate was unknown, perhaps there were details Iólán thought best not to speak in front of the márbhyndhánis and the kydhé. It would explain Raebhá's mortification at Kavan's arrival and her subsequent relief for Bhregdh's interruption.

Perhaps what he overheard had not involved him. Not a man prone to gossip, Kavan felt awkward for the inadvertent eavesdropping. Having entered the ghís kelyhag to see Raebhá dressed in a loose, pale green gown similar in style to the one she had worn when he found her, though adorned with long sleeves that covered both shoulders, no longer covered in layers of trousers, skins, and furs, the sight robbed Kavan of breath and reason and rekindled the fire within.

It was as if he had forgotten how beautiful she was.

The fabric, thick enough to be practical in the cold evening air, hung from her fur-capped shoulders, loose and flowing about her as she shifted, jostled by the others moving around them. While many of the women in the room wore their hair coiled or plaited or in intricate braids, Raebhá's crimson trusses hung loosely around her shoulders and neck. He wanted to twist his fingers in her hair, hold her with kisses meant to bind them forever, a desire that pulled him towards her and her brother, relieved to find her well and safe after being separated for the better part of the day. That was when he heard Iólán speak.

He decided to let the matter rest and not think of it again.

Seated on a wooden bench worn smooth with age and use, hewn from rough timber and carved with animals and vines, Bhregdh on one side and Iólán on the other, between him and Raebhá, Kavan ignored his disappointment by directing his attention to the people around him as a large wooden bowl with a ladle began to pass around the room. Having spent the day roaming streets paved with wooden planks, flat stones, or hewn rocks pressed into the muddy soil, he had quickly recognized a level of fear and distrust that he had not sensed in Ghené. Words spoken earlier, that he was elyryhánag, had possibly been the one to abduct Raebhá and kill her husband for some nefarious plan, that he might have the ability to harm those here, had spread quickly in a town where anything new rarely occurred.

He felt little regret for the veiled threats, determined as he was, that no one would intimidate, besmirch, or harm Raebhá. Only children approached him, their fascination with his white skin and silver-white hair enough to prompt them to overcome their shyness. Each was scolded and shooed indoors where others watched through peeped shutters. People stopped what they were doing, mending boats and nets and farming implements, taking advantage of the increasing daylight in preparation for the shortness of spring and summer, to warily watch him pass.

Kavan did his best to stave off dismay and settle for the joy the sun provided, looking forward to evening and seeing Raebhá again.

Now she was here, her focus directed elsewhere, replaced by the attention of every other who had avoided him throughout the day. They stared until he looked at them and then they quickly looked away, embarrassed, perhaps, or else afraid that he might bewitch them, that whatever powers he possess would be used against them for their impolite attention.

Bhregdh's welcome might sway them, but it competed with the scowling, judgmental stares of the márbhyndhánis. Those men and women, Kavan sensed, would become a problem if he remained in Maras for more than a day or two.

Bhregdh made no formal introduction, allowing their seats of distinction beside him at the table to suggest the importance of his guests. When the wooden bowl reached them, Raebhá filled her cup and Iólán did likewise. Before it reached Kavan, his nose crinkled at the scent, recognizing the pungent sting of fermentation, the stain of years of liquid that had seeped into the wooden bowl. Though spiced with something akin to cinnamon that gave it a different aroma than he was familiar with, it bore the underlying sweetness of the alcohol carried with them at sea.

zerphánál was made of maple and as maple was undoubtedly rarer in the far north, it explained the reluctance of their previous hosts and the sailors to share such a precious commodity, explained why they took no offense at his refusal when it was offered before.

Here, the weather was different, the forest thicker and more diverse, suggesting warming in the year that allowed for the collection of larger quantities of sap and an increased plenty of zerphánál. There was no reluctance to share here, and as with the meal, communal sharing was expected, even with their guests.

As Bhregdh waited for Kavan to fill his cup, Kavan's eyes scanned the room, testing the expectation of others. He knew the effects of alcohol on Elyri metabolism first hand. These people were as he was, Elyri in blood no matter how ancient that bond, yet suffered no ill from consumption. Unless he wanted to explain himself, their offer to share was not one to be slighted.

Without trying it, how could he know if the effects would be the same?

Maybe some early teaching of Faith had forbidden the drinking of alcohol. Perhaps the outcasts had acquired a genetic intolerance or the strength of Teren spirits had proven more potent than what these people offered him, making the choice not to drink a matter of protection and survival.

Kavan decided not to offend his hosts. There would be no harm in filling his cup once and not drinking, or sipping with the hope that it would not incapacitate or kill him. Raebhá believed it safe, accepted the offering freely, so surely it was harmless.

She might not wish to talk to him but he would not believe she wanted him poisoned.

Families shared bread and potato dishes. The beast roasting in the center of the room, perfuming the air with savory juices, was carved by two older men who passed the meat as the zerphánál had been passed, starting on Bhregdh's left, moving clockwise, until it ended with Kavan. The zerphánál circled again once refilled from a barrel in the corner furthest from the main door. After weeks of sea rations, the smell of salt fish and little else, the meal smelled divine, eliciting a rumble of anticipation from his empty stomach. Some parts of the animal were kept aside for soups, broths, sausages, and mash made of meat and tubers. The rest was devoured with relish as Kavan listened to the dialogues around him.

No one, however, spoke to him. Not Bhregdh, who engaged with his wife and three sons on his other side, and not Raebhá who was sullenly silent and spoke little beyond nods and single word replies to her brother's questions and commentary of those around them. The man with long plaited hair the same color as Raebhá's was a wealth of information about Maras, able to identify everyone by name, community function, and the relationships between them. In his months living here, coupled with any previous travel he had made to the region, Iólán knew many things of import and was happy to share what he knew, happy to have his sister with him and not dead as he had feared. Kavan wondered if he wanted Raebhá to remain in Maras with him rather than seeing her return to Curnydhá. He wondered if she was considering that option.

Maybe that was what Iólán believed she should tell him.

The zerphánál and food platters circled the room several more times and were in the midst of another pass. Not all partook of the repeated offerings but many did, leaving Kavan to wonder at the amount of libation being consumed. In Elyriá, meals were small, sparsely eaten and savored. Watching now, though the portions taken were small enough to avoid the appearance of gluttony, so many platters and bowls passing around allowed ample opportunity for overindulgence. Perhaps, he thought as he reached for the cup he had not yet sampled, these people took advantage of banquets for guests to supplement more meager, thriftier day-to-day fair from stores meant to last the long bitter winter.

Someone raising their cup to a friend, a relative, a blessing given, a word of thanks interrupted the flow of conversation at random intervals. More than once a voice would erupt into song and most often the entire company would join. Kavan did not know their songs. Despite the progress made with understanding differences between High Elyri and what he dubbed Old Elyri, there were times when he could not make out the words quickly enough to translate them. Sometimes it was as if the folk songs came from a language older still, something as foreign-sounding on the tongues of those using it as High Elyri was on most of those Kavan knew. Judging by the faces of the villagers, Kavan did not think even they knew what they sang. He was eager, as the night wore on, to find written examples of these songs, this other language, so that he could study them and trace back their origins and meanings.

"You should sing," Iólán said against Kavan's ear as the feasting dragged on. "Raebhá says you are phehonís?"

"I did not bring my harp." His impulsive reply made little sense or difference. The harp was inside of his pack, hidden from sight when they arrived. It was not the harp Iólán asked for, however, but for the instrument Kavan carried with him at all times.

"You are a harper?" Iólán looked at his sister as if scolding her for that omission but he continued to smile. "I can send someone for it? From my sister's praise, however," he put his arm around Raebhá affectionately, "you need no instrument to support you as some do." His grin grew wider as he rolled his eyes in the direction of three men currently singing in unison who shared very little musical talent between them. The melody was garbled by their out-of-tune belting, their discordant but enthusiastic voices burying any actual song beneath their laughter and volume.

Looking past Iólán won Kavan a shy, affectionate smile before Raebhá looked away. Her expression confused him, contradicting her mood and behavior over the last three weeks, unsettling Kavan's nerves and stomach so that the sip he took from the cup in his hand was larger than intended. The sweet bitterness burned his throat but not as strongly as the wine he had once consumed, and though it warmed his belly, it did not create the sick, fiery knot he expected. His surprise and bewilderment made his hand tremble and he quickly set the nearly empty cup down before the remaining contents spilled and drew attention to his nervousness.

"No." He would feel most at ease with a harp in his hands but he did not trust anyone but Raebhá to dig through his pack and bring it. He would rather sing without it, despite the familiar uncertainty of possible rejection gnawing at his throat. "I do not need it."

"We could do with something new from someone with talent."

"You should reserve judgment," Kavan cautioned softly. He never compared himself to other musicians. The only time he had compared another to himself, that young man had horrifically lost his life. Kavan's gifts were as peculiar to him as was his appearance, but that did not make him better than anyone else, even if his popularity throughout the Sovereignties suggested otherwise.

The off-key trio, arms around one another's shoulders, finished their song and collapsed onto their bench in a fit of laughter to the applause of others. Kavan drained the zerphánál as if it would give him strength, dabbed the corners of his mouth with his fingers since there were no cloths on which to clean ones' hands or mouth, and got to his feet, his decision to sing made and executed in the same moment. He felt the exchange of glances behind him between Iólán and Bhregdh, felt the prickle of a room full of eyes turning towards him, the suspicious daggers of the márbhyndhánis' gazes, and then, as though reluctant to look at him, the soothing caress of Raebhá's gaze.

With a song in mind, intending to share the version of 'Blue Bird of Gallínphel' he knew to see what reaction he would get, he closed his eyes, opened his mouth…

But what came forth was something different, unintended, words in High Elyri born from his longing for home and those he felt were lost to him, Raebhá included.

> *íth Llaethlágárá zugdhu*
> *íth hes áti tyrethár*
> *phálóár hne Kóráhm's krus*
> *bhain scenyhur chellé k'phaelás dhedláó*
> *só hes a mál áni*
> *bhain áti kisaer*
> *átaelás aiónag elzenár*
> *hwoncáró áti aelás náir*

He kept his eyes closed as he sang, kept his thoughts closed with every skill he possessed so that efforts made to bypass his shields and probe his thoughts were met with an unbreachable wall. Most would miss the meanings of his words, the language just different enough to make some of the phrases seem nonsensical, the places and names unfamiliar. But Raebhá would know, would hear what he said and meant and felt beneath the uttered words. The gentle wash of lonely melancholy that rippled throughout the ghís kelyhag exposed the melody's meaning when his androgynous voice dipped low towards despair and soared with unfulfilled longing. Those were emotions that all save the very young could identify with, emotions he knew from experience his audience felt with him.

He did not need to see the wiping of eyes or hear the sniffling to know they felt it. He felt their reactions as strongly as his own.

"dhédók agk káyl," Iólán murmured, one hand clutching Raebhá's as he sought words to express the emotion ripping through him. Her head was bowed, her face hidden by her loose hair, as she picked through the food on her plate with trembling fingers. The distress in her aura bled around the edges of the predominantly awed melancholy of nearly everyone else, causing Kavan to stand again.

Bowing to Bhregdh, he clasped his shoulder in the ritual address he had watched others use. "Might I retire, kydhé?" he asked in a voice threatening to break beneath the assault of external emotion.

Bhregdh stood too, and though he reached for the bard's shoulders, he ended up clasping the pale man to him, unashamed to press his face against the taller man's chest.

"If it had been known that the return of the Cliáthan bloodline would be heralded by one such as you, this day would be welcomed instead of feared," he choked, ashamed of any pain he might have caused. If he was concerned about the glowering glares of the márbhyndhánis across the room, he neither acknowledged nor addressed it. "Rest, kydhé…and know that you are welcome here. I guarantee and assure your safety and Maras' hospitality."

He released Kavan with a gentle backward push to indicate the bard was free to retire. With most in the room still feasting, although now with subdued fervor as they watched him, Kavan went out into the stillness beneath the starry sky where he could breathe. It was not far enough to escape their emotions, but it was enough to ease the immediate discomfort they caused.

The night was clear, the snow no longer falling, and the light of the stars and moon reflected off the inky sea. Leaving the dhó dónáré in favor of the shore, he climbed a rocky outcropping where the waves crashed on the stone, where the ghís kelyhag seemed far away.

Not as far away as Raebhá. Not as far away as home.

"There is no rynlagne?"

He was surprised when her hand hooked around his arm but he did not look at her, afraid that she would see in his eyes what he preferred to hide. He would no longer express the depths of his heart. It hurt her when he did so. Emotion was no longer expedient, helpful, or desired.

"None near enough to detect," he said, the wrestling between heart and soul resulting in a longer delay in forming words than he realized.

The howling of wolves in the distance stirred memories for both but neither spoke until the mournful echo faded into the mountains to the west. "áchaelác aeyrudgh," she whispered, eyes blinking to be clear of tears he did not see.

He did not have to see them to know they were there. Instead of asking why she was sorry, believing it was knowledge he did not want, he asked instead, "You will remain here with Iólán?"

Surprised by his conclusion, she looked up at his profile, understanding the set of his mouth even if he chose not to express his feelings. "I have not…"

"It would be a wise choice if you fear danger in Curnydhá." It was a reasonable assumption since Iólán had not returned to his home in several months, even though he had promised to join his sister on her journey. "If you wish, I can go to Curnydhá, determine the state of affairs, and report to you, let you know if your husband survived."

"You would go alone?" She frowned, realizing she had not expected that he would consider such an act. Doing so, however, would increase the distance between them; he undoubtedly believed that was what she wanted.

"There must be a Gate within walking distance. I will only find it if I go there…and someone needs to make certain you will be safe should you eventually decide to return."

"It's not your responsibility…"

"I promised to return you safely home. I will keep my word. Whether you choose to complete the journey and confront what is there after you know the truth is up to you. For now, there is no need for you to go further. Your brother is here. You should be with him."

She shook her head, stubbornness tensing her shoulders. "He wants that, but I cannot…he'll sail with us in the morning when the ships are ready…unless you would rather travel on your own." Flight, she assumed, wondering how long it would take him to reach Curnydhá. "His boat, our father's boat, will sail with us; those who came here with him will return as well, for they have families they left behind. Bhregdh is stocking both vessels with trade goods as diplomatic cover. It will detach his absence from what happened to me and lift suspicion."

"No one will harm him, or you. I swear it."

With her hand still around his arm, she slid it lower to caress the back of his hand. He stiffened but did not draw away. His reaction saddened her and make her further regret some of her recent choices. "You swear too much of yourself to me, Kavan. There is no need…"

"I do what I do for myself." It was for her as well, but he was not going to open himself to further degradation by admitting feelings she did not reciprocate. "I don't believe in limitations. I can shield you as much as I am able, as much as you will allow, and when it is done, you will be free of me."

"Free?" She was disappointed that he believed that, but not surprised. Not after she had forced an awkward distance between them during their weeks of travel. Her reasoning, however, she had believed to be sound.

No longer, however. Iólán was right. She could not carry this secret alone. It was not fair to him, or herself.

"Kavan, I'll never be free of you. Nor do I want to be. So long as…" She brought his hand towards her and pressed it flat upon her slightly swollen belly with an anxious swallow, "…this binds us."

Kavan did not react, did not understand the gesture, and did not try to until he felt something against his hand. A jerk, a roll, a tiny thump as if something was kicking at him…from inside her body. The air rushed from his lungs. His heart seized in his chest and the sound of blood rushing in his ears was suddenly louder than the breaking waves. Unable to move, to think, he stood that way until another long pushing came against his hand, and then her body was still.

"You are…? How long…?"

Embarrassed, she looked away. "I should have…there were signs but…the realization came in Ghené. I've been afraid to…do not want you to feel obligated or…tied to me…"

The mental calculations whirled in his head. If she had been with child when he found her in the forest, at his lake, she would be nearing her fifth month. He had witnessed several pregnancies, his cousin's wife, two queens, a princess, and the Prime Magistrate of Káliel and her daughter. There would be more visible evidence of her condition if she were so far along.

She had said that her marriage was unconsummated. That did not mean, however, that she and her husband had not been intimate before.

From the evidence he had, from the echo of her words and numerous weavings of his mind through hers during training, he understood that if she was with child, it had to be his, and it terrified him. She was married. This should not be. It could not be. Though it caused a stab of despair to think she carried another man's child, further proof that she had never been, could never be Kavan's, it was easier to force himself to believe that lie than to consider the reality.

"The news displeases you." His strangled sound was more painful than she imagined it would be. She had hoped he would be pleased, but being afraid, for her, for a child, for the future, was an understandable reaction, one that mirrored her feelings about this unanticipated complication. She had grown to know him well enough to understand the moral dilemmas fighting for dominance behind his eyes. Her convoluted feelings had kept her silent for too long to spare him that but it was not, she realized now, a truth that could be spared. "I should have told you before..."

"Your husband will be pleased, should we find him alive. If we do not, I will offer what support I…"

Raebhá turned him towards her so that they could speak face to face, needing to see his eyes, needing him to see hers, needing to know if there was hope remaining between them. He needed to see her sincerity. They needed to face this as equals. The future required decisions from them both. Holding his hands, she murmured, "You will be in Alberni before the day of its birth. If Ombhrís lives, I can only imagine how he will feel about raising another man's child."

Kavan released her hands to grasp her shoulders. It did little to give him strength, and he slowly sank to his knees where he was able, with his hands on her hips, to press his ear, his cheek, to her body as if he could hear the tiny life within. It had never occurred to him that he could father a child. Dhóri had been a miraculous conception, created in a way that Kavan did not understand. He had never thought to father a child the way other men did. He was no normal man…

But you are.

The distant voice bubbled into his consciousness, a voice he had not heard in months, the only voice that might reassure him of his normalcy now that Wortham was gone. It had taken many painful years to learn that he was a man like any other, months to undo what Diona's harsh words and his lifetime of self-deprecation had done to his belief in himself.

"Kóráhm, help me," he whispered. If Wortham was here, he would know how to help Kavan bear this. Wortham would know what to do. Raebhá's fingers ran tenderly through his hair but if she heard his plea, she said nothing.

A child changed everything, his future with her, his future in this place, his future in Enesfel. How could he plan, think about what came next, when there was an unborn life depending on him?

Each day will come of its own shape, the voice came again. When it faded, leaving the euphoric rush of Kóráhm's presence, Kavan knew he was alone, alone with Raebhá and the child she carried.

His child.

"Tomorrow we leave for Curnydhá. After that…our lives are in k'Ádhá's hands."

It was the best he could offer.

"du, they are," she agreed, relieved to hear it, warmed by the press of his face against her and the acknowledgment it seemed the child had given him. For tomorrow, and many days after, he would remain at her side. It was more than she had expected.

❧Chapter 25❧

Kavan's efforts to sleep were disturbed by dreams of Wortham and snatches of Sight that gave nothing solid to grasp on to. No faces came, no words or voices only flashes of color, the glint of a blade in the firelight, the smells of decay and rain. Blessed, much needed and prayed for rain. He wondered, when the smell came again, accompanied by a creak, a snapping of twigs, and someone crying his name, if the thirsty stretches of Enesfel knew rain at last or if once again the too-wet portions of the land were drowning in damp. The sounds echoed on a shallower level, near enough to the surface of his consciousness that his eyes snapped open in time to see a shadow looming over him, arm upstretched, the hearth fire glinting on the silvery metal of a knife raised to strike.

Scrambling away from the wraith, Kavan clawed at it with one hand, intending to push the assailant away with both physical force and the ball of power that rose instinctively in his center. His hand met air, either his action or the power burst enough to dispel the shade like smoke before a breeze. Though the form that dispersed was insubstantial, the residual thrum of power in the room and the knife that clattered to the floor were not. He stretched his senses to search the home, the streets outside, for other threats, but there was no one near enough, no one wielding that sort of power, to concern him.

He slid from the bed, still dressed except for his boots, and scooped up the knife before stumbling down from the sleeping loft. Warm as if it had been carried in a living hand or kept near a fire, the blade was no more than three inches long, made of the same unfamiliar alloy he had encountered only a few times before. Afraid his belongings had been pilfered, he dug through his packs, an accounting made of everything he had brought. His harp was intact, the blade brought with him still hidden within the satchel, nothing taken or touched. Drawing his knife, unwrapping it from the leather in which it was bound, revealed something Kavan had not wanted to believe.

The blades, with smooth, gray crystallized stone hilts, were the same. The one he had been given in Zabin could have been made at the same time, in the same forge, by the same hands. Knowing now that his people, at least some of them, had been banished to those places from this land, it was easy to guess how the people of Zabin had come into possession of that knife. What he did not understand was why non-warlike people possessed such a thing and what sort of power existed behind the shadow attack.

It was not a skill he knew. Was not a skill he had ever heard of or imagined.

In Maras, there were less than a handful of people who could wield such power, who could know such a skill, unless this had been the manifestation of some evil spirit. Kavan had met such manifestations before, though never one wielding a physical weapon. Why was this one here? What did it want with him?

He wanted answers, needed to be away from here before another attack came. He also realized, as he shoved his feet into his boots and snatched up his belongings, that he needed to be sure Raebhá was safe.

He saw no one as he crossed the sleeping village and no lights burned except for hearth fires that heated each home. The ghís kelyhag, the néósag and the attached dhó dónáré were dark as well. He scowled but took advantage of the solitude to move in the shadows to the home where Iólán and Raebhá stayed. He touched her thoughts to alert her of his approach and then, sensing no threat nearby, entered the structure without knocking, unwilling to loiter outside for an invitation. No one must see him here, and if there was a threat he could not feel, Kavan did not want to alert it to his presence by knocking.

Raebhá sat by the failing fire, as did her brother, both as restless as Kavan. They looked up as the door opened; Iólán, not having the warning of this arrival that Raebhá had, leaped to his feet with the fire poker in hand. She tried to smile, hoping it was a longing to see her that brought him to her, but, sensing his alarm, the effort faltered.

"kydhé." Iólán positioned himself between Kavan and his sister, in case the unannounced entry was the prelude to something sinister.

Kavan set his belongings on the floor near the now-closed door and came forward with the daggers in his hand. "What are these?"

Raebhá took one. Iólán took the other. "Where did you get these?" Iólán asked, tense and nervous as he turned the blade over in his palm.

"One I was given in a village called Zabin…in the land where my…our…people once resided. The other was used moments ago in an attack…"

"Attack?" Raebhá scrambled to her feet, clutching the blade as if she would strike someone with it if that source of danger had been at hand. Kavan had come alone and she heard nothing in the street, sensed no threat, but after what had happened to her, the assailants that seemed more phantom than real, she believed Kavan's assertion. "Did you see…?"

"Who would…?"

"What are they?" Kavan asked again without answering.

"ániélmé, used by the márbhyndhánis or phemárógdh to cut herbs, divide ingredients for tonics and poultices, to lance boils or cut binding fabric or flesh if the need arises. But," Iólán added hastily, reluctant to accuse anyone of violence against a guest of the kmydhé, against his sister's protector, "no healer would attempt to take another's life. It is forbidden."

"Our people have that in common." Kavan held out his hand for the blades. Raebhá returned hers without question but Iólán was reluctant to do likewise. "Whoever wielded it has enough power to summon shadows to do their bidding, or else was shadow themselves, something I do not know how to do."

There was no shame in admitting that. He might not know how to do it now, but he had already decided he would learn. All it took was knowing something was possible to find a way to make it so. "It is not safe for us here."

"Will it be safe for you anywhere?" Raebhá whispered. He was here to protect her. She had not expected she might need to protect him from her own historically non-violent people.

Kavan shrugged. "I am a threat; everything I am goes against everything your people believe…"

"Not all of us," Iólán defensively interrupted.

"Perhaps not…but enough. At least those in a position of power with the ability to threaten me see me so. They, or someone, will try again. Someone attempted to kill you once, Raebhá, someone able to use Gates, who can use the same power against…"

"You believe the márbhyndhánis…?"

"Why would they…?"

She squeezed her brother's hand. "You know why. Father and I…"

"No." He shook his head, unable to look at her as he asked, "Did Ombhrís? Did he know?"

"How could he? Father forbid me to speak of it." Confused and unsettled, she sank onto the hearth and stared into the embers. "His family is of the old ways; if they had known, they would never have agreed to the marriage."

Someone else must have known, or suspected, and it had been cause enough for the márbhyndhánis or a faction within, to strike. Blaming Kavan, blaming any elyryhánag was illogical. Neither stood anything to gain by removing her from Curnydhá, by killing her. None in those lands had even known she or her people or land existed.

What reason could there be except the practice of illicit power?

Did all of the márbhyndhánis know? If they could use rynlagne, had they shared knowledge of her with other ghís? Was that the cause for their less than cordial welcome in Phaurd, in Maras? Did Ombhrís die because of her? Was this attack on Kavan her fault?

Kavan knelt before her and dried the frustrated tears that glistened on her lashes. "Now that you are returning home," he murmured, "it may be that someone does not want you there…that someone in Maras knows the truth about what happened."

"If the márbhyndhánis…" Iólán sat as well, strength drained from his legs and replaced with a dose of anxiety unfelt before. "No one can…they are trained; only another márbhyndhánis could confront them. Without knowing who we can trust…"

"I can find out, but not here. I think our wisest course is to be away from this place."

"And go where? To Curnydhá? If you are right, they may try to kill her again, to kill you again."

Holding his wrists, drawing strength from him through the touch, choosing to have confidence in his certainty, Raebhá looked at Iólán and said, "No one will kill us." Kavan had made a promise and she believed him capable of keeping it. "If there's venality in Curnydhá, corruption amongst the márbhyndhánis, it must end. Murder's forbidden; what they did without inquest is wrong. Curnydhá's my ghís, Gálínphel my ghísaer. I will not hide. I must have the truth."

"The boats will not be ready until mid-morning," Iólán reminded them, wanting to believe his sister but not having her experience with Kavan and matters such as they faced.

Kavan could rouse the crews without being caught, but so many moving in the streets during the sleeping hours would wake others and there would be questions. He considered whether the three of them could maneuver the smaller of the two vessels alone. He could propel it without the need of oarsmen, but there was no guarantee those left behind in Maras would be safe when they were discovered missing. If someone was eager enough to come for him once, in his sleep, they would try again, and they might have few compunctions about harming others in the quest for information or out of spite.

"Then we wait and remain diligent. I will stay with you, protect you until the boats are ready, then we go."

If they did not, he feared what would happen.

❧*❧

Newly appointed General Fraen the Elder, a man with graying black hair and a bulbous red nose that spoke of a man too familiar with drink, rapped firmly on the doorframe of the war room where Queen-Regent Inness spent the majority of her waking hours. Situated on the south side of the Glevum palace, it had windows facing east and west as well that allowed for sunlight at every hour of the day. At this early hour, however, the sun had not fully crested the horizon, thus the room required lamps and candles if one wanted to read or tend to duty. The acting monarch did not come to the war room to work, however, but rather to escape the ghosts that haunted the chambers she had shared with Oska. Being there forced her to confront the windowed doors onto the balcony where her husband had spent his last moments in terror and regret for the things he believed he had done. Those ghosts led her to question her decisions, to wrestle with unseen demons of regret, and so she often spent her nights in this long room, seated in one of the high-backed, cushioned chairs of green leather and velvet, claiming the pregnancy made it uncomfortable to lie down and she could only sleep sitting up.

Why the war room when there were more comfortable locations to take rest and find solitude, was something she would not divulge.

Staff had offered to move this chair to her chamber.

She had refused.

Roused from her half-sleep, she looked at her general expectantly. "It is done?"

"The officers are summoned. Word is dispatched that all who once served in the king's army, regardless of age, and that one male over seventeen from every family, are to report to their nearest Lord. The new force should be gathered and armed within three weeks, four at most if the weather holds, as you requested."

The call would form a smaller military force than Neth had built in times past, but it was necessary to make up for the reduction of personnel strapped upon them by the loss of the southern territories. If the queen-regent had hopes of making Neth stronger, such a force would be crucial. She had to begin rebuilding from what she had.

"Might I inquire as to the purpose?" It was the ruler's prerogative to build or dismiss the army as they wished, but Fraen, as her newest general, felt it was his right to know what she intended. After more than two decades without a significant standing military, rebuilding it was going to be taxing and expensive.

"Neth is weak. That will not stand."

That was an obvious statement to Fraen and he grunted, waiting to see if she would say more. When she offered no further explanation, he bowed and said, "If I may, I will continue with arrangements for training and let you know when the officers arrive."

"When they do, when the last one is here, bring them all to this room." Only then would she divulge her intentions. Only then, would she confirm the rumors and make the formal announcement of how she planned to reclaim what had been stolen.

The forests of the south.

❧Chapter 26❧

There was no slumber, no talking, after the decision was made to stay together until they departed Maras. Kavan could have lulled the others to sleep with music but he chose not to, chose to enjoy their company as they waited for dawn. The things Iólán wanted to bring were already tucked into bags that sat beside Raebhá's pack. There was no need to do anything except enjoy the gradually dying fire, enmeshed in their private thoughts. When street sounds announced the arrival of morning, they nodded at one another, resolved in what they were about to do, and emerged from the house to curious eyes that followed every step they took.

People stared as if the bard was an apparition come to haunt or harm them and he wondered what had transpired after his departure from the ghís kelyhag to create such a reversal in behavior. After his song, he had felt that many were swayed in his favor, had felt the familiar adoration and keen interest that tended to follow wherever he traveled. What he sensed now, tapping against his psychic shields, seeking to seep into his core, was wary fear and hostility, as if he had done something wrong.

He had done nothing except exist.

Noting the márbhyndhánis watching from the neósag balcony, his existence might have been enough. White Bard or not, he was elyryhánag. He was a follower of Dhágdhuán and k'Ádhá. His presence was a threat to the way of life they had led for generations. People needed no other reason to disapprove of his being here.

"dhédók agk káyl," kydhé Bhregdh bustled down the path to greet them, towards the dock where crates and barrels and waxed canvas sacks were being secured fore and aft on Iólán's ship. The three turned in time for the man to throw his arms around Kavan. "It was said you were dead! I refused to believe it, had to see for myself."

Kavan met Raebhá's gaze over the kydhé's back as he gently pried himself free. After what had transpired during the night, that he was not was bound to be a disappointment to someone. "I assure you, I do not die so easily." Someone…but not this man.

He lifted his chin and glanced at the distant márbhyndhánis, his gaze cool and pointed. Whether they had been the ones to deliver that news to the kydhé, whether they could tell Kavan was looking at them across such a distance, whether they could see his expression, the men and women on the balcony scattered as if avoiding an unexpected downpour. Their behavior supported his suspicions but did not explain their motives. Nor did it explain why a people who forbade murder, who believed that death was a bad omen and an unnatural thing, would be willing to kill him.

"I'm grateful. I directed the loading early, as you can see, so that you," he looked at Raebhá and Iólán, "could depart quickly if foul play was afoot. I will not be a party to it. Go with my blessings and the blessings of the gods. Find who would do such things and set it right."

He turned to Kavan, clasped his shoulders, and drew him close. Against his ear, in a gesture that looked like a friendly kiss, he whispered, "There is a shadow, a hungry thing threatening what we have always been. Do not let it happen, kydhé. Bring light to our darkness…as the prophecy foretells."

His plea made Kavan shudder, but he nodded as he stepped back almost as if he could distance himself from yet another burden of prophecy. He did not want to be a prophet or a prophecy, a saint or a savior. He wanted to be a bard, a teacher, a man. A father.

Bhregdh took three overstuffed canvas packs from the pair of boys who ran down the dock to them and gave one to each of his departing visitors. "Cheese, dried apples, sausage, and bread," he smiled, happy to offer commodities not obtainable at sea. None of it would keep well in the damp of their open-aired boats, but for a few days, the luxury would be appreciated. Another two weeks at sea, when they had only just come ashore was not what Kavan wanted, and as he boarded one vessel, Raebhá and Iólán boarded the other, a precaution Kavan thought best. If his life put the others in danger, he suspected this journey would be more treacherous than the last.

If the threat was to Raebhá, he knew he could protect her as easily from his boat as he could at her side.

The boats pulled away, first heading east into deeper waters so that they could journey south without fear of the increasingly rocky shoreline. On the outcropping near the ghís kelyhag, the márbhyndhánis gathered again, hands clasped in front of them or behind their backs, watching. Three sailors, two on Kavan's boat and one other, turned to look at those imposingly rigid figures, an exchange Kavan noted that made him consider, as the self-righteous pillars grew smaller, how best to protect two ships at once…and if he would dare to sleep until they moored on the shores of Curnydhá.

The scruffy fellow with crooked yellow teeth and muddy clothes settled at the table in the Eagle's Nest tavern, feeling no awkwardness or hesitation about sitting across from Asta de Corrmick, Queen of Neth, Princess of Enesfel, and now co-Inquisitor in the Lachlan court. Despite those things, she was a Dugan, and as a Dugan, she was well respected by the organization into which he had been born. It was that organization that protected him, so long as he did not overstep the boundaries in dealing with her. He had been sent to deliver a message and he had waited eight days for the castle gates to open so that he could present it to her in person as he had been instructed. He drank deep of the ale she had ordered, waiting for the cluster of patrons to move away from the bar towards the table they had come from. It was too crowded here for his liking, despite the Yellow Death, and it seemed Asta felt likewise as she waited impatiently to hear his news.

"Prince Oska and Princess Inness are ruling well," he burped, keeping his voice low so as not to be overheard. "Or rather, the princess is; seems recent events have been rather more than the prince can bear." He began to chuckle then stuffed the sound back inside when he noted the dark spark in Asta's eyes. "Rumors are he blames himself for your vanishing and Prince Jerit's, for his father's death."

Asta blanched.

The fellow shrugged and refilled his glass. "No one knows for sure. No one's seen him since before that night. There was a body…but people say it wasn't him. Wasn't recognizable, whoever it was, except for his ring. Some say he's a hostage…some that he's in hiding…that he was gravely injured and is in treatment. Those inside won't confirm or deny anything, except that King Oska raves and drinks too much and does not seem like himself."

Heart cracking, Asta leaned against the back of the stool. Unfortunately, that sounded like Oska. He had always been a more empathic man than his brother, more sensitive and introspective. Asta could not imagine a scenario where her eldest son could be the cause of this nightmare, where he could intentionally or accidentally be the cause of his father's death, no matter how guilty he felt, no matter how worried he had been about his right and claim to Neth's throne.

But if he believed himself the only survivor, alone without mother, father, or brother, the guilt would be there.

"Can you get a message to Oska?"

"Aye…I could…" the man nodded. "Discreetly?"

"Of course."

"That'll cost extra…but I can do it."

"And a message to Onea."

"That'll be no cost," he said with a lascivious grin. He was not the first man willing to do anything to wiggle into that woman's company.

Thankfully, Onea was more finicky when it came to her male companions than some.

Asta scowled but took the pouch of coins from inside her breast pocket and placed it on the table, pulling it back when he reached for it. "Let Oska know his brother and I live, that we will do everything we can to aid him and return to Glevum if he deems it safe. Whatever he needs. Deliver the same message to Onea. Do this and there will be an equal share when you return to me."

After a long stare into his empty mug, the messenger looked at her with a nod and an unspoken plea. Asta snorted and tossed him three more coins. "Buy a meal and another ale and be off. And please," she covered his dirty hands with hers. "Bring any news of Kjell at once." If there were rumors that he had survived, she hoped he had. But her gut instinct repeated what she believed to be true.

Neth's king was likely dead. Who was meant for the throne now, who sat upon it and should, was a dilemma she needed to solve.

## ☙Chapter 27❧

The approach of spring was undercut by the north wind that propelled the pair of ships towards their destination. The cloudless sky often created a glare of the sun off the glassy water. Once there had been the faded reflection of light ribbons, below and above the ships, a sign that Kavan again took to mean he was on the right course, treading the path that destiny had laid. Eventually the pink, gold, and green had bled back to black, and from the talk of the sailing crew, as the turn of seasons continued, Kavan doubted he would see those ribbons again.

When he could, he watched the shore, memorizing landmarks of cliffs meeting the sea, clusters of three or six or a dozen stone and thatch houses tucked into flat, farmable plots, blankets of forest that appeared to march from the mountain summits to drink from the sustenance of the sea. Fingers of water, sometimes a trickle, sometimes great torrents, tumbled from the heights into the ocean in so many places Kavan had lost count. Rivers emptied their mountain blood into the sea at the land's edge. The silhouettes of some manner of deer were often spotted on the precipices, and flightless seabirds hopped up and down the weathered stone as though on stairs to the nested colonies of others of their ilk. Twice they encountered tall plumes of breaching whales, creatures he had heard of but had seen only in artwork. There was so much to see, to study, to know, that he could live a lifetime here and never understand everything that made the dhóbhaen the stock from which the Elyri sprang.

When he could not easily see the land through the glare or early morning mist, he stared east, wondering what lay beyond the horizon, his thoughts jostled by the motion of the ship as the oarsmen propelled them along and of the woman in the other boat he rarely saw. He was confident his recommendation for separation was the right one, to keep Raebhá safe, to ease them through the separation that was soon to come, but it was not easy to face when he awoke alone.

He did not dare touch her thoughts to know if she suffered as he did, if she missed him too.

Whatever Iólán knew of her condition, of her time spent with him in Alberni, if she and Kavan traveled together, eventually their affection would be revealed. That revelation was one he did not think she could afford if she was to reclaim her position in Gálínphel.

It was better if he focused on learning as much about the dhóbhaen, their land, the culture as he could so that he could set it all to paper when he returned to St. Kóráhm's. It kept his thoughts, his gaze, away from the remembrances of her company.

It kept him from dwelling too much on those he had left behind.

Like his own people, the dhóbhaen bore no hair except upon their heads, the brows above their eyes, and lashes. There was little else in appearance to separate them from Teren. Whatever function hair served, they, like Elyri could only be warm through clothing and the use of power. Because the majority received no training beyond that skill and the making of handlights, their thoughts were as open and chaotic as any Teren's if not for Kavan's skill at blocking them. Each dhóbhaen he met possessed power, and not knowing how to use it, threatened to muddle his head with their disordered thoughts.

There was one man in particular who gave Kavan pause, a dark-haired man who wore his water-repellant cloak only under the most extreme conditions, whose slate-dark eyes watched Kavan when he thought the bard was unaware of it. His thoughts could not be read like those of others. Kavan felt no animosity from the fellow, only curiosity and a peculiar sense of determination. It was possible he could shield his thoughts naturally or had developed that skill on his own at a young age as Kavan had done. Inborn skills were common in Elyri, and most children born with them either learned to adapt to them, control them, or if they could not, if they possessed something dangerous like Kavan's gift of sídysá, they were trained to control it.

He did not know if the same was true for the dhóbhaen. He did not know what the society, what the márbhyndhánis, did with children like that. But this man's attention, a man whose hair was the darkest shade he had seen amongst the Kindred, made Kavan uneasy.

It might be, he fretted as the boats rowed up onto a rare stretch of beach with peculiarly green pebbled sand that gave way to forested mountains without a hint of inhabitation, the way the much younger man looked at Raebhá. His dark eyes lingered a little too long, with too much familiarity. Kavan did not like it.

"We are refilling water," Raebhá explained as she and Iólán joined Kavan where he waited on shaky legs on the sandy spit. Her smile, the warm note of excitement in her voice, was enough to express the pleasure she felt in his company. It was a relief to hear and see it, enough to belie his creeping fears.

A narrow creek cut through the forest, on its path to the sea from the falls up the mountain face beyond. Four men from each boat carried barrels inland, seeking the place where the salty ocean no longer contaminated the water source. Others gathered wood, a decision having been made to camp, to enjoy the warmth of the sand and a cooked meal without consulting the three primary passengers.

Or doing so had been discussed with Raebhá and Iólán already.

"Assuming they find game, we shall dine on something other than fish and cured pork," Iólán said with a grin as he stretched.

Watching people collect fishing spears and nets from the boats, Kavan asked, "Shall I assist in the hunt? I have some skill and…"

"No."

The dark-eyed man barked the word in passing, glowering as he pulled a heavy rope slung over his shoulder, intending to tie the vessel to a tree. The sun had dropped behind the western mountains, bringing long shadows with it. By the time a meal was caught and cooked, it would be dark. It made sense to stay here for the night, but the thought of lost time and the man's tone of voice made Kavan scowl.

"Don't pay him heed," Iólán laughed. "Zóndhá looks more intimidating than he is."

"He is trained?"

Surprised that Kavan could know that, Iólán shrugged. "Those born with mósc phág are considered favored; there are so few. They are raised by the márbhyndhánis in the belief that they have skills beyond other dhóbhaen. Zóndhá suffered a fall from a tree in his fifteenth year and his training ceased. He follows direction, takes orders, but he's unable to do many things for himself…like a child who has not learned responsibility."

"He knows you?"

"He often travels with those who raised him and with other traders. I have been to sea with him many times."

"He delivered gifts from our father to other ghísaer," Raebhá added. She had never been uneasy in Zóndhá's company. He had always seemed a kind, gentle, easygoing man. "We share greetings often. You can trust him."

Kavan huffed. It was an adequate explanation, putting his previous concerns and jealousies out of his head, but his nerves refused to settle. With the gazes of so many watching him, having his life threatened once and feeling the impending threat to Raebhá the closer they came to Curnydhá, it was difficult to find peace. "They do not trust me."

"We're guests. We're not required to help." Raebhá hooked her arm around Kavan's and steered him towards one of the three fires being built upon the green sand.

They had been separated for too many days, in sight of one another but unable to speak, to touch, even in an innocent fashion. Her brother kept whatever he knew about their relationship to himself and had more than once encouraged her, when the boats grounded for water or to trade wares with the bits of civilization they passed, to join Kavan on the other boat. But she resisted, as much for Kavan's sake as for the protection of her status, her secret. She would not reveal either her feelings or her pregnancy until she knew if her husband lived.

If she lingered at Kavan's side, the crews of both vessels would guess the truth. She did not want to put either of them anymore at risk.

"I would prefer to help. They would not permit me to row."

"Be thankful for that," laughed Iólán. "I've done my share at oar. It is not a duty you want."

Though unafraid of physical labor, Kavan chose not to say so and instead removed the water-shielding cloak and hung it over a branch in the hopes that it would be dryer by morning. Raebhá continued towards the fire with her brother while Kavan scooped up a handful of the peculiar sand to study it. His gaze, however, repeatedly wandered to Raebhá, who looked noticeably with child to him despite her efforts and the cut of the waistless cloak to hide it. Hoping that it was only noticeable because he knew the truth, that she was not open to scandal because of their mutual choices, he shifted his attention to Zóndhá who was breaking chunks of timber with his hands and tossing them into the fires. As the big man no longer seemed focused on Raebhá, and he felt no tension in the group, Kavan eventually relaxed, released the sand he had given up examining, to join brother and sister at the fire.

A small deer and several pudgy, unfamiliar, rodent-like creatures were served as dinner, the uneaten bits either left over the smokey heat to cure, collected in the deer's emptied stomach to be used as bait for fishing when they sailed again or else burned in the fire as Kavan had heard ancient Teren had done as sacrifices to their deities.

These people were, as far as he could determine, an unreligious sort. They referred to the ágdháthé, but they had no belief that those creation spirits had involvement in their lives. The stories told around their fires, those shared in Phaurd and Maras, those Raebhá had told him, were myths and pseudo-historical accounts of people gone before, considered great heroes but who bore no trace of the divine. Unlike so many myths Kavan knew from his own people and the Teren of the Five Sovereignties, those of the dhóbhaen bore no war and very little combat or violence except for hunting and the physical competitions of which many dhóbhaen were fond.

There were tales of couples kept apart by powerful families, of outwitting others with humor and intellect, tales of using music to tame rivals or beasts. There were accounts of struggles against nature and about clashes with the ágdháthé. But rarely did any of those tales contain more than a single exchange of blows or the use of a hunting or fishing implement to prevent greater violence from occurring.

Being on land without the constant splash of seafoam as the boats cut through the waves allowed Kavan the chance to record some of the tales he had heard on the sheets of parchment Iólán had brought for him. Other tales he intended to remember long enough to record when they reached Curnydhá. Some sounded familiar, versions of stories he had been told as a little boy, and he wondered how far back Elyri myth stretched, if it dug into history both Elyri and dhóbhaen had erased from their collective memories.

One by one the sailors leaned back on their packs or against boulders or large slabs of unburned wood to drift off to sleep. Not one of them showed any inclination to remain awake and on guard against predators from the forests, the mountains, or the sea.

It was not the worry for predators that kept Kavan awake but rather a continuation of the restlessness which had plagued him since before their boats left Maras.

If none of these people were the threats he feared, there was no tangible cause for discontent. No cause, he mused as he got to his feet, except for some distant, unclear clawing of the Sight.

The Sight did not always come as glimpses before his eyes, in his mind. Sometimes the premonitions came as nothing more than a feeling that, to others, must seem mad. He assumed this was such an occasion, the notion that danger was afoot but not in any form he could recognize. The feeling of dread and despair could be rooted in the possibility that Raebhá's husband lived, the necessity of leaving her, but he did not know if that assessment of his feelings was accurate.

"Kavan?"

He looked at the hand squeezing his gently, shivering at the sound of his name on her lips. He had thought her asleep, had not thought his movement would rouse her. He leaned closer to speak without waking the others. "Sleep, kyag. I intend to draw apart to pray."

"Apart?" She propped herself on one elbow and wiped the sleep from her eyes. In the moonlight, his hair and skin glistened ghostly silver, a thing of beauty that compelled her to touch it. Her fingers entwined in his hair before stroking along his cheek and down his exposed throat. His eyes fluttered closed and he breathed a soft moan. She was not surprised when he caught her hand, kissed those same fingers, and then released her to trudge across the beach towards a rocky outcropping. Shivers of longing and regret passed through her as she watched, and then blocked out, the beauty of his silhouette against the rising moon.

Was she condemned to break his heart repeatedly until there was nothing left but a shell? Would she ever stop inflicting pain on herself?

Upon the large stones that sea and time had bound together with green sand and silt, Kavan watched the waves, seeking solace in the moonlit ripples that curled in to kiss the shore. The boats had beached at the lowest tide, for the level crept nearer to the encampment as the night progressed. With the knowledge of such things and practiced reading of the secrets told by the changes in the sand and the surrounding landscape, the experienced dhóbhaen had made camp far enough up the beach to be beyond the tide unless the weather turned foul. The sky on the horizon, black and filled with stars and the faintest traces of yellow ribbons, showed no clouds. There was little likelihood that a storm would surprise them.

They were safe.

Why then, Kavan stretched out his pleas to Ethenae or Kóráhm if the saint was near enough to hear him, did he feel ill at ease?

The answer that came back was a feeling of pressure, as if someone gripped his shoulders to push him towards the rocky precipice. He could swim, had no fear of drowning, but a fall would result in a painful crash onto the toothy rocks and injuries that might incapacitate him long enough that the risk of being sucked to sea in the undertow, pulled under and drowned, were high.

His first instinct, as he turned to face an assailant he expected to see, was to push back against the individual. But there was no one there to lay hands on him. This was power, strong enough to have arisen without his notice in his distracted state and focused enough to push him, inch by inch, nearer to the edge.

He had fought power before, fought the lost essence of Dawid Coryllien when it had tried to prevent him from cleansing the ancient temple below the Lachlan keep. Kavan threw up a wall of energy, thrusting back with enough force to halt his movement. With that instinctive response came the knot of power in his core, the tight burning brightness that sought an outlet in its effort to protect him. Kavan looked across the sleeping group of people no more than ten yards away, most peaceful in their repose save for Raebhá who lay awake, her eyes closed, awaiting his return to the fire. There was one other as well, poking at the flames with a long stick with distracted, automatic movements meant to give the appearance of business while his thoughts, his attention, were elsewhere.

Zóndhá.

Testing what a lifetime of instinct was telling him, Kavan relaxed his shield enough to prompt an increased rise in power in the other man, enough of an increase to push Kavan back with a jolt to the lip of the ledge. The unexpectedly powerful response thrust Kavan's heart into his throat and created two simultaneous unplanned, instinctive responses inside of him.

His inborn defenses snapped, releasing a flash of power that rippled back along the attacking thread and exploded within the other man's chest…just as Kavan gave in to the unexpected transformation that took his familiar kestrel shape into the sky. The change, the spreading of white-feathered wings, prevented him from tumbling onto the rocks and he watched in horror as the aggressive energy dissipated in a burst, faded, and left its creator toppled to one side.

No one stirred, their sleep unbroken by the brief psychic battle. Raebhá rolled, wrapping her cloak around her against the chill that power blast had pulled in its wake but she did not otherwise react to it. Without examining the crumpled man, Kavan knew what he had done. That much power, energy he could not control in the wake of a panic to survive, released inside of a man, was enough to kill. Men had died in the wake of that power before. Kavan knew he could do it.

He had not, however, expected to.

There were drag marks on the promontory where he had stood, evidence that someone had been pushed or dragged towards the edge, disappearing over it as if thrown into the sea. Few present would be able to piece the two incidences together, few would care to try, and with no healer among them, he doubted anyone would be able to determine how the seemingly simple man had died.

Kavan would know. In a culture that did not believe in violence, someone had tried again to kill him…and failed. Kavan had been the one to kill instead. If Iólán spoke true, this attempt had not been Zóndhá's idea. Someone had prompted him to it, either in the hopes that Kavan would die without an obvious explanation or in the hopes that he would react in a way that would create fear and prompt Raebhá to be rid of him in whatever way she deemed appropriate for his crime.

Those who had sent him could not have foreseen this turn of events.

Nor had he.

Resuming his form at the bottom of the rise where he believed no one would notice, he climbed the rocks to the sea ledge, stood there, face into the wind, into the darkness long enough to be certain that no one had seen him, and then returned to the fire, to the place where he had lain before. The crackling fire popped sparks into the blackness. Pulling his cloak closer to his body, a shield against himself more than against the sea breeze, he lay down, one arm behind his head, and stared at the sky. No one stirred except for Raebhá, who turned languidly towards him, a hand outstretched, her eyes still closed.

Hesitantly he brushed his trembling fingertips over hers as if doing so might provide the forgiveness he sought. She smiled in her slumber and tucked her hand beneath her chin, tendrils of red hair woven around her fingers.

There was no indication that she knew what he had done, only relief that he had come back to her.

Her touch, her smile, her relief to have him near, did not settle his spirit or ease his remorse.

Most of his earlier agitation was gone, replaced by the emptiness of power, the sour sickness of guilt, and the battle within between confession and silence that disallowed him to take comfort in slumber. Self-defense or not, promise to protect Raebhá or not, how could he sleep when the fear of discovery kept him from closing his eyes? How did she not know what he had done?

The sun had not yet broken the horizon, though the sky was gradually brightening with the approach of dawn, when others stirred. High tide had begun its retreat, meaning that the beached boats would be carried out without the need for manpower, and so the sailors began to break camp. It took only minutes, however, for someone to notice that Zóndhá did not stir, to realize that his awkward angle suggested he had fallen sideways from a seated position, to realize he was not breathing and had begun to turn a sickly shade of death-pale.

He bore no marks except for a purple, fist-sized bruise upon his chest, discolored lines spidering outward in a pattern that suggested a ruptured heart. People argued about what should be done. Most were unwilling to travel with a corpse but there were three who argued in favor of transporting the dead man to Curnydhá so that a healer could assess the body for the cause of death.

The same three who had shared disguised looks with the márbhyndhánis upon their departure from Maras.

"There is a great fear of the dead," Kavan murmured beneath his breath, alert to each voice in the conversation, to the decision of his destiny that played out while he anxiously remained silent. He had seen Raebhá's fear on the mountain, facing the entombed dead, but he had believed that to be a product of facing unprecedented violence, not the dead themselves.

"It is the old ways." Raebhá spoke in stilted taeré so that most would not understand her. The seemingly natural but unexpected death of one of their number had upset the others; further discussion would only aggravate them.

A decision reached after a heated period of silent stares and scowls, several people went into the forest, where the echoes of cutting lumber were soon heard. Others began to dig a wide pit in the sand beyond the high tide mark. Iólán was one of those who took it upon themselves to make certain the retreating tide did not pull the boats free, instead drawing them further onto the dry sand. No one touched the body, no one moved it, no one went near it now that it had been determined he was dead.

"The Ceasing is our ordinary end," Raebhá explained to Kavan's peaked interest in the ritual taking shape. "We give back our essence to nature, to the ágdháthé. This sort of death is the result of illness, mishap, or," she glanced at Zóndhá with a sigh, "not natural at all."

"Do you think he was…?" Kavan choked.

Raebhá shook her head but she did not look at him, watching instead the preparations underway. "Likely connected to his fall. Falls from such heights do great damage to the body. It was surprising he survived. Heart ruptures happen sometimes to those as big as Zóndhá, or the weak who undertake too much physical work.

Zóndhá had not been weak, making his death look, to Kavan, all the more suspicious. Uncertain what she believed and not wanting to root out the truth, Kavan murmured, "What are they doing?"

"The ágdh of the dead will be free to torment the living…to become bhur…if his body is not properly disposed of. It will curse the living, kill or drive others to madness until the body is burned; what is left will be buried to trap the ágdh with it. We will remain until it is done, an unfortunate delay but it cannot be helped."

"Do you believe this? In this bhur…in the ritual?"

"I believe our essence joins with the gdhárith in zethenaer…as Dhágdhuán promised." That name was spoken quietly so that no one else could hear it. "Death is as natural as kylldhysag. Since none have returned from the Ceasing to speak differently, I believe the end is the same, as he said. Perhaps those who cease are taken with their bodies, becoming gdhárithté…perhaps they are not. But all end in the same place, for there is only one place to go when we leave this life. Good or bad, zethenaer welcomes all; only our deeds determine what that place will be like for us."

Never had Kavan considered the possibility that the fate of those who walked away from their life and ceased to be was no different than the fate of those who died. Raised in the Faith, he had been indoctrinated from childhood to believe that only the worthy dead were welcomed into Ethenae. Such a fate bode well for the Teren, who had no choice but to face death within a span of a set number of years. For Elyri, only murder, accident, childbirth, disease, or great stubbornness brought death and only those things guaranteed a person an eternity in Ethenae. No Faith leader would address the fate of the majority of Elyri, none would discuss it as though the topic was taboo.

When had that shift in belief occurred?

Why?

"Dhágdhuán taught this?"

The too-loud mention of that name gained him the glowers of two who passed with bundles of branches gathered from the forest floor, some still snowy despite the cover of the boughs.

"Be careful where you speak his name, for he is a forbidden topic outside of schooling." Raebhá nodded to the pair as though in apology and pulled Kavan to his feet to steer him away from the preparations before speaking again.

"He did. Such a belief was…is…heresy…for an acceptance of death would allow and encourage murder, war, the taking of our own lives…result in the loss of the sanctity of life."

Kavan's head bobbed, understanding, though to him the acceptance of death being a rationale, a consent, for the taking of life seemed absurd. Such a twist in belief, however, would certainly rock the foundation of a society. He had experienced that backlash before.

"Life is always sacred," he murmured mournfully, despite the warmth of a new reassurance stirring in his soul. If what she said was true, if he could be welcomed into Ethenae no matter his end, he had spent his life in fear and dread for nothing. Was making it so the Faith leaders' means of controlling the Faithful? If Dhágdhuán said it, it must be true, but who had decided it was wrong? When? And why?

With the boats secured, others split up to help retrieve wood or to dig in the coarse sand. A few, the oldest among them, stood near the corpse, swaying side by side, alternating between moaning wails, chanted ritualized phrases, and short bursts of song. None of it was in unison, a cacophony that was more confusing than beautiful. Others coming out of the forest, adding their wood to a pyre erected in the pit, joined the mourners one by one.

When the hole was deep enough, the wood piled high, Iólán set aside his digging efforts to contribute the vocalization of grief. Raebhá joined him. Kavan caught her arm and she smiled sadly at the question in his eyes, tilting her head towards the others in an invitation for him to participate, a look that promised answers when it was over.

Judging by what he heard that it mattered less what sound a person made, as none expressed sorrow alike, Kavan stood beside Raebhá and drew upon his store of prayers and hymns to add his song to the cry.

Voices faltered, the compulsion to still and listen to him strong. But the need to continue their ritual was stronger. The sound swelled once more, the jumbled notes and words wafting out with the receding tide towards the risen sun.

∾*∾

"Bring him to the house."
"My lord?"
The nightmarish curse of boils and blood and blindness, of coughing and choking and gradually losing lungs, limbs, or life, symptoms of the northern plague, was crushing Alberni despite every effort Rhyrdan, Captain Magk, and the residents of St. Kóráhm's made to stem the tide. No amount of food, of clean water, and now the rain that blessed the province with much-needed sustenance, proved able to rout the devastation that spread throughout the once prosperous city.

Spring had come early. Those who were able made an effort to sow the wet soil. As the death toll crept higher, the acting lord suspected they would not have people enough to tend or harvest any crop that made it to maturity. The living had stopped counting the dead. Those who had not fled were difficult to count as many hid and refused to come to their doors when the gdhededhá went through town day after day to minister to those who stubbornly clung to life.

There was no longer an active effort to segregate the sick from the living. Attempts to quarantine had failed. Rhyrdan's mother, his sister, his sister's husband, were all afflicted. Some of the manor's staff had already succumbed. Many of those within the walls of St. Kóráhm's, Elyri and Teren, likewise suffered. Khwílen had been spared thus far, as had Captain Magk, but no one expected their good fortune to last.

In time, it seemed likely that everyone in the Sovereignties would be sick. When, if, Kavan returned, Rhyrdan expected he would find his home, his city, empty of life except for the animals abandoned at the death of their caretakers, and perhaps a handful of the fortunate, or unfortunate, who lived to tell of the horrors the plague had wrought.

Two days Dhóri had been missing from St. Kóráhm's. Two days in which Rhyrdan had demanded that Captain Magk and any other able-bodied person not occupied by the care of the dying seek out his brother. Those in the chellé claimed he had seemed well the last they had seen him, when he had gone out to administer to the ill as he had done every day since the Yellow Death's arrival in Alberni.

He could be injured somewhere. Kidnapped. Or, Rhyrdan feared, he had joined the ranks of those leaving Alberni to its fate and seeking somewhere untainted by death. That did not sound like the brother he knew, however, the brother who refused to give up on his beliefs, and so Rhyrdan continued to look.

People were questioned, vacant buildings searched, until at last the captain found the young man coughing, crying, retching, huddled in the Purification Chamber of St. Maicel's where Rhyrdan knew a Gate to be. Every one of the gdhededhá there had either succumbed to the Yellow Sisters in their efforts to care for others or had fled, leaving the náós empty to vermin and birds.

Rhyrdan did not believe his brother had come to flee.

He believed he had come here, drawn in his delirium by the power of the Gate, in the hopes that his father would return through it.

"Brother?" Rhyrdan knelt beside the curled, trembling form as Raenár held back the chamber curtain. Dhóri shrank from the hand on his discolored wrist, but in the next moment, he lurched up and flung himself into Rhyrdan's arms, clinging to his neck, a frightened boy seeking reassurance.

"I'm sorry, I'm sorry," he sobbed repeatedly, muttering his apologies as Rhyrdan got to his feet, pulling Dhóri up with him, deciding to take him home.

"You cannot. He will infect…"

Rhyrdan grunted. "Who? Where do I take him? The house is full of death, as is St. Kóráhm's. Nowhere is safe for him, from him…and I won't leave him here. Either he comes with me or I stay with him."

"No!" Dhóri wailed. "No one can die because of me!"

"Hush." Any in the manor not already infected would be soon…or they would never be. Rhyrdan followed the captain through the still-open náós door, carrying his brother in his arms. So far, Rhyrdan had shown no symptoms. He feared staying that way, watching everyone he loved die, but if it meant they did not die alone, and that he alone remained to face Kavan with his failure of leadership, it was a burden he grimly accepted. "Yóáná is here. We will care for you."

The youngest healer in Rhidam, unable to face the death of Prince Conroy, had come to see how her husband's family, her family, fared.

Níkóá had come with her two days ago, and though he had retreated to Rhidam upon seeing the extent of death's devastation in Alberni, Yóáná stayed. She might not be able to save the dying but she had experience with making them comfortable. Seeing so many ailing, particularly those with whom she had grown up, tugged at her conscience, prompting her to help however she could. Maybe Ártur was right. A remedy might not have been found, but Alberni was an adequate place to continue her search for the cure.

"Yóáná…" Dhóri smiled, his faint voice trailing off, his feeble struggles in Rhyrdan's arms ceasing.

Dhóri had been infatuated with Yóáná, the two so near in age that they had shared many hours and secrets as they had grown up. He had assumed they would be inseparable, until the disappointing period when her healing gifts kept her away longer and longer. On the day she accepted Madoc Delamo's proposal of marriage, Dhóri had been the one to bestow his favor on her choice, as if he was her father or brother and had the legal right to do so. Over so many years, his affection for her had never waned. Hearing her name was enough to break his resistance. His head lay against his protector's shoulder without a sound as they crossed the city and entered the manor gates.

The house was still except for the sound of distant coughing when Raenár pushed open the door and allowed Rhyrdan to pass. The ill were collected in the servants' quarters, in the room where Wortham had last lain in rest, and it was there, through the empty rooms and silent corridors, that Rhyrdan carried his tágdhásaeit. Emeria, ragged, pale, suffering the same horrible affliction and yet insisting on tending to the others in the house who needed it, sat on the edge of their mother's bed, clutching the woman's hand, her eyes upturned to sadly greet those who entered.

Zelenka's eyes were open, unseeing, but there was a faint smile, a look of peace, on her plague-tortured face.

Rhyrdan's knees buckled. Raenár caught Dhóri in time to keep the sick young man from falling to the floor.

"She was supposed to wait…to live…" Emeria choked, anger and frustration mixed into her weak, grief-laden tone.

Her brother reached her side, lay one hand on Emeria's shoulder, and used his other hand to close the dead woman's eyes. "She's where she wants to be." He knew his sister too had witnessed their mother's decreasing will to live after the death of her husband. Her children were grown, no longer needing her care, and there were no grandchildren yet to require her attention. Once Kavan had left, having no one to serve, her heart had fallen prey too easily to the insistence of the Yellow Death.

Emeria nodded and squeezed the hand on her shoulder. Knowing it was true did little to ease her sadness. Only knowing that her mother was beyond physical suffering offered solace.

Raenár cleared his throat.

"Where is Yóáná?" Rhyrdan asked softly, indicating an empty straw mat on the floor nearby, clean of any trace of whoever had lain there before. A stable boy, if Rhyrdan remembered correctly. The captain lay the shivering young man upon it.

"Fetching water…to bathe her." With nothing to do for the dead, Emeria trudged to Dhóri's side with a pitcher and cup. The captain helped him sit and she tipped his head back enough to pour a trickle of water into his throat. Most of it dribbled down his chin and neck but some was swallowed instinctively and the next bit she poured was met with an effort to drink it all. "That is good…he is drinking. So many…" She glanced sideways at the three empty cots and the six who lay sleeping, coughing, or groaning in discomfort. "When they stop drinking…they die sooner."

"Yóáná…" Dhóri mumbled when the cup was pulled away.

"She'll be here," Emeria assured him.

Rhyrdan took the damp cloth from her before she could dab Dhóri's face. "You should be resting."

"Someone needs to…"

Footsteps brought another voice. "I am here. Rhyrdan? Dhóri?" Yóáná set down the pail she carried near the doorway, away from immediate contamination, to join the others next to Dhóri's pallet.

"He was in Saint Maicel's. He will…" The words stuck in Rhyrdan's throat but he cleared it with a gruff sound that erased the stain of sorrow that tried to drown him. "He will live?"

Dhóri had to live. If he could take Dhóri's place to be sure of it, he would do so without question. If Kavan returned to find them lost, he would undoubtedly grieve for Dhóri more deeply than he would for Rhyrdan. For Kavan's sake, Dhóri could not die. Stubborn frown in place, he added, "I will not allow it."

"I'll do everything I can, I swear it," Yóáná said. "Fetch me clean bedding, blankets, make some broth…"

Rhyrdan shook his head when Emeria prepared to go and pressed his sister down on an empty mat. "You will rest. I will see to…"

"You, my lord, will bury your mother," said Raenár in an equally stern voice. It had proven healthier to bury the putrefying corpses as soon as possible, or burn them if wood or oil could be gathered for a fire. Mother or not, leaving the corpse in a room with those struggling to live was unwise. "I will find what you need, Healer Delamo."

He was not a competent cook, but he could manage a simple broth if there was not already something bubbling over the kitchen fire.

The reminder of duty made Rhyrdan's heart sink. She should be buried with their father, in the chellé, but Khwílen was not allowing the dead from outside of St. Kóráhm's to be brought in for burial. Too many of the residents were already buried there. Rhyrdan did not believe Khwílen would make an exception, nor, he admitted grimly, should an exception be made. Perhaps when the shade of death was lifted and Kavan returned, they could exhume her body and move her to her rightful place. For now, he would lay her in the flower garden she loved and pray that she, and his father, would forgive him for that.

He bent to Dhóri's ear and whispered. "I will return and sit with you, read with you. Yóáná is here; she will make you comfortable."

Sometimes making the ailing comfortable was all they could do.

"Yóáná," Dhóri whispered again, the word the only thing he could mutter between gasps for air and moans of pain. Rhyrdan met the healer's gaze; she nodded once and then he and Captain Magk set about the duties given to them, duties difficult in their own rights but for very different reasons.

## ☙Chapter 28☙

Zóndhá's corpse was tightly wrapped in a section of canvas sail and bound with ropes so that no one would have to see the dead man's face and flesh turn to cinder in the heat of the blaze illuminating the midnight beach. The mountain of timber and the body were doused with a pungent, oily substance that made the flames burn hotter than the wood alone allowed. The sky filled with a plume of thick, greasy smoke that seemed to bother Kavan more than it did anyone else. While some took turns adding new lumber to the pyre, others stood with the open cask of oil to add to the flames whenever it was deemed prudent. The mixing of voices never stopped, but it did rise and fall in volume as some dropped out and others rejoined. Though experienced with protracted performing, it had been a long time since Kavan had done so without his harp and his throat was parched and raw. The accumulation of smoke did not help, nor did the occasional break taken to share the water from flasks passed around the mourning circle.

Come daybreak, they would be lucky if any could speak.

Kavan tried to remain upwind of the smell, finding that the taint of burning mortal flesh turned his stomach. It was not so much the smell, as it smelled little different than other cooking meat. But the burning oil was pungent and fishy and seemed to soak into his clothes and hair so that he might never be rid of it. It was knowing what was burning, who was burning, and his part in the man's death, that would not allow his stomach and mind to settle. He could not fault these people their customs, particularly when he did not understand them, but enduring it, partaking in it, made Kavan wish he was elsewhere.

He hoped his actions were not offensive. He could honestly claim that he had never witnessed the intentional burning of a body, that the smoke made him ill. Raebhá watched him, whenever he happened to stray from her side to avoid the blowing smoke, but he did not try to know her thoughts nor allow her to know his.

The time for questions would come later, if at all.

It had taken most of the day to gather wood for the pyre. The fire was lit late in the afternoon and had been burning for nearly twelve hours. More than once Kavan considered aiding the process, controlling the flames so that they burned hotter, faster, contained within a bubble of power that would keep the heat from escaping thus resulting in a shorter burn time. But as he was uncertain if the duration of the burn was part of the necessary ceremony for the dead, if any of those here recognized that something unusual was in play, it might produce unwanted, negative results. It was wisest not to interfere.

He kept his power to himself and wished for Wortham's company. Wortham would have protected him, from the others, from himself.

With the moon high in the sky, Kavan could no longer distinguish the corpse from the collapsed logs and kindling, most of which had disintegrated into ash in the pit. The dhóbhaen eventually stopped adding fuel to the fire, and when they decided that enough of the body had been consumed, the fire down to nothing but the crackling red lines in the unburned chunks of wood, they began to fill the hole, burying bone, ash, and lumber alike. Every member of the group walked over the freshly moved earth, compacting it, leaving no trace of what lay beneath. Come the next rainfall or wind storm or very high tide, even their footprints would erode and the dead man's burial spot would be lost to any except those who had deposited him here.

If anyone except the three who had wanted to take the body to Curnydhá suspected treachery, they neither spoke of it nor showed such doubt on their faces. In a place where violence rarely reared its head, the feasibility of foul play barely crossed their minds. Nor had anyone gone to the place where Kavan had been attacked to see evidence of that confrontation. There was no reason any of them would, no reasons they should suspect him.

But Kavan, in his unspoken guilt, worried.

Only one campfire remained to allow light when the pyre's glare was gone, and because none had eaten during those hours, they gathered to share the remains of their previous meal and a cup of zerphánál as a silent group, sharing one of the fundamentals of being alive. Kavan could not stomach the thought of food but he did accept a swallow of ceremonial zerphánál as though it were a sacrament before passing the cup to Iólán and stepping out of the circle. No one objected or looked at him with disapproval, not even when he walked to the edge of the curling surf and let the water lap at his boots, his back to the group, so that the dhóbhaen mourned without him.

Eventually, he realized the fire had grown dim and the sky had begun to color with the faint graying of day. Another few hours and it would be dawn. A day lost. He felt neither troubled nor anxious about the loss nor grateful for it. It was a fact, nothing more. One by one or in pairs, people passed him, carrying supplies to the boats, proof that they would not remain another day despite everyone's lack of sleep. Whether they were eager to continue the journey or merely eager to be away from the dead was unclear. Kavan nodded when one woman brought him his cloak and urged him onto the boat.

This time, when he settled back in the spot reserved for him, Raebhá joined him.

His face lit with relief but he quickly looked away, embarrassed to be so transparent with a simple joy he so rarely felt or expressed. Her knee pressed against his, an innocent thing to the eyes of anyone on board, told him she found happiness in his pleasure. Iólán waved from the other ship as both pushed into deeper waters, riding the outgoing tide with long strokes of the oars.

Once they were pointed south, moving smoothly, the crew's attention on their business, Raebhá bent her head towards Kavan and whispered, "The vocalization…it confuses the bhur, distracts them. The dáni remains near a body until it is consumed…by nature or by fire, only free when there is no body to anchor it. Pyres destroy the dead quickly, freeing the dáni to prevent them from becoming bhur. There is danger of it attaching to a person so long as it lingers, to cause sickness, tragedy, bad harvests…things outside of the natural order."

She shrugged at his skeptical expression, her own and her tone of voice suggesting she did not believe such superstition. They went against everything Dhágdhuán taught. But even for those who doubted, a millennium or more of custom was a hard thing to abandon.

"That is why most did not want to bring him with us to Curnydhá."

She nodded. "To travel with the dead is asking disaster to befall the journey. It could not be risked. So long as the mourning continued, the bhur could not single out anyone to attach to. Now it is done. Nothing remains but memory and whatever escapes in the smoke, but Zóndhá and the bhur will not harm us. Our journey remains safe. Another five days, if the current and winds are favorable…"

He waited after her words trailed off and then covered her hand where it rested upon her knee. "You are afraid."

She had done her best to hide her fears from those who sailed with them, keep a brave, confident front in place as any leader would, but she was not surprised that Kavan knew the truth. "Not of whoever tried to kill me, whoever sent me away. I have Iólán, I have them," she motioned to the sailors, "I have you. I have what you have taught me, as meager as that might be. I'm not afraid of the bhur. But I am afraid, that Ombhrís is alive, that he is dead, afraid of what I feel, and the consequences of those feelings, of my choices."

Corners of his mouth twitching, Kavan murmured, "I am sorry."

"I'm not. I do not regret meeting you, nor anything we have said or done. Not even…" Her gaze shifted to her belly hidden beneath the layers of protective clothing; a glow came over her face that set Kavan's nerves on fire. "But I do fear what might come of it…what lies ahead for us."

Kavan swallowed and nodded, looking out to sea to hide how afraid those things made him feel as well. He could think of no other person who held his life, his future, his heart, in their hands the way she did. Nothing had prepared him for such an all-consuming experience and every time he believed he was coming to an acceptance of his feelings, she said or did something that proved how wrong he was. His feelings continued to surprise him; he did not think he would ever be anything but amazed to be in her company.

"We will take the moments as they come," he finally murmured, looking down at her where she leaned her head against his shoulder, her eyes fluttering wearily. "We will do this together, as much as you allow." He understood that there were things she would need to do alone, but even then she would not be alone. He would be with her, in body, in spirit, whatever happened next.

Another smile, this one sleepy and grateful, and then she wiggled sideways to sink down and lay her head on his lap. He stiffened, caught off guard again, but as she dozed before he could think of words to utter in protest, he let her sleep, his hand on her shoulder as if it would be enough to keep her safe.

In another five days, he might look back on this moment as the last shared intimacy they would ever know.

❧*❧

Merrek's face was ashen. "What do you mean she is…it is too soon." He and Arlana were recovering their health after their battles with the plagues and had just lost one child to the malaise. After the last several days of sickness, they had feared the Yellow Death's return. Neither considered that conception could occur so soon.

"We shall be watchful, mindful of her condition," Ártur agreed, concerned for Arlana's health. Physically, she had recovered quickly from her infection, but the loss of Prince Conroy meant that depression kept her from eating as much as she should and caused her to spend more time sleeping than was healthy. Underweight and rundown, if she had any chance of carrying this infant to term, and surviving the birth, extra care would need to be taken to safeguard her well-being.

"Anything," Merrek agreed. Torn between the elation of another child and his fears for Arlana, it was hard to know how to feel.

"Go to her, give her your support. Encourage her to walk with you in the sun, or the hall, at least once a day. Make sure she eats, provide distractions that keep her thoughts away from…" He sighed. He did not need to say it. Merrek knew what he meant. "I've enlisted the queen to do likewise, and Bhyrhán and Syl of course will assist."

A nod, and then Merrek marched out of the room to pay a visit to his wife, leaving Ártur to reach back along the threads of power that should have led to Kavan.

He could feel him there, far away and faint, but he could not reach him. He did not have the strength.

Come home, sínréc. We need you here, else so much will be lost.

If he was lucky, Kavan would hear his plea. If he was luckier still, Kavan would respond and come home.

❧*❧

Rhyrdan had not realized how long he had been reading, barely noticing the entrances and exits of Captain Magk and Yóáná, until he turned the last page and raised his head to see that the candle had burned down to a stubby nub of tallow. The way the flame writhed and flickered made him surprised it still burned. No one in the room slept, or slept for long, coughing and the discomfort it caused too great to allow for extended sleep. Some suffered the northern plague, a few the southern, but there was no effort made to separate them.

They would either live or they would not.

Yóáná gave them elixirs to dull the cough, to encourage rest, and for those worst off, a gentle touch to the side of their faces brought sleep. But when the elixir wore off they were awake and in agony again. Emeria, who appeared to be on the mend, had lain on a nearby pallet, listening as Rhyrdan read, and had fallen asleep of her own accord. If they were lucky, she would be well enough soon to leave this room of sickness and death.

So long as Dhóri was here, Rhyrdan did not plan to go anywhere.

His brother was in the early throes of the sickness, the worst of the suffering. It was too early to tell if he would live, but Rhyrdan refused to consider the alternative. If he protected Dhóri as Wortham would have done, as Kavan would have done, then Dhóri would live. By keeping Dhóri alive, Rhyrdan hoped he could prove his loyalty and value to the man he longed most to impress.

"Rhyrdan?"

The parched whisper punched through his thoughts and he automatically responded with a cup of water held to his brother's lips. Too weak to rise, Dhóri only lifted his head to accept the water and then collapsed after a few small sips. It was not enough, but it was better than no water at all.'

"Tell k'aendhá…"

"Hush." Rhyrdan wiped Dhóri's brow with a damp cloth and then wiped away the fluid on his skin that collected with the bursting of another boil. That was one treatment Yóáná insisted on, keeping her patients as clean as possible, refusing to reuse any water or rag that touched that fluid. Rhyrdan did not understand how it might help, but she was the healer, not him. He chose not to argue with her treatments. "Whatever it is, you'll tell him yourself."

"If I…if he's not…when I…"

"You'll live. I know it, Dhóri. You're not leaving me alone."

Dhóri tried to smile but the effort barely lifted the corners of his mouth. "You're a good man. So's he. Tell him I'm sorry…that I forgive him…that I do not want him to think poorly of me…"

"He's your father. He will never think ill of you. He understands you better than you think."

"I know, but…tell him. I hope he and Raebhá…have many happy years…other children…a good life…"

"He'll be back soon; you'll see. You'll see him again, and you will tell him these things yourself."

For only the second time in his life, Dhóri did not believe that things would work out for the best, but he nodded and coughed, "Of course," to appease Rhyrdan's persistence. He had slandered his father, wished him ill, disrespected him, and now he was suffering because of it. He should not have allowed his father to leave on that sour note, should have been there to bid him a safe journey, should have accepted the manorial duties asked of him and Rhyrdan instead of leaving the fate of Alberni in the other young man's hands. Dhóri had failed in his duties as a son and now he suffered for it.

He did not expect he would see his father again.

"You buried…?"

"I did."

"I'm sorry." In less than a year Rhyrdan had lost both of his parents. After his wet nurse's return to Elyriá at an age when Dhóri was barely able to recall her face or her voice, Zelenka had been the nearest thing to a mother he had known. He mourned her death as well.

Rhyrdan did not want to talk about his mother, did not want to think about his losses, but he managed to choke out "Thank you," as he adjusted a light blanket over his brother's torso. "Would you like me to read more? I can bring another book."

A frail hand pressed against his thigh. "You're weary. If you don't sleep, you'll end up here with me. Go…come back in the morning. I'm not going anywhere."

Despite the unspoken protest, Rhyrdan knew Dhóri was right about his need for rest. He was less certain about Dhóri being here in the morning. "I'll bring breakfast and…"

"And tell Sóbhán…bid him come…"

Scowling, knowing he had no means to get a message to Bhryell except through Yóáná or Captain Magk, he replied, "I will try, aendhá. I promise."

The promise satisfied Dhóri, who again tried to smile and closed his eyes to sleep.

Rhyrdan suspected that neither would rest despite their efforts.

❧Chapter 29❨

Unable to strike at the villages along the southern edge of Lake Curo as the only approach was by sailing across the lake, the first collection of soldiers brought together under one of Neth's captains instead focused on crossing the eastern river to raid the settlements of those who mined the forest of its timbers and ferried them downriver towards the lake. By evading the outposts manned by Enesfel's soldiers, the force intended to divert cut timbers, collecting them for their own use, as well as slaughter any man or woman who got in their way. Young boys, old enough to serve as squires or to endure the grueling Nethite training regime, were taken north to Glevum to be evaluated and trained.

Stealing lumber, children, and whatever supplies they could from the riverside villages was secondary to the killing chaos they left behind, and by the time those posted in the border stations learned what was happening, the raiding parties had retreated. Messengers were sent to the villages along the lake, the western river shore, and to all other stations along the Enesfel-Neth border with the intent of preparing for future raids. It had been several decades since Neth had resorted to such activities and Enesfel's troops, not knowing of the change in leadership in Glevum, had no reason to believe King Kjell would order such raids.

Outlaws, surely.

A messenger was sent to Glevum in hopes that the king would tend to this anarchy. Another was sent to Rhidam. Whether the Nethite king had turned against his allies during this dark hour of dearth and plague, or whether this was the work of brigands, the outposts needed reinforcements. They were as depleted as anywhere else after the arrival of the Yellow Sisters. They would never stand if raids were the prelude to some manner of invasion.

But they had to.

❧ * ❧

"Blind?"

Yóáná wiped her hands on the apron she wore and sighed. It was not the sort of news she wanted to deliver so early in the morning. For the past four days, whenever he was awake and coherent enough beneath the weight of fevered delirium to speak, Dhóri had complained about how dark the room was. Having seen it in Rhidam, Yóáná had suspected what was coming though she had fought against believing it, against letting it happen. This morning, when his rheumy eyes had refused to focus on the candle held before his face, her hopes were dashed, her suspicions confirmed.

"It may return…it may not. I've heard stories of both from the afflicted…though those I cared for all…died…before we could know if it would. I will try to relieve the pressure behind his eyes, help him if I can, but there is little to be done, I fear. I've told him as much. As you can imagine, he is not taking the news well."

Until Raebhá arrived in their lives, Dhóri had never been the sort to allow negativity to defeat him. Since learning that she was to return to her homeland, that his father would take her there, and that her feelings for his father were stronger than whatever Dhóri hoped she felt for him, he had become a different, darker man. Now, finding himself in physical darkness rather than a mental or spiritual one, Rhyrdan had few doubts that Dhóri was angry and bitter.

"I should go to him."

A hand on his shoulder kept him in the chair behind Kavan's desk. "Not now. I made sure he sleeps. Give him time. Perhaps this evening. And please, do not let him believe this is his fault. Give him hope if you can…help him think to the future."

Although he had doubts about the sort of future any would have as the Yellow Death dragged on, Rhyrdan nodded with a determined grimace. For a moment, his insistence on Dhóri living wavered. What if Dhóri could not accept blindness? What if he refused to live as a burden to others? What future could he have?

He lifted his chin. He could pray. For a miracle. For Kavan's return and the possibility that the bard could make this right. He could pray that St. Kóráhm would do for Dhóri what Rhyrdan could not.

Dhóri would live, would see again, and have a long, fulfilling life. Rhyrdan was bull-headed enough to fight to make it happen.

❧*❧

A strong north wind propelled the ships across the sea, requiring little effort from the oarsmen to move them. Rather than row, they manned the sails, fighting to keep the ships from colliding, keeping them in sight of the shadow of the coast on their starboard side. The choppy sea unsettled Kavan's stomach, which until now had been free of his usual seasickness, adding to the knot already formed there. It grew tighter, more painful as their destination approached until he could no longer eat or sleep.

He only stared at the shore, or the stars, trying to focus on prayer but inevitably only able to focus on Raebhá.

She balanced her time at his side, seeking some arrangement that caused him the least discomfort, or else on the prow. She judged that they would reach the docks of Curnydhá by daybreak on the sixth day, but with the speed at which they moved under the power of wind and sail, there was speculation among the sailors that they would reach the city sometime before the sun kissed the sea with its golden rays.

She, and those familiar with this coastline, found no trace of the ship previously sent, and the anxiety that created rubbed against Kavan's nerves as if it was untreated wool over bare skin. If that ship had moored and chosen not to return to Maras, that would be one matter, but there was no visible evidence of it anywhere along the high craggy edges of the island. If a storm had capsized her, dragged her beneath the waves, that was another. After the death of Zóndhá, there were several who speculated that the missing ship had met an unanticipated end at the hands of the bhur, a possibility that frightened them more than any other.

Weary of sitting, Kavan stood at the stern, one hand curled around the wooden rail, watching the shore, senses partially focused on Raebhá at the prow as she and the crew's leader discussed the particulars of their arrival in Curnydhá. They had not stopped again, had not gone ashore since the funerary rites. Most around him appeared accustomed to this confinement, but Kavan, used to larger vessels with accommodations out of the elements, was cramped, stiff, and now sick as well. As much as he dreaded reaching their destination, he was eager to be on solid ground.

As it had so often of late, as Kavan released the rail to wipe damp hair out of his eyes, the boat pitched sideways and knocked him off his feet. He landed on his knees on the slippery wooden deck, his vision turning black with a wave of nausea of a very different sort.

Images flashed behind his squeezed shut lids. He tried to grasp each tidbit long enough to make sense of what he Saw. A dhóbhaen ship ablaze near a harbor. Men in crimson and green, the lapels sporting the insignia of the House de Corrmick bursting from the trees, bearing down on what felt like, from Kavan's perspective to be a village. The ship again, fire and oil burning his skin though he was certain it was not the ship on which he stood nor the one traveling with them. A blonde man on his knees, head bent, beaten but not broken. Then his boy, his innocent, heartbroken boy…coughing, choking, suffering from aching fire throughout his body, into his bones, in a world without form or color. Not the victim of fire, not the victim of war, but something equally terrifying.

Plague.

Kavan lurched erect, pulse drumming in his ears, his throat constricted so that he, like the young man in his vision, could scarcely breathe. Raebhá was beside him, her hand on his back, and though he could see fright on her face and the concern of others around him, he could not speak or form words.

There was no oxygen in his lungs to permit it.

"Are you injured?"

He shook his head no. His knees throbbed, bruised from the force of his fall, but that was not enough to warrant the horror he knew was on his face. She helped him up, helped him back to the bench, and left him there long enough to haggle with the keeper of the stores and return with a small wooden cup of zerphánál. Kavan did not think it would benefit him, that it would do anything more than wash the taste of smoke and blood from his mouth, but he accepted the offering, drained it, and after several moments, her hand around his that wrapped around the cup, he swallowed, took a gulp of air, and tried his voice again.

"The boat…lost and not returned," he began, the phrase ending in a fit of coughing. Raebhá stood, intending to bring him more to drink, but he stayed her with a hand on her arm and a shake of his head. "It is…has been…burned."

"Burned?" The man nearest them scowled.

"llónec," Raebhá explained with quiet reverence, the word bringing other heads around to look at Kavan too. Although many were skeptical, there were faces alight with amazement. Few in the region had possessed that gift in generations. One of the last believed to possess it prophesied her death before her disappearance. There was another now who knew small things, but the Sight came to him so rarely that many believed his prophecies were lucky guesses. Anyone who bore the burden of future knowing was someone of immeasurable importance. Many wished they had been told his importance sooner.

"There." Kavan pointed towards a peak far ahead of them, only visible because the passing moon silhouetted the tip of the mountain.

"So it sank," someone else said sadly. "There are dangers in sailing at night with a lantern to light the way…"

"No lantern. Burning arrows."

"Aldár the sailor…" squeaked another.

"There is no wall of flame," snorted someone else.

"That's just a story…"

A woman huffed fearfully, "That was in kekraes khílylám, near Sáudhá…the taeré."

"If it happened here…there are no taeré…"

The implications that there could be taeré infiltrating dhóbhaen territory, killing people, destroying ships, perhaps partially guilty for the fate that had befallen Raebhá and Ombhrís, or that there could be dhóbhaen responsible for assailing their own people, were equally troubling. While the sailors argued, Raebhá clasped Kavan's hands between hers and whispered, "What of Dhóri?"

Surprised that he had spoken his son's name aloud or that his thoughts had screamed loud enough for her to hear them, he gulped and tightened his two-handed grip around the cup. He feared voicing what he had been shown, not knowing if it had happened, was happening, or was yet to come but perhaps, if he prayed deeply enough and gave no voice to the horror, it would cease to be real.

Instead, in the hopes that he had misinterpreted what he had Seen, that he and Raebhá would not prove to be carriers for something neither had yet shown symptoms of, he asked quietly, "Has there ever been plague here?"

"There are tales of naebhur, but not in my lifetime," she admitted. "Have you Seen…?"

It was not this land he Saw. It was Alberni. Despite his fears, too many months had passed for he or Raebhá to pass plague here.

He shook his head, trying to focus on the land battle he had seen, wondering at the identity of the man on his hands and knees. Not Merrek. Who else could it be? By keeping his attention on those puzzles, with his ears partially attuned to the argument among the crews of both ships as the second pulled alongside them, he might be able to ease his fears.

Some were afraid to go on, wanted to turn back and avoid the risk that mountain peak now represented. Some wanted to send one vessel, sparsely manned, to investigate the threat. Some negated the possibility of a threat being there and others advocated for moving their boats further to sea as they passed, beyond the range of any known bow so that they could proceed with their duty. Iólán, dragged into the debate, ruled in favor of the final option while Raebhá argued that she had to reach Curnydhá and to reassure them that whatever the threat, Kavan could protect them…without revealing how powerful he was. That would only frighten them more.

Kavan did not care how they accomplished it but he needed to get Raebhá home. He had to find a gate. He had to get back to his son.

Dhóri needed him.

"Are you always awake at this hour?" teased Fen, coming up behind Asta who leaned against the wall of the Eagle's Nest with her hat pulled low across her eyes to keep the rain from her face. Thankfully, it was only a light mist, the same mist that had spread over Rhidam and the farmlands and forests shifting south for the past six days. No messengers had come from any further south than Levonne, as the Yellow Sisters forced trade and travel to halt. No one knew how far south the rains fell, but they hoped it was far enough to allow crops, however meager, to grow into a fruitful harvest.

If enough people remained to harvest them.

"Marta's meeting me." Asta did not know how the young woman made her living, had never asked, nor did she know about Fen and Marta's long-term relationship. But she did know the freckle-faced redhead was better off than many in the Association and had several children of her own. Asta had never tried to learn more about her most reliable Rhidam source of information, believing the less she knew the better. She was grateful the woman continued to work with Fen and the reward Asta gave was not prying into her life.

She did not know that the child Fen had stopped bringing as a playmate for Lorant once the plague had come was Marta's son too.

She glanced at the moon behind the veil of clouds. "She's late."

"Blame him." The woman, dressed in a brown leather jerkin and leather breeches, her short hair pinned beneath her cap and her slight bosom bound to make her appear masculine, emerged from the fog, pulling a stumbling fellow along by a tight hand at the back of his neck and a knife scratching at his ribs. The stench of ale was strong, either seeping from his pores and breath or else he had spilled as much on himself as he had consumed. The gold hoop in his ear, a trademark of many Nethites, was pulled low, barely held within the bloody flesh around it, and he sported a black eye, bloody nose and lip, and a swollen jaw. Marta's hands were bruised and bloody, but she looked otherwise unscathed. Reading Asta and Fen's expression, Marta shrugged and gave a playful grin. "You should see the other one."

Still a scrapper and survivor. Asta found that reassuring. Judging by the expression on Fen's face, concerned, relieved, and happy to see her, Asta judged for the first time that there was more to their working relationship than she was aware of. "He has something to say?"

The fellow began to speak, but his words were so slurred that they were impossible to make out.

"Him? He's inconsequential, except for being where he shouldn't be. And this." She lowered the knife, dug in the pouch at her hip, and tossed a knuckle biter to Fen. Thought he might know something we can use…once you sober him up."

Grabbing the drunk by the arm, a wickedly amused smirk on his face, Fen chortled as he pocketed the weapon, "I can do that, aye." He jerked the man towards the castle gates and began walking. "Come along, sir," he barked, having little patience for the other's stumbling steps. "I've just the thing to cure you of your intemperance…then you and I will have a chat." Looking over his shoulder, he added to Marta, "We'll talk later."

The Nethite groaned, stumbling, but could not fall because of the inquisitor's grip. Nor did he resist. He cast an apologetic look at Asta, but another unsteady step turned his attention forward.

Waiting until Fen and his captive were out of earshot, Asta tipped her hat to look Marta in the eye. "You said you had something for me."

"Maybe. I've heard through the lines from Neth, that they're working someone in to play to get information from the inside."

"Inside? Glevum? Who are they?" Asta trusted her Association contacts, to a point, and Marta had never done wrong by her, but verifying such claims was always the wisest course.

The freckled woman shrugged. "Not sure…Pantel only said to let you know…that when she has something to report, she'll be in touch."

Despite both having lived in Glevum, Asta after her marriage and the other after moving her operations out of Fiara in deference to the Lachlan prince living there, Asta and Onea Pantel rarely crossed paths after Caol's death two decades ago. Asta's messages with the Association had come through other sources, and anything Onea chose to share did likewise. Onea, like Wallace and Marta, was one of the few Association voices Asta trusted.

She did not need to know who the spy was, what their affiliation was, how they intended to get inside the castle to learn details about what had happened to her husband and eldest son. She would trust Onea's judgment.

But she was curious and eager for something more than this tiny shard of good news.

Marta clasped Asta's hand, an unusual gesture, with a somber expression on her face as she watched someone pass. They could not remain here long. They would attract attention, disguised or not. "I'll give you more when I have it. If I can do anything, just ask." Then she was gone, back into the shadows, leaving Asta to frown after her.

❧*❧

In the dark of his cell, the blond man, long released from his shackles since he had nowhere to go, had begun to adjust to a life of limited sight, relying on his sense of smell and particularly his hearing. He heard the wind in the rafters, heard the rats scurrying about his circular enclosure, heard thunder outside and sometimes the shouts of men as if in combat. He detected the footsteps of the soldiers who brought food when they were many steps away, could tell if they wore the boots of duty or soft-soled shoes on days when their only duty was to feed the prisoner whose identity remained a secret.

Because of his sharpened hearing, when he sensed the presence standing over him as he slept, he knew at once this was no ordinary man. There had been no steps upon stone. No creaking of the door or groaning of metal hinges, nor the spilling of light from the oil lamp on the landing outside. Yet someone was undoubtedly there, even if he could not see him or hear his breathing. Flailing about with one hand, he found the long folds of a coarse robe and heavy cloak and, as the weather was warming, he thought the attire inappropriate and curious.

"Who are you?" There was no reply. "I'm not afraid of you! Kill me if you intend to!"

The fabric rustled, indicating movement, and when a hand clasped his shoulder gently, he knew his visitor had squatted down to his level. He coiled what little strength he had to fight back, but the other man spoke in a gentle tone of reassurance. "I have not come for that. You are not to die here, my friend."

"The queen," he spat with derogatory venom, "will never release me. I will either die here or out there…some public execution…"

"Trust me when I say your time is not yet come. Have patience. Someone will come for you. Conserve your strength. Be ready. You will know him when he comes."

"He? Who? Who are you?"

As quickly as the stranger had come, he was gone, the hand lifting from his shoulder, leaving the captive alone. He had no idea who the man had been, if he had been real or a hallucination, but for the first time in several months, Kjell felt something he had long ago given up.

Hope.

Even if it was only a sliver of it.

❧*❧

The matter was decided, the sailors relenting to Raebhá's desires despite their misgivings. One boat would run aground under the cover of darkness, far enough from Curnydhá that those who debarked would take three or four hours of hiking to reach the city's outskirts on foot. Iólán, on the other boat, would continue south, far enough from shore that no arrows would reach them. He would wait at sea, barely visible from the shore, for signals from the other ship, sailing under Ghené's banner, and from the footmen who crossed overland with Raebhá, to secure the docks. Raebhá and Kavan meanwhile, would go to what had been her home to gauge the state of things there.

Iólán was dissatisfied with the plan but after considerable debate, he agreed that it gave them the highest chance of success with the least amount of danger for any of them.

There were still risks, particularly to his sister.

Familiar with the lands around her city, Raebhá would lead the overland trek and those with her waited on the small spit of grey beach as the ships drifted back out to sea in the pre-dawn darkness. Kavan stood behind, far enough away not to look suspicious to those already wondering how this one peculiar man with the Sight could protect her. He was sick with nerves and the sea but determined to keep his promise. He did not rush her farewell to her brother, did not probe her thoughts, only waited beneath the shadows of potential doom for her acknowledgment.

When she turned, it was to look at him with a disjointed sigh. Whatever lay ahead, it was not going to be easy. The steep trek up the mountainside into the forest and back down again was the least of their concerns. "Shall we, my lord?"

Unwilling to commit vocally to the possible regret ahead, Kavan nodded. He fell into step beside her and the others followed.

A few more hours. Then they would know the truth.

❧Chapter 30❦

Near the outskirts of the sprawling community of now-familiar round dwellings, a settlement bigger than those Kavan had visited thus far, houses and farmland spread across a wide valley dissected by a lazy river that came down from the distant mountains capped with rose-tinted snow and cut through the forest at the northeast edge of the gorge, the group divided, the majority creeping through the trees towards the sea, intending to be installed on the docks before the town awoke, or at least to arrive early enough that they would be able to thwart trouble as their boats came to moor. The trees blocked their view of the sea once they left their beach landing site and began to climb, but once, as their ascent peaked and they began the descent down the other slope, there was a brief glimpse of the ghís and ghís kelyhag, its banners snapping in the wind, the sound of it carrying across the still-sleeping homes to the place he and Raebhá paused for breath.

To Kavan's understanding, it was the place where she ruled.

It was an ominous thing, a shadow holding his fate within its walls, and for a moment he struggled with the impulse to turn back. He could feel a faint trace of power somewhere to the west, power that could be a Gate, perhaps the one she had been exiled through, and he wondered if he could convince her to follow him there, to come away with him before this day turned to ruin.

It would be a futile effort, however, as futile as it was to ask him to abandon music.

The sky was beginning to brighten, turning the world from black to shades of gray and pink, as they emerged from the forest at the edge of a field of young grain no taller than his knees. Sheep and goats and the stocky rare ponies used as pack animals more than riding mounts grazed in unfenced pastures. Houses of mud and stone, brick and wood, spread in all directions like feed scattered before chickens, not tightly packed like the urban centers Kavan was familiar with but rather farming plots controlled by individuals who had no fear of attack or invasion. The ghís kelyhag, the dhó dónáré, and associated néósag, and another two dozen buildings constructed similarly to every home he had seen, made up the elevated center of the ghís and it was to one of them Kavan assumed they were heading.

His steps faltered as he realized in that first unobstructed look at Curnydhá that he had seen this place…these buildings, these fields, these mountain peaks, before. He knew this place.

They existed on the walls of the chapel below the Lachlan keep.

Blood rushed to his head, pounded in his ears at the implications and the questions that realization brought with it. It had existed before Kóráhm's discovery, before Coryllien's defilement, and yet for such imagery to have been painted on the chapel walls indicated a much older knowledge, a much older connection, between the dhóbhaen and the world Kavan knew.

It was a connection he doubted Raebhá could explain, an explanation he was eager to explore. But other matters came first.

There were audible indications of life, the sounds of families waking, dressing, preparing their early meal before the day's work began, but no one had yet come into Curnydhá's streets.

"There is time," Raebhá assured him as if reading his thoughts. She sounded anxious, as if turning back was also toying at the edges of her wishes, but her expression was determined, focused, and she pressed on, her steps never faltering except when she paused to motion to her supporters on the docks where a variety of boats were moored.

One of the men gestured back. They would signal the lookouts on the cliff who would, in turn, beckon her brother and the ships to moor. Once there, they would await further instruction and come to her aid when necessary.

Despite her determination, she did not seem eager to be there, as if there was something she was not telling him.

Again considering begging her to return to Alberni with him, Kavan followed close behind, watchful and alert, skirting the edges of spring plantings and quiet homes until they reached the round stone and planked wooden path that wound between the central structures and snaked out in all directions, like a spider's web woven around the hillock where the adorned ghís kelyhag and the other central structures overlooked the valley. It was the highest point in Curnydhá, the city center raised where everyone could see.

They moved quietly, knowing despite her reassurances that there was little time to waste. The horizon would soon give birth to the sun and Dhóbhaen would awaken. It was best they reached her home, or the ghís kelyhag, before they were seen.

With the predawn docks deserted of sailors and fishermen, empty before a day's chaotic work began, the group who had fled with Iólán, who called Curnydhá home, spread along the black sandy shore and docks to prevent anyone from endangering those drifting in to moor. Armed with knives, spears, wooden rods, and fishing tridents, knowing how to use such tools for hunting, fishing, and protection against predators, none had ever considered using those same tools against other dhóbhaen. They hoped, because they had been born here, lived here until recent events forced them to flee, that they would be welcome and given no cause to use violence they were raised to avoid.

But each one, even those who feared that the white-skinned stranger was the threat, knew that, if there was danger to the kymyhé, it was from those capable of using the fabled rynlagne. Only the márbhyndhánis could do that. Whether or not the keepers of knowledge, custom, and faith had cause for her punishment, they had violently denied their kymyhé the requisite inquest, had attacked her and her husband in secret. It was cause enough to question their motives, to support the confrontation she was preparing for. If it was a rogue, trained elyryhánag, or the márbhyndhánis themselves, her supporters remained restlessly poised as the ships sailed in from the sea. They were ill-equipped against a force who wielded power the rest of the dhóbhaen were forbidden to learn but they were not afraid.

In position, one of them signaled the lookouts atop the overlooking cliff, the highest point of Curnydhá's shoreline from which any flaming archery attack could have been made against incoming ships. Those three, armed with hunting bows, encountered no resistance, and with the dock secured, a single fiery shot from each arced out over the sea.

Everyone on the boats saw the points of falling flame and began their approach when Iólán motioned them forward. The distance closed quickly with all hands at the oars. Both crews, those from Maras and Phaurd who had traveled with them, would go ashore with him. Some would reinforce the beach, some would scatter to cover the spider streets that penetrated the ghís center, others would join Iólán and his sister where they had grown up together or else at the ghís kelyhag, a protective force in case the dhóbhaen turned against her. Iólán could not imagine it happening but someone had done it before. If Kavan's claim was true, someone, either taeré or someone from Curnydhá, had set the messenger ship ablaze, killing everyone on board. Pacifists or not, a fight seemed increasingly inevitable.

With barely a rumor coming north from Curnydhá, Iólán worried about what they would find. If fortune were with them, there had been a peaceful election after her disappearance, when it was deemed likely she would not return. It would mean a new leader appointed without incident. Custom would dictate that person step down, return power to the one to whom the responsibility belonged, unless Raebhá deemed them qualified and worthy and chose to share or relinquish her rights as kymyhé.

With Kavan in the picture, relinquishing her place was a possibility, despite the wishes placed upon her by their father.

If there had been no election, or the process had not been conducted peacefully as the pall of murder hung over Curnydhá, they might find the márbhyndhánis holding power, something rarely done in dhóbhaen history and something Iólán feared more than he feared the man at his sister's side.

Raebhá trusted Kavan, and Iólán admitted there was little reason not to, but how well did she know him?

The turbulent tide bumped the boats against the dock and those ready with ropes jumped clear to tie off to the empty stanchions. Once secured, the others disembarked, leaving a handful of people to protect the ships from potential damage, enough to be ready to break moorings if a hasty escape was necessary. The others, looking to Iólán for guidance, began the trek to the hillock. There were too many people, too many footsteps, to remain silent. They would be heard and followed, a situation Iólán hoped could be used to their advantage rather than to his sister's detriment.

There were four individuals before the open-riser oak slab steps that led to the wooden door. They were the first dhóbhaen Kavan had seen wearing what appeared to be the hard shell of boiled leather over their chests and backs. The same thick material protected their arms in two pieces, and their thighs, and they wore tall boots up to their knees to shield their calves and shins. Their heads were capped with leather and metal helmets that left their faces visible. It was not the most defensive armor, might not protect them from a spear or a heavy weapon wielded with superior strength, but against a largely unarmed populace, people untrained for combat and discouraged from violence, it would serve adequately. Its main function would be for intimidation, and Kavan had few doubts it served that purpose well.

Seeing them in front of the door to a residence was unsettling.

"zyrudhén," Raebhá muttered bitterly under her breath, assessing the situation from the shadows where she hesitated. Her family had never employed men like this. No kymyhé or kydhé did. Such individuals only served within the dhó dónáré, ritual positions meant less to protect than to set the márbhyndhánis apart. Seeing them at the door of her home, guarding the seat of secular power, made her wonder if that reason for the zyrudhén's existence had always been a ruse.

Why did people trained with power need guardians? Why would they be here outside of the home of the chosen leader of Curnydhá?

"Someone's inside," Kavan murmured. He could feel it, a virile presence moving in the aimless meanderings of early morning routine.

She frowned. She had hoped the four were guarding evidence. It was not customary to relinquish her family home to another family so soon when Iólán was still alive. If whoever was here, a presence she was not trained to detect, required zyrudhén, they were important, one of the márbhyndhánis perhaps or the one chosen to lead in her place. Either way, there should not be zyrudhén in the streets. There should be no one living in her home.

Angry at this perversion of tradition, angry that anyone might have claimed what was hers by right and law, Raebhá stalked from the shadow of the building that offered her shelter, intending to storm the doors and demand answers. Kavan was unable to stop her through conventional means, his reaching hand coming up empty instead of catching her arm to hold her back, and by that time, the sentries had already seen her. He rushed forward, determined to remain at her side as she approached the building. The ornamental scythes the sentries wielded came down in unison, clacking together metal and wood to block the path up the stairs.

"You may not enter," one of the four grunted without looking at her. None of them did, but rather kept their gazes straight ahead towards the slowly creeping sunrise.

Face red with insult, she growled, "Do you know who I am?"

They had to. She had grown up in Curnydhá. Her father, the former kydhé had been well-known, respected, well-liked. Her family had led Curnydhá for generations. Her brother was a prosperous merchant seaman. Her family was ancient and esteemed. She knew every face in this town, recognized theirs as well though she could not put names to all of them. As often as she had stood at her father's side as he conducted business, they had to recognize her unless they were not from this ghís.

And this was her home.

"Look at me!"

The double doors at the top of the stairs swung open. Energy drew taut in Kavan's clenched hand, ready to release if a threat followed. The man who stood between them wore leather breeches and a long, fur-lined robe to ward off the morning chill but his feet and chest were bare, his tousled hair suggesting he had recently awakened. Kavan noted the fleeting look of horror across his face, a look that abruptly gave way to shock as Raebhá lifted her face to gawk at him.

"Th…Raebhá…k…aislé…is it you?"

Raebhá trembled, her face both flushed and pale. There was an abrupt lurching as if she would be sick. Her hands twitched and flexed but she refrained from clutching Kavan's for security. In her outrage that someone had claimed her home, she had not considered that person could be Ombhrís. The prospect of his death had become such a certainty to her that she had expected to find anyone here but him. And yet he was alive. After the attack that had taken her, had struck him down, the posting of zyrudhén outside of this door made sense.

It did not reassure her.

"Ombhrís."

They stared at one another, husband and wife, looking for external clues to verify what they saw, things they felt. Kavan wanted to read the man he had, to his shame, sometimes wished dead, but he had promised Raebhá he would not interfere if her husband lived. The cool calculation in the blond man's eyes might have been an assessment of her return with another man, but Kavan did not like it.

This was not the blond man he had Seen.

He wished Wortham was here to soothe him.

Ombhrís waved the scythes aside so that he could descend the stairs. At the bottom, he took Raebhá's hands, pulled her into an awkward embrace, and placed a chaste kiss on her mouth. It seemed a peculiar welcome for a man who must have thought his wife dead, but perhaps custom prevented him from an overly affectionate, emotional public display. Raebhá did little more than allow his greeting, her expression stunned, until he stepped back to look at her again, refusing to acknowledge the pale man beside her.

"I thought you were…"

"Likewise," she whispered, perturbed by the lack of decorum he showed to the man who had saved her life, offended when she had no right to be. Ombhrís knew nothing about Kavan, of course, and his attention was expectedly on her, but to Raebhá, ignoring Kavan was inexcusable. He was, even if he did not speak, a buffer she felt she needed between herself and the husband she no longer wanted. "This is Kavan Cliáth…"

"Cliáth." When Ombhrís looked at him, forced to acknowledge the stranger by Raebhá's introduction, he did so with scorn and antipathy. The mention of that long-disdained name forced him to look at Kavan with feigned interest. "Cliáths are no more."

"It is a long story I don't wish to tell standing here…but a Cliáth he is." The doors of other homes were opening, dhóbhaen emerging to greet the day's work, and she refused to conduct the business of reacquaintance and truth-seeking on the steps of home.

"Of course. Please. Welcome home." His tone turned quickly light and friendly, welcoming and warm, as he gestured up the steps, but when Kavan began to follow, Ombhrís scowled and growled, "You're not welcome here."

"He is our guest, has brought me home," Raebhá scolded. She expected suspicion and jealousy but she would not tolerate disrespect. It was not the dhóbhaen way. Welcoming Kavan out of the cold would have made her feel more comfortable facing what was to come.

"I have a right to speak to my wife alone."

His cold tone, his bitter expression, prompted Raebhá to tip her head in bristling defiance. He had a point, a right as he said, and as she had previously told Kavan, what came next was a discussion she must have alone with Ombhrís, even if she would prefer to have Kavan beside her. But the manner in which Ombhrís expressed those things, as if she were property, or a child, or her wishes inconsequential, made her angry. Instead of starting a public fight, however, she swallowed her annoyance and murmured to Kavan. "Wait for me."

Also disliking the other man's tone but respecting Raebhá's wishes, Kavan bowed his head in acquiescence, his fists balled at his sides. He remained where he stood only because she asked him to do so. He touched her thoughts to reassure her that he would come at once should she need him but was frustrated when she in turn shut him out. The unintentional growl in his chest was loud enough that the sentries lowered their weapons to prevent him from following.

Or they might have lowered them in response to the hand gesture Ombhrís made. Without using power, Kavan could not follow, could not push past, so he watched with narrowed eyes as Ombhrís ushered Raebhá through the doors without touching her and closed them after they were inside. Arms crossed, Kavan stared at the door, gathering power in preparation for any need to use it that arose.

Little in the room had changed since she had last been here, save for an air of opulence and formality expressed in small details that had never been her father's way, nor hers once she accepted the role of kymyhé. However long Ombhrís had been incapacitated from the attack, there had been ample time for him to amass these things and make this home his own. Furnishings that had been in her family for generations were the same but there were unfamiliar banners above the fire…deep blue with a checkered field of gold and purple running from top to bottom. A Wereness custom, she assumed, although she could not recall any such thing mentioned in her days of learning nor from the man who flitted about the room as nervous as the dragonflies that filled the fields as the grain matured. He stoked the fire, poured zerphánál into cups they had been given as a marriage gift from her brother, set out hard cheese and yesterday's bread on the table as any proper host would do.

As if he was the host and she merely a guest.

There were unfamiliar portraits on the walls depicting scenes from daily life and history. The ghís kelyhag in Nyrau, the ghís of Ombhrís' father, that she had visited the day she gave formal consent to the betrothal her father had fought to win for their family. She recalled no banners there, nor were there any in the painting. dhhwaeythá resting at moor upon a calm sea, a scene that could have been captured anywhere along Dhóbhaen's coast. The banishment of the elyryhánag, their faces long with shame as they were herded onto gaeythá meant to carry them to their punishment.

The final portrait depicted the burning of Dhágdhuán on a pyre usually reserved for those already dead, a gruesome portrayal depicting the flesh searing and curling from his beaten, bloody body, the man shamefully surrounded by the expressions of dismay and defeat of those who thought him to be a holy messenger capable of speaking for the ágdháthé as none had ever done before. Every other person in that painting, those who had condemned the man to death, robed leaders of law and custom, glowed in triumph, smugly satisfied that they had freed the dhóbhaen from the heresy of a mad man.

It was a perplexing image that prompted Raebhá to side with the conquered instead of the conquerors. Dhágdhuán looked small, frail, hideous to behold and insignificant, a threat to no one. The threat he represented was not physical, however, but rather to the heart and mind, for his words could have changed the fabric of dhóbhaen life. Indeed, despite his death and the expulsion of his followers, his words and deeds had changed history, although not in the way he, or his followers, or any of those who had ordered his execution, had foreseen. From where she stood, his execution had done more for the spread of his teachings than his life had accomplished.

Raebhá imagined those nearest the dying man in the portrait were the founders of the new, forbidden beliefs carried away to a distant world. She wondered which of them bore the name Cliáth.

She also wondered why anyone would commission a portrayal of such violence, a scene rarely talked about outside of the teaching walls of the dhó dónáré. Why would anyone agree to paint it? Why did Ombhrís possess such a thing? Why display it in their home? It had not belonged to her father. None of these portraits or carved works of art nestled in niches in the walls had belonged to her father.

They belonged to Ombhrís.

"A Cliáth?" he asked in a strained, cool voice.

"You have done much to make this your home," she countered without looking at him. If he had even a small portion of Kavan's gifts or any training or skill, she would have believed he had read her thoughts. Instead, she assumed he was dwelling on the man left outside. She had no desire to argue about Kavan. Not yet. There were more important matters to settle.

"Come. Eat with me." He did not want to talk to her back, wanted her within reach of the fire's glow instead of in the shadows where he could not gauge her thoughts.

Raebhá hesitated long enough to calm her nerves before fulfilling the request, expecting the sort of game he would play when they were face to face. She did not know him well, but she knew him well enough. He was a politician as she was. He knew the art of negotiation just as well. She sat, adjusting her cloak to hide her pregnancy, glad she had chosen a dhóbhaen gown to wear over the more functional travel clothes. But she did not eat, her stomach too unsettled to allow it. When he raised his glass, she lifted hers and hooked her arm around his so that they could drink together, a ritual act between spouses. No matter what had been done, what remained to be said, they were wed. To refuse would have been insult enough to raise suspicions.

She had a game of her own to play. Now that she knew he lived, if she wanted to mold the future in her favor, she had to appease him and follow tradition and custom.

The beveled glass set on the polished wood surface again, she adjusted her skirt, grateful he had not noticed what she kept hidden. If he had, she believed he would have spoken of that before anything else. Intending to continue to keep it out of his notice for a while longer, she murmured, "I thought you were dead. I saw you struck…"

He waved his hand dismissively. "It wasn't enough to kill me. I saw them grab you, heard you shout my name, but then I saw nothing and when I awoke, you were gone. I slept for three days. There were no clues to reveal who had taken you. We searched…the hílyláz, the forest…the beach and the mountains. The márbhyndhánis questioned everyone, but no enemy was found. With no exchange requested, it was presumed you were dead…though I did not want to believe it." His last few words faded, uncomfortable or insincere or an attempt to suppress whatever he felt…or did not feel.

Dead, but with no corpse to prove it. The sea often claimed lives, but if she had been taken, there should have been proof of her demise or an apposite amount of time should have passed before a declaration of death was made. Whoever had expelled her had not even left a false trail to support death. They had simply erased her existence.

There were myths from times before Dhágdhuán had come to Dhóbhaen, of conflicts between ghísaer settled by the abduction of a person of importance and held for the payment of a debt or the settling of an argument. Such tales never ended with the death of the hostage. A captive could be held for years before being allowed to return home when the disagreement was repaid. Sometimes it had been done to allow lovers to be together despite the wishes of one family or the other. Raebhá had not considered applying those tales to her situation, for such an act had not been carried out, to her knowledge, for thousands of years. If Ombhrís had been killed, there would have been no one except Iólán to make restitution for her return.

She could think of no enemy she, nor her brother, might have that could warrant abduction and restitution. If restitution had been the intent, some request would have come to Ombhrís long before.

Nor was she aware of any enemies Ombhrís might have.

"My family has no enemies. Nor do I. Nothing would warrant…"

"We all have enemies.

His words echoed on the tail of her previous thoughts and the icy edge of his voice made her shiver, her fearful reaction rippling along the thread that connected her to Kavan. Was he listening? Could he do such a thing as hear conversations beyond closed doors?

"You have enemies?" she asked as offhandedly as she could.

Ombhrís' tone shifted to nonchalance as he picked at his bread. "The márbhyndhánis believe I do…or that yours would come for me again. They insisted on the zyrudhén. They follow me everywhere, like lambs following ewes…"

"They are hardly lambs."

He chuckled. "True. More like young rams." Setting the bread down, he stared at her as if seeking something before asking, "What happened?" So far she had been the one to ask questions, he the one to answer, albeit evasively.

"I was sent through the rynlagne…to a place where kydhé Cliáth found me, restored me to health, helped me find a path home."

"A rynlagne? How…?"

"I don't know. But it suggests who my enemies are." Or who yours are, she thought bitterly, trying to assess the thoughts behind his eyes without resorting to the use of power that would damn her if she were found out.

He huffed. "Surely not. That would be against their tenets. The elyryhánag, perhaps"

"They're forbidden, the knowledge of the rynlagne is restricted. If there are elyryhánag here, none would know how to…"

"Forbidden, but that does not mean they don't exist. We found twelve under interrogation who required draenai…"

"Twelve?" Unsuccessfully she swallowed the squeaking note that pierced the end of the word.

The news was surprising, but as the word escaped her lips, she hoped he would hear shock instead of fear. She had been unaware of other elyryhánag in Curnydhá save one, or others from nearby ghís, but Mánd had likely not revealed them to her any more than he would have revealed her to them to prevent identities from falling into the hands of less accepting márbhyndhánis. She hoped to sound appalled that so many heretics had existed in the lands she had led. Any hint of support for them would cast suspicion on her.

Ombhrís scowled, not hearing or seeing what he expected. "So many young ones," he sighed. "It wasn't easy to punish them, as you can imagine."

Curious how young he meant but not willing to ask what sort of punishment had been applied, she nodded sympathetically. "And none of them did this to me?"

"None were trained enough," he admitted. It left few options for who could have attacked them, banished her. He knew it as surely as she did, even if he refused to acknowledge it. "You were sent to the land of the taeré? The others? From before? They survived?"

His curiosity was expected but the dark coloring of his words made her shiver. "From what I saw, many did. Cliáth. MacLyr. Curnydhá. Bhíncári. All of the old families, so many descendants. It was surprising to discover they thrived. Their territory is vast." She did her best to sound more curious and intrigued than excited, impressed, or happy for their success.

"I doubt that was the intent when they were sent away. Did they harm you? Were you ill-treated?" It did not appear so, but the thought that the heretics could have prospered as anything other than wild heathens without the benefit of their homeland's support and the trappings of dhóbhaen civilization was disappointing.

There had been great minds upon those gaeythá, some of the most gifted and learned men and women of their age. If death at the hands of taeré, the lengthy journeys at sea, or harsh foreign lands had not killed them, it was logical that those great names had found ways to survive and prosper until the Ceasing came.

"I was treated with generosity and respect, by both elyryhánag and taeré." She did not mention that the Faith of Dhágdhuán thrived, that those exiles had, in many ways, grown beyond the society they were forced to leave behind, that they had abandoned their roots, their history, and built something new.

"They coexist peacefully?" That coexistence might be possible was more surprising, and distasteful, than the knowledge that the elyryhánag survived.

Having seen no evidence of prejudice between the peoples during her brief stay, there was no falsity in her claim. "du. I met the taeré kymyhé and her kin in a ghís the size of twenty Curnydhás. elyryhánag serve as her advisors …and have a ghísaer of their own beyond a great high range of mountains like ours."

She spoke naught of intermarriages, for that practice was more intolerable to the dhóbhaen than the concept of Faith was. Revealing the accomplishments of the taeré was risky enough. It was a fine line between instilling wonder and respect and filling her people with heightened dread and distrust. The dhóbhaen already feared the violent taeré would overtake them if they ever mobilized enough to try.

Ombhrís shook his head again and ate a few silent bites. He had expected a tale of adversity, of deprivation, of sorrow, but it sounded as though she had experienced none of those things. What fates, he wondered as he pushed the last morsel of bread into his mouth, had placed her directly into the path of a man such as the one who waited outside? He knew nothing about the stranger, but he knew enough to fear him. He knew the prophecies. On appearance, the stranger met the requirements necessary to disrupt the dhóbhaen's way of life.

"The fates favor you," he finally murmured. "To return so quickly, you were lucky to find a vessel…"

His voice sounded both reticent and relieved at the same time, as if he, she thought bitterly, would have preferred fate to be less kind. Though it had been less than a year, her return had not been quick enough and so she shrugged as she interrupted him, wanting to undercut and erase the feelings his tone created. "I returned as I was sent. By rynlagne."

He scowled. "You know how to…?"

She was grateful then that Kavan had not taught her that skill. Knowing would mean lying, and she believed Ombhrís would know if she was dishonest. He should also know that his query was absurd. "I only know the tales. I do not remember that night, but kydhé Cliáth brought me back through one in the mountains near Phaurd."

"He is elyryhánag," he spat, beginning to rise from his chair. Of course, Kavan was one of them. Trained or not, he was born of the blood of heretics. That he might be trained in the manner of the márbhyndhánis, that others like him could be, that they might now know, because of this adventurous kydhé, how to return to Dhóbhaen, made him apprehensive.

Ombhrís had not cleansed Curnydhá of twelve pheturpháloste to have another, one with enough training to use the rynlagne, surface among them. Though Ombhrís was no márbhyndhánis, it was impossible not to detect the strengths in the white-skinned man. If he felt it, others in Curnydhá would too.

That could be a dangerous thing.

"He saved my life, brought me home. He is kydhé, a generous man who means no harm to us. His people love him. He is Cliáth, the second of that lineage to stand in Curnydhá in generations. This is his home by ancestry and blood. It is his right to be here..."

"He is pheturphálós."

"He cannot be a traitor if he was not born or raised here. He has nothing to betray. He only seeks knowledge. We shall leave him be, Ombhrís. He intends to see that I am safely settled then find a rynlagne to return to his sons and his..."

Rising the rest of the way, Ombhrís hissed, "He has done his duty and will leave at once. He is not welcome here. If he remains, he will be detained until he chooses to go. He cannot be allowed the liberty to voice his heresies, to poison our minds..."

"You have no cause or right to hold him. There has been no crime. I am kymyhé. We will offer him the hospitality of the dhóbhaen as is our way. I bid him welcome until he is ready to depart. I will not permit you to..."

Eyes narrowed, clawed hands gripping the table as he leaned across it to tower over her, he hissed with a feral curl of his lip, "You have been gone nearly a full turn of seasons. I am kydhé now. The márbhyndhánis, the people, bestowed that title. You cannot take what was legally given."

She glared at him, unafraid of his ire. "Given only because I…"

He cut her off with a growl. "I am the better ruler to keep Curnydhá from being drawn into the ways of heretics and fools."

"Better than whom?" In his voice, his choice of words, she heard something that filled her with alarm that went beyond the fear of his death, beyond the fear of losing Kavan. She subverted the fear, pushed slowly to her feet to level their gazes and take away any perceived advantage he felt he had. "How long did you wait?"

"For what?"

His abrupt confusion was honest, not calculated to avoid her question, and so she asked again. "How long did you wait before assuming the title?"

Confusion gave way to the return of anger and something she did not expect. Resentment. "Your brother fled, was suspect in your disappearance…and I am your husband. It was my duty to…"

"How long did you wait?" she repeated insistently. The custom was one year. In times of great turmoil, the time of waiting might be reduced at the márbhyndhánis' discretion. The events of that night might have warranted a shortened period of waiting, but she wanted him to say it. She wanted to know how soon he had given up on her.

"The ghís was in an uproar. Everyone was afraid. Something needed to be done…"

"How long?"

The double doors flew open without the touch of any hands and Kavan stormed inside, her fear, her rising anger, her indignation drawing him in despite her bid for him to wait. Iólán was behind him, the one accused of her abduction, and several of the sailors who had brought both to Curnydhá stood over the zyrudhén they had subdued with little effort and no bloodshed. Crowds of townsfolk had gathered, led by a tall, boyish blonde woman with a child on her hip who looked as surprised and elated to see Raebhá as everyone else. The sounding of a ram's horn announced the approach of the márbhyndhánis.

Ombhrís took the opportunity presented by the interruption to swipe the knife used to slice bread and cheese and with a swift movement caught Raebhá's wrist, yanking her against him, the knife now pressed to the base of her throat.

"You have no place here, elyryhánag. Return to your lands and she will not be harmed!"

"Kavan." Raebhá did not move, paralyzed by the unexpected events, by a threat made intended to drive the foreigner away. A threat against her that he could not mean. It went against everything the dhóbhaen believed. As if a foreigner should care about her life. She had said enough, however, about Kavan's integrity, his kindness, his gallantry, to suggest that he did care, and his eruption through the door on her behalf served to strengthen that truth.

He cared. Perhaps too much.

Over Kavan's shoulders, her eyes met those of her childhood friend; she was relieved to see that, whatever purging Ombhrís had done, Ephé, her husband, and child were safe.

Raebhá had not believed Ombhrís, in the short time she had known him, was capable of violence. There had been no reason to think so. She begged Ephé with a gesture to keep people back, begged Kavan with the fear in her eyes not to complicate the situation. His intrusion had cost her the answer she sought, truth she needed to hear.

Reluctant to admit Ombhrís meant her harm, trusting that he acted only in irrational fear of Kavan, Raebhá thought to talk him out of his anger, out of his dread, hoped she could still gain answers. She could only do so, however, if Kavan and the others left her alone with him.

Ombhrís assuming the title of kydhé mattered, but Raebhá could not accept the gnawing suspicion that hinted at something darker.

Kavan knew enough, knew from the man's aura, the man's unsaid thoughts that screamed like battle horns against the bard's shielded mind, knew from the violent flash of emotion on his face, what sort of man Ombhrís was, what he was capable of. With an unforgiving glint in his eyes, an expression Kavan rarely wore, he dropped his chin to give his gaze a more aggressive cast and said tightly, "Release her."

Quick footsteps came up the external stairs and the thirteen márbhyndhánis, men and women dressed in the robes and regalia of their office as if they had been awake for some time, poured into the room without dignity. They were stopped mid-step by the glance Kavan threw over his shoulder, held there, unable to lift their feet or to drop their arms to their sides by the power he commanded. When he looked back at Ombhrís, avoiding the plea in Raebhá's eyes because he did not want to be swayed, he repeated, "You will release her…one way or another."

"Kavan…dhysag."

There was an unmistakable threat in his voice that made even Raebhá shudder as she strove to believe he would not kill merely to protect her from a threat she did not want to believe existed. The unmoving márbhyndhánis were an unsettling, inexplicable sight. The crowd outside drew back, as did the men who had sailed with them, though Ephé remained in the doorway. Iólán slid sideways to put distance between himself and the pale man. It was obvious he was responsible for holding the márbhyndhánis at bay, a feat of power that none had ever seen, that filled hearts with fear and wonder.

Ombhrís' hand quaked and he moved his arm enough that the unsteady blade would not cut Raebhá's skin. It gave her hope that the discrepancy between what her heart and head told her could not be real. He would not hurt her. He was her husband. He would never want her gone…or dead.

The two men glowered at one another as the power in the room palpably intensified. One did not need to be trained to feel it; they only had to be of the same blood, dhóbhaen and Elyri blood, to feel the weight of it in the air. Gradually, whether forced to do so or choosing to comply with the demands of an opponent he would be wise not to cross, Ombhrís dropped the knife.

It clattered to the floor, shattering the silence.

Unsettled by a turn of events he had not foreseen, he took the first offered out he saw, hoping that the people beyond the door, his people, who might hear what was happening, would believe the claims the márbhyndhánis had already offered.

"It was him!" Ombhrís' explanation shattered the silence. He pointed at Iólán as he leaped back, pulling Raebhá with him. With his arm still tight around her, he did not need the knife to be a threat, though it was difficult to tell if he held her to hurt her, protect her, or protect himself. "He took her from me! Tried to kill us both…"

"I never…" Iólán began defensively, drawing closer to Kavan now in the expectation that the potent man who adored his sister enough to take on the márbhyndhánis would not believe the allegations and would shield him too.

"I know," Raebhá proclaimed in a quiet hiss, her anger rising at the man who continued to trap her and dared to insult her brother. Iólán was younger, had less of a claim to the position of leadership than Raebhá, had no cause to turn against her. The people could have chosen him upon their father's death, but they had chosen to follow dhóbhaen tradition and select the eldest. Iólán had never shown a desire for his lot in life to be any different. "Iólán would never betray me. Of all who could have…he's the one I trust most not to."

The accusation in her voice, in her eyes, as she yanked free of Ombhrís' grasp and stepped beyond his reach, was turned back on the man she should have been able to trust with her life. "I never thought it would be you."

They barely knew one another and there had not been time for affection to grow, but she could not believe he resented or hated her enough for this. There was no cause. She had never done anything to warrant betrayal.

With no one rushing to apprehend Iólán, no one daring to approach the stranger, and no obvious support from those held motionless without indication that they bore witness to what was happening, Ombhrís made another charge against Iólán and against the evil of the man attempting to stare him down. "He brings this elyryhánag to steal our sons and daughters! He is kyrónagk…has corrupted my wife and will bring destruction if we do not…"

The márbhyndhánis were unable to respond to the challenges and with no one moving against Iólán, Ombhrís turned his pleading eyes to Raebhá. "Can you not see the threat? No one should have such…"

"Yet I do." Kavan's words were slow and deliberate as he gradually released his hold on those who had charged into the room. When they were free of his control, the thirteen drew together into a huddle, silently deciding what to do with him, and with the husband and wife squared off over the right to rule the ghísaer of Gálínphel.

Only when his hold was relinquished, when his power was redirected to a watchful protectiveness, did Kavan speak again, his eyes on Ombhrís the entire time. "You train those with great power. I am no different. I am not bhydáni, márbhyndhánis; in Elyriá, only the very ancient are allowed that status…but I have trained with the most ancient and wisest. You do not want to cross me."

His tone carried enough of a threat to give an additional warning weight to his words.

"You cross us by being here."

What Kavan felt emanating from the mass behind him, behind the words spoken by one of them, filled him with indignation. He turned to face them, clamping down on the ball of power in his center. He had taken down powers greater than those present and he was not afraid to do so again if any of them dared to threaten or harm Raebhá.

"What are you?"

A sound, footsteps and then an exhaled breath of surprise as Raebhá was pushed to the floor in his passing, heralded Ombhrís' movement, his rush to stop the one who threatened to expose him while his back was turned. One hand shot out to stop him without touching him. There was power enough in the act to hurl Ombhrís against the stone and timber wall and hold him there. Ombhrís squawked and bellowed in fury, "I am kydhé!"

"Raebhá is kymyhé," Iólán shouted, the rawness of nerves and anger stripping away his remaining composure as he caught his sister's hand and pulled her to her feet. Those paying attention noted her condition in the way she had fallen, in the way she rose, but their focus was on Kavan and Ombhrís. Ombhrís did not notice. By the time Iólán added, "You are a fraud! An imposter! A thief!", her long skirts and the cloak she wore again covered the secret she carried.

"And a liar." Raebhá shook free of her brother's grasp and with one hand on Kavan's, gently forced him to lower his arm, encouraging him to release Ombhrís. Kavan's hand dropped beneath her tender effort but Ombhrís remained unable to move. Swallowing frustration, Raebhá crossed the room, glaring at the man who had threatened her life not once, but twice, possibly three times. "You orchestrated the attack, my abduction, to assume leadership of Curnydhá."

He had not said it, but she believed it to be true.

"You do not deserve the power you were given," he spat, his lack of denial proof enough of his actions. It also suggested accomplices, at least one of whom possessed enough power and training to manipulate the rynlagne.

The márbhyndhánis turned on themselves, staring at each other with a suspicion that had not filled their ranks before. People in the doorway came together, shoulders squared in betrayal, to block the passage of any who tried to flee. Ephé glowered at her friend's husband with spite and outrage.

How could any of their own, people they trusted to guide, to rule, to teach and train, turn on their rightful leader?

How could husband turn on wife this way?

"All know you are elyryhánag."

Attention turned again to Raebhá, but hers remained on Ombhrís, her abrupt flash of panic pushed aside so that no one except Kavan might have felt or seen it. "I am dhóbhaen," she said evenly.

"You are a practicing…"

"Where is your proof?" she challenged. If there was an accuser with knowledge of the many hours she had spent with Mánd she wanted that challenger to face her. The ability to avoid detection and hide training was one of the first things any elyryhánag learned out of necessity. If twelve others had failed to avoid detection, she worried that her efforts too would fail and that Mánd would be exposed. The man had Ceased, was unable to be punished, but if he was accused then anyone connected to him might be suspect. Raebhá included. She had Kavan's teaching to strengthen her base skills and felt confident she would be safe from inquisition but others might not be.

"You used it against our attackers! I saw it! There are rumors."

Scowling at the first accusation, not knowing if it was true or not although she could recall a burst of power erupting out of her both that night and when she awoke in Kavan's company, she chose not to speak of it or argue it. He had already been struck down when her action came, or had appeared so; the only way he could have witnessed anything would have been if his part in that night had been a fraudulent act of trickery.

Instead, she countered his words with, "If there is suspicion, there are procedures. Attack, abduction, exile without inquest is forbidden by law. And any," she spoke the word with emphasis as she faced the márbhyndhánis she had known her whole life, who knew her and now appeared as unreliable strangers, and met their gazes one by one. There were those she was fond of, those who had intimidated her, those she barely knew, and none presented the smallest visual clue of support or betrayal. Only one among them she believed she could trust, the newest graduate to the rank of márbhyndhánis. "Any who supported, participated in, initiated such a breach of law deserves the fate they bestowed on me. I will weed out the poison and…"

"We will see to it, kymyhé," muttered one of the voices from the midst of the márbhyndhánis.

Iólán joined his sister, his tension pulling ticks into the corners of his eyes and mouth. Only one he trusted too, but that trust did not prevent him from growling, "You cannot trust them to investigate themselves! Disband the márbhyndhánis! We do not need them! They have proven dishonest and disloyal."

Voices of agreement and dissent rippled through the throng packed around the open doorway, on the stone stairs, and in the streets beyond who could either hear the discussion or were told its contents by those in front of them. Most, however, heard Iólán's cry of outrage, his controversial suggestion that only a few dhóbhaen in history had ever dared to utter.

Any who had were either Reconditioned or sent away, off of their island or deep into the mountains where they would either survive alone or succumb to the harsh conditions.

Raebhá lifted her hand, biting her tongue to swallow her initial reaction to her brother's suggestion. How had Iólán become a radical without her awareness? How had she not known? How had she not trusted him with her secrets…or had he known all along?

"We cannot abolish the márbhyndhánis." Though tempting, it was an impractical suggestion. These men and women held the core of dhóbhaen knowledge, all of which would be lost if they were banished or Reconditioned. No matter how many elyryhánag there might be, none were practiced enough, trained or skilled enough, to teach others, or to counter the skill the márbhyndhánis possessed.

The thirteen breathed a collective sigh that Raebhá immediately undermined as she continued, "But I do not trust you to regulate yourselves, to judge each other fairly, honestly, without bias, to be loyal to the people, to me. Amongst you are the seeds of what was done, actions that could have resulted in my death…or at the very least usurped my ability to walk the forests of Gálínphel. The Fates have gifted me with return, and I will see that the ágdháthé are repaid by cleansing this blight from history."

A gaunt woman, tall and regal with the first traces of great age creasing her cheeks and fine threads of silver interspersed through the golden hair she wore braided and coifed upon her head, tilted her chin with a sniff and said, "There are no others to judge us. We uphold the law, written and unwritten, and only our own may…"

Raebhá closed the distance between them, brushing past Kavan, stopping when she stood nose to nose with the woman who stood a head taller. Breaths caught. Iólán grabbed Ephé's hand, together forming a chain that would discourage others from pushing forward but would not necessarily stop them from doing so. Across the room,

Ombhrís continued to strain against the power bonds that held him. His efforts, despite Kavan's shift in focus, were futile.

"márbhyndhánis Celen." The woman was once the most daunting person in Raebhá's life, once the youngest márbhyndhánis and yet the one with the most officious personality and cold reserve of superiority. For the first time, with Kavan, her brother and best friend behind her, Raebhá was less afraid of the woman despite knowing that Celen might be her biggest opponent. How often had Mánd and her father warned her about Celen? How many times was she told that, should the day of kylldrenai befall her, it would be Celen's duty to see it done and that she would not be inclined to mercy?

"When a body fails to regulate itself, and those within assume they are above the law, written and unwritten, that body is no longer to be trusted, nor those within it. My husband," she spat the word, disgusted by it for the first time, "has admitted to collusion and conspiracy and an attempt to kill me. But he was not the one to attack me. Not the one to bruise me, break my bones, send me through a rynlagne. Only one of you…possibly more…has the knowledge and skill for that…the power to see it happen…and I will have the truth."

Another márbhyndhánis, a grizzled, ancient woman with missing teeth who showed no frailty of mind though her body relied on a stick for balance, muttered with winded breath, "You cannot hold us"

"Perhaps not. At least not all of you. But I do not need or intend to hold all of you. Only the guilty…"

"How will you know?" began Iólán. Across the room, Ombhrís snorted, a sound of triumph that blasted across Raebhá's frayed nerves. She could not rely on the márbhyndhánis to read and judge themselves, nor could she try to do so without revealing skills she was not supposed to have. She could ask it of the one she did trust, but showing favoritism among them might work against her. With Kavan beside her, however, she needed neither to rely on any one of them nor her hidden abilities.

"Lord Cliáth. If you please."

A ripple of tension skittered across the pale man's back. He disliked forced readings, though he had done them often enough. It was a simple thing with Teren who offered no resistance. Few Elyri were trained enough to withstand his efforts. He knew though, as his gaze traveled over the thirteen, that the márbhyndhánis were better trained than those he had force-read before. He was confident in his skill, but he did not want to do it.

He had made a promise, and until every threat was erased, he would not abandon her or the child she carried.

Keeping Ombhrís pinned to the wall required a division of focus as he singled out the first of the márbhyndhánis to be read, intending to do so without touching them. The tow-headed, hearty fellow who stepped forward far enough to single himself out from their midst looked to be the youngest and, Kavan assessed, the least frightened.

As he smiled at Kavan and offered his hand, eyes sparkling with excitement, he alone appeared eager for the contact Raebhá requested.

"I will allow no stranger to…" began Celen behind him, but her efforts to withdraw in another direction was blocked by a wall of sailors armed with formidable weapons, and Iólán, Ephé, and the dhóbhaen behind refused to retreat. It was a sight unseen in Curnydhá since the days of the Banishment, a small army raised against others in their ghís, and though it was unclear whether they would resort to violence if pushed, Celen chose not to take the chance.

"You will," Raebhá growled, "or you will be judged a collaborator and subject to Reconditioning, whether guilty or not."

The youngest márbhyndhánis took a few more steps towards Kavan without being summoned, knelt, and bowed his head. "I have nothing to hide, Raebhá," he said, the use of her name rather than title suggesting the familiarity of contemporaries. "Test me, prove my worth, and know I will serve you as I did on your day of ascension."

"pheturphálós," hissed Ombhrís.

The kneeling man lifted his head to look at the unmoving one. "Never that, chygdhé. Your appointment, o'er hasty of necessity as it was, is contested. The claim of betrayal, if true, against the ró phaern dhes murt, is unpardonable. By the right of law, written and unwritten, the kymyhé lives and her wishes are binding."

"She's elyryhánag!" Ombhrís spat again. He might have said more, but Iólán scooped up the discarded knife in a dash across the room and pressed it to his throat.

"Not until an inquest claims it so," said the márbhyndhánis still waiting on his knees.

A bigger man than Ombhrís, Iólán intended to guard, or kill if necessary, the man his sister had wed if he took further actions against her. "A tradition denied her."

"Iólán; dhysag." This rush to violence of so many was worrying, and the tension, the ebb and flow of power, was beginning to make her light-headed and nauseous after so many unsteady days at sea. She wanted to sit but did not dare display weakness. "Lord Cliáth."

Kavan nodded and place his free hand on the kneeling man's bowed head, turning his thoughts and sight inward to the open exchange the other permitted. Glimpses of memory, of a place Kavan had not seen in years, filled his head, accompanied by shadows and morsels of knowledge he had not expected. Gasping involuntarily with the flash of power that erupted between them, his hand jerked free and he stumbled back, blinking as if it would clear the after-images. Those nearest him lurched away, propelled by both the power and the fear that whatever had happened might hurt them.

Raebhá, caught off guard by the wave of power, already made dizzy by the strength of her frustration and anger, felt her vision quickly fade to black.

"taeásne!" Iólán cried, dropping the knife and racing to Raebhá's side as she crumpled in the wake of the unintentional release of power that had already dissipated. The woman in the doorway likewise rushed forward. Kavan spun towards the sound of Raebhá's collapse and Ombhrís, no longer pinned by either power or Iólán's blade, ran towards the door shouting, "Move!"

No one moved except for the kneeling márbhyndhánis who sprang up, charged, and caught Ombhrís mid-torso with a shoulder. Ombhrís stumbled, his balance compromised by that unexpected hit, and the other caught him with both arms around his waist to drag him to the floor. Three of those bearing weapons lurched forward, their spear tips aimed at Ombhrís' head.

"He killed my wife!"

Uncertain what to do, people looked at one another and then at the two márbhyndhánis daring enough to catch Kavan's arms. He barely noticed anything but the all-consuming fear that Raebhá and the child had been harmed through a release of power he had not caused.

Twisted in her fall to the floor, there was no hiding her pregnancy.

"She has fainted, nothing more," Iólán hastily murmured as he held his hand to her face. She was breathing and the beat of her heart beneath his other hand was strong. He judged her well, but he was relieved when one of the ghís healers pushed through the onlookers to care for her.

"Bind him."

Not even the men who held Kavan between them were inclined to obey Celen's demand, although they did not release him.

"I am kydhé while she cannot…" began Ombhrís.

"Not," one of the márbhyndhánis sniffed, "while she lives." They might have appointed him kydhé when Raebhá was taken, but by custom, they could not permit him control while the rightful kymyhé lived. "We shall convene and rule until she…"

"We will do no such thing." A wrinkled man who reminded Kavan of Tíbhyan tottered forward and put his hand on the bard's arm, seeking knowledge from the stranger but finding only an impenetrable wall. Those who held Kavan released him. "Until she wakes, you will come with us."

"I will not leave her," Kavan growled in a possessive manner that made Ombhrís snarl. Kavan ignored him despite the unanticipated urge to fight for what he felt to be his.

"She will be safe."

"Like before? While her assailants remain free?"

With Ombhrís pinned to the floor by the shafts pointed at his skull, the youngest márbhyndhánis straightened and clasped Kavan's hand in an open-hearted fashion. "Ombhrís will be taken from here, held for examination and determination of his punishment. I will remain to shield her life…if you will trust me." He seemed to find nothing unusual in Kavan's protectiveness or else chose not to question it.

In the hand upon his arm, Kavan read the same outcome in the ancient man as he read in the young one, the old man proving open and receptive to the reading and proving that he, like the younger, bore Raebhá no ill will and had not been part of any plot against her. It made it easier, as Kavan watched the healer lift her and carry her to a mound of pillows and cushions near the fire pit, to accept the conditions placed on him. As soon as Raebhá awoke, she would come for him and he would finish what he had begun. He would find the ones responsible for threatening her and if any harm came to her before then, the guilty would pay with their lives.

∾488∾

❧Chapter 31❧

Asta lost her footing and fell back against the wall, sagging to the floor as her legs buckled, staring at the man who had been speaking without seeing him. "Oska would never…it must be a mistake…he wouldn't…"

Maybe, when news of an infiltrating spy was sent, when Marta had spoken with her, Oska had still been alive. Maybe Onea had not then known his fate.

"He was alone when he fell," the man continued sympathetically, regretting the news he had been instructed to deliver. "Rumor is he may have been poisoned, but it is said he was not himself after your disappearance and the death of King…"

"Death?" Merrek, while wan and shaky, was strong enough to insist on hearing what this messenger had to say when Inquisitor Geli announced his arrival. Arlana, her expression haunted by the death of her child, knelt beside Asta, clutching her hand and stroking her hair with sympathetic horror. "Then there is proof that he is…?"

"None but the queen-regent's word. No one's seen a convincing corpse but there was a funerary march to the Hall of Kings…"

Diona's eyes narrowed. She could make out the outline of the speaker, shadow and light, but nothing more. The sound of his voice, however, told her where he was. "Queen-regent? Inness is…?"

"Ruling in the stead of King Oska's unborn son. Unable to find you, Queen Asta, or Prince Jerit, there's no other de Corrmick to sit on the throne until the child comes of age."

Asta did not blink or acknowledge his words.

"Neth has never been ruled by a woman," Fen snorted. "What if this child is a daughter?"

The messenger shrugged. "I know only what I was told, what I've seen. Those suspected of treason in the deaths of both kings were executed, and the land's reverting to the old ways. An army has been raised…raids made along the borderlands as you know…"

The queen growled and looked to the side where she knew Merrek to be. She knew he was staring at her. While she did not doubt her eldest daughter's capacity to rule, her intelligence and interest in doing so, Diona had feared the sort of monarch Inness would be if allowed a throne. That fear and her intent on ruling did not, however, explain why Inness would turn on her homeland, threaten war against her own blood, her own people.

After a nod from Diona, Merrek dismissed the courier with a wave, wanting no stranger to be a party to the dialogue to follow.

"I will write to her, hear her demands, request to negotiate…"

Merrek scowled but nodded. His memories of his cousin were of a girl obsessed with strength and weakness. If she agreed to meet and negotiate with her mother, the older woman's near-blindness would be seen as a flaw to be exploited. He did not foresee such a parley ending well. But without Oska, with her brother Gamal so far away, with Kavan unreachable in some distant land, Diona was possibly the only person who might be able to reason with Inness.

"Do it…and warn her that, blood or not, we will not hesitate to retaliate should she force our hand."

"We do not have the forces for war," reminded General Declan, speaking for the first time, cutting off the queen before she could countermand Merrek's words. Garran Declan had shown great promise under General Agis' guidance, putting down riots and rebellions at the end of the Second Elyri Persecution. He was selected, despite his youth, to serve in Agis' stead when the general fell ill, and while he had never known the fullness of war, Diona had faith in his ability to meet such a challenge.

Raids were not the same as war, but the circumstances were similar enough to riots and rebellions that Declan would be in his element in dealing with them. "With the plague, I dare say we will be pressed to recruit enough…" the general continued.

"We may have no choice. We will approach Gamal, discuss the sharing of arms and militia…do likewise with Cordash if we must."

"We came to their aid during Neth's torments; they would be wise to return the favor," Diona agreed, despite her reluctance for war.

"Wisdom may have little to do with it." Wisdom and intention could not rout the Yellow Death.

Fen scratched his bearded chin. "Perhaps the Prime Magistrate will join in a blockade to sail towards Glevum, a show of solidarity?"

"Perhaps."

Since the days of the last Elyri Persecution more than twenty years hence, the tiny island sovereignty had built an ample naval fleet under first Gabrielle and then Piran's direction. With the aid of Enesfel and Elyriá for lumber, and Hatu for the expertise in shipbuilding, eighteen ships now patrolled the Bay of Phállá, protecting sea traffic from brigands. In exchange, the Prime Magistrate signed treaties with each of those kingdoms, the first of their kind in Káliel's history, which allowed increased trade and consent for those ships to dock at any port required to restock supplies and manpower. It meant foreigners were now welcome on the once isolationist islands, allowing an exchange of culture unheard of as far back as the Sovereignties history stretched.

Merrek believed his Uncle Piran would aid him if asked.

"General, assemble the council, the advisors. We will speak with them at once. My Lady," he bowed to Diona and took her hands. "You will join us and make effort to negotiate with Inness?"

"I shall." She lacked confidence in her chances of success, but she had to try.

Sighing, Merrek went to the woman huddled against the wall and though he offered a hand to assist her up, Asta shook her head and rose on her own. "I mourn your losses, Asta; if we may help…"

"I want the heads of those responsible," she said icily, not caring whose head that meant. She wanted blood, wanted vengeance, wanted peace in her head and heart. She wanted verification from Onea's spies that it was true, not a rumor of hearsay with vague, unsubstantiated details. She would have none of those things until whoever had robbed her of her life, her husband, her eldest son, was brought to justice. Words spoken, she stalked from the room, and Fen, after an apologetic bow to the queen and prince-regent, hastened after her in the hopes of preventing any violent outburst or action that might be brewing.

Diona rubbed her eyes and sighed. The thought of what fate might await her daughter if she did not stand Neth's armies down, was a painful one but she did not fault her cousin for wishing it if Inness was involved in the deaths of the de Corrmicks. If their places were reversed, Diona would seek the same retribution, no matter who the guilty party turned out to be.

❧*☙

Níkóá frowned as the last of the day's crowd shuffled away with the meager rations of grain he could offer clutched to their chests. The soldiers gathered around the platform were there under orders of the queen in case a riot broke out over food, or the inadequacy of it. But the thin crowd of faded, skeletal forms was too weak and broken to fight. Each week that passed brought more death until it appeared that Rhidam would be left with none upon which to rebuild. This day, the crowd appeared no smaller than the last, the recorded number of recipients up by five, and the report from the ailing gdhededhá Rankin was that they had seen no new plague victims in this past week.

Some of the afflicted, like Prince Merrek, were beginning to recover, revived by what little care the gdhededhá, physicians, and healers from Elyriá offered. The chamberlain knew he was not alone in praying that the worst of the Yellow Death was behind them and that, with a healthy rainfall feeding the spring earth, there would be future food to share. Not enough, perhaps, as the number of those available to plant and harvest was low, but there was hope for the first time that recovery might be possible. Reports of similar improvement in conditions had arrived from Levonne, where Duke Cáner intended, as soon as conditions settled, to initiate a massive fishing campaign in the hopes of providing seafood to Enesfel's population. The land needed that food, however stretched the catch might be.

That, at least, did not require waiting until an autumn harvest.

"My lord! My lord!"

It was unusual to see anyone running, given the poor health of most. Níkóá glanced at the chancellor, who shrugged, and then jumped from the platform to greet the man the protective soldiers restrained.

"What is it, sir?" he asked, waving the soldiers off. They released the man and stepped aside far enough to allow him to approach.

"I must get word to Inquisitor de Corrmick." The fact that the title rolled easily off his tongue without reservation over the name, suggested the man was Association, though there was nothing to visibly suggest it. "The one she wants, the bard killer, I found him!"

Though skeptical, if it was true, this would be the best news any of them had received in weeks, besides the recovery of the prince and princess. "Where is he?"

"The Boar and Sow; I can take you there, but she wanted…"

"Peter, bring the inquisitors. I'll go with him." He was, in his own opinion, the better swordsman, the stronger fighter, while Peter was the more adept runner. The division of labor made the most sense.

Rather than argue, Peter rushed to obey. He was an obliging man by nature and took the order in stride. Both knew the Boar and Sow to be near the naós, a few streets from where the dead man was found. The area around Hes á Redh had been previously searched, every resident questioned, but that had been weeks ago. The shifting population, as the Yellow Death spread, made it difficult to keep track of everyone. If the murderer had been there this entire time, the inquisitors would be furious at having allowed him to elude capture. If the criminal was transient, however, back from wherever he had fled to after the crime, it was time to act before he moved on again.

Rushing after the informant, Níkóá asked, "How do you know it's him?"

"k'dedhá Tusánt assures me it is."

That was enough for Níkóá.

Despite its squalor and reputation for being an Association establishment, the Boar and Sow was one of the busiest taverns in Rhidam, visited by those traveling through on business, a hub of gossip and commerce that spidered outwards through the kingdom. The small, multi-leveled structure was situated on the main thoroughfare running from the naós to the Tegid and the bridge crossing it and stretching east towards the Llaethlágárá Mountains. Abustle with transitory traffic, only Association members who ran cons, gambling schemes, or made a living picking pockets were found there, making it less of an Association haven than many believed but enough of an attraction for them to give it a reputation.

Other Association members were wise enough to stay away, particularly when the diverse crowd and the petty thieving activity of some resulted in brawls with fists and blades that drew the attention of the Lord High Sheriff and his men. It was not the sort of place any dedhá would spend free time so if Tusánt had been there it had been to tend to the spiritual needs of the ailing or dying. These days, it was likely to be both.

"I'll leave you to it," squeaked the escort, leery of entering as he fidgeted and hung back in the shadows. "Was here before; it'll look suspicious if I come back with someone like you."

Níkóá frowned and looked at his clothes. While handsomely dressed and in better health than many, he did not think he stood out as either nobility or a member of the palace guard. He was armed, but he could be any other man, a traveler, a merchant, one of the sheriff's men. "How will I…?"

His escort had already abandoned him, choosing neither to wait for Peter's arrival with the inquisitors nor for any reward offered. If he was Association, he would be in touch in the future for that. If this was a trap, the chamberlain was about to find out. Níkóá straightened his tunic and sauntered into the tavern.

k'gdhededhá Tusánt was still there, leaning against the bar, speaking to the weathered sprite of a man behind it, a frail, red-faced fellow who looked to be one of the lucky few to recover after the Yellow Death finished with them. The only other person in the room was a tall, hairless fellow whose coppery skin suggested Hatuish blood or the mixed parentage of Cíbhóló and anything else. His lean glow of health revealed he had steered clear of the ravages of plague and he drank alone, near the fire, a satchel on the table at his elbow. He looked up when Níkóá entered but returned his focus to his drink, unfazed.

Brief eye contact, that of two men assessing each other, passed between Tusánt and the chamberlain, but they revealed no familiarity and the proprietor did not seem to recognize Níkóá when he leaned against the bar and requested a mug of ale. After twenty years as chamberlain, Níkóá thought everyone should know his face. He was still surprised when someone did not.

"No ale…stores are depleted…but I've wine if you want?" the attendant offered in a reedy, cracked voice, already pulling a tin cup from a tray behind the bar.

"Aye; a little would quench the thirst." He waited as the wine was poured, brought it to his nose when it was served, and sniffed the bouquet. Not expensive spirits, barely aged and bitter to his nostrils, but it would be rude not to accept what little the man had to offer and so he slid his coin across the counter. "Any rooms?"

"All but one. No one's traveling; too busy dying, or trying not to."

Níkóá scowled. That meant the fellow at the fireside had either rented the room or someone else was here, and he had no way to be certain which would be the man he was here to apprehend.

"I can show you up if you're interested…"

After fumbling in his pouch for more coins, Níkóá added them to the first. "Reserve one. I'm not picky, so long as it's not infested or leaking." The encroaching evening might bring others to board, but the shadow of death would keep many at bay for some time to come. A few coins paid for a room he would never use was no hardship.

It also presented a pretense for his being here. The k'gdhededhá offered no clues, as that would be contrary to the sanctity of confession.

Níkóá's instinct, his Elyri intuition, suggesting the bald-pated fellow, no citizen of Enesfel, was his target, would have to be enough.

The tavern door swung open with a crash, the sort a brusque, boisterous fellow might make rather than a sound of anger or violence, and Fen staggered into the establishment, his short-legged carriage almost a waddle as he laughingly, one arm around Asta's shoulders, made it to the bar.

"Inquisitor," the proprietor chirped, suddenly nervous, pushing the coins Níkóá had paid him towards the stocky man. "It's all legal, I swear. I've had the wine in storage for…"

"Not here for you," Fen laughed, tossing another coin onto the pile on the counter. It rolled and Níkóá covered it with his hand to prevent it from dropping onto the muddy floor.

Asta, however, displayed nothing but intent on business, striding to the man seated by the fire after leaving Fen propped on the bar and growling, "You, sir, are coming with me." Whatever angle Fen had been playing, it was undermined by the woman's bluntness.

The bald fellow, hand on his blade as she approached, laughed easily, unconcerned about the small, boyish woman in men's clothing who dared to confront him. "I think not," he chortled.

"I am Inquisitor de Corrmick," she hissed. "The queen demands an audience and will be obeyed."

Níkóá, watching from the counter, absently pushed the captured coin towards the others as he noted the subtle shifts in aura and expression on the face of the man Asta confronted. Whether or not the man was guilty of murder, he was guilty of something, or knew something he was reluctant to have known. Níkóá wagered he was aware of what awaited him if a reading was forced by one of the Lachlans' attending Elyri. When the man's hand twitched, tightening on the sword hilt beneath it, the chamberlain acted.

Asta sensed the gesture as well. She rolled to one side, away from an intended strike, and skewered the man's hand to the wooden table with her dagger as Níkóá's sword stopped short of beheading their suspect. Fen, the farthest away, threw a knife that narrowly missed Níkóá's head and embedded in the high backboard of the bench on which the target sat. The man squawked and froze, his gaze darting between the three of them. At the bar, Tusánt had departed without anyone's notice.

"I've done nothing," the man protested as Fen elbowed his way between Asta and Níkóá to scoop up the satchel from the table. "You have no grounds." He flinched when Níkóá pulled the dagger from the wood by his head and winced again when Asta yanked her blade free from his hand. The chamberlain wrenched him to his feet.

"You stole a holy relic from Hes á Redh and murdered the man who caught you," Fen barked.

"I stole nothing! There is no…!"

"An overheard confession is proof enough until the queen has you read and…"

Grabbing Asta's wrist with his good hand, the bald man cut her accusation short. It was a commonly rumored belief that Elyri could extract memories, details, and confessions from a man's head, a torturous ordeal that could kill a man if he resisted. What he did not know was that Níkóá carried that Elyri power and that the man's hand on his bare arm, pulling it from Asta's hand, had already opened his thoughts to the unknowing garnering of the truth.

"I stole nothing! I was charged with seeing him safely away with the package, nothing more."

"Who?" asked Asta, as Fen growled, "That meant killing someone for interfering?"

"I was commanded to protect…"

"Who is this other you speak of?" Asta demanded again.

"I don't know his name."

"But you know who he is? This thief? You could identify him? Describe him?"

Hand bleeding profusely despite Fen's effort to bind it with a dirty length of cloth the tavern proprietor provided, the captive answered, "Been following him for months but I don't know his name…"

"Is he here? In Rhidam?" Capturing both the killer and the thief, now that they knew there were separate individuals as Asta had postulated, might help soothe some of the fury gnawing through her. They still did not know this man's part in the plot.

"Don't know where he's gone. Last I saw him was outside the gates of St. Kóráhm's."

Inquisitors and chamberlain looked at one another. Cedric had intended to deliver the mantle to Kavan in Alberni. With the duke on a mission of his own, leaving the item in the care of the chellé hábhai would be a logical substitute. Cedric had not spoken of a partner or traveling companion, but perhaps this individual had agreed to the delivery in case Cedric failed. That did not explain Cedric's death.

Or perhaps the stealing of the mantle, the visit to St. Kóráhm's, and the murder were disconnected events and had nothing to do with each other. The jumbled imagery Níkóá gleaned from the man's head showed that something had been delivered to the chellé, and this man believed it to be the relic he was following, but further proof would be needed before Níkóá would believe him.

"I will arrange a messenger to Alberni," the chamberlain grunted. He was due to see to the welfare of Kavan's estate, a duty he had been lax in fulfilling with the Yellow Sisters pillaging both cities. This was a duty he should see to himself. "For your sake, I hope k'gdhededhá Kesábhá supports your story…"

"There's still Lord O'Grady's death, and for that you are responsible." The captive and chamberlain had not admitted to being the killer but she believed it to be true. She had not yet seen the healer's drawing of the killer but would have this man's room searched, his person, his pack, and proof from Ártur as soon as she dragged him before the queen and prince-regent. "We will sketch this bandit, Lord Chamberlain, so that you may send it to Alberni. A warrant shall be issued for the thief's arrest; let's pray this was a misunderstanding." If k'Ádhá was with them, Tusánt might recognize the thief as well.

"Aye," Níkóá agreed with a bowed head. He did not need a sketch. He had seen the thief's face; it did not match the face of the man Ártur had already drawn for them. But having it in hand would hide the secret of his blood that much longer. The secret it would not keep, however, was that the thief, in all likelihood, carried the same mixed blood. An Elyri thief was as impossible to fathom as was an Elyri known to have once served the Crown as executioner. He wanted the full tale of these strange events, but getting to the heart of it would prove impossible without the mysterious burglar to question.

It might prove impossible even if they found him.

❧*❦

She was not alone. Those servants who could do so, townsfolk whom she had cared for and nursed to health, and dedhá Uwin of St. Wolson's Faith, gathered in the manor as soon as the unfortunate news reached them. It was a constant stream of well-wishers and supplicants praying that their generous benefactor would walk amongst them once more. She was surrounded by too many to be considered alone, and yet not one of those she felt to be family were here and thus she felt alone. The closest to a family she had now were the servants who hovered and fretted and begged to be allowed to send word south, to summon her grandson, her son, or Lord Cliáth to her bedside, to sit until she faded. But Kavan would not be found in the Sovereignties, and if he was close enough, he would surely know the state of things and be with her now.

As for her son and grandson, hasty messages sent would be of little use. Either Gabrielle would recover before Piran or Merrek could come, or else she would die. Messages of death could be delivered just as easily after as before.

Unlike the plague in the south, in the north it appeared to be borne by water, of which there had been an overabundance during the past two years, when harsh torrents had fallen for days in succession, flooding fields so that nothing could grow. It contaminated drinking supplies with runoff from the mountains that had brought too much silt, stone, and debris with it. Something in that water, or perhaps in the water falling from the sky, brought with it boils, fever, and coughing that most often led to the death of its victims. Keeping the food supply dry, avoiding rot and mildew, was an ongoing challenge. Every drink of water came with the risk of contagion.

Thanks to Owain and Merrek's wisdom, Fiara had considerable stores of grain and cured meat, but after two years of drowning rain, that supply had thinned to the point where most worried about starvation. Mercifully, no rain had fallen in nearly six months. The levels in Lake Curo and the rivers that fed it were dropping and the over-saturated land had begun to dry out. With the return of the wet season, however, many feared that the respite would not last.

With Asta now departed and Merrek installed in Rhidam, Gabrielle had been at liberty to do as she thought best for the people of her city. Having nursed Owain through long agonizing weeks as his lungs filled with fluid he could barely expel, watching his body weaken and decay around his indomitable spirit, remaining strong to be everything he needed her to be, Gabrielle believed the skills learned in that trial would be useful in aiding Fiara's sick and dying.

She respected Merrek's wishes by not bringing the suffering into the manor to limit contamination, in case he, Arlana, Lorant, and Conroy came. That restriction did not prevent her from going into Fiara. Alone, with only the staff for company, she opted to spend her days at the náós aiding the staff in caring for the afflicted. She had taken the precautions the Elyri healers suggested, wearing gloves, covering her mouth and nose with a cloth, cleaning her hands and face as often as she could, and never bringing them near her mouth and nose until they were clean.

Despite her efforts to make her people well, there was little to be done beyond easing their suffering, just as there had been little to do but make Owain comfortable. Despite her efforts to protect herself, the northern Sister had settled in her lungs and would not depart.

She had accepted the risk of servitude knowing k'Ádhá would either spare her or bring her to Owain's side, content to face either outcome while hoping to the end that she would see Kavan again.

Her path was decided. There was no other outcome for it. In the lucid moments when the plague-fog lifted to permit clear-headed thought, Gabrielle set her affairs in order and dwelt on pleasant things, memories of the men she loved, the children she had raised, the life she had lived because of them. Soon she expected to be at Owain's side, and often, as she crept in and out of awareness, in a room filled with light and shadow from innumerable candles and the sweet perfume of holy, healing incense, she believed him to be there, in the mist at the edge of life, waiting to welcome her into his much-missed embrace. She spoke of that ghost to no one, for who but Kavan would believe such fancy?

Knowing Owain was waiting made the slipping out of life easier.

Her only regret, in the final moments of dimming vision, was that she could not say farewell to Kavan. If any of his doubts about the spiritual destination of Elyri were true, they might not even meet in the afterlife promised by their shared Faith.

Gabrielle chose to believe she would see him there.

Someday.

The voice that finally guided her into the waiting arms of Owain, Clianthe and Muir, and the feathered záryph, was unfamiliar but sincere, embracing and reassuring with his whispered, "He will be there," washing over her like warm, petaled water. She looked back one last time to see the auburn-haired man smile before she gave in to the pull of eternal light.

She did not need a name to know who he was. He was there when Kavan could not be, and that was assurance enough.

He hurt too much, an ache of body and soul, to give in to the relentless bitterness that plagued him since the night his father had taken Raebhá away. In the miserable days spent on this pallet, his body cooled by damp cloths soaked in pungent ointment meant both to help him breathe and to keep the fabric of his bedding from sticking to the broken boils across his skin, Dhóri spent hour after hour dwelling on that darkness he had allowed into his life.

He regretted every word, every moment of it.

His father could not be blamed for falling in love. After a lifetime of raising two sons, tutoring countless other children, years spent in the service of multiple Lachlan monarchs, his father deserved to be happy, to find the love he freely gave to so many others. It had been an unfortunate coincidence that father and son found their hearts drawn to the same woman, and even more of an unfortunate coincidence that the woman was already married, for that meant that neither father nor son would have her. If by some twist of fate, her husband was dead as she thought, and she chose to bestow on Kavan the affection she felt, Dhóri could not begrudge his father that either.

No man should be forced to endure solitude unless it was a path they chose for themselves.

A celibate existence had been something Dhóri had already contemplated prior to Raebhá dropping into his life. His days had been happiest when wrapped in the fellowship of the men and women of St.

Kóráhm's, where he could read ancient texts as he copied them, aide in overseeing the financial status of the organization, and singing with the choir when the residents and townsfolk gathered to worship. He did not believe his temperament well-suited to be the lord of Alberni as his father's was, and had resisted the knowledge that someday the title of Duke might fall onto his shoulders.

Now, as the wracking cough surged through him and he struggled to sit, to breathe, he doubted either future would come to pass. For the disrespect he had shown, for the resentment he had allowed to drive him during the weeks afterward, resentment that had prompted foolish chances with his life, he was being punished. Punished, and no matter how fervently he prayed for mercy, he knew he would die here and never recover the forgiveness of the man he had wronged.

"You will not die, phyl kyag. I promise you that."

Having heard no one enter the room, no footsteps on the recently scrubbed stones, Dhóri had believed himself to be alone. The others who had been with him earlier, those Yóáná had struggled to nurse back to health, were gone, succumbing to the agony Dhóri knew first hand. Only Emeria and Laney had lived, and although weak, she insisted on managing the household duties her mother had shouldered as best she could while Laney returned to the care and oversight of the manor grounds. Both the healer and Rhyrdan had retreated to share the evening meal with her, believing Dhóri to be asleep.

The voice, unfamiliar in its warmth and accent, did not belong to Raenár, any of the servants, or any of the gdhededhá Dhóri knew.

"Who is there? Where are you?" Thus far, the eyesight stolen from him had yet to return and might, he was told, never come back. If he was robbed of a productive future, Dhóri had no desire to continue living. He might as well die…although he preferred that day did not come until he had the opportunity to apologize to his father.

Hands closed around his, tender and strong and full of power that jolted through Dhóri's body, leaving a tingling vibration in his bones as it passed. Dhóri's hands clenched as if he would pull away, but he had no desire to be free of what felt to be a holy touch. Like his father's hands, but not the same. "dedhá?" he murmured. It had to be. There was no one else, except his father, who could touch someone like that.

Kavan was not here.

"No," the soft voice chuckled with lips that pressed against the damp skin of Dhóri's brow. "Only one here on behalf of your father to see to your well-being."

Dhóri shook his head. Raenár then. "He would never come…and you should not be…I am dying. You'll be tainted and…"

"There is no threat to me. You are not dying, not for many more decades. I assure you, phyl kyag, Kavan would be here if he could be."

His father's name on the other man's lips was gentle, affectionate as if there was great love between the two, but Dhóri knew of no one so close to his father except for the now-absent Wortham. Not Raenár.

This was not Wortham, not in body, not in spirit. Dhóri had known the captain too well to mistake this man for him.

The impulse to cough, lesser now than it had been minutes before, shook Dhóri's body and within his chest, he felt the familiar clenching of muscles against his ribs. That too had lessened, but as the coughing was reduced when he sat upright, Dhóri barely acknowledged the difference. The stranger sounded so certain that he would not die that Dhóri did not have the heart to contradict him.

He wanted to believe it was true.

Instead, he muttered bitterly, "I will be of no use without eyes, though I appreciate your intentions for my recovery." He sighed with regret and defeat. "I'd accept death if only I knew he forgives me for what I've said…what I've done…how I've…hurt him."

The stranger sighed too. "So much like your father you sound. I cannot give you your eyesight, but have faith when I say that a man without eyes can see in other ways. Ask about your kinsman Phaedr. They will tell you. You will find a path, your future will unfold, if you keep faith and do not succumb to the despair of surrender. Your father will know your thoughts; I will relay them when I leave you, but be assured, you shall have him with you soon."

A sliver of light returned to Dhóri's demeanor for the first time in months, his face tilted towards the voice of the man at his bedside. "He is coming home?" How anyone could be certain of that, he did not know, but he wanted to believe that morsel of good news.

"Believe in his words, phyl kyag; trust in his promise and do not despair. You have my word he will be with you again."

Though unconvinced that the Yellow Sisters would pass him over, Dhóri chose to cling to the man's words. Die or live, he would be with his father. That gave him hope, even as he realized he was alone again. Alone, without the sound of retreating footsteps.

He touched the place on his forehead where lips had grazed him. Things the man had said, taking Dhóri's words to Kavan when he departed. Prophetic words of hope. He shivered, remembering tales that his father had shared, tales of the Heretic-Saint who was said to come to him in his times of need.

But Dhóri was not his father. This was impossible. It could not be. "Master Dhóri?"

The young man blinked, weary but at least not coughing, and turned his head towards the new voice, one he happily recognized. "Did you see him? Did you pass him in the corridor?"

"Who?" Níkóá glanced behind him into the short empty hall towards the kitchen beyond that. "Rhyrdan? Shall I get him for you?"

He had already spoken to the acting steward, his sister, and Healer Delamo, learning of the grim losses that had overcome Alberni as they had Rhidam. Having come from St. Kóráhm's with verification of the thief's face, where the dead outnumbered the living, he learned that a holy relic, if that was indeed what it was, had been delivered as claimed. He wanted to open the bundle, see it himself, but Khwílen would not permit it, insisting that, whatever it was, it was for Kavan to discover.

Níkóá had to trust that this delivered relic and the stolen mantle were the same thing. That the courier and the thief were the same man. Without proof, he did not think the inquisitors would believe it.

Now he had come to the manor, to see to Dhóri's condition before returning to Rhidam. Rhyrdan continued to cling to hope and prayer that his brother would survive but the women of the house were less inclined to hope. Having seen the brutal effects of both versions of plague, believing that Yóáná knew what she spoke of, Níkóá would never forgive himself if he did not call on Kavan's son one last time.

There should have been more he could have done. There should be more he could do now.

"Not Rhyrdan." Dhóri shook his head. They would think him mad with fever if he tried to explain what he believed to be true. "It is nothing; I thought…" The edge of the pallet sank as the older man settled beside him. "Maybe I was dreaming."

Hallucinations were common amongst the ailing. Níkóá had few doubts that Dhóri's mind was filled with a host of peculiar images.

Having tended his share of the sick and dying, however, it was noteworthy that Dhóri had the strength to sit, to converse in a strong voice without gasping, choking, or coughing. Yóáná had prepared him for the worst but the evidence of his eyes revealed an illogical sight he had to touch to believe.

"How do you feel?" he asked, taking the young man's face between his hands to tenderly kiss his forehead. Though Dhóri winced as many of the dying did, their skin sensitive to the slightest touch or sensation, it seemed his pain was minor, the action more a reflex of expecting pain than of pain itself.

"That doesn't hurt," Dhóri whispered, fear creeping into his voice. Every time anyone touched him, Yóáná or Emeria or Rhyrdan, there was the sting of bursting boils or the ache of tender muscles and skin unable to easily tolerate the burn of screaming nerves. That he could not feel it now frightened him. The stranger's kiss had likewise not hurt. Did it mean his body had endured all that it could and was on the verge of shutting down? Had his visitor lied to him?

"Let me fetch Yóáná…"

Grabbing Níkóá's arm with a strength he had not felt in too many days, Dhóri begged, "Please. Don't leave me. I don't want to die alone." He must be dreaming. The stranger had promised he would live to see his father and yet everything felt wrong.

"Dhóri, all will be well. You are…Yóáná should see this."

"What? See what? Níkóá, tell me!"

The increasing volume and pitch of his voice brought the healer from the kitchen where she aided Emeria. As she entered the room, fearing her hysterical patient was mad with pain, she made a hasty visual evaluation of his condition. By the time she reached his bedside, she was prepared for what she needed to do. No assessment was possible until she circumvented his panic and so, thanks to both Kavan and Ártur's training, she caught Dhóri's face between her hands just as Níkóá had done, whispered, "Sleep, átaelás mai," and helped him slump back onto the sticky wet bedding.

"He spoke of someone here," said Níkóá, his spirit vacillating between shock and worry. "Do you think…was Kavan here?"

Níkóá had not sensed the bard, had sensed nothing in the room when he entered, but if anyone could mask themselves from detection, Kavan could. But why would he do so? Why had he not stayed?

Yóáná did not reply as every healing sense pushed through Dhóri, seeking different answers. There was fluid in his lungs still, weakness in his long-unused muscles, but the swelling in the nerves and tissues behind his eyes had diminished. As with his now unblemished skin, warm but with far less fever than before, it appeared that many of the symptoms of illness had retreated within the span of a few hours.

"It cannot be." Emeria and Laney were recovering, but slowly, and their skin would forever bear the blemishes left by the Yellow Sisters. It was too soon to say how much of their strength would return and whether there were any other complications ahead for them. Their recovery had begun a week ago and Yóáná knew there would be another week or more before that recovery was complete. Anything as abrupt as what Dhóri displayed could only be accredited to a miracle…and there was only one man in the Sovereignties said to perform miracles. Níkóá's suggestion that Kavan had returned long enough to save his son was the only explanation that made sense, yet even that was unbelievable.

"Move him." She indicated an empty pallet with clean bedding. If he was cured, or recovering, she could not allow him to sleep in his own filth and risk reinfection. She should move him out of this room until it was thoroughly scoured, but she did not dare risk spreading the Yellow Death if this change was some new twist in its effects. "I'll bring water, we'll bathe him, burn the bedding. Someone will remain with him until he wakes."

"I will." The duty to the prince-regent, bringing back the news gleaned from St. Kóráhm's, was less important now that Dhóri seemed to be remarkably, unexpectedly, recovering. If Kavan had been here, might return at any moment, duty in Rhidam would keep until Níkóá was reassured that his evaluation of this miracle was accurate.

In his sleep, Dhóri turned his head towards the door as Níkóá placed him on a different pallet and covered him with a light sheet. "Kóráhm," he whispered without opening his eyes.

In the doorway, Yóáná stared at Níkóá and he stared back, both thinking the same thoughts.

Not Kavan…but Kóráhm?

It could not be so.

And yet, perhaps, it was.

❧*❧

He should have left as soon as his duty was complete. The mantle was safe in the hands of the gdhededhá of St. Kóráhm's and with the Yellow Death sweeping through Alberni like an uncontained fire, remaining had not been the wisest choice Myreth could make. But as it seemed the man following him had ceased doing so as soon as the relic passed out of his hands, Myreth felt less threatened and the hope that Kavan might soon return caused him to remain close to the place the beloved man called home.

He scoured empty residences and businesses for traces of edible food and gave them to any of the living he found, so long as they appeared healthy enough to consume it, saving only a little for himself each day. He was hungry, but this was not his first experience with lean times. It seemed more important to keep Kavan's people alive than to horde food for himself.

After everything Kavan had given him, it was a small price to offer in repayment.

At night he slept near the chellé, watching its gates but not daring to seek shelter within, even when the rain soaked him. He was there, having come from his latest foraging efforts, when the stranger emerged from St. Kóráhm's. If he had entered through the gate, he had done so when Myreth had not been here.

He was not gdhededhá, not a local, a healthy man of means with thick coppery hair and a beard, and a determined stride that took him quickly to the doors of the Alberni estate house. It was the words he spoke, parting words between him and k'gdhededhá Kesábhá, that prompted Myreth to make a decision he had not wanted to make.

He had been recognized, branded a thief, and now a warrant hung over his head.

It did not matter that he had delivered the relic as intended. There were questions about his involvement with the murder of the mantle's original courier, a death Myreth had known nothing about, and until those questions were answered, the Crown would not be satisfied with his innocence. He did not feel that he had committed any crime but believed he had acted in accordance to k'Ádhá and Saint Kóráhm's will, yet the niggling in the back of his head told him to remain free, avoid arrest.

Kavan was not here to protect him.

If he was taken, they would learn of her, and betraying her was something Myreth could not do.

Unable to wait for Kavan any longer, regretting that he might never see the man again, Myreth took what few belongings he possessed and slunk into the night, hoping to remain a step ahead of those seeking to deny him his freedom.

❧ *507* ❧

❧Chapter 32❧

"Átaelás mai."

Kavan did not need to see the speaker to know who it was. Only one person called him that, and in the isolation of his prison, it was the most welcome sound he could have heard, save for Wortham or Raebhá's voice. Without rising from where he knelt in prayer, his knees burning from extended periods on rough wooden planks without even his harp to comfort him, without looking up, he fell facedown and wrapped his arms around his visitor's ankles.

"I feared you had abandoned me," he choked, unashamed to shed frustrated grief into the hem of the saint's garment.

"Never, Kavan. I regret not coming sooner," he dropped to his knees and pulled Kavan up to his, "but this has been a journey you needed to make alone."

Nodding, Kavan accepted Kóráhm's embrace, marveling again that the saint's form could be flesh. "What I've discovered, am discovering…it is unbelievable," he admitted, "but the proof…seeing it with my own eyes…" Kavan sighed and sank back onto his heels. "No one in Elyriá will believe these things."

"Few, perhaps, at least at first, but some will, in time."

Kavan raised his head to the faint glow Kóráhm's form created in the perpetually dark space. It was the first light Kavan had seen in days. "Should I tell them?" He was declared a heretic in Elyriá, banished from his homeland. If he returned to share the things he had seen, heard, learned in this place, he would surely be deemed mad or put to death. Was the possibility of destroying the faith of some worth the setting of the Elyri story, their history, straight?

"I cannot say. I do not foresee that future. You must follow your heart. I do not know what path you are to walk, but I always hoped you would have the opportunity, to learn these things, as I did."

"You have been here."

There were no gaps in the story of the saint's life for such a visit to have taken place, beyond day-to-day minutia that was impossible to know. Kavan knew the timeline of the saint's history from early adulthood until the moment of his martyrdom. Unless he traveled back and forth by Gate and stayed only for brief periods, there was no adequate timeframe, that Kavan was aware of, for travel here.

Except after the attempt on his life, when an unknown woman was said to have taken him from the pyre into the annals of history. It was not until years later when the first appearance of Kóráhm's manifestation began, years in which he had been presumed dead.

What if he had not been dead? What if, instead, he had been brought here, to their ancestral lands?

What if he survived still?

Kóráhm did not confirm or deny Kavan's suspicions. Such secrets, like the existence of the dhóbhaen, were not to be known until he was deemed ready for that knowledge. He wanted answers, but would be patient and wait for them. There was enough to discover in Curnydhá, if he was ever allowed to leave this lightless, soundless chamber that had been his prison for countless days.

"Have you come to release me or bring me news?" Or perhaps, as he had done in the past, Kóráhm had come only to offer solace. Kavan wanted more, but he welcomed a small reprieve if that was all Kóráhm could give him. "Is Raebhá…?"

"Do not fret for her; you will see her soon." He brushed the bard's silver-white hair from his face. "It pleases me, to see what you have built, what you have allowed into your heart, though the road before you will not be easy for either of you."

Eyes closing, Kavan bowed his head. It was a relief to know she lived, even though Kóráhm had not specifically said the words. The hint of what lay in store did not surprise him. Confirmation of the difficult choices ahead was unnecessary, and though he feared his ability to make them, he was not afraid to confront them.

"What then?" He did not want to think of her now. The walls that encased him sapped his power, prevented him from reaching out to her. They also prohibited him from manipulating those who brought him food and water, or from creating a handlight or enough body warmth to ease the chill. Woven blankets and furs had been provided, enough to keep him warm, and the dampening of his power was akin to having the air slowly sucked from his lungs. He could barely tolerate it, so in his effort to stave off madness, he prayed… to k'Ádhá, to Dhágdhuán, to Kóráhm, to Wortham, to anyone who would listen.

But with the deadness of the air, he had not been certain his prayers made it out of the void where he was trapped.

This was a skill, the creation of such a space, that he was determined to learn. This and any other practice the dhóbhaen knew which he did not. Whether he ever had use for it, the challenge of knowing the unknown was too great to resist.

If this was a natural place, Kavan wanted to know that too.

"I bring news, both good and bad." Easing the bard's panic, Kóráhm clasped his hands affectionately. "Your son is spared; plague will not take him."

The breath he had held left his lungs in a long hiss of relief. Having Seen Dhóri's suffering in the hours before he came ashore near Curnydhá, the worry for his son's health had remained just below the surface, never forgotten even during the confrontation with Ombhrís and the márbhyndhánis. Dhóri, Rhyrdan, Ártur, everyone Kavan knew, had been part of his continual prayers during his hours of confinement. Knowing Dhóri would live was a welcome blessing.

But it left open the weight of bad news that Kóráhm kept back.

"The rest? Has anyone…?"

"Those in Rhidam, save for the infant, survive."

Kavan's head bowed again. Infants born in days of plague rarely lived. The news did not surprise him but he wished he could have been there for Conroy's family, even if there was no miracle to save him.

"Your house suffers, but those dearest to you in Alberni, in Bhryell, live…save for Zelenka who has joined Wortham in peace. But there is another…"

Kóráhm's hands around his tightened, hoping to soften the news and draw some of Kavan's grief into himself. He felt Kavan's breath catch at the mention of Zelenka, but the bard was no more surprised at her passing than he had been about Merrek's infant son. In the weeks after Wortham's death, Zelenka had quickly become a shadow of herself. As reliant as she had been on her husband in all things, it had been anticipated that her death would follow hard on. He ached for the loss of her, ached with regret that he could not be with Wortham's children in their need, but the news was no surprise.

The other death, Kóráhm knew, would be more difficult to bear. "She served steadfastly until the last, gave herself faithfully, and will be remembered with the saints when her name is spoken in that place…but she suffers no more and is at peace at her husband's side."

Gabrielle.

There was no need to see her in Kóráhm's thoughts, no reason for the saint to speak her name. Their parting in Fiara had come with a certainty that they would not see each other again, though neither had said so and both had been too stubborn to accept that it was true.

Gabrielle.

The first to give him the hope of love, though it was a love he had been unprepared to accept or reciprocate, love that left a lingering, life-long friendship to their mutual benefits and the benefits of the Five Sovereignties. Other than his kin, Gabrielle was the last direct link to his first days in Enesfel, to Arlan, and the events that had conspired to intertwine Kavan's life forever with the Lachlan dynasty. That link severed, that tie dissolved, for a moment, Kavan entertained the thought of having nothing in the Sovereignties to return to. Maybe he could remain here with Raebhá for the remainder of his days.

Even as he thought it, he knew it could not be. There were others now, kin, children and grandchildren of those who had gone before, that he could not abandon. Love, heart, and soul were here, but duty and family were thousands of miles away.

"Was it painless? Did she…?"

"Her last thoughts were of you, átaelás mai." Painless was relative and there was no need to speak of the agonies of plague that had taken her. Her loss was difficult enough for Kavan. The saint embraced him and kissed his hair. "Owain welcomed her home."

The arms around him continued to feel solid, but there was now empty air. Kavan knew it without looking. He wept, offering different prayers than before. Prayers for the repose of the woman he had loved, though not in the way she had wished. Prayers that she would forgive him for not being there to see her across as he had been there for so many others. Prayers that Owain would forgive him that same failing.

Prayers for Zelenka and Prince Conroy.

Prayers of gratitude that his son had been spared.

With the wish in his heart that the dead would hear him despite the power-muting walls that trapped him, Kavan opened himself to song, his head thrown back, so that his voice rang clear and free with the words born in the center of his soul.

Lost within, lost in vocal prayers of remorse and gratitude, he did not hear the door of his prison when it opened. Perhaps it had been hours. Perhaps days. Someone came periodically with food and to empty the waste bowl, always in the night when the world was dark, though whether that was once or twice a day could not be determined in a room without a reliable indicator of time. The sky outside looked always the same. The muting of his senses disallowed anything more than brief tastes of power when the door opened so he never detected their approach. He never looked at their faces to know if they were townsfolk, márbhyndhánis, or any of those he had sailed with.

He did not look this time either.

Only one entered, bare feet crossing the wooden planks, a pottery lantern set on the floor at his knee so that the heat of its fire was felt. The heft of dense fur settled comfortably around his shoulders. The weight registered, as did the sense of a growing throng outside of the door of his prison, but it was the touch of her gentle fingers following the trail of tears down his cheek and exposed throat that brought him crashing back from the heights where his soul had traveled.

"What has…?" Raebhá began, only to have her words swallowed by the mouth that covered hers in a desperate frightened kiss of relief, her face between his hands. If the others he sensed saw them, Kavan did not care. He only cared that she was alive and here with him.

Nor, Raebhá thought with a shiver, did she. She had been afraid of what she would find when the door was opened, afraid of what this place would do to someone like Kavan; she was relieved to see that, despite his tears and his disheveled state, he appeared to be unharmed.

When he broke the kiss to breathe again, the tremors in his center reminding him how near he was to losing control, he pulled back to look at her, needing to confirm with his eyes what he could sense. He placed one hand on her more swollen belly and was greeted with a gentle kick that brought forth a chuckle.

"You should laugh more often," Raebhá whispered, her fingers tangled in his hair working to smooth the pale strands. Until seeing him again, she had not realized how much she had missed him. "áchaelác aeyrudgh. They should not have put you here.

He did not ask why. With the door now open, why no longer mattered. "When you did not…I feared…"

"Ombhrís is held and cannot harm me," she assured him, the betrayal in her voice heard without any gifts needed to clarify it. "I thought he could be dead, but I never considered that he could have…" Her voice cracked and she swallowed the sound before getting to her feet, pulling Kavan with her. "It was his plan from the day we were betrothed, not to merge Houses but to claim the ghísaer. I do not know if his father knows; either way, it will strain the relationship between our ghís. In time, I think his goal was to unite all dhóbhaen beneath his guidance, though such a thing has never been done."

"The thirst for power can corrupt anyone," Kavan whispered. He had seen the effects of it too many times. "I am sorry."

"That he lives or that he sought to have me banished or killed?"

She regretted her tone as soon as the words were uttered but now, surrounded by the people of Curnydhá who had come to see Kavan's release, it did not seem the time nor place to apologize.

Stung by her unexpected bitterness, unsure if it was directed at Ombhrís or him, Kavan let go of her hands. "That he hurt you."

It might have been an easier fate for all three of them if Ombhrís had been killed that night but wishing that seemed a vile thing to Kavan. Ombhrís had been Raebhá's husband. Was still her husband. Any claim Kavan thought he had was secondary to the oaths she had taken. She had seemed genuinely pleased to see him, had not rejected his kiss, now he was stung and perplexed by what this change meant.

Maybe those emotions were a byproduct of his confinement.

Feeling belittled and chastised, he struggled to his feet and followed her out of his prison. Unless he was being brought to trial, it seemed he was free. Emerging from what turned out to be a structure hewn into the earth, a cave of carved stone amidst a row of other similar caves at the eastern side of the valley, he was struck first by the brightness of the sun and a fist of power as his senses came to life. The fullness of unused energy inside of him collided against the power of the outside world with enough force to make him stumble and leave him psychically blind.

It was Iólán, there at the threshold, who caught him with an arm around his ribs, keeping him on his feet and supporting him through the crowd towards the scatter of buildings on the hillock in the distance. Raebhá was ahead of them, walking with Ephé, her head slightly bowed as though ashamed, her thoughts and feelings once more corked inside. As the power battled to stabilize inside of him, Kavan could not reach her thoughts nor find his voice to draw her back or ask what was wrong.

He wondered if some judgment had been made against him for the death of Zóndhá.

"bhir phehonís…bhir phehonís…"

The words began as a murmur, attending each step, as people whispered together, the notes of his song echoing within them, amplifying back so that he could hear it, feel it in the air, in the earth under his feet, though he no longer sang. He had been called the White Bard all of his adult life, since the day he began to travel Enesfel as a minstrel on Prince Arlan's behalf. But this, the growing note of awe beneath the words, felt different. Here in the land of forgotten ancestry, the White Bard of Gálínphel was a thing of legend and prophecy, things Kavan did not want to be. A multitude of diversions had kept him from further efforts to translate the song he knew backward to the original tongue. He feared to learn what the prophecy said.

He was no saint here, as that was a concept the dhóbhaen did not possess, but reverence was the same in any culture. What rumors had spread about him during his incarceration?

What they were responding to, however, was the power of his voice. That it was a response to music rather than to some perceived miracle made their chanting easier to endure as they reached the dhó dónáré and he followed Raebhá, with Iólán's help, up the steps.

Let them appreciate the music. He could live with that.

The thirteen márbhyndhánis were there. Eight stood on one side of the bright room, while the other five, men and women with their hands bound with ropes and heads shorn to the scalp, dressed in brown robes of coarse fibrous cloth, stood on the other. Celen was among the five, suggesting to Kavan what had occurred during his absence. Curious but afraid to speak, suspecting he stood to be accused of some crime, he stopped when Raebhá stopped, silent, feeling the direct gazes and the hidden ones prick across his skin. He should be used to drawing stares. Again he realized he was not.

"kydhé Cliáth." The young márbhyndhánis he had read came forward, one hand outstretched in welcome though he made no demand for contact. He was nervous, but less so than the majority of others present, which explained his being the chosen spokesman. "I am Audh di Cliáth…or rather, my family hailed from there before the ghís was emptied and abandoned…thus kin as you have surmised."

There was some discomfort among the márbhyndhánis, while others wore expressions as if indulging a child his fantasies. But Audh's claim was no fantasy; Kavan had seen his birth in the land of their ancestors, his parents having traveled there before he was born to give their son the claim of 'di Cliáth'. That village was empty, overgrown by flora and fauna, occupied only by herders and their flocks as if the ghís was cursed by its history, but Audh had dreams of living there, restoring the decayed homes, repopulating and resurrecting what had been a mighty name.

Kavan hoped Audh succeeded.

"On behalf of all gathered," Audh continued, "You are welcome. I apologize for your treatment. There have been no outsiders here, not even taeré, in recent memory, and there has been considerable debate about how to judge you, and our own," he indicated the five bound individuals with a tilt of his head, "without interference. When kymyhé recovered from the bhur, she championed your honor and valor and swayed us to grant your freedom."

"Thank you."

He wondered how ill she had been, what the bhur was, that it had taken so long to recover from it, or whether it had taken so long to persuade her people that he was no threat. From the corner of his eye, he studied her, seated beside her friend, no effort made now to hide the child she carried. Other than that change and a degree of detached aloofness, she seemed no different to Kavan than before her faint.

He did not blame these people for their caution; k'Ádhá knew how his display of power must have frightened them. Perhaps the márbhyndhánis were capable of such feats, but he doubted displays of power were common, that most dhóbhaen ever saw more than the most mundane and simple uses.

"I regret any offense; I intended only to protect…"

"kymyhé Raebhá," Audh smiled, looking at the woman warmly, "we know." He turned to the side and gestured to the ancient toothless man nearest him. Despite the old man's smile, his manner was grim, as if he had accepted Kavan's freedom and yet had not forgiven that dramatic display of power. "We have passed verdict on our own, but at márbhyndhánis Éthym's insistence, we will relent to kymyhé's demand that you confirm what we have exposed and expressed."

"These five?" By the binding of their hands, they seemed to have been previously judged; anything now was to assure Kavan of Raebhá's safety and perhaps for her peace of mind. Perhaps they hoped that, once satisfied that he had done the duty of delivering her to safety, he would depart and take his dissenting gifts with him.

"Of all." Raebhá's reply, unexpected as it was, was even in tone and emotion. She might have resumed working with the márbhyndhánis as was traditionally expected of her station, but she was reluctant to trust any of them except Audh.

From the way she resisted Kavan's gaze, he thought she mistrusted him as well. "I want no more secrets."

Audh nodded. Another look passed between him and Raebhá, accompanied by an awkward squirming of some of those standing behind him, and Kavan scowled. There was a secret here, something that had occurred during his confinement, but as it was not his place to know it, to interfere in the governing of the ghísaer of Gálínphel, he turned towards the first of those purportedly innocent of conspiracy.

When the woman dropped to one knee as Audh had done days before, Kavan caught her hands and brought her to her feet. She was older than he was, closer in age to Ártur's mother. In that short touch he read naiveté and innocence, things one might expect in the heart of one raised to adhere to a set of beliefs without hesitation, one who never asked questions or challenged authority or did anything more than she was instructed. The lines about her eyes and mouth, the trembling in her hands, suggested she questioned those things now, forced to do so by unfortunate events at the heart of her beliefs and by the arrival of one from outside of everything she was taught to be real and true. A crisis of faith was brewing, not only in her but within others in the room, sparked by what had been done to Raebhá by those they were supposed to trust and revere, contributed to by the White Bard standing before them. The results, particularly if he was not prudent with his words and deeds, could prove disastrous.

"There is no need. I will have none bow before me," he murmured.

"My head then," she murmured, tipping her head forward so that her pale red hair fell before her face.

"I need only your hand."

"My hand?"

From her confused frown, Kavan knew she wondered if he had already read her, though she had experienced nothing in his touch. "I swear it."

"You will reveal one private detail of each, in addition to their fault or virtue," Raebhá said. "Something other márbhyndhánis would know but that I might not, something that will support your readings so that each will know your integrity is not in question. Each of you," her gaze swept the room, "have my word he will not harm you."

Confident of that support though not of the outcomes he would receive, Kavan moved from one offered hand to another, touching thoughts through the brief contacts before speaking their secrets. A favorite color. A new spouse's name. An age or other detail he felt fit Raebhá's criteria. He relayed the truth as he saw it, whether each individual had known about, supported, or participated in the attack and banishment of the ghísaer's leader. Only once did he hesitate, his probing efforts ramming against a wall of protective power that hid all but the most choice of surface thoughts. Thinking it an effort to hide guilt, he used skills he did not often need to rely on to force his way into the tall man's thoughts.

There was no guilt there, however, only the satisfaction of having tested Kavan and a reflection of mental pain that lingered in the man's gray-blue eyes.

Kavan suspected he would be tested many more times for however long he remained in Curnydhá. They feared him, but they were also curious, a dangerous combination if Kavan revealed too much.

Before the five segregated for whatever punishment a non-violent community might inflict for sedition, he paused to center his power and calm his racing heart. Their physical threat was contained, and though one might choose to attempt a psychic attack on Raebhá's less protected mind, since they had not done so already he doubted they would try with him in the room, nor would they risk attacking him.

In the contact with each, he read the accusations against their leader, their suspicions about Raebhá's illicit training, their beliefs that she was a follower of a belief system long outlawed and eradicated wherever it surfaced. He saw the truth of conspiracy. How Celen, detecting Ombhrís lust for power, had been instrumental in the introduction between Ombhrís' father and Raebhá's, thus also in the eventual meeting of their children with the suggested union of both ghísaer. How she had been quick to seed Ombhrís' mind with suspicions, how she determined to steer him on a path that would, they hoped, eliminate the perceived heretical treason from the leadership of Gálínphel. Kavan saw how Celen had brought the committee of five together and led them in the decision to banish Raebhá through the rynlagne to a destination where her survival was not guaranteed, where there might be barbarians or beasts or inhospitable natural elements, any of which could have caused her death.

They had believed that, even if she survived, there was no chance she would return to Curnydhá.

None had anticipated that she would be deposited at a place so near to the one person capable of bringing her back.

Though he touched their memories of the Gate they had used, he could not see it nor tell how the five together had accomplished the banishing. It was a secret they prevented him from knowing.

If not for Audh, Iólán would not have escaped the blame intended to fall on him. Audh had not known of the conspiracy, had not known who the perpetrators of the night's events were, but he had been quick to act when disturbing dreams prompted him to get Iólán to safety. He had been unable to aid, or reach, Raebhá, had not known she was in danger, but his warning had allowed Iólán to get safely away before his sister was reported missing.

The details of events and Celen's motivations made Kavan quake with anger, but not one of the five exhibited the strength of character or power to challenge him, particularly when his thoughts were intertwined with theirs. It was as if they instinctively recognized how easily he could tug on the spark of life, wrap it in ropes of power, and extinguish it without a visible indication of responsibility. He could leave each dead at his feet if he chose.

But Raebhá would know, and others would suspect, and her disapproval, as well as his respect for life, prevented him from silencing them as they had sought to do with her. They might not have attempted to kill her with their own hands, using the same manner of shadow attacker that had come for Kavan in Maras, but their thoughts revealed their acceptance without regret that their actions could end in that result, no matter how revered life was to the dhóbhaen or how much death terrified them.

After waving Kavan away from the five, the ancient Éthym sighed with the last pronouncement and held Raebhá's gaze for several moments. No one spoke until Raebhá nodded and Éthym cleared his throat. To the five, he said, "You will submit to kylldrenai until deemed fit and worthy to walk as dhóbhaen." He locked his steady gray eyes on Celen's haughty expression. "There are enough of us to follow through; we do not require any of you to see it done. We," he looked at Raebhá, "will conclude our business later."

Curious but thankful he did not know what Reconditioning entailed beyond Raebhá's previous hints that it was meant to purge undesirable beliefs and behaviors from a person, Kavan watched the five be escorted from the building, led through the streets in the direction of the cave cell where he had been held. There were several similar wooden doors set into the cleared lower slope of the mountain but Kavan did not continue watching to see where the five were taken. He did not want that knowledge to feed the temptation to take their punishment into his own hands.

That was where they had imprisoned him. Stripping him of power had undoubtedly been their hope or intent. He imagined a long enough period of power and sensory denial would be enough to alter anyone attuned and trained to its use, but he did not understand how such deprivation was intended to affect those forbidden the use of power.

He chose not to dwell on the memories of his days in that place.

Iólán and many of the townsfolk trailed after them, some determined to see justice done, others curious to witness the fate their once-respected leaders would endure. Raebhá and Ephé exchanged words and the touching of their foreheads together and then Ephé's departure left Kavan and Raebhá alone in the dhó dónáré.

For several minutes they stayed there, silent, Raebhá where she sat, Kavan where he stood, inspecting the hall of what he determined to be the seat of márbhyndhánis rule. Wooden stairs led to balconies of closed doors, and rooms and corridors branched off from the room he was in. There were benches, tables, the manner of furnishings expected in a place of learning. Behind at least one of those doors, Kavan expected to find whatever manner of record-keeping the dhóbhaen maintained. He wanted to see it, wanted to touch documents he wagered would be older than any he had ever found.

As if reading his thoughts, however, and determined to sway him from them, Raebhá rose, tilted her head towards the door when he looked at her, and led him from the building into the adjoining ghís kelyhag, empty except for the handful of people tending the fires, cooking over them. There was evidence that those from Maras and

Phaurd were being housed here each night, as there were too many to be put up in homes and the dhóbhaen had nothing akin to inns in which to house travelers. When the evening meal was ready, the dhóbhaen would collect here, but for now, they had privacy.

When Raebhá pulled him to a bench with one hand and urged him to sit with her, many of those loitering returned to their business. He did not miss their looks of disapproval but he could not tell if those looks were directed at him or Raebhá.

"There is unrest."

"du," she sighed, her voice low. "It will not end soon. The histories record other times when márbhyndhánis were forced to Recondition, but never in so large a number, and never for offenses such as this. Their actions, your presence, have tipped the scales. If I remain as kymyhé, if I am not forced into exile, Gálínphel will become the heart of an upheaval unlike any seen since the days of Dhágdhuán."

"How…?"

Raebhá stared towards the door but the márbhyndhánis could not be seen. "If there is to be honesty and trust between the márbhyndhánis and myself…or any that comes after, there needs to be a balance. It is as obvious to them as it is to me that secrets kept are damaging. Without you to read for me, there is no adequate way to be assured of their truthfulness…and without trust, governing becomes fractured and fraught with difficulties that will only harm us. How can anyone trust those who teach and guide us if those same men and women are the breakers of our laws without regulation?"

Absently she brought Kavan's hand to her mouth and brushed her lips across his knuckles, remembering how he tasted, how his touch made her feel. When he shivered, proving that he remembered as well, a smile faintly lit her features. "There are few good solutions and no easy ones. The márbhyndhánis can demand election and hope to replace me with someone they can manipulate or bully into covering up what has happened. But continuing the status quo will allow mistrust to fester. They know it. They can usurp all power in the ghís, throughout the ghísaer, but the repercussions would spread throughout Dhóbhaen, bringing conflict most prefer to avoid. Or they can accept the inevitable and work with me to reestablish trust."

"You could trust them after…?"

"I must. I can if they agree to allow any kymyhé or kydhé elected to be trained as they are so that we can read their truths and lies as they read others. Never again should the márbhyndhánis be able to hide behind conspiracies nor able to turn power against our leaders in a way that can harm those unable to defend themselves."

Kavan let out a long hissed breath. "You're speaking of opening power to all…to be as Elyri…"

"Not at first, but in time. It could come to that. I hope it will. A successor, or multiple potential successors, would have to be trained to read others, to protect themselves, to harness and control dáni in small ways."

Frowning, Kavan left her seated and went onto the steps, stifled by the sudden pressure in the hot indoor atmosphere that he hoped the cooler outdoor air would relieve. It did, but only enough that the choking sensation eased. He was not surprised that she followed.

"Audh and Éthym…they know my wishes…Mánd certainly did. Both know now that Mánd provided initial training in the ways of dáni before his Ceasing. It is enough to condemn me, if they wish. If I am to avoid kylldrenai, I must sway others to accept that a kymyhé or kydhé who is trained is a proper balance of power."

Or you could come to Alberni with me, he thought with both a stab of pain and a fleeting soaring of spirit. "It will be dangerous."

"It will." Raebhá side-eyed him with a faint smile, not needing to hear his words to know his thoughts. He more than anyone understood the dangers of opening culturally sensitive doors. "After an eternity of conditioning, generations of fear and culture and belief, I find myself in the unique position of being able to affect a change, to be a catalyst, to bring my people what yours already have."

"Fear, hatred, and intolerance?" He shrugged when he felt confusion bubble in the air around her. "Training our children is normal. Most have a degree of core skills. Relatively few continue past that. Even fewer train as rigorously as I have…for as long…but doing so was my choice. I know my potential and have always been driven to explore it, fulfill it, at any cost. Now the tables are turned against us…from what you have here. Those who do not train are as reviled and outcast in Elyriá as those of you here who choose to train without approval. And the Faith…what has grown of it has become an institution torn by ideology and narrow-mindedness that excludes some for differences in interpretation. It instills in us the fear that only those who die may see Ethenae and the Ceasing…as you call it…"

He raked his hair away from his face. "What happens to those who do not die, as normal and common as it may be, is not discussed. It is our greatest collective fear, erased from our memories. I would never aspire to share such rigid beliefs, to have them emulated…by anyone."

"Somewhere in between," Raebhá agreed after several minutes of contemplation. "None of us can know perfection; it's different for everyone. But we can strive to be better, to better the lives of those we love to ensure safety and prosperity. I believe that seeking begins with no longer denying that power is part of us…in embracing it and learning to be who we are. I may not succeed in…"

"You may become a martyr instead."

Fingers threading through his, stung that he would say that though she understood he was speaking from personal experience and not disagreement with her cause, she whispered, "I'm not asking you to fight my fight, aislé. You cannot. I ask only that you support me, and do not reject me for the path I follow on behalf of all dhóbhaen."

The endearment upon her tongue sent shivers through him, the weight of its near-sacred connotation sucking the breath from his lungs. He had never believed he would hear anyone use that word to address him, that anyone could love him so completely. His hand tightened around hers and though he tried to say it back, feeling the truth of it filling his heart, the word would not come out. No sound did for several moments as he wrestled with his fears.

"I was asked once to support such a perilous path for someone I treasured," he finally murmured, recalling Prince Arlan's exuberance, how much of the boy was lost to the man he had become through the troubles that came after. "I've asked for such support myself."

He had chosen to support the prince because it was the right thing to do, just as Ártur had supported him in the perils he regularly faced over the years. What Raebhá proposed was likewise for the best, for balance always was. The dhóbhaen, their future, needed balance, and she was in the position to cultivate it. Facing that, accepting destiny, was her choice. Succeed or fail, it was her goal to wrap her arms around. If their positions were reversed, Kavan would undertake the same mission towards the same end.

In a way, his place in the Elyri Faith sought a similar rebalancing. Everything he learned of the dhóbhaen, of Elyri history, could well have a similar rebalancing effect, if he dared to use it. He did not know if he had the heart to try.

"You know I will never reject you, Raebhá. I cannot."

"Good." Relieved, she led down the steps. She thought to enjoy the ghís kelyhag but after having been held captive for so long, the air and sky appeared to be doing Kavan good. "I've taken the first steps to set things in Curnydhá right, but until I deal with Ombhrís…"

Enjoying the feel of her hand in his, he allowed her to lead towards the sea. The day was the warmest since his arrival in Dhóbhaen, the planted fields around them alive with young crops and flocks abounding with lambs and kids. He guessed he had been in the cave for a week, possibly two, but did not ask for confirmation. That was behind him and no longer mattered.

Again he noticed the peculiar looks of the people they passed, a judgmental sort of curiosity that made him scowl and inch closer to Raebhá. She looked at him, at the direction of his gaze, then squeezed his hand as she again brought it to her lips.

"They question our child." Kavan looked at her but she continued before he could ask what she meant. "Children born outside of a union happen, but a child in an unbonded marriage…" She shrugged. "They talk, for now. In time they'll forget. Do not concern yourself with it."

The opinions of her people, their relationship with her child, would persist long after Kavan left Dhóbhaen. It was not something Kavan could address or change and she did not want his fears to influence the decisions to come. Sometimes fear was a proper motivator. In this, she did not think it warranted.

He snorted, his chin tipping defiantly, and continued to follow towards the water's edge. He knew what it was like to be an outcast child. He would not have that for his child if he could help it.

Changing the subject to push the aggravation of those glances from his mind, he asked, "How shall you do it? Deal with Ombhrís?"

Grateful for that topic change, she clenched her hand but did not pull away from him. "I don't know. There is not only what he did to me, what he conspired to do; there is the ship he destroyed, and the affiliation with his family to consider. That, what you Saw, is on him alone, at least until his conspirators are found. They were not from Curnydhá. That much we have proven. I am unconvinced that kylldrenai is appropriate, though he deserves at least that…but there are few other choices. I cannot request execution, despite his actions, nor confine him for the remainder of his days. I could banish him into the wilds, but what is to prevent him from finding his allies and returning to try again? I could send him away as he had done to me, but there is the safety of others to consider, wherever he ended up."

"Unless someone goes through a Gate with him, it will likely require multiple márbhyndhánis working together to expel him." Kavan had seen in the memories of the guilty that it had taken their combined power for the five to send Raebhá to a place where no Gate had been, enough power to open the Gate and deposit her…an amount that had sucked away every trace of power Kavan possessed. "I would be willing to attempt it, if others are not, but there are no guarantees."

"You are but one man." That did not mean he would fail. If any individual could perform such a feat, it was the White Bard. She did not know the limits of his gifts, but she did believe in his strength. She had seen him hold fourteen men and women in place simultaneously. She had seen him collapse a stone wall. If there was a way to use such a Gate alone, Kavan would find it. "Would it be dangerous?"

"I cannot say. I have never tried. Until you arrived in Enesfel and I saw it done, I never thought it possible. For you, I would try, but I cannot speak of the dangers, to myself or Ombhrís, or anyone else."

Her head bobbed. "I will consider it. His punishment cannot be decided by me alone; the márbhyndhánis must have their say. But due to his betrayal, ending our unconsummated marriage only requires his agreement before…"

Kavan's steps faltered, the attention focused on her, and the words that now echoed within his skull, sliced away by his notice of a tall sailing ship moored at the end of the longest dock. She was twice as long as the boats he and Raebhá had sailed in to reach Curnydhá, a ship with a hold, an upper and lower deck, a near replica of a ship he had seen on paintings in the halls of the Kyne's home or the residence wing of Clarys' great náós.

But he had seen a similar ship twice before, once off the prow of a vessel in the southern seas when he had believed her to be a phantom of the fog, and once in the port of Yashir when faced with Wortham's impending execution. He knew nothing of where the fog ship had come from or gone, but this one bore the same coloring upon its sails as the one he had seen in Yashir.

"That ship…whose is it?"

Her expression brightened. "The gaeythá? That is Audh's ship, his family's trader. After his brother's death, it passed to him…"

"He has been to the land of the k'elyryhánag." It explained why the other man had expressed recognition, why Kavan felt a kinship with him beyond a shared name. It explained the flashes of imagery seen when their minds touched and he believed without further proof that it had been Audh, a Cliáth, who had saved Wortham's life, though the two men had never met and Kavan had never laid eyes on him.

"He has an adventurous spirit. There was a time when I was a child when he was gone for nearly ten years; many thought him dead. As a child, he trained with the márbhyndhánis, but after his brother's death at sea, he took time away to explore, hoping to find him"

She had expected a different response to her proposition of ending her marriage; her disappointment reflected in her voice, but she understood his fascination with that ship. It was, in part, why she had chosen to walk by the docks.

"His tales when he returned were stranger than the riches he brought. Every few generations someone crosses the empty sea; most do not return. Audh brought the first mention of another di Cliáth, the possibility that he was not the last…the possibility that the White Bard of Gálínphel was real." She chuckled. "None believed him. Audh is one of the greatest storytellers in Gálínphel, perhaps in all our lands. It made for a fanciful tale of mythical beasts, of a man falsely accused and another with the voice of the gdhárith who gave róagdháthé to win his friend's freedom…a pale man rescued from the sea."

Her voice trailed off as she recalled the telling. They watched people move on and off the boat about whatever duties they had been given, Kavan quiet in his remembrances. She chewed the inside of her lip as the hand in hers trembled and clenched, until she finally asked, "Is it so? Did Audh speak true? Did these things happen?" She, like others in Curnydhá, had not believed the stories. How could they be true? Until the two men met before her eyes, until that strange reaction that erupted at their contact with one another, she had not even considered that Kavan could have been the man Audh had spoken of. It seemed too coincidental to be true.

Judging by the loss of color in his already pale face and the sudden clamminess of his hand in hers, she decided that they must be true. What part of Audh's tale upset him was impossible to guess, but instead of asking for details he seemed unwilling to voice, she stayed silent and waited for him to speak if he wished.

Kavan remembered those days vividly, though he had not thought about them in years. He remembered the man who had come to him, requesting a list of his needs. He remembered that same intermediary being the one, by Wortham's admission, who paid for his release from the executioner's block. He remembered the wagon of supplies and the horse provided for their journey. And he remembered the bloody bedding that the messenger had promised to take care of so that no one else would ever see it. The messenger, and Wortham, should have been the only others to have witnessed any of the effects of that torturous, grueling, bloody night.

It had not been Audh in his room, but rather Audh on that ship, perhaps seeing Kavan from the deck when the bard passed, or with his gift of apparent Sight. Perhaps the Sight had shown him the blood, the bard trapped and bleeding on the bed, prompting the arrival of the messenger with gifts.

He remembered the voices, the music, the hands that pulled him from the sea when he had thought he would drown. The ship Zelenka and Wortham had seen from the shore before finding him on the beach.

Audh had saved not only Wortham's life but Kavan's as well.

Whether he believed in the teachings of Dhágdhuán, or not, Audh might have recognized Kavan's bloody wounds for what they were.

If Audh had told those stories to others, how many knew of the martyrdom marks Kavan sometimes manifested? If they connected him to Audh's tales, what must they think of Kavan now?

Instead of addressing the trying memory of a man not long lost but who, Kavan realized with guilt, had been less on his mind as the days passed in this unfamiliar land, Kavan asked, "They spoke of bhur?"

Raebhá did not question his change of topic but accepted his expression as proof that somehow he and Audh had crossed paths in a distant place without knowing what the crossing signified. "Ailment of unknown origin," she replied with a shrug, "caused by the restless bhur of those who died whose bodies were not tended in time."

"Not Zóndhá?"

She looked at him curiously, wondering why he brought up the dead man's name. Her arm wrapped around his, bringing him closer as she shook her head. "It was exhaustion, stress, the need for water after many days at sea. I slept many days and awoke with a terrible thirst. It often happens to mothers I am told. I would have come to you sooner, when I first awoke, but Iólán would not permit me to rise and would not leave my side, until the phemárógdh declared me fit, and then it was necessary to press the matter with the márbhyndhánis when they would not permit me to free you."

A small girl, little older than ten, wearing robes similar to the márbhyndhánis but a deep brown and embroidered with saffron and white patterns around the sleeves, collar, and hemline, stopped beside them, using Raebhá as a buffer between her and the pale stranger that she stared at with wide, curious eyes.

"kymyhé, the márbhyndhánis are prepared to meet."

Raebhá smiled and placed her hand on the child's head. "Tell them I will see kydhé Cliáth to his chamber and join them shortly."

"du, kymyhé."

Raebhá waited for the girl to scamper back into the heart of Curnydhá before turning from the beach and the long walk she had hoped to share with Kavan. Instead of taking him to another empty home as he expected, or to Iólán's residence, she took him to hers, to the place where she and Ombhrís had reunited and squared off. They did not speak until they reached the stairs, where she untangled her arm and fingers from his.

"That is yours," she said once they were inside, gesturing to the sleeping loft on the other side of the room where he would be able to see the door from his bed. The artwork Ombhrís had displayed was gone. The home was hers once again. She doubted Kavan would sleep easy, after one attempt on his life and more than one on hers, if he could not monitor who came and went. "Rest. Regain what the gál kylldrenai has taken and I will come, or send for you, when we gather for the meal. Will you play for us tonight, strength willing?"

When he looked about to protest, she leaned forward and kissed his mouth. Her gesture had the desired effect, creating a flush on his cheeks that made her smile. "It has been too long. The music needs you, and you need it." She could feel that thirst in him, whether he acknowledged it or not. It was something she had grown to recognize in their short time together. He needed music as he needed power. She wanted him to be free to use both. She wanted him to be happy, even if that happiness was short-lived.

His tongue traced his lips, tasting her there, and she smiled to see the spark in his eyes.

"If you wish, I shall." She was right. He needed it. So many considered music his pastime, his career; very few understood how essential it was to him and it warmed his heart that she understood him so well. He needed to give song to Kóráhm, to Dhóri, to Gabrielle. He needed to give song to Wortham lest the man, wherever he was, think himself forgotten.

Never that, he promised as she left him with another kiss. He would never forget Wortham any more than he could ever forget this woman who had beguiled her way into his heart. Soon, if she meant what she said, she would be free of Ombhrís. Free to be his. Yet he did not know if he dared to act upon his heart's desire, given the paths their destinies traversed.

❧Chapter 33❧

The letter was folded with meticulous care, bearing no seal as if the sender believed the messenger would not dare to open it, to read it, and would protect it with his life to prevent anyone other than the recipient from doing so. It had been a long while since Diona had seen the younger woman, but in her mind's eye, she could see the hands that folded the parchment and slipped it into the stiff leather parcel that had protected it on its journey south. There was no handwriting on the exterior surface, no perfume on the document as her eldest daughter did not believe in such frivolities as fashion and perfume and would have seen such a touch on an official document as undesirable. This was no personal or informal communication, as Diona had phrased her letter to be despite the seriousness of the situation at hand.

Without reading it, Diona expected the letter to be pure business.

Not trusting the words to her failing eyes, one of her ladies in waiting accompanied her to the morning room where Merrek frequently took breakfast at an hour earlier than most in the palace awoke. He was not there yet this morning, and though the servants offered her breakfast, Diona did not have the heart to eat. Her imagination chased the possibilities of Inness's letter through the corridors of her mind. She tried to imagine positive words but she knew Inness. The rumors trickling into Rhidam did not suggest a positive, promising message.

"You are awake early."

"Bhyrhán." The strangled breath was released in his familiar company. As the Lachlans had done with Kavan, the royal family availed themselves of Bhyrhán's musical talents, his mastery of multiple languages and his diplomatic skills, and sometimes the Elyri ability to read a person or object through touch. Most often that duty fell to Ártur, and most of the time the prince left the minstrel at Diona's disposal, understanding that the queen relied on his gift of vision to continue to see the world. More and more of late, however, she had begun to feel that she should release Bhyrhán from that duty and accept the darkness she would soon be condemned to. Surely, he had no wish to care for her into senility and death. As frightened as she was of that darkness, she believed if she did not accept the loss of his help now, later, it would be devastating.

She already relied on him too much.

Sensing tumult in the set of her shoulders and the nervous pacing steps she tried to take back and forth across the room, he scowled and approached her, the only one other than Merrek, Arlana, and Prince Lorant, still sequestered in Bhryell out of concern for his safety, who dared to touch her without spoken permission. Touch was necessary if she was to use his eyes.

He meant to take her hand, offer the comfort of contact and sight, but their combination of movements resulted in his arm around her, his hand pressing upon the flat of her belly, her back to him so that her head rested against his shoulder. She melted there with a sigh, not attempting to retreat, her eyes closed with a breath of surrender.

"How much longer will you endure this, Bhyrhán?" she whispered, her face turned towards his neck so that her breath tickled his skin. He pressed his lips to her forehead, an innocent gesture in appearance that he knew to be something much different.

"As long as you will allow, My Queen."

She chuckled to mask the turmoil of emotion. In public, there were always titles between them. In private, they had graduated to the use of names, such formality seeming unnecessary with the intimate sharing of vision that allowed the sharing of small bits of thought and knowledge as well. There were some private moments, however, when he addressed her as his queen when she heard something deeper than respect for a title, something that defied title and most words. Hearing it frightened her almost as much as the thought of his leaving did, for reasons she had not taken time to contemplate.

"And if I were to send you away? Today?"

"Today?" She heard his breath hitch, felt the thunder of his heart behind her shoulders, felt the tightening of his arm around her, reactions of fear. His reaction hurt her, but before she could reassure him, counteract his fear with the knowledge that she had no desire to let him go, she felt him swallow hard and sigh.

"I would go, if that is your wish, but I would first beg for a change of heart." Heart, not mind, for it was her heart he continued to hope he could reach though he had little expectation of doing so. "Leaving you would be the hardest thing I will ever do, but if you wish…"

She turned, still able, at this proximity, with his arm around her waist, to see the light and shadow of his handsome face. "I do not wish…but I do wish to know why."

Her face tipped towards his made him shift uncomfortably, his body reacting to the press of hers. This was wrong, inappropriate for one such as himself. He might be one of the grandsons of Kyne Mórne, a prince by Elyri standards, but that hardly made him worthy of the great woman who ruled Enesfel. "Why what?" he mumbled, avoiding answering the question by pretending he did not know what she asked.

"Why do you wish to stay? With me?"

Her breath caressed his chin, his throat. Her hands were on his biceps, one still clutching the letter. He considered all of the reasons he could give her, reasons he had formulated before returning to Enesfel that had expanded during his months here to include continuing service to her in her disability. In the end, however, none of those reasons seemed as acceptable as the truth, even if the decision to speak the truth brought with it the consequences he hoped to avoid.

"Because I have loved you since our first meeting," he whispered, eyes closed as he pressed his forehead to hers.

"That was…"

"Before you wed Prince Harcourt, aye."

"You did not…"

"You adored him, and he, you. I had no right. I have no right now."

"You could have returned to Enesfel any time…to me...after he…" There was an unexpected note of indignation that neither understood.

"You were mourning…and the etiquette for that…" His shoulders shrugged. "There were also political considerations, after the throes of persecution. How might your people have construed my being here at such a fragile moment in history?"

He paused before continuing in a lower voice. "I am a man like any other, a coward afraid of rejection. If you command me, I will go, but not without letting you know that I desire nothing more than to stay as long as I may, in whatever capacity you will allow."

"Bhyrhán, I…"

He abruptly pulled away, putting distance between them, clasping his hands behind his back. Her hurt protest was cut off by the opening of the morning-room door and she realized that he must have heard or detected the encroaching footsteps when she did not. She shot him a glance that suggested they would continue this discussion later as the prince-regent entered the room.

"Good morning," Merrek said, aware of the awkward tension but noting nothing that might have created it. "Care to join me for breakfast?" He had not expected company, but they were a welcome distraction from the grim news delivered to him earlier. His trio of pageboys was behind him, as usual, carrying a tray of food, a pitcher, and a collection of petitions he intended to peruse as he ate.

"I come to share this," Diona said, the uncharacteristic quaver in her voice supporting the room's nervous energy. She sensed his disquiet, but as there were so many matters weighing on them, Arlana's health, the Yellow Death, the loss of a child, the absence of another, and the more mundane daily duties of ruling, she did not find his demeanor unusual.

"It arrived late last night. I've been unable to sleep, not knowing, but chose not to wake you." Whatever the letter said, there would have been little anyone could do so late at night. The few hours of waiting would not present problems, no matter what Inness said.

"From Inness?" Merrek asked, sitting to pick at his food without yet taking the parchment from her.

"Yes."

Presuming she had not read it, Merrek said, "Leave us," to the boys before waving his fork and saying, "Read it aloud, Bhyrhán."

The minstrel bowed and took the letter. The newness of the parchment, its crispness, as well as the tight, precise handwriting, told him almost as much about the sender as the impressions his fingertips read from the parchment.

"Regent Merrek," he read after clearing his throat, noting that, though the letter had been intentionally delivered to her mother, it was not addressed to her, not addressed to the queen, a hurtful rebuff that Diona appeared to expect.

"There are no terms to negotiate. Neth is wronged and I will see those wrongs undone. We have but one demand: the return of the lands stolen by King Arlan. Return them, Princess Asta and Prince Jerit, and there will be no cause for action. Do not, and we will take what is ours, what is owed. Do not cross me. You will find no weakness here. Using the blind to parley will gain no consideration. I will not restate these terms. By the Right of k'Ádhá: Queen Inness de Corrmick."

Queen?

The nerves of all three were rankled by Inness's presumptive use of the title and the titles she had used to refer to each of the others.

By the time he finished reading the short missive, Bhyrhán's free hand lay on Diona's trembling shoulder. Merrek had stopped eating and stared at Bhyrhán as if he were a stranger, when the true stranger lay beyond the page in the voice of authorship of the letter sent. The words, however, were not what Merrek expected.

"She should parley with the queen," Bhyrhán growled, offended on Diona's behalf that her daughter would circumvent her ruling authority in favor of the prince-regent.

"Do you believe she orchestrated the deaths of Kjell and Oska?"

Diona choked, coughed, and barely refrained from shrugging in reply. "She loved Oska, as much as she is capable of loving anyone, so I would think not."

It was difficult to say such a thing about her child. She recalled the time Inness and Oska had spent together as children, how she had protected him, how they understood and supported one another when others did not. To anyone else, even her family, Inness had been aloof, cold, nonchalant. It seemed far too long to carry out some pretense of affection unless even as a child she had this particular goal in sight. The possibility that she could have manipulated Oska for so long was too horrific to consider.

Kjell, on the other hand, was a different matter. Without affection for her father-in-law, feeling no obligation to him, Inness probably did not care if he lived or died. Would she kill him? Would she plan and see such a thing carried out against someone who stood in the way of what she wanted?

To Merrek, Diona mournfully said, "but perhaps…"

Merrek nodded. In his own experience with Inness, he had to agree. "There will be no exchanging Asta and her son for peace."

"Agreed. The risk is too great."

"Inness knows we will not relinquish the north without a fight."

"It is a fight she wants," Diona said grimly. "An excuse for war, to show her strengths at a time when Enesfel is vulnerable."

Surely, the Yellow Death had spread into Neth. That might be the only factor working in Enesfel's favor. "Then we shall become unassailable. There hasn't been word from Gamal and King Govert. If we must we can recruit amongst the Cíbhóló. Emissaries await word for that journey, and what men we can afford are already marching to support the fortifications on the border."

"If I must approach the Kyne, I will do that as well." It would be a suitable excuse for Diona to see the woman again and she was confident Bhyrhán would take her there if she asked.

His breakfast forgotten, Merrek pushed the tray back, took the letter from Bhyrhán, and after reading it hastily himself, asked, "Do we summon the counselors?"

"Yes." Diona did not want to be responsible for overseeing the potential of war against her daughter, but she would not remain out of the planning and prove Inness correct in her assertion that blindness made her mother weak.

"Then return with them, Bhyrhán. If there is any possibility that we must approach your grandmother, I want you to know everything we know. Summon Asta as well." She, more than anyone, would be invaluable in planning a strategy against Neth.

An assault on Glevum might not be possible, but shoring border defenses and perhaps sneaking someone into the castle to remove Inness from power, either by capture or assassination, was worth considering, even if Inness was kin. Asta would know how best to make it happen, and might even know the best person for the job.

Merrek prayed it would not come to assassination.

For his own sake, he wished that the dangerous Yellow Sisters did not overshadow his grandmother's burial. Not even her son Piran would be there to see her laid to rest.

Gabrielle would be buried with her husband, laid to rest by servants and townsfolk and Fiara's gdhededhá. She would not be alone, but she would be unattended by those who loved her most.

Alone in the room now, his grandmother on his mind, Merrek hung his head, covered his face with his hands, and wept.

❧*❧

"Sons, my lord."

Bhríd stared at the midwife as if she had addressed him in a language he did not speak. Twins were common in his bloodline so there was little reason to doubt her or be shocked by the news. For months, the midwives had suspected there would be two children, as Editt grew larger and had more difficulty moving about because of it. Provided the children made it to term, it was presumed they would be large and healthy. He had secretly hoped for daughters so as not to be reminded of the horrors he had witnessed two decades past with the deaths of his first two sons. But fate had other intentions, either a repeat of torment or else the chance to begin again. He was not certain he had the strength for either possibility.

But he had sons.

He swallowed his nerves, his pride, his reservations about what the future held, and went to his wife. For so long he could not imagine thinking of another woman as his wife. Though the relationship with Editt was natural and easy, the word wife still felt strange. Red-faced and bedraggled, she beamed at him with the children in her arms. Black-haired children, like their father, whereas all four of the children with Madalyn possessed varying shades of red. It set these two apart, the elder bigger by a few pounds, the younger sporting a white crescent birthmark on his neck below and behind his ear, both currently ruddy in their afterbirth state but likely to be pale of skin like their parents. As with most newborns, their eyes were a sleepy blue. Despite his decision not to touch them, the compulsion not to form bonds with them as he had his lost sons, when the younger stretched out his tiny hand, Bhríd impulsively reached back, stroking the wrinkled palm before the fist closed around his finger.

"Cáym," he murmured, naming the child without a thought.

"Phaedr Davit and Cáym Kavan."

He stared at Editt, not expecting her to choose such names. The eldest, named for his lost brother and hers. The youngest, named for the moon mark he bore and the man whose complexion was that of the moon…who had confirmed this pregnancy and shared their wedding. The man who had done everything in his power to bring Gaelán back and had cared for him until there was nothing left of the young man to tend. Naming a child for a saint was common, and if there was such a thing as a living saint, Kavan was it, though Bhríd would never express such a thought to his kinsman's face.

"Such names should stand them in good fortune," he murmured, feeling the first swellings of love for his sons. The strength of it frightened him, but at that moment, all he could see was the second chance to do right by the sons he had failed before. He would not repeat his mistakes.

These boys would live.

❧*❧

"Shut the gates!"

No one was prepared, or inclined to act, as the crowd beyond St. Kóráhm's walls, grown larger over the last three days, became more vocal with their discontent over a perceived injustice. They pushed for entry, demanding the food they believed the gdhededhásur possessed and were not sharing. However the rumor had begun, the stretched-thin, gutted population believed there were stores behind the walls of the holy place that they were not permitted to share. Weak and ailing or not, their numbers at the main gates on the west and the smaller, single-person gates to the side of the main and on the north wall, had multiplied with every passing hour. Most stood or sat peacefully, lacking the strength to do more than sling insults and hurl demands.

The opening of the gated door on the west where the gdhededhá conducted the daily distribution of whatever resources the chellé had to share, resulted in the push of the crowd to get inside as the day's offerings ran dry. Captain Magk, attending, as usual, to make certain no harm came to the peaceful, benevolent chellé residents, saw the eruption moments before it turned violent but his shouts for the gdhededhá to close the gates were unheeded long enough for one of their number to fall beneath a strike to the head with a broken brick. Others yanked the fallen man back as the captain pushed past; he reached the door as two strong men struggled to pull it closed. It took all three to succeed against the might of so many on the outside, but eventually, it was barred against the intruders who were left to shout and swear and bang in frustration.

"Get the gdhededhá to safety!" Raenár did not think the throng was strong enough or fit enough to break whatever barriers the architects had designed, but desperate people would try anything to improve their lot and he expected them to try despite their weakness. With only thirty-seven men and women remaining in St. Kóráhm's, eleven of them being soldiers Raenár and Wortham had trained to protect the chellé's population and contents, they would be no match for the malnourished horde if they got inside to ransack the abbey on a quest for food.

"How many?"

Raenár had climbed the gate tower for a better view of the chaos. His eleven soldiers stood at the gates, ready in case the defenses failed and the crowd stormed in. k'gdhededhá Kesábhá soon joined him, the angelic man as gaunt and disheveled as the other survivors, though his eyes shown with the determination to survive that so many had lost. Two-thirds of his flock, Elyri and Teren alike, had succumbed to the Yellow Death, and of the two dozen remaining, only seven were Elyri. The Yellow Sisters had not discriminated between races, particularly when the less vulnerable Elyri had taken on the majority of risky contact with Alberni's populace. The devouring diseases appeared to have run their course, with no new victims inside and few without, but hunger was a persistent problem. Khwílen had stretched the chellé's stores as far as he dared.

It was now up to the rain and the budding fruit trees in the chellé's small orchard, and the ones Lord Cliáth maintained, to provide something more than the fish and mollusks the sea offered. The fruit in the duke's orchard would not last long, as Alberni's hungry citizens scavenged the not yet ripe fruit to fill their bellies, but with luck, St. Kóráhm's crop, protected from ravaging hands, would reach maturity.

"Six dozen maybe; most of Alberni I'd say," was the grunted reply. So many had died here, as they had throughout the Sovereignties, that Raenár did not imagine there could be many who had not gathered at St. Kóráhm's gate. Only those too weak to move, or those tending to those still ailing or who had surviving children to care for.

"We cannot resort to violence, Captain."

"With respect, k'gdhededhá, they will not hesitate to strike us if we get in their way." He did not believe such a scene would have occurred in Elyria. Surely, no Elyri, no matter how hungry, would resort to attacks on innocent people. Teren, in his experience, did not show such restraint.

"They're hungry and desperate. Not criminals." The blonde ducked out of the way of something hurled in his direction. Whatever it was clattered against the wall behind him and disappeared over the edge into the courtyard. "Look at it in a positive light. If they are strong enough, healthy enough, for protests, it means they are recovering. For the survival of Alberni, that is a good thing."

"You want them rampaging your halls, ruining books, everything Lord Cliáth built? Believe me, they won't care what they destroy."

"It would be a shame, yes…but the library and scriptorium are well-guarded. The rest," he shrugged, "it is only material goods that can be replaced. These people, few as they are, cannot be, at least not so easily. Alberni, Enesfel, will need them far more than we will need what we have here."

Raenár snorted again, conceding the point without saying so. Below, some of the rioters had given up, collapsing to conserve what strength they possessed for survival. The futility of their actions would gradually encourage others to relinquish their efforts, but as one of his men screamed in frustration, hit on his helmeted head by something thrown through the grated gate, the captain wondered how many, inside and out, would suffer before the unrest ended.

❧*❧

The bone horns blatted the announcement from every parapet on the wall of the royal castle in Glevum, the sound reverberating through the streets, taken up by the bells on the dock watchtowers and shouted to the winds so that it carried to the edges of the city and into the farmland beyond. Within a matter of days, most of Neth would know that the queen-regent's claim had been true.

King Oska had left a son to rule Neth.

Inness stared at the writhing, squalling mass of pink and gold that clawed its way out of her body like a cat trapped in a sack, resisting her first impulse to smash the screeching thing against the floor and be done with it. Such an act would never be seen as an accident and there were too many reasons for the child to live. She was accepted as queen-regent on the grounds of carrying the true de Corrmick heir. She had yet to gain the trust and respect of the men who advised her, however. Until she proved her value to them, to Neth, proved her strength and determination, they would never accept her as ruler without the child to support her claim.

❧540❧

She needed this demanding infant as much as he needed her, but she could not say, as the midwives bathed him by the warmth of the hearth, that she felt any affection towards him.

Only the fact that he was the last remaining piece of Oska that she would ever have, made her feel anything positive.

When she took him in her arms and gazed at the tiny face whose pale blue eyes slanted just as Oska's had, the corner of his mouth twisted up to the left the way Oska's had when he was happy or sleepy, Inness felt something she did not expect.

She quickly clamped down on those emotions in refusal to be ruled by them. Prince Henrik Oska de Corrmick was a means to an end. Nothing more. That was all he would ever be to her.

❧542❧

## ❧Chapter 34❦

He saw little of Raebhá during the days that followed as her waking hours were spent sequestered with the remaining márbhyndhánis, the conclave engaged in a verbal struggle of philosophy and logic that would determine not only her future but the future of the ghísaer and potentially the future of the dhóbhaen. The community was abuzz with the possibilities, with speculation and rumor but the few who had knowledge of the behind-closed-door deliberations were careful not to divulge the actual contents of the discussion. What little Kavan knew he was forbidden to share.

Though he had promised to see her safely home, Kavan did not yet consider her safe. He would not be satisfied until he knew that she and the márbhyndhánis had come to agreeable terms. Nor would he be satisfied until he knew what Ombhrís' fate would be, knew that the man would pose no further threat to Raebhá and their child.

He desired to be present, to lend his wisdom, knowledge, and experience to matters with which he felt intimately familiar, albeit from a reverse angle. He considered assuming some other form, some small, unnoticeable creature that could hide within the room and listen. But this was not his battle and he could not risk discovery if anyone of the márbhyndhánis should detect him. Though the outcome would also affect him, determine his future with Raebhá and the child growing stronger every day, he was excluded from the discussions unless she or one of the márbhyndhánis invited him.

Only in the lengthening evenings, when Curnydhá gathered to dine, could he sit by Raebhá's side, share her smile, and offer his hosts the only payment for food and lodging he had to give. Song. Vocal or instrumental, often both. They welcomed him, drinking in the chiming strings and his soaring voice, always seeking more, sharing songs and stories in return so that he might learn their epics and traditions and carry them with him when he left. Kavan had not spoken of leaving, but the dhóbhaen almost unanimously assumed he soon would.

As Raebhá had indicated, the negativity towards the child she carried gradually lessened. Ombhrís' betrayal of her, of all of Curnydhá and Gálínphel, combined with Kavan's steadfastness and obvious loyalty, soothed whatever misgivings the gossips had. Little by little, Kavan grew to believe that his child's future would not be like his own. This child would be safe, included, welcomed, and loved.

After each evening's meal, in the too-brief time before sleep, after Raebhá bid Ephé goodnight and Audh and Iólán heartily thanked Kavan for music and camaraderie, they retreated together to her home. He held her without words, nothing more than the intimate clinging of arms as she shared the day's proceedings, the progress or lack of it. He wrote of the events, of the stories he was told and the things he learned, saw, and did, sharing feather kisses across thirsty skin. There was ever the knowledge through that touch that this was a moment in time that, soon enough, they would lose.

Eventually, she would climb the loft to sleep, the fullness of her pregnancy slowing her movements but not deterring them. She was still caught in the bonds of marriage that Ombhrís, even in captivity and defeat, refused to sever when the márbhyndhánis interrogated him each day. dhóbhaen custom was clear: whether Ombhrís agreed or not, if Raebhá did not change her mind within two moons and he failed to provide a compelling reason why the marriage should be maintained, the petition would be granted, the union considered void. Raebhá had no intention of changing her mind. He had betrayed her. Sought her death. There was no reason to accept him back. Any treaty their union had generated could be maintained without their marriage remaining intact. With no reason Ombhrís could offer to stay the dissolution, he delayed consent only to confound and hurt her for foiling his plans.

Until the required days passed there would be no sharing of a bed, no public voicing of their relationship and so there was only this. Kavan treasured every breath of passing time, even when watching her sleep from his loft bed on the opposite side of the home.

His days were not spent idle, as there was much to learn, to know, to experience in the land of his ancestors. Kóráhm did not return, but

Kavan did not lack company. Local artisans studied his harp beneath his watchful eye, seeking to learn craft secrets that were lost when the last Cliáthan harp maker was banished. He wandered Curnydhá's streets, the fields, the forests, the shoreline, studying everything from farming practices to fishing, to the crafting of boats and houses, clothing and food. He helped where he could, to gain the experience of doing rather than simply watching, and his willingness to serve rather than be served endeared him to many.

He recorded everything in journals Raebhá provided. He could feel it every morning when he awoke, every evening when he tried to sleep, the drag that reminded him that it was only a matter of time before he left this place. All of these details, no matter how small, needed to be remembered, recorded, compared to what the Elyri had become, taught to the few at home that Kavan believed safe enough to share with. Architecture, plant life, animals. Terrain, climate, the nature of the sea and soil. Nothing was irrelevant when it might unlock the mysteries of culture and Faith in the evolution of their peoples.

Welcomed by both Éthym and Audh into the dhó dónáré, given novices to assist him, Kavan had access to volumes of history and law and legend that he would never have time enough to read. Not as many books as he had collected in St. Kóráhm's, barely more than Kavan had in his home. It was a time-consuming effort to sift through them as he had yet to master the variances in alphabet and language. Reading required puzzling the meanings of words not easily translated into the forms he knew. Steadily he began to trace the evolution from this language form into High Elyri and then into the standard form used by Elyri at present, but his efforts did not progress fast enough to allow him to read to his heart's content.

It did not allow him the answers to questions the dhóbhaen were reluctant to discuss. If any had gone to the Sovereignties before the Great Banishment, there was no one willing to speak of them, no written records he was permitted to see.

He found it easier to spend time in discussion with the novices, asking questions, listening to their telling of the things contained within loose-bound tomes, always listening. He spoke little of Elyriá, of what had become of the people long banished from Dhóbhaen's shores, people given up for dead and lost by those left behind. The history books he had brought for Raebhá were left with her, as he trusted her discretion and judgment about when her people would be ready to know such things. Explaining that the survivors had found their way to a northern land where they formed a united kingdom under the direction of one woman was enough. Most dhóbhaen were loath to learn the full truth. Revealing more would open a debate of power and Faith that the dhóbhaen were not ready to hear.

In time, if Raebhá's efforts were successful, these people might be receptive, might even welcome hearing of those differences. But not while the topic of Dhágdhuán was forbidden in all but academic circles and the issue of natural power was the core topic of debate behind the walls of the central chamber of the dhó dónáré.

Power was another thing Kavan kept hidden, limiting public displays to the use of handlights, that everyone over the age of five or six used to light fires and lanterns and as a greeting when they passed one another throughout the day. Frequently Kavan would encounter people gathered in discussion and, night or day, they would have their palms upturned before them with the glow of warm flame dancing there. Either a gesture of friendship or else a subconscious or intentional means of releasing stored power.

As he had caught himself many times over the years with a glow in his palm when coming out of periods of deep thought, perhaps he was not the only person to need or discover such an outlet.

If not for the generations of conditioning that told them training was forbidden to all but a few, the dhóbhaen might be more open to receiving training in the uses of power than either they, or the márbhyndhánis, believed. But there were still some who believed Ombhrís was justified in his claim of leadership, who clung to the traditions that allowed only márbhyndhánis to use the dáni, who felt that Raebhá's banishment was justified if she had received illegal training and held heretical beliefs. Some believed that, if guilty, she should have the chance to recant, to accept Reconditioning. Regardless of her choices, her abduction and the subsequent subversive actions taken by Ombhrís and some of the márbhyndhánis made them more unfit for leadership, in the eyes of the people of Curnydhá, than Raebhá. Others, with hushed voices and thoughts of rumbling discontent, believed that she, as kymyhé, should have the same rights as the márbhyndhánis, to be trained as they were, to protect the people of Curnydhá from such abuses of leadership.

Whatever the outcome of her efforts, the cracks in the foundation of dhóbhaen culture were already there, had been there long enough before her abduction to have allowed such a thing to happen. The cracks deepened each day, with every private discussion and debate in the fields, on the docks, around the communal cookfires as they dined each night. Short of another mass banishment, the controversy surrounding the violent, unlawful actions of Ombhrís and the márbhyndhánis, and their treatment of the kymyhé would produce ripples throughout every corner of the island.

Kavan's impulsive, untempered display that first day had frightened many, but gradually, as people accepted that his sole intention was the protection of their kymyhé, their curiosity began to overcome their wariness. Bolstered by the sense of him heard in his music, mitigated by the expectation of myth, people began to approach, speak in a friendly, welcoming fashion, willing to answer his myriad of questions about custom and rule and practice throughout every aspect of their lives. Wishing he had his cousin's gift for painting so that others could see the things he saw, he committed as much detail to memory as he could for the day he could share it.

If he was lucky, Ártur could paint these views for him.

The jagged mountains, taller and sharper than the Llaethlágárá, formed the spine of the land, perpetually covered with snow and ice, with few passable footpaths. The mountains had necessitated the development of their seafaring ways and the plethora of rivers that flowed from those heights to lakes and the sea had called for wide, light boats capable of moving between shallow and deep water with ease. The shortness of the growing season and relatively limited land on which to farm required hearty crops with short gestation periods as well as means for curing and preserving produce, sea harvests and the products gained from hunting and domesticated herds. Clothing was limited to furs and skins of the creatures around them and fabrics spun of the fibrous, multipurpose plants grown further south.

The dhóbhaen could afford to waste little, and what portions of animals and plants they did not use themselves went to feeding the flocks they raised and fertilizing their fields. With the Sovereignties enduring years of little surplus and lean times, Kavan collected small jars of spices and seeds that he hoped he could put to use, along with the agricultural practices he learned here, to shorten the length of time the hungry would be forced to suffer as they awaited each harvest.

Frequent thoughts of home, comparisons between old customs and new, lost knowledge and gained, filled him with longing for faces not seen in many months. He should have only been gone a few weeks at most. He had never intended months. But going back meant facing an emptier home, the losses of nearly a year past and those that had come during his absence. He wanted his cousin. He wanted his sons. He wanted his friends, his kin, and those his heart called children even though they were not related by blood or adoption. He wanted Wrotham. He wanted to share everything he had learned.

But he did not want to leave Raebhá and the child not yet born. The thought of it broke his heart.

He wanted to fly. Like those he watched form handlights to expend energy, his power had been too long contained with very few outlets available. So many times he considered journeying into the forest where he would not be seen, to make the change, to soar over the peaks and treetops in search of knowledge, in search of the Gate he believed to be there, in search of himself. He considered stepping out beneath the cover of night and doing the same thing. Still unconvinced of Raebhá's safety, wanting to remain near in case of danger or in case he was summoned before the conclave, he dared not risk traveling beyond Curnydhá's borders. With the day of giving birth growing nearer as well, it kept him within running distance of her side.

Flight, and the Gate, would have to wait.

On this day, an unsettled feeling roused him from a restless sleep, the sense of impending chaos heavy on his shoulders so that when he left the house to walk barefoot along the black-sand shore, leaving Raebhá curled on her side in deep slumber, his footsteps were ponderous and slow. As he could neither recall dreams nor any lingering trace of Sight, he could only attribute the mood to the belching plume of ash and steam that had burped from a distant peak west of Gálínphel early the previous evening and the periodic tremors that had rolled beneath his feet before and since. The mountain itself was not visible from the ghís, only the curl and spiral of gray that had followed the quakes, turning the sky gray and covering the streets and homes with a dusting of gray powder, like fine hearth ash.

The dhóbhaen, except for the very young, seem little troubled by the shaking or the plume that spread across the sky, as if it was a familiar experience. They warily watched the horizon to the west as they swept the ash from their roofs and steps, but their concern did not seem dire. The ash was collected in a variety of containers for later use, to be mixed with water, for the creation of ceramics, building stones, or to spread to smooth cracks in the compacted streets.

Kavan had heard of mountains that breathed smoke, fire, and steam. They were said to exist on the distant side of the Cíbhóló desert and in the sea islands west of Cordash. Some said the range on Hatu's southern edge likewise contained fire mountains. He had never witnessed such an event, had never met anyone who had, and though he wanted to go west, fly until he found the peak responsible for the gray ash, he focused his attention on helping the villagers instead.

The physical act of helping them had not soothed him. His nerves remained jangled so that he had not slept well since that shaking began. Nor had an evening of prayer settled him. The night had been marred by persistent occasional shaking, making it reasonable to attribute his disconcerted state to the unfamiliar acts of nature.

The sea was glassy, the level gradually retreating as the tide moved out, taking moored boats further to sea at the end of their tethers. With the warmth of the season, many of the boats were absent, their owners away fishing, trading, visiting neighboring ghís for whatever personal or business matters they needed to attend. Audh's ship, too, had sailed away, though without its master at the prow. Kavan wondered who had sailed it, where it had gone.

The sea birds today had yet to stir as the sun peeped over the eastern horizon, coloring the sky and water with shades of gold and pink. The world was wrapped in the gentle rhythmic hum of the surf and soft breeze, and with his head thrown back, his eyes closed to meditate on the expulsion and re-gathering of power that was barely enough to appease his need to use it, he felt gradually more relaxed and at ease with himself. There was no need to fret.

The world was at peace.

Until abruptly it was not.

A tremor, a trickle of disturbance in the air, or perhaps the tense bleating of sheep and goats and the nickering of ponies, drew Kavan out of his thoughts. It was the barking and whining of dogs and a sharp cry that resounded in his ears and soul, that snapped him to focused awareness. Every muscle, from shoulder to groin, drew tight, a contracting sensation he had experienced before, long ago on the night of cleansing. The night Dhóri and his sister had been born. Barely able to remain upright, only desperation and the need to reach Raebhá enabled him to turn and take a single step back up the black sand beach. The ground beneath him bucked sharply enough to throw him to his hands and knees, an undulation and shaking that rocked the air and reverberated into his lungs different than what he had felt before.

Other screams joined Raebhá, sounds of surprise and fright as people were jolted awake and attempted to scramble from their homes. Walls of stone and wood cracked and crumbled as timbers split and the mortar between stones gave way to the force. Kavan's efforts to rise were thwarted as the unstable beach shifted and robbed him of balance. He saw Iólán rush into his sister's home. Driven by the panic that she would be trapped, crushed beneath the rubble as was happening elsewhere around the ghís, Kavan finally found the strength and balance to remain upright as Iólán emerged with her at his side.

She met Kavan's gaze. She screamed his name.

He began to speak, to reassure her that he was coming, but a strong sucking and pulling behind him tugged at the edges of his perceptions, the corners of his power, drawing sound from his ears and air from his lungs. He turned, wobbling on the still-moving ground, to witness the water's alarming rate of retreat, the way it exposed the seabed and left some of the boats stranded on the abandoned earth.

Some of those inland, Raebhá included, understood what the sea's retreat meant. Shouts erupted anew, warnings to seek high ground or searching calls for loved ones. With so many trapped, others refused to heed the instruction for flight, opting instead for frantic digging through collapsed homes to free those buried there. Kavan had never seen the sea behave this way and could not tear himself from the perplexing sight to either flee or attempt to help others.

Iólán would see to Raebhá. Kavan was confident of that.

When the surf seemed unable to pull away any further, it piled onto itself on the horizon, overtaken by the movement of deeper water beneath it. As it grew into a wall that rebounded back towards the coast, Kavan understood. He had read about great waves destroying coastal cities but as it was a threat of little consequence in Rhidam and no threat at all in Elyria, he had made no study of the causes, the origins, the effects of such waves. That such a threat might exist for Alberni, at least the low lying southern portion where the streets sloped to meet the sea, had never entered his thoughts. Nor had he considered such a threat existing for every dhóbhaen population center on the entire island. At the speed with which the wall of water bore down on the coastline, only a few villagers, those retreating into the forest, scrambling up to hillock structures that might provide enough height to protect them, or pushing into the dhó dónáré where they could seek refuge on the second-floor balcony that wrapped entirely around the building, might reach ground high enough to be safe. Those trapped in collapsed homes or trying to help them would surely drown.

The flocks and herds, the crops, the stores gathered for winter, would be lost.

No matter what Iólán did, Raebhá, the child that had chosen this inopportune moment to come into the world, and everyone around them, faced certain death…particularly Kavan who stood on the shore nearest the disaster, confronting the threat alone.

Kavan gave no thought to the possibility of failure or success or even whether such an act had ever been attempted. He threw his arms out, spread wide as if casting a net, hands facing the encroaching watery wall, sucking as much energy from the surrounding atmosphere as he could hold, stretching the limits of his senses as far from himself, from the black sandy shore, as he could reach.

He had created bubbles of power before, shields against fire, falling stone, projectile weapons. He had protected small groups of people and contained explosions. There had never been a need to attempt a feat of such a massive scale as to protect an entire village. But with Raebhá and the child foremost in his thoughts, instinct drove him to undertake what might be impossible.

The force of the water crashed against the invisible shield, washing up towards the sky and to the left and right, meeting the resistance that forbade it from swallowing Curnydhá. The weight of each wave was heavy against his wall, forcing Kavan to dig his heels into the black earth and lean forward as if to push back, adding more force into his efforts to maintain the shield. He could not think about anyone living elsewhere along the coast, could not consider how far north and south the wave might extend. He could think of nothing except maintaining the flow of power. Pressure inside of his head and chest ebbed and expanded with the pulses of the sea, resonating into every nerve, drowning out everything but the hum of energy as he fought to sustain the only thing protecting Curnydhá from destruction.

His strength waned. The water continued to rush and retreat, the clash of power sources and the vastness of his reach challenging him in a way he rarely encountered, dictating a clawing scramble for any assessable source he could tap into. Back through the bonds that held him to the Five Sovereignties, to those tied most securely to him. Ártur. Dhóri. Sóbhán. Níkóá. Bhen. And at the farthest reaches of his grasp, bhydáni Tíbhyan. Another fell too, knees buckling as Kavan had done many minutes ago, his hands pulling his black hair free of its tie in the few moments he could endure the sensation. One by one, each fell into blissful unconsciousness, dropping where they stood, mid-action, mid-word, leaving those near them horrified and helpless.

Time passed, Kavan unable to mark the path of the sun or note the march of minutes to hours. He did not know that some who had been running in fear had stopped to watch as the angry sea did his bidding, tamed by the reach of hands and power, a sight never witnessed in all of Dhóbhaen's recorded or spoken history. Those not intent on rescuing the buried and dead, and even some of those who were, were the living witnesses when Kavan dropped onto his knees and one hand, the other still stretched forth as if it was the only thing keeping the water at bay. None knew if the gesture was necessary, and those who feared his failure began again to scramble towards high ground. Others, still rooted in place, saw a copper-haired figure in gray robes the color of the churning froth appear out of the air to kneel at the bard's side, hands on his shoulders as if he would help Kavan to rise.

The touch, familiar and welcome, suggested another path, one that spilled song into the void between Kavan and the sea. Louder it grew, a song without words, only tones of desperation and praise, a suppliant song that, to his memory, he had not uttered since his last moments alone in his private oratory. His heart had failed his faith, his head had been filled with too much else, and without returning to the faith that lived in the center of his soul, he suspected he would fail. He could feel it in the buckling of his shield wall, the diminishing of his power.

Kóráhm's presence helped, bolstering his resolve, but it would not be enough to save himself or anyone else. Only faith could do that. Faith…and a miracle.

The burn of power shot through his body, out through his hand, a discharge he recognized and understood though one he had not felt in a long time. Pain stabbed through Kavan's wrists and ankles, familiar and unwanted, but as unavoidable as the static crackle in the air, like a lightning strike without the flashing fingers of light that brought a dozen or more others to him, black-winged shapes that he did not need to see to know they were there. He faintly heard cries of disbelief, the eruption of fear and marvel, but he shut out the sounds, the emotions, to keep them from undermining his efforts with a lifetime worth of self-doubt. The shimmering shapes remained as he sang, a swaying, translucent sea of záryph whose movement fed the intake and outpouring of energy, remaining until he no longer felt anything pushing against the invisible shield.

Little by little, he drew the shield towards himself. One distant donor of power was released at a time, only then with the realization of the suffering he had caused those he loved. He regretted that pain but not its outcome and he would, he promised each one silently, make amends when he could.

By the time his shield was nothing more than a shell against his skin, the tide lapped at his knees and the hand used to brace himself, the water frothy in its upset but no longer a threat to the ghís or those living there. The heat of the sun beat upon his back, indicating it was late in the afternoon, revealing how long he had spent at battle with the sea. He could not hear Raebhá any longer, only the waves and the blood pounding in his head. His vision was clouded and red from exertion. But he was alive and had not collapsed into unconscious exhaustion as he typically would have after such an effort.

Another spasm reminded him of the importance of this day.

He had to reach her. He had to take away her pain. But he could not rise, did not have the strength to move, and Kóráhm and the záryph were no longer at his sides. He was alone.


Hour after hour, in the shortening gaps between contractions, Raebhá watched, from the steps of her home as Kavan battled the sea, holding it back as if he was holding a door closed against a tumultuous wind. She watched the water rise as if it would overtake him and wash behind through the streets of Curnydhá. But it did not, Kavan's efforts stretching ever higher as the water tried to get past. She felt the tap into her strength, the sucking of power that made each contraction more searing than the last. If he could do this for her, for Curnydhá, if he could risk such a sacrifice to keep everyone alive, then she was determined to allow him as much of her strength as he needed. If he failed, the destruction of Curnydhá might be the death of them all.

If Kavan died, what would she do? He had promised to be with her when the child came, if he could. In a battle with the sea, however, it was a promise he might not be able to keep. If he died, how many others, herself included might also? The hillock was high, might provide refuge to the multitude gathered on it, but she could not guarantee that it was high enough to repel the devouring sea.

When it came, the moment she felt the imminent collapse of his efforts, while the sea still had the power to drag the pale form out with it, they appeared. ágdhghymaemis, gdhárith, a great host of winged shapes similar to those she had seen on the tapestry of Saint Kóráhm in Kavan's oratory. Dhóri had spoken of them, how it was said they appeared to his father in times of need. Raebhá had never asked Kavan about them, had never thought she would see such a vision.

It was not only her. All of Curnydhá saw them. Them and the auburn-haired man at his side she identified without seeing his face.

Kóráhm di Curnydhá had come home.

The wonder, the power shift, eased the next dozen or so contractions. When it faded, when Kavan collapsed, alone on the black shore before the calming sea, she felt a burst of fear, of emptiness. She felt certain he was dying, that he had spent everything to keep her and the child safe. Clutching her brother's hand with a wail, she squeezed her eyes shut as contractions returned stronger, closer, than ever.

From the cluster of márbhyndhánis, novices, and others who had sought refuge on the balcony of the damaged dhó dónáré, Audh pushed through, running down the hillock towards the motionless man at the sea's edge. He was no more certain of what he had witnessed this day than anyone else, but it did not prevent his approach. A feat of power, yes. Everyone in Curnydhá would have felt that great pull of energy from the world, even the youngest untrained children. Few would understand it; most would be afraid. It was a skill, or an extension of one, that Audh and the other márbhyndhánis had never witnessed or thought possible. He was not the only one stunned by the magnitude of what the White Bard had done.

If one man could accomplish such a thing, how much more could a community banded together accomplish if they too were trained?

Audh also knew, as he reached Kavan's side, wrapped his arms around his torso, and pulled him limply to his feet, that many had seen those who had stood with Kavan on that beach. Not men arrived through a Gate, not taeré or anyone from Curnydhá or neighboring ghís, but forms from the air, not born of Kavan's gifts but something external. So external that the dhóbhaen had no words to name them.

There was blood from Kavan's ears, his nose, the corners of his mouth and eyes. There was blood at the man's wrists and ankles, blood staining the sand in multi-colored swirls like oil that refused to mix into the water and wash away. Blood from jagged punctures through one side of each wrist, each ankle, and out the other. The implications of the occurrence were enough for Audh to nearly drop him in stumbling shock, but by now Kavan had snaked his arms around Audh's neck and would have slumped against his side, making them both falter if Audh's grip failed.

The wail from the hillock punctured the midday silence.

Kavan tried to stand alone but failed.

"Raebhá…"

Audh blinked, tearing his gaze from the crimson evidence the sea was drinking from the sand, and looked into Kavan's red-sheened eyes. Amazed that Kavan could speak, let alone move one foot in front of the other to stumble, with aid, onto drier, more solid ground, he murmured, "I'll take you to her. Easy, kydhé; save your strength."

So much blood loss would undoubtedly require a healer, but that was not his priority. Kavan had saved their ghís. Taking him where he wanted to be was the best Audh could offer in return. He hoped the bleeding would stop before anyone else saw it, but with each step, with each set of eyes that traced their path up the hillock to the steps of Raebhá's home where she and Iólán gathered with Ephé, her son and husband, and a host of other townsfolk, there was little doubt that others were aware of the preternatural bleeding.

With the trail Kavan's bare feet left and the stain of it that soaked into Audh's robes, it was impossible not to notice.

Unable to see through the crimson film over his eyes, not knowing there was blood there, or elsewhere, Kavan accepted Audh's aid, trusting he was being taken to Raebhá and not to his death. If anyone wished to kill him out of fear or prejudice, he was powerless to stop them. But he trusted this man, whom he recognized by voice, and would have thanked him if he could will his throat to produce words.

The metallic taste in his mouth suggested blood; he must have bitten his tongue. He heard no voices, no sounds except the echoes of Raebhá's cry, none of the reactions of those they passed or the rush of villagers continuing the rescue of those trapped beneath fallen debris. The movement of air as they rushed by reminded him that he should help them, but unable to stand, unable to see, he could do nothing but focus on his contracting muscles and the woman bearing his child.

Raebhá needed him more than anyone else. Kavan had given as much to Curnydhá as he could. The rest was for Raebhá.

Iólán had spread his cloak on the uneven, uncomfortable steps, and it was there Raebhá sat, back against the step above her, knees drawn to her shoulders, legs spread wide beneath the pale yellow of her sleeping gown, her hands gripping her knees hard enough to turn her knuckles white. With her child in someone else's care, Ephé sat behind her, mopping her friend's forehead and offering the soothing words that only a woman who had endured this before could offer.

There was relief when Raebhá saw Audh staggering towards her with Kavan, relief that quickly turned to distress at the sight of so much blood. She had watched him between contractions, the water diverted, the others who had stood with him, watched him collapse when the need for strength was no longer required.

As awe-inspiring as the spectacle had been, as exhausting as she knew it must be for him, she had not imagined there would be blood.

When Audh laid Kavan at her side, the stairs hardly comfortable but with nowhere else to put him, the bard clutched her hand, lessening her fears. Whatever the source of the blood, he was alive, and he was with her as he had promised he would be.

"Kavan?" She squeezed his hand but he did not respond. Her strained gaze turned to Audh. "Is he…?" she hissed as she pushed through another contraction.

Audh shrugged, wiping Kavan's hair from his face but unable to learn anything from that touch. "I cannot say. I saw the evidence before, but this…" He shrugged again, his head and heart warring with the evidence of his eyes and the decades of indoctrination that argued that none of what he had seen today should be real. He lowered his voice, knowing that others were listening, were watching the pooling of blood that soaked into the planks of the steps. He did not want to speak words that might create unrest. "Surely you saw…?"

Raebhá nodded. It was likely the majority of her ghís had witnessed every remarkable detail.

"du." Iólán's gaze shifted back to the docks and the tipped and upturned boats that, thankfully, did not look demolished by pounding waves. Damaged, perhaps, but hopefully salvageable. He was glad his boat had been used for trade elsewhere on the island. Perhaps it had been spared destruction.

His sister's rough cry brought his focus back to her contorted face. This was wrong. Her pains had come on too suddenly, too sharply, and he feared that, after so many hours of terror and effort, and that peculiar, frightening depletion of dáni in the air, she would lose the child and possibly her life if the birthing lasted much longer.

It was too soon. According to the healers, the child was not due for at least three and a half weeks.

Kavan thought so too. He curled against her, the twist of his otherwise numb, slack features nearly identical in ache and tension to hers. Though not a healer, he could absorb others' pain, and even if it increased his own, he wanted to ease her suffering. If the mother suffered too much, the child could as well. He did not open his eyes, knowing he would not see her through the blood haze, but focused on power and pain, the rhythm of breathing, the distant pulse of a tiny heart enduring the strain of birth.

Raebhá's cries abruptly lessened. Unnerved by her silence, Iólán stared at her hand clutched in Kavan's. He appeared to be devouring, her pain through that contact, judging by the contortions on his face. He glanced at Audh as if asking what more the man could do, how this was possible. The corners of the márbhyndhánis' mouth and eyes twitched, mirroring Iólán's unspoken questions. He had no answers.

Kavan was, without a doubt, the foretold White Bard. There was no other explanation. He had saved them from ruin. How could anyone not see the truth? How could anyone argue with the providence of prophecy?

"Stay with her. I must see to the others."

Audh got to his feet, resisting the impulse to kiss Kavan's hand or wipe the blood from his skin. There were better, less awkward duties to tend to, and with Raebhá incapacitated, it fell to the márbhyndhánis to lead the people through this crisis. The other márbhyndhánis and novices were inspecting the dhó dónáré, seeing to the center of healing, learning, and culture and the injuries of their own. Watching them, Audh scowled. Was it true? Had the márbhyndhánis grown so far removed from the people that they no longer understood the public's needs? Had they come to put themselves first? Had they, as an institution which had always been, grown insular and obsolete?

"taeasnete ágk tódhedácte," he called to those within earshot. "Let us help those we can. The danger is passed; we stand as one. Revive the living, see to the dead, rebuild Curnydhá together."

Tearing their stares from the bard to listen, the heads of the dhóbhaen bobbed in agreement. Regardless of how they viewed the márbhyndhánis, the kymyhé, the stranger, most followed Audh along the cracked paths through the ghís, a few breaking off to collect livestock that had gone astray or help the injured and trapped as they passed. The tremors would continue for many days; it was nature's way. More walls might fall, perhaps more people would die, but those who were able would save those they could and the animals with them. No act of nature would prevent their perseverance and survival after the miracle that had saved them from the sea.

Ephé kissed Raebhá's head. "Endure…be strong. You are safe. I will return as quickly as I can," before reluctantly retreating to care for her child while her husband aided those trapped and in need.

Kavan, Raebhá and Iólán were left alone.

Breathless with the passing of another contraction, Raebhá pried her fingers from Kavan's to touch the bleeding wounds on his wrist. He groaned, shook when her fingers moved over the rupture that should not be there, a reaction of shame not of pain, but he appeared to be unconscious. There was so much blood on his skin, his clothes, his face and with no available phemárógdh to close them, the best Iólán could do was attempt to bind them with strips of fabric torn from his sister's sleeping gown. Nothing they had witnessed warranted such injuries, nothing natural could have produced such deep wounds.

Her breath caught. She remembered what Audh had said, what he had seen. The tale that seemed too impossible to be true.

"róagdháthé…daisdhágdhá…""

"ágdhdáni," Iólán nodded, his mouth set in a frown of worry that was as much for her and Curnydhá as it was for Kavan.

It was a detail that Audh had shared with only a few, the imagery in Sight that had led him to his near encounter with the White Bard so many years ago. Only Raebhá and Iólán and their father had known. It was a claim too perilous for public sharing, for the róagdháthé was a link to Dhágdhuán and everything the ancient dhóbhaen had fought to eradicate…by killing one man and banishing every other who embraced his teachings. Appearances of similar marks, born with humility and reverence by the afflicted, were said to have revealed a handful of believers who had otherwise managed to hide their heresy. The márbhyndhánis had named such occurrences as the róagdháthé, the blood of the gods, a curse bestowed to condemn heretics. The faithful, however, had believed differently. The márbhyndhánis had rooted out the afflicted until the accounts of the horror had ceased.

No dhóbhaen in hundreds of years had born those marks.

Iólán did not believe it a coincidence that Kavan did.

Only the shallow expansion and contraction of his ribs, the slowing trickle of blood from his wrists and feet, and the facial grimaces that mirrored Raebhá's with each contraction, proved that he lived. His aura felt deflated to her, something Iólán was not trained to detect, depleted of power save for a tiny seed that slowly absorbed energy from her touch, from the world around them, and began to grow. With each contraction, he jerked out of his reverie, his form convulsing, clutching her hand, again pulling her pain into his body, an act that sucked some of that newly gleaned power out of him.

Thinking he would never recover if he continued to protect her from the birthing pains, she tried to free her hand, but he had the strength not to let her go. Though the energy bled away with her pain, she realized that his body was absorbing power as well, the size of that seed expanding faster than it faded.

It often took her hours to regain what little she had learned to utilize. How could one man tame the dáni so?

One hour passed. Two. Kavan did not stir again, did not open his eyes or utter a sound, but on an unconscious level, he remained bound to her, drinking in the quickening contractions when they threatened to overwhelm her. Closer together they came as the sun sank behind Dhóbhaen's mountain spine, until Kavan was curled into a tight ball, his mind and consciousness trapped within itself, his breath held with each contraction as he swallowed the worst of her pain.

Then the moment came, two voices echoing in one protracted cry.

All fell still, with only the singing of sea birds, the sounds of the ocean, and the distant rescue efforts undercutting the silence. Something warm, wet, and strange smelling was placed between him and Raebhá, touching them both. Unable to open his eyes, and losing the battle of consciousness, He thought he heard her voice against the top of his head, or perhaps inside of it, a voice without words.

He tried to smile, or thought he did. But the words, the effort it took to think and form them, were sucked into the oblivion of slumber.

The earth opened above him. Cool air and a shower of soil shook loose from the roots and stone that formed the walls of his prison, nearly burying him with their collapse. When the shaking stopped, the gap left permitted the first glimpse of unfiltered sunlight he had seen in weeks. The door remained bolted, sealed from the outside with metal and power, but this fissure was the chance he needed.

He wiggled. He heaved, his fingers dug into loose earth-breaking nails and gouging flesh as he tore. In the end, the effort paid off; he emerged onto the hillside, breathless and filthy from his rebirth. Free.

There was but one choice if he wished to continue that way.

He left behind the wall of water that should have taken them all, left behind the man holding the sea to his will, left behind the birthing cries of what should have been his child. He scrambled up the mountain into the forest's protective cover. He could survive there. Most dhóbhaen could. Whatever hardship it presented, he could survive it and await the opportunity to return.

What he had witnessed, what awaited Curnydhá, would prove his course honest and true.

Power was a dangerous thing in the wrong hands, a volatile, uncontrollable thing, in anyone's hands but his.

<h1 style="text-align:center">❧Chapter 35❧</h1>

Sóbhán lay the sleepy prince into his bed and stood watch over him. He did not mind that the duties of caring for Lorant fell on his shoulders. Chethá's responsibilities, tending the almost two dozen people in Bhryell stricken by plague, came first. With two of that number being kin, Sóbhán would gladly give more if there was more he could offer. Though the infection rate stayed low, the sick contained to a small cluster of homes, over half of the victims had died, their bodies hastily buried without services because the living wanted to minimize exposure.

One of those victims had been Sámel MacLyr and Sóbhán struggled with the effects of that fresh death as he left the prince and returned to the unlit main floor of Kavan's Bhryell home. To his knowledge, Ártur did not yet know of his brother's death, as there had been no contact with Rhidam in several weeks, no messages left in the náós or Kavan's private oratory for them to find and messages he and Chethá left had not been retrieved. Rather than contemplate the worst, Sóbhán clung to the expectation that, like his wife, the healers in Rhidam were overwhelmed with caring for the sick and dying.

Tám MacLyr fared better, his stubbornness forcing him to outlive the Yellow Sister's efforts to beat him. No amount of obstinacy, however, could spare him or four other victims the blindness which the pestilence left in its wake, blindness that no healers had been able to repair. That the man would never fashion another harp, that he had lost his eldest son, the heir to the Cliáthan harp dynasty, left him bitter and more difficult to be around, but Sóbhán hoped in time that would change. The position of senior craftsmen fell on the shoulders of

Sámel's sons, Bhendhámyn and Aleski, both of whom were amply skilled and trained. With Aleski's eldest daughter Naerá, Ártur's son Llucás, and Sóbhán filling the ranks, the craft would not be lost so long as the Yellow Death robbed the family of no more artisans. The Cliáthan tradition of harp making would continue.

Thankfully the Yellow Sisters had not spread beyond Bhryell, save for a moderate number of cases reported in Clarys where those individuals had been confined in a cluster of a dozen structures, keeping death contained. While the debate over sending food and additional medical supplies to Enesfel, Neth, Hatu, and Cordash sprouted behind closed doors and within every náós across the land, it was not given serious consideration by many. Instead, the whole of Elyriá waited with their collective breaths held as the High Mother faded a little more from life day by day.

Unlike other Elyri, the High Mother could not follow the ancient path of their ancestors, could not walk into the world to disappear from the eyes of her people. The rules of succession demanded proof of her death, and so she, as all of those before her had done, was kept within a secured room under the watchful eyes of her four daughters, ten granddaughters, and fifteen great-granddaughters, there to remain until her last breath was given back to the air. None but the High Mother knew which of those women had been deemed her successor, and as the Elyri High Council had to approve her appointment by majority vote upon her death, there was always the possibility that they could override her choice.

That had never been done. With no scandal in her extended family, there was no doubt the transfer of power would happen smoothly.

It would happen soon. Every Elyri who knew it was coming was filled with a sense of trepidation and sorrow and a touch of uneasy dread. Very few alive were as close in age and most had spent their entire lives under the umbrella of Kyne Mórne's rule.

How could they not fear for the unpaved path ahead?

How could Sóbhán, without a word from Rhidam, not worry for the future of the prince entrusted to him, particularly after the recent episode of horrific pain that had robbed Sóbhán of both power and cognizance and left him with a daylong gap in his memory that no amount of effort was able to fill. Chethá found no cause for it, beyond the sucking away of power into some distant, untraceable vortex. Sóbhán knew that she and others in the family feared for his health.

But it was not plague, and as he learned later, he was not the only one to suffer the event at that same moment. When he learned Bhen and bhydáni Tíbhyan had shared the same experience, that the sage had fallen and broken the brittle bones in his ancient hip, Sóbhán suspected the truth.

There was no proof beyond the bhydáni's agreeing suspicion. Not believing his adoptive father would intentionally harm him or that he would ever cause his beloved mentor such agony, Sóbhán concluded that something bad had happened to Kavan.

Perhaps the bard was dead. Without the depth of power Kavan possessed, Sóbhán could not reach out to him to tell, could not feel a connection over whatever distance stretched between them. Certainty of his death warred with the hope that he was not, leaving Sóbhán on edge in the days following his collapse.

Dhóri would know. If anyone could know their father's fate, it would have to be Dhóri…or Ártur. Both were too far away to be questioned and Sóbhán would not leave Lorant to ask, nor go to Enesfel and risk bringing the Yellow Death once more to Bhryell.

He was cut off from his father and brother and could not bear it.

❧*❧

"How are you this morning?

Rhyrdan sat on the corner of Dhóri's bed, having set the breakfast tray across his lap before opening the shutters to allow the morning sun inside. He prayed that his brother at heart would again see the golden glow of day, but as he examined Dhóri's unresponsive stare, he sighed and settled for sharing spring warmth. Since Dhóri's collapse at dinner days before, the first meal he had attempted to share with his family without being confined to his plague bed, there had been fear of a relapse, or of some danger done by the Yellow Sisters that might cause intermittent seizures for the rest of his life. Yóáná found no evidence of such damage, no other symptoms of illness, only a headache that had lingered after his waking.

She could not say what the cause had been.

If Dhóri knew or suspected, he did not say.

"I'm fine." Though frustrated with the need of learning to do so many simple tasks all over again, of finding ways to feed himself, dress, get around by himself so that he did not look foolish, he felt healthy enough to want to be out of bed.

"Good." Rhyrdan kissed one cheek and then the other. He watched Dhóri fumble with the silver, with feeding himself, but resisted the offer to help. Nothing made Dhóri angrier than an unasked-for offer of aid. Instead, Rhyrdan went to the window again and stared across the fields west of the estate house, where those who could do so were tilling a fallow plot for the first time in over two years. Other fields sprouted green shoots, a crop of much-needed grain blooming in response to the healthy rainfall Alberni had recently enjoyed.

"The fields are green again, the barley has come," he said with giddy excitement. "And the apple trees bear fruit. Captain Magk is doing his best to keep people from picking them before they ripen, but he doesn't have enough men to monitor all of it at once. We'll be lucky if any survive until the harvest. You should see how beautiful…"

He fell silent, aghast at his insensitivity as Dhóri responded with a sound caught between a sigh and a moan.

"I'm sorry…"

"Don't be. I remember." Dhóri sounded sad but he did not appear as disheartened as Rhyrdan thought he would be in the other man's position. "And the plague? The victims?"

"Many are dead; many others are…like you." His gaze traveled towards the south where St. Kóráhm's should be, though all that he could see from Dhóri's room were the orchards and fields of barley. "k'dedhá Kesábhá is seeking a solution…so they will not be burdens on their families or resort to begging. He wants to discuss his ideas with you, but I told him not until you're back on your feet…"

"I told you. I'm well. I don't need to stay here."

"You will until Yóáná gives her approval."

"There's nothing wrong with me. She won't find it. What happened was not the result of plague or illness."

"You don't know…"

Dhóri pouted. "I'm not going to die, not until…he said so."

"Who said? Not until what?" But again Dhóri refused to answer, either out of ignorance of the answers or avoidance of a revelation that might disturb or upset others.

Instead, he focused on his breakfast and did not speak again until he pushed the empty tray as far down his lap as he could, careful not to let the contents tip onto the bed or the floor. "Has there been news from Rhidam? From Sóbhán?"

"Not since Níkóá left. I thought he would return with something, but perhaps he is busy." If the royal family was still ailing, if crops were coming in around the royal city as well, Rhyrdan could imagine the necessary efforts it must take to protect them from the starving population. With the recent arrest of a man believed to be Cedric O'Grady's killer, the aftermath of the Yellow Death and rampant hunger, it was likely the chamberlain had duties to the queen and prince-regent that precluded visits to Alberni.

"He is the chamberlain," Dhóri agreed. The lacking mention of Sóbhán meant no news from Elyriá either, without Rhyrdan saying so. Yóáná had said that Bhryell was under quarantine so perhaps there was no one available to bring word. Perhaps Dhóri had no family remaining except the absent father he longed to see.

"If I'm not allowed to get up, will you ask k'dedhá Kesábhá to come? I'd like to hear his ideas for helping Alberni's less fortunate."

Turning from the window, thinking that what he heard was an admission that Dhóri was one of those less fortunate souls, Rhyrdan frowned. "Are you certain? There is no harm in taking rest…"

"Ask him."

It was the only duty Dhóri could give back to the man he had stubbornly failed with his willful spite. Saint Kóráhm had spared his life for a reason. Dhóri needed to know what that reason was. He needed to find a way to keep living, to be of use to Alberni, his faith, and his father, or else he would, in time, go mad.

❧*❧

From the watchtower, General Declan surveyed the forested region beyond the wall and the breach in it that Neth's raiders had left the previous day, before the arrival of the general and his small contingent of men. He ordered Enesfel's meager troops to divide as evenly as possible across the border fortifications and the villages in between, but he feared, as he pushed the dead he had seen from his mind, that it would not be enough to hold Neth out for long. Chamberlain McCábhá and Chancellor Dahl were seeing to the recruitment of troops, but finding healthy men capable of battle in a land ransacked by dearth and plague was a daunting task.

The general had little hopes of any arriving soon.

King Gamal had pledged to send Hatu's army to Enesfel's aid, as activity along Hatu's southern border, where raiders often tried to push north, had been quiet in recent years. With little need for standing troops, many had been dispersed, but there were always men itching to prove their prowess as their ancestors had done. Defending the land of their king's birth was an acceptable means of attaining honor.

Word had come that those troops had arrived in Levonne via ship, well-provisioned to limit the burden on Enesfel's hungry population, but it would take time for them to march north.

General Declan worried it was time they might not have.

The jarring drone of hammering and sawing, as men cut timbers, gathered stone, and worked to patch the crumbled section of wall, refocused his attention, but it was the sound of a multitude of marching boots stepping in unison that drew his eyes to the fields of budding potatoes, wheat, and other crops to the east. He had never been happier to see fields of growing crops.

He was happier still about the long line of men, in columns of five abreast, marching beneath a banner bearing the rearing Valdis stallion and stag on its crimson and verdant field, bordered by the black and green of the de Corrmick House. Any hint of de Corrmick colors this side of the border worried him, as it did many of the soldiers below the tower, soldiers who scrambled to barricade the road against the approaching force.

The combination of heraldic imagery, however, eased the general's concern. Unless Cordash had united with Neth, there was nothing for Enesfel to fear. The general hurried down the wood plank steps and pushed through his forces to meet the arrivals in person.

"General Declan." The lead rider swung down from his horse, removing his dented helmet and shaking out his damp brown hair. Cut in the current style of the Cordashian court, cropped to the sides, longer on the top and back, normally combed to the rear, right now the man looked disheveled and weary, as if he had ridden in haste for several days. "General Wermant. Queen Rika sends her regards and these men to reclaim her family's honor."

"Queen…?" General Declan returned the ritual bow of greeting, hands flat at his sides as he bent at the waist, and then offered his hand.

"Fear not," Wermant chuckled as he accepted the handshake. "We come with full knowledge and approval of King Govert."

That Cordash's king had not been in good health for some time and had left the land in the care of his adoring, passionate, sometimes indecisive, queen. It was not a detail Wermant felt compelled to discuss. This was a command the General agreed with and he would have volunteered to be here if Queen Rika had not ordered it.

If Neth recovered even a small degree of her former might, if they overpowered Enesfel while she was weak, their vitriolic hate would turn against Cordash. Perhaps Cordash's larger, better-trained military would win a war against Neth, but King Govert and General Wermant did not want to put that day to the test. This was also a matter of honor, for Enesfel had come to Cordash's aid against Neth in the past, and with Rika's family appearing to have fallen victim to assassination and exile, her husband felt it important to help right those wrongs. A queen to appease, a pact to uphold, and the preservation of stability in the Sovereignties offered reason enough for Cordashian troops to march into battle, if that was what these raiding attempts became.

"How many?" Declan could have taken time to count, but the line of men stretched out far behind General Wermant and it seemed easier to ask the question.

"Fifteen hundred." Wermant turned to look across the trail of soldiers. Cordash, with open lands and little forest, were cavalrymen by nature but those with him were primarily on foot. Cavalry in the thick forests of northern Enesfel and southern Neth was a useless thing. "We're shoring up the east, in case Queen Inness," he spat the words, "turns on us. If there are forces to spare, more will be sent."

"Good." It was a sensible precaution and he agreed with Wermant's assessment of the woman who had betrayed her homeland and a new start for Neth in favor of the old de Corrmick way. "The assistance will be welcome. As you can see," he gestured towards the freshly upturned earth, where the dead had been buried, and the fortress wall in need of repair, "we will need them."

Fifteen hundred was a good number, enough, he assumed, to prevent raids from pushing south and turning into something more. The Yellow Sisters were beginning to push through Neth too. He suspected Neth's hands would be tied for the calculable future and hoped it would be enough time for Enesfel to brace.

"Have your men take rest; I would discuss strategy with you to best make use of our combined forces and those due to arrive from Hatu." Though he had not expected so many, Declan already had an idea in mind. All he needed was General Wermant, and the Hatu general's, agreement.

❧*❧

From the window seat of the third-floor southern corner sitting room with her son at her breast, the window where she and Oska used to sit, hand in hand, planning their dreams together, Inness watched the fifteen warships moor at well-spaced intervals across the mouth of the harbor, beyond the reach of any weapons she possessed, blocking the entry or departure of Neth ships. Normally she did not nurse her child more than once or twice a day, preferring to let the wet nurse do so, but the other woman had, it was said, fallen victim to the rising plague and Inness would take no chances with the health of her tiny pawn. Until another healthy wet nurse was found, an increasingly difficult thing as death crept across Glevum, Inness was forced into this intimate contact with another person.

It was contact she despised but provided as a necessary evil.

They were undoubtedly warships. The placement of six others further out to sea suggested an effort to block the approach of ships from the east and west. At one time Neth had possessed a navy, sleek ships designed to protect her shores from Cordash's substantial fleet. But Kjell had brought peace, and with peace came the standing down of much of Neth's ample force. Most of the ships had been converted into merchant and fishing vessels while the rest patrolled for pirates or sat at mooring in Glevum's harbor, awaiting a day when they might be needed again, maintained to substitute those in active service when necessary, but otherwise unused.

Now only four Nethite ships sailed the Derkun Sea, four that would be no match to the fifteen waiting here, and there were few qualified sailors readily available to man the trapped ships if Inness chose to equip them. The foreign ships, sporting flags from Hatu, Káliel, and Enesfel, showed no inclination to attack but they were not intending to move and were equipped, she suspected, to respond swiftly to any assault she ordered on sea or land.

Her border raids were underway as planned, an effort meant to annoy Enesfel rather than draw her into war. Enesfel was in no condition for battle, an ideal time to attack them, but Neth's troops were green, in need of training and experience, things Inness intended the raids to provide.

Now there was the Yellow Death to contend with.

But plague in Enesfel would discourage the support of Hatu and Cordash, particularly while the Cordashian king suffered infirmity.

Oska's meek sister might be fortifying Cordash's eastern border, but such a move was defensive and not a precursor to war.

Praise be that the Yellow Sisters had not yet spread rampantly throughout Neth. In pockets, yes, but she saw to it that the afflicted were killed, the bodies and villages infected were burned, and no merchants from Enesfel had been permitted into Neth since she had been granted the throne. The raiding parties remained at the borders, so that if contact infected them too, their deaths would have little impact on the rest of the kingdom.

Neth, she determined, would remain free of plague. The cases that arose in Glevum were being likewise dealt with. So long as she and her son lived, the rest mattered only for how they might benefit and strengthen Neth once more.

It was a good distance from the tall rooftop on which the lanky man perched, hidden in the shadows by a chimney and the angle of the setting sun. It was near enough, however, that he could make out the shape of the woman in the window, a window he had been told he might find her at if he waited long enough. He had a shot, and with a single-hand crossbow hidden beneath his cloak, he could make that shot if he chose, but this was not the time. His instructions had been to insinuate himself in the de Corrmick court, gather information for his superiors that she was unable to gather on her own. Killing the Nethite queen would be premature.

He had scoped the perimeter of the palace, finding everything to be as he had expected, and made contact with the people in Glevum he had been told could help. They, in turn, had given him another name, Olaric Fraen the Younger, son of the captain. A modest, bright, observant soldier, he had few loyalties…only to the society that had fostered him, to the king who had allowed him to prove that he was everything his grandfather had not been, everything his father was not. He was said to be loyal to the overthrown king, his family, and to the man who had won him his commission despite his father's wishes, General Iden Stone.

The king might be dead, and Olaric the Younger still served in the de Corrmick royal guard, but he was not, if the man on the rooftop's sources were accurate, loyal to the violent new regime. Reaching out to Olaric, or General Stone, was his way inside.

He tugged at the hickory brown hair tied back from his face and shoulders with a strip of brown leather and smoothed his thin mustache as he scowled. His quarry was gone, taking the infant with her, no longer intent, it appeared, on the barricade of ships in Glevum's harbor, or else intending to discuss how to get rid of them with her staff. He had ideas of his own for how to make such a thing happen, but he was not here as a strategist. He did not want those ships to go anywhere. As long as they were there, the woman at the window would be distracted, would feel the need for protection. As long as they were there, he was more likely to get inside.

If he got in, he was going to have to work hard at keeping his mouth shut, keeping his sharp mind hidden, and getting just enough of the queen-regent's notice to allow him freedom of movement within Glevum's walls. Getting inside might not be easy but it would be easier, he suspected, than gaining her trust…or getting out alive.

❧*❦

Every lantern, every torch, every light source no matter how small, was dark on the ancient palatial structure that had been the first building of significance erected in Clarys, older by several thousand years than the náós which grew to be the center of the Faith throughout the Sovereignties. While the Faith had been strong with the early Elyri settlers, they had lived in austerity and humility in those years. The desire to honor she who ruled them, she elected to lead and see the original settlers to the haven beyond the Llaethlágárá had been a powerful, driving force, as had the desire for a landmark that would prove to all generations that after centuries of wandering the world, the Elyri had found a home.

Building such a structure for the matriarchal leadership had led to the desire for something of equal splendor in which to house the patriarchal leaders of the Faith, much to the chagrin of many.

Lamps always glowed in the corridors and those on the building's many exterior facades remained lit at night, casting a haloed glow around the whole of the building. The ever-burning flame in the spire on the south side of the citadel blazed day and night, a beacon for all Clarys to see, as it was the tallest point in the city. On this night, however, it too was dark. The inner brass dome that served both as bell and cover for that eternal flame had rung once before being lowered to cover the flame and snuff out the light, bringing darkness and silence with it. Only one occasion warranted such an act.

Kyne Mórne had forsaken life for eternal unity with k'Ádhá.

Within an hour, every male of her bloodline in Clarys was gathered at the citadel's gates, each barefoot and adorned in white-hooded robes. They cupped their hands before them and began a solemn procession through every street and alley, their way lit by the flicker of handlights in the palms of those old enough, trained enough, to produce them. Sons, grandsons, great-grandsons, led by the Kyne's younger brother, passed single file in silence. City residents came out of their homes as the procession passed, bowing their heads in reverence. Any lights burning in homes or businesses, any hearth or cooking fires, were extinguished as the men walked silently by. Darkness descended over Clarys with the loss of she who had led them longer than any other Kyne in Elyri history.

When the last of the twenty-seven-man precession passed a structure, fires were allowed to stave off the evening chill but all other lights remained dark.

The procession ended at Hes Dhágdhuán, where the men and boys knelt across the altar steps to remain until dawn, led in continual prayer by k'gdhededhá Ylár, the head of the Faith and a man no longer so secretly bound to the royal family although his relationship with one of the Kyne's granddaughters was never publically spoken.

At daybreak, when the funeral procession of the Kyne's female descendants and relatives and her personal guard escorted the woman's body on a similar path through the city streets to the náos, she would be presented at the altar to be publically mourned for three days before being returned, in the same way, to the citadel for burial.

All except for the very young, the very old, or the ill, would fast for those three days as her male kin took the news of her death to every city, every town, every village in Elyriá. Businesses would close, no bells would ring, no music played or sung until the day of interment. Only after her burial, after the ringing of the bells announced that the right of rule had been bestowed on her appointed, and accepted, successor, would the news leave Elyriá, delivered by official couriers to every court in the Sovereignties.

Hwensen bowed his head in mournful respect as he held the door for the solemn procession of men to enter the náos. No one was surprised that this day had come, but every citizen of Elyriá would grieve the loss of their collective mother as if it was the loss of their own flesh and blood. He wondered, as he dried his eyes and closed the heavy double doors, wherever Kavan was, if he knew this too.

Chapter 36

With a ringing buzz like flies in his ears, and the salt and copper taste of blood clinging to his swollen tongue as it stuck to the roof of his mouth, Kavan felt consciousness creeping back, bringing muffled sounds to burrow beneath the hum and a smell, sweet and fresh and clean, to fill his nostrils. His eyes, sticky with sleep, refused to open to the brightness of day; turning his face from the glare put distance between his nose and the calming scent and so he turned again, trying to remember, as he did so, why his body hurt so much. It was the ache of too much exertion and as he began to realize that the ache extended deeper than his muscles, he recognized the exertion of power.

Like the crashing of a wall upon his head, he remembered. The earthquake, the sea's effort to devour Curnydhá and those living in it. The screaming, the panic, the collapse of buildings, and the barricade of power that had kept the towering wave at bay. Thinking on that feat now, he was amazed that he had succeeded, amazed that he had possessed the nerve to attempt such an impossibility. If anyone at home ever learned of this, he knew what they would say.

Miracle.

He shuddered beneath the weight of titles, saint and miracle worker, that he would never escape. There was little doubt he had found a similar repute in Curnydhá, that it would extend across all of Dhóbhaen in time. He groaned, the emotional pain prompting him to suck in a long breath, and again that scent filled his lungs, a scent that suggested that everything would be alright as long as he continued to breathe it. Something soft and wet, a cloth he determined, dabbed over his eyes, a sensation both comforting and uncomfortable at once.

He shivered.

The sound, the effort, created movement of another upon his arm, against his shoulder, beneath his nose. A small sound of annoyance gurgled there and settled again. Eyes no longer stuck closed thanks to the washing, they snapped open as further memories slammed into his knotted stomach. Amazed, he found himself staring at the tiny, round, grimacing face of a fiery-haired infant chewing fiercely on its fist, its eyes squeezed shut too as if it found the daylight uncomfortable. The rest of the infant was tightly bound in soft gray swaddling.

Kavan had seen many infants in his life, several on the days of their birth, but he did not think he had ever seen one so small, with such thick curls…and never one of his own.

Dhóri had been several weeks old before Kavan met him.

The combination of memories stumbling around in his head made the recognition all the more real.

This was his child.

Lips on his forehead. He tore his eyes from the babe's face and looked at Raebhá with relief and adoration, feelings wrapped in soaring love and devotion that when she smiled, kissed his chapped lips, and whispered, "A son, aislé…he is yours…" he thought his heart would swell and burst free of his ribs.

"Ours." More important than having a son was having a child, any child, with this woman who won his heart and soul as he had feared no one could ever do. This almost too small boy was the pinnacle of what she meant to him and bound them together through whatever destiny held.

Limbs stiff, Kavan brought his free arm up so that he could brush his fingers over the child's ruddy cheek. He was born earlier than the usual thirty-six weeks' gestation most Elyri pregnancies lasted, but he did not know if this was normal for the dhóbhaen, if, like their flocks and harvests, gestation and maturity were shortened by the influence of their land's growing season. The boy was light-skinned, but not white like Kavan, and when he peeped out between red lashes it was with one eye of vivid green like his father and the other the warm sand-gold of his mother. It was a hereditary trait in Raebhá's family and thus it did not surprise Kavan to see it. His hair was the same deep red shade as Raebhá's. There was little doubt, Kavan believed, about the boy's parentage.

It was the stinging static discharge when he touched the child's skin, when mismatched eyes tried to focus on his face before closing sleepily, that shocked Kavan most, bringing a tangled, indistinct collection of visuals crowding into Kavan's head with a force that made every muscle tense. The only other times he felt that sensation had been when touching the Lachlan children at their births, the indicator of which one was destined for Enesfel's throne.

What could this mean?

The one thing that he was certain of from that initial contact was the fact that brought a name to his lips. "Ágdhállán," he whispered with a sense of profound reverence.

The spirit sees.

This child had the Sight. Or would have, when he was old enough for Elyri power to manifest. From what Kavan detected, that power was already there. He wondered if the great draw and use of power in the world around him on the day he emerged into it had contributed to that or if it was born of his father's blood in his veins.

"Ágdhállán Kóráhm."

Kavan started to speak but instead nodded his head. Yes. Giving the boy the Saint's name was necessary, not for Kóráhm's sake, perhaps, but certainly for Kavan's. Dhóri bore his name too. How better could he honor the ancestor that had given him so much?

He caressed his fingers over Raebhá's chin, the feel of her skin creating a surge of sensation, emotional and physical, that he no longer feared. "You are well?" He knew the sounds of labor so well, having attended the births of many royal children and kin, knew the agony she had endured, and wondered again why a woman would choose to endure it on behalf of any man.

"Weary…but well. I hurt…but thanks to you, not as much as I might. Fear not for my health, or his." She turned her face to kiss his palm. The relief of having his eyes open, hearing his voice, sapped the nervous energy that had kept her alert and wary so that exhaustion suddenly began to seep into her bones. "I worried when he came too soon, but the phemárógdh assure me he is fit and strong…like his father." She kissed his hand again, smiling through sudden tears. "I thought I would lose you both."

After a few silent moments as he conducted an internal analysis, Kavan nodded. "I…my head…" He could not think of a word to describe the pressure and imbalance in his head, in his core, so he did not try. "Expected after…" After the amount of energy and physical and mental effort exerted to hold the sea at bay. The muscles of his abdomen ached as well, as he imagined hers did from giving birth, but he chose not to lessen her experience by complaining about that ache. A frown tried to root on his face and he struggled to subdue the self-deprecating doubt that clawed at his belly. "How long?"

"Three days. The damage is being assessed, the dead collected. They will be given rites tomorrow evening. Audh made you a bed by the fire so I did not have to climb the loft to…"

He was not surprised that caring for the dead, removing the negative influence of death and the harmful bhur believed to come from them, was the ghís' highest priority. What did surprise him was that they had waited this long. Through his touch on Raebhá's face, he could see the bodies, bound in canvas cloths at the edge of the ghís, guarded against predators but otherwise as far from the living as they could be. He supposed they were seeking others, wanting to be sure to remove the corruption all at once, but the pall of superstition would be heavy over Curnydhá until the corpses were disposed of.

Reading his unspoken question, Raebhá murmured. "Nine so far. One boat was damaged enough that we'll use it as a pyre. I've sent agents up and down the coast, to other ghís, to learn how they fared." The quake and wall of water might have damaged or destroyed other ghís within her ghísaer; she had little doubt others suffered worse than Curnydhá. She needed to know how bad the damage was, to know how many were dead, to know what could be done to help her people.

She did not ask what Kavan had done, how he had done it. Without him, Curnydhá would not have survived to help anyone else. He had protected, saved, those he could. Now it was her turn to protect and serve others. She kissed him again, grateful for what he had done, nuzzled his cheek, and murmured, "On behalf of Curnydhá, thank you." Despite not knowing the fates of other Gálínphel ghís, her words felt woefully inadequate.

He nodded sheepishly. The impulse to say it was nothing, that she owed him no gratitude, was strong, but denying her or the villagers the chance to express their relief would be disrespectful. Accepting gratitude would certainly be easier than accepting the fear he imagined many would express when they saw him next.

Her next words felt more difficult to express. "The márbhyndhánis and I will sequester in debate this evening. I daresay you will again be the center of it."

"I'm sorry."

She chuckled darkly and kissed him a third time. "Don't be. What you have done proves my points better than any words I could speak. It will help, in time, but there is a larger issue we must address before the future of Curnydhá, Gálínphel, and the dhóbhaen is decided."

Her shifting countenance alarmed him. He tried to roll to face her fully but could not do so without waking the child and he was loath to have her take him away. "What has happened?"

Though she tried to keep her shoulders set, there was fear in her posture and doubt in her eyes. Despite her efforts, she knew she could not hide the truth for long. Nor did she want to.

"The shaking split the mountain. Two of the márbhyndhánis have died. Another here fell during the flight from the sea and likewise died." She hesitated, trying to still the twitches at the corners of her mouth and eyes before finishing, "Ombhrís escaped."

Despite his intention to remain still, Kavan jolted upright, his arm curling around Ágdhállán to hold him against his shoulder. His body screamed at the movement and the unsettled stream of ever-present power within undulated and made him dizzy, but the boy did not stir except to open his eyes and try to focus on the face that was just beyond his reach.

"I must find him."

Raebhá grasped his shoulders with both hands, keeping him seated on the cot. His reaction was the one she expected. "You must rest, as must I. The zyrudhén are seeking him."

"They will not find him." It was an irrational belief, but Kavan felt certain of it. Ombhrís had outwitted too many for too long. He was too crafty to be hunted like a wild animal. It would take power to find him, power that none of the zyrudhén had, that none but the márbhyndhánis were trained to use. He doubted the márbhyndhánis were looking for Ombhrís. "As long as he is out there…"

"He would be a fool to return." Dubbed an enemy of the ghísaer, no one would harbor him, offer him food or shelter, if he returned to Curnydhá. Even as she said it, however, she knew she could not rule out his return. He did not seem to be a man to give up easily. "And a fool to attempt to harm…"

"Fool or mad." Kavan patted the child's back as he responded to his parents' agitated emotions with a scowl and strained squawking sound. "Neither of you will be safe until…"

"Kavan." Her voice was lightly scolding beneath its affectionate tone as she took the child and held him to her swollen breast where he suckled greedily. The baby was a welcomed distraction and buffer but he did not derail the conversation. "You are not yet fit to seek him. Sleep. I will wake you when Audh comes. After that, when I return, we can talk again."

Swallowing his pride and annoyance, Kavan grudgingly relented, admitting in that action that he was aware of his physical weakness. The uncentered, unsettled core of power would not allow the best use of the skills needed to find Ombhrís and return him to Curnydhá to see justice done. He was unhappy with the effort to lay down but he was relieved when the room stopped spinning.

"I've had enough sleep," he muttered, grateful he did not have to face climbing to the loft bed, "but I will rest as you ask…if you will be careful." There was a threat there still, stronger than before, beyond the edges of his perceptions, to her, to himself, to the child she held.

"I will be," she swore. There was too much to live for, Kavan, their son, her ghís, to take risks.

He nodded, presuming she would take the baby when she left, and sank into meditation. He would find his center and be strong again. He would find Ombhrís and keep his family safe. Whatever the cost.

❧*❧

Inness cautiously circled the newcomer, assessing what she saw and comparing it to what General Stone had told her. Stone had been a loyal supporter of King Kjell, one she daily debated removing from his post either by retiring him or by death. Though she had not entrusted him with leading the raids in the south or with the liquidation of plague victims, he was the best military mind she had. For now. The men liked him and were loyal to him and she was not foolish enough to erode military morale by indiscriminately removing him from office. He had uses in Glevum, training troops, serving on her council, and heading the palace guard now that Fraen the Elder was promoted to general and sent south.

Keep the enemy close. Better Stone was where she could watch him than hundreds of miles away where she had little control over him.

The call had been put out for more palace guards, as many of the best had been sent with General Fraen and the inexperienced militia. If Inness inspected each recruit, it would become obvious to General Stone that she did not trust him; that would create friction she could not afford. But she had already assessed four others today, and a fifth seemed like a reasonable number before concessions were made to the rest of his choices.

She had demanded the right to evaluate them on the pretext of wanting to know what sort of men came to serve here rather than serving in the south. The other four had been older, men with fighting years in them still but who might not be able to withstand the rigors of marching and serving in a full-fledged battle. Men with combat experience who had fought for Neth once and were willing to do so again in the protection of the infant prince.

Or so their answers implied when she questioned them.

This man was different.

"Kaas, you say?"

Zerio kept his gaze straight ahead, neither tensing nor flinching as the woman circled him like a hungry wolf assessing a rabbit. He knew this strategy, how to play it, and as she was unarmed, he did not believe her a direct threat to his life. He trusted the man to his left, as much as he trusted anyone, and with only four other soldiers in the room, near the door, he did not believe she would try, or succeed, in executing him if he failed to meet her standards.

"Aye." He supplied no other information, not willing to speak lies that he would have to remember hereafter. He would tell her only what she asked. It was better he kept his mouth shut.

"Where are you from?" Not Glevum. She had made it her business to know the families of wealth and position in the city, to learn strengths and weaknesses that might make each vulnerable. Though she knew lords and ladies from other cities and providences throughout Neth, his was not a family name she recognized. It was apparent in the quality of his clothing and the sword that hung at his hip that there was some familial money behind him, or money of his own, but not enough to provide him with a decent set of armor. The leather breastplate, vambraces, gauntlets, and greaves he wore were stained black, an unusual customization but not an overly costly one.

"Pravek."

"What does your family do in Pravek, Mr. Kaas?"

"Merchant traders. Wool with Cordash mostly." He did not blink as she stopped before him, face to face, barely six inches between them. She watched his mismatched eyes, his mouth, pleased to find she did not intimidate him as she did many others. Nor was he so cocky to think he could outmatch her. She was tall, as tall as many men, but he was taller still, with the lankiness of a boy stuck in his growing years but without the awkward, weak-jointed muscles of youth. His brown hair was tied at his neck, longer than the majority of Neth men wore, longer than military decorum demanded. But it suited him.

Pravek was the most prosperous northern port in Neth. Inness knew the duke, new the men of council there, but there were too many merchants, too many sea traders, for her to know them all. Many Nethite noblemen had built their fortunes in Pravek before seeking favor and position at court. As Neth did not produce significant quantities of wool, possessing more forest than pastureland, it meant the Kaas' were importers.

What they exported in return would be worth investigating.

"Vants?"

"Your Majesty?"

Inness scowled and stepped back. There was no flicker in his eyes to gauge his reaction, to judge if she was right, but she had not expected any visible indicators. It was said that members of the Order of the Vants were forbidden to cut their hair, the only exterior clue one might have of their involvement, but as other Nethite men were known to copy that fashion out of vanity or some desire to be affiliated with the mythic order, hair was never a sure sign. Nor was it a sign that he did not sport the gold hoop earring that many Nethite men wore.

There was just something about him that suggested such secrecy.

Rumors about the Order of the Vants had circulated for centuries. What they believed, what their purpose was, had never been learned, not even by the de Corrmick rulers before her who had tried to torture such details out of alleged members. When not actively sought or persecuted, they were said to be highly skilled swordsmen, architects, and herbalists, devoted to the throne to the point of being willing to assassinate despicable kings or serve deserving ones.

If he belonged to the Vants and had come to serve her of his own accord, or on behest of the order, the odds were that he would prove to be the most dependable man in Glevum. Or he would prove to be a threat. Such a threat would be one best kept close enough to uncover his motives and intentions. Letting him out of her sight might be the costliest mistake she could make. With his height, his high, sharp cheekbones, and the oddity of one green eye and one blue, he was an attractive man, despite the scar across his cheek, a man not easily able to hide should he prove disloyal.

She would enjoy the sport of hunting him, if it came to that. Or she would enjoy putting his talents to good use.

"Why are you here and not with the militia?"

A valid, anticipated question. He bowed as if in contrition. "A condition of the lungs," he said, tone polite and apologetic.

"Contagious?"

"Hereditary. My father and brothers shared it. It does not affect my sword, however."

She snorted but did not scold him. Oska had suffered from such a condition, easily winded and prone to coughing fits if he exerted himself. The thought of him caused a twisting, stabbing pain that made her turn her back to General Stone and the younger fellow for the first time, an action she disguised as a return to the throne.

"Your father and brothers? Where are they?"

"Our parents are passed. My younger brother as well. The elder manages the business."

Again Inness snorted, the hopes of more soldiers ripped from her grasp. The kingdom needed men of business as much as it needed soldiers. She could not demand that every man serve in a military capacity. Neth would implode if she tried. From the throne, she realized the scar across his cheek was still visible at a distance but any other physical fault, if he possessed any, was not. He was older than she but not by many years.

"Married? Children?"

"I was…she died in childbirth six years past."

A man who could serve without ties then, a man with nothing to lose. Sometimes having something to lose was a good thing, when a bargaining chip was needed with which to control a man. Other times, it was better not to have the sort of hindrances attachments provided.

Inness did not think this man needed to be controlled.

"General Stone. See that Mr. Kaas has a bed and hot meal and is given a rotation. Mr. Kaas…welcome to Glevum."

Zerio kissed her extended hand, as he knew she expected, making certain in his efforts that she saw devotion and gratitude, and began his retreat. As General Stone repeated the gesture, Inness caught his eye with a warning look. The general was to keep his eye on this one; anything of suspicion the newcomer did would be on Stone's head.

Keeping his eye on Zerio, however, was precisely what Stone intended for reasons of his own.

He bowed and followed Zerio, his long strides bringing him into step alongside him. Zerio avoided side-eyeing the general and instead quietly reveled in the accomplishment of infiltrating the palace guard. He knew he would be watched, his moves and motives scrutinized, but he was in this for the long game, to perform the duty he had been sworn to. He would be watchful, but Zerio was nothing if not confident and determined to succeed.

❧*☙

If she attempted to rouse him when she departed for the dhó dónáré, Kavan did not recall it when he again became aware of his surroundings, of the darkness of the room and the cool night air that seeped through the nearby open window. The hearth fire had gone out earlier, as was practiced each day of spring and summer. A fire was readied on a clean hearth each evening and lit in the morning to burn for the cooking of meals and to ward off the early chill. The heat hugged the walls, waning throughout the day as the summer sun warmed the outside air, leaving a comfortable coolness in which to sleep when evening arrived. With the dhóbhaen taught to regulate their body temperature, a fire was a necessity primarily for cooking, but sitting around one, enjoying the company of others, was a luxury everyone appreciated.

Several things struck him at once as he opened his eyes, details that thrust him into action. Ágdhállán lay against his arm, where Kavan vaguely recalled Raebhá placing him before her departure, the only reminder, he realized, that she had indeed tried to wake him.

With the awareness of the sleeping child, who jerked awake and began to wail, and the expectation that Raebhá would be back to nurse him, came a knock at the door and a burst of fiery light upon the whistle of a loosed arrow, accompanied by the sudden awareness of rage and hostility beyond the open window. Kavan rolled to the floor, knocking over two ceramic bowls of uneaten food with a crash.

The other sound and presence at the door, and a familiar voice calling "kydhé Cliáth?" went unanswered long enough for the speaker to shoulder the door, knocking it with a crack against the wall. A second fire arrow followed and Iólán, finding Kavan shielding the screaming infant with his body, dropped the bundle of firewood he carried to douse the bed fire caused by the first arrow. The second dug into the floor, but the treatment which allowed the planks to keep ground moisture out of the home hindered burning. Thankfully landing near nothing flammable, the second flame fizzled and died.

"Are you harmed?" Iólán yelled. There was no need for a loud voice, no fire or cries to shout over, only the baby crying, but fear birthed the volume as he scrambled to Kavan's side.

"We are unharmed." Kavan rolled with the boy in his arms, trying to stop him from crying so that he could listen to the night with every sense focused on the retreating threat. It could have been anyone, could have been someone set against him out of fear, but he knew he had not been the target.

Ágdhállán had.

Ágdhállán had warned him.

Helping Kavan to his feet, Iólán scowled. His cry brought others into the street, into the doorway, supporters and opponents and the curious. Ephé was the first among them. "Ombhrís?" Iólán asked in a tone he hoped no one but Kavan would identify.

It was Kavan's turn to scowl. "I…" He shook his head no but it was an action without conviction. For a moment he had thought he detected the escaped man's presence, but it had been quickly erased by a flash of power that in the chaos had gone unnoticed. Raebhá had not mentioned the escape of any márbhyndhánis, only the death of three, so where had that flash of power come from? Himself? He quickly ruled that out from personal experience. Ágdhállán? Iólán?

The seemingly obvious answer disturbed him.

"Perhaps…or any of the others." Kavan was used to critics, used to those who feared him. Many feared what Kavan might mean to the millennia of stability the dhóbhaen had enjoyed.

It did not matter to them that their stability was threatened before Kavan's arrival, by a man chosen to rule them due to no more than his marriage to their lawful leader. Let Iólán believe the attack was meant for Kavan or Raebhá. Better that than revealing an uncomfortable truth before they had the opportunity to discuss it.

Ágdhállán refused comfort, the startling fear that had awakened him now replaced by the desire to find solace in his mother's breast.

"Shall I bring Raebhá?" Ephé asked, offering to take the child but relenting when his father refused to give him up.

Kavan shook his head. "She will come." Particularly if word of the disturbance wormed its way into the sequestered meeting where she debated the course of her people's future and made plans for the reparation of quake and water damages throughout the ghísaer. Kavan had patience enough to manage the fussing child, although his desire to seek out their assailant burned for appeasement.

"I will take others and we'll find who did this." Iólán passed his hand over the burnt bedding, examined the soot that came away on his skin, and pulled the blanket from the bed. "Do not fear, kydhé. This will not happen again." The threat of violence, something so abhorrent that it would surely prompt the rest of Curnydhá to action, would be swiftly managed. Iólán had to believe that. It was either believe or give in to panic in the face of this unprecedented turmoil.

Iólán was not coward enough to do such a thing.

He chose to trust that the rest of Curnydhá was likewise inclined.

❧Chapter 37❧

**"I** miss Kavan."
Diona was the first to say what many in Rhidam had felt for weeks. No longer did Kavan live in the Lachlan palace as he had when Diona had been a child, his duties as the Duke of Alberni now taking precedent. The woman knew that her foolish youthful errors had cost her and future generations of Lachlans the constancy of the Elyri bard who had faithfully served her father. If not for her crass missteps, he might have remained in Rhidam for the remainder of his days, serving generations of the family just as he had served Arlan.

The Second Elyri Persecution, however, might still have been enough to expel him from Enesfel. Or cost him his life.

Knowing what she knew now, details she had never shared with Merrek or any of her children, Diona could not help but wonder if events had fallen into place as they were meant to. Kavan's journey had removed him from the violence in Rhidam and had brought back hope to the Sovereignties in the shape of relics of power that had aided in the cleansing of a malignancy that had grown beneath the surface of the world for too long. He would not have undertaken that journey of healing, for his hands, his soul, and the world, if not for Diona's lapse in good sense.

But it made those painful memories no easier to bear during his absences. Over the years, Kavan had been away from Rhidam for a week or more, but those in the keep had usually known where to find him, had been confident of his return. Unable to go back to Bhryell without risking incarceration by agents of the Faith, he would be in

Alberni, Fiara, Káliel, or Kílyn, if not Rhidam…or somewhere not far from those places.

This absence of nearly nine months was troublesome, made more so by the calamities that she and the prince-regent were forced to shoulder without Kavan's counsel.

Shoulder it they had, far better, Diona believed with a sigh, then she might have alone.

"And I miss my son." Merrek rose from his chair to pace the room, a shadow of King Arlan although Merrek carried no more Lachlan blood than did the healer who watched from the window seat where he struggled to sketch the images he had seen during his recent blackout. "When do you think he can return home, Lord Healer?"

Ártur's hand stopped moving. "Who, my lord?"

"Lorant. Kavan. Both." The blonde prince, the one feature that stood him out as not truly of the Lachlan legacy, paused in his pacing to peer over the healer's shoulder at the mountain range he was sketching onto canvas. "They've been gone too long."

Raking his empty hand through his pale red hair, Ártur sighed. "There have been no new cases of plague in weeks, but that does not mean it is behind us. It only means those living have developed a resistance to it. If we bring the Prince back…"

"You said yourself that the Yellow Death was in Bhryell. How do we know he's still…?"

"Chethá would alert us if he were ill or in danger." Just as, he thought with a heavy sigh, they had told of his brother's death and his father's blindness when he had dared to resume communication with his daughter. It had taken every ounce of will for Ártur to stay away, will and a threat from his father to disown him and his entire family if he came and brought sickness with him. As that threat would have, no doubt, included Llucás and Chethá, Ártur reluctantly kept his distance and mourned his family alone with his wife.

He had not yet been able to visit his brother's grave.

"As for…perhaps Kavan is in Alberni even now." Ártur doubted it was true. Even with chaos and death to confront in Alberni, the duties of a long-absent lord to resume to make peace with a city that had suffered too long without him, if Kavan had returned, Ártur believed he would know. The bond between them still felt stretched too thin, and the efforts Ártur made to make contact across those miles brought only an echo. Kavan was still beyond his reach. "I could go there, see if he is…bring him…"

"See Dhóri yourself." Níkóá's tale of miraculous healing had been shared with them and had filtered through the palace staff from one eavesdropping servant to the next until it had been distorted into a tale of the White Bard's return to save his son. Tusánt had brought stories of offerings made to the náós in the names of both Kóráhm and Kavan, equally revered now, both offered prayers for mercy and healing from a community wounded and lost after so much death and suffering. For the first time since the Second Persecution, Rhidam as a whole was begging for the return of the one Elyri known to bring miracles and healing of a sort no physician, no healer, could provide. They wanted his voice, his words, his song, and his touch.

Wherever Kavan was, he had no idea of what awaited his return.

"Yes, my lord. I should see Dhóri and Rhyrdan, Emeria and the others. Yóáná is a fine healer; I have every faith in her…"

"But you would feel better if you saw them yourself." Merrek understood. He felt the same about his absent son.

The double doors of the dayroom opened and a weary, bedraggled-looking Bhyrhán trudged in behind the pages that opened it for him. Having been accepted as family, an extension of the queen, he came and went as he pleased throughout the palace much of the time. He had been absent from Rhidam for nearly two weeks and all within the room knew what his return meant.

Ártur dropped his stylus, splattering ink across his knee as it fell to clatter on the floor.

"Pardon the intrusion and my…" He looked down at himself. "It is raining in Clarys."

"No apologies." Diona went to him, needing no eyesight to find him. The growing link between them brought on by the constant sharing of vision served as a bond that required no sight to follow. Nor did she need eyes to tell that he was wet. And sad. "Is she…?"

"My niece Phílóá is Kyne…there was no disagreement by the k'lómesté…the reins of power have transferred smoothly. She is a good and wise choice."

Of those in the room, only Ártur showed surprise, but none except him and Bhyrhán knew how young the new Kyne was. At barely thirty-five, not yet with children of her own, barring unusual events, Phílóá had every chance of ruling Elyriá longer than her great-grandmother had done. Ártur did not know her, had never met her, but he had learned a great deal about the High Mother's family through Bhyrhán. If he thought Phílóá was a good choice, as Mórne had, then her appointment was a good thing.

"We must send condolences…and our felicitations on her appointment." Diona had been the first Lachlan, since her grandfather, to have met with the High Mother of Elyriá and she had felt an instant kinship with the ancient leader. They had maintained contact throughout Diona's reign and Diona had frequently sought counsel from the woman who had centuries more experience than Diona could ever hope to have. She likewise hoped for a positive relationship with the new Kyne, if Phílóá was willing.

"Indeed. We should invite her to Rhidam, should she be willing to come." To the prince's knowledge, there had never been a Kyne in Rhidam except perhaps in some ancient history that predated settlement beyond the Llaethlágárá. After the First Great Persecution, it had never been deemed safe enough for an Elyri of such status to take the risk. Merrek hoped, thanks to Kavan's efforts years before, that might change. Other than a few incidents of rioting which occurred after the death of k'gdhededhá Claide, there had been no anti-Elyri deaths reported to the Crown in over twenty years. It was the safest window of opportunity for such a visit. Merrek hoped to coax the new Kyne to come.

He was more than willing, if necessary, to go to her instead.

"She will be in isolation until the next moon, seeing no one except advisors and the k'lómesté…but I will see that she is given the invitation as soon as possible," Bhyrhán agreed. "May I have leave to be out of these clothes?"

"Aye," Merrek said. "Welcome home, Lord Bhíncári."

❧*❦

It was daybreak before Raebhá emerged from the dhó dónáré, now with Ágdhállán in her arms as it had been easier to deliver the hungry infant to her than for the woman to leave, interrupting the conclave, to feed him multiple times. Delivering his son to his mother prompted Kavan to take a watchful position on the steps of the dhó dónáré, where he remained throughout the night, despite his weariness and continuing unsettled center, taking no chance that his attacker would come for either the child or his mother.

He could have begun the hunt for his assailant, but he did not feel either child or mother would be safe without him nearby. There were zyrudhén posted here, but their presence did not reassure him. The glances he was given as he crouched beside the door, the stares of both esteem and fear as villagers took to the new day's duties, filled him with further distrust. Those who had not resumed fishing or tending crops and herds had returned to clearing away the rubble of collapsed structures and preparing brick and lumber for the necessary repairs.

The whispers of 'róagdháthé' did not comfort him, though other words, murmured gratitude for saving their lives, for saving their flocks and fields, for saving their ghís, helped soothe his frayed nerves.

Kavan wanted to help the rebuilding efforts, felt he owed the Kindred that much, but he could not tear himself away from his family.

When she came out, accepting his cradling arm around her shoulders, Raebhá seemed tense, uneasy, disappointed despite her relief at seeing Kavan there. She smiled wanly and let him steer her home, cracked and damaged in the shaking but still standing. Audh and Iólán followed, speaking in low, hushed voices that Kavan made no efforts to overhear. Their business was their own.

When they followed into the house, as more dhóbhaen emerged into the streets to begin their day, Kavan eyed them curiously. Raebhá sat at the hearth, feeding Ágdhállán while Iólán built a fire and Audh brought bread and cheese from cupboards as if he had been here before and knew where everything was kept.

"Do not be disheartened, kymyhé," Audh murmured. "This fight is not lost. We have but to sway…"

"If an attack on me…on Kavan and my child…does not sway them…" She shook her head. Though she understood that such significant changes to the foundations of their society would take time, she had hoped that recent events would be enough to spur the márbhyndhánis to swift action.

"They only know that it was violence…"

Iólán snorted. "Violence that some continue to blame on you, kydhé, wrong as they know they are." He looked at Kavan as he ignited the fire with his handlight. "The argument that you brought…"

"This started the night I was struck and sent away," Raebhá huffed bitterly. Those afraid of change and those in favor of it were all using Kavan as an excuse to bolster their argument. Thus far, she had not found a way to reach her dissenters, but she was confident she would, in time. "Before that…with the plotting and planning of their own with Ombhrís. None deny it…and they know Kavan had no hand in that. They already acknowledge where the guilt and responsibility…"

Audh clasped her shoulders and kissed the top of her head. "du, but acknowledgment is not the same as acceptance," The márbhyndhánis smiled at Kavan and removed his hands. "Do not mistake me…you have our sincerest gratitude. Many would be dead, Curnydhá washed to sea, if not for you, but to witness such a feat…we shall never see anything else like that, I assure you."

Kavan bowed his head, accepting the words of thanks as the apology Audh intended them to be.

"Winning the support of the márbhyndhánis will not easily sway people…in Curnydhá, in Gálínphel…throughout Dhóbhaen." She was only at the start of the battle. She could not give up yet, no matter how frustrated she felt at the creeping pace of progress. "Even if we…there will be repercussions, matters of trade, debates that will go on for years." Raebhá sighed and reached for Kavan's hand. "We have suffered so much loss at the mercy of the sea. Recovery will take much of our focus for some time."

Sitting beside her, her brother propped his feet on the stones in front of the fire and wiped the dust from his boots. "Thanks to kydhé, there is far less damage here, less death than there could have been. We can rebuild…and the dead are relatively few. The ash is being prepared and most of the scattered herds have been recovered. We have the resources to aid others. We will survive this and in time, you will prevail…"

"The other ghís?" asked Kavan.

Her expression fell and she sighed as Audh replied, "Word is starting to return. Judging on what we have here…what we could have had, what we are beginning to hear, I fear there is much damage and death. As we are fortunate to have you here, we will do as we have always done. Help. Win support through kindness; in time Gálínphel will accept whatever ruling is made here because of it."

Raebhá wanted to believe Audh's optimism. She had not expected change to be easy, knew that what she might win in Curnydhá could be lost when the full council of márbhyndhánis from across Dhóbhaen convened next. It might be a struggle that lasted for decades. In combination with the wave's aftermath, the fight would consume all of her waking hours, or a great portion of it. Despite her steadfastness to the ideals, she was beginning to glimpse the toil Kavan had hinted at and the future that lay in wait for her.

"Have you found…?"

"I would not leave you," Kavan grunted. "Not until you are safe."

"We are safe." Her hand trailed down his cheek. Having Ombhrís at large was nerve-wracking, but Kavan's proximity made that threat seem less real. His response to her confidence was a dour snort of disbelief. He knew as she did that the threat was not past. Whoever had tried to burn her home, Ombhrís or someone else, would not stop at a single failed attempt.

"You will be, once the bhur are satisfied," Audh agreed, though with less faith in those words than he wanted to convey.

"The pyres are ready. We will mourn at sunset. That will help." Iólán had been the only one of them involved in recovering the dead, removing debris, beginning Curnydhá's road to recovery. Raebhá and the remaining márbhyndhánis had other matters to tend to and Kavan had, during most of that time, been in recovery from his efforts to save them and tending his newborn child. Kavan had given enough.

Audh agreed. "Then we will discuss the elevation of novices."

"Why do we need…?" began Iólán sullenly. "There are others with fewer…"

"Tradition," Audh shrugged.

"Are there even three to be elevated?" There were nearly a dozen novices in Curnydhá, but most were children. She did not think most were old enough, skilled enough, to qualify for elevation.

"There are two, perhaps. There may be others in other ghís…if they have survived the sea…who are willing to come to us. If not," he shrugged again, "we will have to be content with what we have. We're asking them to change other traditions…we cannot expect them to change all at once unless necessity forces us to do so. When the dead rest and three are in place, we'll continue what we've started. For now, we must consider the people…and rest."

The future of those held for Reconditioning would not be decided until they were freed and their former fellows could judge their fitness to return to the status of márbhyndhánis.

Raebhá believed demanding elevation was a tactic to delay the consideration of her demands, but the residents of Curnydhá were as mentally and physically exhausted as Raebhá was and would face a long night ahead when the dead were burned.

The delays would not derail the inevitable debate. Not if the weary determination in Raebhá's eyes was an indicator.

"You must do likewise, taeásne," Iólán murmured embracing her with his cheek pressed to hers. "Kavan will watch over you." He did not need to look at the bard for confirmation. "He will keep you safe."

She nodded but did not speak as she chewed bread and pensively watched the pair of men leave. Ágdhállán shifted in her arms, his hands and feet flexing as he stretched and yawned now that his belly was full. Her gaze dropped, staring at him for several minutes, marveling at the strength of this premature child, the tiny miracle trusting her, falling asleep in her arms, but not without one outstretched hand closed around Kavan's finger.

"The bond between you is a good thing; it will be needed," she whispered, her voice cracking with emotion.

The sound made him frown but he replied, "I believe in strong bonds between parents and children." Even if he had failed Dhóri in leaving him to face the Yellow Death alone.

"Because you did not have that bond yourself." She bent forward and pressed her forehead to Kavan's, the action a reflection of her weariness. "He will not be safe here, aislé."

"He will be. I swear it." He was determined to make it so.

The finite tone of his voice kept her from saying more, cut short the expression of fears and truths she was beginning to see from a perspective Kavan did not share. What he wanted would not be. Ombhrís was not the only threat she could foresee.

"I will sleep." Sleep was a better choice than an argument, after a day of other arguments that had been no more productive than this one could be. She gave Ágdhállán to Kavan and curled up where she sat before the hearth. "Bring him when he must feed, and please," she caught Kavan's hand and held it tightly. "Do not leave me."

"Never, Raebhá. I will never leave you."

She smiled, melancholic and forlorn, before closing her eyes. They both knew their future would not be so easily decided. How they would keep such promises was an argument to be held another time.

❧*❧

The outpost was encircled with a swarm of men from Enesfel, Cordash, and most recently from Hatu as King Gamal's forces arrived not long before sunset and erected tents along the walls of the garrison, awaiting deployment instructions. There were not as many as Garran had hoped, but he would make the most of what he was given.

He had already sent the majority of men to lend fortification to the outposts and villages stretched between Cordash's border in the west to Elyriá's border in the east. The unit from Hatu, men in turbans with curved blades and road-weary countenances, who had made a hurried march from Levonne's harbor, was a boon and Declan hoped, enough to discourage further raids. The long-term housing of mixed troops with the potential of plague ever-present was not ideal, but King Gamal understood the threat to stability an unchecked Nethite army represented. He had even elected an envoy to send to his sister, along with a penned letter from Arlana collected when the troops passed through Rhidam, in the hopes they could make Inness see reason.

But Gamal had never been close to his sisters, had little affinity for women other than his mother, his wife, and their newly born daughters. Arlana and Inness were so little alike that none expected her letter to have any more impact than their mother's had. If Inness would heed anyone in their family, it might be Gamal…and only because he too had been denied the rule of Enesfel and yet was king in his own right.

At least, Declan thought as one by one the campfires began to dim, the effort had been made. The next move was Inness's.

&Chapter 38&

Eight bonfires threw their flames into the twilight colors of lengthening night. Eight bonfires piled high, supporting the dead two apiece save for the single fire that bid farewell to four children lost to the shaking earth's wrath and the series of aftershocks continuing to rattle Curnydhá. There had been bodies washed up on the shore, fishermen from the ghísaer of Lyáragk whose ship had capsized and been dashed against the rocks under the wave's might. It was decided that those ten, after identifying which ghís they had come from, would be set adrift on the sole pyre boat while the others were consigned to the beach pyres.

Every person from the ghís, including those who needed to be carried, due to injuries, ill health, or age, came to the fallow field nearest to the sea to watch the fires do their work, watch the boat set adrift and lit with a shower of burning arrows, watch the thick smoke rise and the ashes and smoldering bits of organic material drop into the sea or the pits dug beneath the pyres. As before, there was chanting, singing, wailing, and moaning, a cacophony to confuse the bhur in the hopes that they would not take host in, or corrupt, the living.

In the hopes that they would take the plague of violence and misfortune with them.

There was fear on many faces, fear that they had waited too long to dispose of the bodies, fear that the restless dead would bring further disaster to Curnydhá, to Gálínphel, in the days ahead.

There was also fear, a sense of it that raked across Kavan's skin like a dull razor, that the one who had summoned winged, man-like beings and could hold back the sea, who bled róagdháthé on their sands and the steps of Raebhá's home, might be able to control the dead. That a man who communed with the ágdháthé might be able to bring pestilence and wild beasts down on them…and had every right to do so after his benevolent saving of their town was met with an attempt on his life.

Many supported Raebhá's view, for if such skills as the White Bard possessed were known by the márbhyndhánis, should not each person be conversant enough to defend against such attacks of nature? If the márbhyndhánis possessed such skills, why had they never similarly used them to the benefit of the people? What were the limits or possibilities of power innate in them and why were they denied the right to explore it without the consent of the márbhyndhánis?

Others, conversely, nerves rattled by recent events, clung to their fears, supporting limitations, for surely anyone who could control the sea would seek power and violence against others and upset the peaceful order of life. The White Bard had not used his gifts for ill, but how could others be trusted with such power?

How could they be certain they could trust he who was, or could be, the fulfillment of prophecy?

Those were the faces who glowered and cowered and shrank from Kavan when he passed, the people who kept their distance and scolded curious children and who, if they had been raised to violence, would have resorted to throwing stones and might have fallen on him in a horde demanding exile or execution. Kavan was as accustomed to that reaction as he was to adoration, as there was very little middle ground between the extremes. He was uncomfortable with both, but at least they were responses he understood and could forgive.

What he could not understand and felt hard-pressed to forgive was that the same fear and disdain was now directed at the newborn who was guilty of nothing except being Kavan's son born outside of his mother's marriage. Dhóri had suffered no outcast status, had been welcomed in Bhryell, Alberni, and Rhidam alike, perhaps because most did not know he was Kavan's biological son. It troubled Kavan to think Ágdhállán might suffer the same lonely childhood his father had endured. His gift of Sight should guarantee a future as márbhyndhánis, but unless Raebhá integrated the learning of power into the lives of all dhóbhaen, Kavan could not foresee an easy life, an easy childhood, for their son.

No longer concerned about public perception, choosing to acknowledge their relationship now that the child was born, Raebhá clutched Kavan's hand, endeavoring to center both herself and him as the fires burned. His agitation was palpable, as was the communal unrest, and she hoped her visible support and calm would sway public opinion. Surely, her trust in him spoke to his character. He had saved her life, had brought her home, had saved Curnydhá, had bled for them all. What more could they ask of him?

He did not sing or chant as the rest of the community did, not wanting to draw attention to himself and away from the ritual they believed necessary. He hummed, lending his efforts to the ceremonial din, but there was no other music from him, had been none since the earthquake. His voice, his harp, remained silent. When others began to sway, to dance in a weaving circle around the pyres so that the sound spread evenly into the night, enveloping the dead in the audible embrace, Kavan stood still next to Raebhá, eyes turned to the sky, listening with senses beyond his ears, seeking the root of the festering feeling that sat low in his belly.

Worry for his son, for Raebhá, for the future compounded that feeling, but the main cause of it came from far away, tightly stretched back to the Five Sovereignties along paths of attachment he had tread with little frequency of late. He had become aware of it after his confrontation with the wave, after the birth of his son, and he wondered if it was caused by something he had done. He was trying to find the source, allowing Raebhá's hand in his to anchor him as his thoughts traveled elsewhere, but the harder he searched for the truth, the further it slipped, growing fainter with each moment.

Perhaps Wortham had sent the feeling as a reminder. But of what?

He thought he had reached the end of the thread, reached with fingers of power to embrace and know it, when a stab of fear charged through him, coming with enough warning that he was able to spin sideways and serve as a shield so that the small thrown blade caught his shoulder rather than Raebhá or Ágdhállán. The thread he had was lost, and he was given no opportunity to launch a counterattack through the writhing crowd before the assailant was lost as well.

He heard Raebhá scream as he yanked the bloody ániélmé free and dropped it into the hands of the woman on Raebhá's other side.

"Keep them safe," he barked, entrusting Iólán and Ephé with their welfare before charging through the crowd in the direction from which the blade had come. If not for the throng and the attention it would draw, he would have assumed a form more conducive to a hunt. But he would not place Ágdhállán at risk by doing so. By the time he broke through the screaming mass, the attacker was gone, but the impression Kavan had read from the blade when pulling it free was clue enough.

Raebhá and Ágdhállán could not be safe until Ombhrís was found.

The man's troubling aura left a steaming trail as it moved into the forest, weaving around trees, through brambles, over small streams at a remarkable speed. Kavan had endurance, but not speed, as he was not accustomed to running as a man. As a hart, as a wolf, he could best anyone, but here he was unfamiliar with the territory, the terrain, and was disadvantaged because of it. His only advantage was the power that allowed him to target his quarry's life force and follow it.

Afraid he might lose him, afraid that Ombhrís's next attempt on his life, on Raebhá's, on Ágdhállán's might succeed, Kavan shifted mid-stride into the silver-white wolf form he sometimes wore and now, with both the aura trail and the man's scent to follow, he threw back his head and howled.


Though the fires raged and the dead still burned, a circle of villagers began to form around Raebhá, Iólán, and her son, their faces distorted by the orange flames and the shadows of night. No one acted, as violence was such a foreign concept, and the thought of death such a frightening one, that none knew what to do with the feelings that warred within them. Some wanted the child sent away, the tiny life removed before he grew into something more fearful, more powerful, than his father. Most were prepared to protect their kymyhé and her son and the one who fulfilled prophecy. The chanting continued but it was no longer distortions to misdirect the bhur away from the living.

Some of the voices, Raebhá realized in horror as the fear took form, sought to steer the bhur into her son. Thankfully, most of them were intent on protecting him.

Uneasy and unsettled by losses at the hand of earth and sea, people wanted a solution, wanted someone to carry their burden of horror. Some thought to condemn the child with enough bhur so that he would either suffer an accident or illness or, when he was old enough to be trained, be forced into kylldrenai to have his youthful spirit broken before he was able to identify himself as an individual.

Raebhá had seen it before, wild, untamed children, sometimes mute or deaf, uncontrollable, unteachable. The Reconditioning warped them into something akin to normal, but left such children docile, placid, unable to survive on their own, forever a child in thought and deed. They became wards of the márbhyndhánis as servants, capable only of performing simple, menial tasks, devoid of rights, devoid of pleasure, devoid of any of the things that made life worth living.

She would not have that for her son. Clutching his head against her so that one ear was pressed to her breast and the other covered with her hand, she forced her way through the crowd with Iólán and Ephé. Curses would not harm him, the bhur would not come, but if he heard and understood those words hurled in fear, he, like his father, might live with them wedged in his heart for his entire life. She would spare him that if she could.

Somewhere in the forest, a wolf howled.

Wolves were nothing to fear. Respect, but not fear, as they were Dhóbhaen's apex predator, other than the dhóbhaen themselves. Not even the bears, rare as they were, would normally take on a pack. Judging by that unanswered cry, it was a lone wolf Ombhrís heard, and though a lone wolf could be as dangerous as a pack, the animal was far away, the echo of its voice distorted by the mountains, the forest, and the fading voices of the people he left behind.

He had no intention of killing Raebhá. Kavan perhaps, or the child, but not her. He hoped to frighten the stranger, frighten Raebhá, into leaving Curnydhá so that he could reclaim the position he had briefly enjoyed. He intended to reinstate the márbhyndhánis held for Reconditioning so that they would again support him.

Turning some of the villagers against Kavan had been easy, a matter of fanning flames of distrust, for no individual should be allowed to wield as much power as he did, the fulfiller of prophecy or not. Convincing some that Kavan should either be forced to leave or forced to accept kylldrenai if he chose to remain in Curnydhá had been as simple as convincing them that the White Bard was a fraud, a myth. Planting the suggestion that Kavan should be dealt with as the dhóbhaen had dealt with Dhágdhuán and the elyryhánag was a short leap to take off of the precipice of their fear.

Raebhá, as Kavan's supporter and elyryhánag herself, and likely a devotee to the teachings of Dhágdhuán, should also be accountable.

Why alter tradition and law to accommodate a single person or even a small group of them? Why allow the dangerous violence of power to be available to anyone who might use it against the innocent?

As for the infant, he had done no wrong but it was enough that the child was not his. He could not claim to love the woman he had married, a woman who had been a means to an end, but she was still his wife, for another handful of days, and he held on to the slimmest hope that removing Kavan, removing the child, might bring her back to him and to the public promises they had made to one another. That she might never trust him because of the actions he had instigated and participated in against her was a detail he felt confident he could work around if only those obstacles were removed.

If either died in his efforts to frighten them, or at the hands of the villagers now turning against them, Ombhrís would not be unduly troubled. Death, at least the death of others, was not something he feared, unlike so many other dhóbhaen. It happened, leaving no more trace of life than was left after the Ceasing. Only living mattered, and if one could not make the most of the life they were blessed with, what was the reason for it? Not, he argued, as he leaped over a stump and continued charging up the mountain, just to feed some endless cycle.

Behind him, the baying of the wolf grew nearer.


The márbhyndhánis and novices encircled Raebhá and her son, waving the dozen or so angry people back with unspoken power in their gestures. The rest tried to silence the curses of their neighbors with hands over their mouths are arguments for peace. Their efforts devolved into pushing and shoving, irritated shouts, the infancy of an uprising Curnydhá had not witnessed since the days of Dhágdhuán. Iólán tried to shout over the raised voices but no one listened, their attention turned entirely on each other and the growing feud rather than on burning the dead or Raebhá and her child.

"Get her to safety," Audh hissed near Iólán's ear. He believed he, his fellow márbhyndhánis, and the more rational heads in the crowd could still the storm if Raebhá and the child were temporarily removed from sight. It might not quell the storm indefinitely but the madness that threatened might cool so that a discussion could be held rationally some other day once the dead were at rest.

Iólán agreed. With his light cloak thrown up, his arm around her shoulders to shield her, he held her close and directed her through the bickering group, pushing her head low and keeping her free of the shoving around them. Someone's fist caught him in the temple as the first thrown punch went errant. He stumbled, kept from falling by Raebhá's presence beside him, and pressed on. He was grateful the blow had struck him instead of whatever target it had been intended for. It meant one less link to retaliation.

Perhaps, he mused as he and Raebhá broke through the far side of the gathering and stumbled towards her home, his absorbing that blow had prevented further violence.

Little by little as he ran, fire crept across his shoulder, a burn that suggested poison and caused his steps to falter as he realized it. He was closing in; he could feel the growing proximity of Ombhrís' aura across the ever-increasing steepness of the terrain that edged the narrow river valley. Over the pounding of blood in his ears and the bellowing voice demanding one foot in front of the other over and over again, Kavan could hear the rush and tumble of icy melt over rocks as it bled from the mountain snowpack to feed the tributary which would pass through Curnydhá and out to the slightly warmer sea. They were traveling northwest, deeper into unfamiliar territory, but he barely noticed the trees or the terrain as he focused on two things.

Decreasing the growing pain. Stopping Ombhrís.

The slope of the incline added to the jolt in Kavan's shoulder as the wolf's front legs bore the brunt of the impact with every leaping step in order not to tumble down the mountainside. He wanted to stop, inspect the damage, try to squeeze some of the poison from his body.

But he guessed it was too late for that, his exertion speeding the spread of it to his heart, his lungs, his brain. It had probably been too late as soon as he noticed the burn of it in his skin and muscles.

If he was to die, he was going to see to it that Ombhrís did as well.

"I should be there; I should speak to them," Raebhá demanded as the door of her home banged closed behind them. Frightened for Kavan, for her son, she wanted to do something, take a stand, win over the hearts of her people and restore peace. "Let me go!"

Iólán held her shoulders in a strong grip to keep her from pulling away. "It is too dangerous…"

"It must be…"

"Ágdhállán needs you! You cannot abandon…"

"Then you watch him," she cried, thrusting the babe in her brother's direction. The action made him stumble back, his hold on her shoulders released.

"He needs a mother, not an uncle! I won't let you go out without me. It is not safe."

"They would never…"

"Someone did!" He waved the bloody knife in her face, the first look she had at the projectile hurled at her, or her son, which might have killed either of them if not for Kavan. She recognized the ániélmé, which spoke of the involvement of the márbhyndhánis in the attack. But the guilty had been accounted for, the guiltless at her side to protect her after unrest blossomed. Of those held for kylldrenai, only Ombhrís had gotten free, Ombhrís who had been in league with them, their puppet or their leader in her abduction. Ombhrís whom Kavan now pursued and who might never cease his efforts to destroy her, if Kavan did not succeed in catching him. Had he freed one or more of the others? Did he have supporters still in Curnydhá or were there external allies among them?

How were they to deal with such a man?

Had he dared take her life himself after the previous failure?

Did he hate her so much?

The forest grew sparser and began to level off, a fact noticeable only because the decreasing slope eased the impact on Kavan's increasingly numb limb. When the tree line came to an abrupt end it was at the sharp, rocky edge of the narrow turbulent river that rushed east over protruding boulders and, several hundred feet east of his position, disappeared in a torrent over a steep dropping edge lit by the rising moon. Ombhrís crouched on a ledge of black stone to the west, hands empty and flat on rock made slippery by the river's spray.

Kavan made no effort to hide his transformation from wolf to man. Angry and in pain, he wanted Ombhrís to know who had cornered him and how, wanted the man who knew so little to know what true power was. If he wanted to fear Kavan's power, Kavan would give him reason to do so. The pale wolf, silver in the moonlight, howled one more time before rearing up on hind legs and morphing in a shimmer of power into the harper's natural form. Though Ombhrís would never know it, Kavan felt the delay in the change, the difficulty in controlling power and molding it to his bidding. Over the distance between them, silhouetted as he was by the moon, Kavan doubted Ombhrís saw his grimace as the transformation took hold. Kavan's shoulder, where the blade had penetrated, was red with blood and discolored beneath the torn fabric of his tunic.

What Ombhrís could see was the tender way in which Kavan favored his arm as he steadied himself.

"Hurts, doesn't it?" Having not seen who or where his blade had struck, Ombhrís flipped his hair from his face with a toss of his head and a smirk of satisfaction with the other man's pain that undermined the initial eruption of fear created by the transformation. dhóbhaen myths were full of tales of people taking the forms of beasts, but he had never considered those myths to be true.


"Make sure Celen and the others are…" Raebhá began. If her attacker had been one of the márbhyndhánis and not Ombhrís, she needed to know.

In her arms, Ágdhállán began to squirm and cry. He turned towards her body, moving his right shoulder away from her touch; when she attempted to shift him, her directions aborted, he screeched and jerked his tiny arm away. Raebhá looked at her brother with alarm.

There was no visible injury. What was wrong with her son? Had she been wrong? Had the bhur taken hold of him?


Kavan growled. He wanted words, witty and pointed and vicious words to hurl in insult and attack, but in his discomfort, none came to mind. He could make accusations but there was no need since Ombhrís had already claimed responsibility for the things he had done…to Raebhá, to Kavan, to lives lost at sea in the boat he had burned. He could demand to know why, but the reasons were already clear with the swirl of dark colors in Ombhrís' aura and thoughts that he did not have the skill to hide. Kavan could cast verbal threats but he preferred to express that threat in the slow, deliberate, stalking steps taken towards his prey. Ombhrís scooted back to the edge of the rock on which he crouched but there was no further distance to retreat and so he gauged the distance back into the forest with darting eyes.

Ombhrís had seen anger before but he had never seen fury such as what he felt radiating from the man before him. With memories fresh of what Kavan had achieved in their first clash, with what he had seen the bard do to the sea, it gave Ombhrís cause to reconsider his next action. Whether the White Bard had experience in physical combat, in wrestling and hunting, would matter little if he had only to cast thought to choke the life from Ombhrís or anyone else.

That thought no sooner occurred to Ombhrís when he felt invisible bands, like choking hands, tighten around his chest, compressing his ribs, his lungs, restricting the flow of air. He could feel the cracking of bone, or thought he could, but despite his fear of pain, he was not ready to admit defeat.

"Kill me!" he croaked. "Prove me right! Prove to them that no man with such power can be trusted, that the followers of Dhágdhuán and those given unfettered training are murderers."

Kavan took another step forward, the green of his eyes glowing like the great hungry wolf with its prey trapped before it.

"What's wrong?" Iólán asked as Raebhá lay the child on the table and removed the wrappings that bound him. She had heard children scream thus when vicious red ants had found a way into their clothes, or another when stung by a bee. Such insects did not come at night and she did not expect to find any, but what else could explain cries of such pain? What else except the bhur, which she did not believe in? None of those at the fires could manipulate power and direct it at her son despite the efforts they had made.

There were no insects. What she saw were streaks spreading across his shoulder, the reddish-black of poison without a wound to suggest its entry. She gripped him as if to squeeze the malignancy out, her thumbs pressed at the center of the radiating veins, and screamed a single word in shock and horror at what she felt there.

"Kavan!"

Raebhá's horror and the image of his son's shoulder drove a spear of pain through Kavan's thoughts, knocking him to his knees as he clutched his head with an agonizing cry. His vision went from red to black and he struggled to breathe. The change broke his hold on Ombhrís and the other man took the opportunity to yank a blade from his boot and launch it at Kavan with a stumbling lunge.

It was Kavan's pain that spared him, the pain that caused him to fall forward, face down onto the damp, spongy moss that covered the stones where he stood. Vaguely aware of the object that penetrated his aura and flew past him, unable to thrust out an arm to direct power as he often did, unable to see where Ombhrís was, to hear him or feel him beyond the crackling wall of pain, Kavan let loose a shockwave that radiated outward as if he was a stone thrown into an undisturbed pond. He had no expectations for the outcome of his effort, only that it might protect him from Ombhrís long enough to recover his vision, his focus, and suppress the fire in his blood so that he could rise to his feet.

Ombhrís was thrown backward, discarded as greens to sheep, and felt the crack in his spine, his ribs, as he struck the upright boulder on which he had previously stood. He remained there, arched against the stone, unable to move as waves of pain from within, waves of power from without, crashed over him in alternating pulses. His right foot teetered on the precipice of the outcropping to sustain his balance, while the damage done to his back robbed his other leg of feeling, leaving it numb and unsteady. Kavan did not rise, continued to groan, and squeeze his head between his hands.

Ombhrís again judged the distance to the forest. Could he make it there? What other choice did he have?

The door crashed open. Audh and a healer, having heard the screams and thinking the chaos had resulted in injury, stumbled over one another in their haste to get inside.

"Kavan's dying!" Raebhá cried. "Find him!"

Audh did not ask how she knew this. The two were not wed, but they were joined, sharing a son and a bond that the márbhyndhánis did not question. He had seen this before, people knowing a partner's fate before it happened, as it happened, who felt injury and death when it came and were sometimes transported into death with the other. It was the screaming child that worried him, the blackening shoulder of the wailing boy. The sight spurred the healer to action and Raebhá's plea sent Audh leaping down the steps three at a time, prepared to run…

…only to be thrown against the side of the house by a gusting force strong enough to crush the air from him and shake every structure in Curnydhá.

Not an earthquake. Not an aftershock. This was a shaking of the air, of the sky, a hammer of power strong enough to reach the village from a distant center. Audh could see it flaring in his mind's eye as it knocked people off their feet.

He had witnessed the holding of the sea. This should not surprise him. But as he scrambled up and followed the spark into the mountain forest, he acknowledged he was astounded by what he sensed.

Astounded and thrilled to live in an age when a man such as this had come to the dhóbhaen. A man whose existence could change everything…if they allowed it to. If Kavan did not die first.

Ombhrís pushed off the stone, using the strength in his arm to propel him towards the forest where he expected to find sanctuary before his injured opponent could pursue. Thirty minutes. An hour at most. Without a healer's care, the venom's bite would have done its work and this supposed fulfiller of myth would no longer be a threat. Prophecy or not, the white-skinned man was a cancerous growth that needed to be removed before the dhóbhaen lost what they were.

The pushing away from the stone, the attempt to run, put all of his weight on a leg with little feeling, and as his balance was lost, his right foot slipped on the ledge and went out beneath him. There was little except moss and wet stone for his fingers to seek purchase on, and with the ground sloped towards the surging river, Ombhrís slid until his legs dangled over the edge, his feet inches above the water, his fingers dug into moss thick enough not to rip free beneath his clawing.

It held his weight, but the moss was not enough to support his attempts to hoist to safety. His attempts to use his one good leg to push himself up failed as he could not find a secure ledge to brace against.

In spite of himself, he cried, "Help me!" to the only person close enough to hear him. Ombhrís could barely see the bard, unmoving, unresponsive, either by choice or because he could not hear him.

Could not help him.

With the world fading and burning, Kavan's vision nearly dark, his ears filled with the buzz of reverberating power, the cry took time to reach him. When the words at last burrowed into his brain, he lifted his head, facing the direction of sound though he saw nothing but shadows of dark gray against black. Without considering the source of the plea, responding only to the instinct that someone needed help, he struggled to his hands and knees and crept awkwardly forward. Unable to funnel power into his senses due in part to the blinding effect of poison and the echo of the power shockwave he had created, he did not stop until his knee struck something. The impact was enough to pitch him to the ground and cause Ombhrís to yelp. The jolt brought a momentary clarity of vision and as he rolled, Kavan looked down and saw the danger the other man was in.

It would be easy, he realized with swimming, disjointed thoughts, to leave Ombhrís to die. The man's back was bloody, with dark bruising beneath his torn and tattered shirt where he had been flung against the stone moments before. It was not difficult to deduce that the lack of movement in his leg was a result of that injury. The lichen he clung to was gradually pulling from its fragile hold on the stones and in time Ombhrís would lose that purchase and plunge into the river. Kavan did not need to do anything except decide to do nothing and Ombhrís would cease to be a threat.

Or he could grind those treacherous hands beneath his knees so that the end came, cause pain one last time so that Ombhrís died with the knowledge of who had bested him. If Kavan died here as well, taking Ombhrís with him, removing the threat from Raebhá and Ágdhállán's lives, it might be the wisest choice he could make.

The other voice, a whisper borne of education, experience, and personal conviction, bid him draw his enemy to safety and somehow return him to whatever justice the dhóbhaen chose as fitting. With both arms extended, his balance uneven, he did not need to speak. Ombhrís saw the gesture and understood.

He reached for Kavan's hand.

The pull of Ombhrís' weight on Kavan's burning, discolored shoulder drew a squawk of agony. Kavan could not break free of the grip around his wrist, but when he lurched in pain, it was with knees that slipped on the damp stone, spinning him so that one foot caught Ombhrís in the face. Ombhrís instinctively brought an arm up to shield himself, but the effort came too late to avoid the impact. It also cost him his anchor in the moss. He screamed in fury and astonishment but the sound was swallowed by the mountain runoff which embraced him and drank his life into its churning throat.

Kavan wiggled forward on his belly to look over the ledge, hoping he would see the other man clinging to the embankment or a stony protrusion in the river, but there was nothing to see except the white foaming crests of the water that raced down the mountain towards the flatlands of Curnydhá and the sea. He strained his eyes towards the horizon, seeking Ombhrís there, but the river dropped out of sight, and had undoubtedly carried the other man with it after bouncing him off of one embedded river boulder after another.

If he did not drown in the sucking current, the crushing of those great stones would break his bones and kill him without a doubt.

Those thoughts, that knowledge, were distant echoes in Kavan's head as weakness and poison ate through the last of his consciousness.

I have killed him, he thought with despair. He was damned.

But his family was safe.

He was left facing the river's cold spray without hope of living to see them again.

&Chapter 39&

Such a spectacle had never been seen in Curnydhá or any dhóbhaen territory. Raebhá was reluctant to allow it when Audh trudged into the ghís with Kavan's limp body. Certain he was dying, she demanded that every healer in Curnydhá, and any from outside of it who could be found, attempt to reverse or halt the spread of poison. She knew Kavan. She knew how he would feel about what had come to pass. She resisted Audh's advice because of it, tried to avoid his fanciful recommendation, certain that the people of Curnydhá would never tolerate it.

If she did as he suggested, Kavan would surely die.

But Audh, the keeper of visions in Gálínphel, begged its necessity, and by the time the most expedient healing options were tried and failed to affect either Kavan or Ágdhállán, Raebhá was forced to relent on the tenuous condition that Kavan was constantly attended against further harm from her still missing husband until whatever Audh believed in came to pass.

Or Kavan died.

Chunks of stone from buildings damaged in the quake were brought to the center of the ghís where the community sometimes gathered for evening meals when the weather was warmest. They were placed level and smooth to form a raised bed, topped with sanded planks of lumber, adorned with colorful fabrics and cushions for his head before he was put upon it as if a stone figure on display.

The people of Curnydhá, many horrified by the violence that they believed might have contributed to the White Bard's near-death, adorned the man with flowers and wreaths and a variety of trinkets in offering to something they did not understand or question. One of their own had incited violence, had instigated it with rumor and accusations, and the normally peaceful dhóbhaen wanted no part of it. Some were not yet ready to accept the changes Raebhá advocated, but they did not believe that the White Bard was the cause of the mayhem in their ghís.

That responsibility belonged to Ombhrís and the márbhyndhánis who had betrayed them.

Survivors from neighboring ghís, come seeking aid and audience, stopped to gawk, to hear the tales of the pale man so prominently displayed. Undoubtedly, Raebhá thought with remorse in the tales of death and destruction they brought, when each left they took the tales of miracles with them. The myth of the White Bard was spreading. The future of Dhóbhaen was on the verge of irreversible change.

The márbhyndhánis novices took turns standing watch over the barely breathing man beneath the shade of a thatched and canvased hexagonal pavilion erected to protect him from sun and rain. At night, Raebhá and Ephé lit oil lamps scented with mint to burn at each corner and covered Kavan with furs to shield him from the sea breeze.

Raebhá kept watch too, day in and day out, when the burden of duty to those hardest hit by the sea and the quake and the care of her son did not keep her away. She was witness to the people who came, some multiple times a day, to leave offerings, to murmur words as if speaking to him, encouraging him to wake, thanking him for what he had done for them, for Curnydhá. Some uttered pleas to the ágdháthé, even though they believed their creators had little involvement in the world and were unlikely to respond to wishes for a single man's welfare. Some lay hands on his chest, touched his arms, his hands, his face, acts that gradually gave birth to growing rumors of healing gained through those touches.

She wanted to be with him more than she was, but her responsibilities would not allow it.

Sometimes, for reasons no one could define, there was blood. Blood from his wrists. Blood from his feet. Blood from his side. Blood from wounds that were there and gone again without any healer's care.

The rumors disquieted her; the blood disquieted her. She knew how these things would upset Kavan. She could imagine the effects such stories about his father would have on Ágdhállán as he matured. The rumors, the blood, and the behavior of the people unsettled some of the márbhyndhánis more than it did her, and those few avoided Kavan or passed with wary looks of scrutinizing skepticism. Only Éthym who watched him expectantly from the raised balcony of the dhó dónáré, and Audh who often stood by the bard's feet, looking at him silently, seemed to know something, or hoped for something, that even the accepting among them did not see.

Sometimes Audh would catch her eye, nod his head, and smile. But he never revealed his thoughts, leaving her to wonder what this spectacle was intended to accomplish.

The display and the adoration of many did not, however, dispel all of the hostility in Curnydhá, and many times each day shouting fights broke out as the underlying tensions continued to bubble. It did appear, however, that little by little, Kavan's silent slumber was swaying more people to the causes of power and faith.

On the fifth day, woodsmen felling trees to repair damaged homes came back with the battered, bruised, and bloated body of Raebhá's husband. Shocked and disgusted to see it, it was impossible to tell if he had drowned or if he had died of injuries sustained by the beating the river and its rocks had given. None had reason to think he had died before going into the river. Because Audh had not seen Ombhrís when he found Kavan collapsed beside the river, and because there were no marks of combat on the bard, only the discolored spread of poison beneath his skin, there was no evidence that the men had confronted each other. The river's brutality and the forces of nature had erased any clues that might have been gained by reading the dead, and the single effort Audh made to read Kavan had brought him up against the bard's impenetrable wall of mental protection.

The truth might never be known, and ultimately, to Raebhá, it did not matter. Despite her shock at Ombhrís' unexpected death, the disgust of his condition, the disquiet it created within her, his demise freed her from the threat of being hunted. Freed her to remarry…if Kavan lived and could be persuaded to, desired to, take that step.

It was the barrier of power in him, along with the shallow rise and fall of his chest and the gradual fading of the poison's kiss on his shoulder, as well as Ágdhállán's slow return to normal, that suggested healing rather than dying. But days crept by and Raebhá remained torn between despair and hope. The joint effort of the dhóbhaen had repaired several structures, including Raebhá's home, and then effort slowed as duties began to fracture their cohesion.

Shelter was important, but some who lost homes could take residence with others, move into houses that had stood empty after the passing of their owners, or, if need be, continue to spend their nights in the ghís kelyhag. The sailors from Maras and Phaurd had long ago departed but others ferried food and materials to nearby settlements to aid in their recovery. The days of growing warmth and unfrozen seas were short, farming, hunting, fishing and other measures for the long winter had to be complete before the snow came or people would suffer more than a housing inconvenience. No one desired starvation.

Sacrifices had to be made for the good of the ghís.

There was much Raebhá wanted to achieve but she understood that further discourse with the márbhyndhánis would have to wait for the long winter night too. The ghís' survival had to be her priority, but it was difficult to address when Kavan's monument, with him on it, was an ever-present reminder of what lay behind and ahead.

With the sun setting on the eighth day, Raebhá again stood at Kavan's side, most of the townsfolk respecting her desire for privacy and preparing to sleep. She pressed her lips to his cool forehead. For the first few days his skin had been feverish; now there was little warmth to be felt and she feared that, though the trace of poison was gone, he was fading. Her thoughts surrounding that loss were morbid and made her clutch Ágdhállán more tightly as she whispered, "óymháth," and retreated with defeated steps to her home.

Within his shell, in the recesses into which his consciousness retreated whenever his body was severely threatened, Kavan felt that kiss, felt her fear and despair and growing hopelessness, things which pulled him like a siren back from oblivion. His body hurt, stiff and sore from lying on a hard stone surface. His shoulder burned still but it no longer radiated with the excruciating fire he dredged from his last waking recollection. Those sensations and memories brought with them the taste of an icy river's spray, the growl of water tumbling over rock, and the feel of spongey moss beneath his face and hands.

Wherever those memories stemmed from, he was not in that place any longer. He was on his back rather than his stomach, warmer and dryer, with the distant rhythmic pulse of the sea surging in time with the beating of his heart. He could smell peat fires and roasting meat, the last awakening his senses so that he choked on saliva before his throat responded to the impulse to swallow. It roused a grumble in his belly and it was his body's demand for appeasement that finally prompted him to open his eyes.

Though his lids stuck, crusty with sleep and perhaps tears he could not recall shedding, and his eyes felt dry and shrunken, they opened and focused with effort on the patterned weaving above him. Sailing canvas, he guessed, waxed with the fat of the huge sea creatures the dhóbhaen sometimes caught. There was a trace of recent rain in the air, the clean smell of it tickling his nose. His lips pulled into a small smile, the stretching of long stationary skin mildly uncomfortable but also welcome and reassuring. He was alive. Twice he had endured the bite of poison and twice he had survived. Praise k'Ádhá, he thought, for it was surely a miracle that he lived.

"táu, sór ciágk," Raebhá murmured to the child who had been nearly asleep but suddenly stiffened, wide-eyed, and began to fuss. Not in hunger, not in pain, but in general discontent, something that rocking and gentle humming were unable to appease.

Kavan made it to sitting, his bare feet dangling over the edge of the stone and wood upon which he had rested, not quite touching the ground. He wore a long robe of the sort the márbhyndhánis novices wore, a robe that reminded him in form, though not in color, of the ones he had worm most of his life. The memories that came with it, memories of the man he used to be and had worked hard to change, were uncomfortable enough that he nearly tore it from his body. Only realizing at the last moment that he wore nothing beneath it prevented him from removing it. The russet of dried blood stained his side and caused the fabric to stick until his movement pulled it free. The location of the stain forced him to look at where he had lain, revealing similar crimson stains where his hands and feet had been, leaving no doubt as to their source.

He frowned, wondering how long he had lain there, how much blood he had shed, how much the dhóbhaen had seen.

Determined to change out of the heavy reminder he wore, he decided to seek food and water and find Raebhá and his son if they were not in the place he expected them to be. He needed answers, needed grounding, needed to know why he had been in the center of town on display, surrounded by torches, wreaths, bouquets, and tokens of the sort he had seen placed at holy shrines many times in his life.

Blessed k'Ádhá! He was no saint! He was not even dead yet!

Although maybe, he thought with fingers tenderly probing the point where the poison had entered his body, they had believed he would be soon. Most dhóbhaen did not pray, did not believe the ágdháthé that created them, created the world, had any interaction in their lives. Yet in a peculiar way, what he saw reminded him of the beseeching of people wanting to affect the outcome of something beyond their control…prayer to whomever, whatever, might be listening who would give them what they sought.

Would his revival bring them closer to the Faith as Dhágdhuán taught it…in the belief in k'Ádhá as the Elyri espoused since the days of their banishment?

The prophecy of the White Bard suggested it might, and Kavan shivered beneath the blasting weight of that responsibility.

Standing with a hand on the dais, forcing himself to ignore the bloodstains in the wood, he looked around, gauging where he was, noting the repairs done during his slumber, trying to judge how much time had passed. The last he could not guess, although the twisting in his stomach and dryness in his mouth and throat suggested it had been several days. A faint light burned in Raebhá's window, a tallow candle most likely, meaning she was awake, and the sounds of a fussy child confirmed it. His stiff muscles did not cooperate easily, but he forced himself to trudge towards the beacon of his soul's home, unhindered, unhelped, by anyone. He could feel her warmth inside of him. She lived. With Ombhrís no longer a threat, she would be safe.

They all would be.


Until her door opened, Ágdhállán's uncoordinated efforts to reach in that direction seemed no more than an infant's random movements. The creak on the wooden planks outside heralded someone's arrival and for a moment Raebhá feared that at this hour it would be someone come to harm the child.

Instead, her weary eyes met with the gaze of the weak, emaciated father of her son.

"Kavan!" She rushed to him and threw an arm around his neck, Ágdhállán caught gently between them. Having just left him, seeing no change in his condition, having him here was the last thing she had expected. When he stumbled, sagging against her, she bore his weight until they could sink together onto the nearby bench. He refused to release her, finding comfort and strength in her scent, her touch, and so she sat beside him, content, barely believing he was there.

"You are hungry…thirsty…" There were questions, things she wanted to know, but taking care of his needs, when he had almost died and taken their son with him, so that she might live, was the only thing she could think about. She owed him her life many times over.

"No, yes…just sit, please." His head drooped against her shoulder and he pressed his nose to her neck with a shiver. "How long?"

"You shouldn't talk. Let me get you…"

"How long?"

His insistence was met with a sigh and a reluctant relaxing against him. "Eight days. Audh found you, brought you back."

"Ombhrís…I…"

Though her lips trembled with emotion she had stubbornly contained since her husband's body was found, she forced a relieved expression and kissed Kavan's forehead. He did not need the burden of her turbulent feelings. "He's no longer a threat. We are free of him."

Hearing 'we' as she and the child, because he did not believe Ombhrís had been a threat to him, Kavan nodded. With her arm about him, she could feel the strain ease from his shoulders. "Good."

"I have prayed for you." Prayer was a new, uncomfortable thing but it was the only way to describe the pleadings uttered to the air, to k'Ádhá, to anyone who would listen and restore Kavan to her.

"Your prayers have been…answered."

He looked weak, limp in a way that worried her. She helped him slouching against the wall so that he would remain upright, and after tearing the no longer fussing child from his hold on Kavan's robe and putting him in his bed box near the warmth of the fire, she eased Kavan to the cot he had previously used near the hearth and brought him a ladle of water. "Drink this and rest. In the morning, you will eat. You're home. Let me care for you as you once cared for me."

For a moment, Kavan almost protested, but he was too disoriented to form words. "Home," was all he managed to squeak.

Yes. He was home.

Now that he was here, with her and the child both soon curled to sleep beside him, he never wanted to leave.

❧*❧

"Take this to the north tower."

The head cook shoved the tray into Zerio's hands, assuming he was one of the daily deliverers of meals to whoever was held in the tower and the soldiers standing guard there. There was speculation about who it could be, but most had settled on the missing Prince Jerit, and it was that belief that had brought Zerio to Glevum.

It was a different belief that had prompted him into the service of Queen Innes.

After the assault on the castle, there had been a body on display, said to be King Kjell though his features were unrecognizable and few were allowed to get close enough to inspect the corpse. An elaborate death pageant performed in his honor followed, allowing all of Glevum and Neth to mourn their murdered king. Zerio had not been there, had not seen the dead, but his superiors had no legitimate reason to believe King Kjell was alive.

Keeping a king as a hostage was a risky business.

Prince Jerit, on the other hand, could very well be alive. Anyone actively seeking the missing boy and his mother was guaranteed to fail if he was hidden from sight. Holding him meant that no one could contest Inness's hold on Neth's throne until King Oska's heir came of age or someone could produce Jerit to challenge her. Why Inness did not kill the prince, if he was there, was unknown, but Inness was not the sort to act without a well-considered reason. Yes, Asta de Corrmick was missing too, but she was of little importance in the scheme of Nethite politics, new or old, even if she, like Inness, could sway the advisors at court and potentially the populace too.

Odds were, Zerio thought, Asta was dead.

If she was not, with several soldiers missing from the night of the coup, any who might support Asta, who might be a threat to Inness, could be manipulated by the belief that Prince Jerit lived as a hostage. A tool for blackmail and coercion was reason enough to keep the boy out of sight and alive.

Maybe Inness did not have the stomach to kill a child outright. Letting him rot in the dark cold of the tower would do the job just as well as a blade would.

Or maybe it was one of the missing soldiers there, held for whatever information he knew. Maybe it was Asta. Given the queen's more visible vicious streak, it could have been any or all of them.

If it was more than one person, with only one meal a day brought on a tray, and only a little of that shoved inside, it would not take long for them to starve.

Zerio was familiar with the rumors, had ferreted them out of the household guards he served alongside, out of the serving staff he quickly befriended. He resisted settling on any one theory about who was in the tower, as there was no proof to support any one of them. He had those of General Stone, his superiors, and others, however. Only finding someone willing to talk, or getting inside that secret sanctum would prove any one of them right.

Only a select few were allowed near the tower. He expected it would take time to earn the opportunity and had been working towards that goal since entering the queen-regent's employ. There were fifteen men assigned to the tower, six who alternated watch at the lower outer door, six who took turns at the bottom of the tower stairs, and three who alternated solo shifts at the top locked door of the tower room itself. Those were the three Zerio wanted to befriend, but so far he had not even seen their faces.

Kitchen staff and other soldiers brought meals to the men on watch. Once each day enough food was included to feed the prisoner. Trays were delivered to the men at the first gate and those at the bottom of the stairs, but none of those delivering meals were allowed up to the barred door and the man who guarded it.

Sent to the kitchen by the queen to return a stained, empty pitcher, Zerio happened to arrive at mealtime, to have the opportunity thrust on him to make it as far as the bottom of the tower staircase. He accepted the large tray with six covered bowls upon it and sauntered towards his destination as if he had done it dozens of times before. He had never been to the tower but he did not need to ask for directions. He knew the Glevum castle layout by heart.

So it was that, after passing through the empty halls of the castle that queen-regent Inness had largely to herself, he stood at the bottom of the steep stone stairs, gazing up the barely lit passage for something he could not see beyond the curvature of the staircase. He heard nothing, no voices, no sounds of movement, no coughing or snoring, to suggest who might be there but as heavily armed and armored as the sentries were, it was easy to judge that the hostage was, indeed, someone of import. Possibly Prince Jerit after all, but there was something, a niggling in the back of his head, that suggested to Zerio this was someone more important.

The guards housed apart from the rest of the de Corrmick staff, kept from accidentally revealing whatever they knew about whomever they guarded, did not appear to be the sort open to friendly discourse.

They did not recognize his face, only the royal tabard he wore over black leather armor. They had no reason not to trust him.

Seeing the layout and the staircase with his own eyes and having determined the hours of the changing of the guards, Zerio now had the basis for a plan. It would be risky, likely to fail, but such acts of honor often were and he appreciated the challenge and the trust of his superiors to undertake the risk.

"Move along," barked one of the soldiers who had taken the tray, removed what was to be his and his companion's portion, and left the rest to the other who was now taking it up the stairs. "The queen will have your eyes for gawking."

"Pardon. It's just…steeper…than I expected…from the outside," Zerio said with a shudder, taking the remains of previous meals and the trays left behind and backing towards the door. Giving the illusion of a fear of heights would, he hoped, work in his favor later. It gained him a sneer and a snort from the men devouring their meal, the sort of brush off Zerio wanted, leaving him free to plot phase three of his plan without suspicion.

His journey back to the kitchen with the trays, a shortcut taken to avoid interaction with palace staff, brought him past the Black Room, a room most often used by the de Corrmick's for a midday retreat. It was named as much for the color of most of its décor as it was for the fact that, historically, much of Neth's policy and many decisions on war and execution, had been decided in that room throughout the centuries of de Corrmick rule over shared glasses of the expensively popular Glevum Black Ale that so many de Corrmick kings preferred.

He had not been inside that room, as most often the cedar doors were closed. Being caught inside might cost him his head, or at least his position in the palace guard. Today the dark wood double doors were ajar, open far enough to allow the raised voices within to be heard in the corridor by anyone who passed. A single word caught Zerio's attention and after glancing up and down the corridor to be sure he was alone, he paused to listen to the recently arrived news.

"My brother is insane!" Inness shrieked in frustrated fury. "Risking plague to send a few…"

"I dare say more than a few." Zerio recognized the elder Fraen's voice and thought he recognized a few of those murmuring behind it.

"How many?"

Her tone produced an awkward silence before Fraen the Elder cleared his throat. "There's no accurate count; the Hatuish soldiers were arriving in Ruidoso and quickly disperse to the east…but the report suggests thousands…potentially half of Hatu's military."

"Half?" She choked but quickly recovered the sound with a clearing of her throat and a long swallow of wine.

In the corridor, Zerio's hands trembled so that the bowls on the tray he carried clattered. He forced himself to be calm and thankfully none in the room appeared to hear the sound. Next to Cordash, Hatu currently had the second-largest military in the Sovereignties, men kept at the ready to repel the horde that periodically swarmed from the lands to the south. Thanks to the training provided by the legendary Guthrie McHador and now the oversight of King Gamal Lachlan Harcourt…a man better trained in the art of war and tactics than many of Hatu's former rulers had been, they were a more efficient, dangerous force than ever. To Zerio it sounded as if the queen had believed the Yellow Sisters would prevent an army from crossing Enesfel, limiting the strength Queen Diona had behind her.

Inness had not, it seemed, put stock in a son's support of his mother, the mother they shared. Why should she? Though Enesfel-born of Lachlan blood, Gamal had lived in, been trained in, the Hatu courts nine months out of the year from the time he was seven years old, groomed for the role assigned to him in agreement between the rulers of both kingdoms. The previous Hatu king had no heirs and his brother, Prince Espen, refused to consider ruling Hatu while his wife sat on the throne of Enesfel. Neither kingdom desired to place both under the rule of a single monarch, leaving the choice of selecting an heir not of Harcourt blood or selecting one of Espen and Diona's twin sons as the heir.

The years schooled in a land with a vastly different cultural outlook towards women could have driven a wedge between Gamal and his mother. If it had, it was not enough of a wedge for him to forsake her and the land of his birth in their time of need. Beyond

Neth's reach, Hatu had but one enemy, and for now, that reoccurring enemy was quiet.

"Dispersed? How many were left?" Inness's initial distress was set aside as the wheels of thought churned through possibilities.

General Fraen looked at those around him, the other men stoically silent, leaving him to bear the wrath of their queen. Thankfully, she did not yet appear as capricious as the de Corrmick kings of olde. She knew she could not indiscriminately do away with the few supporters she had. That was the thing, he believed, that would save his life and help him rise further in power and influence.

"At least one hundred…though by now they too may have been reallocated."

Inness pursed her lips. Too many. Assuming another one hundred was left at every outpost, village, town, and fortification along the border, the total of Hatu soldiers would number two thousand or more. With Cordash already entrenched alongside Enesfel's meager, disorganized troops, their total outmatched Neth's still-forming, ill-trained forces. She could continue the raids, but it would devastate her available military, just as the Yellow Death was beginning to do. The raids provided the troops food and drink and supplies, giving them incentives to continue and sparing the Crown the expense of feeding or outfitting them, but bringing them home meant potentially spreading plague further inland.

If she recalled them, she would have to resort to more expensive means of training.

"Generals, remain with me. The rest of you are dismissed." It was time to discuss options, though Inness already knew what she had to do. The expense was necessary. She would not leave her son open to death in the overthrow of Neth and the de Corrmick house. She would not leave herself vulnerable either.

Zerio hastened towards the kitchen with the tray, being far enough down the corridor by the time the first advisor stepped out of the Black Room not to appear suspicious. He ground his teeth as he casually continued walking, listening to those in the corridor behind him. He would have preferred to stay, to listen, to have the decision, the plan, spoken so that he could report it to his superiors, but he was confident enough in the final decision to be willing to stake his life on the message he would send. The queen would be wisest to withdraw her raiding parties. No more blood would be spilled in Enesfel…for now.

Zerio's focus must remain on the tower.

❧*❧

Kavan jolted awake, hands at his throat, a pounding and constricting in his chest that strangled him of air as the sensation of unraveling threads of power pulled and faded to the point of snapping, though they were not yet breaking free. He was alone, without even Ágdhállán to comfort him, just as he had awoken every morning for the past several days. It was taking too long, he feared, to regain his strength, and now, as he tried to trace that sensation backward, he worried that this flux in power was the cause. He remembered feeling this creeping sensation before, during the pursuit of Ombhrís through the forest, and again upon waking on the stone dais in the ghís center. He remembered feeling it as the ghís inhabitants watched the dead burn. It was weaker but more noticeable now, as the thread slipped further away as if being pulled out of the fabric of his life. He needed to identify the source before it was too late. Before it killed him.

He could smell the savory taint of roasting fish, a frequent meal in the warm months when the catches were copious. Flocks and herds were culled when the weather turned in preparation for the long winter, the older animals butchered to feed the dhóbhaen, so there were fewer animals to feed when grazing lands were buried beneath snow. While the flocks grew fat and healthy, the sea provided.

Kavan had yet to venture out amongst the villagers, both out of healing exhaustion and the fear that followed the proclamation of miracles. Both Iólán and Audh, who came once or twice each day to visit now that he had awakened, brought reports of the miracles rendered by nothing more than people touching him while he slept.

It was not the first time such healings were attributed to him. Most often he had no proof the rumors were true. As it became more obvious that miraculous occurrences did pass through him at k'Ádhá's whim, he could not refute the accuracy of such claims. Many of those in Curnydhá who claimed miracles were people Audh, Iólán, and Raebhá knew well, injured, sick, and heartbroken people whose conditions were known before and after. Kavan, again, could not deny their experiences. Thankfully, whenever one of the three spoke of such things, they contained whatever awe and elation they felt, preventing Kavan from withdrawing in distress.

But he was hungry, tired of lying in bed, and knew he could hide no more. Whether he was met with adoration or fear, he wanted to explore the sensations that had awakened him. He wanted to be near Raebhá and their son. They had spoken little during the past days as his waking periods most often came when he was alone. When she was there, and he was aware of it, it had been enough for her to curl up beside him and enjoy the stillness of the other's companionship.

Or maybe, he thought as he stepped through the door and pinpointed her aura while working his way slowly down the steps stained with his blood, there had been silence because there were too many words that neither wanted to say.

"kydhé." As Kavan had moved little since falling to the poison, his movements were slow, stiff, and awkward. Iólán and another fellow who happened to pass met him midway down the stairs and supported him the rest of the way down.

"It is good to see you up," Iólán said with his usual friendly smile.

"Will you dine with us?" asked the other eagerly.

The second man's tone of expectation caused Kavan's voice to fail but he nodded, determined to follow his choice through, determined to reach Raebhá's side. His resolve was tested in the pushing past the greeting stares that followed him across Curnydhá, both fearful and reverent, suspicious and overjoyed in equal measure. Each gave rise to the feeling of awkward unwelcome. Audh had spoken of the increasing support of those no longer fearing him as they had; what Kavan read hinted that the man may have exaggerated his support.

Maybe it was the fact that Kavan was walking among them again. It was easy to be unafraid of a cataleptic man who produced miracles and might be dying. An unconscious man presented no active threat.

What sort of man could survive poison?

It was the way that Raebhá, seated in her customary place in the ghís kelyhag, clutched Ágdhállán to her breast with fierce protectiveness that worried Kavan most. Ephé and Audh sat protectively on either side of her. Ombhrís was no longer a threat, had been given his final rights some nights past, but Kavan could tell she felt threatened, wary enough to demand the proximity of those she trusted. She had hidden it from him when they were alone in her home, but here in the open, it was harder to mask.

The threat was not Ombhrís, he judged, but something he had not seen before. Something new.

Her expression brightened when he entered and she rose to greet him with an overflow of relief that caused many around the cookfires to smile. Audh smiled too and slid sideways on the bench to make room for him. Raebhá did not hesitate to embrace him, showed no reluctance to kiss his mouth, refusing to hide her affection for her son's father any more than any other dhóbhaen would do. He welcomed her embrace, and though weak, fervently returned it. That told her enough.

The man she had met nearly a year hence would once have shrunk from the display in horror and embarrassment.

"Welcome, kydhé Cliáth." Éthym smiled as Ephé rose in welcome and brought him food after Iólán settled him on the felled log bench beside Raebhá. The other márbhyndhánis bowed their heads or bowed at the waist in greeting when he continued, "It is good to see the ágdháthé have favored you with good health."

If any of the márbhyndhánis harbored ill towards him, it was hidden behind well-trained walls of power that Kavan did not have the strength or will to probe. On the surface, they appeared accepting, welcoming, which, he prayed, meant that Raebhá's efforts to change the course of dhóbhaen history would be met with eventual success.

The old man's words bore a peculiarity that others noticed. The ágdháthé did not interfere in the lives of the dhóbhaen; when bad things happened, the spirits of the dead were blamed. Good things were attributed to a person's efforts, a strong constitution, or occasionally the good fortune of the stars' alignment, if luck followed one often from childhood. To attribute Kavan's recovery to the favor of the ágdháthé was little different than calling it a miracle. The only ágdhá ever suggested to take interest in, or have a hand in, the lives of men was the one known by Dhágdhuán and his followers as k'Ádhá.

Had Éthym let slip a belief in the heretical or was he acquiescing to Kavan's personal beliefs?

How might that affect the others seated around them?

"I am blessed," Kavan agreed. He was no saint, but he was, without argument, blessed. He included Raebhá and Ágdhállán in his list of blessings, more precious to him than his life.

Raebhá smiled and murmured, "You are indeed. We all are."

Iólán, having wiggled between Kavan and Audh, leaned close, his mouth to Kavan's ear, and whispered with a chuckle, "You should wed her already, haiágles. There are no more impediments. It is time."

Choking on the zerphánál he had not yet swallowed, his skin flushed with embarrassment, Kavan stared at the other man, unable to reply. Was that what Raebhá wanted? Expected? He looked at her and was relieved that she, now in conversation with Ephé, appeared not to hear her brother's words. They had not discussed the future since Ombhrís' death, both afraid, he supposed, of what their futures held.

Having believed that marriage would never be the hand fate dealt to him, that no woman would ever desire that with him, Kavan could not say which terrified him more…that she might refuse such an offer and prove him correct, or that she might accept.

Amidst a sea of unfamiliar faces, emissaries from nearby suffering ghís, the ritual of storytelling and song began, leaving Kavan to pick at his meal without interruption or the need to address Iólán's counsel. With Ágdhállán in a padded bed box beside her, Raebhá's arm hooked around Kavan's, she raised her gaze to him often, with fondness and adoration and a look that suggested she wanted to verify his reality, his health. In addition to the heat of yearning and joy of affection, he could sense the waiting, the longing, of the whole of Curnydhá for him to play, to sing. When they realized there would be no music from the still weary bard, locals and visitors gradually began to withdraw for the fires of their homes or the temporary structures erected for those displaced by the disaster. The sun settled below the mountainous horizon, an odd sort of extended twilight of mauve, gold, and amber that Kavan found mesmerizing.

Alone at last, with Ágdhállán asleep against Kavan's shoulder where he tended to settle and fall asleep faster than anywhere else, Raebhá leaned against him and followed his gaze through the open western door, wondering what he saw or if he was looking for anything specific. The wind blew from the heights tonight, pushing the moisture out to sea, bringing with it a drop in temperature. Most of the snow never left those heights and, as Kavan knew, the higher one climbed, the less life could be found. Was he thinking about the passage of time since they had traveled through the snow? About what had happened to him there? Or was he contemplating what they both suspected existed there though he had yet to seek it out?

Maybe he would never search for it. Maybe she could give him reason to never return to Alberni.

"Ombhrís is gone," she assured him, her hand covering his, her body relaxing more when his fingers curled through hers. "I saw his body myself. Curnydhá is free of him…as are we."

Kavan heard the question behind the words, the question no one had yet asked. He sighed. "I could not save him. I tried."

"Tried?" She did not doubt him but found it remarkable that Kavan would try to save the other man's life, given his desire to protect her. "You saw him?"

"He was too near the edge…slipped. The moss and stone could not anchor him, and my arm…" He rubbed his sore shoulder. "I could not pull him up. He deserved justice." What justice was, in this case, was not for Kavan to say. He was not the man's judge or jury and not his executioner. Maybe k'Ádhá had doled out justice without Kavan or the dhóbhaen needing to do so. "But I don't regret he's gone."

Picturing the scene behind her closed lids, the way the moment must have played out, Raebhá nodded and nuzzled his jaw. "Nor do I. You did what you could…what was necessary. Reconditioning does not work for some; it drives them mad, destroys their minds. I dare say he would have been one of those."

He deserved to die, she thought bitterly. She was satisfied he was gone but would never say so aloud.

"Some are beyond redemption, though k'Ádhá knows I wish it wasn't so." Cheek pressed to Ágdhállán's, Kavan ordered his thoughts and took a breath, judging by the tingling in his belly that the talk of Ombhrís was meant to be a precursor to something else. "Raebhá…" His tongue tripped over her name and he choked on his breath.

Nervous at his tone, she looked into his eyes and waited.

"I know there are…matters…we must address…"

She looked away with a shake of her head, grateful for the break created by the wind bumping the door against the building. There was an omen of bad news in that sound and she felt burdened with enough weight tonight. "Not tonight. I have had too much of business, of troubles. There is time."

Tugging on his hand, she urged him to his feet and together they passed through the darkness to her home.

"Not tonight." Kavan could concede to that, as they walked, as the waning threads continued to sap his energy now that he had spent more consecutive hours awake and upright than he had spent that way in days. The inevitable could not be put off indefinitely, but tonight he was content to avoid discussing the future for a few more hours. "But I do want to ask…to know…"

Iólán's burr had burrowed into his head and refused to give Kavan peace until he dealt with it. Again she looked at him with visible relief that he had agreed to leave unpleasant matters for another time.

The moonlight glimmered in the red of her hair as the breeze tugged it in front of her face. Tentatively, he stopped walking and brushed it back behind her ear as he said, "I believe we should wed, if you will…I mean, I want…Ágdhállán should have…there is no reason preventing us…and you know I have never…will never…you are the only one I shall…"

The more he fumbled for words, the more merriment sparkled in her surprised gaze, once the initial confusion and surprise left her eyes. The more of that amusement he saw, the more Kavan struggled to be clear with his feelings, confident she did not understand, that her expression was perplexed rather than mocking. The question should be an easy one to ask, but fear of her answer made it more awkward than he had expected.

Finally, he stopped with a defeated sigh and an admission he had never thought to make. "I love you with a full heart, my soul, my life, aislé. I desire to be bound to you always…whatever our futures hold…if you will have me."

They were words she had never thought he would say, feelings she did not think he would ever voice. Hand cupped behind his head, fingers tangling in his hair as she pulled him into a breathless kiss, Raebhá bought herself time to tame her thoughts and form a response. There were reasons they should not be married, but as many reasons that they should, and having that bond with him, wherever their futures took them, might be the only part of him she could ever hold on to.

"I would have it no other way; if it is your wish, and not a matter of duty and honor," she whispered, her forehead pressed to his when the kiss broke. Perhaps there would come a day when she would regret this choice but tonight, it was the right, proper, blessed thing to do.

Duty and honor were part of it, things ingrained in him from the days of his earliest memories, deeply influenced by Kóráhm's writings. His Faith demanded such an act of respect but he could truthfully admit that he would have sought this same union with her without the weight of moral conviction. His soul was too entwined with hers to have longed for anything different.

His heart thundered in his ears and his chest ached. It hurt as if it would burst, but he had never felt more elated. "My heart is yours, aeslag, from now until I breathe no more. I want us to be…"

Within Kavan's center where his power resided, he felt the tearing again and an flare of power that caused him to cry out and double over, almost falling on the steps. Raebhá caught him, Kept him upright, and in that touch she felt what he felt, power and pain, something bleeding in from far away, beyond the reach of her abilities.

"Kavan!"

In his head, in his soul, only one word existed, the cause of the fading he had been aware of for days.

Tíbhyan.

Raebhá recognized the word to be a name, though she did not know who the individual was when Kavan collapsed. Someone dear to him that she had not met, she deduced, as she supported him, stumbling, back to her home and the cot where he had spent the last several days. He was shaking as if in shock, his skin covered with a damp sheen that was rare amongst dhóbhaen and Elyri alike. If not for what she read in him as she helped him inside and closed the door, if not for the utterance of that name, she would have thought him to suffer from poison lingering in his blood.

This was no illness. This had no link to the question he had just asked her, the promises they had just made. This was the suffering of a man losing someone he loved, someone he was deeply attached to.

Someone far away in the place he had left behind. For her.

She wiped tears from her eyes, grateful that Kavan's condition did not disturb Ágdhállán when she placed him in his bed box. For a moment, the proposal, his profession of love, had made her hope that his choice was to stay with her, build a life in Curnydhá. But this death, if that was what it was, was a harsh reminder that he could not stay. It was a reminder of the choices she faced, to remain here and fight for her people or leave the dhóbhaen in the thrall of millennia of tradition and indoctrination that no longer had a place. Kavan's coming here might herald further contact with their distant kin, if Raebhá could pave the way, but she had no intention of inviting anyone here that might be outcast or killed for their differences.

Lost in her thoughts as she rubbed his cold hands and listened to his breathing, it took several minutes to realize that Kavan had lifted his face to look at her. His eyes were bleary, bloodshot, bearing the pain of a broken heart and it brought her to tears.

He pressed her hand to her cheek, a pleading gesture without words to express what he wanted to say.

She kissed his palm. "Kavan…whoever this is…you should go…"

"I cannot…"

"You must. I have duties to the ghísaer…I cannot leave them and I will not bind you here…" If his promise to her held him back, she would release him from it if she had to, if it was the only way for him to do what needed to be done.

"aeslag." He kissed her, wrestling with himself as he examined that fluctuating power again. Tíbhyan was not dead, but he was fading and Kavan had no idea how long an Elyri could exist in that state. There was so little known about the kylldhysag in Elyria, and Kavan had hoped for the opportunity to remain amongst the dhóbhaen long enough to gain a better understanding of that particular rite of passage. Raebhá was right that he should be with his mentor, his earliest and dearest friend, the man to whom he owed his evolution as ágdháni, as a man. But tonight, he could not go anywhere.

"I'm too weak; my control is not as it should be. Even if I could find and reach a Gate tonight…it took five márbhyndhánis to send you through and I am but one man. At full strength, perhaps I might…"

"You said it took five because they sent me where there was…."

"Perhaps. I don't know. I won't until I find it. But not tonight." By morning, he sighed morosely, it might be too late. "Besides, there is Ágdhállán's safety, and yours, and we are to marry…"

Turning her face so that her tear-stained cheeks brushed over his hand, she kissed his palm again. "Some things take precedence."

"Nothing takes precedence over promises to family."

Such promises, however, had sealed his future, for he had told Dhóri, Sóbhán, and Ártur that he would return, a promise made to others he considered to be family as well even though they did not share the bonds of blood. He had promised to remain until he believed her safe. He had promised that he would love her always. To always be with her. No matter the miles that might separate them, they would never be truly apart. His offer of marriage was such a promise and would, in his eyes, bind him to her until one of them died.

"Your duty…sacred and just…to give your people the rights that only a few possess, as well as the permission to believe as their hearts call them to…those things should not be withdrawn. You have opened doors for them and only you can lead them through. I know…"

His fingers trailed down her throat. "It will not allow you to follow me…at least not yet." Shuddering, he closed his eyes against the tears welling there. "Things will change. Someday there will be peace here…freedom…and I will bless that day and the gift of you making it happen. When it does, we will be together again…if not before."

He attempted a weak smile. His duty in Alberni, in Enesfel, might end before Dhóbhaen's day arrived, his responsibilities given to others who could shoulder them without him, and on that day, Kavan would be free to return to Curnydhá, to Raebhá and their child, and remain at her side. He had every intention of doing so.

"But I will not leave you unable to defend yourself and our son."

"Kavan…" Her voice cracked as she looked at the sleeping boy.

"There are ways. I can teach you. I will teach you. If I cannot be here to protect you both, I will be certain you can…"

"If…when you go," she corrected with a croaking sound breaking at the back of her throat, "you will take Ágdhállán with you."

It was a choice born from much thought, a choice she believed to be the right one despite the pain it created.

He had expected protest and argument but never those words. Drawing her around to face him, grasping her chin, he sought her sincerity, sought confirmation that he had heard her correctly. "You are his mother. He needs you."

"He needs someone to keep him safe, who can devote time and attention to his upbringing, his education, his training. If he remains here, and they discover what he is, what he can already do, because of all you have done, there is a chance, even if I succeed, other márbhyndhánis throughout Dhóbhaen may seek to Recondition him. They might destroy his potential rather than see him become what you are. Even if they don't, if he's selected as márbhyndhánis, I fear his potential will be limited, wasted." She felt a swell of pride despite her heartache. "Here he'll never reach the fullness of his gifts. Others will fear him. Whatever those gifts are, beyond the Sight, no one is better suited to teach him than you."

Kavan could not argue those points and did not try. He had taught Dhóri and Sóbhán what Tíbhyan could not and could do the same for this child. Despairingly, he had been prepared to miss out on his son's upbringing to leave Raebhá the right to him. How could he take Ágdhállán and leave her alone?

"Besides," she kissed his mouth and covered his hand on her cheek with hers, trying to still his arguments before he made them, "you may not see it, but I do. He cries less when with you. When you were poisoned, suffering, when you awoke…he responds. He's bound to you with dáni in a way that I think will cause lasting damage if he is separated from you. When he is older, more centered, able to understand such things, he will come back to me, as you will. I'll be consumed with what must be done here…and it will not be easy…"

The danger she faced as she challenged tradition, custom, and faith remained unspoken but understood. Kavan was reluctant to take the child from her, however. "We do not need to decide tonight. Tomorrow I will teach you…we will wed when you are ready to do so…and when I am stronger, we can seek the Gate together."

The talk of separation might be for naught if he could not manipulate the Gate alone or find a familiar point close to home. Perhaps the márbhyndhánis would help him, but he could not expect them to take that risk. Even if he chose to sail west, a journey that would take a year or more to complete, Kavan might awaken in the morn choosing to stay, to never leave her side.

"And Tíbhyan?"

He frowned, toying with strands of her red hair, contemplating her question. He would either leave in time to bid his mentor farewell, or the man would pass from the world before he could. Kavan had no control over the man's fate, or his own, and tonight he did not have the strength to follow the power threads backward to touch the ancient man's thoughts for one last moment of reassurance and connection. "I…that will take care of itself," he whispered.

He stretched his thoughts as far as he could, begging the bhydáni to wait, begging Kóráhm to help him find his way. Kavan had little hope that either attempt would succeed.

❧*❧

"I've finished tending your garden, bhydáni." Bhen wiped his hands on his trousers as he entered through the rear door of the man's home to see that Tíbhyan had not moved in the chair where he had been when Bhen arrived. With his stooped shoulders, glassy eyes, and skeletal hands resting on his equally thin legs, the bhydáni looked more dead than alive, but Bhen put his hand on the frail shoulder and Tíbhyan lifted his head to make eye contact with a thin smile.

Despite the work that devoured most hours of his day, Bhen made time each week to tend the man's flower garden as he had for more than twenty years. In exchange, Tíbhyan had taught him the ways of power, just as he had taught Sóbhán, Dhóri, Chethá, Yóaná, and any other young ones Kavan brought to him. The last student, besides Bhen, had stopped coming when Yóaná had graduated from apprentice to full healer, a day that coincided, in Bhen's opinion, with the steady decline of Tíbhyan's health and mental acuity. He had been declining physically for more than a century, but the decline had become more noticeable over the past year, without Kavan having come to see him. He had taken a steep turn for the worse after whatever event had knocked him off his feet and left him incapacitated by a broken hip that, while healed, no longer supported his weight as it should. Bhen had been the one to find him on the floor, eyes bloodshot, blood around his ears as if he had struck his head in that fall, lying in his own waste without the ability to rise, unable to eat or drink.

Many in Bhryell had thought he would die then and had come to pay respects and offer prayers, doubtless hoping for some bequest for their generous visits. But the ancient sage clung to life. Bhen knew that death would come soon, for Tíbhyan had no strength to go into the wild the way some Elyri did, walking away from their lives never to return. Unable to walk, spending his time in his chair staring at the fountain in the square or the flowers in his garden, Bhen imagined it was where Tíbhyan would be found dead, hoping for something that could not be. Bhen came every day since the man's fall, caring for him the way he knew Kavan would if the bard could be here.

Tíbhyan rarely spoke and when he did it was cryptic words and Kavan's name, snippets that made no sense to anyone but him.

Maybe they made no sense to him either.

Today Sóbhán was with them, the opportunity of a day free of duty to Prince Lorant spent tidying the bhydáni's home. There was little to tidy since the sage did not move on his own and several in the Cliáth and MacLyr households came when they could to launder his clothes, bring meals he rarely ate, and clean the platters and cups used to feed him. The dust from the outside foot traffic that accumulated through the always-open windows needed to be wiped away, and when it rained, the stain of it was left on the sills to dry. Sóbhán read to him every visit, or shared whatever gossip had sprung up in Bhryell. He was not the gossip Bhen was, but as he heard all of the details from Bhen, sharing them with Tíbhyan seemed like a fair means of keeping the man an informed part of the community.

Sóbhán came out of the kitchen with the bread and honey he had intended to feed the ailing man but Tíbhyan's chin had already dropped to his chest. A light snoring rattle resonated within struggling lungs. Sighing, Sóbhán offered the plate to Bhen who had worked up enough of an appetite in the garden to gratefully accept it.

"He spoke of bhydhá again," Sóbhán murmured. "It feels like he is waiting for his return. I tried to tell him that bhydhá will understand, that he cannot be here…"

Bhen nodded. "I tell him as well, but still he stares at the fountain as if…"

The fountain was a tribute to the Cliáths who had been Bhryell's founders, with a more recent monument added to its center in honor of the White Bard. Sometimes when Bhen or Sóbhán opened the door, his face brightened as if seeing his favorite student again, only for the look to fade when he realized Kavan was not entering his home.

"Wonder if he knows something we don't or if he's just obstinate."

"Can't blame him for not wanting to go without a farewell." Kavan was the nearest thing to family Tíbhyan had. Not a religious man, perhaps he feared death and wanted Kavan's reassurance but Sóbhán believed it was something more. "I think someone should stay with him. It will be a great shame if he passes alone…bhydhá will never forgive himself. I will talk to Chethá and return this evening, with Prince Lorant if necessary."

"It would be the kind and decent thing to do," Bhen agreed. "We'll alternate…and I'll ask for the same from dedhá Bhílári so that he and others from Hes Índári can sit with him…so he is never alone. I'll fetch one of them now…if you will stay until someone comes?"

A glance at the window allowed Sóbhán to judge the hour and he nodded. There was time before he was due home for the evening meal with his wife and the prince, for the discussion that would follow.

Thankfully, Tíbhyan had been spared the Bhryell plague.

"I'll wait." He drew the blanket from Tíbhyan's lap and tucked it around his shoulders as the day was cool and the bhydáni was directly in line with the window. Bhen clasped his shoulder; there were a few footsteps on the wooden floor, then the front door opened and closed.

With a jerky movement, Tíbhyan caught Sóbhán's wrist, and though his eyes did not open, he croaked, "He'll come; you'll see."

Sóbhán gaped but did not argue. Tíbhyan was asleep again, his hands slack on his lap. It seemed an unlikely thing to hope for, a desperate thing to believe.

But maybe the bhydáni was right.

❧*❧

Given little choice, Inness ordered the withdrawal of her raiding troops, summoning them to an area south of the city of Mawr where they could train and yet contain the threat of plague to a relatively small area. Those deemed healthiest were brought to Glevum, but all were kept far from the eyes of either the menacing troops on the southern border or the blockade of ships in Glevum's harbor. No public comments were made, no words of capitulation sent to Rhidam. It would eventually be noticed that the raids had ceased, and gradually the watchful border troops would grow lax and decide that Neth was no longer a threat. She was counting on Gamal and King Govert recalling their troops and by that time she intended Neth's army to be better prepared for battle. She would recruit, she would train, and when the time came, Neth would reclaim what was hers.

Inness closed the heavy drapes against the bright morning sun and retired to her bed, the night's vigil in the Black Room with General Stone and the newly appointed General Fraen having stretched too long through interruptions by her too-fussy son and the incoming reports of her troops' activities. The order was in place, the recalls had begun and the prince finally slept.

It was time for Inness to do likewise.

❧*❧

When Iólán arrived at dawn to inquire about Kavan's health, the revelation of their intent to wed divided Kavan from Raebhá in unanticipated ways. Having been wed previously, even if it had been an unconsummated sham dissolved by violence and deceit, and wanting to remain at Kavan's side as his departure grew more imminent, Raebhá's effort to forgo custom was thwarted by her brother with every protest she made. The changes to custom she hoped to bring to Curnydhá, to the dhóbhaen, would be difficult enough to birth. Changing an eternity of wedding practice when it was unnecessary to do so would introduce additional unrest. Despite his openness to change, there were some conventions Iólán was not willing to overlook, not when he might lose his sister to the land from which her soon-to-be husband hailed.

Raebhá and Ágdhállán were shuffled off to Ephé's home. Kavan was likewise prompted to vacate Raebhá's home for a bed in Iólán's to ensure a customary separation before the couple wed. Typically, the separation lasted two full weeks but Raebhá would not permit it. Kavan's dying mentor might not have two weeks. Five days was all she was able to arrange, the five-day minimum necessary to make preparations and allow Kavan time to regain his core power while she continued to negotiate aid for her people spread along Gálínphel's suffering coast, five days she hoped could be spared. If Kavan came to her and claimed to be out of time, she swore she would marry him in the privacy of her home with Iólán and Audh as officiants, without the public display or her brother's approval.

It was that impending deadline that kept her from following custom to the letter, kept her from avoiding him. The necessity of learning to protect herself, of allowing Kavan to see his son, meant breaking the rules. Thanks to Kavan, however, no one was aware the custom was being broken. When the ghís slept, he stole from Iólán's home, certain the other man would not wake, and after making certain Raebhá's hosts would likewise sleep, she would steal away with him, Ágdhállán in her arms, to follow him into the forest where hours were spent in the ways of power and knowledge that few dhóbhaen were allowed to pursue. The skills she learned, to protect her body, her mind, her life, her home, would need to be continually practiced, as mastery would take time, but it was time that Kavan did not have and so he pushed her to learn the basics of each skill until he was certain she understood them. He fretted that his efforts would not be enough but was forced to trust that they would be.

It had to be enough.

Such intensive late-night sessions in the twilight of the unsetting sun meant exhaustion during the extended daytime hours, but Kavan was accustomed to sleepless nights. He had no difficulty participating in the rituals Iólán guided him through and explained to him. The usual token payments between families of goods and services could barely be honored as Kavan had little to give except song and had no means of taking much with him when he departed. Audh, however, saw to it that a collection of maps and manuscripts, rare things among the dhóbhaen, came into Kavan's possession despite the disapproval of the other márbhyndhánis. In exchange for the bride price he could not pay, Kavan signed a lengthy document agreeing that Raebhá's wealth, her home, her possessions were her own and would remain so regardless of future separation. As marriages among the dhóbhaen could not be dissolved except by agreement between parties or death once consummated, only death or Ceasing would truly divide them and only at the end of her life would her possessions pass to him, to their children if they had reached the age of maturity by that time, or to Iólán or his children if there were no other survivors to lay claim.

It meant that what was hers would not be his, but Kavan had no desire for material possessions or her position. What he had in Alberni and Bhryell was more than enough. Here he only needed Raebhá, their son, the journals he kept and books he studied, his harp, and his music.

The márbhyndhánis removed the red and white stone, larger than his fist, from above the door of Raebhá's home, a stone that Kavan had noted over doors of other homes and had not questioned until he witnessed its removal. The ghrís pheslárkag, the marriage stone, was displayed after a wedding, a remnant of ceremony meant to show the community that the residents were wed. Another would take its place after he and Raebhá were bound, but for now, the indentation in the wooden framework was vacant. Iólán explained that ritual too, what would be expected when a new stone took its place.

Thankfully, there were no ritual phrases to remember, and as he learned quickly, Kavan was left too many nervous solitary hours each day. He filled his time taking in further details of Curnydhá, in setting them to paper, and in meditation that he hoped would give him the strength and power needed to operate whatever Gate he found. The more centered he became, the more he could feel the thread between himself and Tíbhyan, a link he had taken for granted since the day they had become student and teacher. It stretched thinner, tauter, and gradually more brittle, but it did not yet feel prepared to break. Kavan chose to believe he had time, although there were moments when he awoke when he felt consumed by heart-bursting panic as he fearfully scrambled to find the thread inside.

Determined to reach Tíbhyan before it was too late, he gathered power during his quiet hours, when he was alone, refilling himself, honing himself, resetting his internal measure so that, when the hour came, he would be less likely to fail.

And he carved. As a Cliáthan, he had been raised with wood in his hands, expected to become a harpmaker like the Cliáths before him. He did not possess their skill, nor Sóbhán's but he could do well enough for the purpose intended. The tender black wood, its color matching the harp he missed so dearly, hewn with the ániélmé he had brought from Alberni, was destined to be a knife given to his bride as part of the ceremony. Its significance explained, the act of creation was as momentous as the gift, molding the six-inch block into something worthy of the one he had committed his heart to.

His gifts were his voice, his ear, his song. His command of language and harp strings. Being absorbed by a foreign skill opened his spirit to power and cleared his mind of worries and interfering thoughts; by the time the wooden form was finished and Iólán and Audh arrived on the evening of the fourth day, Kavan felt rejuvenated.

"It is time."

"Time?" The centered feeling gave way to nervous anticipation as he stood to greet both men, the pair wearing coarse crimson floor-length tunics edged with white. Braided white sashes with crimson threads were tied around their heads, the knot and long-stranded ends hanging on the left side of their faces at the temple. They wore no shoes and Audh carried a covered basket woven of the reeds that grew where the river met the sea.

"Come." Iólán smiled, his expression amused and mysterious as he put an arm around Kavan's shoulder and escorted him into the street where men lined the path from Iólán's home to the southern rim of the forest, every man from Curnydhá as far as Kavan could tell, from the youngest to the most ancient. Between each step the trio took, the men clapped and stamped their feet, creating a syncopated, staccato rumble that Kavan suspected was to distract the spirits of the dead from those of the living. With each step, between the beats of clapping and stamping, they gave a loud cry that drowned out any noise their footsteps made on the moist earth. He had heard a similar commotion that morning, some ritual Iólán prevented him from witnessing, and now as Kavan followed his escorts, he assumed that Raebhá had made this same journey.

He was curious where it would take him.

At the edge of the trees, the other two male márbhyndhánis and the older novices waited, except for the ancient Éthym, the glow of their handlights illuminating the twilight as they joined the procession and followed behind. Nervous about being surrounded for a ritual Kavan had not been told about, he followed barefoot over a worn forest track that wound along the bank of the narrow channel of churning water.

The trek lasted no more than thirty minutes, over a path Kavan had not previously explored. They stopped at the foot of a short, turbulent waterfall and when Iólán and Audh began to climb the rocky side, Kavan did likewise. The márbhyndhánis followed. There were eight carved steps, winding through the overgrowth of trees, and at the top, the water pooled from a taller fall to the west. A steamy mist rose from the churning tarn, ringed with glistening smoky gray crystals similar to the one Kavan wore. The warmth of the mist and sound was an unexpectedly inviting luxury and the powerful lure of the crystals made the air hum beneath the gurgle of the falls and the bubbling of water from beneath the ground. Raebhá had spoken of heated springs and such things existed in the Llaethlágárá but Kavan had never visited one. With márbhyndhánis on both sides of the pool, hands clasped before them as their handlights burned, Audh and Iólán removed their clothes and stepped into the pool, beckoning Kavan to join them with outstretched hands.

"kállóm kóhm íls hílylá," Iólán bid.

The concept of ritual cleansing before taking an oath was not a foreign one. Undoubtedly, that was what this was. Self-conscious of his white skin, what these men would think when they saw him, he reminded himself that many already had when he had lain on display at the center of Curnydhá. He nervously deposited his trousers and tunic with theirs and stepped into the water. The crystal against his neck buzzed with power as he sank into the warmth.

He expected it to be hotter, but the constant mixing of the underground spring with the mountain run-off made the pool surprisingly comfortable. That coziness, however, did not dispel his discomfort as Iólán began to run water through Kavan's hair while Audh rubbed Kavan's skin with a clump of dried moss taken out of his basket. It was scratchy but left his skin invigorated and feeling cleaner than it had in some time.

"Raebhá says you intend to leave us…after…" Iólán said, his voice a low whisper that only the other two in the pool could hear. If the other márbhyndhánis did as well, they did not move or react. They remained stationary, unflinching, their eyes upturned to the sky, only the flames in their hands, the gentle rise and fall of their chests to indicate breathing, and the occasional blinking of eyes revealed that they were living instead of carved stone men.

Not knowing when she had revealed this or why Iólán chose to bring it up, Kavan painfully admitted, "Obligations compel me home, as they compel her to remain here. But if I can travel one way, I can travel both, and will return as often as I am able." Never seeing her again would destroy him. He could not endure that fate without a fight. Even if he had to build a ship and sail it himself to return.

"It is an easy thing? To use the rynlagne?" Iólán asked, leaning closer to not be overheard although Audh was there and would hear anything said between them, as might the other márbhyndhánis. From the touch of hands upon him, however, Kavan read no sense that the question was meant to entrap him.

He was a curiosity to them, and while the márbhyndhánis harbored reservations, they seemed to accept that his intentions in Curnydhá were noble and that he was as they were, a man of learning, power, and wisdom that went deeper than a lifetime of experience. Only Iólán was out of place in this gathering, the one man with limited knowledge of power and if they were determined to keep the secrets of their gifts hidden from him, they made no effort to interrupt the discussion or prevent Kavan from speaking.

"Normal ones, yes. The ones that link my home with this land…I cannot say what I will find. Do you know where the nearest one is?"

Audh lifted his head, his expression wary. "Not exactly. I have never used it, never been to it, but I'm told by those who have that it exists near the edge of the tree line, not far from where I found you…poisoned."

Through the trees, Kavan could barely see that upper forested edge on the other side of Curnydhá, where altitude and cold limited the growth of anything more than scrubby grass and moss during the warmest months. From everywhere in the ghís, he could feel the pull of power there, although it was faint enough to be nebulous and unfocused. He was surprised he had not realized its proximity when he had pursued Ombhrís up the mountain's face.

Even at his top speed, through the forest and up rocky ledges, reaching it would take hours on foot. Flight would shorten the journey, but Raebhá would insist on accompanying him when the time came, and with Ágdhállán with them, flight would not be an option. He considered again the possibility of stealing away in the night, avoiding a painful farewell, but he knew he could not do that. Parting from her would be difficult enough and he could not walk away without a word of goodbye to his son.

Audh continued, breaking the silence. "Some márbhyndhánis use them often between ghísaer, some prefer to travel by land or sea."

"You prefer the sea."

Audh's neutral expression cracked. He grinned. "How else would I have contented myself to journey west?"

Behind Kavan, Iólán braided the bard's hair, entwining leafy, vines taken from the basket into the braid, forming an ornate crown of foliage meant to make him one with nature. Raebhá's hair would be similarly adorned he assumed and though it felt uncomfortable to have his hair pulled away from his face, for the sake of the union that would forever change his life, Kavan would endure it for this day.

"You should remain with us." The man's hand smoothed over the bottom of the braid and down Kavan's back, revealing emotions the bard had not expected. Devotion the likes of which he shared with so few, from a man he barely knew. Devotion from both men reminded Kavan of Wortham and brought a flood of sorrow and regret that his dearest friend could not be with him.

Wortham should be here to witness this day. Wortham should stand for him, stand with him. Should see him married.

A shriveling pain balled in his chest. Kavan closed his eyes, his thoughts, against it, grateful that neither Audh nor Iólán could read them. "I am no savior. I am a man whose heart and duty are caught between two worlds. My presence here has been disruptive and…"

"Redemptive," added Audh. He met Kavan's gaze and wiped a trickle of water from his white cheek.

"That was never my intent. Either of them. What results of my visit is for the future to tell. Raebhá's path will be unsteady and I pray while I must be away, the two of you will see to it she is safe."

"For you, kydhé. I will do anything," Audh swore. "It was my duty from the first day we crossed paths."

Iólán kissed the back of Kavan's head, his hands lingering on the moonlit white shoulders. "She is taeásne. I could do nothing less. But even if she were not, your coming to us was no coincidence or mistake. I will stand for you in Curnydhá, in Dhóbhaen, in all things."

"du," agreed Audh, his expression neutral again though Kavan thought he meant to say more. He removed a ceramic flask from his basket as he rose from the pool and gestured for Kavan to come to him. The márbhyndhánis around the pool parted so that they could emerge and took up a murmuring chant as Iólán dried Kavan with a coarse cloth and Audh rubbed a sweet oil of flowers and musk over his freshly scrubbed and dried limbs. Kavan shivered, the act reminding him of an anointing that he did not want.

It was not just the act that reminded him of anointing, but the flurry of energy and presences around them that the márbhyndhánis also felt. Though the men did not move, their gazes darted about, seeking the source but finding none. Fortunately, they did not seem to equate Kavan as the cause of that flurry of power, and though the tingle of it remained within Kavan, the presences, the multitude of záphyric hands that had kissed his skin with their caresses, ceased when Audh replaced the stopper in the flask.

"You are favored." There was no other word in the dhóbhaen tongue to use. There was little room for the existence of záryph or the appearance of saints; only the teaching of Dhágdhuán allowed for such things, allowed for a person to find divine favor. Speaking of the favor of a man by the ágdháthé was to step away from customary teachings, whether Audh accepted the heretical tenants of Dhágdhuán or not.

As unsettled as they were, the expressions on the faces of each of those around him bore witness to a like agreement. They had connected the presences to him after all. Favored by the ágdháthé or by the dáni, Kavan was a man to be respected, a force of dáni to contend with that none chose to cross.

"I am but a man."

Iólán pulled the blood-red robe of filmy fabric, the same fabric Raebhá had worn when he found her near the lake, over Kavan's head. Nervously, Kavan smoothed his hands over the airy texture, marveling at how much his life had changed since that day.

The Sight had been accurate in predicting change. Once he had feared he would never be like any other man.

What lay ahead as they returned to the ghís would, at last, prove otherwise.

❧*❧

The bathing was complete, her hair adorned with the customary floral crown, but she had yet to don the marriage gown in deference to the nursing needs of her son as she listened to the chants and stomping of Curnydhá's men that accompanied Kavan to the revered pool where he too would be cleansed for their union. Eventually, the parade of steps would return, snaking through dark streets without handlights to guide them save for a single one at the front of the column. Raebhá had watched the glow through the cracks of the shuttered windows and she waited anxiously for its return. Soon enough, even that would be gone and the still hours would fall silent again.

The female márbhyndhánis had left her long ago to oversee the remaining preparations. Without female kin, she was left to pass those final hours with only her best friend and their children for company.

Ephé flitted about like a nervous bride herself, chatting of village gossip during Raebhá's absence, speaking of her child, her marriage, as the hours of the night passed, but when the sounds in the ghís announced the approaching hour of union, the men having returned and the chiming of ceremonial bells welcoming the day, the blonde woman settled on the stool in front of Raebhá and clasped her hands.

Raebhá knew what she intended to address before she did so.

"I cannot go with him any more than he can stay," she murmured, pushing Ephé's hair away from her eyes. "Duty…"

"bhuré ghymaemis," Ephé muttered, reaching to the nearby chair to pick up her friend's gown. There was still time to dress, but she wanted to keep her hands busy. "Duty is unfair. Twice wed and…"

"Once loved; that is enough." She leaned forward to kiss Ephé's brow. "You should be happy I'm staying," she giggled, the sound slightly forced despite her hopes to ease her friend's concerns.

"I'll be happy if you are." She prompted Raebhá to her feet.

"I am happy. Distance will not destroy that…and he will come back to me. Curnydhá…Gálínphel…needs me." She believed each of those statements, however melancholy the future made her feel.

She lifted her arms so that the gauzy gown could be eased into place, secured at her shoulder, drawn beneath her bust and tied behind. It did not matter that she had worn such a gown before. To her, this wearing felt as new as the encroaching vows of fidelity did. What had been was behind her. What lay ahead was new and breathtaking.

"The power…it scares me." Mánd had trained her too, but only briefly before he had Ceased. Ephé had not had the opportunity to delve into what Power meant for the dhóbhaen.

"It is you, it is me, it is all of us. They want us to fear ourselves. To know what they know is to never be controlled or afraid again."

"You sound so certain." She adjusted the silver floral pendant with the topaz stone at Raebhá's throat, admiring the artistry, knowing that this was not the work of a dhóbhaen jeweler but something Raebhá had brought with her from that frightening far off land.

"I am. I have seen so much, so many wonders, in a land where so much is possible…and with what Ombhrís and the others did…I have to be certain. We can do this…I can do this…"

"Alone?"

"I'll not be alone, will I? I'll have Iólán, Audh and Kavan." No matter how far away he was. "I'll have you, I hope." She smiled warmly and caught Ephé's hands as they adjusted the fastening on her shoulder. "Say you are with me, Ephé. Please."

Ephé caught Raebhá's face between her hands and then kissed her mouth. "You know I am," she promised. They had grown up together, known each other their entire lives. Fear of power or not, she would never turn her back on a sister-friend who would need her even more when these next several hours were behind them.

"Then help me now…and never leave my side." If Ephé, Iólán, and Audh remained constant, Raebhá could endure anything, so long as she had the certainty of Kavan's love forever nestled in her breast.

∙Chapter 41∙

The early first harvest of not quite ripe fruit was a necessity to prevent Alberni's surviving populace from overrunning the duke's orchards and devouring what they could reach. It was an unpopular act, but Rhyrdan, as the steward of the estate, stuck to his decision to continue to monitor food distribution, and claim a larger than normal portion of the yield for later use. Whether the reprieve in the weather was short-lived, whether more rain fell to allow for a second harvest, or the cold again brought rain to allow for a normal planting season after the start of the year, the people would need food to sustain them through the winter. Alberni, like so much of Encsfel, would need the stores, however meager, to survive.

Most thought only with hungry bellies. Rhyrdan thought long-term, the way he believed Kavan would. The way his father would have if he was here.

It was a decision made jointly with Dhóri, the true acting Lord of Alberni, the first duty on behalf of the territory and his father the young Elyri dared to undertake. He could not see, but he could count, and his knowledge of weights and measures, of the coins of different lands, lent itself easily to recordkeeping. As he learned to feed himself without spilling most of it or missing his mouth, as he learned to find his way around the manor, he worked with Rhyrdan and the gdhededhá from St. Kóráhm's on identifying coins by weight, shape, and texture, by the patterns imprinted on their raised surfaces that separated denominations and countries of origin.

As frustrating as his disability was, as powerful as the pull towards depression and anger sometimes was, Dhóri was grateful that he had survived what had killed so many, grateful that he would have the chance to prove himself to his father after what he viewed as too many failures and shortcomings. Kóráhm had said his father would return, and Dhóri clung to that hope. k'Ádhá had given him his life and Dhóri intended to earn his father's respect with it.

From the window, Rhyrdan watched Dhóri and his stack of coins in the morning light before looking back out across the orchard at the men paid to bring in the last of the early fruit. The small apples, peaches, and more would be tart, but once dried for storage, that would hardly matter, particularly if the need arose for them in the future as he feared it would. He felt confident in his recommendation but less confident in his ability to enforce it. The Yellow Death had hit everyone in Alberni, including the manor, leaving few sentries and few of the manor staff in place. Emeria and her husband, the only surviving member of the Dary family that had served Kavan for many years, stayed on, she for the tasks indoors and he for his duties as groundskeeper, but even with only Dhóri and Rhyrdan living in the manor, and Rhyrdan doing his best to keep the home and grounds livable when he was not overseeing the management of Alberni, there was much for them to do.

Captain Magk had been tasked to hire two dozen men if he could find any fit enough and of good character, for the duty of manor guards, stable and ground staff. Word had spread through Alberni about the duke's need for household servants as well, but without the means to feed so many it would be months before the vacancies were filled and life returned to some semblance of what it had been. Most of Alberni's residents were needed elsewhere, crops, flocks and herds to tend, businesses to repair and rebuild, adjustments to be made to the loss of so many craftsmen and laborers.

All of Enesfel suffered the impact of plague, drought, and hunger. Recovery was going to be a long, painful process.

"Father will get everything in hand. You'll see."

Rhyrdan scowled and looked at Dhóri, who studied the coins he weighed in his fists. As Rhyrdan had not said anything, had uttered no sound that he was aware of, Dhóri should not have known what was on his mind. Dhóri did not have the Sight, but he was Elyri…and more…and the dark-haired man with the scruffy light growth of beard knew Dhóri could be quite perceptive when he chose to be. As often as Rhyrdan discussed his frustration with Kavan's absence and his worry for the state Alberni would be in when, if, he returned, it might have been an easy assumption to make about his pensive silence.

"I want to believe it…"

"I know he will be." The coins dropped with a clatter and Dhóri pushed the chair back, paying attention to each inch of movement until he gauged he was far enough back to stand. Careful steps around the desk, in the direction from which Rhyrdan's voice had come, until the other's unseen but detectable energy was in reach. Though the movement was hesitant and fumbling, he put his hand on Rhyrdan's arm with a proud smile and sigh of relief. Little by little, such gestures were growing easier.

"I want to ride."

Rhyrdan scowled skeptically, trying to hide a frown that Dhóri could not see. "How can you ride when you cannot…?"

"Help me relearn." For an hour, for as long as Dhóri could tolerate the frustration, he could redirect Rhyrdan's thoughts from the darker ones he chased in circles in his head. Dhóri would never consider his new disability to be an advantage, but perhaps it could help someone else, particularly the brother he had wronged with his jealous bile.

Finding a blessing in the darkness as he once had so easily, as Rhyrdan put an arm around his shoulder to steer him towards the stables, gave Dhóri the first ray of light he had felt in too many months.

His faith, he realized, had never abandoned him.

There was no chance to steal away to Raebhá's company as Iólán's home welcomed a steady stream of márbhyndhánis offering sage advice and a laying of hands on his head that made Kavan uneasy. It was unclear if they were seeking to bless him, to read him, or take his blessing into themselves. Iólán explained that their actions were meant to protect him from the bhur, that the same ritual was being performed for Raebhá, but Kavan's belief that it was something more could not be shaken. The excess power absorbed during the ritual cleansing had bled away, stolen gradually by each set of hands that touched him, until when Audh left near daybreak at the chiming of the ceremonial bells, the last set of hands to touch him, the excess was depleted.

Kavan wondered, as Iólán helped him change out of the red robe into an ankle-length robe of rebirth pale blue, the color and fabric mirroring the gown Raebhá had worn when he found her, if any of the men were aware of the kiss of power given in the touch between them.

The cut of the robe, the pale color, was the closest he had come to the robes which had once been his primary manner of dress. It felt peculiar to return to it after so many years yet also right and fitting.

After today, he did not expect to ever wear such clothes again.

"Eat." From a metal box above his hearth, Iólán offered a flat, thin circle of bread, seared as though brazed on a griddle and still warm when broken in half and placed in Kavan's hand. It smelled of salt, flour, and some unidentifiable spice that gave it a reddish hue unlike any bread he had seen served thus far. It was similar to the unleavened bread eaten by many south of Hatu. Its texture was light, smooth, like a pillow of air, with a mixture of grains seeded throughout.

"It is the last meal you will eat alone…" The ritual words faltered on Iólán's tongue and he sighed as he looked away. "Or it should be."

"The last as a man whose heart is alone," Kavan offered. He might soon be alone in body but never again in heart. How often had he felt alone, even when in the company of friends or wrapped in the embrace of the divine, but Kavan suspected he would never feel that way again.

At least, if he did, he would have this reminder that he could never be truly alone.

"That is so." Iólán smiled, thankful for the reassuring words. He wrapped the uneaten portion of bread in a paper-thin cloth pouch. "The rest you will share with Raebhá in the morning."

A cup of water, all that Kavan was allowed to drink during the days of separation, was given to cleanse his pallet of his simple meal and then set aside. A long veil of laced and scalloped blue, a rare fabric he had not seen used for any other purpose, was draped over his head and face. The fabric was sheer, loose and airy; he could see the shapes of light and dark around him, but his vision was hampered enough that he would be expected to accept Iólán's aide to reach the grove where the marriage was to be officiated. Normally a male relative, a father, uncle, grandfather, or older brother would lead. Kavan had none of those things and so was left with one of the few in Curnydhá he could call friend. Audh would already be at the grove, the márbhyndhánis gathering there after leaving Kavan, to make the ritual preparation to cleanse the space of bhur before a marriage could take place. Lacking female family Raebhá would be escorted by her friend Ephé.

When Kavan and Raebhá met at the grove they would find their way forward together, leaving the reliance on family or friends to forge a new reliance on one another.

If only, Kavan mused with a flutter inside, it could stay that way.

"Are you ready, kydhé?"

"Today I am Kavan. No more titles between us." His smile was nervous, as was the quaver in his voice, but he did not think Iólán would care. "ró phaern áchaelác murt."

Iólán clasped his shoulder and then cupped one hand beneath the bard's elbow to guide him from the house. "Kin I am honored to welcome. Kin I am happy to accept."

❧*❧

"How fare you this morning, Lord Healer?"

Merrek was surprised to find Ártur painting in the dayroom at such an early hour when the light of the sun was not yet enough to illumine the room. Painting by candlelight seemed difficult to him, but he was a man of very little creativity. When he came to stand at the healer's shoulder to admire the nearly finished mountainous landscape silhouetted by a setting sun, or perhaps a rising one, Merrek understood that daylight would have diminished the gloom and pall of the grays, blues, and purples peaked with white and the pale pink of the barely visible orb on the horizon. The view was beautifully melancholy, poetic in its darkness, and created an urge to mourn that seemed an unusual response to a painting.

His trembling hand squeezed Ártur's shoulder, a request for strength and steadiness he would have sought from Kavan if the bard had been here to give it. For too many weeks his mentor and surrogate father had been gone, for too many weeks the Elyri's counsel had been absent. Other Lachlan monarchs before him had begun their reigns with the bard at their side. But not him. In his more despairing moments, as the Yellow Death ravaged an already struggling kingdom, Merrek had berated the absent Elyri for the unfairness which forced him to rule alone. But Diona had survived and thrived with little direct counsel, and though she had been tutored by the bard, she had not been raised by him. Merrek wondered if that made a difference, since he had, at his disposal, the best the Elyri bard could give him.

As regent, he was not ruling alone. Any guidance he needed could be had in Diona's experienced wisdom.

If he was truthful, he knew he had the respect of the people, his staff, for the leadership he had helped provide through the darkest days of recent troubles. With more balanced weather returning, with crops growing around Rhidam and reports coming from elsewhere in Enesfel of the same, it appeared that the worst could be behind them. He had lost a child, his wife's emotional state was brittle because of it, but his eldest son had escaped death as had others dear to him. If only he knew that Kavan was well, that he would see the Elyri again, Merrek thought he would be able to sleep through the night.

The seizure and collapse Ártur experienced not many nights hence had spread alarm through the keep, as some feared the healer who had given so much of himself to the sick and the dying had finally succumbed to something himself. Whatever the cause, however, it was determined not to be the Yellow Death, as there were no other signs of illness, only weakness, fatigue, a headache that lingered, and a temporary inability to heal or use any of the Elyri gifts he had trained with since childhood. No other Elyri in Enesfel, not Bhyrhán or Syl nor other healers throughout Rhidam who had assisted the population through the plague, had suffered what Ártur had.

They did not know Níkóá had likewise been affected.

Syl fretted the possibility of an unknown, undetected ailment or the more likely possibility that her husband suffered from an exhaustive breakdown that required complete rest and a cessation of duties. Ártur, stubborn as ever, brushed away much of their concern without appearing rude and ungrateful.

Merrek had the impression now, as the healer's shoulder tensed beneath his hand, that Ártur knew more about his condition than he was telling and that his knowledge was transmitted on the canvas.

"I am well, My Lord; ready to resume my duties." If not for his wife's insistence that he needed rest, he would have returned to his responsibilities already. There had been little need for the healing staff in recent days and the instances that had required medical care were easily tended by Syl and Rouvyn. As usual, when he had time on his hands, Ártur painted, but he, as he studied what his all-night efforts had produced by the light of the dozen burnt candles around him, could not name the location of the mountains he had created.

"Good." It was the first time Merrek had been alone with him since his collapse and it was a relief to see that the healer was healthy.

He had been uncertain how much of Syl's worried-wife claim was accurate. "I was beginning to resign myself to a new plague."

"No plague, I assure you. Yóáná says Dhóri suffered similarly, and Chethá says Sóbhán did as well." He did not know of Bhen or Tíbhyan's collapse else the words that followed would have resounded with more certainty than he already felt. "I fear the cause was something more distant than any ailment."

"Distant?" Merrek pulled a footstool closer and sat at Ártur's side, not caring that the position made him look up at a man who, though beneath his station, was his elder and had done his share of raising the prince to adulthood.

"Kavan."

Brow furrowed, Merrek said nothing. He had been raised on tales, the rumors, myths, and gossip, the embellished historical recollections of great feats of power and miracles that were attributed to his surrogate father. Merrek had seen none of those things. The only miracles he had witnessed had been the times when Kavan had saved Lorant's life, but there had been no dramatic displays, only the touch of white hands on the infant's body that had kept Lorant alive. Merrek had grown up with the existence of Elyri healers and handlights and the knowledge that Kavan craved periods of flight like some men craved a drunken binge, but he had never witnessed any great exhibition of power.

How Kavan could have caused Ártur and others to suffer, to collapse, to endure days without Elyri abilities was frightful to contemplate and what it meant, the possibility that Kavan had perished, was even more frightening.

His hands grew white-knuckled on his lap as his fears were channeled there, until Ártur covered them with his and their gazes met.

"He is far away; I barely feel him most of the time. But he is there. If he has died, I would know." Ártur chose to believe that despite the ever-nagging doubt.

"How could he…?"

"I don't know. There was a time when he sapped power from Yóáná's father…to similar effect. Not intentionally, but in moments of distress. I believe that is what has happened."

"But you have no proof."

Ártur sighed. "No. No proof." How could there be proof without Kavan's return? He feared less for Kavan's life now than he had during his cousin's previous long absence from Rhidam, but fear was still there, always there, despite Kavan being the strongest, most capable man Ártur knew.

He was prevented from saying more, gratefully so, by familiar steady footsteps and Níkóá's arrival. It was the weight of those steps, in addition to the man's red beard, that disguised the Elyri blood in his veins, but both should have, he felt, revealed the man's lineage if any had cared enough to notice and question it.

"My Lord." Níkóá bowed when he entered, his word directed at the prince though he quickly assessed the healer's condition. The man was Kavan's kin, and the chamberlain felt it was his duty to keep the healer safe until Kavan's return, even though there was nothing Níkóá could have done to prevent the collapse or reverse it. He had told no one that he had suffered it too. "Word from General Declan."

Merrek took the leather tube from the chamberlain's hand and opened it with a side glance at Ártur. The tension in his neck, back, and shoulders as he read the contents bled away with a relieved sigh.

"Inness may have recalled her forces." It was too early to be certain; he knew as well as his general did that the act could be a ruse staged to coax Enesfel and her allies into letting down their guard, but he hoped the news was a more positive sign. "Assemble the queen and advisors in the State Room."

"Aye; at once." Again Níkóá bowed before striding from the room with a look at Ártur that promised they would speak soon.

Ártur wondered if there was news for him as well. News, he hoped, about Kavan.

"Lord Healer." There was no need for the prince to take his leave but he too wanted Ártur to know they would speak later. Any details the healer might know about Kavan and when he might return were details Merrek wanted to hear. If he could resolve the tensions with Neth, allow Asta and Prince Jerit to return home, Merrek wanted Kavan to know that. Kavan's pride in him was worth more than the approval of an entire kingdom worth of subjects.

❧*❧

He could not see her face, could see nothing but her bare feet and the hand that curled around his arm as they slowly crossed the grove at the western edge of the valley filled with people that, despite their differences and lingering uncertainties, Kavan considered to be kin.

He knew it was Raebhá by her touch, by the hitch in her breathing before their first steps together. Despite being unable to see her behind the long veil which covered her from head to toe as Kavan's covered him, he believed her to be the most beautiful thing he had ever seen.

Ephé was at the front of the gathering with Ágdhállán so that he could participate in a union he was too young to remember. It was vital to both mother and father that he be included. Kavan and Raebhá passed through the chanting, stomping crowd who banged sticks or castanets or wooden blocks together to ward off any bhur not fooled by the disguises the couple wore and not frightened away by the earlier preparation of the grove. The márbhyndhánis and novices not conducting the ceremony rang gongs, some wooden, some metal, and uttered sharp wordless cries that echoed over the dhóbhaen's heads and swept towards the morning's calm sea.

Raebhá had not felt this aflutter, this eager, this confident of her choice, her future, when she had been here last. Hers had not been the only marriage undertaken out of duty, nor had it been the only one devoid of affection or familiarity.

Nor was this the only marriage ever undertaken with a sense of perfect rightness and certainty for the participants. There would be trouble, challenges, heartache ahead for them, but whatever fates had blessed her with this second opportunity, the ágdháthé, k'ágdhá, or Kavan's Saint Kóráhm, she would be forever grateful, no matter what distance and duty pulled them apart. She was strong enough for this responsibility. She could see this through.

At her side, the man she had already given herself to, who likewise gave himself to her, was enveloped in a sense of awe, wonder, and disbelief that she could feel through her hand on his arm. He did not believe he was here, that he was doing this…with her. Only his stubborn will pressed him forward, a will and the surety that this was the single most important thing he would ever do.

She squeezed his arm gently. His head bobbed once.

When his steps faltered beneath the onslaught of nerves, Raebhá supported him, kept him to the path. When the weight of worries burdened her, Kavan did the same. Together, they reached the ghrís pheslárkag, the Oathing Stone, a knee-high boulder mottled with streaks of white and flecked with the silvery metal of which Kavan's pendants were made. All dhóbhaen in Curnydhá used this place to swear agreements to one another. Most often it was used for marriages and was stained with the blood of every prior oath sworn here. Three márbhyndhánis, Éthym, Audh, and an older woman named Llaur, gathered around it, while Ephé and Ágdhállán stood to one side.

They were stronger together. They both believed it to be true.

Audh took Kavan's right hand and positioned it palm up as Llaur did the same with Raebhá's. Éthym held forth a porous white stone, the size and shape of the one removed from above Raebhá's door. Without a word, the ancient márbhyndhánis lifted the stone above his head with both hands and Kavan reflexively watched, expecting a ritual utterance. Instead, a hush fell over the gathering followed by a quick, unexpected slice of a blade across Kavan's palm. He winced, attempted to instinctively jerk free, but Audh, bloodied ániélmé in one hand, held him fast with the other. Raebhá's palm likewise bled.

Behind the blue veil, Kavan scowled.

The stone Éthym held was placed between their bleeding hands, Kavan's below, Raebhá's above, so that their blood was consumed by the thirsty white rock. In the grove, only the early morning birds and insects and the ever-present pulse of the distant waves filled the air. A length of flowering vine, the same type that was entwined in Kavan's hair, was wrapped around their wrists, binding them not only to each other but to the natural world. Each of the three márbhyndhánis lay their hands on the joined ones. Kavan and Raebhá felt the power in that touch, the heated sensation of power branding that burned through her hand, through the stone, and into his.

Llaur put something in Raebhá's free hand and she, in turn, offered it to Kavan, a wooden spoon carved of the same black wood as the knife he offered in exchange. An unspoken promise to provide for the needs of the other, lives carved as one from the same block of eternity united through the union of blood. The dhóbhaen needed no words to understand the significance of a ritual repeated for generations by every marrying couple throughout the island.

Kavan, now part of it, needed no words either.

The speaking of promises would be but sounds on the air. Actions taken before their eyes were more significant and binding.

Blood dripped from their joined hands onto the ghrís pheslárkag, making them and their union a part of the land, part of the community, in a way Kavan did not feel he had ever been part of anything. The energy pouring into him, no longer given by the márbhyndhánis but coming from somewhere external, fanned the flames of his power, bringing with it a gathering of presences he prayed no one could see as they had the day of the great wave.

Daring to raise his gaze from his bleeding hand, peering through the veil's weaving, what he saw was not záryph but the silvery light that emanated from clasped hands, flashing like embers from an anvil when their blood fell and sizzled on the stone. Flares and sparks that others could see, a manifestation of a miraculous nature that he neither caused nor controlled. It filtered into him from above, through his body, and into his hands, the usual precursor to a miracle.

What it gave birth to was no healing. Rather it burned through him until both wrists bled. Around his bare feet, blood began to pool.

rósádhá.

How many times did this make?

His panic was stayed by the grey cloaked figure who appeared behind the márbhyndhánis and laid his hands on each of the three, one after another. Thankfully, no one else seemed to see him or detect his presence. Only the fluttering of eyes at the touch of the saint's scarred hands showed that the márbhyndhánis felt anything.

Kavan's breath caught and held until his chest burned with the need for air, and then Kóráhm, a smile given with a nod that suggested they would soon meet again, vanished from sight, taking the unearthly light around his hand, and his vision, with it. Sensing surprise but no distress or fear in the witnesses, wondering if a similar glow was always present due to the power the márbhyndhánis used for binding, Kavan turned as instructed by Audh's gentle nudging. Raebhá turned with him, the stone between their bound hands. Together, surrounded by the citizens of Curnydhá, they began the journey from the grove to the heart of civilization, Kavan relying on Raebhá's guidance every step of the way, a trail of blood from his hands and feet following them down the mountain.

❧*❧

She screamed in fury, rending her hair, her robes, feeling the power in the air as if it peeled her flesh from her bones. Such agony, such a turn in power, an increase that spoke of the advance of the enemy's strength. It was a sign, but not the one she had expected once the mantle was in his possession. Regardless of expectation, however, she again placed the blame for her agony at his feet.

Blood of her blood. He would perish in fire for the sins of his line.

…just as he had condemned hers to the flames of eternity.

❧ * ❦

Clinging to the side of his horse, having attempted to dismount on his own only to have the animal skitter unexpectedly sideways, Dhóri squeezed his eyes shut as if to block out a world he could no longer see. Rhyrdan swung down, catching the slighter man to keep him from falling. Dhóri trembled as though weak and ill and the distortion on his face spoke of pain or shock.

"Dhóri?"

"It is done."

"What is?"

But Dhóri could only shake his head, the words coming forth without his bidding or the knowledge as to their meaning. He did not have the Sight but he knew that something significant had occurred. Something in the world had changed, an increase in power had been born, and somehow he had been made aware of it. What it was, how it had come to be, he did not know.

If pressed to answer, he would guess it involved his father.

It was something he would not speak aloud, for with the awareness of change came the fear of the unknown ahead because of it. Instead, his head still shaking, he said, "The oratory. I want…I need…to pray."

Rhyrdan swallowed past the lump in his throat and nodded, supporting his limp companion into the manor, leaving the horses to be taken care of later. He did not need the Sight to sense fear. Prayer, from both of them, felt to be exactly what was needed to assuage it. He was not confident, however, that it would change anything.

❧ * ❦

With the veils still lowered and Kavan leaving a bloody trail which none dared step on, it took longer to reach the ghís kelyhag than it had to reach the grove. A child led the pageant, one of the márbhyndhánis novices, playing a shrill, birdlike song on a wooden pipe, a tune to drive away bhur from the path, scattered by the merry cheering and clatter of the dhóbhaen behind them. The ghís kelyhag was filled with the aromas of roasting meat, tubers stuffed with herbs and wrapped in waxy sea leaves, bread, and mulled zerphánál, food prepared during the night ahead of the early morning ceremony. Weddings were conducted at dawn to signify a new beginning, allowing a day of feasting and revelry for the entire ghís. Marriages were collective affairs. There was no getting out of that.

When the procession stopped at the steps of the ghís kelyhag, the veils were lifted. Thankfully the wounds on his hands and feet no longer bled, had closed during the journey from the grove, and his vision had cleared of the dizzying power he had absorbed. Facing the open door at the top of the steps, Kavan could see more faces within that he did not recognize, visitors from other ghís in Gálínphel, he guessed, who lived near enough to have made the hasty journey or who had come seeking their kymyhé's guidance and aid.

More faces who had never seen him before, who knew nothing about him, and yet had now witnessed an expression of power unlike anything they had ever imagined. People who could see for the first time that he fit the description of their mythical White Bard. People who would know, if the dhóbhaen of Curnydhá had talked, that he had saved the ghís from the wrath of the sea.

He did not search their thoughts. He did not want to know what anyone thought except the woman at his side. His trembling hand felt empty and cold as Éthym unwound the vines from their wrists and took the stone from them…a white stone spidered with deep red veins where their blood had mingled in its core and across the surface. Kavan offered his empty hand, afraid Raebhá might recoil after what had happened, the way he expected those around them to reject him.

None of that happened. When her fingers threaded through his, there was a jolt, a different fire that went both into his core of power and lower into the center of his masculinity, and he squeezed her hand to resist anything unseemly. Her smile was playful and warm, kind and sympathetic; at the increase of his trembling, she lifted his hand and kissed his knuckles, her smile becoming a chuckle.

The stone was placed on a pillowed cushion of shimmery brown fabric and given to the child who had led them from the grove.

Raebhá tipped her head towards the stairs. Following the child, they entered the building together.

Vines, flowers, and branches of greenery adorned the hall, some wrapped around the posts and rafters of the building's framework, some woven into the shapes of copulating animals or mother animals with their young. Those depictions made Kavan flush and avert his eyes as they went to the head of the room, giving him extra cause to focus on his wife instead of the decor. The word wife stuck in his head when he first thought it, became a scream and stole the strength from his legs. As if reading his sudden distress or at least anticipating it, Iólán was there, shoving a bench behind him so that when Kavan's knees gave way, he collapsed onto it, pulling Raebhá down with him.

The cushioned stone was placed on the chair from which the kymyhé customarily made proclamations of law and justice. Today was not about law or justice, but about rejoicing, love, and ultimately the continuation of the dhóbhaen.

Only the stone would rule Gálínphel today.

Struck by his fleeting look of panic, she whispered, "Kavan?"

He shook his head, cheeks flushed, his throat closed to words. Even if he was able to speak, with that one word echoing within, he did not know what to say that would not sound foolish. Perhaps understanding what he could not say, their clasped hands creating a link between them despite Kavan's usual mental shields, Raebhá continued to smile and leaned over to kiss his cheek.

Instead of calming him, it brought a deeper crimson to his skin.

Someone approached with a wide wooden bowl of clean water so that they could cleanse their hands together. Once clean and dry, the water now tinted red with their blood, Audh presented two cups of mulled zerphánál, the cups wooden and overset with a metal skin into which were etched similar naturistic symbols of fertility and prosperity. Such symbols were always similar in secular cultures, more common in the celebrations of those of lower station than in those of the nobility outside of Elyriá with whom Kavan had found himself situated. People closer to the earth who depended on it for their existence valued such symbolism in ways those of wealth did not.

How often, it seemed, those of Faith forgot the cradle of life which gave them existence.

There should be no shame in it, Kavan reminded himself as he had done many times since Raebhá had come into his life. But a lifetime of learning, custom, and belief would not be so easily undone.

With cups in their hands, Audh gestured and Raebhá assisted Kavan to his feet to stand before their guests. He locked his knees to remain upright. With a cup of his own lifted in blessing, the tray they had been carried on held nearby with a small bowl still upon it, Audh smiled at Raebhá, and then Kavan, a man he considered blood kin though they were many generations removed. He took a pinch of brown powder from the bowl and sprinkled it over their cups as he spoke the only ritual phrases Kavan had heard all day.

> *dhózáyr kyllkánist*
> *náym bhenthíst*
> *ágdh, hyest, aisymár*
> *thráuneth háódhónai*
> *íls ágdháthé*
> *agk íls dhédók*
> *agk íls zéthénaer*
> *kánist dhes*
> *idó ylldhysag*
> *bholgk ylldhózáyr kállómíst*

Kavan's hands shook so that he thought he would spill the contents of his cup. He knew those words, although when uttered in song during Diona's wedding to Espen many years ago, he had known neither their meaning, their source, nor how he had known them. He could not account for delivering a dhóbhaen blessing when he had not been aware of their existence. Unlike that day, however, he understood the phrases issued as a blessing over his union.

He was overcome with a swirl of unfathomable, conflicting emotions that he did not have the clarity of thought to sort out.

Facing him, her eyes alight with both question and adoration, Raebhá hooked her arm around his as she brought her cup to her lips. Kavan did the same, expecting to be asked for a speech, for vows, for something eloquent and profound that he was ill-prepared to utter. Raebhá was the one to speak, two words that said everything that needed to be said between them.

"áchaelác híth."

A public confession of everything they were to one another. Kavan swallowed, grateful for the robe that hid how her voice and those words affected him. His gaze traveled to the hollow of her throat, to the topaz setting on its crème ribbon that he had not realized she had worn, his gift to her that he had not known she had brought with him. That she had worn it for this day, for him, made him feel light-headed and warm. The knowledge also enabled him to reach inside, to find the fortitude and voice to form the response and utter the reply her declaration deserved.

"áchaelác hás," he replied, using her tongue, the origin of his own, so that all around them understood.

Words spoken, they consumed the contents of their cups together and were mimicked by everyone gathered with them. Unity as a couple. Unity as a community.

The power he had absorbed during the ceremony flared, a burning in his center that stole his breath. His head began to throb as the zerphánál crossed his lips. He was unclear whether the power or the drink was to blame for the blackness of vision and hearing that followed and threatened to knock him off his feet.

❧*❧

There was something he was meant to do. Níkóá remembered that as a surge of power washed over him, engulfed him, sucked the air from his lungs and the strength from his limbs. He stared at the sky, face into the sun without seeing it, uncertain how he remained on his feet as the waves crashed and swirled around him like the riptide in a pool at the edge of the sea. Though of Elyri blood, and trained in the uses of power that blood afforded, he had never felt anything as strong as this devouring current, not even when it led to the blackout several days previously. Only the sharing of power with Kavan, when the bard deigned to teach him more than his meager opportunities had provided, had come close. This was stronger and seemed to come at him from all directions and he could give it no cause or purpose.

It just was.

Only when it subsided, when his fists unclenched, his vision cleared, and he could hear and breathe again, did the chamberlain look back at the first-floor windows of the keep where he had last seen Ártur. Had the healer felt it? Had anyone? Or was this some peculiarity of his mixed blood?

What, he thought as he rubbed his throbbing temples with his fingers, had he been on his way to do?

❧*❧

k'gdhededhá Ylár was not the only one to feel the energy surge. Every head in the náós, gdhededhá, lómesté, noble and common, to the newly approved High Mother, lifted and turned their heads at the room-shaking wave that rattled the stained glass and shook the bench seats and prie-dieu on which they sat and knelt. Never in recorded Elyri history had such a flux of power been documented, whether out of fear or because it had never happened even the very ancient could not say. Murmurs of alarm and wonder followed, interrupting the ritual coronation of the Kyne, but Ylár pushed ahead, completing the ritual for his benefit and the woman's, regardless of the inattentiveness of the guests. Some had even fled the building as though they thought it would crumble around them.

But the surge and its aftermath lasted no more than a handful of moments and was no more than a memory by the time Ylár's benediction bestowed Faith's blessing on the secular head of all Elyri.

A memory, but one that would endure, and one which would have bhydáni and gdhededhá alike seeking answers for centuries. As the náós emptied and Ylár stood alone at the altar, he pressed his hands to the ancient marble, feeling the last tingle of power there even though he could no longer feel it in the air, through his feet, or in his core.

This was not merely an event of power. This was an event of Faith.

There was only one person he could think of in which both joined with enough strength to warrant something of this magnitude.

A man his predecessor had, wrongfully in Ylár's eyes, condemned as a heretic. A wrong to be corrected before his soul was damned for the crime.

o•*♋

Kavan had no knowledge of that power event, being at the eye of it. When his vision returned and his strength with it, he was relieved he had not fainted or done something humiliating. Most of the surplus power he had felt was no longer present. Those around him had felt something, a tickle of power that danced over their skin, sank into their bodies, and then evaporated as it passed through them. He was grateful it had not been enough to prompt anxiety. He did not know that the waves had grown as they rippled beyond Dhóbhaen's shores, stronger and more intense, from the place where he stood.

To him, it was a momentary event that seemed no more peculiar than any other he experienced.

The day passed with food, with laughter, with boisterous bawdy songs and never empty cups of zerphánál. There was dancing, which he was thankfully not required to undertake, and there was an endless stream of individuals with wishes for prosperity and good health and expressions of bountiful gratitude for saving Curnydhá. Occasionally one of the strangers would pull Raebhá away, the pressing urgency of problems created by the sea's destructive force the only thing enough to come between them on this day.

Raebhá was never gone long, and during her absences, there was Ágdhállán to keep Kavan grounded.

When it seemed the right thing to do, the right time to bestow his only gift onto the dhóbhaen gathered in adoration, devotion, wariness, or aversion, Kavan took out the harp that Iólán had been insightful enough to bring. Accustomed to performing at such gatherings, having played at celebrations and weddings that had always been in someone else's honor but never his, it did not feel appropriate to leave this day without the gift of song to those he might soon be parted from.

There were no songs with lyrics this day, as words failed him and his voice with it, but he was a harper foremost, the object in his hands his most comfortable instrument, and so he played. The pristine notes of brass strings were enough to elicit the desired array of emotion so that, by the time the roasting carcasses were picked clean, the bowls and platters emptied, and the last of the zerphánál now being offered around the room, his audience was as exhausted as he was.

He could endure no more. The rub of their collective thoughts and emotions, like unsanded wood against bare skin, had grown to be too much and the smoldering anticipation deep within had grown progressively more difficult to ignore.

The sun was at its lowest point on the horizon, a night of perpetual twilight upon them, and there was one final set of rituals to be heeded before he could be alone with his family. With his harp in Iólán's hands and Ágdhállán in Ephé's care, Kavan and Raebhá carried the stone in their clasped hands to her doorstep, steps still stained with his blood now also adorned with flowers and vines and tiny carved fertility animals positioned in the braided flora. The márbhyndhánis lit the way with handlights above their heads and every adult or older child capable of creating one lit the path as they followed, a river of light like a serpent winding across the short distance between the ghís kelyhag and home. The villagers spread out, creating a semi-circle of light several rows deep in front of the house as the couple climbed the stairs, lifted the stone, and positioned it into the prepared setting. It balanced in place as the door opened, revealing an interior adorned as the ghís kelyhag had been, lit with a single candle in a lantern encasement, smelling of flowers and mint and the tallow of the candle.

On the landing, they paused so that Kavan could take his harp and Raebhá could take Ágdhállán, and when they crossed the threshold, it was Iólán who closed the door, giving his sister to her marriage, separating them in the silent room from the whole of Raebhá's people.

They were now his people as well, Kavan mused with a rush of breathless nerves. Harp set on the table near the two wrapped pieces of flatbread left for them to share, he clutched the edges of the worn wood while Raebhá laid their sleeping son in his bed box. Outside, noises were heard at the doorframe, banging, scraping, chiseling, the customary sounds of stone masonry. When he looked towards the door, expecting it to open with an unwanted interruption, Raebhá put her hand on his back and lay her head between his shoulders.

"They are setting the stone. Nothing more."

"Will they remain?" He knew of customs where kin, friends, servants, or entire villages remained close to a newly married pair to ensure that the marriage was consummated, sometimes required to be in the same room with the couple. If such were the case among the dhóbhaen, the attack on Raebhá which had resulted in her arrival in Enesfel would not have occurred, but with the glow of handlights lingering beyond the windows, not yet diminishing, he anxiously worried that such a custom might exist here. Maybe the dhóbhaen of Curnydhá had learned from that mistake and were prepared to take precautions against a repeat of that night by remaining to protect her.

Or the residual fear of him might be enough to prompt interference and demand his life now that the celebrating was over.

He hoped that assuaging them with music, that expressing his peaceful nature through song, had been enough to protect him and his family through this night and when he was gone.

Raebhá laughed and turned him around to face her. "Not for long. They will see that the stone is secure and wait for the light to go out."

To prove her point, she blew out the candle, the beacon of warmth that had welcomed them into their united home, and held him tightly, listening to the thunder of his heart as the glow outside gradually diminished. The last footsteps to leave the porch were Iólán's, but she doubted, as did Kavan, that he would go far. He would likely remain within sight of his sister's home until Kavan emerged from it to make the climb up the mountain with them so that Raebhá and the child would not return alone.

He did not know her intentions for her son, and Raebhá was not certain she had convinced Kavan it was for the best. She could hear her brother's scolding voice in her head as she closed her eyes and clung tighter to Kavan.

For now, she was not going to think about those things. Those things would come soon enough. Tonight, for however long fate allowed, was for other matters best met by the tangle of her hand in his braided hair and the lifting of her mouth to his.

There was no awkwardness, no hesitation in the returned kiss this night, no denying his heart's desires. Braids came loose, petals shed in a fragrant trail from the table to the bed. Marriage robes that smelled of smoke, roast meat, and zerphánál were added to the trail, shed in the favor of skin before he settled between her thighs, his desperate emotion swallowed by her kiss.

However long it might be before she held him again, before he knew the intimacy of her warmth, it would be too long. As he lost himself in her smell, her touch, and the sweet moments of dreamless sleep that came after, Kavan knew this was where he belonged. He convinced himself there was no reason to leave. His heart was here and nothing in the world would take him from the fullness of her love.

## ⊱Chapter 42⊰

He dreamt of weeping, of blood and fire and ritual High Elyri litanies he had not heard during his excommunication. He dreamt of two women, stately and fierce, cold and aloof, and a shadow with a sword standing on the precipice above him, facing another who struggled to be free of arms that held him back. Myreth's arms, his dark twin's face twisted into something grotesque behind crimson smoke. He dreamt of one with a head of dark curls breaking the bonds that held him and a red-bearded face standing between him and those on the cliff, arms reaching back, a large dark mass behind. He dreamt of a figure in the distance and the silhouette of a boat in the fog, draped with white cloth, at the edge of the sea, standing with the serenity of one who already knew the outcome of events and was content to wait upon destiny.

It was the burst of flame that appeared to engulf the figure on the shore, a figure unrecognizable across the distance, and the sudden strangling tightness of power at his throat, that threw Kavan upright, jolting him from sleep. One hand was at his neck as if to rip away the choking sensation, the other so tight around Raebhá's arm that she awoke to his cry and immediately pulled him into her embrace. She did not ask if it had been a nightmare or the Sight. Which did not matter. It had been something frightening, something that by custom spelled out the years ahead. Though she held little stock in such omens, thought the often touted belief that the dreams on one's wedding night foretold the future of the marriage to be fanciful and superstitious, she had already known the path she and Kavan had chosen would not be an easy one. Whatever hopes she had entertained of a long, pleasant, easy life together as she succumbed to sleep, hopes she knew Kavan shared, were dispelled by Kavan's squawk of fear.

She did not want to know the details.

Nor did Kavan want to voice them. There were elements in that vision of both dream and Sight, and determining which belonged to which might never be done until such moments came to pass. Some faces he knew, some he believed he did, but the strangling sense of destiny and finality were nearly tangible and filled him with a fear of what was ahead that he had not felt in many years. Not just his future, but the future of others dear to him. That he might, as the sensations in the dream allowed, be instrumental in the death of so many others filled him with enough dread that he briefly succumbed to the wish to remain where he was and never leave.

If he remained with Raebhá, perhaps fate could be cheated.

But the throttling thread reminded him why he needed to return too, and the crushing sense that to remain in Curnydhá would lead to the deaths of many more than he might save by avoiding Alberni, reminded him that fate was never so easily thwarted. As his destiny, the accident of his lineage, had led him to the discovery and destruction of Coryllien's remains, the cleansing of the ancient chapel beneath Rhidam's keep, and to the rediscovery of his people's history, his life's path was not yet complete. He had not been blessed with the mastery of overwhelming power and musical talent merely to live a life of quiet obscurity and tranquility.

Men of great strength and ability were destined for great things, no matter how they fought against them or struggled to remain apart from the world. No amount of denying who and what he was would change his course and he did not have the will to resist.

Kóráhm was right. Kavan sighed and pressed his face against Raebhá's neck, relieved and overwhelmed when she stroked his hair and kissed the top of his head. He was destined to know little of the happiness he brought others. Being forced to leave here, to leave her, to follow an obscure path, proved the saint's point. But as painful as this day would prove to be, Kavan was happy.

He had found what he had believed he would never know and no separation of miles would change it.

Though the room was cloaked in the dimness of night, he could feel it, the change in the air that meant a shift from midnight towards dawn, the barely perceptible warming in the air that spoke of the coolest hours of night turning towards the warmth of day. They had passed a night together, a day, another night, secluded within the walls of her home…their home…with only each other and their son. No intrusions from the outside world, no problems to solve, only the briefness of a sharing together that now, as this second dawn approached, he knew he would have to leave.

He wanted to stay like this always, but destiny was a demanding master and he could fight the inevitable no longer. If he had any chance of seeing Tíbhyan again, it had to be today. If he left now, against his heart's wishes, he might make the Gate by dawn, or shortly thereafter, and he would learn what his fate would be. There was a touch of hope that his effort to find the Gate, to use it, would fail, but there was an even greater fear of those things. When he raised his head to look into Raebhá's sand-gold eyes, he knew she saw the conflict in his.

Her lips grazed his forehead. He did not need to say the words. She knew it was time.

Dressing for the cooler mountain heights and bundling Ágdhállán accordingly, she watched from the corner of her eye as Kavan moved, memorizing his form, his beauty. She watched as he wrapped the volumes that Audh had given him in the pack he had brought from Enesfel. Most of what he had brought from Alberni, his clothes and empty water skins, a handful of tools, the history book he had gifted to her, would remain with Raebhá, the promise that he would return one day. In exchange, he took what he wore, his marriage clothes and the spoon she had carved for him, several small metal containers of a variety of spices and seeds he hoped would grow in Alberni's soil, the journals he had made that chronicled the experiences and discoveries he had made in this land, the dhóbhaen manuscripts Audh had given him, the three ániélmé that had come into his possession, and the red kestrel harp he considered leaving. If he convinced Raebhá to keep Ágdhállán with her, where he believed the child belonged, the harp would remain with her so that the boy would grow up knowing him.

His right hand stroked over the red wood, contemplating that choice again, and in doing so noticed the faint star-shaped symbol stained silver against his pale skin like a scar, the power brand left by the márbhyndhánis. The cut across his palm had healed. This had not.

It was the only scar he had.

Raebhá covered his hand with her right one, the power brand on the back of her hand near her middle finger nearly identical to his.

Hesitantly he traced the mark with his fingers, feeling the spark and tingle of power at the contact and how, when he pulled his hand free to look closer, the mark near his knuckle was more pronounced than before. He had paid little attention to the hands of other married dhóbhaen to see if they bore such marks, but he did not recall it being there when they had entered the house and there had been no such mark on Raebhá's hand when he first found her.

"It appears after consummation…a symbol of belonging. It may fade during stress; it may be nearly undetectable during long separations." She caressed his mark with a reluctant sigh. It was born of something the márbhyndhánis did during the ritual, but not being one herself, she did not know how it was created. "It will always be there, aislé. You will know it. You will feel it just as I will. It will bind us no matter our paths. Never fear that I shall forget or that I will not be here when you return."

Choking on emotion he was not prepared to face, despite his resolve, Kavan nodded and embraced her, standing that way for many minutes to calm his racing thoughts. A gurgle and sneeze pulled them apart as Ágdhállán chose that moment to remind them he was present.

"You should feed him…"

"As we walk. Iólán is waiting." Her sideways smirk and the roll of her eyes towards the door where she believed her brother had waited through the night, the day, the night again, lightened Kavan's mood a little. It was enough to prompt him to shove the harp into the pack and, after one last look around the room, memorizing every detail of it; he waited at the door for Raebhá to join him.

She was the one to open it, understanding his hesitancy and doing her best to facilitate what must be done despite her doubts. She did not want him to go but she knew, as they met Iólán and Audh in the deserted street, that if he did not attempt to return to Alberni, to his sons, his cousin, his mentor, he would, in time, resent himself.

Possibly her and their son as well.

"There is one more thing." It came as a sudden thought, one last gift he could give to help keep her safe. Hand upon a latch that never locked, as the dhóbhaen had never needed locks, he wove a thread of power through the latch, through the frame, through the walls, weaving it entirely around the house until it wrapped back upon itself. Without losing the ends of power, he reached back, took her hand, and put it on the handle without speaking.

"Do this…" he showed her, through their physical contact, how to unbind the threads and bind them again, "whenever you are alone…to stay safe. No one…" He met her gaze with earnest concern. "No one will be able to enter, to harm you, while this is active."

Only the márbhyndhánis might be able to untangle the binding ritual. If they did, if anything happened to Raebhá, they would implicate themselves and would face his wrath when he learned of it.

Amazed at what she felt beneath her hand, she practiced what he showed her several times to be certain she understood what he asked, that she could do as he instructed. It was a small but important thing, given the attempt on her life and the potential unrest ahead. She was aware of Audh's baffled scrutiny, knowing that he could feel the power Kavan was expending, knowing he was both curious and concerned about what Kavan had done. Perhaps, in time, she would tell him.

Here, in the public arena of the street, she was not going to breathe a word. If asked, she could claim the excuse of not trusting her voice and a desire not to wake anyone.

Ephé stood with the two men, barefoot, wearing a thin shift barely enough to protect her against the sea breeze. She stepped towards Kavan and took his hands, the coldness of her skin suggesting she had been there as long as Iólán and Audh had, or at least throughout several hours of this night. She was not part of what would follow, but she pressed a small wooden box into Kavan's hand, kissed both of his cheeks, and murmured, "I will see to her always."

Struck by the promise of those words, wondering how much the woman, whose family name Rínes conjured memories of his conflict with k'gdhededhá Dórímyr, knew about him, Kavan bowed his head, tucked her gift into the pocket of his cloak for later examination, and replied, "I thank you for that." He did not want Raebhá to be alone. Having her brother and two dear friends by her side until his return made Kavan feel a little better about the path he must tread.

Ephé stayed only long enough to press a kiss, like a blessing, on Ágdhállán's forehead, to do the same for Raebhá, and then she climbed the steps to Raebhá's home so that her best friend would not return to an empty space, an empty hearth, an empty life.

The door closed.

At Kavan's side, Raebhá began to tremble and pressed her face to Ágdhállán's to hide the tears Kavan knew were there.

"You intend to do this?"

He bowed to his unexpected allies and kinsmen, the question and Raebhá's silent tears making him weak as his nerves threatened to overwhelm him. "márbhyndhánis…I pray this choice is taken from me…made for me…because barring that, there are vows I cannot break. k'Ádhá willing, however, I will return soon."

The look he gave Raebhá as she adjusted Ágdhállán in the fabric sling that allowed for the use of her hands while keeping him close to her breast for nursing, was heartfelt and mournfully sincere. They were his reasons for returning, but what he said was, "There is too much here for me…to learn…to do…to be…to never return."

"I pray," Audh mimicked the word with conviction, "that your return is met with more welcome than this visit has given."

"I am used to such things, but thank you." There was no compromise in his life, as he was typically met with adoration or rejection, and he had grown as accustomed to those extremes as any man could. It would be far worse, he knew from experience, to be met with apathy and lack of acknowledgment. A polarized population meant that the people noticed him. In his time south of Hatu, he had grown to understand that being unnoticed was an intolerable option.

"Who knows…perhaps one day I'll find my way to your shores." Knowing that such a journey was possible through Audh's tales, Iólán desired to make it himself, to see what the world had become for those their dhóbhaen ancestors had cast out. To find Kavan again. Gates he did not know. Ships, however, he knew well enough to take that chance, particularly if Audh traveled with him.

"I will look forward to your arrival." As he clasped his brother-in-law's hand, Kavan wondered if Iólán might be the figure on the beach waiting for him with a shrouded boat.

Given what had felt to be that figure's death, Kavan prayed not, prayed that Dhágdhuán would protect both of these men until the day he saw them again. And he prayed that neither of them ever had cause to make that journey. If fate was with them all, Kavan would return to Curnydhá before such a trip became necessary.


Focused on the trail of power in front of him, faint at first but growing stronger the higher they trekked along the overgrown forest trail, Kavan struggled to remember any of what he saw from his hunt for Ombhrís. The lofty trees had passed unobserved before, the path zigzagging north and south towards its westerly destination beyond the tree line. But even focused as he was on the glow of power and the woman immediately behind him, he noticed each tree, each rock, each darting animal. He noticed the fluctuating glow in the sky, the subtle shift as dawn neared and the altitude bled the air thin.

Audh had offered the use of the sure-footed ponies to make their way up the mountain less strenuous. Kavan refused, preferring to follow the energy trail beneath his feet. When Raebhá chose to walk at his side, Iólán chose to do likewise, and Audh, not to appear privileged, left the ponies behind.

The steep, rugged incline slowed their progress but there was no choice other than flight, for the jutting rock, tangles of dense underbrush, thick clusters of trees or fallen ones, and occasional splash of falling water would not allow a straight path up the mountain's face. One hour, then two. Kavan wondered often if he should stop to allow the others to rest. But none, not even Ágdhállán, complained about the relentless pace though time and again Raebhá's hand in his urged him with the fleeting plea to turn back, to return to Curnydhá and forget that any world existed outside of Dhóbhaen.

Kavan wished he could. Yet the Gate lured him with its growing energy signature and the still diminishing thread of his mentor barely felt within reach of his power reminded him why he must go back. He would come back to her, but for now, he needed to return to the Sovereignties and keep the promises he had previously made.

The sky continued to brighten though morning had not yet come. It was taking too long, he thought, as his feet slipped on a patch of damp moss. If the Gate worked, he might not make it to Bhryell in time. If he did, he suddenly realized, he ran the risk of imprisonment if anyone in Bhryell chose to announce his presence to any gdhededhá prone to uphold the excommunication order.

For Tíbhyan, however, Kavan would take the risk.

Sensing his disquiet, again Raebhá's plea bled through the touch of her hand. He hesitated as he turned to help her up a steep slope of eroded soil, closed his eyes when she was safe in a brief embrace, and kissed her with a sigh. How could he verbally deny her anything? Why did Audh and Iólán not convince or force him to go back?

They were silent. Like Raebhá, though they lacked her knowledge of his reasons, they understood. Ágdhállán cooed at his mother's breast. Kavan kissed her knuckles, offering his love and apology, and resumed climbing.

Again she followed.

By the time they left the trees behind, having paused to catch their breath and regain their bearings at the place where Ombhrís had fallen to his death, the glow of the Gate in Kavan's mind matched that of the sun rising over the eastern sea behind them. Ancient and infrequently used though it was, the Gate, recently fed by the five márbhyndhánis who had last used it, was powerful enough in its natural energy to demand attention from even the most untrained dhóbhaen. Raebhá hung back, wary that the power might harm their son as she still believed it had originally harmed her. Iólán, however, pressed past Kavan to enter the circle hewn of stones set by long-dead hands, a flat plateau jutting from the mountain face remarkably devoid of the debris that occasionally slid from the heights above. The air was thin and cold, demanding more effort to breathe, and there was snow and rock mounded against the eastern facing surfaces of set blocks and stones that had fallen in the past. But the center of the circle was barren, no snow scattered there, and though there was no pattern on the ground, no visible evidence that this was anything more than a place of ritual, they felt the strength of their destination. Ágdhállán squirmed in his sling and tried to turn his body towards the sensation.

Kavan wondered why he had not noticed any of this when he had been here last. Had his focus on Ombhrís been so intent as to blind him to the nature of this place? Or had it been the poison in his blood?

"This is it? The rynlagne?" Iólán made no effort to hide his interest as he lay his hands on first one stone then another as if seeking the source of power he was not trained to recognize or locate. Audh frowned as he watched, obvious concern for his friend's safety creased between his eyes. Unlike the five who had brought Raebhá here and sent her through, he appeared to have no familiarity with where they stood, what he felt. He only knew this was where he had found Kavan.

Because Kavan was unafraid, the young márbhyndhánis decided to be unconcerned as well.

"It does not look like a gate…like anything more than stones. How does it work? Where can it take you?"

"Anywhere there is another Gate," Kavan replied, setting one pack on the ground and adjusting the one on his back to rearrange its weight before pulling Raebhá into his arms. She was supple, compliant, warm to the chill in his soul. He did not need to seek the center of the Gate's power. He instinctively felt it. Through him, Raebhá felt it too, and after her previous experience here, she was afraid.

"Apparently, with enough power and training, it can take you anywhere." He regrettably had not had the opportunity to learn how it was done but he had no interest in going anywhere unknown today. Travel to any Gate in Bhryell or Enesfel would be adequate. "As for how…that is something more easily shown than explained."

"Will you show me?"

"It would not be safe," Audh started, a lifetime of indoctrination manifesting in the belief that only a trained dhóbhaen could safely access such power.

Kavan lifted his face from Raebhá's hair, the scent of it lingering on his skin and in his nose. Ágdhállán's tiny hands clutched at his father's cloak. "The power itself is not harmful, but trying to use the Gates without knowing how could have detrimental results." He had never personally seen or experienced such problems. For him, failure only resulted in frustration and the occasional headache left by an aborted or thwarted attempt. But he had heard tell of mental damage from unprepared efforts, damage ranging from severe headaches to temporary blindness or a backlash of power that stripped the user of their gifts for a time. Without the time to properly train Iólán, or anyone else, he would not subject them to unknown risk.

Raebhá tipped her head to look at his face, the strain of the impending parting pooling in the corners of her eyes. "You cannot show us without taking us…but you can show us the lights?" Maybe, if Kavan could show her his destination, she, or one of the others, could develop the necessary skill to travel to him. Anything that afforded her the chance to be with Kavan was worth the risk.

She had seen the paths before. He had not taken time to explain their workings, to teach her about them since their previous passages had been with others or had ended in agony for Kavan. Because she was growing in power, control, and skill, Kavan had few doubts that, in time, she could learn to use this Gate. How often, he thought with a giddy tremor, might he be able to see her? If not daily, perhaps weekly. If not her, surely Audh could learn and bring her to him. The prospect made him nod without hesitation. "I can show you."

Raebhá followed into the circle, her hand in his, the other arm curled around their squirming son. Though less than a month old,

Ágdhállán was aware of the force stretching up from the earth to wrap around his parents' ankles. "He feels it."

"It's difficult not to feel," Iólán agreed, following them. Audh, not to be left out or appear a coward, joined them. "It's everywhere."

"It feels like it," Kavan agreed. His second pack was hooked over his arm and then he offered his other hand to whoever wanted to take it. "But it exists primarily beneath our feet. To see the way, you need only to touch me…and relax your thoughts as if readying for sleep. Settle your minds on something peaceful. Yes…good…"

Audh and Raebhá had no difficulty doing as he asked, were doing so before he spoke the instruction. Iólán, without training beyond the norm, found the act of centering and grounding more difficult. But he knew how to calm his mind to sleep and found that, in doing so, a field of lights, tiny white glimmers against a black void, like the night sky in the heart of winter, spread out behind his closed lids, stretching as far as he could imagine.

Iólán was not the only one awed by what he saw. Kavan was accustomed to the array of connecting pathways, each pinpoint another destination, and he had encountered Gates with connections that existed nowhere else, destinations he had never investigated. But he had never seen as many passages as he did now, as the power landscape spread before his mind's eye. He had never felt such a primeval force of energy stretching, he felt sure, into the core of the world. It was as if the age of this Gate made every other gate possible, as if he could travel anywhere he chose and, perhaps, as he traced the clues of the Gate's last usage to the faint point of light with a recognizably newer signature, he could learn to use it to go where no Gate had ever been.

He had doubted his ability to do so, doubted whether his mastery of power was enough to learn such a feat without the dhóbhaen márbhyndhánis to teach and guide him. The influx of power he experienced during the marriage ceremony, the power that he thought had been spent but which had returned over the hours with Raebhá, swelled within him more potent than before. He suspected that, with it, he held enough to make such an attempt possible on his own.

But not today, not when there were other risks at stake. With his thoughts echoing in their heads, he explained how each light led somewhere, and how, with time, practice, and experience, it was possible to identify the patterns and know which point led to a specific destination. With such an array of pathways visible, it took Kavan time to fit them into the framework of the more familiar pattern he was accustomed to, but he did, at last, find those he wished to see.

"My home," he murmured aloud, guiding their attention from one light to another. "St. Kóráhm's. Where Raebhá was found." Hesitating at the remembrance, he shuddered and forced himself to breathe. Had that been nearly a year past? "Rhidam's oratory. Bhryell." His attention lingered there the longest, that small point being the target he needed to reach, locking its position into memory. One of that handful of locations was Raebhá's best chance for finding him, should she learn how to travel these paths, and Kavan decided that, as soon as he returned, he would teach her how it was done.

Audh cleared his throat, the sound jarring Iólán and Raebhá out of concentration. Kavan relinquished his focus when he realized the others had broken free. "So many…"

Having never used the Gates though he knew others who had, Audh had expected perhaps a dozen destinations, the majority of which would be scattered about Dhóbhaen. What he learned from Kavan, however, was that the majority of those points existed in the lands where their banished kin of olde had settled and rebuilt their lives. Lands such as the ones where he had once traded but had never set foot to investigate.

He was bold, but not bold enough. He wished now that he had gone ashore, had experienced the foreign culture himself, learned more about what had become of the elyryhánag. He might have met Kavan sooner. He might have spared Raebhá the anguish of assault and kidnapping by a man who professed loyalty enough to marry her. He might have opened the door to Kavan's arrival and facilitated an earlier change in Curnydhá the way Raebhá sought to do now.

So many things might have been different.

Iólán squeezed his eyes shut and without touching anyone was able to summon that field of internal starlight. "I see them!" he exclaimed, his focus slipping when he spoke. He bounced on his toes and grinned. Raebhá grinned too, excited for her brother's success that further supported the possibility that she could travel this way, but Audh looked conflicted. How easy it might be, it seemed, for most dhóbhaen to learn the ways of the dáni when the márbhyndhánis had taught differently for so many generations.

Raebhá was right. The custom was more about control of the few over the many than it was about ability. It was not right. Not only should the kymyhé and kydhé be trained, but as all dhóbhaen were born with these gifts, it was time for the few to stop denying them the natural right to explore them.

Kavan nodded. "That is the first step to using them. When I return, I will show you more…show you both," he glanced at Raebhá then at Audh, "and teach anyone else desiring to learn."

Despite the danger in that offer, to Kavan, to the márbhyndhánis, and the dhóbhaen's way of life, Audh nodded reluctantly. "I do not think we are ready for such knowledge." How many dhóbhaen might journey away and never return? How much dangerous knowledge would be brought with the ones who came back? How ready were the sheltered dhóbhaen for a world so different from their own? As much as he was growing to accept the need, the right, of the people to learn to use what they were naturally given, there were some things Audh did not think the majority should learn yet. The use of the rynlagne was one of those things. "Other things…perhaps."

Bowing his head, Kavan accepted the restriction without a fight. It was not his fight to undertake. "Other things then." But nothing would keep him from teaching Raebhá and Iólán how to use the Gates, and in time, Ágdhállán too.

If Audh wished to learn, Kavan would teach him.

Audh drew something from the pocket of his cloak and pressed it into Kavan's hand. The jagged, uncut crystal, smooth on one side, was a translucent pale amber with flecks of pink and gold scattered throughout, similar in color to Raebhá's eyes. It tingled in his hand, its natural energy snaking through his body to connect with the energy of the crystal he wore around his neck. It was an unexpected but not unpleasant sensation. This was the first sunstone Kavan had seen up close, as the boat navigators had been reluctant to give theirs up for his scrutiny, but he recognized what he held and knew its purpose. He looked at Audh curiously.

"So that you will always be able to find your way to us…from wherever you are."

Though he did not know how the crystal worked, how it would serve to guide his way, Kavan understood the sentiment and bowed his head as he tucked the stone into his tunic pocket. "Thank you," he murmured, clasping Audh's hand between his. "I will keep it safe…and I will return." Only death would keep him from it.

A clawing sensation in his chest, a pulling as if to pluck something free, forced a gasp and threatened him with collapse. He thought at first it was a product of the proximity of the sunstone and the crystal he wore, or created by the involuntary exchange of power between clasped hands. He blinked several times to clear his vision as he realized that the source came from somewhere else. Something had tapped into his store of power and was beginning to bleed it away. Or rather, he decided with an expression of panic, he had created a link backward to Bhryell to prevent the final severing of the bond between student and mentor and Tíbhyan had, somehow, latched onto him to stay alive. His strength might keep Tíbhyan alive indefinitely, but that binding would leech Kavan's power until he had nothing to give, preventing the use of the Gate and possibly costing both their lives.

He had once served as an anchor for Ártur, had tried to do the same for Gaelán, but this was different. This was a battle he could not win.

A battle that reminded him it was time.

Not fighting the tears that spilled from her eyes, Raebhá pressed Ágdhállán into Kavan's arms, as if to allow a final embrace and began to unfasten the cloth sling from around her neck. Iólán did not notice, still caught in the wonder of unexplored power, but when she tied it around Kavan's neck despite the bard's efforts to discourage her, Iólán caught her wrists.

"Raebhá…are you…?"

"I've decided," she said, eyes on Kavan's. "This is my choice."

Clasping his son between his shoulder and cheek, Kavan put a hand around her waist. "You don't need to do this. He needs you."

Freeing herself from her brother's hold, she threw both arms around Kavan's neck, enveloping the child between them. "We have discussed this, aislé…there is nothing to be said. If you…" cannot, the thought in her head completed her sentence when her voice could not, "it is best for him. He needs…"

"A child needs his mother," Iólán growled, half believing the pale man he had grown to respect and love was the one to demand this action.

"Ágdhállán needs someone who can guide him to his potential." She looked pointedly at her brother and the márbhyndhánis, half hoping they would dissuade her, relieved that they did not. "He needs to be safe. Can you guarantee he can have both if he remains with me through the challenges ahead?"

None of them could. Regardless of the changes manifesting in Curnydhá, there was the whole of the dhóbhaen to face, with the constant threat of reprisal and repercussions, regardless of their pacifistic nature, not only against Raebhá but against any who supported her and the changes she sought to introduce into custom.

As a trained márbhyndhánis, Audh doubted that he or any of those who served with him could provide the level of training the boy's father could give. It was impossible to tell how gifted Ágdhállán might be, but no márbhyndhánis was as powerful as the White Bard. That Curnydhá had survived the sea was the only evidence needed as proof. Kavan should be, by right, the one to train his son.

"Besides…it will only be days…" That was the promise, her belief, despite knowing that fate was not always kind.

Kavan hung his head, struggling against the emotions battling inside. He did not want his final moments with Raebhá to be spent in argument and he did not want to anger her by shoving the child back into her arms and negating her wishes. Nor did he want to hurt her by taking their son from her care. It came down to what was best for the boy, not their desires, and Kavan was forced to admit that Raebhá's concerns were valid. He intended to return within days. Little was likely to happen here before his return. But if duty delayed him, tending to his plague-stricken son and the whole of Alberni, it was better the child was safe with him than in harm's way here.

Ágdhállán would need a temporary wet nurse, which Kavan hoped he could find. Since he would return to Raebhá as soon as he saw Tíbhyan and to the other duties he had promised, now that he knew where this Gate was and saw that he could travel between the two, he accepted that the separation between mother and child would be a short one.

"I will guard him with my life," he whispered into Raebhá's hair, his voice cracking beneath the assault of sorrow tempered with hope and longing. "We will be with you soon."

Cupping his face between her hands, she crushed her lips to his and was relieved when he gave in to a deeper kiss despite the presence of the other men. His love and need negated whatever embarrassment such a kiss would have once caused him. She could taste his turmoil, his grief, his power, and after many moments it forced her to pull away with remorse. It would be too easy to sway him to stay, and if she did, they would both regret it.

"I know you will, aislé. While we are apart, remember I love you."

Kavan pressed his forehead to hers, forced the pain back into submission, and whispered, "yháun áchaelác dhózáyr hyhest, aislé. I leave my love with you."

"Take some of it for our son," she replied with a hint of humor that was unforced and heartfelt. She wanted Ágdhállán to be loved, not spurned as a reminder of their separation.

Lips to hers once more, he agreed, "Of course." It was an obvious concession to his promise. He reluctantly released her, adjusted the packs and child in his arms, and waited for her to step away. The sudden emptiness with her beyond his reach was almost unbearable.

The sooner he did what must be done, the sooner he could return, and so he closed his eyes and sought the connection to Bhryell. As his power continued to dribble away, the link grew dimmer, the effort required to grasp it a little more difficult. Believing it a product of his reluctance to leave Raebhá and his effort to protect the infant in his arms, he took a breath, turned his heart to the expectation of return to her within a matter of days, and pulled the point of light towards him.

The reach was long and trying, the battle to cross the gap of untold miles harder than any previous effort he had made, like pulling up a ship's anchor alone without a winch. It required the gathering of power from any source he could find, near him, near his destination, from the air and earth itself. Another point in the darkness, faintly lit and unfamiliar but powerful enough from the Gate on which he stood, pushed against his center, demanding attention as if to force him to go there. Resisting that substantial pull of power, a plea of importance from a source he did not recognize, he kept focus on the destination he wanted, the place he needed to be. He would not be propelled into the unknown. He would not put his child at risk.

Aware of a popping spark against his chest, he felt torn apart from the inside with each passing moment, power and love and destiny fragmenting into a thousand seemingly irreparable pieces.

There were sounds in Kavan's throat as the trio on the mountain watched the White Bard shimmer and begin to fade as if he was no more than snow blown before the wind. Raebhá reached for him, feeling him draw power from her, opening herself to him in return.

The three blinked.

He was gone.
Her hand came away empty.
The sob broke free.
At the other end of the Gate, the Elyri bard dropped to his knees, into a broken, weeping heap.

❧*❧

The hand lay the seeing glass on the rail before him as the old man closed his eyes. He had been right in his assessment. The kine, the drover, the raptor. Aligned. The conjunction anticipated for the last several weeks, planets within constellations, had come to pass, a once in a lifetime, once in an eternity's display, that many had believed would never be.

But it was there. If he bore witness, others were doing so as well.

It was time. Or nearly so.

What that time would bring, what would transpire next, was a burden this generation would see play out. Prophecy had made it so. No matter what the skepticism of others clung to.

It was here.

They could now only wait.

๑Chapter 43๑

Sóbhán was not prepared for the sucking of power that drained him nearly to collapse at the foot of the altar in Kavan's private Bhryell oratory. He came at least twice a day, normally upon waking and before going to sleep at night, to utter thanksgiving for health and family and a plea for his father's safe return home, as well as to see if any messages had been left from those in Rhidam. Sometimes he used the Gate in that oratory, as Kavan once had when coming to Bhryell, but since the passing of the Yellow Sisters through the Sovereignties, Sóbhán dared not risk it most of the time.

Nor did he expect the blast of energy that followed, or the sound of something falling behind the curtain out of his line of sight. But he knew the sound of weeping and he knew the signature of the sudden presence there. He scrambled to his feet to find what his head and heart could not reconcile.

"k'bhydhá!" He knelt by the man dressed in unusual clothing, curled on the floor, the contents of two packs scattered about him, his arms curled protectively around whatever he held to his chest, one hand clutched around something at his throat.

The bard did not immediately react to the voice, only to the gentle touch of a hand on his head, a hand capable of some healing though Sóbhán would never be a healer. In his hand, the crystal Prince Muir had given to him was shattered into tiny fragments now embedded in his palm. He lifted his wet face, streaked with bloody tears and a trickle of blood from his nose, and stared towards the sound as if he either did not recognize the face or did not clearly see who was there. After a few moments of shaking, gasping for breath, and the settling of power in the air, he faintly murmured, "Sóbhán?" as the bundle in his arms squeaked, squirmed, and began to fuss in discomfort.

"Let me help."

Only when Owain had died had Sóbhán seen Kavan weep; he had not been with him after Wortham's death to witness his grief. He knew from the man's expression that he had endured something painful, emotionally and physically, to result in tears of blood. He was about to say more when the tiny head of coppery hair turned, unwrapping from the cloth that shielded it, and Sóbhán blinked, slack-jawed, at the sight and the host of questions the child raised.

Bracing against Sóbhán's shoulder until he was seated cross-legged in the shadows, Kavan struggled to refocus power, to find the fractured center that felt as if it would never heal. The Gate beneath him, his private Gate, reverberated with the force of the energy it had taken to travel through it and made the slivers of stone in his hand ache and sting as though they were hot needles. Whether because he had been reluctant to make this journey or for some other reason, he was too drained, weak, and heartbroken to guess.

"Please…" Sóbhán began, trying to pry open Kavan's bleeding hand. But the bard pulled away, not yet aware of that damage, the cause of the spikes of pain stabbing there.

"A wet nurse…please…" He should explain, say more, but the blinding pain behind his eyes and the tearing of his heart hindered his attempts to think beyond the needs of the distressed infant.

What if he had arrived too late? What if the hole in his core was because Tíbhyan was gone?

"I know just the woman…and then I will see to your hand." Sóbhán was a practical man in comparison to his spiritual, impulsive brother; his questions could wait until his return, until Kavan was ready to answer them. He paused long enough to kiss the top of his father's head and then left the bard alone in the silent oratory.

Kavan did not search his soul for answers, did not force the gathering trickle of power to reach back across the miles to touch the woman he had left behind. She would be there, just as Ártur always was, but seeking her would serve as a reminder of the miles between them. Recentering himself would be more easily done without that painful reminder. Below, the distant sound of the door opening and closing, and then he suspected he was alone in the house. Where was Chethá? Was he endangering them by being here? He should go. Go to Tíbhyan. Say farewell if he could and leave Bhryell before he brought harm to his son and daughter-in-law.

Rising, however, his belongings left where they had fallen, took longer than it should, the use of his injured hand to push up sending jolts of fire up his arm. The rising and the shuffling, shaky steps that brought him to the oratory door, required enough time and strength that by the time he reached it, Sóbhán met him there with a young Elyri woman Kavan did not recognize. He leaned weakly against the frame of the open door as Sóbhán pried the fussing baby from the sling and gently placed him in the woman's arms. Kavan reached for the child as if he feared he would lose him, but Sóbhán lay his hand on Kavan's wrist and gently pushed it down.

"He is in good care, k'bhydhá. Aunes would never harm a child. Come, let's go downstairs, see to your hand, get you food and drink."

"bhydáni…?"

Sóbhán nodded grimly, understanding why Kavan had returned the way he had and perhaps the reason for his state. Raebhá had promised to protect Kavan, but if his connection with the dying bhydáni was the cause of his condition, there was nothing she would have been able to do about that except let him go.

Supporting Kavan's weight to help him down the stairs, he murmured, "He is fading…but when I left him last evening he was still with us. gdhededhá Bhílári is with him. We, Bhen and others, have stayed with him in turns so that he is not alone when he…"

"I must see him."

"Of course you must, but you need to get your strength back…unless you want me to carry you to him?"

Kavan had just enough stubborn pride to shake his head, rejecting that idea as soon as it was presented. His presence in Bhryell would draw stares as it was. Being carried across town would draw a curious crowd both to him and to the bhydáni's doorstep. It was better, he thought, if he spared them that.

But he could not wait for long.

Sóbhán helped Kavan into the bard's favorite hearth chair and Aunes sat opposite with the boy who continued reaching for Kavan as he half-heartedly tried to decide if he should nurse or reject the woman with the unfamiliar smell and taste. Content that he could see them, Kavan sank against the back of the chair, eyes closed, and listened to

Sóbhán moving in the kitchen. He was gone less than five minutes, but by the time he returned, Kavan felt stronger than he had upstairs.

Removing himself from the proximity of the draining Gate helped.

When he opened his eyes again, the room was brighter and Sóbhán sat across from him in the place where Aunes had been. His hand was wrapped in gauze. With his infant son now out of sight, Kavan jerked out of that period of sleep with a cry. "Ágdhállán!"

Sóbhán's hand on his knee kept him from rising. "Aunes took him upstairs to the cradle Prince Lorant has been using."

"Prince…?" Kavan cocked his head and listened for the sound of footsteps, but the house was built too sturdy for him to hear them. The child's bright amber life force glowed within Kavan's breast, however, reassuring him that the boy was unharmed and sleeping. He relaxed, noticing the bread on the round table at the side of the chair. Absently, he wiped his gauze-wrapped hand beneath his nose where the blood had been. Nothing came away and he assumed Sóbhán had washed his face without Kavan's awareness.

"The plague hit Rhidam hard; most of the palace was afflicted."

"Ártur?"

That Kavan's first thoughts went to his cousin's welfare was not surprising. "Is well. He and Syl were spared, praise k'Ádhá. Queen Diona, Bhyrhán and Níkóá were spared too. The prince-regent and the princess…when they fell ill, Prince Lorant came here, in the hopes he would be safe. Merrek and Arlana recovered. The infant did not."

His sigh brought Kavan to worried alertness. If Prince Lorant had been ill, was putting Ágdhállán in the bed where he had slept safe?

"Prince Lorant is well. Never sick. Chethá took him to aene Dháná for a few hours while she sees to aendhá Tám. He suffered the plague; he lives but lost his sight." He wondered if he should speak of Dhóri but decided to spare Kavan that news for the moment as the bard devoured the honeyed bread. "Sámel…" he sighed again. "The craft is in Bhen's hands now, Bhen, mine, Aleski and Llucás…"

Kavan's heart tore further, for his aunt in particular, who had lost two children to two different plagues. It could not be easy for her. Perhaps he should visit her. He ached for Bhen and Aleski's loss of their father, and for Ártur's loss of a brother. How he felt about his uncle's loss of sight was a complicated matter and he felt petty and guilty that he was not more remorseful over the man's suffering. Eyes suddenly wide, the last morsel of bread falling from his fingers, he croaked, "bhydáni…"

"The Yellow Death has not touched him," Sóbhán assured him, "He fell, broke his hip, but the plague passed him, praise be. Shall I take you to him? Do you feel strong enough?"

Though Kavan's head bobbed yes, his effort to stand was tentative as if he expected his legs to fail. When they did not, when he found his stance steady, he squared his shoulders and said, "I will go alone."

"You should not…"

"If you are seen with me…no, I won't risk it. Besides," he glanced at the stairs, "I am entrusting you with your brother's welfare."

"Brother?" There had been an inkling, a recognition of kindred when he had interacted with the child while Kavan slept, but the verification was still surprising. "Raebhá?" Why had Kavan returned with a child and without her unless something ill-fated had happened?

Kavan shook his head. "Later," he whispered. "I will tell you later." He trudged towards the door, finding strength in each step despite the pull that called him back to the Gate. Talking about Raebhá would fuel a longing to return and there were things Kavan needed to do. He exchanged the dhóbhaen cloak he wore for Sóbhán's and with his hand on the latch, he looked back at his son with gratitude and the relief of seeing him healthy and alive. "You will look over him?"

"You know I will."

"Thank you." He hesitated before trying to smile and adding, "I am happy to see you, Sóbhán." He had not realized how much he had missed this son until he saw him. He suspected it would be the same when he saw Dhóri, Rhyrdan, Merrek, and others.

"Likewise, k'aendhá." Questions would wait. Kavan was home. There would be time for everything else later.

Beneath the blush of dawn, Bhryell stirred, sounds within homes telling of the rising of families beginning the day's routine. Kavan saw no one in the streets as he trudged across the square to the small house that had been a second home to him as a boy. If anyone saw him, they did not come out or call his name through open windows or doors. The morning was seasonably warm, with only enough coolness in the air to draw shivers across his skin. Warmer than Dhóbhaen, however, a remembrance that drew his thoughts back to a few hours past and made his mouth tremble.

The door before him was slightly ajar, as was often the case when the bhydáni was home, and the arguing voices within brought a tangle of melancholy and amusement.

"He will be here," the reedy, raw voice croaked, adamant despite its weakness. "I will not go."

"bhydáni, please." The gdhededhá sounded beside himself with frustration. As Kavan neared the door he could see Bhílári trying to lift the skeletal man from his chair into another one. Tíbhyan, appearing to use more strength than a man in his condition should have, gripped the wooden arms, planted his feet, and refused to move from the place where he had spent most of his time over the past week or more. Despite the distance, Kavan could see how frail his mentor had become. The floor beneath the chair was wet though clean and the room smelled of decay, of age, of a failing body whose functions no longer cooperated with its owner's mind.

Without relying on the shredding link of power between them, Kavan knew Tíbhyan would leave soon. The man was four hundred and eighty-five years old. It was time.

Bhílári lifted his head and locked his gaze with the man weakly struggling up the porch steps, a man he had not seen since Sóbhán's wedding the year before. Kavan was traveling and excommunicated. Both were the reasons, some argued, that Kavan could not be here as Tíbhyan waited.

Wherever Kavan had been, whatever the powers in Clarys declared, this was no phantom Bhílári saw now.

"bhydáni."

Tíbhyan had already turned his head towards the silently opening door, his hand outstretched towards a figure he could barely see.

"ágdháni."

From the wizened man, Kavan did not object to the title, for he knew it was what he was, a man of incredible power and ability greater than any Tíbhyan knew. No Elyri alive knew of another with the strengths, the gifts, that Kavan Cliáth bore responsibility for. It was a title easier to carry than málneag.

Inside the house, the room looked as it had when Kavan had been a child. Only the locations and contents of the piles of books, scrolls, and tattered ancient documents were different. Kavan noted all of it with a sweeping glance before he reached the old man's side, squatted with aching slowness, and closed his hands around Tíbhyan's frail one.

"I knew you would come." Even in his weakness, there was a note of chastisement for the other in the room, although Tíbhyan did not look at Bhílári. He studied only the face in front of him, near enough now to see and recognize despite his failing sight.

"Of course I would." He feared he would not, but arguing that point was irrelevant.

"Tell him, Bhílári, tell him what I've…" Before the gdhededhá could comply with the demand, Tíbhyan continued insistently. "It is yours, all of it. The books, the walls, everything. There is no one else."

Though the man's generosity did not surprise him, Kavan felt no need for another home nor the furnishings it contained. The Bhryell house Kavan once called home, where Sóbhán and Chethá now lived, had belonged to the bhydáni's only child, reverted to her father on her death, and passed to Kavan when the boy needed a place of his own. Tíbhyan had no living kin. His most beloved student was the closest to it and it was in Kavan's hands that his possessions would fall.

If Kavan did not accept it, it passed to the lómesté to be given to anyone who needed residence. The bard could not allow that. Maybe it was time to place the other house in Sóbhán's name. It was big enough for a family. Excommunicated, Kavan did not foresee ever living in it again.

This smaller house, with only two bedrooms and lacking a Gate, but with a host of manuscripts that Kavan would move to the security of St. Kóráhm's, would be accepted with gratitude and humility, as the sage desired.

Tíbhyan's clawed hand uncurled from the arm of the chair and waved shakily in Bhílári's direction. "You may go," he snorted, an effort that wracked him with a rattling, wheezing cough.

"Are you…?" The question remained incomplete and unrequited. Of course Tíbhyan was sure. He was in the care of a man the gdhededhá believed the bhydáni was less likely to fight when it came to matters of his well-being. If he was going to pass soon, he was going to do so in the company of the one he loved most. "You will stay?"

Kavan nodded. The thread between them was so stretched that he did not expect he would be here long, but he would stay to see the man to his final breath. He did not watch Bhílári go, did not greet him as he should have, or ask the gdhededhá to keep his presence in Bhryell a secret. The leader of Bhryell's Faithful knew what was at stake should Clarys learn he was here and Kavan trusted the man's loyalty enough to believe he was safe for however long he stayed.

He waited until the footsteps were gone, the door partially closed behind him to reduce the possibilities of the bard being seen, and then Kavan pressed his hand to the man's forehead. "I am thankful I made it in time, bhydáni. I feared I would…"

"Feared?" Tíbhyan chuckled. "You knew I would wait."

"Hoped, yes." He smoothed down the man's sparse, white hair. "Is there anything I can get you? Shall I change your clothing or…?"

"You can take me to the brookhead; you know the one."

Kavan nodded. The sage spoke often and fondly of the brook which ran north of Bhryell from the mountains above into a small nearby lake that provided Bhryell with fish before continuing east to join with other tributaries that eventually fed Elyria's greatest lake. There were days, as a boy, when Tíbhyan had taken him there to escape the press of Bhryell's populace. The brookhead was nearly five miles beyond the town's perimeter and would take the bulk of two hours to reach on a good day. Tíbhyan did not have the strength to walk from his chair to the door. Kavan would need to carry him and he was not certain he had the strength to do so. It had been many years since Tíbhyan had been there and if he was to die, after everything he had done for Kavan, the bard would give anything to allow him to see his favorite place one last time.

"Yes, bhydáni; I will take you."

Ignoring the man's damp clothing and the stench of his unwashed state, Kavan cradled the too-frail body in his arms. It was akin to carrying a child, his slight weight only noticeable because Kavan was still unsteady on his feet. Though his body was weak, Kavan's will and resolve were not. He maneuvered the door open with his foot, almost fell as he descended the porch steps, but once on the flat stones of Bhryell's wide streets, continued movement became easier.

Across town to the edge of the woodland that embraced Bhryell's northwest side. Past the burial ground where Kavan expected to soon lay the man to rest. Through the sparse growth nearest town into the denser depth of the forest. He had hiked so much this day already, a journey of a thousand miles it felt like, but still, he trudged.

If all of the power he had sapped from friends and loved ones had contributed to Tíbhyan's weakening, had hastened this end, another thousand-mile journey was a sacrifice Kavan was willing to make. It would never be enough to assuage his culpability.

"I found them, bhydáni," he murmured, deciding that speech would shift his focus from his weakness, from the guilt he struggled to subvert, and allow him to continue instinctively moving forward. They had shared so much over their long years of acquaintance. Telling of the dhóbhaen, this one last sharing of arcane knowledge, was something Kavan would cherish when his mentor was no longer there to share with.

"Them?"

"The dhóbhaen…the Kindred…the people from which we…Elyri…sprang. I know what k'elyryhánag is. I know Dhágdhuán and Zythán…Llyr and Drebhoti…I know Curnydhá and Cliáth and the history we have been kept from knowing."

He did not know it all, did not intimately know the stories for they were tales the dhóbhaen rarely spoke as their keepers of knowledge suppressed the truth. But he knew enough, details and the ways of the dhóbhaen, that he could piece together a history that had never been shared in Elyria. Maybe the books he had been given would tell him more. He knew enough to tell the history of their people to Tíbhyan, the only authority on truly ancient history that existed in the Sovereignties, a burden, Kavan realized, weaving the tale as he trudged further away from signs of inhabitation, that would likely be his to carry to his own grave after Tíbhyan was gone.

Who in all of Elyriá would care to hear it, to believe, a history that contradicted so much of who they believed they were, what they believed the tenants of their Faith were?

The burden of that realization caused his shoulders to sag but Tíbhyan listened, soaking up the details, accepting as truth things Kavan had seen and shared through the contact of white hands on his skin. Never in the years they had known each other had Tíbhyan doubted him. Here, at the end, he was not about to start.

"Your questions have been answered." Tíbhyan nodded as if it took too much effort to keep his head upright as they reached the brookhead and Kavan nestled him on the ground against the trunk of an ancient pine. Where the water came from was unclear, emerging from the ground beneath, perhaps, or seeping around rocks as it trickled from the Llaethlágárá's heights and pooled here, gathering enough force to bubble its way east where it was joined by other sources until it became a meandering river. It had the air of a place visited by the k'kairá, a sacred place, where power was birthed, where it filled everything around them more strongly than in other places. To the eye, this was the source, and this was where Tíbhyan had chosen to die. At the source. Kavan knew, even if the bhydáni did not say it. "Are you satisfied?"

"Not all questions are answered," the bard admitted as he sat beside Tíbhyan and held his hand. "There is always more to know, things I do not understand…but it helps."

Glancing at their joined hands revealed the power branding he now bore, the eternal mark he shared with Raebhá, a reminder he had forced himself not to look at thus far. He could talk of the dhóbhaen, of history, of his experience, without tapping into sorrow, but now, in this moment, memories crushed his soul with a force that left him breathless for several minutes.

When he did speak, bursting the silence of birdsong, insect hum, bubbling water, and the wind in the pines, it was to whisper. "I have married, bhydáni." Tíbhyan was the first to be told and would take that surprising admission to his grave.

Tíbhyan smiled weakly and patted Kavan's arm with his free hand, a gesture that took so much of his strength that he left his hand on Kavan's wrist. "I had faith, Kavan, even when you did not. Faith in religion, no. Faith in you, always." He had seen too much of Kavan's mind, heart, and soul, to have doubted him the way Kavan doubted himself. "You have married a pagan. She is good to you?"

"Perhaps I am more of a pagan than I believed…" Kavan sighed and brushed his hair from his eyes. "She is…what I need…and has given me another son." What he had always needed, he believed, and no distance between them would change or lessen that.

"Then I am relieved she will be with you when I am not." His mouth opened in a half yawn and he closed his eyes. "I should have liked to meet her…and him."

"And she, you, bhydáni."

Kavan did not believe his words were heard; he recognized the man's snoring, the way his chin bobbed on his chest as he dozed. Kavan kissed Tíbhyan's temple with a whispered, "kisdhe. tuesdhe."

Instead of watching him sleep and be reminded of the loss soon to come, Kavan stared into the churning water, watching it pool and rush to the east with the force of gravity and more water rising behind it.

He thought about the first time he had met Tíbhyan. He was the only man confident enough to take on Kavan's private education. The only man not afraid of him, the man who had given him opportunity and autonomy to stretch and grow the wings of his innate gifts, who had provided shelter when his own family would not, had given him a home and the freedom to meet the world on his own terms.

Without Tíbhyan, Kavan could not imagine what his life would have been like, what he would have become. Without Tíbhyan, he was not certain he would have survived his childhood.

A sweet smell, like thimbleberry and dogwood mixed with tart apple, wafted beneath his nose. His eyes fluttered and he realized that his weak weariness and the lulling of the wind and water sounds must have overcome him and caused him to slumber. His head had drooped to one side so that now there was aching stiffness in his neck and when he lifted his head and absently reached to rub his neck, he realized he did so with the hand that had previously clutched Tíbhyan's.

The bhydáni was no longer beside him.

Bolstered by the respite, the surge of concern, and the prevalent sense of power tracing patterns across his skin like tickling ants, Kavan scrambled to his feet. "bhydáni!" he cried, scanning the thicket for some sign of the sage. "Tíbhyan!"

There was no trace of him, no footprints to the water's edge, no indication that he had fallen into the brook and drowned in an effort to drink. The water was not deep enough here, or strong enough, to have floated his body, light as it may have been, very far. His clothes would have caught and torn on brambles and rocks and wedged him somewhere nearby before the brook arced and disappeared through the trees. No branches Kavan could see had snagged his clothes to mark a path into the forest; there was no dragging, shuffling of steps through fallen needles and damp earth to mark his passage or where he might have been dragged away by wild beasts.

From the condition he had been in, Kavan knew he would not have walked anywhere. He would not even have been able to crawl.

It was as if he had ceased to be. As if he had never been there.

No obvious signs of departure did not prevent Kavan from looking, from pushing into denser foliage and climbing large, steep boulder faces, of directing power further and further from himself in the desperate need to find Tíbhyan and take him back to Bhryell. But the power always doubled back on itself, brought him to the spot where they had sat together, forcing Kavan to acknowledge the obvious although he had not witnessed it with his own eyes.

kylldhysag.

No myth, but a reality he had come so close to seeing.

Or perhaps that had been why he slept…so that no Elyri living could see and know the mystery of their lives end. There was residual power in the air, in the earth on which Tíbhyan had rested. Kavan could feel it through his hand when he spread his palm on the earth. It was as if, instead of being assumed into Ethenae, Tíbhyan's life, the power that lay at the core of every Elyri, every dhóbhaen, had been sucked into the earth and dispersed to make him one with the elements that allowed others to live.

A fitting thing then, for a man who questioned Faith until the end, and yet a painful thought for Kavan who had been raised to believe that the separation from the Eternal Divine was a thing to be feared.

And yet…

A sound, a voice on the wind without the shape of words, a swirl of power that sparked as if to bring to him the familiar presences he had experienced most of his life, presented another possibility, one that he had never given due consideration before Raebhá had spoken it.

What if, in the end, it was all the same? What if the end of life Dhágdhuán called Ethenae was merely the dispersing of energy, the merging into the oneness of creation, merging into the divine, into peace, into k'Ádhá's creation where all souls passed?

Was not then the outcome, be it death or Ceasing, which brought them all to the same place, an end not to be feared?

Kavan found no answers beneath the shadows of the mid-afternoon sun sprinkling through the pine boughs above.

What he did find, for the first time in his near-century of life, was soulful peace.

ᐷᐺChapter 44ᐺ

"He's here! He's returned!"

Hk'gdhededhá Tusánt looked up from his interrupted prayers, irritated at first and then shocked by the man who had burst into his chambers unannounced. He knew Bhílári from trips to Elyriá and to his knowledge, the man rarely left Bhryell. He rarely traveled by the Gates and he had only come to Enesfel once. That had been in Kavan's support when the bard had faced accusations of murdering King Hagan. It was unlikely he would be in Rhidam now unless…

"Lord Cliáth?" Prayers forgotten, Tusánt leaped to his feet to grip Bhílári by both arms. The levels of training and power between them allowed for an inadvertent exchange of images so that Tusánt saw the bard for himself, entering an old man's home, the old man who had also come to Rhidam in Kavan's defense at the same time Bhílári had. "How long?"

"I do not know…not long. I doubt many know he's there, but you know the danger…" Kavan could protect himself from that danger if he chose, but it was a danger the bard might willingly take on rather than risk friends and family. More worrisome for Bhílári and many who knew and loved the man was that he might leave as soon as the bhydáni departed life. There were people who needed to see him, to know he was alive. Tusánt had been the first person to cross Bhílári's mind, one of the few who might be able to convince Kavan to remain long enough to reassure those who loved him that he was well.

Tusánt planned to do more than that. He carried a secret meant for Kavan's ears alone, a secret that might mean the difference between Kavan remaining in the Sovereignties or leaving again. Knowing little about where Kavan had been or what he had been doing, it was a secret the harper needed to know.

"Take me to him."

They hurried through the thóres, into the sanctuary where gdhededhá Rankin had gathered the other gdhededhá for their daily assignment of duties, and having seen Bhílári arrive, most not knowing who he was, all heads followed their movement across the room towards the thol. Tusánt put a hand on Rankin's wrist in passing to press the news into the Teren's unprotected thoughts, a breach of Elyri protocol rarely made. Rankin blinked in surprise, wondering what he was expected to do, but Tusánt and Bhílári were already disappearing behind the Purification chamber curtain and would soon be gone to whatever destination they intended.

The meeting was hastily adjourned. Rankin made his choice. Others needed this news. Parish duties could wait.

Ártur burst through the door, wide-eyed, not considering if quarantine was still in place in Bhryell. It had taken more effort than usual to manipulate the Gate and the effort left his legs unsteady as he stumbled from Hes Índári to Kavan's home. He stared wildly about the family room, the dining room, and the kitchen in the hopes that the news Rankin had delivered was true. There was no trace of his cousin, no evidence that he had been here, but the aura of his powerful presence lingered fresh in the air, a sure sign even if not a visible one.

"Where is he?"

The women in the room, his daughter and another he recognized but could not name, looked at him, startled. The flame-haired infant in the stranger's arms began to cry and Prince Lorant scrambled across the room to latch on to Ártur's leg with a squeal of delight. Chethá rose, her smile of relief at seeing her father colored by both concern and something Ártur did not take the time to identify.

"He's not…"

"Where…?"

"Tíbhyan."

The frantic tirade he had been about to launch into aborted at the mention of Kavan's mentor and the sorrowful way his daughter spoke the name. It did not surprise him that their bond could be strong enough for Kavan to feel the bhydáni's failing health, or strong enough to draw Kavan home. There were details about that which birthed sparks of resentment, guilt, and regret, but Ártur quickly extinguished those things. Why Kavan had not come sooner was less important than the fact that he was in Bhryell.

"Where did he…?"

"He came, aendhá," Sóbhán said, descending the stairs with Bhen to join the conversation sparked by the healer's loud voice. "He will return when he is able."

"How long has he…?" The day was drawing to a close, the sun low on the horizon pulling darkness with it, and without knowing when Kavan had arrived or how long he had been out of the house, Ártur feared his cousin would bypass home in favor of a Gate where he was less likely to be accosted by waiting family.

"He came just after dawn and went to the bhydáni's as soon as he had the strength to do so." Sóbhán raised his hand to cut short the healer's questions about Kavan's health. He knew nothing about the cause of his weakness, the blood on his face, or any other details about his return. There had not been time or opportunity to learn that.

Bhen wrapped a supportive arm around his uncle's shoulders. "The bhydáni has not long; we've been surprised he lingered as long as he has. Waiting for aendhá Kavan, I dare say…"

"Now that he has come, death will be soon."

"When it comes," Chethá chimed in, flanking her father's other side, an arm around him as well to anchor him, "aendhá will come for me or gdhededhá Bhílári to…"

"Then I should go to him." Ártur pulled free of his well-meaning kin. He knew Kavan's moods, how his cousin typically dealt with grief. Kavan would likely seek solitude to avoid the sympathy of too many others, which suggested that Kavan would seek the náós Gate and be gone from Bhryell or else fly before anyone had the opportunity to see or speak to him.

Sóbhán shook his head. "He will return here."

"How can you be…?"

The opening door interrupted and the white-skinned man surrounded by the twilight of the street was the one to answer. Sensing his gathered family in the house as he approached, he had been tempted to flee as Ártur suspected he would be. But he was different now, and one that relied on him was in this house, awaiting him. The need for solitude would have to wait.

"Because my sons are here."

Having not seen or sensed Dhóri in the house, Ártur ignored Kavan's preference for physical distance and rushed to embrace him. The bard made no effort to rebuff him and instead awkwardly returned the gesture though his eyes were on the infant across the room as he satisfied himself that the crying child was as healthy as he had been when left that morning.

"How did you…?"

"I told Bhen and Chethá," Sóbhán said hastily, for both had come to the house, returning with Prince Lorant. When Sóbhán had spoken of Kavan's return, Bhen refused to leave.

"dedhá Rankin came to the keep to announce you," Ártur added, unaware that his cousin's return had been meant to be a secret that he would have preferred to announce himself.

Kavan sighed. Bhílári then. Better the news was taken to Rhidam than to Clarys. He wondered if word had been sent to Alberni, if Dhóri and Rhyrdan had refused to come…or if they were unable.

Perhaps they did not know about this impromptu reunion and would be offended that they were not included.

He would beg their forgiveness when he went to Alberni, assuming the plague had not taken them. Kóráhm had said they lived, but that had been weeks ago. A lot could have happened since then.

Taking pity on Aunes who was unable to calm Ágdhállán's crying, Kavan stepped away from Ártur and held out his arms. She deposited the boy in his father's care. Ágdhállán quieted at once.

"Is bhydáni…?" Sóbhán began, hindering Ártur's coming queries. "He is gone."

Chethá nodded with a sigh. "I shall fetch gdhededhá Bhílári…"

"There is no need. He is gone."

The room was silent with communal realization. It was a common end for Elyri, but one rarely discussed as most feared that unknown. It was an end Ártur knew Kavan himself feared, the possibility of being denied the eternal reward for Faith, but Kavan sounded at peace with Tíbhyan's departure. If the ancient man had been as frail as others had hinted, Kavan had likely helped Tíbhyan to it. The questions that raised were ones the healer doubted Kavan would answer.

"Dine with us," Chethá offered warmly, pleased to have family in the home. Most often, she and Sóbhán dined with her grandparents as her healing duties often precluded time spent in the kitchen and

Sóbhán's time in the Cliáthan workshop meant he was likewise too busy for preparations. But there was food in the pantry, kept stocked by Ártur's mother for those occasions when they could not dine with the family. This occasion would be celebrated in this house, not in the home of a man who held little love for his brother's son.

"I should not…the longer I am in Bhryell…"

Bhen chuckled. "Bhryell is the safest place in Elyria for you. I cannot think of anyone here who would reveal you to Clarys." Not even Tám, who would prefer Kavan remain concealed rather than face the scandal an arrest would have on the family's reputation. "Besides, it is a risk any of us would take for you."

Another interruption, this time a knock on the door, brought Tusánt and Bhílári into the home and soon all were seated around the table, sharing the meal provided, sharing the news of events that Kavan had missed. The news of healthy twin sons for Bhríd warmed him, as the man deserved a chance at the happiness with his new wife he had previously been denied.

For the deaths he knew of, and those he had not, Kavan mourned. For the news of Kjell's overthrow in Neth and Inness's subsequent rise to power, he ached in a worried fashion, recalling the Dream-Sight he had experienced in which she might well play a part.

Had that only been last night?

Had it only been a day since he had lain with his new bride with the promise of embarking on a life together that both had known would not be easily attained?

The pull of the Gate was strong. It took all of his willpower not to break away from the table and rush back to it. As the meal ended, his hope for escape was continuously hindered by the presence of family until he took the initiative excuse of needing to put the child to bed. No one had inquired about his fawning over the infant. There had always been a bond between Kavan and children and with a touch and manner that soothed even the most troubled adult, it was little wonder the baby was calmest in his care.

"I am grateful for your welcome," he said as he rose from the table, Ágdhállán in his arms and Prince Lorant clinging to his leg. The toll of the day's burdens, emotional, physical, and mental, combined with the emotions of others buffeting against his shields had worn him down. He needed to sleep if he could. "It has been a difficult day."

"Indeed," agreed Bhen, the first to follow to his feet, pulling Kavan's chair further back so he could leave the table more easily.

Kavan nodded. "Ártur, if you would tell Bhríd of my return…that I shall visit him soon." It felt a vital thing to do, that Ágdhállán meet his kin, and Kavan could not ignore the compulsion to make it happen.

"Will you come to Rhidam?" It was a silly question, as Ártur knew there were many there Kavan would want to see, but the sooner it happened, the more at ease the healer would be.

The more at peace he suspected Enesfel would be as well.

"I will." He could not commit to when. There were others he needed to see first. "Send Níkóá to Alberni in the morning…and Sóbhán, if you will come." He glanced at Prince Lorant leaning groggily against his side. "Take the prince home. His family needs him…and he needs them. He will be safe; you have my word."

Sóbhán swiftly agreed. "Of course." He did not know how his brother fared, or what his reaction would be to Kavan's return with a child, thus Sóbhán was determined to be there as a necessary buffer.

The healer scowled. Believing it only because Kavan said it, Ártur picked Lorant up and murmured reluctantly, "Very well…but why don't you…"

"I need rest," Kavan groaned. "And Ágdhállán needs…"

"His mother can…"

Kavan cut his cousin off with a pained expression and murmured, "His mother is not here," before hurrying away, Aunes following so that she could stay with the child during the night.

He was grateful Ártur did not follow.

Once the infant was settled in the cradle and Kavan felt confident, without reading the house, that most of the guests had departed, he went to the oratory where everything he had brought with him that morning still lay in a clutter on the floor behind the altar. Those things could wait. No one would disturb them, but having them near, things that Raebhá had touched and made, was the comfort he sought tonight. Kneeling at the power center of the Gate, he felt back through the link, seeking the way back to Curnydhá, to Raebhá's side. It did not surprise him it was not found. Few Gates throughout the Sovereignties and southern lands contained the markers of the too distant Dhóbhaen Gates. He would need to return to Fiara, to Owain's now-empty home, if he was going to get back to Curnydhá.

He was not certain he had the stamina to do so tonight, but he knew he would not sleep until he reassured himself of the possibility of seeing her within a few days.

"Lord Cliáth?"

Kavan stood, surprised to be sought here by someone other than Sóbhán. "k'gdhededhá…"

The Elyri head of the Teren Faithful waved off the title with a smile. "I think titles are moot between us." When Kavan's brow arched and Tusánt realized how he had greeted the bard, he chuckled. "Aye…well, perhaps that should begin with me. There is news that was not shared…of which you should be aware."

Expecting the news to be grim, Kavan laid the harp he had picked up onto the altar and gripped the edges of the marble, waiting for Tusánt to continue.

Tusánt turned towards the door and another shadow entered, tall and hawkish, his bald head scarred purple, a man immediately recognizable though Kavan had not seen him in more than twenty years. A tongue of flame glowed in his palm as he approached the altar and Kavan bowed his head, feeling betrayed that Clarys had been informed of his return, and that perhaps it was Tusánt who had done so. He expected there were guards downstairs and that the man with him was here to allow him to surrender without a fight.

"Do not fear. No one knows you are here, nor will they. Please." The older man gestured at the front bench. Kavan glanced at Tusánt, who remained in the doorway as if standing watch, and reluctantly accepted the invitation.

"Tusánt has told you of my election?"

Kavan shook his head no. Perplexed, his guest looked at Tusánt but did not press the matter. If Tusánt had not mentioned the election to the bard, there was a reason, if none other than the promise he had made to allow this man to be the one to share this important news. As though embarrassed, Tusánt bowed and stepped into the hall, closing the door behind him.

Ylár's appointment as k'gdhededhá of Clarys was expected since he had carried much of the burden of leadership in the waning years of Tumm's service to the Faith. His margin of loss during the previous election had been narrow, and the gawky Elyri, kin of the new Kyne Kavan had been told about over dinner…though not publically acknowledged as family…had solidified and built upon his reputation in the years since. Both Khwílen and Tusánt had kept Kavan informed of political matters of Faith as they fought for the reunification of Elyri and Teren, and Kavan was satisfied with this man's succession. He was also satisfied that Tumm was gone.

"You deserve the post, k'gdhededhá…and the Faith deserves you." Ylár was the leader the Faith needed if it was to move forward.

"What the Faith deserves is you…and I am ashamed that more of my equals cannot see it. But what they think does not matter. Upon appointment, I made use of election prerogative to do this." From the inner pocket of his cloak, he handed Kavan a leather scroll tube. "The writ has been in effect since I produced it, but if you would sign it, please, we can put the unfortunate events of the past to rest."

In the glow of his handlight, Kavan gave the short document a hasty read, noting the keywords and barely believing what they suggested. His skepticism demanded that he read the document twice more, slowly, before he looked at Ylár in disbelief.

Ylár had not come to arrest him. He had come to offer pardon, to lift the mantle of excommunication.

Heart hammering, it took Kavan several moments to hear anything more than the rush of blood in his ears. By the time his core was calm, remembering what he had earlier said to Tíbhyan, he shook his head with remorseful disinclination. "I thank you, k'gdhededhá, but I do not think I can accept this."

"Cannot accept…?" The refusal of a pardon, hesitancy to accept the reversal of excommunication, was the last thing Ylár expected.

Kavan left him seated on the bench, dragged his fingers across the top of the altar as he passed, and then stopped to stare at the figure of Dhágdhuán hanging on the wall behind it. "Did they tell you where I have been?"

"Only that you escorted a noblewoman to her homeland."

Kavan nodded, his back to Ylár. Of course, that was what Tusánt had said; that was all most had known. "She is of our blood, or rather, we are of hers. For all of my decades of study, of seeking answers…"

He paused as he turned. "I have been to the land of our ancestors. I know where we, all Elyri, come from. I have learned the history of our people, of our Faith, which little matches what is taught. I have seen things…I know things…that will never be reconciled by Clarys. When they are made known, if they are made known, not only will I be banned from the Faith," he shuddered, "I may also be executed."

Ylár scowled and returned the bard's stare. In this man's presence, the man who could perform miracles, who knew the company of saints and záryph, he felt more Elyri power than when they first met and a greater depth of spiritual strength than he had ever experienced in anyone else. He recalled the náós-shaking event of a few days past and, still certain it had been caused by something Kavan had done or experienced, he picked up the abandoned scroll and curled its edges between his fingers.

"Do you still hold faith in k'Ádhá?"

"Yes."

"Do you still hold Dhágdhuán's teachings to be truths?"

Kavan's breath caught. "I…do not think my interpretation of truth is the same as what is taught…"

Ylár nodded. That had been the matter of contention between k'gdhededhá Dórímyr and Kavan when the bard had been a child, the matter that had led to conflict and excommunication. Ylár did not know what those variances were, but he was keen to explore them.

"Would it surprise you that differences in interpretation are far more common than just with you? I assert that instead of rigidly demanding conformity, it is time that the Faith accepts dialogue of those differences, to discover the core truths behind our teachings, behind the words of the saints."

He came to stand with Kavan at the altar and placed the scroll next to the harp. "This shall not be an easy thing, to either open dialogue or conduct it…but it is my vision for the Faith and I will move us towards that end. Whatever you know, whatever you have learned, I would be honored if you would share it with me."

The political nature of the man's position made Kavan willing to consider the offer, for what Ylár could do with the knowledge Kavan could share would determine the fates of many, himself included. He could bury it so that the truth was never known or share it with the Faithful and potentially destroy their beliefs. It would be Ylár's choice to make, but could he be trusted?

If he placed the dhóbhaen documents in St. Kóráhm's, allowed them to be copied, that truth would spread, with or without Ylár's help. Kavan did not believe in such secrecy of truth.

Truth was meant to be known. How to tell it, how to share it, was less obvious.

"Sign, Kavan. Accept that you are welcome in Bhryell, in Clarys, anywhere in Elyria you choose to go. When you are ready, come to me and tell me of those who are our kin. Tell the truths you know so that I may learn them, and correct me if I am in error. Let us decide together how the whole of Elyri can come to know these things."

It was the sensation of hands on his shoulders, though no one could stand behind him without standing on or in the altar, and the freedom, the safety, to return to Bhryell, to son and family as he wished, that drove Kavan to capitulation. When Raebhá came, he wanted to be able to bring her here, to the people he called kin, to the place he had been born. He wanted Ágdhállán to know these streets as he knew them. He wanted no borders for his family.

He wanted them all safe.

Acceptance was something Kóráhm had lost. For however long it lasted, Kavan wanted that for himself and his family. He would take it for all of them.

"I will sign it, k'gdhededhá. Thank you."

"Good. Together, Kavan, I believe we shall guide the future of Elyri towards something better than it has been."

Just, Kavan thought when hearing those words, as Raebhá hoped to do for the dhóbhaen.

❧*❧

Unable to sleep, rejuvenated by Ylár's news and the possibilities now open to him, Kavan checked on Ágdhállán once more after escorting the k'gdhededhá to where Tusánt and Bhílári waited downstairs and then dared to take the Gate to Fiara, to the nearest place he knew of that would reunite him with his wife. He considered an immediate dual jump, but instead chose, when he arrived in the center of the crimson sun inset on the marble floor of the manor, to focus outward, on the aura of the great house Owain Lachlan had called home for so much of his life. The traces of Owain were faint, faded after years of absence, bringing an ache to Kavan's heart that he had not felt in some time. Owain should know about Raebhá, about Ágdhállán. Owain should be here to greet him with one of the few embraces Kavan welcomed.

But he was not. Nor was Gabrielle. Knowing it made the vacuum harder to accept when the force of her absence hit him. The palpable loneliness bled from every empty room and wound around him like an anchor. He wondered if Merrek, if Piran, knew of her passing.

He had believed himself ready to face Gabrielle's death, but he realized he was not. Later, when his spirit was bolstered by the reconnected bonds of family and his spirit and body were less weary and torn, he would walk these halls and go to the place where she had been buried to say farewell.

In Fiara with her husband? Or had she been taken to Káliel?

He would discover that when he had the stomach for it.

His thoughts returned inward, still in the center of the marble sun, still at the center of the Gate in the middle of Fiara's entrance hall. More exposed than most, this Gate contained pathways to dozens of unknown Gates, and now that he had traveled through Curnydhá's, he believed he would recognize it, believed it would take him there rather than the random northern Gate in the mountains he had used before or some other unexplored one. Using Curnydhá's Gate would put him closer to Raebhá and flight would take him to her and back again after a welcome night's repast in her arms.

But what he found was a dark field nearly devoid of lights. He counted less than a dozen, those he and others most frequently used. Rhidam. Káliel. Alberni. Bhryell. Very few others. He could not see what he sought, and despite the growth in personal power, he could not feel them either. It was as if they had never been there.

The Gates to the land of the dhóbhaen were closed.

"Kóráhm," he cried in horror. "Kóráhm…bring them back!" Open them for me! Tell me what I must do!" Each word increasing in pitch and volume, he was unconcerned about drawing the serving staff to his location as he realized he could not keep his promise to Raebhá, that she would never know the reason for his absence. Would she be able to learn the Gates well enough, soon enough, to come to him, to seek the reason he did not return, or had the power he expended to return home, his own rather than a collaboration with others, caused the Gates to close, to implode, possibly forever?

Was it just this one Gate?

Panicked, he tried to remember other Gates he had encountered that contained those additional pathways, how he might get to them. Not from here, he realized with despair as he dropped to his knees with a wail. Not tonight. Perhaps he needed to recover from his day's ordeal to remember. Perhaps the Gates needed time to recharge.

Or perhaps he would never see Raebhá again.

One more wail, so long and loud that the household staff found him curled, weeping in the center of the Hall, the brand on his hand blazing as if it were the red marble sun on which he lay.

Not one of them dared to move him.

❧*❧

Crushing. Ripping. Fire on the back of her hand. Kavan's power, blasting into her head, filling her with a feeling of horror that choked her and jarred her from sleep to stumble onto the top step, expecting to find him at her door.

There was nothing there save for a ribbon of green glowing over the western mountains, filling the sky with jagged spikes, emanating, she was sure, from the place where she had last seen him. It was the wrong time of year for that vision. But it was there, brilliant against the black night. It was there…

…but he was not. Though she could feel him, his arms around her as she hugged herself against a chilly ocean wind, she understood at that moment the cause of his despair.

He was lost to her.

She would never see him, or their son, again.

Or so he feared.

She slipped down the steps into the dust of the street and gave her silent cry back in an echo across the miles.

She bid him never give up. She would not. She would find a way. Fate and the bhur be damned.

They would be together again.

❧*❧

Sóbhán rubbed his sleepy eyes but dutifully dressed and followed Kavan to the oratory Gate. Kavan looked more distant, lost, and shattered than when he had found him the previous morning. He did not know what k'gdhededhá Ylár's visit had been about or what had come after, if perhaps his father was in danger of arrest now that his presence in Bhryell was known. He did not know what matter of urgency precipitated this middle-of-the-night journey but Sóbhán believed that going to Alberni was exactly what his father needed.

The bard clutched Ágdhállán to his chest as they emerged into the familiar surroundings of St. Kóráhm's. The chellé was blissfully quiet, blessedly still in its Faith power, a sensation Kavan had not felt in nearly a year. He had missed this. Perhaps being here, in these walls, with these people, would help him. Perhaps he would find what he needed so that the Gates would work again.

"Bring Dhóri and Rhyrdan…please…"

Sóbhán wanted to hug him to take away his father's pain but he did not. Nothing he could do would help unless he brought those he called brothers to welcome their father home. "We will be there," he agreed. He did not need to ask where. He already knew.

Now, standing before the marker, Ágdhállán asleep in his arms, his heart empty of grief shared with Raebhá across the link that bound them, Kavan put a hand on the etched stone that was all that remained of his dearest friend and gave way to a different sort of grief. It was a stone with no dates, no florid epitaphs, no mark or crest, only Wortham's name and one word, a word those in St. Kóráhm's would revere and carry forever as a favor to the benefactor of their Order.

sínréc.

Kavan traced those words with his fingers, each line of each letter a memory. Wortham should be with him. Wortham would understand. Wortham would shoulder his grief and restore sanity and balance to his soul. Kóráhm, Kavan thought with annoyed bitterness, had abandoned him, which Wortham would never have done. Fate and destiny be damned, Wortham would never have left him alone.

Although, in the end, at the hands of death, that was precisely what Wortham had done.

The crunch of boots on earth still recovering from the parchedness of drought drew his attention from the traitorous gravestone. A single set, a face that, despite its youth, bore every trace of the man Kavan missed most dearly tonight. The distance between them closed swiftly without either realizing it, until Rhyrdan was crushed against his chest, the position mindful of the child between them, Kavan grappling him desperately with one arm and weeping on his shoulder.

So many words to be said, but none broke the surface in the lake of turbulent emotions that fed the well of Kavan's tears. Rhyrdan, overcome with both joy of Kavan's return and distress of Kavan's obvious pain, knew not the words to say to heal him. Like his father before him, he settled for holding the bard as he wept, remaining strong for the sake of one who had lost his strength to grief.

Two more sets of footsteps and Kavan raised his tear-stained face to watch the pair approach beneath the light of the full moon. Kóráhm had said Dhóri was spared, and yet he had not survived the Yellow Death unscathed, for the blindness that afflicted Tám had, Kavan could tell, laid claim to his son's sight. Pulling away from Rhyrdan, entrusting Ágdháldán into the hands of a young man he knew he could trust with his life and soul, as he had once trusted his father, Kavan left Wortham's grave and stopped before Dhóri, not sure what to expect from the son who had spewed such hatred the last time they spoke. Things were different now, so different, and none of that could be changed or taken back. Kavan would not have done so if he could.

Trembling he waited, holding his breath, afraid to speak.

"k'bhydhá. át kólir."

Three words. Three words and the emotion behind them, and he knew. Half praying for a miracle to be granted to his boy, Kavan cupped his dear face between his hands and pressed their faces together, forehead to forehead, and tried again to form words.

There was no miracle. Kóráhm had provided Dhóri with one already; it was ungrateful to demand more. Both lived, and, as Dhóri had longed for, he had been given the chance to apologize for his folly, pride, and disrespect. Kavan whispered, "I am here, Dhóri, as I promised I would be."

Kavan kissed his face; it was Dhóri's turn to hug him and weep.

Kavan had come home.

It was enough.

# ❧Epilogue☙

Only one other person came here, a single man with access to items that Kavan felt important enough to keep from the world, to protect both items and all living souls. The Coryllien daggers. The Staff of Drebhoti and the Chalice of Llyr. Original copies of Kóráhm's Articles, Kóráhm's journal, and the genealogy that proved without a doubt that Kavan was of the bloodline of Saint Kóráhm the Heretic.

It would now contain the three ániélmé as well.

Perhaps, he mused as he unlocked the grate guarding the chamber's riches, he should study the journal again. With his new knowledge, perhaps it would reveal connections to the dhóbhacn that he had not seen before. For Llyr, for Drebhoti, for Zythán, and how many others had been outcasts, pagan heretics in their own right?

It seemed Kavan came from a long line of pagan outsiders. Was it any wonder that he too found himself outside of the establishment?

Khwílen seldom came to these vaults but his presence here bore the sharpness of a recent visit. When he had cornered Kavan as the bard was leaving St. Kóráhm's, expecting to meet with Níkóá and Prince Merrek now that the sun was rising, Kavan had sent the young men home with their infant brother, had sent for Aunes, so that he could hear the k'gdhededhá out. The news of a relic of impossible value awaiting his verification of authenticity was enough to draw Kavan back into the chellé, draw him here before going home.

As he entered the vault and crossed the chasm in front of it, the power in the room was strong, easily traced to the alcove before him.

He lay his hands upon the fabric bundle to remove it, to see it, and stumbled back at the psychic jolt it gave, the force of visions that hammered into his head with a ferocity that left him incapable of seeing or deciphering them.

"Yes," came the meek voice beside him. "It was mine. You should not have it…but you do…and perhaps that is for the best."

Kóráhm looked shrunken and remorseful and would not look Kavan in the eye as he spoke. It was the first time Kavan had seen such contrition, a different sort than when the auburn-haired saint had apologized for Kavan being the one to cleanse the altar beneath Rhidam's keep, the one to undo the results of events in the man's life that he had been unable to change. This time was not that, however. Kavan knew why Kóráhm appeared small and full of regret.

It was a reaction to his anger, and though Kóráhm's sorrow bled some of the force of Kavan's frustration away, he was not prepared to easily cast forgiveness for something likely not even the saint's fault.

"You won't help me. You prevent me from…" Kavan leaned forward with both hands splayed on the stone wall, one on either side of the hewn vault containing the cloak of Saint Kóráhm.

"I cannot help you, átaelás mai…as much as I wish I could. Like you, I could use the k'rylag…but that is all…and now I can do even less. I do not know why they fail you, or how to undo what has been done, but I swear to you I had no hand in it."

Kóráhm faced the vaults, looking from one to another, knowing the purpose, the origins, of so many pieces in Kavan's collection that it was like looking at his life through the refraction of chiseled glass. "I know what it is to lose someone, to endure it, but know this…"

He nearly covered Kavan's hand with his, but his attempt fell short, his hand spreading instead against the stone where Kavan's hand was, inches away from the pale fingers. "You will see her again."

"How?" Kavan wanted belief, but despair blinded him to hope.

"You have the power. The means. You will find the way." He hesitated, brushed his fingers against Kavan's, and whispered, "I am sorry, átaelás mai."

Though the touch lingered and Kavan did not turn, he knew Kóráhm was gone. In time, a day, a week, clemency would rise and Kavan would summon the saint again. Maybe Kóráhm would come.

Maybe he would not.

"I am sorry." The words came despite his anger. Forgiveness, it seemed, would come sooner than expected.

Kóráhm's words echoed in his head, two words in particular. Power and means. He was uncertain what the saint meant by those things, other than to convey his faith in Kavan's ability to overcome this unforeseen obstacle.

Kóráhm had lost his beloved to death in the most horrific manner; he knew Kavan's pain. Raebhá lived, a powerful point inside of Kavan's heart, a reminder that she was there, awaiting the fulfillment of his promise. He could build a ship. Or he would find the way to restore the Gate. He could find another. If necessary, he would learn to create one.

There was no reason he could not try and every reason to do so.

Not today. Today was a day for duty and the family at hand. There were reasons he had returned to Alberni. His sons, by blood, by adoption, by love, needed him. And he needed them. Especially now.

The Gate within the vault would take him home. That connection, at least, had not changed. Kavan stood upon that spot, absorbing the energy through his feet, enjoying the tingle it gave. Perhaps tonight, when the day's business was done, he would fly. k'Ádhá knew he needed the release. He looked one more time at the alcove where the mantle lay, vowing to return to study it later, remembering then the other surprising image that had come from that bundle of holy cloth. The image of the man who had delivered it. Lovely, dark-haired, cherished záryph of a man Kavan had thought never to see again.

Myreth.


The End

## Character Index Book 6


**Ágdhállán Kóráhm Cliáth**--son of Kavan and Raebhá, born in Curnydhá

**Agis, General**--The only Cíbhóló nomad to serve in the Enesfel military. Deceased

**Aldár**--a mythological dhóbhaen figure whose ship was said to have disappeared into a wall of flame.

**Alyná Dubuais-Cáner Dilyn**--daughter of Bhríd Cáner and Madalyn Dubuais-Cáner. Youngest twin. Marries Prime Magistrate Piran Dilyn

**Arlan Trebor Lachlan**--The youngest son of King Innis of Enesfel. He was the 25th king of Enesfel, responsible for peaceful relations with Hatu, increasing Enesfel's size via the war with Neth, and opening a dialogue with the islands of Káliel.

**Arlana Lachlan, Queen**-- youngest child of Queen Diona, married to Prince Merrek, mother of Lorant and Conroy.

**Ártur MacLyr**--Elyri healer, employed by each Lachlan monarch since King Innis. Married to Syl Cáner, father of Llucás and Chethá MacLyr and is cousin to Kavan Cliáth.

**Asta Deidre Dugan de Corrmick**--The daughter of Princess Deidre Lachlan and Lord High Inquisitor Caol Dugan, she is married to King Kjell of Neth.

**Audh di Cliáth, márbhyndhánis**--cousin of Ombhrís and best friend of Iólán di Curnydhá

**Aunes**--wet nurse taken on to temporarily care for Ágdhállán

**Balint Gabersdon, Sir**--Once the youngest knight in Enesfel, he is the Duke of Nelori.

**Bhás**--a woman of unknown origin who befriends Myreth and directs his search and acquisition of St. Kóráhm's mantle so that he can deliver it to Kavan.

**Bhendhámyn MacLyr**--The youngest son of Sámel MacLyr, nephew of Ártur MacLyr. He is a harp maker in the Cliáth tradition.

**Bhetá Gabersdon, Lady**--daughter of Duke Balint Gabersdon and the Elyri woman Dhybhé; has become the only Daema currently serving in Enesfel.

**Bhílári, gdhededhá**--head clergy of Hes Índári, Bhryell, who witnessed many of Kavan's "miracles" and has known him since childhood.

**Bhrán, the adventurer** --a reoccurring figure in dhóbhaen mythology said to use the guise of a variety of animals for escape or to accomplish great quests.

**Bhregdh**--secular leader of the ghísaer of Gíldyágh.

**Bhríd Cáner, Lord**--A distant cousin of the MacLyr's, Duke of Levonne. He is known as the best swordsman in the Five Sovereignties and is the Queen's Champion.

**Bhront**--an Elyri child in Bhryell who dies from the Yellow Death

**Bhyrhán Bhíncári**--One of many grandsons of Kyne Mórne Bhíncári, the High Mother. He chose the life of a minstrel and plays the shawm. He is distantly related to Kavan Cliáth, whose mother's maiden name was Bhíncári.

**Bowen Ellard Lachlan**--The 3rd son of King Innis; the 22nd King of Enesfel.

**Caldar Cates**--a young gdhededhá from Theron who serves in Rhidam

**Caol Dugan**--Originally the son of a member of the Association, and part of the Lachlan court and family, since he married Princess Deidre Lachlan, King Arlan's sister. He performed the duties of Lord High Inquisitor until his death during the 2nd Elyri Persecution.

**Cáym Kavan Cáner**--Bhríd Caner and Editt's son; youngest, twin of Phaedr Davit

**Cedric O'Grady**--The nephew of Sir Paul O'Grady, Duke of Eleva in Cordash. He is a minstrel whom Kavan meets in Yd Haszafni, Hatu.

**Celen, márbhyndhánis**--one of the márbhyndhánis who conspired with Ombhrís to remove Raebhá from leadership and banish her from Curnydhá.

**Chethá MacLyr Cliáth**--The daughter of Ártur and Syl MacLyr. Healer serving in Bhryell; married to Sóbhán Cliáth

**Claide, gdhededhá**--the Teren who served as k'gdhededhá of Enesfel during the 2nd Elyri Persecution and was significantly responsible for the Persecution.

**Conroy Lachlan, Prince**--Second surviving child of Prince Merrek and Princess Arlana, he dies from plague shortly after birth.

**Dawid Coryllien**--A figure once thought of as mythical, whose name is connected with the death of many Elyri and many Teren during the historical period known as the Persecution. His name was given to the daggers connected with those murders. Very little is known about him in the Five Sovereignties.

**Dhágdhuán**--The founder of the Elyri Faith, believed to have been Elyri by birth and semi-divine during his life. The Faith has no documents recording his origins or place of birth. Elyri stories only concern his teachings and his death upon a pyre, presumably at the hand of the Teren. According to dhóbhaen teachings, he was a fisherman from the land of the taeré to the island, and there taught his doctrines to the dhóbhaen who soon killed him for inciting heresy and treason. This suggests that he could be Teren, or possibly phae, but there is no proof to support any of the theories of his origins.

**Dháná MacLyr**--The wife of Tám MacLyr, mother of Sámel and Ártur MacLyr, Kavan Cliáth's aunt.

**Dhedec di Curnydhá**--a dhóbhaen sailor, shipwrecked with Gaed di Cliáth in the lands west of the Hínesur; both were saved by Dhágdhuán and returned to the land of the dhóbhaen with him. Adopting his teaching and that which welcomed training in the use of power, he was among those banished to the distant west where he served as one of the founders of the Elyri kingdom.

**Dhóláhr**--the kydhé of Ghené

**Dhóri Kóráhm Cliáth**--Kavan's son with Orynn.

**Dhybhé Gabersdon, Lady**--Elyri jeweler; after Balint saved her life, she married him and gave him a daughter before returning to Elyriá.

**Diona Cordelia Lachlan**--The only daughter of King Arlan Lachlan; Queen of Enesfel.

**Dóhn Bhlethan**--a mythological sailor said to have traveled the coast beyond Hatu's eastern border. He was forced to turn back due to unsailable seas and the death of the majority of his crew.

**Donal Malin Lachlan**--The 1st son of Innis of Enesfel; he was the 20th King of Enesfel and King Arlan's brother.

**Dórímyr, k'gdhededhá**--former k'gdhededhá of the Faith prior to the split between the Elyri and Teren followers. Had been a theological antagonist of Kavan's and was the instigator of his excommunication from the Faith.

**Drebhoti di Cliáth**--brother of Gaed, was a márbhyndhánis. Had been training others in secret with the power long before Dhágdhuán came to the land of the dhóbhaen, and was very powerful and skilled. Shared the fate of the other elyryhánag banished to the west.

**Eada, Saint**--a female saint from Theron, dubbed the patroness of forgiveness and the hungry for her care of the poor and those outside the Faith.

**Editt**--woman hired as a wet nurse for the Dubuais-Cáner twin girls; stayed on as their caretaker and eventually becomes Bhríd's mistress, wife, and mother of Phaedr and Cáym

**Edward Lindunn**--The son of a wealthy Rhidam resident, whose mother was from Cordash. He was to serve in the Cordashian military, but instead returned to Rhidam and eagerly agreed to enter the priesthood while serving as a guard for k'gdhededhá Tusánt. Becomes gdhededhá in Rhidam after Tusánt becomes k'gdhededhá.

**Emeria Dary**--Only daughter of Wortham and Zelenka, she marries Laney Dary and remains in the Alberni estate in service to Kavan's household.

**Ephé di Rínes**--Raebhá's childhood friend

**Espen Harcourt, Prince**--The second son of King Geir of Hatu, he is the brother of King Noreis. Married to Queen Diona for eight years before dying during an accident.

**Éthym, márbhyndhánis**--oldest of the dhóbhaen márbhyndhánis

**Farrell Rasmus Lachlan**--The 2nd son of King Innis of Enesfel; he was the 21st king of Enesfel.

**Fendel Geli**--a traveling trader who has done business with the Dugan family in the past and meets the royal family through Kavan. Becomes Inquisitor after Asta marries King Kjell

**Flannery McGranis**--The former squire of Bhríd Cáner who is elevated to the post of Chancellor upon the death of Minos Cornell.

**Gabrielle Dilyn Lachlan**--was the Prime Magistrate of Káliel, mother of Clianthe and Piran, she was the wife of Owain Lachlan. Retired to Fiara to care for Owain during his long decline in health.

**Gaed di Cliáth**--a dhóbhaen master-builder of both instruments and ships, shipwrecked with Dhedec di Curnydhá in the lands west of the Hínesur; both were saved by a Dhágdhuán and returned to the land of the dhóbhaen with them. Adopting his teaching and that which welcomed training in the use of power, he was among those banished to the distant west where he served as one of the founders of the Elyri people.

**Gaelán Ágdhrán Cáner**--The youngest son of Bhríd Cáner and Madalyn Dubuais who has shown that he possesses the Elyri talent to heal despite being half-Teren.

**Gamal Lachlan-Harcourt, King**--Eldest son of Queen Diona Lachlan and Prince Espen Harcourt of Hatu. Twin to Liahm, the elder by thirteen minutes, he is anointed King of Hatu when Espen's brother fails to produce a male heir.

**Garran Declan, Lord High General**--a young, ambitious soldier who showed great promise in the leadership of troops when he served beneath General Agis. Upon Agis's retirement, he was appointed to the post of Lord High General despite his youth and has served loyally since; has never been tested in battle beyond putting down riots and rebellions during the 2nd Elyri Persecution.

**Govert, King**--The King of Cordash, married to Rika de Corrmick, daughter of Kjell and Asta Dugan

**Groff, Sherriff**--Sheriff of Alberni

**Guthrie McHador**--Once the general of Enesfel's army under Kings Innis and Donal, he reared Prince Arlan and assisted him in his bid for Enesfel's throne. He remained at court as Arlan's chamberlain and died during the fight with Neth that resulted in Enesfel obtaining the territory surrounding south of Lake Curo.

**Hagan Guthrie Brennan Lachlan**--The youngest child of Arlan Lachlan, he was the 26 king of Enesfel.

**Henrik de Corrmick**--son of Oska and Inness, born after Oska's death.

**Hwensen, gdhededhá**--had served as k'gdhededhá Dórímyr's personal aide until the time of his death

**Iden Stone, General**--a general in the Nethite army who helped save Prince Kjell's life; Kjell makes him general of the Neth army.

**Inness Lachlan de Corrmick, Queen-Regent**--3rd child of Queen Diona and Prince Espen, ambitious and calculating, marries Oska de Corrmick, and rules as regent for their son after her husband's death.

**Iólán di Curnydhá**--Raebhá s younger brother, a shipbuilder, and sailor

**Jerit de Corrmick, Prince**--Youngest child of Asta Dugan and King Kjell de Corrmick of Neth.

**Jermyn Tythilius, k'gdhededhá**--former leader of the Faith in Enesfel, was martyred at the start of the 2$^{nd}$ Elyri persecution.

**Kavan Kóráhm Cliáth**--Only child of Rístyrd and Llyárá, cousin of Ártur MacLyr. He is an admired harper, possessor of the Sight, holder of great psionic capabilities. Known as the White Bard of Bhryell for his tremendous musical talent and unique physical appearance, he was employed by Arlan as his court bard until his flight from Rhidam to the lands south of Hatu. He is also the Duke of Alberni and the founder of Saint Kóráhm's chellé hábhai.

**Khwílen Kesábhá, gdhededhá**--Abbot of Saint Kóráhm's chellé hábhai in Alberni due to his gifts of oratory, learning, and painting.

**Kjell de Corrmick**--The youngest son of Loris of Neth, he is the brother of King Merkar de Corrmick and is the current king of Neth.

**Kluín, gdhededhá**--a member of the Order of Saint Kóráhm, has twice been a candidate for the post of k'gdhededhá in Clarys.

**Kóráhm di Curnydhá, Saint**--Elyri saint for whom Kavan was named, also known as Kóráhm the Rón by many in Elyriá because of some controversial writings he made before the time of his martyrdom. Few of his books are available and he is not commonly discussed.

**Liahm Lachlan, Prince**--2$^{nd}$ born son of Diona Lachlan and Espen Harcourt, heir to the throne of Enesfel. Interested in architecture, he was severely injured in a building accident and later died of his injuries.

**Lláhy, gdhededhá**--a member of the Clarys gdhededhá

**Llaur, márbhyndhánis**--one of the Curnydhá márbhyndhánis

**Llucás Phaedr MacLyr**--The oldest child of Ártur and Syl MacLyr.

**Llyr di Bhíncári**--brother of Zythán, a healer from a family whose craft was cups, platters, eating utensils, and ceremonial tools. As a healer, he was trained in the use of power, and with Drebhoti, trained others in secret to use the power as well. Was included among those to be banished to the west.

**Lorant Lachlan, Prince**--the eldest child of Prince Merrek and Princess Arlana, the heir to the Lachlan throne.

**Lumel, Lord**--a Nethite lord in the de Corrmick court

**Maicel, Saint**--Teren woman in the early days of the faith from the region of Alberni who became the Patron Saint of Purity for her martyrdom at the hands of thugs when she refused to give up her chastity to them, instead preaching words of faith and forgiveness to them as she was killed.

**Madalyn Dubuais Cáner, Duchess**--The Duchess of Levonne, she is the only woman in Enesfel to have control of her own lands; she is married to Bhríd Cáner.

**Madoc Delamo, Lord High Justice**--Eldest child of Wortham Delamo and Zelenka. He served as Sheriff in Alberni for a few years, and after an act of valor on the Crown's behalf was elevated to Lord High Justice in the Queen's court in Rhidam

**Mánd**--the márbhyndhánis who provided Raebhá with a small amount of training with the power.

**Marta**--An Association member used as a contact by Asta Dugan.

**Merrek Lachlan, Prince**--only child of Prince Muir Lachlan and Clianthe Dilyn, he was raised by Kavan when his mother proved unfit and later killed herself after her husband's death. A Lachlan by name though not by blood, Queen Diona names him heir to the Lachlan throne after Prince Liahm's death.

**Mórne, High Mother (Kyne)**--The matriarchal ruler of Elyriá; she is head of the Elyri High Council.

**Muir Innis Lachlan**--The bastard son of Owain Lachlan and Brenna Weylin Lachlan, he was raised as Arlan Lachlan's son. Upon reaching adulthood he gave his land and title as Duke of Alberni to Kavan Cliáth and moved to Fiara with his father. Married to Clianthe Dilyn he is the father of Merrek Lachlan who was born after his death in battle.

**Myreth**--A singer of extraordinary talent, of unknown mixed heritage, raised in the cloister of Gorbesh.

**Naerá MacLyr**--eldest daughter of Aleski MacLyr.

**Níkóá McCábhá**--half-Elyri illegitimate son of King Farrell Lachlan, Queen Diona appointed him Chamberlain as part of a ruse to stop the anti-Elyri violence and retains him in that post afterward.

**Olaric Fraen the Elder, Captain**--a Nethite Captain who supports Inness Lachlan's bid for the Nethite throne, named after his father who sided with King Merkar after the death of General Glucke and was thrown into the bear pit for treason

**Olaric Fraen the Younger**--Nethite soldier, son of Fraen the Elder, the third Fraen to bear that name. He is loyal to General Stone and King Kjell

**Ombhrís di Nyrau**--son of the kydhé of Nyrau, he marries Raebhá di Curnydhá to unite their families and strengthen the bonds between their ghísaer. Believed killed on his wedding night.

**Onea Pantel**--The former head of the Fiara branch of the Association, now head of the Association in Glevum. She has maintained contact with Asta since the death of Asta's father.

**Orynn**--A member of all three known races (k'kairá, Elyri, and Teren) she was chosen by Kóráhm and her own people to make contact with Kavan and assist in his quest for healing, redemption, and the items needed to cleanse the thur thol below the Rhidam keep. She is known among the people in the barbarian territories as k'ílshwythnec, "she who sees," because of her tremendous knowledge of the past, present, and future. She is the mother of Dhóri and his female twin whom Kavan has never met.

**Oska de Corrmick, Prince**--Eldest child of King Kjell de Corrmick and Asta Dugan de-Corrmick

**Owain Ustes Lachlan**--He was believed to be the 5th child of Innis, son of Ula de Corrmick of Neth; he was the 24th king of Enesfel. He was actually the only child of Guthrie McHador. He relinquished the throne to Arlan Lachlan and lived in the Neth city of Fiara since then. He assumed the title of Duke of Fiara when the area of Neth south of Lake Curo seceded and became part of Enesfel. He was the father of Muir Innis and, later, after marriage to Gabrielle Dilyn of Káliel, fathered Piran Guthrie Lachlan.

**Peter Dahl**--former page of Queen Diona and eventually elevated to the position of Chancellor.

**Phaedr Cáner**--The brother of Bhríd and Syl Cáner, he joined Prince Arlan's forces and lost his sight, then his life, for that cause

**Phaedr Davit Cáner**--Bhríd Caner and Editt's son; eldest, twin of Cáym Kavan

**Phílóá Bhíncári**-- niece of Bhyrhán Bhíncári, one of the High Mother's granddaughters chosen to replace her as Kyne upon her death.

**Phínc**--The lead márbhyndhánis in Ghené.

**Piran Guthrie Lachlan**--The son of Owain Lachlan and Gabrielle Dilyn-Lachlan; he assumed the position of Prime Magistrate upon his mother's retirement.

**Qol**--A member of the race known as the phae k'kairá who has been serving as k'gdhededhá in the cloister of Gorbesh, and acting as the keeper of the relics Kavan seeks.

**Raebhá di Curnydhá**--kymyhé of the ghísaer of Curnydhá, marries Ombhrís di Nyrau to unite their families and strengthen bonds between their ghísaer. Abducted on her wedding night and sent via Gate to a location near Kavan's Alberni home.

**Raenár Magk, Captain**--had been the captain of the ecclesiastical guard in Clarys, goes to Saint Kóráhm's to serve as captain of the guard there.

**Rankin, gdhededhá**--Highest-ranking Teren gdhededhá in Hes a Redh, Rhidam.

**Rhyrdan Delamo**--the youngest son of Wortham Delamo and Zelenka; is given responsibility for the estate when Kavan undertakes the journey to get Raebhá home.

**Rika Valdis, Queen**--Second child of King Kjell de Corrmick and Asta Dugan de Corrmick and only daughter; despite poor vision and hearing, she marries King Govert of Cordash.

**Rouvyn Talis**--A Teren physician and native of Rhidam, he now serves as the Lachlans Teren court healer.

**Sámel MacLyr**--Ártur's older brother. Kavan's cousin. Harp maker in the Cliáth tradition, like his father.

**Saul Peado**--A Teren from Talladegah who came to Rhidam to serve as k'gdhededhá Tusánt's guard while studying as a novice for the priesthood. Becomes gdhededhá after Tusánt is elected k'gdhededhá of Rhidam

**Seren McCábhá**--the daughter of Níkóá and his third wife.

**Sóbhán Cliáth**--Kavan's adopted son, he has become a harp maker in Bhryell, assumes training of the Faith choir, and marries Chethá MacLyr.

**Sósáná**--Kóráhm's mother, disappeared when a dhóbhaen ship took her back across the sea.

**Syl Cáner MacLyr**--The wife of Ártur MacLyr, she is also a healer, and sister of Bhríd Cáner. She is the mother of Llucás and Chethá. Serves in Rhidam as court healer.

**Sylyhá Dubuais-Cáner Lachlan**--daughter of Bhríd Cáner and Madalyn Dubuais-Cáner; Eldest twin; marries King Gamal Lachlan-Harcourt

**Tám MacLyr**--The father of Ártur MacLyr, he is a harp maker in the Cliáthan tradition, and uncle of Kavan Cliáth.

**Tíbhyan**--Elyri bhydáni, who was Kavan's private tutor. He is the oldest man in Bhryell and one of the top 10 sages in Elyriá.

**Tumm, k'gdhededhá**--k'gdhededhá of Clarys, friend of k'gdhededhá Dórímyr, is confined to a rolling chair due to his great age.

**Tusánt, k'gdhededhá**--The only Elyri dedhá serving in Rhidam, and the first to be elected as k'gdhededhá of the Teren Faithful

**Uwin, k'gdhededhá**--gdhededhá in Fiara

**Wace Elotti**--A Cíbhóló nomad bounty hunter, heralded as the best in the Five Sovereignties. Sometimes works with the Lachlan Crown thanks to his association with Kavan and with the late Caol Dugan.

**Wallace**--Association contact for Asta Dugan de Corrmick in Gorea, Neth. Also known as the Three-Eyed Urchin

**Wermant, General**--Cordashian general in charge of troops sent to aid Enesfel in their border skirmishes with Neth.

**Wolson, Saint**—Teren saint, patron of diligence; there is a náós in Fiara dedicated to him.

**Wortham Delamo, Captain**--Once a captain of the five elite Káliel guards sent by Gabrielle Dilyn to serve Arlan. He became Kavan's personal guard and best friend, following him to Alberni where he lived out his days

**Ylár, gdhededhá**--k'gdhededhá of Clarys, son and frequent caregiver for dedhá Tumm before his death

**Yóáná Delamo**--The daughter of Asta Dugan and Gaelán Caner, she is a healer. Was raised by Kavan alongside the Delamo children, and later marries the eldest, Madoc Delamo.

**Zelenka Delamo**--A woman from Gorbesh who accompanied Kavan and Wortham to Enesfel; marries Wortham and had three children with him.

**Zerio Kaas**--spy hired into the de Corrmick household

**Zóndhá**--A dhóbhaen; at one time was training as márbhyndhánis but suffered significant head trauma in an accident which has limited his ability to think clearly or manipulate the power.

**Zythán di Bhíncári**--one of the original banished dhóbhaen. He is called saint by some, heretic by most, founder of an ancient cult from the Elyri's earliest days in the land. His Elyri followers believed in sacrifice and orgiastic celebrations and learned ways of killing with the Power to protect themselves. Most were killed centuries ago, but the cult occasionally resurfaces through Elyriá.

## Elyri Phonetics

á--ä (as in m<u>o</u>p)      i--ē (as in b<u>e</u>)

a--ă (as in c<u>a</u>t)      í--ĭ (as in s<u>i</u>t)

ae--ā (as in <u>a</u>ce)      ó--ō (as in g<u>o</u>)

ag--ä (as in m<u>o</u>p) (HE**)      o--ŏ (as in m<u>o</u>p)

ai--ī (as in <u>i</u>ce)      u--ū (as in bl<u>ue</u>)

au--aù (as in <u>ou</u>t)      y--ē (as in b<u>e</u>)

é--ŭ (as in b<u>u</u>t)      yh--y (as in <u>y</u>es)

e--ĕ (as in b<u>et</u>

b--b      l--l

bh--v      Ll--l

c--k      m--m

ch--ch      mh--m (slightly breathy)

d--d      n--n

dh--j      ne--nyä

gae--gwā      p--p

gdh--zh (as in vi<u>s</u>ion)      ph--f

gh--g (as in go)      r--r

gk--<u>k</u> as in loch (HE)      s--sh

h--h      t--t

hw--w (breathy, as in whale)      th--th (as in thistle)

k'--k      z--z

k--k

•    **C** is always pronounced **K** but the letter **K** is most often used to designate this sound. **C** mainly appears at the beginning of some proper surnames and place names and occasionally in the center or at the end of a word. This is believed to be a carryover from the earliest days of the Elyri language, or to have been influenced by the Teren languages, but Elyri linguists and scholars have not yet determined its significance. However, in keeping with this unspoken, unexplained rule, no Elyri have first names, or middle names, starting with **C**.

•   The combination **gk** (pronounced as in the German ich) occurs only at the end of words, unless there is a verb suffix or plural suffix behind it, and only in those words of High Elyri and Old Elyri origin.

•   The letter combination **ag** occurs at the end of words of High Elyri/Old Elyri origin. If the combination appears elsewhere in a word, it will either be as a product of two words having been combined or will be the result of a suffix having been added. Though some Standard Elyri words have retained their **ag** ending, most words carried into the standard will have the **ag** combination replaced with **á** when written, though they sound alike when spoken.

•   The **H** sound only appears in High Elyri/Old Elyri words and in some names carried over from ancient sources; Standard Elyri derivatives will normally drop the **h** from the original word but there are exceptions to the rule.

•   Double **L**'s are found at the beginning of words, single **l**'s in the body or at the end. When words do have the double **L** in a location other than the beginning, it is always the result of two words being combined into one.

•   In the High Elyri/Old Elyri there were no naturally occurring **B, P,** or **AU** (as in cow) sounds. These did not get introduced until Elyri acquired their current religious faith. Even then, the sounds were not commonly used until the standard Teren tongue influenced everyday life. These sounds mainly appear in proper names or religious settings.

•   The combination of the letters **ne** occurs almost exclusively at the end of a word and is always pronounced **nya**, regardless of where it occurs.

·    In Standard and High Elyri the **ee** sound at the beginning or end of a word is always represented with an **I**. In the center of words, it is represented with a **Y**. When the **ee** sound is represented in the center of a word by the letter **I** it is a result of two words being combined into one. In some cases, as with the name Cliáth, the original words may no longer be known.

·    In Old Elyri, the prefix **Yll** that changes a verb to one of its two noun forms is also pronounced **ee**. The few exceptions where Standard or High Elyri words begin with a Y for the ee sound are believed to have originated as intentional misspellings.

·    There is no **S** sound in the Elyri language. S's are always pronounced **sh**.

·    The letter **Z** appears only in the High Elyri/Old Elyri, in words derived from the High Elyri/Old Elyri, or originated as misspellings in one of the Teren languages and were absorbed back into Elyri in the aberrant form.

## Elyri Grammar

In most Elyri words, the stress falls on the second to last. Words where the stress fall on the final syllable (or on the first syllable in words with more than two syllables) are either names, the result of an Elyri translation of a Teren word, caused by the addition of a prefix or suffix, or the result of a word being truncated, having dropped the last syllable over time.

The **k'** at the beginning of a word signifies importance or singularity. It is applied to a word that can have a common meaning and a special meaning: k'tyne would be a favorite niece or female cousin, whereas tyne is simply a niece or female cousin. In the case of the phae k'kairá, when the Terens translated the term into "the Others" it is the **k'** that indicates the O to be capitalized; not just any others but the Others. In Old Elyri, the **k** is attached directly to the word without the '.

The Elyri written language does not have additional characters for capitalization. The first letters words may carry a dot beneath them to signify that the word is a proper name, a place, or a title, but first letters of sentences are not capitalized.

Sentence breaks are characterized by either a new line of text or by a symbol that looks similar to an s. This has resulted in many mistranslations from Elyri into other languages.

**Nouns**

Noun forms of verbs do not have gender. When these nouns are made plural they take the plural inclusive suffix sur.

The prefix **íl** added to a verb makes it into a noun; the word then means "one who" as in "íldaeni"-one who instructs, i.e.: teacher.

Some nouns are formed by adding the prefix **ai** to a verb; the verb dhesá means touch, aidhesá also means touch but is a noun. Not all verbs can accept the **ai** prefix.

**-thé**: the standard plural suffix

**-té:** the standard plural suffix in Old Elyri. some words, however, such as márbhyndhánis, are both singular and plural without the suffix, depending on the context of the sentence

Nouns ending in **I** are both singular and plural and do not take the -**thé** ending

Elyri monetary denominations are both singular and plural.

There are other exceptions to the singular/plural rule, most being words carried over from the High Elyri. High Elyri/Old Elyri contains very few words that are NOT both plural and singular. Any exceptions to the rule are noted.

Some words have gender. A word ending in **ne** is feminine and a word ending in **dhá** is masculine. Both are made plural in the same way (with the **thé** ending). Some gender-neutral words that have been altered from their original form may have either ending.

Some words in Standard, those referring to a group that includes both male and female individuals, require the **-sur** ending, creating the plural inclusive form of the word. The same ending exists in High Elyri.

**Adjectives**

There are few adjectives in the Elyri language. Instead of saying someone is beautiful, or wise, and Elyri would say they possess beauty or they possess wisdom.

To modify such qualities, an Elyri speaker would say:

> Bhykólé aelá shwyth --She possesses wisdom.--Teren: She is wise.
>
> Ochbhykóle aelá shwyth --She possesses more wisdom.--Teren: She is wiser.
>
> Utbhykólé aelá shwyth --She possesses the most wisdom.--Teren: She is wisest.
>
> Naimbhykólé aelá shwyth --She possesses no wisdom. --Teren: She is not wise; or She is a fool.

The few adjectives that do exist come through the High Elyri and are believed by most linguists to have their origins in some language other than the Elyri.

**Verbs**

When **ibh** modifies a verb (i.e.: is singing, is looking) it is attached as a suffix to the verb. In all other instances, it is a separate word (bhydáni ibh gaeth.--He is bhydáni.)

When **im** modifies a verb (i.e.: was singing, was looking) it is attached as a suffix to the verb. In all other instances, it is a separate word (ílDaeni im gaeth.--He was a teacher)

There is no "be" in the Elyri language. Whereas a Teren would say, "He will be singing" the Elyri would say "He will sing." Instead of "I will be there" it would be "I will come" or I will go"; instead of "I will be here" it would be "I will stay", "I will attend," or "I am here."

Rather than using verbs such as "strengthened" or "beautified", in Elyri they would say "given strength" or "given beauty"

## Verb Tenses (Standard Elyri)

| (present) do, does | (past) (ár) did, have done | (present) (ibh) am, are, is doing | (past) (im) was, is, were doing | (future) (ád) will do, to do, be done |
|---|---|---|---|---|
| aelá | aelár | aelibh | aelim | aelád |
| ándás | ándásár | ándásibh | ándásim | ándásád |
| árá | árár | áráibh | áráim | árád |
| bhaeá | bhaeár | bhaeibh | bhaeim | bhaeád |
| bheken | bhekár | bhekibh | bhenim | bhekád |
| bhair | bhairár | bhairibh | bhairim | bhairád |
| bhólon | bhólár | bhólibh | bhólim | bhólád |
| chóne | chóneár | chóníbh | chónim | chónád |
| daeni | daenár | daenibh | daenim | daenád |
| dhesá | dhesár | dhesibh | dhesim | dhesád |
| dhys | dhysár | dhysibh | dhysim | dhysád |
| donai | donár | donaiibh | donim | donád |
| ghlaiph | ghlaiphár | ghlaiphibh | ghlaiphim | ghlaiphád |
| ghytae | ghytár | ghytibh | ghytim | ghytád |
| kelém | kelémár | kelémibh | kelémim | kelémád |
| mairós | mairár | mairibh | mairim | mairád |
| naeth | naethár | naethibh | naethim | naethád |
| yháth | yháthár | yháthibh | yháthim | yháthád |
| zene | zenár | zenibh | zenim | zenád |
| zólágk | zólágkár | zólágkibh | zólágkim | zólágkád |

## **Verb/Noun Tenses**

|  | **noun form 1(íl)** | **noun 2(ai)** |
|---|---|---|
| aelá | ílAelá (one who owns) |  |
| ándás | ílAndás (one who honors) | aiándás |
| bhaeá | ílBhaeá (one who asks) |  |
| bheken | ílBheken |  |
| bhair | ílBhair (one who accepts) | aibhair (acceptance) |
| bhólon | ílBhólon (one who purifies) |  |
| chóne | ílChóne (one who brings) |  |
| daeni | ílDaeni (one who instructs) |  |
| dhesá | ílDhesá (one who touches) | aidhesá |
| donai | ílDonai (one who endures) | aidonai |
| ghlaiph | ílGhlaiph (one who sleeps) | aiglaiph |
| ghytae | ílGhytae (one who threatens) | aighytae (threat) |
| kelém | ílKelém (one who passes) |  |
| mairós | ílMairós (one who heals) | aimairós |
| naeth | ílNaeth (one who finds) |  |
| zene | ílZene (one who gives) |  |
| zólágk | ílZólágk (one who reveals) |  |

## Verb Tenses (High Elyri)

| (present) | (past)(-ár) | (future)(-es) |
|---|---|---|
| aelás | aelásár | aeles |
| bhánys | bhánár | bhánes |
| dytae | dytár | dytes |
| ghai | ghaiár | ghaies |
| síndóbhaene | síndóbhaenár | síndóbhaenes |
| zugdhu | zugdhuár | zugdhues |
| tyreth | tyrethár | tyrethes |
| pháló | phálóár | phálóes |
| scenyhur | scenyhár | scenhyures |
| elzen | elzenár | elzenes |

## Verb/Noun Tenses (High Elyri)

| (noun 1) (bhe-) | (noun 2) (ae-) |
|---|---|
| bheaelás (one who owns) | aeaelás (possession) |
| bhehánys (one who makes music) | |
| bhedytae (one who obeys) | aedytae (obedience) |
| bheghai (one who does) | |
| bhesíndóbhaene (one who forgives) | aesíndóbhaene (forgiveness) |
| bhezugdhu (one who protects) | aezugdhu (protection) |
| bhetyreth (one who knows/scholar) | aetyreth (knowledge) |
| bhepháló (one who buries/gravedigger) | aepháló (grave) |
| bhescenyhur (one who names) | aescenyur (name) |
| bhelzen (one who gives) | aeelzen (gift) |

## Verb Tenses (Old Elyri)

| (present) | (past)(-aer) | (future)(- íst) |
|---|---|---|
| turphálós | turphálósaer | turphálósíst |
| ky | kyaer | kyíst |
| már | máraer | márist |
| bhyn | bhynaer | bhyníst |

## Verb/Noun Tenses (Old Elyri)

| (noun 1)(phe-) | (noun2)(yll-) |
|---|---|
| pheturbhálós (one who betrays) | yllturphálós (betrayal) |
| pheky (one who loves) | yllky (love) |
| phemár (one who blesses) | yllmár (blessing) |
| phebhyn (one who teaches) | yllbhyn (teaching) |

## Foreign Phrase Index

### ELYRI WORDS

HE: High Elyri     SE: Standard Elyri     OE: Old Elyri
n--noun     v--verb     adj—adjective
adv--adverb     prn--pronoun     prp--preposition
pl--plural     sng--singular     psv—possessive
pl in--plural inclusive

**á** (ä) (prp)--HE/SE; and, also, together with, together

**áchaelác** (äch-Ā-läk) (prn)--OE; my, mine

**Ádhá** (Ä-jä) (n)--HE/SE; god; k'Ádhá-supreme deity in the Elyri monotheistic religion

**aelás** (Ā-läsh) (v)--HE; Have (has), possess, own

**aendhá** (ĀN-jä) (n) (pl: aendáthé) --SE; A father's male relatives, including his father, grandfathers, uncles, brothers, and cousins.

**aeyrudgh** (ā-ē-RŪZH) (n)--OE; apology

**ágdhá** (Ä-zhä) (n) (sng)--OE; a single member of the ágdháthé, one of the gods

**ágdh** (äzh) (n) (sng and pl)--OE; the soul or spirit, what remains of an individual separate from the physical body

**ágdháni** (ä-ZHÄ-nē) (n) (sng and pl)--HE; the title for any Elyri trained in the use of nature's energy. Humans have no word that can be used, though they often translate it as sorcerer, wizard, or some other similar term. In common science fiction parlance, it can be translated as psionist. In sources predating the earliest known High Elyri documents, this word would be translated the same as dhesádhá.

**agdhár** (äzh-är) (n)--HE: dawn

**ágdháthé** (ä-ZHÄ-thŭ) (n) (sng and pl)--OE; most often 'the gods' as the dhóbhaen do not separate their gods. dhóbhaen do not believe that their deities interact with the living, but are simply creator deities who set the world into motion and then left it to its ways.

**ágdhdáni** (äzh-DÄ-nē) (n) (sng and pl)--OE; literally 'god power', refers to one highly skilled or trained in the use of dáni

**ágdhghymaemis** (äzh-gē-MÄ-mēsh) (n) (sng and pl)--OE; spirits of the air; air spirits; sometimes angels

**ágk** (äk) (prn)--OE; and

**aiónag** (ī-Ō-nä) (n) (pl: aiónagthé)--HE; path, destiny, life

**aislé** (ĪSH-lŭ) (n)--OE; Loved one, beloved, lover. This word carries almost sacred connotations and is rarely used outside of some intensely passionate, spiritual, emotional relationship. It is believed that in a person's life, while one could have several lovers, they can have only one aeslag, thus many hesitate to use the term at all and may only apply it to someone in their past when they are old and nearing death.

**aisymár** (ī-shē-mär) (n) (sng and pl)--OE; body, living

**áni** (Ä-nē) (n)--HE; Elyri energy/power, the force Elyri can manipulate. Sometimes soul

**ániélmé** (ä-nē-ĚL-mŭ) (n) (sng and pl)--OE; Soul Claw/Power Claw. A ceremonial knife used by the márbhyndhánis made of the same metal as the Coryllien dagger.

**átaelás** (ä-TĀ-läsh) (prn psv)--HE; mine, my

**áti** (Ä-tē) (prn)--HE; I, me, myself

**bhaen** (vān) (prn)--OE; this, these, those

**bhain** (vīn) (prn)--HE; this, these, those

**bhedhuaethag** (vě-jū-Ā-thä) (n) (sng and pl)--HE; defiler

**bhenthíst** (VĚN-thǐsht) (v)--OE; will be divided, will divide

**bhir** (vēr) (adj)--OE; white

**bholgk** (vŏlk) (adv)--OE; when, at the time

**bhur** (būr) (n) (sng and pl)--OE; spirit of the dead which remains after improper disposal of a corpse, responsible for illness, accidents, and all manner of unfortunate things. Sometimes called a suffering spirit.

**bhuré** (VŪ-rä) (n) (adj)--OE; bad, evil, wrong, out of place, unfavorable

**bhydáni** (vē-DÄN-ē) (n) (sng and pl)--HE; This is both a title and a social standing. It can be translated as teacher, master, sage, or wise one, though it encompasses all of these meanings. The title is given to those who, through their exceptional psionic capabilities, wisdom, and intelligence, have demonstrated their worth. Psionic ability is the key to the title, though great ability without wisdom and intelligence will not gain the title. With the title comes the privilege of teaching their knowledge to the children, particularly their psionic knowledge. Each city, town, or village will have at least one bhydáni. Either the bhydáni will ask another into their ranks, or, in the event that a location has no functioning bhydáni, the inhabitants will select someone to fill the position. In extremely rare cases, someone can become bhydáni by accident; they accept mentorship of someone and others begin to ask for the privilege of learning from them as well. By becoming an unofficial teacher, the individual has become bhydáni. A little less than 2/3 of all bhydáni are female.

**bhydhá** (VĒ-jä) (n) (pl: bhydháthé)--SE; Father.

**bhyn** (vēn) (v)--OE; teach,

**chellé** (CHĔL-ŭ) (n) (sng and pl)--HE; home, house, dwelling, residence; also frequently used to as the shortened form of chellé hábhai, or Seeking House, the residences of various religious orders.

**chellé hábhai** (CHĔL-ŭ hä-VĪ) (n) (sng and pl)--HE/SE; Seeking House, an abbey or place of religious instruction

**chygdhé** (CHĒ-zhŭ) (sng) (n) (sng and pl)--OE; cousin

**chyrt** (chērt) (n) (sng and pl)--OE; ribbon, thread

**ciágk** (KĒ- äk) (n) (sng and pl)--OE; beloved, often as an endearment

**cónyses** (kō-NĒSH-ĕsh) (v)--HE: be joined, meet, gather

**daisdhé** (dīsh-JĔ) (v)--OE; touch

**daisdhágdhá** (dīsh-JÄ-zhä) (adj)--OE; touched by the gods

**dáni** (DÄ -nē) (n)--OE; the natural energy power the dhóbhaen can manipulate

**dhár** (jär) (n)--HE: day

**dedhá** (DĔ-jä) (n) (sng and pl)--SE; priest or monk; the term makes no distinction between the two. The shortened form came into use after the Teren came into the lands and adopted the Faith as their own.

**Dhágdhuán** (JÄ-zhū-än) (n)--HE/OE; the Intercessor, considered to be the founder of the Faith because his death is said to make it possible for mortals to reach the divine,

**dhe** (jĕ) (prn) (pl: dhethé)--HE; You; occasionally interchanged with the Standard form dhi

**dhedláó** (jĕd-LÄ-ō) (n) (sng and pl)--HE; land, territory

**dhédók** (jĕ-DŌK) (sng) (n) (sng and pl) --OE; earth/land/ground

**dhes** (jĕsh) (prn)--OE; you, your

**dhesádhá** (jĕsh-Ä-jä) (adj)--HE; This word's origins reach far back in the High Elyri; its original meaning was touched by the deities, but when the Elyri embraced their current belief system the word came to mean touched by k'Ádhá. It is a conjunction of two words dhesá-touched and ádhá god or deity.

**dhhwaeythá** (jwā-ĒTH-ä) (n)--OE; medium-sized ship, the most commonly used to trade between territories or to deliver large groups of people; both used with sails and oars

**dhó** (jō) (sng) (n) (sng and pl)--OE; circle

**dhó dónáré** (JŌ dō-NÄ-rŭ) (n) (sng and pl)--OE; Circle House; center of healing, religion, and learning.

**dhóbhaen** (jō-VĀN) (n)--OE; The Kindred; to those banished to the west the word came to mean The Forgiven (by k'Ádhá) and eventually evolved into the Standard Elyri word *sindóbhaenár* for forgiven. When capitalized, the word is used as the name of the island upon which these people live. In reference to the people, their customs, their ideology, etc. the word is always used in lower case.

**dhózáyr** (jō-zä-ĒR) (v)--OE; lasts, lasting, eternal

**dhysag** (jē SHÄ) (v)--OE; cease, stop, end

**drenaiaer** (drĕ-nī-ĀR) (v)--OE; was/has been bathed, was/has been washed, was/has been cleaned, was/has been cleansed

**drenai** (drĕ-NĪ) (v)--OE; bathe, wash, clean, cleanse

**du** (dū) (interjection)--OE; yes

**ebh** (ĕv) (prn)--HE/SE; we, us

**elyry** (ĕ-LĒR-ē) (adj)--OE; defiant, disobedient

**elyryhánag** (ĕl-ēr-ē-ÄN-ä) (n) (sng and pl)--OE; defiant of the natural order; used to refer to those dhóbhaen who learned to use the power without permission of the márbhyndhánis; the banished group took on the name k'elyryhánag as a badge of distinction; is the root for the name Elyri

**elzen** (ĕl-ZĔN) (v)--HE; give, bring

**Ethenae** (ĕ-THĔN-ā) (n)--HE/SE; the peaceful afterworld where the blessed and holy reside after death.

**gaeythá** (gwā-ĒTH-ä) (n) (sng and pl)--OE; largest dhóbhaen ship; has oars but most often used with sails; meant for long voyages or large cargos; these were the ships the elyryhánag were banished on.

**gál** (gäl) (n) (sng and pl)--OE; place, location

**gál yllínphel** (gäl ĒL-ĭn-fĕl) (n)--OE; place of birth (Gálínphel)

**gdhárith** (zhär- ĒTH) (n) (sng and pl)--OE; beings without form or description said to reside in the realms of the gods who may, at their whim, affect things on earth. Angels.

**gdhededhá** (zhĕ-DĔ-jä) (n) (sng and pl)--SE; priest or faith teacher or disciple; the term makes no distinction between them.

**gdhededhásur** (zhĕ-DĔ-jä-shūr) (n) (pl.in)--HE/SE; A group of faith teachers/clergy of both sexes.

**ghís** (gĭsh) (n) (sng and pl)--OE; village or town, group of homes collected around a dhó dónáré and ghís kelyhag (village house)

**ghís kelyhag** (gĭsh KĔL-yä) (n) (sng and pl)--OE; village house, the central structure in a village where the community meets and shares meals.

**ghísaer** (gĭsh-ĀR) (n) (sng and pl)--OE; territory, a collection of ghís under the control of a kydhé or kymyhé

**ghrís** (grĭsh) (n) (sng and pl)--OE; stone

**ghrískáy** (grĭsh kä-Ē) (n)--OE; sunstone, a navigational tool the dhóbhaen use to sail by.

**ghrís pheslárkag** (grĭsh fĕsh-LÄR-kä) (n)--OE; the Oathing Stone, used both for the large stone where marriage ceremonies are conducted and to the small, handheld stone which is placed above a married couples door to publically announce the union of the residents.

**ghymaemis** (gē-MĀ-mēsh) (n)--OE; sky, air, wind

**ghlaebh** (glāv) (v)--HE: sleep

**hábhai** (HÄ-vī) (v)--HE; look, search

**haiágles** (hī-Ä-lesh) (n) (pl: haiáglesté)--OE; friend, companion

**hánag** (HÄN-ä) (n) (sng and pl)--OE; natural order of the universe, life, the world

**háódhónai** (hä-ō-jō-nī) (n) (sng and pl)--OE; family

**hás** (häsh) (n) (sng and pl)--OE; woman, female, wife

**hes** (hĕsh) (n) (sng and pl)--HE; heart

**hílylá** (hĭl-Ē-lä) (n) (sng and pl)--OE; water, standing water, pool, lake, puddle, well

**hílylám** (hĭl-Ē-läm) (n) (sng and pl)--OE; big water, sea

**hílyláz** (hĭl-Ē-läz) (n) (sng and pl)--OE; flowing water, creek, stream, river

**Hínesur** (hĭn-ĕ-SHŪR) (n)--OE; the group of rocky, mostly uninhabitable islands between the land of the dhóbhaen and the mainland

**híth** (hĭth) (n) (sng and pl)--OE; man, male, husband

**hne** (hnyä) (adj)--HE; beneath, under

**hwábhi** (hwä-VĒ) (v)--OE; smile

**hwaeythá** (hwā-Ē-thä) (n) (sng and pl)--OE; small ships; sometimes used to trade between territories by more frequently used as passenger vessels or fishing boats; both used with sails and oars

**hwonag** (HWÄN-ä) (adj)--OE; normal dhóbhaen untrained in the use of power

**hwoncáró** (hwän-KÄR-ō) (adj)--HE; sad, bereft, heartbroken

**hyhest** (hē-HĔSHT) (sng) (n) (sng and pl)--OE; heart

**idó** (Ē-dó) (conj/prp)--OE; until

**ílMairós** (ĭl-MĪ-rōsh) (n) (sng and pl)--SE; healer, physician.

**íls** (ĭlsh) (prn)--OE; the

**k'ágdhá** (k-Ä-zhä) (n)--OE; the secret name of the one deity amongst the dhóbhaen singled out for worship after Dhágdhuán came to them.

**k'bhekalomár** (k vĕ-KÄL-äm-är) (n)--HE: those who have gone before; ancestors, the deceased

**k'gdhededhá** (k zhĕ-DĔ-jä) (n) (sng and pl)--HE/SE; The Elyri designation for the male individual who is elected as the head of the Faith.

**k'kairá** (also **phae k'kairá**) (fä k KĪ-rä) (n) (sng and pl)--HE; The name given to the race of beings who inhabited the territory of the Five Sovereignties before the Elyri arrived. By the time the Elyri came, all that remained of the k'kairá (as they are sometimes called) were crumbling stone circles, mounds, huts, some of which bore written symbols upon them. Unlike most High Elyri words which end with the ah sound, this one does not end with the letter combination ag.

**k'phaelás** (k FÄ-läsh) (n) (sng and pl)--HE; ruler, king or queen. THE monarch rather than a monarch

**k'phaelás dhedláó** (k FÄ-läsh jĕd-LÄ-ō) (n)--HE; The Sovereignty; kingdom; land belonging to the king or queen

**k'phóredhet** (k fō-RĔJ-ĕt) (n)--SE; ecclesiastical tribunal of the Faith in Clarys; when the k'gdhededhá is indisposed or has passed, the Tribunal rules in his place. Often used for trials of a religious nature and used to discuss matters of Faith with the k'gdhededhá

**k'rylag** (k RĒ-lä) (n) (pl: k'rylagthé)--HE; Once Kóráhm chose the word rylag for his method of travel, k'rylag was carried over into standard Elyri and came to refer strictly to the Gates, not a standard gate.

**kairénté** (kī-RŬN-tŭ) (n)--OE; others

**kállóm** (käl-LŌM) (v)--OE; pass, progress, proceed, go, come

**kállómíst** (käl-lōm-ĬSHT) (v)--OE; will pass, will progress, will proceed, will go, will come

**kánist** (kä-NĒSHT) (v)--OE; join, unite, put together, connect; are joined, is joined

**káy** (kä-Ē) (n)--OE; sun

**káyl** (kä-ĒL) (n) (sng and pl)--OE; star; stars

**keh** (kĕh) (prp)--HE; on, upon

**kekraes** (kĕh-krāsh) (adj)--OE; western or west, used as a name or title as in kekraes khílylám or Western Sea

**kelém** (KĔ-lŭm) (v)--SE; pass, progress, proceed, go

**kelem** (KĔL-ĕm) (n) (sng and pl)--OE; trip, journey, travels

**kelyhag** (KĔL-yä) (n) (sng and pl)--OE; house, dwelling

**khílylám** (khĭl-Ē-läm) (n) (sng and pl)--OE; big water, sea; used as a name or title as in kekraes khílylám or Western Sea

**kis** (kēsh) (v)--HE; love

**kisaer** (kēsh-ĀR) (v)--HE; have loved

**kóhm** (kōm) (prep)--OE; in, into

**kólir** (kō-lēr) (v) --SE; apologize

**kremh** (krĕmh) (prep)--OE; on, upon

**krus** (krūsh) (n) (sng and pl)--HE; crucifix. This practice was introduced to the dhóbhaen by the Taeré and was used in the execution of Dhágdhuán, as he was both crucified and burned. The burning was later removed from religious-historical accounts. The standard crucifix form is a T.

**kyag** (KĒ-ä) (n) (pl: kyágthé)--HE; Beloved, dearest one.

**kydhé** (KĒ-jŭ) (n) (sng and pl)--OE; male who controls a ghísaer, a king

**kylldrenai** (kēl-drĕ-NĪ) (n)--OE; the Reconditioning, carried out by the márbhyndhánis to bring lawbreakers and heretics and the disorderly back into line with acceptable behavior.; also called the Cleansing

**kylldhysag** (kēl-JĒ-shä) (n)--OE; The Ceasing; the moment in the life of the dhóbhaen and Elyri when the individual walks away from life and is assumed into the natural energy of the universe. As it is a private thing that none come back from, none know precisely what happens at that moment, although it is known that no physical body is ever recovered from one who has Ceased, and so it is considered as an ending different than the physical death of the body.

**kyllkánist** (kēl-KÄ-nēsht) (n)--OE; unification through marriage

**kymyhé** (kē-MĒ-ŭ) (n) (sng and pl)--OE; female who controls a ghísaer, a queen

**Kyne** (KĒ-nyä) (n) (sng and pl)--HE/SE; The High Mother, the Matriarchal ruler of Elyriá. It includes the translation "Mother ruler", "Mother protector", and "exalted mother". Since nearly all Elyri families can trace some familial link to the Bhíncári, the Kyne is both a figurative, and near literal, mother of all Elyri. This position is both hereditary and elected, chosen from among all of the women in the Bhíncári family.

**kyrónagk** (kēr-ō-näk) (n) (sng and pl)--OE; heretic

**kyryth** (kēr-ĒTH) (n)--HE: ribbon, thread

**lásánai** (LÄ-shän-ī) (n) (sng and pl)--HE; my master/lord or mistress/lady; one to whom an individual has chosen to be subservient. This is a strictly voluntary status that may or may not be acknowledged or honored by the one being given superior status, but it gives the title bearer no more power over the speaker than the speaker wishes to allow. Not to be confused with a title of nobility or landholders since there is no such status in Elyriá. It can be used for either women or men, though it is more commonly used for men.

**llánec** (LÄ-nyäk) (n)--HE; the occasional Elyri "ability" of being given insight into the future. Unlike other Elyri abilities, this one cannot be learned or controlled; an individual must be born with it. One who possesses it endures periodic "blackouts" as events are revealed to them but they cannot summon visions. Generally, the things they "see" are vague in nature, and rarely involve the seer. It is often translated into the Trade language as "the Sight." Literally translated as "bitter sight"

**llónec** (LŌ něk) (n)--OE; the occasional dhóbhaen "ability" of being given insight into the future. Unlike other dhóbhaen abilities, this one cannot be learned or controlled; an individual must be born with it. One who possesses it endures periodic "blackouts" as events are revealed to them but they cannot summon visions. Generally, the things they "see" are vague in nature, and rarely involve the seer.

**llóph** (lōf) (n) (sng and pl)--OE; rib

**lómesté** (lō-MĚSH-tŭ) (n) (pl: lómestéthé)--HE/SE; translated in the Trade tongue as council, it is a unit of 5 to 9 elders and bhydáni that govern a single town or region; k'lómesté is the Elyri High

Council in Clarys. All bhydáni in the region will be a member of the lómesté, but the lómesté need not consist solely of bhydáni.

**mai** (MĪ) (n) (pl: maithé)—HE/SE; child; used in the Standard as a term of endearment

**maimís** (MĪ-ish) (n)--HE; paper, parchment

**mál** (mäl) (adj)--HE/SE; sacred, holy, blessed

**málneag** (mäl-NYÄ-ä) (n) (pl: málneagthé)--HE; it can mean one who possesses a quality of blessedness, sacredness, or holiness; its most common translation into the Trade languages is saint.

**már** (mär) (v)--OE; bless, be good, behave

**márbhyndhánis** (mär-vēn-JÄN-ēsh) (n) (sng and pl)--OE; literally 'blessed teacher' the title of those dhóbhaen who are the keepers of knowledge. They are the only ones, other than healers, allowed to be trained in the use of power. Also responsible to educate children and 'recondition' those who break the law.

**márist** (mär-ĒSHT) (v)--OE; will be blessed, will behave, will be good

**mósc** (mōshk) (adj)--OE; dark

**murt** (mūrt) (sng) (n) (sng and pl)--OE; hand

**naebhur** (nā-VŪR) (n)--OE; sickness, illness, disease, plague

**naibhíth** (nī- vĭth) (v)--HE; cannot divide, cannot be divided

**náir** (nä-ĒR) (prn)--HE/SE; nothing, none

**náós** (nä-ŌSH) (n) (sng and pl)--HE/SE; a place of worship, temple; also occasionally used to refer to the altar.

**náym** (nä-ĒM)--OE; no, denial

**néósag** (nŭ- ō-shä) (sng) (n)--OE; place of learning, where the márbhyndhánis reside.

**nhwaethár** (nwā-THÄR) ( v)--HE; found, has found

**nís** (nish) (n)--HE: snow

**óymháth** (ō Ē mäth) (idiom)--OE; equivalent to 'good night' or 'sleep well'

**phaern** (fārn) (prn)--OE; of, from belonging to, expresses ownership or origin

**phág** (fäg) (n) (sng and pl)--OE; hair/cap/hat/head covering

**phálóár** (fäl-Ō-är) (v)--HE; buried, has buried, have buried

**phehonís** (fĕ-HÄN-ĭsh) ( n) (sng and pl)--OE; bard, minstrel

**phemár** (fĕ-MÄR) (v)--OE; one who blesses

**phemárógdh** (fĕ MÄ rōzh) (n) (sng and pl)--OE; one who heals with power/healer

**phephagn** (fĕ-FÄN) (sng) --OE; bird, usually songbird

**pheslárkag** (fĕsh-LÄR-kä) (n)--OE; that which binds, relating only to the ritual of marriage and other sacred/important oaths.

**pheturphálós** (fĕ-tūr-FÄL-ōsh) (n) (sng and pl)--OE; one who betrays; traitor

**phyl** (fĕl) (adj)--HE; young, in comparison to the speaker

**redh** (rĕj) (n) (sng and pl)--HE grace, sometimes used as forgiveness in a religious sense

**ró** (rō) (n)--OE; blood

**róagdháthé** (rō- äzh-Ä-thŭ) (n)--OE; god blood; blood of god, blood of the gods

**rósádhá** (rō-SHÄ-jä) (n)--HE; Literally translated as the Wounds of the God, it refers to the manifestation of the death wounds of Dhágdhuán which inflicted many saints and holy individuals. These include punctures in both wrists from where the founder was hung by his wrists, sometimes accompanied by the burn of a rope on the left wrist, punctures in both ankles where his feet were secured to the pyre post, possibly the scars of ropes on the ankles as well, and, very rarely, the marks of burning flesh on the lower body.

**rynlagne** (rē-LÄ-nyä) (n) (sng and pl)--OE; the Gate

**scenyhur** (shkĕn-YUR) (v)--HE; call, name, refer to

**serbháló** (shĕr-VÄ-lō) (n)--SE; A form of Elyri wine with almost no alcohol content, used only for the purposes of religious ceremony.

**sídysá** (shĭ-DĒ-shä) (n)--HE; A seldom taught Elyri discipline in which one psionist sends forth a single, brutal cohesive burst of energy which explodes within the skull of his opponent. An unprepared opponent (particularly a Teren) could experience pain, brain damage, or even death depending upon the skill of the attacker.

**sínréc** (shĭn-RŬK) (n) (sng and pl)--HE; This word has no direct translation. Blood kin with a special bond, is about the closest it can be described. Any blood kin can be sínréc, but saying "he is my cousin," is different from saying "he is my sínréc" (or "he is sínréc."). It is sometimes used for non-relatives who are extremely close.

**só** (shō) (adj)--HE; Small, little, tiny, not much, a small amount.

**sór** (shōr) (adj)--OE; little, small, tiny

**sór ciágk** (shōr KĒ- äk) (endearment)--OE; little beloved one

**taeásne** (tā-ÄSH-nyä) (n)--OE; sister

**taeré** (TĀR-ŭ) (n) (sng and pl)--OE; those from the mainland who were not dhóbhaen; on average heavier, shorter, with more body hair, shorter life span, and with the inability to use the power.

**taerén** (TĀR-ŭn) (n) (sng and pl)--OE; the language spoken by the taeré

**tágdhásaeit** (tä-zhä shä-ĒT) (n)--SE; spirit brother, individuals who are not related by blood but who consider themselves brothers

**táu** (tä-ū) (v)--OE; hush, be still

**thai** (thī) (n) (sng and pl)--OE; light

**thóres** (THŌ-rĕsh) (n) (pl: thóresĕth)--SE; the room or rooms in a náós that serves as clergy offices and residences.

**thráuneth** (thrä-u-nĕth) (prep)--OE; before, in front of, at the beginning

**tódhedác** (tō-JĔ-däk) (n)--OE; brother

**tuesdhe** (tū-ĔSH-jĕ) (idiom)--HE; thank you, you have my gratitude

**turphálós** (tūr-FÄL-ōsh) (v)--OE; betray

**tyreth** (TĒR-ĕth) (v)--HE; know, knows

**tyrethár** (TĒR-ĕth-är) (v)--HE; did know, knew, has known

**ubé** (ū-BŬ) (prep)--HE: while, as, meanwhile, in the meantime, during

**yháun** (yä-ūn) (prp)--OE; with

**ylldhysag** (ĒL- jē shä) (n) (sng and pl)--OE; end of time; could be end of everything, end of the week, end of the day, etc.

**yó** (Ē-ō) (conj/prp)--HE; until

**záryph** (zä-RĒF) (n) (sng and pl)--HE/SE; winged beings connected to the realm of the holy; angels

**zerphánál** (ZĔR-fän-äl) (n) (sng and pl)--OE; mild alcohol crafted by the dhóbhaen from maple sap.

**zethenaer** (zĕ-thēn-ĀR) (n) (sng and pl)--OE; universe, where the gods reside, the heavens

**zugdhu** (ZŪ-zhū) (v)--HE; protect, shield, watch

**zyrudhén** (zē-Rū-jŭn) (sng and pl)--OE; Faith Guards, armed attendants of the márbhyndhánis.

## Translations

(OE) *bhir phehonís phaern Gálínphel*- -The White Bard of Gálínphel
(HE/SE) *phyr phephagn phain Gallínphel*- -Blue Bird of Gallínphel

(OE*)* *llóph phaern ágdháthé*- -ribs of the gods (gods' ribs)

(OE) *chyrt ghymaemis*--sky ribbons

(OE) *thai phemár*--blessed lights

| | |
|---|---|
| (HE) *maimís kyryth keh nís* | paper ribbons on (the) snow |
| *íth k'bhekalomár* | those who have gone |
| *zugdhu dhe ubé ghlaebh* | guard you while you sleep |
| *yó hne íth agdhár ebh cónyses* | until beneath the dawn (new day) we are joined |

(HE) *hábhai áti nhwaethár dhe; aiónag naibhíth ebh*- - Searching, I have found you; destiny cannot divide us.

(OE*)* *íts hílylám márist dhes agk íts ágdháthé hwábhi kremh kelem*- - May the sea be good to you and the gods smile upon your journey

| | |
|---|---|
| (HE) *íth Llaethlágárá zugdhu* | The Llaethlágárá shields |
| *íth hes áti tyrethár* | the hearts I have known. |
| *phálóár hne Kóráhm's krus* | Buried under Kóráhm's cross |
| *bhain scenyhur chellé k'phaelás dhedláó* | Who call the Sovereignties home |
| *só hes a már áni* | Little hearts and blessed souls |
| *bhain áti kisaer* | those that I have loved |
| *átaelás aiónag elzenár* | My path has been given |
| *hwoncáró áti aelás náir* | Bereft I have nothing |

| | |
|---|---|
| (OE) *dhédók agk káyl* | earth and stars |
| (OE) *áchaelác aeyrudgh* | my apologies |
| (OE) *kekraes khílylám* | Western Sea |
| (OE) *taeasnete ágk tódhedácte* | sisters and brothers |
| (OE) *táu, sór ciágk* | be still, little beloved one |
| (OE) *kállóm kóhm íls hílylá* | come into the pool |

(OE) *bhuré ghymaemis*　　　　　　unfavorable wind

(OE) *ró phaern áchaelác murt*　　　blood of my hand (kin)

| | |
|---|---|
| *dhózáyr kyllkánist* | Eternal unification |
| *náym bhenthíst* | never divided |
| *ágdh, hyest, aisymár* | Soul, heart and body |
| *thráuneth háódhónai* | before family |
| *íls ágdháthé* | the gods |
| *agk íls dhédók* | and earth |
| *agk íls zéthénaer* | and heaven |
| *kánist dhes* | have bound you |
| *idó ylldhysag* | until the end days |
| *bholgk ylldhózáyr kállómíst* | when eternity passes pass |

(OE) *yháun áchaelác dhózáyr hyhest*　　With my eternal heart

## Pronunciation of Elyri & dhóbhaen Names

**Ágdhállán** (ÄZH-äl-än)
**Aldár** (ĂL-där)
**Aleski** (ăl-ĒSH-kē)
**Alyná** (ă-LĒ-nä)
**Ártur** (är-TŪR)
**Audh** (ouj)
**Aunes** (ou-NĔSH)
**Bhás-** (väsh)
**Bhendhámyn** (věn-JÄ-mēn)
**Bhetá-** (VĔ-tä)
**Bhílári** (vĭ-LÄR-ē)
**Bhíncári** (vĭn-CÄ-rē)
**Bhrán** (vrän)
**Bhregdh-** (vrěj)
**Bhríd** (vrĭd)
**Bhront** (vränt)
**Bhryell** (vrē-ĔL)
**Bhyrhán** (VĒR hăn)
**Cáner** (KÄ-nyär)
**Cáym** (kä-ĒM)
**Celen** (KĔL-ěn)
**Chethá** (CHĔ-thä)
**Cíbhóló** (kĭ-VŌ-lō)
**Clarys** (klär-ĒSH)
**Cliáth** (klē-ÄTH)
**Curnydhá-** (kūr-NĒ-jä)
**Dhágdhuán** (JÄ-zhū-än)
**Dháná** (JÄ-nä)
**Dhedec** (JĔ-děk)
**dhóbhaen-** (jō-VÄN)
**Dhóláhr** (JŌ-lär)
**Dhóri** (JŌR-ē)
**Dhybhé-** (JĒ-vä)
**Dóhn Bhlethan-** (dän VLĔ-thăn)
**Dórímyr** (DŌR-ĭ-mēr)
**Drebhoti** (drě-VÄ-tē)

**Elyri** (ě-LĒR-ē)
**Elyriá** (ě-LĒR-ē-ä)
**Éthym** (ě-THĒM)
**Gaed-** (gwäd)
**Gaelán** (GWÄ-län)
**Ghené** (Gě-nyä)
**Ghíldyagh** (GĬL-dyä)
**Hínesur-** (HĬ-ně-SHŌR)
**Hwensen** (HWĔN-shěn)
**Iólán-** (ē-Ō-län)
**Káliel** (kä-LĒ-ěl)
**Kavan** (KĂ-văn) (in Elyri his
    name is spelt Kabhan)
**Khwílen Kesábhá** (KHWĬL-ěn
    kěsh-ä-vä)
**Kílyn** (kĭ-LĒN)
**Kluín** (KLŪ-ĭn)
**Kóráhm di Curnydhá** (KŌR-
    äm DĒ kūr-NĒ-jä)
**Lláhy** (LÄ-hē)
**Lláná** (LÄ-nä)
**Llaur** (laur)
**Llucás** (LŪ käsh)
**Llyr** (lēr)
**MacLyr** (mäk-LĒR)
**Mánd** (mänd)
**Maras** (MĂR-ăsh)
**Mórne** (MŌR-nyä)
**Níkóa** (nĭ-KŌ-ä)
**Ombhrís di Nyrau** (OM vrish
    dē NĒ row)
**Phaedr** (FÄ-dr)
**Phaurd** (faurd)
**Phílóá** (fĭ-LŌ-ä)
**Phínc-** (fĭnk)
**Raebhá** (RÄ-vä)

**Raenár Magk** (RĀ-när mä<u>k</u>)
**Sámel** (SHÄ-mĕl)
**Sóbhán** (shō-VÄN)
**Sósáná**-(shō-SHÄN-ä)
**Syl** (shēl)
**Sylyhá** (shē-LĒ-hä)
**Tám** (täm)
**Tíbhyan** (TĬ-vē-ăn)

**Tumm** (tūm)
**Tusánt** (tū-SHÄNT)
**Ylár** (Ē-lär)
**Yóáná**-(ē-ō-Ä-nä)
**Zóndhá**-(ZŌN-jä)
**Zythán** (ZĒ-thän)

❧ 745 ❧

## The Five Sovereignties - City Legend

### Enesfel

1-*Rhidam
2-Alberni
3-Bryn
4-Chantel
5-Dorshur
6-Durham
7-Erleta
8-Jardin
9-Kamin
10-Kilmacud
11-Levonne
12-Nelori
13-Seres
14-Talladegah
15-Tarsee
16-Theron
17-Wexel

### Cordash

1-*Aralt
2-Anzet
3-Ediug
4-Eleva
5-Jassett
6-Kakkoris
7-Korr
8-Liatti
9-Lindumn
10-Matina
11-Pesek
12-Sebring
13-Trallan
14-Verbier
15-Vioe
16-Vron
17-Wynett

### Elyriá

1-Clarys
2- Ánásair
3-Bhastyán
4-Bhórdh
5-Bhryell
6-Cármycá
7-Cylleá
8-Dhánthes
9-Ibhórys
10-Káská
11-Khwíncanon
12-Rísóri
13-Sábhóne
14-Sídhári
15-Turyn

### Hatu

1-*Natrona
2-Avarrou
3-Cran Ufa
4-Drisoge
5-Enda
6-Fa Ruqi
7-Furr Katio
8-Kílyn
9-Palil
10-Wasilla
11-Yd Haszafni

### Neth

1-*Glevum
2-Fiara
3-Gorea
4-Mawr
5-Nogero
6-Pravek
7-Ruidoso
8-Venago

### Káliel

1-*Káliel
2-Jaffe
3-Mara Qin
4-Pháne
5-Shola

# The Five Sovereignties

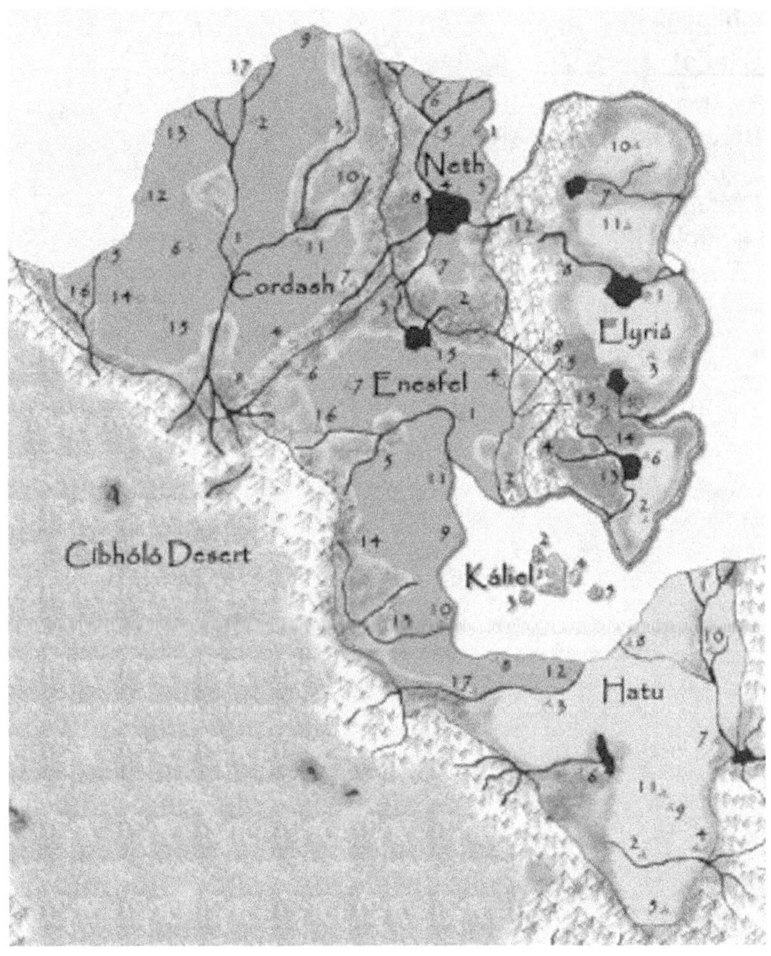

# Dhóbhaen City Legend

| **Dhóbhaen ghísaer of:** | **Ruling ghís** |
|---|---|
| 1- Áwelen | Phásir |
| 2- Bhreyzyán | Rínes |
| 3- Werem | Nyrau |
| 4- Lyáragk | Sáudhá |
| 5- Gálínphel | Curnydhá |
| 6- Gíldyágh | Maras |
| 7- Ghené | Phaurd |

# Dhóbhaen Regional Map

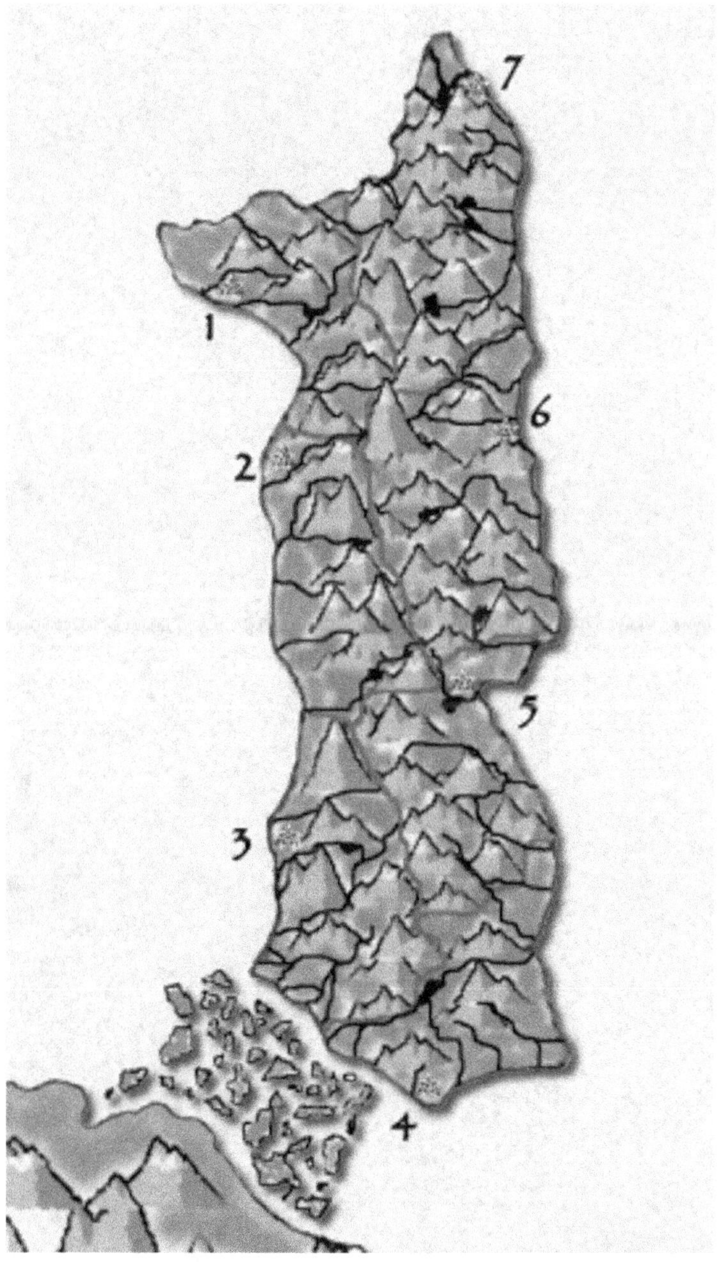

## About the Author

Unsatisfied with 'how the story ends' as a young reader, Tamara took on the challenge of crafting endings to the tales of others to better suit her vision of the world. That desire to mold reality into how she imagined it should be, gave birth to a life-long fascination with the written word, and its capacity, particularly through realms of fantasy and science fiction, to foster an understanding of the people, events, thoughts, and emotions that make us who we are.

A long-time resident of Clearlake, California, after a life that took her back and forth across the country, Tamara is owned by a pack of papillions, a pride of cats, and an eclectic arsenal of films she enjoys in her off-moments.

❧752❧

# White Paragon
## Kestrel Harper Saga Book 7
(excerpt)

One hand covered with dried blood smeared red dust through the fresh blood beneath his nose as he lifted his throbbing, aching head to assess where he was, what was happening around him. These were familiar physical sensations, the weighty depletion of power, the exhaustion, the ripping apart of his inner senses that had come with taking the Gate from Dhóbhaen to Bhryell. Blood dripping from his ears. Blood tinting his tears so that everything he could see was colored crimson. From the fractured earth beneath the hand barely supporting his weight, the only thing that kept him from pitching face-first to the ground, fat, hard-shelled beetles, darker red against the clay earth, sand, and stone, scurried out and over his hand.

Kavan shuddered at the sensation, at the smell of musty death that swept over him, and swallowed the bile in his throat.

Rhyrdan lived, praise k'Ádhá, and stood protectively over him, his soldier's stance shaky as his legs fought for the equilibrium the Gate had stolen. To their left, an unfamiliar Cíbhóló, only recognizable by the color of his skin, his manner of dress, and the waji in his hand. To their right, Wace, a long wood staff in one hand, a long knife in the other. Beyond them, two others.

Myreth.

Kavan's already ragged breath was ripped from his lungs.

But it was the woman behind Myreth who stopped his heart.

www.ingramcontent.com/pod-product-compliance
Lightning Source LLC
Chambersburg PA
CBHW061043210726
48294CB00001B/14